American Jackal

A TROY STOKER, M.D. PSYCHIATRY THRILLER

DR. FRANCIS BANDETTINI
MATT NILSEN

Naoband, LLC
Baltic, South Dakota

To Naomi

To Julie

First Naoband, LLC paperback edition January 2015

ISBN: 0692271287
ISBN-13: 978-0692271285

Cover design by Heather and Jason Steed of Targa Media

Visit TroyStokerMD.com

 @TroyStokerMD

facebook.com/TroyStokerMD

ACKNOWLEDGMENTS

We want to thank Dr. Dave Auch for his military and historical insight. We express appreciation to Naomi Bandettini for her edits, insights and late night meals. Peter Bandettini, Ph.D., Section Chief Investigator in the Laboratory of Brain and Cognition, as well as the Director of the NIH Functional MRI core facility, has been generous with his time and knowledge for sharing his invaluable expertise in fMRI technology. Sandy Brende's keen eye saved the day, when we discovered some editing defects. Detective Scott Schovaers taught us about some key police procedures. Whitney Borup challenged us with additional insight into framing a story and creating a hero. Thank you Targa Media for your help with our publicity, book cover, website, and marketing. There are also numerous other friends in the military and civilian life, along with new acquaintances, who will remain anonymous. You provided extremely valuable insight. We owe you our sincere gratitude.

Dr. Bandettini wishes to thank his patients for providing him always with a continuing learning experience. As he wishes to express, "It is my deepest hope that in my continued working with all of you who may read this book that we all come to realize that we are really helping each other in this journey through life."

PROLOGUE, STOKER, 1992

The unconscious patient was an injured Airborne Ranger. Only eighteen-year-old medic, Troy Stoker, was keeping him alive as they raced in a jeep back to the temporary airfield southeast of Laredo, Texas. A tourniquet was slowing the bleeding, but not enough. Stoker further restricted the hemorrhaging by applying direct pressure to the shredded femoral artery. "Radio into the first aid tent," Stoker instructed the driver. "Tell them I've got a major compound fracture and this guy is bleeding out. We're going to need that doctor and air evac immediately!" Stoker watched his unconscious patient's chest rise and fall. "Now's the time to fight, Soldier. Just keep breathing, man."

"Troy! The aid station says the bird just left! The general is using it as a transport!"

"Tell the doctor to order it back!" Stoker yelled.

"The doctor left with the general on the helicopter!"

"Tell them to call them back! We need the doctor and we need the chopper!" The ranger's chest continued to rise and fall—a good sign—as the driver radioed again.

"The radio man says you can't issue those kinds of orders, Corporal!"

"I don't give a damn if it's an order or not an order. It's just the right thing!" Stoker thought about his dilemma. "Let's pull this jeep right up in front of his cozy little sunshade. You take over this wound! I can take an officer's reprimand, but I can't live with this man dying."

Forty-five seconds later, the driver skidded the jeep to a stop right in front of the radio operator's sunshade. "Call back that helicopter!" yelled Stoker as the driver jumped back to the patient and took over the first aid. "This man is about to die!"

"I can't!" protested the radio operator, as he watched corporal Stoker jump out of the jeep with bloody hands. "I have orders from the general to—" Stoker's gory hand reached for the radio and the operator lurched back in fear.

Stoker took over the radio and hit the transmit button. "Deathstalker, this is Medic Alpha Six. Over."

A moment later, the pilot responded to Stoker's call. "Medic Alpha Six, this is Deathstalker."

"Roger," Stoker said. "I'm a medic with an Airborne Ranger in critical condition requesting you turn that helicopter around. I need medevac and I need that doctor. Over."

"Standby, Medic Alpha Six," came the pilot's reply. Silently, Stoker waited and hoped while lethal seconds ticked by. "That's a roger, Medic Alpha Six." Relief flooded through Stoker. "Ground control. This is Deathstalker. Landing site clear, over?" Stoker started to hand the blood-covered radio microphone back to the radio operator, but he would not touch it. So Stoker shoved the device to within three inches of the radio operator's mouth, turned his head to glance at the empty landing zone, and started to key the microphone so the squeamish radio operator could issue the response. The nauseated, mute radio operator stuttered a few times. Stoker yanked the microphone from the radioman and held it within an inch of his lips. He looked at the frozen radioman with disgust. "You're a disgrace as a soldier." Stoker again keyed the microphone. "Deathstalker, you're clear for landing." The broad-shouldered medic threw the microphone on the ground in exasperation, and ran back to attend to his patient.

Five minutes later the helicopter descended from the sky as Stoker and two others approached with the patient on the gurney. They had inserted an IV and were administering saline, but his pulse was still weak and his breathing labored. The doctor was the first to exit the helicopter and he ran for the patient. Stoker gave a crisp report over the roar of the helicopter rotors and engine, and the doctor took over.

"Medic Alpha Six!" bellowed the mature voice of a man who knew how to cut through the clutter of aircraft noise. Stoker snapped to attention and he issued a salute with his blood-covered hand. Stoker expected to feel fear. But oddly, he only felt serenity. He had done the right thing, even if it cost him solitary confinement or worse. "Call the MPs!" ordered the general. "Corporal, I'm placing you under arrest!"

"Sir, yes sir!" Stoker said.

Then from inside the helicopter, the voice of the doctor called out. "Arrest me, too then General. This ranger should be dead. On top of that, I was supposed to be here to save him. This young corporal did medical things today that some of our ten-year sergeants couldn't do—including persuading our helicopter back. If he's not a hero, General, he's got the potential."

PROLOGUE, RIVERA, 1992

The visiting colonel was a complainer. The humidity and heat of the El Salvadorian jungle was hard on this pencil-pushing desk jockey. As a result, Captain Errol Rivera despised this visitor and his assignment of piloting the guest around. "So, Captain, what will you do when you return stateside?" the colonel yelled above the blades of the UH-1 Huey helicopter skimming two thousand feet above the jungle.

"I'm checking into a mental hospital where nobody can find me, and there I'll learn the coping skills necessary for an eternity in Hell, sir!" shouted Rivera mockingly while considering the horror of the hundreds of people he'd killed in Central America. Today, Rivera's job was dull, however. His assignment was simply to fly this colonel, who was actually an accountant with a default military rank, around El Salvador to tally up American assets and military personnel remaining from the Salvadorian Civil War. The boredom had opened Rivera's mind to poignant, painful introspection.

"There are limited coping skills for navigating Hell, son," replied the colonel seriously.

"It's not the bad people that I've killed, sir. They deserved it. What's punching my express ticket to Hell is the evil I perpetrated by killing kids, by killing women, the folks you accountants label as collateral damage, Colonel," explained Rivera. "There must be a special place in Hell for people like me, and I need—" The radio interrupted Rivera as he pressed one earphone to his ear. After listening for a moment, Rivera announced, "We've got injured back at the base. They need immediate medical evacuation." The seasoned helicopter pilot banked the chopper around for the return. "Ground Nine, this is Swift Sword. Roger that. Returning to base. Over."

"Hey, wait! You get permission from me before you turn around!" demanded the colonel.

"A mine exploded, sir. One dead. Two wounded," replied Rivera.

"Are the wounded critical?" asked the colonel.

"No, but one is serious. He is currently stable—for now," replied Rivera.

"American or El Salvadorian?"

"I don't know, *amigo*. You're asking a *Cubano*. I love everyone."

"Look Captain, I've got an itinerary. You tell them to stabilize those guys on the ground, and you can come back for them after you've dropped me off in forty minutes." Rivera ignored the colonel and punched the throttle for emphasis. "Are you ignoring a direct order, Captain?"

"No, sir. I was ignoring you momentarily while I consider your direct order," Rivera said, turning his attention to some navigation systems for a few seconds.

"I will court martial you, Captain!"

Rivera smiled confidently and sent the helicopter into a rapid five hundred foot descent. After leveling out, he turned to the accountant who also happened to be a colonel, who was now very nauseated. "*Now*, I'm ignoring your order! I'll see you at the proceedings, sir."

Rivera repelled the dozens of insults, threats, and orders for the rest of the flight. When he landed his helicopter, a team of waiting soldiers loaded up a man with face and neck trauma, who was breathing mostly through a tracheotomy tube. The colonel was too angry to care about the injured. The other casualty climbed in under his own power. His left hand was heavily bandaged. "Thanks for coming back, Captain" he exclaimed. "They say I only have an hour or two to get these sewn back on." In his right hand, he was holding an ice pack containing his severed fingers.

Sixty days later, and back in the United States, Rivera had been discharged from a Veteran's Administration psychiatric unit, and he was now reporting to Fort Sam Houston to attend his pretrial hearing. The event lasted twenty-six minutes. During the hearing, the surgical notes from the physicians who treated the injured soldiers explained how a twenty minute delay would've cost one man his life and another man at least two fingers. The judge immediately exonerated Rivera, slammed down the gavel and made a hasty exit for his chambers. Once the judge was alone at his desk, he removed the top ten sheets of Rivera's personnel file, and faxed them to a little-known fax number. His note on the cover sheet read:

> *This one's got the goods and availability for the special training you've been selectively offering. Definitely not your average soldier. Call me ASAP. I'll explain.*

Twelve hours later, Rivera was back in his barracks, reflecting on his past life, his present situation, and the vast unknown days ahead. Rivera knew that the medications from the VA were slowly but surely helping to pull him out of his depression. With the proper and good use of the medications, the therapy was much more effective, and they were helping him to realize some paths in his life that he may want to take. He truly appreciated his psychiatrist, who not only listened to him, but also was able to very gently make changes to his medications. Each change seemed to help him incrementally in an overall positive direction. Rivera reflected on the recent death he had prevented by defying the colonial's order, as well as the man's fingers he had saved during his final days in El Salvador. Yet, he was hurting because of the many good people he had killed, accidentally.

At that moment it really sank in that Rivera had done much more good than harm. Rivera started to remember all the lives he had saved, villages he had defended, and families he had kept intact, and his pulse quickened. Deep down he knew that he helped many more good people than he had killed.

Over the last few weeks, he had started to realize a sense of fight that was awakening within him, and he was feeling stronger. The talks with his psychiatrist and pastor were starting to make more sense, and he started to realize that he must consider the possibility of redemption in some way, shape or form.

Eight days after his pre-trial hearing, Rivera picked up a phone, drew in a deep breath, and dialed the number for his commanding officer.

"Colonel Franks." The man's voice that answered the phone was stereotypically gruff.

Rivera shifted in his seat. It was time to jump back into the action. "Sir, this is Rivera."

"Well, hello Captain. Congratulations on your successful pre-trial hearing victory, and putting that Pentagon accounting pussy in his place. They don't give medals for that kind of bravery, but it sure left an impression on the brass."

Rivera smiled and sat up taller. Recollections of respect for his C.O. washed through his memory. "Sir, I'm ready to return to service. But, can you assign me someplace stateside where I can gain medical skills and save lives?" he asked. "I need that now, and it will give me some time to prepare to take the Medical College Admission Test. I know people think I'm crazy, but this is what I'm going to do. I have to go to medical school—period."

"Yes Captain Rivera, of course. But I also got a phone call from somebody I think you should meet," the commanding officer said.

"Who's that?"

"I have orders not to share any information over the phone. But I will tell you that it's much bigger than you, the Army, or me. You need to have a very private conversation with this person, and I guarantee that you'll be signing some nondisclosure agreements."

CHAPTER 1

JANUARY, SIOUX FALLS REGIONAL HOSPITAL

Troy Stoker, M.D. passed quickly through the emergency room doors as he had done thousands of times during his work as a physician at Sioux Falls Regional Hospital. But, this time was different. It was not his normal confident stride that moved him through the doors to perform a psychiatric consult. On this occasion, two emergency medical technicians propelled him on a gurney, and Stoker was affixed to it with a strategically woven scheme of Velcro straps.

Stoker was only vaguely aware of his surroundings. Just minutes ago, he had lost more than two liters of blood, and he had lost it fast. Stoker had felt the terror of fading to unconsciousness while confronting the possibility of bleeding to death. Thankfully, the EMTs arrived moments later, stopped the bleeding, and started an IV to temporarily replace some of the blood that now stained the carpet on his office floor. Despite the shock, nausea, and pain all competing for his attention, he was uncomfortably aware of the Velcro straps across his forehead and chin that immobilized his spine. The tie-downs impeded his every effort to move, talk, swallow, and breathe. It was Stoker's turn to be a patient, and he felt a deep vulnerability that disagreed with the independent spirit he had enjoyed for decades.

For only the second time in his psychiatry career, a patient had attacked him, and this time the man managed to injure him. Unfortunately, his patient, Tom DuPont, had been strong, paranoid, and motivated that afternoon. It was the first time Dr. Stoker had ever reached for the Taser he had fastened to the bottom of his office chair. Tonight the device saved his life.

As Dr. Stoker torpedoed atop his gurney through the emergency room hallways, he gasped for air. Yet, even with all the pain and discomfort, he managed to find some mental capacity to appreciate his decision, months ago, to remove the .40 caliber pistol that used to reside secured to the bottom of that chair.

The emergency room physician Dr. Simmons ran alongside the gurney. "I never imagined I'd see the day when Dr. Troy Stoker would come through our doors all beat up. I'm truly flabbergasted." They wheeled him into a trauma bay and Dr. Simmons began listening all over his torso with a stethoscope. "How many guys jumped you?" Stoker managed to hold up a single index finger. He was in too much pain to be proud, and he never made excuses.

Every few seconds Simmons would find a new spot to situate his stethoscope. "Good news, Troy. As you probably guessed, you have a small hole in your lung. And, the good thing is it's not a large pneumothorax. Give me a minute and I think we can have you breathing one hundred percent better."

Down the hall in another exam room Stoker could hear his violent patient who had arrived in a separate ambulance. The paranoid and agitated Tom DuPont was yelling psychotically. "I am not a spirit! I am not a spirit! Do you hear me? Do you understand me? I demand to know your mission!"

Just forty-five minutes earlier Dr. Stoker had been welcoming this patient, Tom DuPont, into his office in downtown Sioux Falls for a one o'clock appointment. It was their sixth visit in the last three months. Until now DuPont had progressed well in his battle with schizophrenia, in which he experienced mumbling voices that were only present in his head. The medication, Abilify, had helped him tremendously. However, when Tom mixed illicit substances with his mental illness, he could aggravate his condition and override the medication that normally kept the schizophrenia in check.

After the first session, Tom had agreed to sign a contract with Dr. Stoker promising to stop his alcohol and substance abuse. If he neglected this agreement, Dr. Stoker would not see him for any further visits. DuPont had signed the document with conviction and determination. For ninety days DuPont had taken the Abilify and remained sober, a fact he confirmed with a signature from his Narcotics Anonymous sponsor for Dr. Stoker, after attending his meetings two times each week. DuPont had also reached a significant decision point by recognizing his need to cut out the cocaine and tequila as a means of self-medicating his schizophrenia. However, this particular afternoon Dr. Stoker had no idea that Tom DuPont was experiencing his first meth rush in months.

Right after DuPont checked in with the receptionist, he walked back to the bathroom and snorted a couple hits to offset his anxiety about visiting with the psychiatrist. Needless to say, the dopamine rush the chemicals induced was the last thing Tom's already active brain needed.

At the beginning of the therapy session, Dr. Stoker noticed that Tom was indeed more energetic than usual. Tom wanted to vent about recent frustrations. Instead of sitting comfortably, as he had done in the other visits, Tom was standing up and pacing about the office as he ranted about the circumstances of his life and recent events. Something was not right, and Stoker was on guard.

Tom's manic behavior set off alarm bells in Dr. Stoker's head. Ten minutes into the appointment Tom's rage reached a frighteningly disruptive level, which Stoker recognized as an elevated danger sign. But with a firm, friendly, and authoritative voice, Dr. Stoker gave Tom instructions to sit down. Twice the psychiatrist redirected him into more constructive thought patterns. However, twenty minutes into the appointment, Tom refused to sit and he shouted his complaints with the rage of a badger. Now fully manic and psychotic, he swung his arms and cleared off a bookshelf. Then he punched a wall, burying his hand into the drywall. Next Dr. Stoker dodged Tom's roundhouse, but failed to avoid the large coffee table Tom flipped over as if it were a blackjack card. As the corner of the table struck Dr. Stoker just below his right shoulder, he heard a pop and felt the intense pain of air rushing into his pleural space. Tom's next weapon was a wooden office chair. He hurled it at his doctor, and Stoker raised his arms defensively and blocked the blow. But as the sharp edge of the chair leg impacted his left forearm, the angle and force of the glancing blow tore back a flap of flesh from his inside forearm and severed numerous blood vessels. Suddenly, Dr. Stoker was bleeding profusely.

Stoker fell toward the ground and somehow managed to roll toward his chair where he could reach for his lifeline. When Tom reared up like a grizzly bear, Dr. Stoker knew he only had one option for getting out of this alive. The look Stoker saw in DuPont's eyes at that moment was the same look he'd seen before, dozens of times, working on acute psychiatry units. This patient was completely psychotic and the voices were so loud within his brain—the voices commanding him to kill. Troy Stoker, M.D., was trained to recognize that expression in his patient's wild eyes.

Dr. Stoker reached his arm out while ignoring thunderbolts of pain in his chest and grasped the Taser. With a swift motion he pointed the weapon towards Tom's chest and pulled the trigger. As every muscle in the psychotic patient's body contracted, Tom fell to the floor with his head whipping sideways and smashing squarely alongside Dr. Stoker's knee. Another shock of pain emanated briefly from his knee, but quickly faded, as the horrific pain of his collapsing lung demanded all of his ability to feel pain. Then Stoker's vision tunneled and blurred. His panic was stunted by the darkness of unconsciousness that enveloped him.

At some point Stoker returned to a vague, bewildered consciousness in the presence of two EMTs who were lifting him from his office floor and onto a gurney. The ride in the ambulance was only a blurry memory. But since arriving at the hospital, Stoker's consciousness was returning on a minute-by-minute basis.

Dr. Simmons reached into a drawer, pulled on some gloves, donned a surgical mask, and started giving instructions to a nurse. "Marnie, please prep Dr. Stoker there on his right side. Let's deal with this pneumothorax so Dr. Stoker can get back to breathing normally. Our surgical consult, Dr. Singh, should be here any second."

Stoker wheezed before he gulped another breath of air. He still felt a slight panic with each difficult breath. "Let's get this show on the road, Doc."

Dr. Simmons sat down beside Stoker and did a little more listening with his stethoscope. Marnie quickly set out a few supplies and then proceeded to swab Dr. Stoker's chest with Betadine. Within a minute the surgeon arrived.

"Hello, Dr. Stoker. My name is Dr. Singh. I'm on call for general surgery and trauma this evening. I'm also the chief resident."

"No explanations," whispered Stoker. "Let's aspirate!"

"Okay, say no more," Dr. Singh said.

Dr. Singh moved gracefully and efficiently, evidencing quite clearly that he had performed this procedure hundreds of times. The young surgeon from India listened to Dr. Stoker's abdomen with the stethoscope, gently touched a few spots on his chest, and then proceeded to insert a respectable sized needle into Stoker's chest. As he gently threaded the needle just about halfway between Stoker's right nipple and his fractured collarbone, it eventually reached a depth that produced a soft hiss. As the misplaced air escaped Stoker's chest, he started to breathe easier. With each breath he could inhale a little deeper. Within seconds the pain in his chest subsided substantially. Now, the pain signals from the nerves in his knee started to make their way to his brain, but they were much weaker. With two more minutes of work, Dr. Singh skillfully finished the procedure.

"Oh yeah, now that's progress," whispered Troy Stoker. "You know, Dr. Singh, you're one cool cucumber and I appreciate your good work. Thank you." Stoker repositioned his head on his pillow and rearranged that IV tubing running along his arm. "I'm back from the dead, once again. That's the most dead I've felt since Yugoslavia," referring to his relief work during his time as an Army medical officer in the late 1990s.

"Well, Dr. Stoker, now that you're stable, let's see if we can talk you into a consult on that forearm and collarbone, and an x-ray on that knee," Dr. Simmons said. "Let's call in the on-call orthopedic surgeon."

"Who's on for ortho tonight?" asked Dr. Stoker through his oxygen mask.

"It's Stintson," replied Dr. Simmons.

Dr. Stoker grimaced. "Who's on for ortho tomorrow?" Stoker asked.

"Stephano, I think."

"Um, can we put this knee on ice until tomorrow?" Dr. Stoker asked with an air of sarcastic diplomacy.

"Good call," replied Dr. Simmons with neither sarcasm nor diplomacy.

It was a well-known fact that Larry Stintson was an orthopedic surgeon of poor integrity and questionable ability. He had an uncaring outlook toward people and a deep devotion to money and power. Indeed Dr. Stintson was a powerful man. Due to his generous political donations, some old high school connections, and family notoriety, he had been appointed as the president of the South Dakota Medical Board. This position was largely due to his good fortune of being born into a family that was a South Dakota medical dynasty. His mother had been a trailblazing female general surgeon, and within his extended family of siblings, uncles, and cousins there were more than a dozen other doctors. Most of them practiced in Sioux Falls, but few referred patients to him.

Stintson's nickname around town was the "psychopathic surgeon," and the thought of the man operating on Stoker caused him more consternation than his collapsed lung had.

Fifteen minutes into his recovery, Troy Stoker's wife, Allie, burst into the trauma room with guarded concern in her eyes. She was accompanied by the Stokers' good friend, Dr. Errol Rivera, whose intense worry for his friend was evidenced by the purple blood vessels bulging out from the side of his head, which were easy to see thanks to his high and tight military haircut.

Stoker was grateful that Allie had not seen him at his worst, although it's not as if she couldn't handle it. Allie was stoic by nature, and he had never seen her bristle at injury or illness. Still he knew his condition a few minutes earlier would've bothered Allie—at least a little bit. Rivera, on the other hand, was not a typical physician. He became deeply emotional about pain as well as social injustice, the value of history, the Second Amendment, and Ron Paul. "Who did this to you?" Rivera asked.

Stoker motioned with his head. "The disembodied spirit a few doors down." Allie and Rivera acknowledged the commotion coming from down the hall, but still looked at Stoker with confused looks. "He was my patient and now they're treating him in one of the rooms down the hall. I got caught in the crossfire between the raging voices in his head. Something tells me his tox screen will tell us the rest of the story; and I suspect that we'll find that a methamphetamine overdose flooded his neurons with dopamine and fueled his psychosis."

"Hey, Stoker. Forget your psychiatry talk and babble," Rivera said. "That punk's lucky to be here in the hospital, or about now he'd be wondering where his throat, eyeballs, and testicles went."

"Yeah. For now he'll just have to get used to his new tattoo," Stoker said referring to the mark left by the Taser. "It looks like a black widow bite."

"You used the Taser?" Allie asked with a tone of awe and disbelief in her voice.

" Affirmative. First time."

"Wow! Seven point five million volts. That's ECT Stoker style," Rivera said. "I like it!"

"No. That's 'Say hello to my little friend,'" Stoker said in an atrocious Cuban accent. While his accent was poor, his humor hit a bull's-eye with Rivera, who emigrated from Cuba to the United States as a child. In Rivera's work at the Veteran's Administration Medical Center he often took advantage of one-liners from the movie *Scarface*. Rivera's odd mixture of testosterone-propelled strength, wittiness, and interpersonal warmth created a mystique that surrounded him in the medical community. His history also supposedly contained deep, dark secrets people spoke about in whispers.

When Dr. Simmons returned he ordered a series of x-rays and told Stoker about the game plan. "I'm going to have them take an x-ray of your collarbone and ribs and also take a picture of your knee. You may have a tibial plateau fracture," Simmons said referring to a fracture just below the knee. "After that, let's discharge you home to get some rest."

"What? You're not going to do an ortho consult on him?" protested Rivera.

"Not with Stintson on ortho call," interjected Stoker before Dr. Simmons could say anything.

"Oh yeah. Let's get you out of here," insisted Rivera. "I'm not letting that whack job work on the man who helps all the whack jobs."

"Whack job?" challenged Stoker. "Now that's the pot calling the kettle black, Rivera."

Rivera smiled. He was comfortable with his edgy personality. "Who's on for ortho tomorrow?"

Rivera never got an answer. Stoker's breathing stopped instantaneously, and again, darkness enshrouded him faster than he could piece together his next thoughts. Before he could form words or reach out to grab Allie's hand, consciousness vanished.

CHAPTER 2

CHELSEA CROSSING, SIOUX FALLS

Ann Higgins was relieved to be back in her comfort zone. It was Friday afternoon, and Ann was selling real estate—an activity she had set aside for the last few months as she had been on the campaign trail with her husband. She was showing homes to some of her friends in a new development, Chelsea Crossing, a large-scale planned community in Sioux Falls. It was a slice of paradise with homes built along golf course fairways, or in close proximity to swimming pools, walking trails, fishing ponds, and parks to create a familial wonderland. Chelsea Crossing even had its own elementary school. Ann and two other financial partners were the developers on the project, and it was Ann's job to sell all of the new homes.

She was thrilled to be back from the campaign trail—a successful campaign. Her husband of twenty-three years had emerged the victor, and was now the Lieutenant Governor-elect of South Dakota. Ann had never expected Kent Higgins to be a man of power or stature in the community. She had fallen in love with him all those years ago because he was kind, honest, and sincere. Back then, she even had her doubts about his ambition. After all, his life's dream was to teach high school history. But a lot had changed in almost two decades.

In college, Kent had not only studied history, but he had also earned a degree in respiratory therapy. He knew supporting a family on a teacher's salary would be difficult, so he made ends meet by picking up two weekly shifts as a respiratory therapist at Sioux Falls Regional Hospital. During the summer, he picked up every extra shift he could; and his co-workers loved him, because it meant that the other respiratory therapists could take much-needed vacations.

Ann had just handed her clients some brochures that included a map of Chelsea Crossing and pictures of families swimming, playing at the park, hiking on the trails, and golfing. "I want to show you a home that is similar to the layout and square footage you are talking about. It's out on Bryant Way." Ann opened her car door and climbed into the driver's seat, while her clients jumped into the back seat of her comfortable SUV. "Now this one's already under contract," she explained as she pulled out of her office parking lot. "But, if you like it you could build something similar to it—with your custom choices, of course."

Ann and her clients made small talk as they drove through Chelsea Crossing. Ann was one of Sioux Falls top real estate agents, and she was also the CEO of her own successful realty franchise. Her participation in the Chelsea Crossing development partnership was going extremely well. Life could not have been more perfect for Ann Higgins. But it had not always been this way.

Three years ago, as a new CEO and high-sales realtor, Ann Higgins experienced some serious problems. She prided herself on being on top of each detail. She insisted on micromanaging everything. However, after a near-nervous breakdown, she received some professional help. She started seeing Dr. Troy Stoker, whose psychiatric therapy and carefully managed medication helped her out of her obsessive-compulsive pattern of micromanagement.

"There are good things about your obsessive compulsive tendencies," explained Dr. Stoker in a therapy session. "You pay attention to the details. But, this micromanagement is swinging you too far to the perfectionist side and you're draining yourself of your energy and your ability to function efficiently. We can find strategies to decrease these symptoms."

Ann followed Dr. Stoker's recommendations. As an obsessive-compulsive person, she followed his care plan to the letter. Consequently, Ann started taking medication, hired a new chief operating officer and a dynamic executive assistant to attend to more of the businesses details. With their help, she re-focused her energies on key transactions, and she dedicated her time to her natural strengths, sales and developing new business. She was happy again, and today was another satisfying day out with clients.

As Ann and her prospective buyers pulled onto Bryant Way, the couple in the back seat commented that they liked how the homes on this street backed to waterfront property. "If you like living next to the water, we still have a few similar lots available." Ann knew how to help people dream by opening their minds to the possibilities. "Some people prefer living close to swimming and fitness, others want to be able to walk to a tennis court in a minute or less, and others want to be right by the park for their kids."

"Close to the golf course is all I need," the young husband said as Ann pulled the car into the driveway at 5644 Bryant Way. They got out of the car and walked up the front steps to the front door. Ann grabbed onto the lock box that was hanging on the doorknob and entered the combination that opened the device. She took out the key, unlocked the door, and ushered her clients into the home. As always, she started by showing them the kitchen.

"As you can see these owners have chosen just the basics. There is nothing special about the flooring, appliances or countertops."

"We would definitely be doing some upgrading," interjected the woman client.

The arrival of the three uninvited guests to 5644 Bryant Way did not go unnoticed. Frank Thompson was working next door at 5660 Bryant Way. He happened to be an employee of the firm that recently purchased both of the homes as investment properties. He was certain that the bosses would never want the lieutenant governor-elect's wife snooping around their new properties. The bosses had plans for 5644 and 5660 Bryant Way—the kind of plans that somebody such as Ann Higgins could quickly derail. Frank took out his cell phone and sent a text.

> *Ann Higgins and two others just walked into 5644 Bryant Way.*

The response arrived rapidly.

> *Get rid of them. Tell them they're trespassing. Must leave immediately.*

Thompson placed his phone back in his pocket, hastily exited 5660 Bryant Way, and paced across the lawn.

Ann showed her clients the bedrooms, bathrooms, living room, and the rest of the living spaces. "Let me show you the unfinished basement." The trio began walking down the stairs. "It is nothing spectacular, but you can envision how you could use some space down here for a man cave, additional bedrooms, storage space, or whatever you would like." Ann and her guests walked into the plain, cement-dominated architecture of a dimly lit basement. She turned on a light and the couple wandered through the space. "That's interesting," commented the man pointing to the corner of the basement. "Do you build all of your basements with those intense trenches and drains? Is there a big problem with the water table here?"

Ann Higgins was surprised by what she saw in the corner of the basement. The cement floor was sloped into a gravel-filled corner, which contained a large drain. "Actually, no. I didn't realize they had made this upgrade in this home. It is highly unusual, and completely unnecessary in my opinion." Ann Walked to the corner, squatted down, and ran her finger along the PVC drainpipe and black grate that was covering it. "This is called a French drain, and I am intrigued. I don't know why it is here. They are popular in states such as Louisiana and Florida where, like you say, water tables are high. There is no reason to have one here in Chelsea Crossing or almost anywhere in the greater Sioux Falls area."

Ann stood up and looked around. Immediately, she noticed that there were extra electrical outlets installed along the walls as well as an additional set of water hookups for a clothes washer and dryer. "Why would anybody need two washing machines and two dryers?" wondered Ann aloud. These strange additions fueled her curiosity. A small mystery was unfolding before her. To spend so much money in the unfinished basement, but not upgrade carpet and appliances in the true living spaces made no sense to Ann. As she further surveyed the basement, she noticed that the owners had opted for an on-demand hot water system instead of the conventional tank-style hot water heater. Ann was momentarily fascinated with the unit, and she reached up to open the door covering its pipes, electronics, and mechanics. As she pulled the door open, a scroll of paper fell from the inside of the door and landed on the ground.

Ann picked up the scroll and unrolled it. She examined the hand-drawing but struggled to understand its meaning. She rotated it 90 degrees, and then another 90 degrees, and then the space became clear. It was a depiction of the very basement she was standing in. She recognized the placement of the staircase, heating, and air conditioning systems, as well as the still unexplained water spigots and power outlets. However, this drawing contained so much more. She saw numerous lines, boxes, notes, and other symbols that she did not understand.

Somebody had some plans for this basement; and while Ann Higgins did not understand them, her intuition told her there was something troublesome in this home's future. Fortunately for Ann, even with alarms going off in her head, she knew she could not panic in front of her clients. The new source of stress mysteriously brought her mind into focus. In situations where most people would have been overridden by anxiety and panic, Ann was clear-headed. "I think we need to leave," stated Ann frankly to her clients.

She took out her phone and started snapping pictures of the plans. She took pictures from afar that captured the whole image and then she took pictures of different sections up close to capture all of the detail. She knew that she could piece it all together with her computer if she needed to.

After she had taken a dozen pictures of the hand-drawn sketch, she carefully replaced it within the metal cabinet of the on-demand hot water heater. Then she took her phone and snapped off another two-dozen pictures of the basement. "All right, I think we're done here." Ann motioned for the couple to climb the stairs. Once on the main level, she directed them to the front door and rushed them outside. As they stepped out on the front stoop, they met Frank Thompson who came charging up the driveway with authoritative body language.

"Hey, aren't you Ann Higgins?" His tone was confrontational.

Ann was not one to be intimidated. "Indeed I am. What's your name?"

"My name is not important. The problem here is you're trespassing! You need to leave immediately."

"Well, sir," responded Ann, "before this home closes; I just wanted to show it to my clients as an example."

"Actually, Mrs. Higgins, we closed on this unit last week."

Ann realized she'd made a mistake by showing a home that was someone's private property, but she did not let it fluster her. "Then, I am sorry for the misunderstanding." Her apology was sincere but not pandering. "I did not know that the owner had taken possession. Why didn't the key box get removed?"

"Now, that's a good question," responded Thompson in a sarcastic and disrespectful tone. "Isn't that your job, Ann?" Thompson's accusation set off Ann's micromanager anxiety. Somebody on her team, whom she had trusted, had failed in his assignment. She remembered how she never overlooked these details, back when she did it all. There was going to be hell to pay at the office on Monday.

Ann fumbled a little to place the key back in the key box. "I'll take the key box with me right now." Ann placed the device in her purse. "Besides, we were only in there for a second. Once we saw the drab kitchen, I knew it was an uninspiring example of craftsmanship for my clients." As they walked to the car, Ann called to the man. "Hey, Mr. Unimportant Name!" Thompson looked at her surprised. "It was a simple mistake, and this is a friendly neighborhood. You might consider adjusting your attitude a bit around here."

"Lady, if you knew my employers, you would thank me for the courtesy I've exercised today. In case you didn't get the memo, we closed on the house next door, too. Now get off our property."

Ann stepped into her car and chauffeured her clients away. "I'm sorry about that situation."

"No, don't worry," chimed in the male client. "But, there is something out-of-the-ordinary going on there. I'd keep my eye on those two properties. What do you have on the *other* side of Chelsea Crossing?"

CHAPTER 3

SIOUX FALLS REGIONAL HOSPITAL

Errol Rivera was slapping Stoker's face. "Stay with me here, Troy! *Ay!* Wake up, *flaco!*" he yelled as he glanced up at the heart rate and blood pressure monitors. "Allie, how come your wussy husband can't keep his blood pressure up? The *loco* is freaking us out." Rivera turned to Allie for a moment and explained. "His blood pressure just dropped, so he's taking an involuntary nap. It's no big deal. This just happens sometimes after patients lose a lot of blood."

For the first time in their marriage, Allie Stoker was worried for her husband's life, and she was not going to stand idly by. From her vantage point, Dr. Rivera was under reacting. "Well Errol, stop with the lecture and do something about it!"

Rivera reached underneath the exam table, pulled a lever, and elevated Stoker's feet. "Relax, *sardina*. The only way your beast of a husband will ever die is when I stab him in the heart with my grandma's silver cross." Rivera reached over to Stoker's IV and opened the valve all the way, allowing the maximum flow of saline solution into Stoker's blood stream.

The nurse rushed into the room. "What's going on in here?" She had been alerted by a blood pressure alarm at the nurse's station.

"Oh Marnie, my friend here is entertaining us by terrifying his wife! I just raised his feet and opened up his saline a little. He should be returning to consciousness momentarily." Rivera continued to aggressively slap Stoker's face.

"So no defib paddles?" Allie asked with uncharacteristic alarm in her voice.

"Only if you *really* want to. I suggest slaps in the face, instead. His blood pressure's improving, his pulse is strong. And believe me, this is nothing." Rivera looked at the unconscious Stoker. "Hey, *amigo*! Hey, you're such a tough guy!"

Troy Stoker snapped back to consciousness, thanks to Rivera's appropriate response. The face slapping was probably a factor, too.

"Welcome back, *princesa*," joked Rivera. "Now you have me to thank for saving your life! You owe me dinner! You're taking me to that restaurant, *Carnaval*."

"What was that?" Stoker asked with a groggy voice. "Why are you touching me, Rivera? Are you going all, what do you call it, *maricon* on me? Get your stinkin' hands off of me."

"See Allie? Didn't I tell you? Your man of steel thinks he's funny just because he can insult me in my mother tongue. This *yuma*, with fourteen Spanish words in his vocabulary, still manages to recall one of them when he's half out of his *loca cabeza*." Rivera slowed the flow of the IV, and took a look at the blood pressure, pulse, and other readings on the monitor. Then, he turned to Allie. "Here's what happened, Mrs. Stoker. Troy lost a little blood. The monitors say he's fine. I touched him a little bit to wake him up, and *bang*! He's up. Now let's get out of here before he insults me again! Don't worry. He's good. He's going to be fine. We're out of here."

Stoker sat up a little taller. "Yes. Get me out of here. I think you're enjoying this weird slapping too much. Is this an old technique they taught you in medical school, or what?"

Turning to Stoker, Rivera smirked as he stood and headed for the door. "Hey *guapo*, we'll see you soon. I'm going to tell Dr. Simmons to get you on the discharge fast-track."

CHAPTER 4

Nothing helped the intense man with striking blue eyes sharpen his mental focus or keep his priorities in line like assessing his investment portfolios. He often did just that on Friday afternoons. He was a neat, orderly man. His desk was perfectly straight and his secretary in his Pierre, South Dakota office helped him keep meticulous records. He liked things to match and he liked to "make all the pieces fit together," to the point of obsession.

For example, a few years ago, he was sick of using shaving cream, soap, shampoo, conditioner, deodorant, and cologne that all had different scents. To his discriminating sense of smell, the fragrances often clashed. So, the tidy, intense man purchased a dozen bottles of his favorite cologne and asked a compounding pharmacy to create all of the toiletries with the same fragrance. Now he smelled excellent on a consistent basis. With a subtle, steady, and commanding scent, he perceived that he caught more female attention, too.

During his career—the one that the IRS, his family, few friends, and the public knew about—he had contributed to a 401K, bought stocks, bonds, and mutual funds, and invested in some apartment complexes. The state of South Dakota paid him reasonably well, and his recent election would further improve his lifestyle. An accountant or banker would value his known net worth at a little more than $1 million. It was easy to check on the current status and performance of these investments with just about any web-enabled computer or device. It was all online.

However, the intense man had only a general idea of his *true* net worth. After all, he could only look up *some* of his hidden assets on his small laptop computer. Only he, his accountant and right-hand man, Ron Cunningham, and an IT consultant residing in Reno, Nevada knew about this small device, which was the window to his world of a completely different conglomeration of enterprises. This computer used an encrypted wireless signal to tap into a virtual private network. If anybody were to attempt to hack him or spy on him digitally, they would get jumbled data and a digital footprint that made it look as if he were accessing the Internet through a Wi-Fi hotspot in a seedy Los Angeles neighborhood—the kind where people tended to rent rooms and small apartments on a pay-as-you-go basis with all leases being verbal and notoriously flexible.

His offshore bank accounts totaled more than $2 million, but thanks to the protections afforded by the laws of the state of Nevada, the intense man did not find offshore banking as appealing and mandatory as he had once assumed. He had another $4 million of laundered funds in a corporate bank account in Las Vegas. Even still, bank accounts were so boring and intangible. He was a man who loved to touch, hold and caress the fruits of his labors. It had been years since he'd counted up all of the gold bars and diamonds he owned. He received quarterly reports on the restaurants and pubs his syndicate owned, and he loved the results. He had purchased the gold and diamonds, a little at a time, with small cash investments—dirty money, of course. He had filled two safe deposit boxes in Pierre; and according to his underlings, he now owned one in Sioux Falls. Banks in Cancun, Mexico and two Caribbean islands each housed some of his assets within cement and steel safe-deposit fortresses.

He also owned tracts of farmland, which he always acquired in a distressed state. His agricultural businesses had been ninety-nine percent grain and feed and one percent marijuana. But now, the marijuana was gone. When the United State Drug Enforcement Agency and local sheriff departments started using high tech helicopter surveillance equipment to scan cornfields and detect cannabis growing, intermingled with corn, it drove the commander out of the pot producing business. Still, the land parcels were worth holding from a financial perspective. Even without the high profit margins of marijuana production, he just loved the power of owning thousands of acres of the most productive farmland in the world. He also learned that barns and farmhouses were some of the last places on earth law enforcers would search for the offices of online identity thieves. The intense man with the deep blue eyes was now overseeing a ring of more than a dozen staffers, using digital cloaking from rural locations, to create falsified lines of credit and sign up for fraudulent credit cards that the commander would use to fatten up his portfolio on a daily basis.

But, the biggest question mark in his portfolio was the value of his small but lucrative "factories" that now produced one of the most demanded substances of the current day and age. The commander's labs produced modest amounts of what drug addicts used to call ice, speed, crank, wash, Tina, gak, or jib. Now the popular stimulant was known by dozens of nicknames. Soon, the intense man's new properties in Chelsea Crossing would be quietly manufacturing whatever the locals wanted to call their meth at the moment.

The intense man was also looking to the future, and heroin had made a ferocious rebound in popularity. Poppy fields in Mexico and Columbia had made opium plentiful, and science had helped heroin chemists radically increase its potency. With hits of heroin selling for about the same price as a high-end cup of coffee, people were using it ravenously. The intense man's portfolio now included poppy farms in Mexico. But, he wisely decided to avoid financing any cross-border smuggling operations. Instead, he was financing some research and development on synthetic heroin that was starting to look promising.

He loved the money, the power, and the risk he lived with every day. Each of his factories we're churning out about $4,000 per day in product. It was a small enough operation to keep the police from noticing, and a large enough business to increase his unofficial income by hundreds of thousands of dollars per year. His net worth from his "creative" side-ventures exceeded $17 million. Nobody else knew, besides his accountant in Reno, Ron Cunningham.

As the intense man used his small computer to account for the week's identity theft earnings and meth production, a small cell phone vibrated in his pocket. This was a phone he used rarely, so he answered quickly.

"Hi Commander," Harry Klein said. Commander was the title everyone used to address the intense man. "One of my workers out at Chelsea Crossing reports that Ann Higgins is out snooping around." Klein, a project manager within Green Growth Ventures, worked with the commander almost daily by telephone, but had rarely met with him in person, and only in Reno. Klein assumed that the commander was based in Reno, and he had no idea that the commander was sitting in a government office in Pierre, South Dakota, just a few miles away.

"Two things. Where did she go? What did she see?" the commander demanded.

"She was inside of 5644 Bryant Way, but we don't know if she went into the basement," Klein said.

"Idiots! Who's responsible for the situational awareness of this operation?"

"I've been overseeing the real estate deal and Frank Thompson's work," Klein admitted. "There are at least four other people in the chain of command between you and Thompson, so you're well protected by many layers of relationships, sir. While this Thompson guy knows we're not the nicest people in South Dakota, he has no idea what's really going on in those homes."

"Okay, here's the plan. First, don't touch Ann Higgins. But, I need a tail on her twenty-four hours a day. I'll worry about her in my own way. Second, no more work on those basements for at least a month. If anybody asks you or Thompsons what's going on in those basements, just tell them the new owners are overly cautious about flooding. Tell them that they had a bad experience years ago that still haunts them."

"Sounds good, Commander."

But, the commander was not finished with his instructions. He loved to hear the sound of his voice booming off the walls of his office. "We can start up operations there when people have forgotten about this little incident. Also, Ann won't dare snoop around anymore. Now we own those properties; and we can hide behind our legal rights to privacy and due process. Let's just hope Ann loses interest in anything she may have seen. We're just days from the inauguration. After that, some of my friends will have even more access to Ann, and I suspect we can find out what she did or did not see."

"Yes sir, Commander."

"And Klein." The commander lowered his voice to a growling whisper. "You're a moron. Your security has been sloppy and you've mismanaged a simple thing like removing a key box—a device that could potentially give dozens of people access to our little venture!" The commander paused for effect. "After we've cleaned up this mess, you're assigned to the farm in Arkansas, and I'm stripping you of your project manager title. You need a little reminder about how good you've had it, and how important it is to watch your back and cover your tracks."

"Yes, sir," Klein said.

"What's the label we put on our security consciousness and procedures, Mr. Klein?"

"Situational awareness, sir."

The commander hung up on Klein. He had lost all interest in his legitimate and criminal financial portfolios. All of his mental energy was now focused on solving the "Ann Higgins" problem.

CHAPTER 5

NEAR MITCHELL, SOUTH DAKOTA

Brian Berg coasted southbound along Interstate 29 in the large Chevrolet sedan he had checked out from the South Dakota state motor pool. Berg had been on the job as an investigator for the South Dakota Medical Board for about a year. At the time he was hired, the circulating rumors whispered that the previous investigator departed quickly and under questionable circumstances.

This afternoon, Berg was returning to Sioux Falls from another "investigation." A South Dakota resident, Veronica Hansen, had filed a complaint against a family practice doctor in Aberdeen, Harold Slade. In her letter to the South Dakota Medical Board, Mrs. Hansen outlined a long story of sorrow, toil, and pain due to a back injury. Hansen had visited Dr. Slade when she could bear the pain no more. Her complaint stated that Dr. Slade scarcely acknowledged her situation, and she accused him of neglect for prescribing ibuprofen and acetaminophen instead of morphine or something stronger for her pain. Even after a week of tearful and pleading phone calls, the apparently heartless Dr. Slade still refused to prescribe the narcotics that she felt she needed to dull her severe pain. The complaint letter concluded that Mrs. Hansen only achieved relief after visiting an urgent care center one night, where a physician assistant offered her deliverance by writing a prescription for oxycodone.

Berg interviewed Dr. Slade about the incident at 1:00 that afternoon. He was more than happy to explain his side of the story. However, this meeting was a mere formality, since three weeks earlier Slade had convincingly defended his actions in a well-written letter. Upon learning of the complaint against him, Slade dictated the letter that explained that he had consulted with Mrs. Hansen, in his office, three times that week. When her pain complaints escalated, he referred her to both a back surgeon and a pain management specialist in Sioux Falls. Mrs. Hansen had refused to keep the appointments. Instead, she chose to refer herself to an urgent care center and exhibited significant drug-seeking behaviors.

The physician board member who reviewed the case, quickly concluded that Dr. Slade had been more than appropriate with his treatment and referrals. Nevertheless, the South Dakota Medical Board was a political machine, and it needed to constantly prove its supposed value. Even with all of this overwhelming evidence that the prudent Dr. Slade was blameless, this case was an opportunity for the South Dakota Medical Board to show the complaining patient that the state was indeed looking out for her best interests. Berg believed in the "never let a good crisis go to waste" notion that was often repeated around the offices of the South Dakota Medical Board. Every citizen complaint was a crisis. It was an opportunity for Brian Berg and the medical board to show all of the other bureaucrats that they were doing their job. It was also important to flaunt just how important they were within the elaborate scheme of state government. Status was the currency of choice in South Dakota state politics, and the medical board had made excellent strides lately in improving its visibility.

Today Brian Berg was about to score another victory for the board. While Dr. Slade's defense against his patient's complaint was airtight, his medication records were not; and Berg was about to turn it into the perfect exploitable crisis.

"Thank you for a moment of your time, Dr. Slade." Berg closed the file folder and slipped it into his backpack. "I will report my findings back to the board. You can rest assured that this matter will be resolved in your favor."

"Not a problem," Slade responded.

"Oh, Doctor. Would you mind if I check in and say hello to your nurses before I leave?" Berg asked.

"Of course not," Slade said. "Be my guest."

That I will, thought Berg as he walked down the corridor to the nurses station. He approached the tidy desk where the nurses and medical assistants made phone calls, managed medical records, updated their Facebook statuses, and kept track of medication, lollipops, and birthdays. He honed in on the most homely girl. Missy was the name on her nametag.

"Hi, Missy. My name is Brian Berg. I'm the *chief* investigator for the South Dakota Medical Board."

"Okay . . . Hi. Um, what can I do for you?" responded Missy, who happened to be a young medical assistant.

"Yeah, I was just meeting with Dr. Slade about a matter. You know, it's kind of routine stuff. And, I need to do a narcotics count and look at your medication logs. Can you please show me where they are?"

"Um, sure." Missy pulled out a white binder. "Here's the log, and we keep all the medications over there," she said as she pointed to a cupboard and refrigerator.

"And, how often do you count the narcotics?"

"Every morning and every night."

"When was the last time *you* counted them?" Berg asked. His question was a snare.

"Oh, it was my turn last Friday," replied Missy naïvely admitting that she had broken the law. Only a person with a license, such as a doctor or nurse, was allowed to perform and document a narcotics count. Medical assistants could not.

Berg examined the narcotics log and quickly found last Friday. The hastily scribbled initials were, "JB, RN."

"Who is JB, RN?" Berg asked.

"Oh, that's Jennifer Boyce, our nurse. Sometimes the MAs count the medications, like on a really busy day, and the nurse signs off on our counts." Missy had just divulged another critical piece of information that Berg would use against the practice.

"Is Jennifer here? I'd like to talk to her." *Wow! This Missy is not the brightest*, thought Berg. She had no idea of the traps she was walking into. *It's rarely this easy*, he thought.

"Yup. Hang on. I'll go find her," Missy said. "Who did you say you are again?"

At that moment her brain answered her own question, and the reality of her situation sank in. She came to the dreadful realization that a government inspector was standing before her, and she had already given him a head start on his investigation.

"I'm Brian Berg, *chief* investigator for the South Dakota Medical Board," he replied.

As he saw the panic on her face, adrenaline surged through his veins. He loved this moment when fear overpowered the minions of medical offices out in the backwaters of South Dakota. This was when Brian Berg felt truly alive.

Missy retreated without saying another word. Berg knew he had a few opportune moments, so he dug back into the medication folder that Missy had so freely granted him access to. This was a well-maintained record. But, he had rarely seen perfect records. All medication records contained opportunities for Berg to exploit.

His finger followed the pages backward. December, November, October, September, August—Bingo! On August thirteenth the nurse had failed to initial the narcotics log that evening. July, June—Bingo again! Another missing set of initials for June twenty-second. That was all he needed. His foot was in the door.

Strike one! thought Berg. *The missing initials on August thirteenth. Strike two is the missing nurse initials on June twenty-second! Strike three's my sweet new friend, Missy, admitting that medical assistants perform the narcotics counts and the nurse just signs her initials! These nurses are failing to ensure that a nurse or other person with a license perform the medication counts. Yes!* This gave Berg some great ammunition for his favorite activity, writing letters of concern.

Just then, Jennifer Boyce arrived at the nurse's station. "Hi, umm, Missy said that you wanted to talk to me? Something about an inspection?"

"Hi Jennifer. I'm Brian Berg, *chief* investigator for the medical board." Berg lifted up the medication log for emphasis. "Yes, I'm doing a little inspection here of your narcotics counts and a few other things. Dr. Slade pointed me in this direction."

Berg's rush resurged as a glint of steel appeared in Jennifer Boyce's angry eyes. *Oh, yes! This one's a fighter! How I love the fighters! From the naïve Missy to the defiant Jennifer Boyce, RN! An emotional bungee jump!*

"Now wait a second here Mr. Berg! What gives you the right to come in here and—"

Brian interrupted. "First, Dr. Slade pointed me in your direction. Second, South Dakota law gives the medical board power to investigate you. Here are a few papers to back me up." Berg removed an envelope from his backpack. "Here's my card and a copy of my badge. Also, here's the law. I think they call it Chapter Thirty or something like that. You can go online and look it up yourself. But, these documents let me inspect your records and count your pills and stuff."

Boyce picked up the papers and glanced briefly at the law. After six seconds of reading the legal document, she knew she could not interpret the legalese on the spot. "Just what do you propose to do?" she asked. "Before you touch a thing, I think I'm going to need to run this by Dr. Slade and our lawyer."

Berg was not about to wait for anyone. Nobody was bringing him off of his power trip. "Like that document says right there, I'm just looking at your medication logs and counting your narcotics." Berg walked over to the medication cabinet and refrigerator. "I'm going to do it right now, and I don't need anybody's permission." He smiled arrogantly. "Get your lawyer down here if you want. I'm glad to include him, and Dr. Slade, too. But first, I need copies of these pages of your narcotics log."

Berg removed the pages he wanted. "I just need June through December, and I'm happy to reimburse you at thirty cents per copy. Can I use that copy machine right over there?"

"Absolutely not!" shot back Boyce. "Not until I've spoken with our attorney."

"And who might that be?" Berg asked.

Jennifer Boyce stammered and stared blankly at him. She had no idea who Dr. Slade's attorney was. Missy, who had been standing about five feet from the desk with a look of terror on her face, just shrugged her shoulders.

"Look, Jennifer. This is just routine stuff," Berg said in his disingenuous, calm voice. "It's just counting and checking. There's no SWAT team here. I don't arrest people. I just don't get why you're resisting a routine inspection that happens every day all across America. I'll be out of your hair in five minutes. Let's just get a few copies for me here, and count through your narcotics together." Berg paused for a moment and looked the nurse in the eye very seriously. "Unless you want me to bring in the big guns. I'll bring a whole team to do a head-to-toe audit of your practice." It was a lie. Berg had neither a team nor a system for performing a huge audit.

Jennifer Boyce thought about it for a moment. "I'm sorry," she said. "I think I over-reacted."

"That's okay," Berg said. "Now, which medication do you want to start with?"

"Morphine injectable vials," replied Boyce.

As they counted, Berg worked hard to keep track of the numbers, but he was actually focusing on expiration dates on the medication vials. So far their counts were spot-on which was no surprise. However, toward the back of the refrigerator, they pulled out a vile of morphine that had expired just two days ago. *Strike four!* Berg thought.

After quizzing Boyce about letting the medical assistants count medications, he reveled in issuing her and Missy a moderately stern verbal warning. Then, Berg walked over to the copy machine—this time without asking—and copied the log pages he had previously requested, plus a few more.

Berg snapped a picture of the expired vial of morphine with an old digital camera. "I need to get my findings back to the board so we can prepare a final report and some other correspondence," Berg said. "This expired vial, the missing initials, and the practice of nurses delegating the narcotics counts are all mild to moderate issues. I think you really need to step up your plan around here, Jennifer."

Berg tossed the camera and copies into his backpack and then turned to the nurse to fabricate some final official-sounding statements. "Look, I'm running short on time. If I had time to stay, I would also ask to look at your OSHA logs. I would inspect your HIPAA compliance and audit your x-ray suite, too," Berg said with lust in his voice. He felt a rush when he saw how the mere mention of more inspections filled Missy's and Jennifer's faces with distress. The truth was, Berg had never inspected anything related to OSHA, HIPAA or x-ray in his life. He wouldn't know how. "But, I think this is enough for today," he said. "If you have any questions, please call me at my office. The number is there on my card."

Brian Berg turned around, walked to the door, and exited Dr. Slade's office. He made his way across the icy parking lot to his state-issued sedan, unlocked the doors, climbed in the car, and started it up. "Shock and awe!" yelled the medical board investigator, as he clumsily backed the car out of the parking space. During the last ten minutes, he had yet again experienced the thrill of putting a nurse in her place, reducing a medical assistant to the point where she could barely control her bladder, and legitimizing the status of his state government job. He craved a cigarette, which he pulled from his pocket, and lusted for a Big Mac Meal, purchased on his State of South Dakota credit card. "Super-size me!" he yelled aloud as he threw the car into drive. "Woohoo!"

CHAPTER 6

As Ann Higgins left Chelsea Crossing's main thoroughfare and pulled onto the main county road, she didn't notice the late-model minivan following her from three hundred yards back. Harry Klein was already on her tail. He would undertake the assignment of keeping tabs on her until he could turn it over to one of his underlings in a few hours.

Ann had dropped off her clients at their car, and now she was headed for home. What started as a few curious observations about twenty-five minutes ago, now occupied her thoughts as a small mystery. By nature, she was an imaginative person and she conjured scenarios in her mind about what she had seen in the unfinished basement of 5644 Bryant Way. However, at that moment Ann Higgins had no idea how deeply her minor misstep would disrupt her family, the government of South Dakota, and her psychiatrist, Dr. Stoker.

Using her hands-free earpiece, Ann dialed her mom as she traveled down the road. "Hi, Mom. How are the kids?" Ann's parents had been involved grandparents during the last few years. They helped by picking the kids up from school, by shuttling them to and from activities, and by helping them with their homework. It was a good arrangement. Tonight was Friday night, and three generations would spend time together by going tubing at Great Bear Recreational Park, eating at HuHot Mongolian Grill, and perhaps heading to the theater if they could find a movie that would appease three generations.

"Everyone's fine, dear. Todd won his hockey game," Ann's mom replied. "Meet you at the tubing hill at 5:45?"

"Yes. That sounds wonderful. I need the fresh air."

Ann and Kent Higgins had never intended to be wealthy or politically powerful. Their goal in life when they married more than two decades ago was simple: To raise great kids and enjoy doing it. So, a few years later, when political and financial success started competing with their simple dream, Ann and Kent began to search for a solution. Kent had just been elected to the city council in their city, Brandon, just a few miles northeast of Sioux Falls. Ann's real estate career was also taking off.

After a month of consideration, Kent had decided that he would leave teaching, keep his position on the City Council, and spend a year as "Mr. Mom." Over time, they would wait for options to open up for their careers, which also allowed them to raise great kids. On the night they made that decision, they took Ann's parents out to dinner and announced their plans. When Ann and Kent told them that Kent would be leaving his teaching position to spend more time with the kids, Ann's mom piped right in. "Absolutely not. Your dad's going to retire from the machine shop."

"I'll turn in the retirement papers tomorrow," Ann's dad said. "They've been offering an early retirement package for the last few months. Now, I'm convinced that it's time for me to take it."

"And I'm cutting back to part-time at the grocery store," Ann's mom insisted. "We'll help you take care of the kids."

"Mom. You know you're not ready to retire," interjected Ann. "You're close, but don't you need to work another three years or so?" And then, a brilliant idea hit Ann. "We'll pay you two thousand dollars per month to take care of the grandchildren. Also, we'll go trade in your thirteen-year-old Buick on an SUV, tomorrow."

The deal was struck, and the grandparents were on board. Two weeks later Ann's dad walked out the door from the machine shop for the last time—thrilled that his bride of forty-five years was picking him up in the new Tahoe.

After Ann ended the call with her mother, her mind immediately turned back to the bizarre basement she had seen on Bryant Way. She needed to get back to her office and think about what to do next. She thought about calling some of the other subcontractors to see if they knew about the strange construction. However, Ann felt that this was one of those occasions when she needed to check things out on her own.

As Ann arrived at her office, she turned off her car, walked to the front door, and let herself in. As she sat down at her desk her phone synched wirelessly with her computer. Within seconds, copies of the pictures of the basement on Bryant Way resided on her computer and on a cloud-based server.

Ann typed a password into her computer, and opened a simple image management program. She located the pictures she had taken, and used cutting a pasting to meld together a single fairly good rendering of the rough construction drawings she had found hidden in the water heater. She saved the new file with the name Bryant_Mystery.

Ann then opened her email, attached the new file to an email to Scott Lewis, a private investigator she had used a few times to check out some real estate title work that did not seem right. The email explained that this was a sensitive and private matter. She asked Lewis to help her figure out what the construction plans were for, and then she requested that he call her.

After sending the email, Ann ignored the 147 new emails that waited for her. Ann knew that opening just one email could end up distracting her and making her family wait for her at Great Bear for tubing. As she had learned to do in therapy with Dr. Stoker, Ann shut down her computer, put her phone in her pocket, and headed out her office door. "Let the team tackle the emails," Ann said aloud. Dr. Stoker had helped her learn to delegate and trust.

A few minutes later she was pulling into a parking spot near the base of the night-lit tubing hill. She parked alongside her parents' Chevrolet Tahoe, stepped out, and then exchanged hugs with her parents and kids before receiving a kiss from her husband, Kent. Finally, she was spending time with her family. During the first ride up the tow lift, her excited son told her about the hockey game. Her daughter, Joanna, explained how a close friend had broken up with her boyfriend. Also, she talked about how all the Democrat kids in social studies were still upset about the Republicans winning most of the state elections.

Ann asked kids about their recent test results as well as upcoming school projects. Like most other American families, there were some high scores to report, with some rather average scores mingled into the results as well. Todd eventually admitted that he was earning a C in Spanish.

The soon-to-be lieutenant governor was also listening in. "And, why *Señor* Todd was your *nota* so bad *en español*?" His friendly smile told his son that he was genuinely concerned.

"I just don't get *español, Padre*," replied Todd. "It's stupid language. Why do they have to conjugate all those verbs?"

"We conjugate verbs when we speak English, son. It was hard for you to learn English, too. You'll get better at *español*."

As the group approached the top of the hill, Ann's phone rang. The caller ID told her that her private investigator, Scott Lewis, was trying to reach her. Ann chose to ignore the call. Instead, she climbed on a tube and invited her daughter to join her for the ride. Together, they launched down the run and felt the thrill of plunging down the snowy slope. Ann and her daughter shared screams and peals of laughter as they glided over the snow and eventually came to a stop at the foot of the hill. Ann cherished every second.

Fifteen minutes later, Ann's phone rang again. It was Lewis, and she disregarded the call. Ann Higgins was enjoying the time with her family, the rush of tubing, and the cold wind against her face. Her husband and children deserved her undivided attention. And, she deserved to relish time with them while breathing the crisp air and experiencing the pristine evening and beautiful stars in the sky.

CHAPTER 7

It was 7:35 p.m., and Ann was struggling to enjoy her chicken and vegetables at HuHot Mongolian Grill. Her mind was on the mysterious Bryant Way basement; and the fact that she had now missed six phone calls from Scott Lewis was adding to her distractibility. So, she sent Lewis a text informing him that she would call him in fifteen minutes. At that point, she turned her attention to savoring the conversation with her family and finishing her meal. Fourteen minutes later she excused herself from the table and called.

"This is Lewis."

"Scott. I'm sorry I didn't get right back to you, I've been—"

Lewis cut her off. "Do you have any idea what you're looking at, Ann?"

"I'm hoping those new owners are planning a laundromat." Ann emitted a small, nervous laugh to punctuate the comment.

"Ann, that's no laundry." Lewis was speaking in staccato, worried tones. "I'm no drug expert, but I've been searching online, and I'm ninety-five percent sure that your drawing is a future meth lab."

"Oh." Ann was momentarily speechless. Her mind flashed back to all of the campaign appearances she had made with Linda Horton, the woman who would soon become South Dakota's first lady. Horton was deeply passionate about ridding the state of South Dakota of methamphetamine, and other illicit drugs. It was her crusade. For Linda Horton going on the defensive against illegal drugs was *not* a publicity stunt. Then-gubernatorial candidate Richard Horton had promised to give his wife *carte blanche* access to law enforcement and healthcare officials. She wanted to make South Dakota the least drug-friendly state in America, and she had pledged to help recovering addicts. Even though Richard Horton was not yet governor, the fifty-two-year-old Linda Horton was actively charging ahead on her mission. Four days ago, she participated in a drug raid in Rapid City. Every week she was meeting with her adopted heroin support group in Pierre and sharing sincere hugs and tears with the participants. She had attended the trials of three drug dealers and glared at them from the gallery. She chronicled all of her activities on her wildly popular blog.

Now, as the lieutenant governor's wife, Ann found herself smack-dab in the middle of a potential nightmare. Within a few days or weeks, there may be a functioning meth lab operating in a community she had worked so hard to build. The potential paradox of the situation was distressing.

"I don't know where this lab is or what your connection is to it," Lewis said, "but, you should call the police."

"No way." Ann took charge of the situation. "Don't you dare call the police. Don't move a muscle until you've heard from me or Troy Stoker."

"You mean that psychiatrist?" Lewis asked.

But, there was no reply to his question. Ann had severed the call and was already looking up 'Stoker' in her phone's contact list.

CHAPTER 8

Troy Stoker was back at home sitting on the couch in the living room. His leg was propped up and iced, his arm bandaged, and his torso still tender. The narcotic painkiller oxycodone they had given him for pain in the ER was wearing off. Breathing was a little painful, but his knee was killing him.

Allie Stoker was working on her computer from her quaint desk in the living room. She swiveled her chair around and saw her husband grimacing from the pain. "Come on, Troy. Let's just fill this prescription so you can sleep. A day or two on narcotics won't kill you."

Stoker winced as his knee throbbed. "800 milligrams of ibuprofen. Let's start with that. We can add some Tylenol in a couple of hours." Troy adjusted the ice pack so it directed more cold to his knee. "I had no idea they were giving me oxycodone at the hospital. They must have snuck it in on me. I prefer to avoid narcotics, when I can."

On the surface, this exchange about pain medications appeared to be a wife who was concerned about her husband's pain as well as a man who was willing to tolerate some pain. But, just below the surface, it was a friendly contest between two lovers. Allie Stoker had perhaps the highest pain tolerance her husband had ever encountered, and he was slightly jealous of her strength. She had suffered kidney stones, a hyper-extended knee, and a slipped disk. Allie Stoker he had tolerated the pain in each instance using only over-the-counter medications. So now, how could the mighty bow-hunter, avid backcountry skier, and a man who chopped wood to heat his home, succumb to the pain and fill the prescription for narcotics? While Troy Stoker did not possess the pain tolerance to rival the stoic Allie of Nordic descent, tonight would not be the night that would knock his toughness credentials down a notch. He would not take a narcotic.

Allie brought him the ibuprofen. She also brought him some milk and a slice of whole-wheat bread so he did not take the anti-inflammatory medication on an empty stomach. Stoker pulled out his laptop and started sending emails. The first email was to the detective in charge of the Sioux Falls Area Drug Task Force. Stoker was the consulting psychiatrist to the task force, and he often strapped on a bulletproof vest and accompanied the team on drug raids and other drug enforcement activities.

He was a potent member of the team. When the task force raided a home, the police stepped in to find the criminals, and Stoker stepped in to find the victims. As a psychiatrist, he supported the children and other innocent family members at this moment of intense trauma. When their worlds were falling apart, Stoker was entrenched in their ordeal, building bridges that saved lives, families, and souls. Other psychiatrists thought he was a fool, getting up at 4:30 a.m., and walking into dangerous situations—all without financial compensation. For Stoker, providing hope and a lifeline, precisely in their great moment of need, was deeply satisfying—a benefit that never arrived in a check or showed up on a financial statement.

Stoker's email informed the task force lieutenant that he would not be available for the next week or two.

His next communication was a text message to a cross-country skiing buddy canceling their tour for tomorrow. This was deeply disappointing to Allie, too. She was an excellent skier who usually conquered the course much faster than her husband or anybody else who joined them.

Finally, came the hardest cancelation of all. Stoker sent another text message to his best friend, Errol Rivera, canceling their bow-hunting trip for next Thursday. Because Dr. Rivera had accompanied Allie to the hospital earlier that afternoon, it was already obvious to him that the hunt was off. However, Stoker felt like he needed to confirm the painful fact, and he suggested a date to re-schedule the excursion. Fortunately, the x-ray of his knee was negative for fractures and Stoker hoped he could hunt again in a week or two.

Allie walked over and sat down on the loveseat about three feet from her husband. She was scanning the paper—an activity that could only interest her for ten minutes or so. Stoker decided to interrupt her reading. "So, Allie, my love. Enough about me, because my issues have dominated the whole afternoon. Why don't you tell me about you?" teased Stoker.

"Well let's see, I'm five foot three, I love winter sports, and I was really looking forward to kicking your trash tomorrow on the trail," Allie said.

"So, has this hostility toward men hurt your relationships in the past?"

"No, it has only helped me ferret out the wussies."

"Like the ones who have to take narcotics for their knee injuries?"

"I thought we were talking about me." Allie playfully flung the newspaper toward Troy. "Quit redirecting the conversation to you."

"Oh, yes. Let's get back to your narcissism."

Allie stepped over, punched him in the shoulder, gave him a gentle hug, and briefly teased him by nibbling on his ear. "Too bad you're out of commission tonight. I was hoping to show you a little more hostility."

Stoker started to respond, but his phone rang and interrupted the conversation. Usually Stoker would ignore phone calls during conversations with Allie, but the name appearing on his caller ID surprised him. Allie peaked over at his phone. "Oh, look. I knew we should've sent a congratulatory note to the lieutenant governor and his wife," she said.

"Mrs. Lieutenant Governor," bellowed Troy Stoker as he answered the phone. "Congratulations on your victory."

"Thank you Dr. Stoker," replied Ann Higgins.

"It takes a little effort for those of us on the far-right to utter such a phrase. You centrist-Republicans captured those votes by waffling on issues and swaying over a few center-left voters who like Governor Horton's conveniently revised positions on food stamps and Medicaid."

Ann sensed that Dr. Stoker was, for the most part, joking, so she decided to refute with some wit of her own. "Thank you, Troy. Your *qualified* congratulations mean a lot. For the next election, I'll look into kicking a few more kids off of food stamps so we poll better among your Tea Party friends."

Stoker laughed. "Perhaps cutting benefits to obese kids is the solution. You should focus-group that."

"In all seriousness Troy, please remember that my husband is quite conservative. The two of you probably see eye-to-eye on most issues. There were many issues that Kent challenged Richard Horton on, including welfare. And. . . " Ann paused for a moment remembering that Dr. Stoker prided himself on not accepting government money. "Hey, Troy? Did you really opt out of ObamaCare again?"

"That's right. No funding from the regime for me." While Dr. Stoker did not participate in government healthcare programs such as Medicare and Medicaid, he gladly treated Medicare and Medicaid patients. Stoker preferred to treat patients for free instead of taking money from a system that created a paradoxical, subtle welfare system for physicians.

After a few short years of ObamaCare, many health insurance companies had failed. Payment delays to doctors were unprecedented. The health plans that remained in business struggled to keep up with the regulatory burden as well as the cash flow crunch created by a government that failed to confront the economics of medicine realistically.

Stoker didn't worry much about the money. He stayed focused on his track record of keeping patients out of the hospital and helping people reclaim their mental health. His phone rang dozens of times a day because people knew that Stoker cared deeply and helped immensely. He was actually staying in business as a solo psychiatrist—a feat that astounded psychiatrists who sought refuge from the ObamaCare storm by joining large physician practices.

"Medicare and Medicaid started as well-intentioned programs," Stoker said. "Now, they are bloated government welfare organisms that serve too many people and ensnare would-be rugged individualists."

"And your practice is doing all right without ObamaCare, Medicare and Medicaid?" asked Ann.

"My practice is just fine. I enjoy working with my patients and I get paid enough. Sure, it's less than it used to be, and the money from insurance flows in a lot slower. But, I'm also free to pay more attention to cutting-edge psychiatry research and outcomes. That helps me filter out a whole bunch of government noise." Stoker punched a button to turn on the speakerphone and it relieved a little pain in his arm to set the phone down on a pillow. "Allie and I would like to host you and Kent one evening for dinner. Let's see just how conservative Kent is." Stoker rolled a little to his left and found some temporary comfort. Allie could see his discomfort and anticipated his need by bringing him a Bluetooth earpiece and attaching it onto his ear. Troy winked at Allie in a gesture of thanks. "But Ann, I don't suspect you called to talk about politics or ObamaCare. What's going on?"

"Troy, there's a situation I really need to discuss with you. You've helped me so much before, and I know that you work with police drug teams. So, could we just talk through this right now?"

"Absolutely. Tell me what's going on, Ann." Stoker activated the earpiece." You have the floor and my total attention."

"Well, I found a house out in Chelsea Crossing with some interesting plumbing and electrical work in the basement. I also found a hand-drawn construction plan of the space that looked suspicious to me. I sent the drawings to a private investigator and he thinks they are plans to build a drug lab in the basement."

"Do you still have this drawing?"

"No. I just took pictures."

"Okay. Show them to me. Do you have them with you? Do you have a copy with you?"

"Yes. I'll email them to you."

"No, don't do that. Let's keep this off email for now. You never know who may intercept your email. I'd like to see these pictures in person." Stoker had forgotten about his pain and discomfort. The news of the soon-to-be lieutenant governor's wife stumbling upon an illegal narcotics lab had his full concentration. "Because you and your husband are days away from the inauguration, you may want to avoid calling the police for the time being. There are some strange undercurrents with local law enforcement right now. Something's wrong in the world of Sioux Falls drug enforcement. Calling the police could result in leaks and misunderstandings about you, Kent, and your Chelsea Crossing paradise. The liberal media would have a heyday with such a story, and you would never get the correct facts into the hands of the public."

"Troy, you know I'm not one to sit still," Ann said. "I don't want to wait this out or pretend it will go away. If we don't call the police, what else can we do?"

"I have some friends I trust, and you should feel comfortable sharing this information with them. Their due diligence and assertiveness will get results that will speak for themselves. They will know exactly when to call the police and how to set up a swift resolution."

Stoker was already assembling the team in his mind. His first thought was to recruit a lawyer, and he knew just the person. "Do you know Holly Glover, the attorney here in town?"

"No. I've never heard of her."

"She's in private practice, but takes on some overflow on drug prosecutions. It makes up about forty percent of her practice these days. You should retain her."

"Okay. Done."

"She's going to charge you about two hundred and ten dollars per hour, just so you're aware."

Even though Ann had become a wealthy woman, she still had frugal habits. "For now, that will be fine, but I'll be watching her to make sure she doesn't run up a bill."

"Of course. She's a good lawyer, and most attorneys would be tempted to run up a bill on a real estate executive and wife of a hotshot politician. But, not Holly." Stoker opened the calendar on his phone. "What does your day look like tomorrow?"

"First, my husband Kent is *not* a hotshot," contested Ann. "Second, my morning includes waffles for breakfast and indoor soccer in the morning. I will be attending a dance performance at five o'clock that evening. But between those times, I'm at home reading through the mail and reports I've neglected for months while campaigning."

"Good. Let me see when I can get Holly to join us. Do you mind inviting your P.I. friend? His skills may come in handy."

"Yes. I'll call him."

"I'm sorry about the expense you are about to incur for all of this. I may or may not keep track of my hours, too," stated Troy. "However, my invoice may just get lost along the way somewhere—especially if we bust some meth cookers."

"Thank you, Troy," Ann said.

"No problem." As Stoker was navigating his calendar on his phone, his leg tumbled off of the pillows. A thunderbolt of pain shot up his leg, and the inhaling gasp of pain was clearly audible as the air traveled through his vocal cords and sinus cavities.

"Are you okay, Troy?" Ann had heard the brief but pronounced response, and her instincts told her it was an expression of pain.

Stoker smiled to downplay his pain. "Yeah. I'm fine. I just had a little injury earlier today that I'm nursing back to health." Anticipating that Ann would ask about it, he pre-empted her question. "It's nothing worth bragging about, so it's certainly not worth talking about." Stoker decided not to move his leg until after he finished this phone call. "Now Ann, there are a couple more people I'll be bringing to our meeting tomorrow, and I'll tell you their names and introduce them then instead of saying much over the phone."

Ann was initially amused by Dr. Stoker's apparent paranoia about telephone communication. "That's fine. I trust you on this." As she heard her own voice expressing trust, her amusement vanished and she realized that it was vital to avoid discussing her circumstances on the phone.

"Great, Ann. I'll get back to you."

Stoker hung up the phone and called the attorney, Holly Glover. She picked up after two rings. "Dr. Stoker. Are you refusing to give psychotic patients their medical records again?" Glover cajoled with guarded humor in her voice.

"No, Holly. Dr. Stintson and those guys at the medical board have not bugged me today. You know they only work a half-day on Friday."

"Stintson and a few other board staffers only work a half-day every day," joked Glover. "Now, why are you interrupting my Friday evening?"

"I may have a new client for you."

"I'm going to be honest with you, Dr. Stoker. You have not been the best source of clients in the past. Many of them are minors who have no money. And, I seem to recall three or four recent cases you sent me. They were adults who had burned through half of their gray matter with crack, meth or some other substance."

"Well this client is an adult, I doubt she has ever used drugs, and I promise she can pay." Stoker paused a moment. He had referred dozens of paying clients to Holly Glover. She was a caring individual and talented attorney. Stoker knew that her bosses had conditioned her, from day one, to sniff for money in every phone call. With the next sentence Glover captured that scent of the dollar her partners coveted. "Her husband will be inaugurated lieutenant governor in a few days, and it's your job to help us get to the bottom of a possible meth lab in her multi-million dollar real estate development."

"Ann Higgins?" The question was almost a statement. "It just so happens, I'm available if she needs to meet tonight."

CHAPTER 9

SIOUX FALLS REGIONAL HOSPITAL

Dr. Stintson, president of the South Dakota Medical Board, loved being the on-call during the weekend. As the go-to orthopedic surgeon on Friday nights, he could expect to treat victims of bar fights and car crashes. Saturdays tended to attract more athletic injuries and snowmobile and ATV accidents. Sundays were sort of a mixture of Friday nights and Saturdays, but with fewer bar fights. Weekend follies helped marginal orthopedic surgeon, Larry Stintson, M.D., make a comfortable living. His poor reputation generally precluded other doctors from referring patients to him, so he managed to scrounge up business by being on call as much as possible at the two hospitals in town.

It was somewhat uncommon for doctors to work at both hospitals in Sioux Falls. Many of the physicians in the area were employed by one of the two health systems and that allegiance led them to admit patients to their employer's hospital. The business rivalry was robust, and it tended to draw lines and create factions. However, Stintson still worked at both hospitals. Because he was in private practice, instead of being employed by a health system, he could pull off this small feat. Also, he had friends in high places. They helped him get on the orthopedic surgery call schedule at both hospitals.

Dr. Stintson was certainly the least qualified orthopedic surgeon to treat trauma cases on the orthopedic call schedule. Truth be told, the hospitals preferred to use orthopedic surgeons who had completed a trauma fellowship to cover the emergency room on-call schedule. The extra year of post-residency training in trauma made them better surgeons. Their patients had better outcomes than Stintson's patients. Nevertheless, Stintson still managed to bribe his way onto the trauma schedule.

On the nights when Dr. Stintson was on call he waited excitedly at home, at his office, or in the doctors lounge for patients to arrive. He loved treating fractured wrists, hyper-extended knees, strained backs, broken legs and shattered ankles. Much to the horror of the medical community, he also operated on complex spine and pelvis injuries instead of referring them to the proper specialists.

Injured patients automatically trusted the doctors they were assigned in the emergency room. What choice did they have? Their destiny and doctor choice was dictated by the call schedule. Little did patients know, when they met Dr. Stintson in a trauma or exam room, they were about to experience medical mediocrity and financial torment.

Tonight, Larry Stintson decided to wait for patients from his office. He would lie on his couch, in his scrubs and watch movies on a screen that dropped down from the ceiling. He enjoyed the female companionship of a mistress, Katerina. She was in awe of his power and his money, and she was also a big fan of an occasional hit of meth or MDMA. Stintson was proud of himself for keeping her "under control." He shared the illicit substances with Katerina in relatively small doses, and just once or twice a week. He gave her the psychedelic, relaxing high of ecstasy one day and the pleasurable rush of meth a few days later. He was fairly certain that this strategy kept her from developing an addiction. Stintson never participated in the highs or rushes when he was on call, but he would occasionally party with her on other nights.

On this particular Friday night, Katerina was an hour into a hit of Molly, and Stintson was forty-five minutes into a 1990s military action movie, when a text from the ER arrived. The message informed him that a patient had arrived with a lower extremity fracture. Stintson persuaded Katerina to drink about eight ounces of water, and then he left for the hospital. Seven minutes later he walked through the ER doors, logged into a computer terminal, and read some facts about a morbidly obese forty-seven year old woman who had slipped on some icy stairs. The notes from the emergency room physician pointed out that she had taken a theatrical fall, and her ankle was obviously broken. The note also stated that her injuries probably also included torn ligaments and tendons. Dr. Stintson was elated as he turned and walked to her room with an optimistic spring in his step. The complexity of the case would generate a hefty bill. Arriving at her door, Stintson reminded himself to act empathetic and sorrowful at his patient's plight.

"Hello, Mrs. Jensen. I'm sorry about the fall that brought you to the hospital this evening." Stintson has recited similar lies thousands of times, while masking his delight with fake sorrow. Pain contorted Ms. Jensen's face, and tears took turns leaking from her right eye and then her left. "I'm Dr. Stintson, the orthopedic surgeon on call, and I'm a big fan of pain medication."

"Oh, please! Yes. Stop the pain." Mrs. Jensen's eye produced more tears, and the desperate look on her face matched the begging in her voice.

"My favorite technique, in which I've been specifically trained, is called a block. It will work within about sixty seconds to deaden your pain. But before I give it to you, I need you to sign my regular consent documents. You know, the lawyers insist on all of this paperwork. I swear, they just don't get it, you know. They never consider how much pain people are experiencing in emergency situations."

The patient grabbed the documents quickly, even while whispering, "Thank you, Doctor. Just tell me where to sign."

"There's also some financial and arbitration paperwork, as well as my document about handling your insurance and payments. Will you please sign here?"

Again, the patient complied rapidly, and much too naively.

Moments later, Dr. Stintson was injecting the painkillers lidocaine and bupivacaine into the major nerve roots of Mrs. Jensen's leg while she winced and cried out in pain. "Give it about a minute. The relief is just moments away." Dr. Stintson was right. A few seconds later Mrs. Jensen's grimaced face finally relaxed.

"Thank you, Doctor. Thank you." Now the tears that flowed were tears of relief. In her eyes, Larry Stintson was a miracle worker. However, little did she know she had just signed documents that would create a legal and financial headache, which would compromise her sanity and solvency for the next few years. Within the nine pages of documents, Ms. Jensen had just acknowledged that Dr. Stintson did not have a contract with her insurance company. Nor did he have contracts with Medicare, Medicaid or any other insurance company. The document bearing her signature also made it clear that Larry Stintson, M.D. did not accept payment from insurance companies. She had also unknowingly agreed to pay the excessive fees that Dr. Stintson set, and she would pay them to him directly. She was free to file her own claims with her insurance company, after the fact, and keep anything they paid her—which the document made clear would only be a fraction of the amount she would pay Dr. Stintson for his services.

The second document Mrs. Jensen signed was an arbitration agreement. This small piece of paperwork protected Dr. Stintson from lawsuits, which would have otherwise plagued him due to his shoddy surgical skills. At the instant patients signed the document, they waived their right to a jury trial. If a patient wanted to pursue a malpractice claim against Dr. Stintson, the paperwork required that the parties enter into arbitration with a panel of three individuals who would decide the case. Dr. Stintson would choose two of the arbitrators and the patient could choose one. This process stacked the three-person panel in favor of the doctor.

In six years, Stintson had been brought to arbitration seven times. Dr. Stintson had emerged the victor six times. The fourth time, he paid $17,200 in damages to settle the dispute one day before the scheduled mediation session. Of course, the mediation agreement also included gag clauses prohibiting the patients from discussing the case with just about anyone.

Doctors and administrators knew about his dirty tricks, but they met resistance any time they tried to bring a complaint or lawsuit against him. The only entity that had the power to stop or sanction Dr. Stintson for his deplorable medical practices and heartless approach to patient relations was the South Dakota Medical Board. However, the board's intervention was unlikely since Dr. Stintson himself was head honcho there. Sometimes other doctors questioned Larry Stintson's skills or ethics. Almost without fail, they were investigated aggressively by Brian Berg within weeks. Dr. Stintson was effective at making life miserable for those who tried to address the harm he inflicted on some patients.

Mrs. Jensen was comfortable and had signed the documents, yet Dr. Stintson maintained his façade of kindness. After all, he still had to talk his patient into surgery. "You've got a bad fracture here, Mrs. Jensen, and we need to fix it in the operating room. In about two hours, I can have everything put back together. After that, if you'll give your body about four weeks to heal, I suspect you'll be almost as good as new." Stintson explained a few more things in medical speak that his patient did not understand. However, a few minutes later, she had consented to the surgery and her gurney was rolling toward the operating room.

Two hours and fifteen minutes later, Larry Stintson emerged from the operating room having completed numerous fusions and reattachments. By his calculation, he would bill Mrs. Jensen about $7,000 for the surgery and she was contractually obligated to pay it all. Unfortunately, her insurance company would probably only pay her back about $1,700—assuming she had met her deductible already, which wasn't likely since it was January.

Stintson was in a hurry because another orthopedic injury had come into the ER while he was in surgery. He walked into the recovery room and carelessly explained to a heavy-eyed Ms. Jenson a few things about the procedure. Then he left her and practically race-walked to the emergency room to meet his next patient. As he entered the room, he saw a thirty-two year old woman sitting up on the exam table. Her right forearm was wrapped in a bandage. Her husband accompanied her.

"Hello, Mrs. Sun. I'm Dr. Stintson, the orthopedic surgeon on call. I'm sorry about the fall that brought you to the hospital this evening." Again, he was pretending not to be excited. "I hear that you fell while you were ice-skating?"

"Yes. It's just one of those things. And, please call me Renee. I think I've fractured my radius and ulna."

Stintson was slightly surprised that she knew the names of the forearm bones. "You must work in health care or have a really great memory from an anatomy class a few years back," joked Stintson. "Most people don't know those terms."

"No. I work as a paper-pusher in a pretty boring cubicle. The ER doctor told us the names of the bones. We looked up a few more things, on my phone, while we were waiting."

"Oh, yes. And speaking of waiting, I'm very sorry—"

"Don't worry." Renee was calm and relaxed. "They told us you were in surgery."

"Alright. Well, I'm a big fan of pain medication, so let's start there."

"I don't have much pain," explained Renee. "I don't think my fracture is that serious. Besides the ER doctor gave me a pain pill about forty-five minutes ago."

"Okay, well then, before I treat you . . . Oh wow." Stintson looked at her forearm with an expression of fake surprise. "I think we may need to take you into surgery before that gets any worse." Stintson's statement was medically inaccurate. He knew that the right thing to do, with this particular injury, was to splint her fracture and wait a few days for the swelling to go down instead of rushing into surgery. But if the doctor gave this patient some time, she might do some research, find out about Stintson's reputation, and find a different surgeon. "So, before I treat you, there's a little paperwork I need you to sign." Stintson took out the first document and turned to the signature page. "You know, it never ceases to amaze me how the lawyers just insist that this paperwork is *so much more important* than the actual care." Stintson pointed with a pen to the signature line. "I'm sorry to bother you with this, but it is just the usual stuff. You know, I promise to take care of you. You promise to pay me. Arbitration and dispute resolution."

"Did you say arbitration?" Renee was no longer calm, trusting and relaxed.

"Well, yes. You know. I guess it's all the rage these days to speed things up in arbitration instead—"

Renee interrupted Dr. Stintson and snatched the paperwork out of his hands. "Where's that arbitration agreement?" Stintson tried to answer her, but Renee had already found the document and was reading it. Her husband stood from his chair, and stepped over next to his wife, before she said, "So Dr.

Stintson, I see here that this signing this binds me to arbitration. You get to pick two of the panel members, and I get to pick one. But, we split the costs of arbitration equally. Is that correct?"

"Well, I don't know. It's just the standard agreement they give me."

"That who give you?"

"My attorneys."

"Who are your attorneys?"

"Well, Dirk Roland is the guy I work with the most."

"That explains a lot." Renee said with contempt as she and her husband continued reading through the document.

"So you don't have contracts with insurance companies?" Renee's husband asked.

"No. I prefer to deal directly with my patients," Stintson said. "Look, I'm the president of the South Dakota Medical Board. I have impeccable credentials. I no longer fight insurance companies. I am modeling the new way for my fellow physicians. That mantle of leadership has fallen on me. Doctors are seeing how to keep insurers from getting in the way of practicing medicine."

Renee was unimpressed with Stintson's speech. It smacked of misdirection and propaganda. Her index finger was traveling over lines rapidly. "Actually, according to this paragraph, it looks like the objection you have with insurance is the fact that they keep you from making exorbitant fees. Can I see your fee schedule?"

"I don't have a copy with me," Stintson said flatly.

"It should be an exhibit in this document, Doctor." Renee stood up and took a small step toward Stintson. "So, what would you charge to fix my fractured radius and ulna? Don't they call that a distal radius fracture?"

"Yes. That's a term for it, and the charge depends on how bad it is."

Renee, obviously bothered, pointed at her swollen arm. "Let's just say it's this bad. Let's assume it's non-displaced. How much?"

"I don't know," stammered Stintson.

"How much was the last one you did that looked like this?" Renee stepped toward him again, and Stintson stepped back. "Give or take two hundred dollars?"

"I don't recall. My billing gal handles all of that."

Renee winced. "Your billing *gal*?"

"Girl, um, I mean, clerk. Actually, I think her title is billing specialist."

"So, your billing *gal* handles sending out the bills, but she won't file my insurance claim?"

"That's the problem with healthcare." Stintson was starting a speech again. "Patients are not in charge of their own destiny." Renee Sun wanted no part of Stintson's next speech.

"How many times have your patients filed arbitration complaints with you?" Mr. Sun asked.

"I'm not supposed to answer that. According to my attorney, it's not a fair question." Stintson watched as Renee put the documents in her purse. He was completely confused. "Who are you? Is this some kind of audit?"

"I'm a two-bit paralegal who can see right through you. I'm going to review your document and check your credentials online. I *may* call you back."

Renee and her husband walked out of the exam room and into the hallway. They were silent for the first few paces, and then her husband made a suggestion. "Let's go up to the orthopedics floor and ask the nurses about this Stintson guy."

"A brilliant idea." Renee thought for a moment. "Do you think that they will speak to us honestly?" Then she answered her own question. "All we need is one honest person." They walked to the main elevators and pushed the button. As they waited a man with a hospital employee badge arrived to also take the elevator. "How do we get to the ortho floor?"

"Take this elevator to the third floor, and then turn left. Just follow the signs from there." Then the employee noticed Renee's arm, and he looked a little confused. "Are you okay?" he asked. "Pardon me for being nosy, but you look like you could use more treatment before you get to the floor."

The doors opened, they stepped on, chose their floors, and watched the doors close. "Thanks for your concern. We just met with Dr. Stintson—"

The man could not hide his alarm. "The orthopedic surgeon?"

"Yes, and frankly his paperwork and mannerisms concerned us. We're going up to the orthopedics floor to ask around about him."

"Let me save you a trip. I'm a scrub tech in the operating room. I work with him a couple of times a week. He's a horrible surgeon." The doors opened, and the man walked off the elevator with them unexpectedly. "Look, that's a simple fracture. Even Stintson could fix it just fine. But, you don't want to do *business* with him."

"You mean he sends you a bill and you have to pay it all?"

"Wow! You read the fine print. Congratulations" the man said. "His patients end up paying four to six times what they would pay a doctor who is on their insurance plan."

"That's criminal!" said Renee.

"I think if people dug a little deeper on Larry Stintson, they would find out that he *is* a criminal." Then the man looked at her arm. "That arm can wait. They usually don't operate for a few days, until your swelling's gone down. So, look on your insurance plan and find an orthopedic surgeon who specialized in hands and arms. You'll be glad you did because most of the surgeons in town are fantastic." With that thought, the man bolted through a door, and up a stairway.

The elevator chimed and the door opened. Dr. Stintson walked out.

"I'm glad I didn't sign your crazy document, you fraud." Renee looked him in the eye with confidence. "Because now I can go down to the *Argus Leader* and tell one of my reporter friends about my experience this evening." Renee turned and stepped into the elevator. "A little advice, Stintson. Get a spray-on tan in the next day or so. Your pasty mug alone will indict you on camera."

CHAPTER 10

It was Friday night, and Sarah Haslam was on call, yet again. As a second year psychiatric resident she spent many weekends and evenings on call at Sioux Falls Regional Hospital, which was to be expected. In her first two hours, she had made an appearance on the acute psychiatry floor to adjust some medications. Then she went to the birthing center and consulted with a new mom who was experiencing a dissociative disorder. The trauma of delivering a child, the jubilation of intimately attaching to that child, and the overwhelming sense of responsibility of being a new mother had wreaked havoc upon the emotions of this twenty-four-year-old woman. Subconsciously, the new mother was disassociating—a defense mechanism whereby she emotionally detached or completely ignored the issues.

Dr. Haslam loved these consults because they were easy and efficient, and she would not have to form a lasting relationship with this patient. Sarah Haslam hated forming relationships with patients. Frankly, she hated the effort involved in almost all relationships. Haslam would see this patient one or two more times before she went home. From there, the new mom's obstetrician and a local psychologist would take over the case. Someone other than Dr. Haslam, would sit in long, tearful sessions with her and provide the necessary therapy.

Dr. Haslam left the birthing center and made her way back to the psychiatry unit. As she approached the doors, her phone vibrated twice indicating she had yet another text message. This one was from the ER requesting her presence to evaluate and admit a psychotic male in his mid-forties.

"I just love these crazies." Haslam was shameless enough to speak her mind out loud. "Welcome aboard South Dakota Psycho Cruise Lines." She did a 180-degree turn and started walking toward the ER. She traveled two flights of stairs and passed through a couple of hallways to get there. As she approached the large swinging doors to the ER, she felt a slight adrenaline surge. She loved this moment as well as the next ninety minutes that would ensue. She was about to introduce herself to a completely helpless person in a psychotic state. For the next few hours and days, she would make virtually all of the decisions in this person's life. She would dictate the medications he took, where he slept, and the people he could or could not talk with. She could even impose dietary restrictions. Haslam would issue orders for therapy, and he would have to follow them. If he refused to follow her orders, she could restrict his activities, remand him to his room, and even have him put in restraints.

Sarah Haslam *loved* being a psychiatrist. She had the power to write orders, and a team of nurses, social workers, psychologists, technicians and other minions would carry them out. But, perhaps the most fascinating aspect of her job was pharmacology, which in Haslam's deluded mind, was just a fancy word that meant working with drugs. The young resident felt a rush from prescribing those few basic medications that could transform a person's behavior within the first few hours of admission. It often helped that the patients also had a few hours to get alcohol, cocaine, speed or whatever substances out of their system. However, Haslam seemed to lose interest in patients after a few visits to their rooms. Other medications took days or weeks to produce results. Watching this slow, cumbersome metamorphosis was the opposite of excitement and Haslam loathed this aspect of psychiatry.

Today her patient was occupying an exam room toward the back of the emergency room. Dr. Haslam, accompanied by a nurse named Monica, knocked on the door and let herself in. "Hello, Mr. Martin."

The patient, eyes closed, issued no verbal response, but did nod his head to acknowledge her presence.

"So how many paramedics, nurses, and doctors have asked you, 'How are you today?'" asked Haslam.

"A few," grunted Martin.

"Idiots. All idiots," Haslam said. "When you're obviously experiencing a living hell, why do people ask you that? Can't they see how you're doing? How did they even let these people out of junior high?"

Doug Martin laughed one of those through-the-nose laughs. It was just a single, short exhale.

"Yes," continued Haslam. "They are disconnected enough from reality to ask a person how he is doing while he is bleeding out an eyeball or the bone from his forearm keeps poking him in the ribs. And then they take it upon themselves to determine that a patient needs a psychiatrist. I've tried to point out the problem there, but they still don't see it."

Martin smiled, but only slightly.

"My name's Doctor Haslam, but most people call me Sarah." This was not completely true. Patients could call her Sarah and so could other doctors. But, nurses and everybody else called her Dr. Haslam at her insistence. "So, you've had a disappointing hour or two. Would you be willing to tell a perfect stranger that story?"

"Well, it's like I told everybody already," said Martin. "I get mixed messages from the TV in my mind. Sometimes it's the channel where our ancestors offer us the protection from the Chinese." Haslam pretended to listen with interest to Mr. Martin's severe symptoms of psychosis, while also reviewing his tox screen and other documentation created by the ER doctors. Haslam noted the possibility of delirium, but overlooked the potential acute medical problems affecting Martin's brain. "As we made it through the wilderness and into the badlands we had to use extreme caution and our ancestors were all around us. They were our protection. You know, the Chinese have nukes but they don't want to use them because they want our natural resources. But that would also alert the NSA. So we decided to fight them like the Philistines, just like the olden times of the Bible."

Indeed Doug Martin was experiencing full-scale psychosis, but at least he was not currently violent. The real story, evident from the notes in his medical chart, was that Martin had a DUI a year ago. Once his employer found out about the conviction, he lost his job as a truck driver. He was now working as a cook at a fast-food restaurant, which he considered beneath him. He was deeply depressed, but he had never talked to a doctor about his condition because he didn't know that he was depressed. It was common for people to live for years with depression without recognizing it.

After working the breakfast and lunch shifts at the restaurant, Martin stopped off at a liquor store and picked up a fifth of tequila. He arrived home to see his ninety-one pound wife on the couch sleeping. Tina Martin worked nights at a truck stop. She tolerated the measly nine dollars per hour pay because her employer provided excellent health insurance. During last night's overnight shift she had scored some crank in a casual transaction, which nobody else noticed. They never did.

Doug and Tina Martin turned on the TV, which they would largely ignore for the next few hours, and partied. Their eleven-year-old son Alex had an Xbox and a television in his bedroom to keep him occupied for the next few hours — or days if necessary. The pantry contained a half-empty box of Captain Crunch, an almost full box of Lucky Charms, and an unopened bag of Cheetos. In the refrigerator there was milk for the cereal, Code Red Mountain Dew and a jar of pickles. Alex would be fine.

When the sun went down just before 5:00 p.m., the Martins were living it up. Around 7:00, chaos began. One thing led to another, and by 8:05 p.m., Doug Martin was smashing shop windows on Minnesota Avenue. At 8:12 p.m. he was being pinned to the icy-cold asphalt of Minnesota Avenue by two Sioux Falls police officers. The tequila, Doug Martin's depression and a bad batch of methamphetamine combined to induce a full-blown psychotic break, which had landed him in handcuffs and in the ER.

"Well, Mr. Martin, I'm also thinking that in addition to the Chinese and the TVs in your mind, the tequila and meth have also mixed up the channels. So, I'm going to have you stay here with us this evening as our guest, and we'll take good care of you."

No response from Martin.

"Monica, I'm going to admit Mr. Martin to the fourth floor psychiatry unit," declared Dr. Haslam to the emergency room nurse. "I see here an order from the ER doc for 1000 micrograms of cyanocobalamin. Was that administered yet?"

"Yes, Doctor," replied the nurse. "About an hour ago."

Cyanocobalamin was just a fancy name for vitamin B12. It was protocol at Sioux Falls Regional Hospital to administer vitamin B12 to intoxicated emergency room patients. This simple medication could minimize the odds of developing Wernicke's encephalopathy, or brain damage from alcohol poisoning.

"Will you get us a bed upstairs, Monica?" asked Dr. Haslam.

"No problem," she replied. "We already let them know that this guy would probably be admitted."

Dr. Haslam knew that she had a few minutes before the psychiatry floor would give them the green light to admit Mr. Martin. So she walked out of the nurse's station and found the nearest computer terminal and logged in. She pulled up the template on the computer for admission orders and proceeded to set up a plan to diagnose and treat Mr. Martin over the next forty-eight hours or so.

More than anything, Mr. Martin needed sleep, so she first ordered fifty milligrams of quetiapine to be given to him upon arrival on the psychiatry floor, and each night thereafter. She instructed the nurses to call her if he did not fall asleep by 3:00 a.m. She also gave the nurses an order for ten milligrams of zaleplon. However, this was a PRN or "as needed" order. If the nurses decided that he needed the additional medication, they had the option of giving him one to two tablets per night. Dr. Haslam generally trusted the nurses on the psych floor. But she could never fathom, in her narcissistic mind, that a nurse would ever develop even a fraction of the judgment of a doctor.

She wrote orders for a nurse or technician to check Mr. Martin, just to make sure he was breathing, every fifteen minutes during the first night. Other orders included arranging for neuropsychiatric testing and sending a social worker to evaluate his home situation.

She decided that she would do all the rest of the dictation, paperwork, and computer-based tasks up on the psych floor in a few minutes. But, for now she had some time to burn, so she went on to Facebook and caught up with her circle of friends, checked out some Twitter feeds, and soaked up some news headlines.

The psychiatry floor still had not called for the patient, so she took a minute to jump into her personal email account and shoot off a quick email to one of her friends from medical school. The friend was also completing a psychiatry residency. This particular friend had matched to a prestigious residency in St. Louis. Haslam's email contained a harsh criticism of most of the attending psychiatrists, and certainly the residency chair who oversaw her work in South Dakota. Haslam perceived them all as incompetent. She used her personal feeling to make the judgment instead of clinical reasoning. She concluded that she would certainly need to complete a fellowship at a more renowned institution to round out her educational experience and make up for the deficiencies of her current environment.

After sending the email, Haslam logged out of the workstation, made her way to the physicians lounge, and purchased a Mountain Dew. Just as she picked up a copy of the newspaper, her cell phone vibrated and the text arrived informing her that a bed was available on the fourth floor's locked inpatient psychiatry unit.

While walking back to Mr. Martin's room in the ER, Dr. Haslam summoned an emergency room tech and the on-call crisis worker to join her in transporting Mr. Martin to the fourth floor. "Okay sir, let's take you upstairs and introduce you to the nurses who will be taking care of you for the next few days."

Mr. Martin acknowledged her statement with his customary nod of the head, still keeping his eyes closed. Dr. Haslam lifted the side rails on his bed, removed the heart monitor cuff from his left arm, the oxygen monitor from his finger, and made sure that he was not attached to any other devices. She unlocked the bed brakes with her foot, grabbed one of the side rails, and began to wheel Mr. Martin out of the room.

The emergency room technician grabbed a hold of the other side of the bed and added a little more force, propelling Mr. Martin down the hallway toward the elevator. A few steps from the elevator, the social worker, Mary, caught up with them and instinctively grabbed onto Mr. Martin's bed to complete the team that would accompany Mr. Martin up to the fourth floor.

As Dr. Haslam and her team arrived at the door to the secure psychiatry unit, they pushed the doorbell to request entry. A few moments later, a beep informed the team that someone on the other side of the door had recognized them through a security camera and granted them admittance. The door swung open automatically, and the team traveled through the door around a corner and passed the nurse's station. They approached a second secure door that Haslam opened with a four-digit code, and entered the room everyone called the intake room.

"Who do we have here?" asked Pilar Torres, the charge nurse for the evening, and a veritable ninja in the world of psychiatric nursing.

"This is Mr. Douglas Martin, a thirty-two-year-old male, chauffeured to the ER in the back of an ever-so-luxurious Sioux Falls Police Department car," explained Dr. Haslam. "After consuming a respectable amount of alcohol, as well as some methamphetamine, which we suspect was not prepared according to the usual recipe, Mr. Martin decided to go for a walk. His travels took him a few blocks from his home. Apparently at some point, Mr. Martin reached a state of agitation and excitement, wherein he decided a little vandalism would be in order.

"Fortunately Mr. Martin had the wisdom to swing his baseball bat at some windows along Minnesota Avenue. We're pleased to report that he selected no human targets to engage in his extra-curricular activities. Mr. Martin has a history of drug and alcohol abuse. I'm also diagnosing him with depression and I'm going to work on ruling out schizophrenia and other related disorders. What did the nurses from the ER tell you, Pilar?"

"He got the vitamin B injection, and I have his blood and urine tox screen results. I'm also noting his high blood alcohol level. It's 1.5 milligrams per deciliter—twice the legal limit. It will take us another day or so before we get the amphetamines out of his system," Torres said. "We'll push fluids and wash out the meth."

"Great. It couldn't hurt—I guess." Dr. Haslam was always making these condescending remarks toward the nurses. *Great suggestion, professional babysitter*, she thought in her narcissistic mind. Haslam hated suggestions. She wanted to have total control and make all the decisions. On the weekends, the attending physicians were rarely around, and a resident, like Haslam, could rule the roost in the hospital. "Mr. Martin should have most everything out of his system by the time the attending psychiatrists and social workers show up on Monday. So, let's set him up for some neuropsychiatric testing on Monday or Tuesday to include a substance abuse evaluation." Haslam loved these moments when she could rattle off orders like an army general. "Also, make sure he's set up with a social work consult sometime between Monday and when he leaves. My guess is the psychosis he experienced tonight was not just the booze and pills talking. I bet we find a little crazy lurking just under the surface, so I'll be back tomorrow morning."

"What about labs?" Torres asked.

"The usual stuff."

"What about the thyroid? He's thirty-two-years old, and his hormones may be a bit out of whack."

"No. We don't do thyroid voodoo here," shot back Haslam. "Have you been frequenting the bars with Troy Stoker too much?"

"No. But, I listen to the psychiatrists who have a long history of producing amazing results for their patients," shot back Torres.

"No thyroid tests." Haslam stood up abruptly with indignation in her eyes. "Doctor's orders. And more importantly, don't you be pushing any of that thyroid and hormone junk medicine here on the acute psych unit. If Stoker and other loonies want to do their cute little lab tests in their cozy little offices, that's their business. But here, we have *real* sick people. It's not their hormones, or they would be given a shot in the butt and admitted to the medical floor."

Dr. Sarah Haslam turned her back and left Torres and her team to care for Mr. Martin. Yes, Haslam loved psychiatry. She was large and in charge. Unfortunately, Haslam was overlooking the fact that her residency advisory committee had just issued her a second serious performance warning. The committee had been watching Sarah Haslam carefully during the last nine months and they had seen no improvement in her attitude or her psychiatry skills. More alarmingly, her bedside manner had become even more curt, cold and condescending. Sure, she could charm a patient for a day or two with a little humor and some painted-on personality. But, by day three Dr. Haslam had frequently managed to assume the role of drill sergeant over her new patients. Dr. Haslam's residency was not progressing well. It was not progressing at all.

CHAPTER 11

WALKER, SNOW, ALLEN AND TROUT, SIOUX FALLS

Holly Glover, attorney at law, occupied prime office space on Main Street in Sioux Falls. She was a relatively young partner with the prestigious firm of Walker, Snow, Allen, and Trout. After graduating summa cum laude from Howard University, she attended Harvard Law School and quickly gravitated to healthcare law while also maintaining a healthy interest in civil rights law. Her firm catered to a clientele of businesses, banks, real estate professionals, and doctors. It also had a division that ferociously prosecuted crime and corruption; and the partners prided themselves on taking on numerous pro bono civil rights cases. They were defenders of the Constitution and rugged individualism. They hated government and public relations stunts that lined the pockets of other law firms around town. They shunned divorce and personal injury cases.

Glover's new partner status with the firm afforded her privilege and latitude, such as booking one of the partner conference rooms on a Saturday morning and forbidding non-partner attorneys from entering the room during sensitive meetings. At 9:30 a.m. Glover welcomed Ann Higgins, Dr. Stoker and private investigator Scott Lewis. The conference room was adorned with traditional mahogany walls and a beveled glass door. But, this state-of-the art conference room lacked the traditional bookcases of legal books and stately portraits of the firm's founders. Instead, the room was extremely high-tech. It included a large computer monitor mounted on the wall and sophisticated telecommunications equipment. Glover's firm even swept the room for bugs on a regular basis.

"Good morning, everyone." Holly Glover was clearly running the meeting. "I want to begin by stating that *some* of the contents of this meeting are protected by attorney-client privilege, but not all. So, please don't assume that you can say anything and it will never come back to haunt you. Also, you should not discuss this meeting with anybody without me present.

"I will be the sole note taker and recorder of this meeting. If there is something you wish to ensure we include in the notes, please ask me to include those facts. I discourage you from taking notes. Instead, please lend your full attention to engaging in our discussion today. Individuals tasked with action items will receive an email with those action items from me by eight o'clock this evening."

Doctor Stoker was the next person to speak. "I've also taken the liberty of inviting Errol Rivera and another friend of mine, who we affectionately refer to as Z. They will arrive at ten o'clock, so I suggest we get started and see if we can get to the bottom of what's going on here."

"Let's start with those pictures," Glover said.

Ann opened her computer, and Glover handed her the HDMI cable that connected to the large monitor. One by one, Ann projected the pictures she had taken and the graphic she had spliced together from a few of the different photographs. "So these are the two drains. And, over here are two sets of spigots, a hot water and the cold water in each set, supposedly for two washing machines. But, there are none of those 240-volt outlets for dryers present. Look at this picture here." Ann showed them the picture of the wall that contained numerous electrical outlets. All of them were the traditional 120-volt sockets. "But the rest of the drawing, well, I just don't understand it."

"Unfortunately, I've seen a few of these." Lewis had been eager to chime in with his private investigator expertise. He had been subconsciously waiting for a moment to make an impression. "There's no doubt in my mind, that somebody intends to cook meth in this spot, and these guys mean to do a good job and run an efficient operation."

For the next few minutes Stoker and Glover walked the team through the process of manufacturing or "cooking" methamphetamine. They explained why a dual drain system and the extra hot and cold-water sources were a distinct advantage. They pointed out how extra electricity would help this lab produce efficiently.

"So the only question that remains is, why do these underground water lines appear to be running either to or from the fishing pond?" Lewis asked.

"I speculate that this is a stroke of genius," Stoker said. "This manufacturing process creates hazardous toxins, and disposing of all of those byproducts is dangerous to the surrounding area. Destroying a house or hurting the environment doesn't concern these scumbags. However, getting caught worries them immensely, and sending *some* of their wastewater out to a pond instead of down the drain will help them stay off the radar screen. That pond flows into a creek and it would be months before anybody noticed plants dying or other effects."

"One of the ways we catch meth cooking criminals is by monitoring the sewage flow from their homes," explained Glover. "You would be surprised how easy it is to snake in a camera through the sewer system just far enough to monitor the outflow that comes out of washing machines, shower drains, dishwashers and the like. Of course it requires probable cause and a warrant."

Stoker continued the explanation, describing how a long, constant trickle of water coming out of a home's sewer system indicates it may be a meth lab. In contrast, when the authorities monitor the sewage coming out of a normal house, water flows for a few minutes during a shower, for a few seconds during a flush, or for about three minutes as a clothes washer or dishwasher drains. But, few homes have sewage exiting consistently for an hour or more, as required in the production of methamphetamines. Stoker speculated that this system took advantage of the fishing pond and allowed the meth cooks to jettison a fair amount of polluted water out to the fishpond. It would be months, or maybe even years, before the effects of those chemicals would show up in a seventeen-acre fishpond.

"That's it! Yes." Ann Higgins interrupted Stoker. "They own two homes. Wait a second and let me tell you my thought." Ann stood up and paced as she thought for a moment. Then, she turned back and leaned over the table. "That Frank Thompson guy who got on my case yesterday for trespassing, mentioned that the owners also bought the home next door. With two homes they can alternate production as well!" Ann said. "That would let the meth cooks hide the sewage discharge even more. Does that sound crazy?"

"Isn't that convenient?" said Glover. "An excellent observation, Ann. I bet that is exactly what's going on."

"So, now what do we do?" asked Lewis.

"Scott, we may need your help with a little snooping. But, we're going to rely on Z and Dr. Rivera to call the next surveillance shots," Glover said. "They'll be here in a few minutes and we'll get down to some details at that point."

"We need to keep watching what is going on inside that house," explained Stoker. "No crime has been committed yet, but we're pretty sure it will be."

"Unfortunately, those homes are private property, and we cannot access them without a warrant," explained Glover. "We may need to get creative about monitoring activities from the outside. We can watch the construction teams and deliveries."

Stoker turned to Ann. "With your permission, I could monitor chemicals flowing out into the pond, which is Chelsea Crossing property."

"Permission granted," Ann said.

"When do we involve the police?" Lewis asked.

"For now, we will not involve the local police." Stoker surprised Lewis with his snappy answer. "Something's not right in the world of Sioux Falls police drug enforcement. I don't know what it is. Cases seem to fall through their fingers. Somebody's tipping off the criminals. Let's lay our own traps and see what happens."

Holly Glover agreed with Stoker and then leaned into the group with a dire expression on her face. "I'm about to share with you some confidential information. Drug interdiction and the greater Sioux Falls area has been challenging of late. I follow these cases as a hired prosecutor. I take the overflow the State's Attorney's office cannot handle. I've seen four cases where we watch potential meth houses and dealers for a few days or weeks. Once we gather enough intelligence to start asking for search or arrest warrants, the labs and people disappear.

"The timing is uncanny. This is no coincidence. The police suspect that somebody in their own ranks or somebody with a position within the legal system is tipping them off. As somebody who prosecutes a fair number of drug cases, the police have even come to my office to ask me some tough questions. They wonder if I'm the leak."

"That's horrible," interjected Ann.

"Oh, no. I know better than to be offended. There's a lot at stake, and they have no good clues. But, I don't mind saying that the police have been aggressive about questioning me. They've also interrogated other prosecutors and every member of the vice squad. The heat is on to find out why the meth trade has the upper hand right now in Sioux Falls."

"As an attorney, Holly has some latitude about when she decides to make her knowledge available to the police," explained Stoker. "Let's see if we can help her gather, and then hand over, a thick dossier of incontrovertible facts in the next few days."

It was 9:58 a.m., and Glover called for a short break. Standing up, she stepped toward the door. "I'll check the waiting room for Z and Dr. Rivera."

Ann opened her bottled water and looked across the table at Scott Lewis, the private investigator. The look on his face said, *Wow! The coach has put me into the big game.* He was excited to add a little variety to his life, which consisted mostly of documenting adultery. He had photographed couples going in and out of the same seedy Sioux Falls hotels hundreds of times. His life of boring P.I. work looked like it may finally get interesting.

Glover returned to the conference room accompanying Dr. Rivera, and another man who was five feet eight inches tall, sporting a stubbly beard and hair that was long and dark. His Levi's were worn, and his New Balance shoes looked amazingly comfortable. His crisply laundered Canali dress shirt with a subtle blue stripe looked starkly out of place with his other clothing choices. This was the man known as Z. His clothing choices were only slightly brilliant, but his domination of all things technology was thoroughly brilliant.

Holly Glover made introductions and had everyone sit down around the table. "Z is a freelance IT specialist our firm uses." She shot Z a look of partial disapproval. "We use him sparingly, however, because his hourly rate is higher than our lawyers. Z was involved when we completed this building two years ago, and he helped install our new IT system with the upgrade."

"He's done some security and IT work at my office, too," Stoker said. "Nobody encrypts a smart phone and wireless network like Z."

"We appreciate Z particularly for his security skills and his discrete tendencies," said Glover. Z waived courteously but said nothing, and Glover continued on. "Z is going to use some of his smarts to help us keep an eye on the homes on Bryant Way," Stoker explained. "Later today, two paralegals from my office will accompany Z on a tour of another home that is for sale on Bryant Way. One paralegal will pose as a real estate agent. Our second employee will pose as his spouse."

Z perked up and uttered his first words of the meeting. "The hotter one gets to be my wife, right?"

The room broke into laughter, and Glover brought the meeting to order by smiling and countering Z's lighthearted remark. "Not if you keep interrupting my meeting." Z smiled, but there was just enough tension to put Glover back in control. "Scott will put his P.I. skills to good use and be in another nearby car as a lookout. As part of the tour, Z and the paralegals will walk along the shore of the pond."

"At opportune moments we will place some listening devices and small, external cameras that will camouflage in with the snow," Z said. "That will give us a chance to watch what's going on from the outside and do some listening."

Stoker chimed into the conversation. "Ann, what you discovered here may be huge. I want to be straight with you. Over the next few weeks, I bet we're going to see a meth lab or two go live here. And, if busting a few meth cookers was all we were interested in, we would not take all of these measures."

Ann Higgins looked back and Stoker and said, "You're trying to see if you can somehow flush out some of the higher ups and find out who is behind all of this."

"This is risky business," Rivera said.

"While I cannot anticipate all of the risks, I'm not going to run from trouble. You do what you need to do, and I'll watch my back the best I can," Ann said.

"We'll all watch our backs," Rivera said.

"That is precisely what we need to do," Glover said. "There's a big fish out there, and we just need to know little bit more to catch it."

"Let me be frank with you," chimed in Rivera. "The Sioux Falls Police Department is jam packed with talent. The vice squad rivals teams in Minneapolis, Des Moines, and many other Midwestern cities. But, right now they're scratching their heads because somebody in a high position is sabotaging their investigations."

"Now, Scott." Stoker turned to the private investigator. "We need to let you in on a little secret. Dr. Rivera here is a successful physician who practices full-time at the Veterans Administration hospital. However, his military experience has prepared him to tackle some, well, let's just say, weekend warrior assignments outside his practice of medicine."

"I'm not swearing you to secrecy," stated Rivera sternly. "I'm ordering you to it. I occasionally receive assignments from Washington D.C., but they never come from named federal agencies. You're not allowed to tell anybody about my assignments, including this one." Then Rivera turned to Ann. "Even the lieutenant governor should not know we're acquainted." Rivera paused for a minute and furrowed his forehead. "Actually, for now, *especially* the lieutenant governor should not know about me and any of our work together."

"There's been the looming potential for a large-scale federal DEA investigation here in Sioux Falls. This new lead has prompted me to reach out and encourage them to move forward. The complexity of this operation, the apparent money involved, and the potential scale of the meth manufacturing have me convinced that this investigation needs to occur. It would be wise to pursue it unbeknownst to all state and local authorities."

Z took his turn explaining to Ann and Scott. "We're reading both of you into the case because, well, you already know too much. But, more importantly, Ann, you can help give us access to places and people that we did not know existed before yesterday. I realize this puts you in a difficult place. For now we're asking you to keep a secret from your husband, who just happens to be the lieutenant governor."

"I understand. I hate it emotionally, but I understand it intellectually."

Rivera looked at Ann with kind eyes, but spoke with a stern voice. "That's just the way it has to be. We cannot function any other way." Then turning to the whole group, Rivera stood up. "This is turning into a highly classified operation.

We will cease this operation immediately if our operational security is compromised in any way. Any questions?"

Everyone in the room was motionless and silent. After a few seconds, Stoker spoke up. "Then, we're done here." Everyone else stood and filed out of the room. Ann Higgins was anxious to get back home. She was not driven by a timetable or "to do" list. She needed the secure feeling of being home. Instead of lingering after the meeting, she made a hasty exit from the law office, went out into the parking lot and got in her car.

As Ann Higgins left the parking lot, a man inside a small SUV with dirty blond hair and pronounced acne scars noticed her leaving the building. It was his job to notice where she went and what she did. Once Ann had pulled out of the parking lot and had traveled about thirty yards down the road, the man in the SUV pulled his car into traffic and followed her. He speed-dialed a number on his phone and issued his report the moment the other person answered. "Higgins is on the move."

"What was she doing in that place?" Harry Klein was talking from his hotel room where he'd been lamenting his forthcoming reassignment to the farm in Arkansas.

"I would say she was meeting with her attorney, but I also saw that shrink, Troy Stoker go in there just before her. So, I'm not quite sure."

"Well, did you try to get any information with that bag of surveillance toys I gave you?"

"Yes, sir. I tried, but I couldn't pick up anything." The man with the dirty blond hair had mainly tried to use a special microphone to listen for Ann Higgins's voice, but he could never find it. "That place is a black hole of silence. Somebody designed it that way. These damn lawyers are good. They surprised me this time."

"Just stay on her. Tell me anything you can find out." Klein was issuing commands out of desperation. He could not afford to provide the commander with an inadequate report. "Let's hope it's a lot more good information the next time you call."

CHAPTER 12

MINNEHAHA COUNTRY CLUB, SIOUX FALLS

In a few days they would be the four most powerful men in South Dakota; and here they all sat on a Saturday morning. Governor-elect Richard Horton was flanked by his soon-to-be Lieutenant Governor Kent Higgins. On the other side of the small table sat the man would soon be the secretary of state, Allen Miller, as well as the next attorney general, Steve Hewitt. They were gathered in a small meeting room in the Minnehaha Country Club in Sioux Falls. The outgoing administration had been slow to facilitate meetings at the South Dakota State Capitol in Pierre. This did not bother governor-elect Horton, because he had already decided that his administration would be doing a little more of its work from Sioux Falls. The outgoing administration was refusing to help the state's new leaders because of the bad blood that had built up during the campaign.

The state's four incoming executive officers were engaging in yet another highly productive strategy session. They wanted to hit the ground running and give the voters exactly what they asked for, incarcerating more criminals and defending low tax rates. It had been their battle cry during the campaign and it was now their mandate. These four men were going to show the rest of an increasingly left-leaning nation how God intended the U.S. of A to operate and thrive. "Within two years we'll be joining North Dakota, Arizona, Nevada, Colorado and Utah as one of the fastest growing states in the country," Governor Horton said. "People with a work ethic and common sense will be fleeing here from Illinois, Wisconsin, Massachusetts and Oregon. They'll be sick of seeing their neighbors sit around all day watching cable TV and eating food-stamp-subsidized potato chips. They'll be a little weary — not from working their fingers to the bone because that is what they love to do — but from paying so much of their hard-earned cash into a system that doles out benefits with a Santa Claus mentality."

Allen Miller, the man who would soon be secretary of state, chimed in. "They don't want to live in a state where the welfare lines are staffed by people who will gladly process applications in English or the language of your choice. They're sick of paying for it. All of those hard-working, independent and law-abiding people will want to be here in South Dakota. Now let's make this happen."

This was the sixth time this team had held their Saturday strategy meetings. The first meeting concentrated on identifying attorneys who were tough on crime and who could join one of the many State's Attorney offices around the state on a full-time basis. More importantly, there were talented attorneys who would never leave their private practices, but would proudly work as private contractors prosecuting cases for the attorney general. These hired guns would never consider joining the ranks of government attorneys, but they had a passion for the courtroom. For some of these lawyers, it was the ego-massaging thrill of hearing their own voices booming off of the walls in a well-apportioned courtroom that drew them to the work. There were also a few private-contract prosecutors who were passionate about putting away the bad guys and keeping the streets safe in their corners of South Dakota.

Incoming Attorney General Hewitt had a list of fifty such attorneys throughout the state, and he had already agreed, in principal, to contract with most of them. However, Hewitt insisted that all methamphetamine-related work was to be done internally by state-employed assistant district attorneys whom he would oversee personally. The governor heartily endorsed Hewitt's plan and mandated that bringing methamphetamine under control was to be one of the new attorney general's highest priorities. Hewitt pointed out that he was passionate about the methamphetamine issue, and he wanted to focus his time on putting hundreds of methamphetamine labs out of business in South Dakota.

The last item on today's power meeting agenda was the upcoming inauguration. "Sioux Falls delivered the vote for us, so we need to reward our constituents here. They really put us over the top. So, we're going to hold the inauguration right here in Sioux Falls."

The governor-elect nodded to Kent Higgins, signaling that it was his turn to speak. "We've booked the Sioux Falls Convention Center," chimed in the lieutenant governor, "for the inaugural ball. But, we'll take our oaths of office at Falls Park right alongside the water, whether the river is running or frozen. It will take place at noon on Inauguration Day."

"I don't give a damn if it's thirty degrees below zero," said the governor-elect. "We're tough, rugged people, and we need to show the people how tough we can be."

"I love it," exclaimed the attorney general. "None of this stuffy three-piece-suit-and-tie pageantry. We'll wear real men's clothes."

"I'll order mine out of the Cabela's catalog, and I'll shine up my great grandpa's Sterling silver bolo tie," Horton said. "We'll show South Dakota that we're men of action braving the storms and enduring the cold as we take our oaths beside the pristine falls. It says we love our state, and we love our country—in rain or shine, in hot or cold. Now that's showing the progressives some progress."

All four men laughed, but it was really the governor who was indulging in a large belly laugh. As his laughter died down he turned to the attorney general-elect. "Now Steve, I know you enjoy living in Pierre, so please don't be offended if we spoil the people of Sioux Falls a little bit. This town has a lot to offer, and I hope you'll get to know it a little bit more."

"Oh no, Governor. I've done a fair amount of work here in my time. I love Sioux Falls already."

CHAPTER 13

The farmer's name was Robert Nichols, and his handler had just put him on call. "You might have to fly up to Sioux Falls." Ron Cunningham, a man the farmer spoke with almost daily, was explaining the problem. "We have a situation, and I think we're going to need your help taking care of it."

"And, it might require some dirty work?" Nichols loved the idea of doing a little dirty work.

As a farmer, his life growing cash crops in Arkansas was solitary and angry, and that was exactly how he liked it. Nichols had lived this way for years. But now his life included money, thanks to the intense man with piercing blue eyes, the commander. It also included spending a fair amount of time in South Dakota, which was fine during seven months of the year.

Nichols had married his high school sweetheart at the age of nineteen. Due to his violent and controlling tendencies the marriage was over by the time he was twenty. He'd married two more times—the last being a mail-order bride. But, neither of those marriages lasted more than six months. His abusive beatings had landed his last wife in the hospital, and landed him three weeks in jail and on a year of probation. Of course, he attended more than a hundred anger management classes, but they did him no good.

Fortunately, two of his wives had been wise enough to use birth control and had never conceived a child with Nichols. Also fortunate, the third never informed him that he was indeed a father—at least biologically. She quietly slipped off to Atlanta, had the baby, and gave her up for adoption to a warm and sincere couple offering the little girl love, a good home, and kindness throughout her formative years.

Robert Nichols hated just about everyone and he had a vast list of people he blamed for his failures. According to this crude Arkansas farmer, his banker had oppressed him financially. He also perceived that some of his failures were due to underhanded tactics by "those Mexicans, Vietnamese and other migrants." The Democrats had impoverished him with taxes and overwhelmed him with regulations. His parents had failed to provide him with guidance in life. Each of his wives had failed to satisfy him on many levels.

More than a decade ago, when the commander conducted an extensive background check on Nichols, he learned that Nichols was the problem. The hired investigators learned that the rural banker who managed the farmer's mortgage had actually worked very hard, and made many concessions to help him keep his farm. Nichols had been greedy and careless with money. His parents had taught him to work, provided him with tutors during high school, and saved more than $80,000 for his college education. Nichols had the intelligence, but he would not study. He dropped out of junior college before he could complete a single semester. Had it not been for the family farm, Nichols may have spent most of his life working for minimum wage.

The commander walked into Nichols's life at his darkest hour and laid out a plan. "I'm offering you eighty-three thousand dollars for ten percent of your farm." The well-dressed stranger sat at Nichols's kitchen table. The farmer had just been released from jail, and he had missed some mortgage payments on his farm. Life was bleak, and the commander seemed to be the miracle Nichols needed. "Over the next thirteen years I'll buy out the rest of it for seventy-eight thousand dollars per year. You'll keep your share of the profits and maintain ninety percent of the control. But at the end of year thirteen, it's all mine, and I decide which employees I want to keep." The commander had found the desperate farmer by bribing a banker for a list of upcoming foreclosures in the area. Nichols was the easiest target on the list.

The farm-saving deal sounded reasonably good to Nichols. He was just days away from the shame of a foreclosure and homelessness. The commander sipped the mint julep Nichols had unexpectedly produced from within his rickety kitchen. The commander pointed to the signature line on the last page of the contract and then laid down the pen. "But, before you sign, you must agree that there are just a few decisions I get to make starting today. And, it's critical for you to keep some secrets. You've got to keep your mouth shut about our partnership. If you keep quiet, you'll be around to cash your last check. And also, don't go asking me, or anybody else, a bunch of questions. Just learn as much as you can along the way."

Fear immediately seized Nichols that night at his kitchen table, but he'd been in enough bar fights to know how to mask fear with bravado. He had no idea how the new man might afflict him if he failed to keep silent. He sensed that this new person, the commander, had the means and capability to cause him intense pain—or even a miserable death.

"I'm in." Nichols masked his fear and looked the commander in the eye. "Whatever you need, I'm in." He signed all of the paperwork, but understood almost none of it.

"I think your farm is a perfect place to grow one of America's favorite plants."

"What's that?"

"Usually it's imported from Mexico and sold in baggies—but never sold in stores."

Nichols smiled. "I'm already a big fan of your product, Commander."

The commander did not return his smile, but instead remained serious. "If you keep your mouth shut, do what I say, don't smoke the pot, and work your butt off, you will quietly become financially comfortable."

"Okay." Nichols wiped the smile off his face while lamenting that free samples were not part of the deal.

"Oh, yes. I also expect for your celibacy trend to continue, at least here on the farm. No wives, girlfriends, boyfriends or any other types of relationships that can compromise the confidential nature of our little enterprise, here," the commander insisted. "But, if you go out of town, have all the fun you want."

That next February, Nichols started a small crop of Cannabis plants in a greenhouse on his Arkansas farm. A few weeks after his spring corn planting, he carefully interlaced the plants with his budding crop. In August the commander sent two men to harvest the plants. The whole year's crop fit neatly in the back of their rental van.

A few weeks later, the commander showed up on a Saturday afternoon. He handed Nichols a check for $78,000. "That's for next year's payment. I now own twenty percent, *partner*. And, here's a bonus." The commander handed him a thick manila envelope. "Take a look."

Nichols opened the envelope and inside he saw a large wad of cash.

"That's five thousand dollars," explained the commander. "It's my way of saying thanks. Just make sure you spend it a little here and a little there. Enjoy some nice meals, but always at different restaurants. Make your next truck payment with cash. Use cash for every other gasoline fill-up. Enjoy a weekend gambling in Memphis, but at a few different casinos. You know, you need to do these kinds of things to make sure the IRS never notices."

From that moment on, Nichols was fully invested with his new pal, the commander. His assistance, compliance, and silence was now bought and paid for. This relationship continued like clockwork for the full thirteen-year agreement. At the end of the thirteen years, Nichols was directed to turn the title to his farm over to Green Growth Ventures, LLC of Reno, Nevada. He was also offered a modest-paying job as the farm manager and was allowed to remain living in the home. The commander showered him with perks to make up for his low wages. The cash bonuses continued, and Nichols also got to attend frequent business "meetings" in Florida that included fishing charters, booze, flattering female companionship, NFL football games, amazing food and Cuban cigars.

Sometimes the commander joined Nichols aboard a fishing charter. He used the opportunity to reinforce the no wife, girlfriend, boyfriend or other relationship issue and to remind Nichols how important secrecy was in their relationship.

Then, almost overnight, things changed. The naïve farmer, Robert Nichols, got a new handler from Green Growth Ventures. Ron Cunningham, who was now, apparently, the commander's right-hand man, started issuing the orders to Nichols from out of the main office in Reno, Nevada. For the next few years, Nichols conducted business as usual on the farm. He remained angry and alone—and he could not have been happier. He particularly liked jumping on airplanes and doing dirty work for the commander as his handler in Reno was directing him to do today.

"You know I'm ready," Nichols said to Cunningham.

"Even for the cold?" the handler knew his man well. He knew Nichols always had his overnight bag packed. He also knew how much the farmer from Arkansas hated the cold.

"Sure, I hate the temperatures in South Dakota in January, but I love to see the coyotes so ravenous."

CHAPTER 14

His name was Jason Moore, and he was a social worker, which meant that he was supremely confident in his abilities to resolve psychological issues, navigate the legal system and manipulate the medical establishment for the good of society's many victims. When he opened his email that morning, the report of Dr. Stoker using a Taser on a patient was in his inbox, and he made it his highest priority—even though few people cared about his priorities.

When Moore stepped into Dr. Stoker's office an hour later, he waited ten feet behind the reception desk and observed a patient negotiating with the receptionist, Tamara. "I'm just dropping by to pick up new prescriptions," the patient said.

Tamara asked her to have a seat. "I'll try to work this in with Dr. Stoker. Can I please ask you to call ahead next time, sweetie? That helps us take care of you faster." Tamara was a master negotiator and she used her skills to help Dr. Stoker avoid interruptions and optimize his time helping patients. "I'll see if Dr. Stoker can sign these between patients," Tamara said.

Moore, the always-observant social worker, looked around and noticed a kindly looking couple, probably in their mid-fifties, seated on a couch together and waiting. A preppy middle-aged drug rep was seated in another chair, and was reading Men's Fitness magazine. The social worker unconsciously cast his eyes down at the floor and failed to recognize how quickly he had ceded alpha status to the drug rep. He briefly considered the discrepancy in salaries and the unfairness of their worlds. *This guy probably has a bachelor's degree in basket weaving, and he's probably making seventy thousand dollars per year. Here I am serving humanity at a lousy thirty-six grand, and I have a master's degree from the University of Minnesota*, thought Moore. He pursed his lips for a moment and then clenched his fists before turning back toward the front desk. "Screw him," he whispered softly under his breath.

Finally, it was Moore's turn to talk to the receptionist. As he presented his business card, from the South Dakota Department of Social Services, he was fully aware of the smug expression that graced his rather plain face. "I'm here on investigation, and I need to visit with Dr. Stoker," Jason Moore said without any additional introduction or greeting.

"Let me check in with him when he finishes with this patient," responded Tamara. Dr. Stoker had trained her specifically how to respond when health inspectors, process servers, and investigators presented at the office. Most doctors thought that calling an attorney was the best thing to do in these instances. Stoker had simply laid down policies and practices based on basic civil rights. Tamara rarely needed to use the tactics on legal and government people. However, they tended to work surprisingly well on overly aggressive drug reps and sales people.

Moore's hypersensitive feelings detected the non-committal tone in her answer. After all, she only agreed to check in with Dr. Stoker. "Great. But, after you check in with him, I will be able to see him, right?"

"That's up to Dr. Stoker. But, as you know, patients come first. You may have to make an appointment and come back. What can I tell him about the investigation?"

"I'm not at liberty to discuss it with anybody but Dr. Stoker."

"Well, for you to assert that *liberty*, you may want me to pass along a detail or two. Is this about one of our patients?" She was reading a list of questions taped just under the counter where she could see them anytime. It happened to be the same counter the leisurely Jason Moore was leaning on.

"Yes."

"Are we the target of this investigation, or is this collateral information for an investigation on another party?"

Moore's spine stiffened, and he stopped leaning on the counter to stand upright. "I'm afraid I cannot say," answered Moore.

"Actually your body language said enough." Tamara was squarely in charge of this conversation now. This was one of the many reasons Dr. Stoker appreciated her so much. "Despite your being afraid, Mr. . . . . "

"Moore."

"Yes, Mr. Moore. This sounds serious. As *afraid* as you are to state your intentions, Dr. Stoker will want me to send him a message with key information about all of your darkest fears. Many times I've heard him turn people away who will not disclose their intentions."

"He has to talk with me. I'm an investigator from South Dakota."

"That may work on some people, but not here. We're pretty familiar with the Fourth Amendment, and we've trained ourselves extensively to ensure that government people abide by it."

Moore's mind went blank. In spite of all of his undergraduate and master's degrees, he was completely unaware of the Fourth Amendment. It had been a few years since high school civics.

"So, are we being investigated, or is this collateral information for an investigation on another party?"

"I'm looking into an incident with Dr. Stoker."

Tamara slid a small sheet of paper along the counter toward Moore. "Please write the associated patient's name here. Please do not say it out loud." Moore hesitated and searched for words to rebut, but Tamara spoke before he could protest. "We certainly worry about privacy. Just write that name right there."

Moore decided not to argue. And he scribbled Tom DuPont's name on the paper and slid it back. Although Tamara was acutely aware of DuPont's attack on Stoker last Friday, she showed no emotion as she read the name. "Thank you. I'll send Dr. Stoker a message and push this patient's record to the doctor's computer."

"Do you think he'll see me?"

"It's hard to say. Let's just wait and see. Why don't you go ahead and have a seat." Moore chose the seat furthest from the well-dressed drug rep.

After about five minutes, Dr. Stoker emerged from his office. Today he was using a cane to compensate for his injured knee as he accompanied his patient back to the front desk. After recommending the patient return in two months, and busying Tamara with making that appointment, Dr. Stoker turned to the other patients in the waiting room. "Hello, Mr. and Mrs. M!" He used only their initials to respect their privacy. "I'm sorry about the limping. I can't decide if I limp more like Master Yoda or like that Dr. House guy on the TV."

"You definitely walk more like Yoda," joked Mrs. M.

"It's time to get caught up with each other." Stoker anticipated Mr. M's first question. "And, no. I still have not bagged my buck this year. I'm way behind."

"When was the last time you bow-hunted, Doc?" Mr. M asked.

"It's been weeks, and that's a problem," Stoker said. "Now, before you get up off of this marginally comfortable couch, I'm going to ask you to hang on for a few minutes. I need to visit with somebody from the government who has overlooked a courtesy that the rest of us extend to each other—an appointment."

Stoker turned his head and stared Moore straight in the eye. "You've got five minutes today, but next time I expect an appointment—or a signed search warrant." Stoker limped back to his office. Moore watched Stoker for a moment, and decided to follow him. "What is this about?" Stoker asked with firm diplomacy as Moore entered his office.

"I'm investigating the incident with Tom DuPont."

"For the love of Pete, man! Don't you believe in privacy? You just broadcast the name of your agency's client and my patient. What if somebody out there in my waiting room knows him?" Then he motioned with his hand, "Can you please close that door?"

Moore obeyed, and then elected to sit down without being invited. The social worker launched into an apology. "I'm sorry, Dr. Stoker. I was just answering the question you asked me."

"Yes. But, I thought the state would send somebody who was trained and aware of patient privacy. What are you? Some kind of paralegal?"

"I'm a social worker with the Department of Social Services."

"A social worker? You're trained as a mental health professional, and you overlooked the fundamentals of confidentiality with a patient we hold in common? You have four minutes remaining. And, you're lucky that I'm probably too busy to report your HIPAA violation. I may have to disclose to Mr. DuPont and ask him what he wants me to do about it, though."

Moore hesitated for a moment, and considered ignoring the remark and continuing with his investigation, before he decided to apologize one more time. "I'm sorry Dr. Stoker. I should've been more careful. I don't know what else to say."

"Say no more. Let's talk about Tasers and ambulance rides."

"I've been sent here to investigate the incident with Tom DuPont," stammered Moore. "The man you electrocuted."

"So we're focusing on the Taser part?" Stoker asked.

Moore hesitated and began to backpedal. "Oh, no. We want to talk about all of it. I do need to cover the Taser, however."

"What else to you want to cover? Your statement about *electrocution* was quite telling. You're here in an attempt to implicate me, Mr. Moore. Is your mind already made up?"

"Oh, no, no, no. I'm an impartial investigator. This is all just routine stuff."

"So, what else, besides the Taser part, do you want to cover?"

"All of it," Moore said.

"Such as?"

Moore squirmed before he answered, "Well, let's start at the start."

"Sure, but before we go to the beginning of the story, what do you think the ending looks like?"

"I really don't know. I hope you'll tell me, Doctor."

"Well, there's a reason I'm wearing a bandage on my forearm and limping around with a cane this morning, I would hope those observations gave you some obvious clues. There's a hint about how the story ends." Stoker lifted up his cane for emphasis, and gave Moore a stern look. "You know about the Taser. What else do you know?"

"I know you went to the hospital," replied Moore.

"Why?"

"I, um well, I guess I know about your leg and arm, but I'm not aware of the full extent of your injuries."

"Where did you get your information so far?" Stoker asked.

"From another social worker at the hospital."

"And, he or she did not tell you anything about my injuries?"

Moore hesitated. Indeed, the other social worker was only excited to report that Dr. Stoker had used a Taser on a patient. "Well, Dr. Stoker, I see your point. The report I received was biased. It reported the Taser incident only. So, let's cancel out some of this bias. Tell me what else I should've learned. I'm happy to consider both sides."

"If you inquire at the hospital, you'll learn that Tom DuPont's tox screens, both blood and urine, showed that his physical manifestations of tweaking were certainly caused by a high dose of recreational amphetamines. A few minutes into our exam, Tom attacked me using a table and a chair as weapons. Check in with the hospital. You'll find a list of extensive wounds that I suffered—all prior to using the Taser. I withstood his attacks before defending myself. If you do your homework, you'll see that the law allows a person under an imminent threat to defend himself with force. I went two steps beyond imminent threat before I reacted. What more do you need to know?"

"So, what happened when he attacked you?"

"Do you know what a pneumothorax is?"

"The term rings a bell," said Moore.

"Tom DuPont collapsed my lung and almost caused me to bleed to death. Incidentally, I now have a few units of a stranger's blood coursing through my veins, thanks to the wounds Mr. DuPont created. So after those injuries, I used the Taser."

Moore scratched a few notes on a legal pad while he furrowed his brow and exaggerated his concern. "I'm certainly glad to know that, Dr. Stoker. I'm sorry about your injuries."

Then Moore looked up from his notepad. "So, do you have any guns here?"

"I used to. Some very effective ones," Stoker answered with calm conviction. "I'm on my private property. I have a right to keep and bear arms. Even as a psychiatrist, I retain that right. Many psychiatrists are killed by patients each year, Mr. Moore. Despite what your mental health left-wing training may have brainwashed you to believe, I can have weapons, and I can use them when my life is threatened."

"Can I see the Taser?"

"The short answer is no," responded Stoker with a pause. "The long answer is, you can see the Taser if you proceed with life-threatening violence against me." Stoker leaned forward and looked Moore intensely in the eye. "Mr. Moore, I allowed my assailant to attack me on Friday. That is a much higher standard than the general public, who only has to *recognize* they are in a state of imminent danger. For example, if you felt an imminent threat to your life as you walked to your car after work, you would have the right to use a weapon. In my office, I wisely waited until Tom DuPont proceeded with violence against me. That is how Tom DuPont ended up injuring me first." Stoker lifted his cane a little bit and pointed it in Moore's direction. "Stuff that in your little report."

"Oh. All of this is still preliminary for any sort of report," said Moore.

"What's your email address?" Stoker asked.

Moore handed him a card. "It's right here on this card."

Stoker took a moment and typed a few keystrokes on his computer and clicked the mouse a few times. "There you go. Your inbox now contains an email from me with all of the legal and case law information you need to include in your report. While I'm an expert psychiatrist, I'm also an amateur student of history, the Constitution and the law. Two constitutional law attorneys have trained me on the proper use of force. If you would like to consult with them, on your dime, their contact information is in that email, also.

"My reaction on Friday was disciplined and planned, according to my rights, as well as the rights my attacker. I have always dreaded the possibility that such a day might come when I would have to exercise my right to self-defense. I hoped it would not. But, I needed to be ready. If I hadn't been prepared, right now I would be dead." Stoker sat forward a little more in his chair and pointed directly at Moore. "Did they tell you that a large proportion of my blood volume stained this carpet during that attack?"

"No. But, you still cannot go around using Tasers on patients."

"Did you say *patients* with a plural 's' on the end?"

"No. I am just speaking in general." Moore hesitated, confused by his own words.

"Really now. How many other *patients* have I used a Taser on?" Stoker asked.

"Well, none. But, I was just—"

Stoker cut him off. "Showing how you really perceive the world? What's really going on here?"

The social worker asserted an air of authority and tried to regain his momentum. "We fear an emerging pattern, and we need to prevent—"

"Emerging pattern from one event? Unbelievable!" Shaking his head, Stoker said, "It's obvious you've not been listening to me." The doctor stood from his chair and reached for his cane. "Let's have you go back to your cubicle and review the email I've sent you. After that, you just *might* understand. I indeed can use the Taser on a patient or anybody else who acts a certain way. Now, let me show you something on your way out." Stoker limped toward the door. "Follow me." Moore followed the doctor out of his office, and wondered why Stoker was walking toward the waiting room?

"Here is a lesson in what it is like to live in a free nation." Stoker's voice was calm as he stepped to the door. "Please leave my office—my personal, private property."

"I'm investigating you, and my questions are not answered yet," Moore snapped. "This interview is not over."

"I've voluntarily answered all your questions. Some of them more than once. Now, leave my property and don't come back without an appointment. You can bring a warrant, too, if you can obtain one."

"Dr. Stoker. I am an investigator for the State of South Dakota, and you must—"

Stoker held his index finger up to his lips and limped toward Moore while looking him directly in the eye. "For the third time, leave. You are now trespassing. I can and will remove you."

Moore hesitated briefly, broke the stare, and spoke up into the air. "You must answer my questions."

In a split second, Stoker dropped his cane, rapidly maneuvered to Moore's side, grabbed him by the collar of his jacket and shirt with his right hand, swung open the door with his left hand, and firmly pushed the unsteady social worker out onto the sidewalk. "I really believe in appointments!" called out Stoker before he shut the door and locked the deadbolt.

The patients in the waiting room applauded. "Now that's what I call government waste reduction," Mrs. M said. The drug rep, who had been waiting for more than an hour because he did not have an appointment, was dumbfounded.

"Bravo, Dr. Stoker," Tamara said. "I'll watch through the window to make sure he does not linger in the parking lot. If he doesn't leave, I'll call our next patient and ask her to come to the back door."

"He'll leave. He can't wait to get back to the office and file a report." Stoker smiled and hobbled toward the reception desk. "Will you please send him an email a little later today, and tell him how to contact us for an appointment? Let him know we appreciate his interest in fairness and the rule of law."

The well-dressed drug rep had recovered from his initial shock, and he collected enough courage to interrupt Dr. Stoker. As the man approached the doctor, Stoker immediately pivoted on his good foot toward Mr. and Mrs. M who had been waiting. "I think it's finally your turn. Why don't you go back to my office? I'll meet you in thirty—no fifteen seconds." Then Stoker turned toward the drug rep. "Let's see that device of yours. Let me sign it. Give the samples to Tamara."

"But, Dr. Stoker—" The drug rep tried to get in his latest sales speech.

Stoker elevated his voice and spoke right over the top of him. "These people have already waited long enough, thanks to somebody else who wanted to give a speech." Stoker picked up his cane and glanced out the window. "On my time and my property no less." Then he limped toward the drug rep. "I know the efficacy of your antidepressant." He made air quotes as he said "antidepressant" and continued talking so the well-groomed man could not interrupt him. "All the thirty-nine patients I've given it to, according to your titration schedule, vomited it up, period. I have adjusted the titration schedule to lengthen the ramp-up time significantly from your recommendations. Now, the four patients I have allowed to remain on it have no side effects. However, they also have no *good* effects, either—so far. I think they believed your slickly produced magazine ads, but now they're realizing this antidepressant is a dud."

The drug rep silently handed the doctor his iPad, which Stoker signed. "Leave the samples with Tamara. Thank you. This is definitely the ninth most effective antidepressant out on the market these days. I'll probably write a script or two per year. Please see me again in three hundred days." Stoker began hobbling toward his office.

"That is definitely a Dr. House limp, you grump," Tamara said with a sweet smile.

"Act this way, Master Yoda would not," Stoker joked as he limped back to his office with his patients.

CHAPTER 15

"Dr. Haslam, this is the third time you've met with this residency committee to discuss issues that have us concerned." Dr. Penny Denning, chair of the department of psychiatry was conducting the meeting. Four other psychiatrists from the committee flanked Denning. Sarah Haslam sat alone on the other side of the table. "We're *not* here to discuss just one or two small issues. We've got some major problems to straighten out—"

As was her habit, Sarah Haslam interrupted. "Dr. Denning, you know as well as I do that none of this is fair." Haslam was defiant. "Look around. Have you seen how the other residents don't include me?"

"Yes. You've alienated them, and you need to take responsibility for how you pushed them away, Sarah." Dr. Denning knew she could only be frank with Sarah Haslam. This perpetually troublesome resident only understood bluntness. "You fail to complete your documentation and our attending physicians are encouraging me to expel you. Your interactions with borderlines and other difficult patients are harsh and inappropriate, especially for a psychiatrist. Yet, you persist in trying to fault your fellow residents for your shortcomings. You've also blamed the department administrator, nurses, social workers, and even the computers for your problems."

"These idiotic electronic medical records are a waste of time! I spend my whole day pointing and clicking and searching interminable lists of diagnostic codes." Haslam was defiant. "Oh, please give me another lecture about medical necessity and how the Office of Inspector General and FBI will bring down fire and brimstone upon us, and throw us all in jail, if we fail in our quest to actually find a logical diagnostic code and click it." Now Haslam was on a sarcastic rant tinged with a little stress-induced psychosis.

The residency committee had identified her severe personality disorders, including narcissism in the first month. Moreover, the stress of residency had brought out some psychotic tendencies. By month two, they had also concluded that Sarah Haslam showed a strong possibility of borderline personality disorder—a diagnosis that was troubling to the residency committee. These seasoned psychiatrists lamented that they had overlooked her psychological troubles when they interviewed her for a residency slot two years ago. Haslam had displayed charm, wit and intellect back during the residency selection process.

Haslam continued her stormy dialog. "Wow! These computers and all their 'meaningful use' are really speeding up patient care and making us better doctors."

"Enough, Sarah!" Dr. Marty Sinclair said. He was the residency mentor specifically assigned to Haslam, and he let his anger show through. "Since you've managed to piss off everyone in the hospital, we've decided to change up your rotation schedule and send you out into the outpatient psychiatry world." Dr. Sinclair raised his index finger, pointed it at Haslam and gestured with it to punctuate every third or fourth syllable. "And, let me be clear. This is a last-ditch effort to save your residency. We are all hoping and praying that a miracle happens out there as you leave the hospital for a while and work with a psychiatrist in private practice. Perhaps you will find your calling in office-based psychiatry. Because frankly, treating hospitalized people with acute mental illness is not a competency you currently possess."

Dr. Haslam said nothing as she looked Dr. Sinclair directly in the eye with an emotionless poker face. Dr. Michelle Upton, another residency board member took over the conversation. "On Wednesday you will report to Dr. Troy Stoker's office and begin your first outpatient psychiatry rotation".

"What? No! Troy Stoker?" The news hit her like a head-on collision and she was stammering. The members of the residency committee were trying to conceal their surprise at her reaction to this well-intended decision. This was the first time they had ever been able to get through to Sarah Haslam, to interrupt a process of self-directed, know-it-all arrogance. This surprise turn of events was penetrating her fabricated hard mental exterior. But in reality, her brain was screaming, *They're rejecting me! I'll reject them before they reject me! Nobody is going to hurt me!* Accordingly, Haslam's rebuttal was passionate. "That Stoker guy does nothing orthodox. I mean, does he even practice psychiatry? You're going to send me to hang out with a babysitter of depressed housewives and ADHD-riddled teenagers?"

"We're sending you to learn from the psychiatrist with the best outcomes in the community for schizophrenia and bipolar disorder," Upton said. "And his work with the police drug interdiction team is phenomenal."

Haslam argued back with desperation in her voice. "Sure. His outcomes appear excellent because he gets all the easy cases. The hard ones get admitted here."

"You could *not* be more wrong, *again*," Sinclair said. "Your pride and narcissism blind you from developing any wisdom and seeing things as they really are." Dr. Sinclair removed her glasses and set them on the table while folding her hands together. "Let me tell you something that nobody wants to talk about. Most of us psychiatrists wish we could build a practice like Troy Stoker's. He takes many patients nobody else will. He connects with his patients and they trust him. Then, they get better."

Dr. Denning chimed in. "There are hundreds of people in this town who are living full lives thanks to Dr. Stoker's hard work and talent."

"New patients enter his office divorced, unemployed, neurotic, suicidal, catatonic or psychotic, and weeks later their hope is back and they're on the road to recovery," said Upton. "Stoker's got a gift."

Dr. Sinclair interjected, this time with his voice devoid of anger. "I'm an excellent psychiatrist. But, I admit that I'm green with envy about the pure talent that man possesses."

Now it was Haslam who was showing signs of anger. "Why are you giving me a sales pitch about Troy Stoker? This is a doctor who thinks that psychiatry is based primarily in the thyroid."

"A gross misrepresentation, which I can almost guarantee you'll take back in a week or two. Wait until you see what is really going on," said Sinclair. "Use this time to learn how to connect with patients and cut through bureaucratic red tape. Stoker is a master at getting patients the treatment they need when insurance companies try to shift treatments to fit their budgets."

Dr. Denning took over the conversation. "During this rotation, I want you to see yet another example of a doctor who cares deeply about his patients. Try to emulate and understand him."

"I hear the guy's a nut, driving around in that old four-wheel-drive from the 1970s," Haslam said.

Dr. Denning recognized that Sarah Haslam's criticisms were subconscious attempts to undermine this upcoming rotation with Stoker. She was already building a case to defend her future failure. Denning knew she must stop

Haslam's self-damaging dialogue, and she tried to reframe Haslam's perspective, even though she strongly suspected that it was a losing battle. "Indeed, he's his own man. He's fiercely independent and rather extroverted, but it works for him because he's also sincere. Let that sink in for a moment, Sarah." Everyone was silent. Even Haslam knew not to interrupt during that moment when a thought was supposed to be sinking in. Eventually, Dr. Denning spoke up again. "And Sarah, you need to learn a thing or two about classic cars. Stoker's Bronco runs better than the new SUV I bought last year."

Dr. Stoker was indeed a unique individual. He drove a 1976 Ford Bronco, but he did most of his commuting on a bicycle. He even rode his bike over the snow-covered roads during the harsh Dakota winters. Most doctors in the community admired Stoker's tenacity. Yet others, like Haslam, labeled him as eccentric or wacky. Stoker was also a self-described "preparedness enthusiast" who stored some extra food and fuel and planted a large garden every year. His solar panels and wind turbines provided about seventy percent of his home's power. Some doctors made rude remarks to Stoker about his alleged doomsday or Armageddon outlook. But, when he recounted his experience of watching people starve in the Balkans during an Army tour of duty, the thin smiles of derision and snide remarks often melted away.

Stoker's desire to be ready for hard times had its roots in his profoundly troubling experience as a U.S. Army peacekeeper and medical officer in the former Yugoslavia during the late 1990s. Seeing the horrid conditions the Croatians endured during the Serbian siege made Dr. Stoker resolve to always be prepared for tough times. Now, a small hideaway space in his basement also included some legal weapons, food, firewood and a seed collection.

The 1976 Ford Bronco was Stoker's treasure because he loved its simple, sturdy mechanics. It was highly modified under the hood and inside the cab. The bodywork was finished in a black matte paint, which enshrouded top-rated UL-752 NIJ level III flexible Kevlar ballistic panels. Any casual observer would never notice the shields, which were impenetrable by most caliber ballistic rounds, up to forty-four magnum. The black exterior, including wheels and wheel covers, blended perfectly with the darkness when parking at a trailhead for a nighttime cross-country ski. Stoker had also equipped the Bronco with rock-hard struts, and a carbon nanotube composite rollbar, which was ten times stronger per unit weight than the stock rollbar. Again, other physicians rolled their eyes at the car that thoroughly satisfied Stoker.

But none of his preparedness possessions meant as much to him as his cherished hunting bow. He had never enjoyed hunting with a rifle. Years back, he concluded that hunting with guns seemed a little unfair. The challenge of bringing down a deer or elk with a bow and arrow was invigorating—and the bow-hunting season was longer, too. Combining the bow and arrow with his cross-country skis gave him access to game that average hunters never considered. He could enter a forest quietly instead of alerting and scaring the game away like so many hunters did by using a traditional four-wheeler earlier in the season. A fish and game warden once complimented him on the timing of his late-season hunts. "You're helping us thin the herd at the perfect time of year. Removing another buck or two in December or January greatly improves the chances of survival for the rest of the herd."

So, while Haslam and some other doctors labeled him as eccentric, Troy Stoker did not care. He was happily married and satisfied with helping his patients mend their problems. Living was deeply fulfilling for the man whom the amateurish resident, Dr. Haslam, had just labeled a "nut."

Dr. Denning stood up to signal that the meeting's end. "So Sarah, your rotation with Dr. Stoker begins next week." Before Haslam could ask any other questions to interrupt the momentum of the decision, Dr. Denning redirected her thoughts. "I've covered your call and other assignments. Take the days off between now and Wednesday. Recharge your batteries before your rounds with Stoker. Because Sarah, if you can't make this rotation with Dr. Stoker work, your residency is over."

Haslam failed to acknowledge how grave Dr. Denning's last statement had been, and all of the psychiatrists recognized her dismissive attitude immediately. Dr. Sinclair decided that Haslam needed to hear the message again. "If you screw this rotation up, Sarah, where are you going to be in eight weeks?"

Haslam's eyes widened and she stammered. "I don't know. In my apartment, I guess?"

"Do you know how to apply for unemployment?" Sinclair asked. "Do you know how to apply for a job as a lab assistant at a hospital? Because that's the kind of work residency drop-outs do."

Haslam did not answer, but it was evident that the questions were penetrating her thought processes.

"What happens if you excel during these next few weeks?" Sinclair asked.

Haslam smiled a grin tinged with narcissism and delusion. "Then I've proven you all wrong, and I'm back to being the best psychiatrist in the world."

CHAPTER 16

OFFICE OF TROY STOKER, M.D., SIOUX FALLS

Ann Higgins made herself comfortable sitting in a chair in Dr. Stoker's office, just like she had as a patient many times in her past. Unbeknownst to Stoker and Ann Higgins a thick-necked short man with dirty blond hair sat a few yards away from Stoker's office attempting to eavesdrop on their session. Harry Klein's goon worked from the second row seat of a Ford Explorer, unrolling the window about an inch, and pointing a sensitive unidirectional microphone toward the window of Troy Stoker's office.

"Thanks so much for seeing me, Troy. I could really use your help. All of this is weighing heavy on my mind. Sometimes I think I'm delusional that somebody's building a meth lab in my planned community. Is that crazy?"

The microphone was only picking up portions of the conversation, and the short man could only hear about half of the discussion so far. White noise generators that Stoker had installed just above the inside each of his office windows blocked the sound waves from the conversation between doctor and patient. Usually the specialized microphones could filter out the white noise, but they weren't working well tonight.

Cursing under his breath, the short man reached over the front seat to the ignition, and turned off the car. *Perhaps that will reduce noise interference just enough*, he thought. It was sixteen degrees at 6:04 p.m. With the car's engine off, and no heater running, the next hour of surveillance would be uncomfortable to say the least. He tried again to pick up the conversation and the microphone was now working much better.

Stoker was now relating a recent experience to Ann. "Actually, about six months ago I saw a patient who told me about meth labs being built in his attic. However, in his case it turned out to be his paranoia, and we worked through it. So, let's hear about these interesting events that appear to be *actually* going on."

"I wish I was delusional right now. I'm truly concerned, and it's hard for me to figure out the likely consequences stemming from my visit to that home on Bryant Way. I mean, has my visit there put me or my family in danger?"

Now the snoop could hear the conversation better. Without the noise of the car's engine and heater, his high-dollar equipment was cutting through the white noise. The audio was not perfect, but the short man could hear through the privacy protection white noise well enough to capture the most important facts.

"Ann, I've known you for quite some time, and I know that you're not delusional now," Stoker said. "I do think you're anxious and possibly fearful about what could be going on—but you're not delusional."

The short man, who still suffered the indignation of the scars that acne had left on his face as a teenager, did not have the time, or frankly the skill, to set up recording capabilities. So, tonight he would have to resort to a notepad and rollerball pen and take notes about this conversation.

"What am I going to do, Troy?" Ann asked with exasperation.

"Now, these feelings that you have are real, according to what you've told me and to the facts I saw. Let's take a good look at this. What did you experience?"

"Basically, I went into a basement in Chelsea Crossing, saw some uncharacteristic plumbing and electrical work, found a strange construction drawing, and with some help from my friends, concluded that someone is building a meth lab in the community I've worked so hard to create."

"I see evidence that all of that is true. You took some great pictures, Ann. You thought on your feet."

"All right Troy, so what should I do next?" Ann looked out the window for a moment but failed to notice the Ford Explorer. "What's my next step?"

"Why are you asking me, a doctor, that question? I'm a healer."

"Because psychiatrists are supposed to know the answers," Ann said.

"Thanks for the compliment. We've been through some of your hard times, and you've gotten better. I appreciate that sentiment. These things are a bit different. There's a lot more at stake here for you, and this appears to be a new level of concern."

"You know me," Ann said. "What do you think?"

"Give me more of your thoughts so we can at least begin solving what appears to be a serious problem. Give me some more facts and let's talk about this." Stoker said as he stood up, walked over to his coffee pot, and offered coffee to Ann even though he knew she would decline. You know a little bit about my work as a doctor and my time in the military. I've run into a lot of people, and I know some really nasty bastards, who—believe it or not—are actually my friends in some way shape or form." Stoker said this with slight grin and laugh as he topped off his coffee mug.

"What do you mean, Troy? I'm not following you."

"No seriously, Ann. Those friends I introduced you to are some hard-core characters. I would not want to be on their bad side. Let's put it this way. They're good guys with some bad habits, so to speak. They're quite good at doing nasty things for good reasons."

"You mean Dr. Rivera and Z?"

"Yes. They are my *amigos* in bad times and in good times. And I love them like brothers." Stoker sat back down and leaned forward toward Ann. "So, are you convinced? Will you trust them as I do?"

"Whoa, Dr. Stoker. I don't know. I don't plan on robbing banks anytime soon," Ann said. "Tell me your plan, and I'll let you know my thoughts."

"You know Ann, I recognize that you have high anxiety about things you sometimes cannot control in your life. I know that stumbling into a meth lab must make you feel completely out of control. So, I do understand how you must feel about this situation. It must really bother you, and I understand. And I *do* understand!"

The short man listening from the SUV was stunned about how much Ann actually knew. This information would alarm his bosses. He had been tasked with finding out what Ann Higgins knew. At this moment, it was crystal clear. What was also abundantly clear was that Dr. Stoker and some of his "*amigos*" knew a lot about the Bryant Way operation. This was getting messy.

Ann spoke next. "Dr. Stoker. My anxiety is off the charts because I don't know who I can trust. Can I trust the police? I don't know who's involved with this Sioux Falls drug mess."

The man in the van smiled. *No cops yet!* he thought. *And, who are Rivera and Z?*

"Troy, you're the psychiatrist here. What's happening in my mind? I'm seriously worried and concerned for my safety."

"Okay, what do you want to do here, Ann? Do you want to call the police?"

"No," she said. "I agree it's not time for the police yet." Ann thought for a moment. "I want to inform my husband and tell him this whole story. I also want to hire some private security for my family and me." With that simple decision Ann was centered and more focused. She trusted Dr. Stoker. Her intuition was speaking and she was listening. It took her a long time to learn to trust her intuition, and she was realizing this indeed was a strength she could use in this strange situation. Ann could feel her anxiety lifting, and her thoughts clearing. "I'm also going to give your friends, Rivera, Z, and their professionals, the time they need to find out who's behind all of this."

Professionals? What professionals? thought the man in the Ford Explorer.

"Badabing, badabang! Wasn't that easy?" Stoker said. "You're good, Ann. What did you need me for?" Stoker leaned back in his chair casually. "But, of course, I have a few more patronizing questions."

"Okay, shoot," Ann said.

"Envision three to four weeks from now, how do you think this is all going to work out?" Stoker asked. "Let's not forget our subconscious. Let's visualize a good result. Can you do that?"

"I envision arrests," Ann said.

Good luck, thought the man in the van.

Ann continued explaining her visualizations. "I also envision my family in safety."

"Only if you keep your mouth shut," the short man muttered from his increasingly cold vantage point in the SUV.

"I anticipate that the problems in Chelsea Crossing will be diminished by those arrests."

Stoker allowed silence to linger for a moment to ensure he did not interrupt Ann's visualizations. After a moment, he stepped in to support her as a therapist. "So, you came to this appointment wondering if your thought processes were logical. Were they?"

"Yes. The facts were there."

"Now, where has your logic led you?"

Instantaneous relief graced Ann's face, and she smiled slightly. "I have a plan, and I'm in control."

"Listen, Ann. This is serious stuff, and you've done amazing at mustering your strength and power. We don't know who the bad guys are right now, but we really should rely on these professionals. They're good."

"Let's do that," Ann said.

"In summary, are you okay—at least for now—that the police are not involved? Because, I want you to know, these friends have already tapped into federal resources that tackle these very issues. Let's keep just that thought in our minds right now."

The man listening outside panicked at the mention of federal resources.

"How do you feel about your decision to tell your husband about this?"

"We share everything. He is part of me, and I want that part of me to know what's going on as soon as possible."

"Tomorrow, let's get you, your husband, Dr. Rivera, and me on a secure phone call. I'm concerned that lieutenant governor might feel duty-bound to have a knee-jerk reaction and call the police. I think Rivera can talk him out of it."

"The earlier, the better," Ann said.

"Okay, Ann. Let's do it. I'll be in touch with you. I hope you feel a little bit better about these issues. They're serious, but we'll get through them."

Ann thanked Dr. Stoker, and he walked her out to the waiting room and front door. As Ann Higgins briskly walked to her car, she didn't notice the lone SUV parked on the road. There was nothing out of place about it. Ann slipped into her car, started the engine, put it in gear, and pulled out into light traffic. As she drove by the Ford Explorer, she noticed the outline of a man inside the Explorer, and her subconscious mind anxiously filed away a memory of the out-of-place person. *Must be Stoker's next patient*, she assumed in her conscious mind.

CHAPTER 17

Back in his office, Stoker picked up the phone and dialed Errol Rivera. "Hey Rivera, I just met with Ann Higgins. I think she could be in a lot of danger and we really need to let her husband in on this."

Rivera responded to Stoker's recommendations. "Actually, we've been following her, and she's safe for now. The bad guys, whoever they are, do not know how much she knows, and . . . " Rivera paused mid-sentence. "I just got a text from Z. He wants to join our call."

Stoker waited for ten seconds as he wondered how Z knew about the phone call. Then Z's voice came on the phone. "Dr. Stoker, I want you to say as little as possible. I don't think your office is secure at this moment."

"Got it," Stoker replied. This new revelation about somebody listening in on his session with Ann Higgins concerned him. But, he also knew that whoever was listening could only hear the words he said. The infiltrator would miss Z and Rivera's side of the telephone conversation.

Z continued. "Let me connect a few details and issues for you. As Rivera just told you, we've been following Ann. But, I think our mystery criminals just found out how much Ann knows."

"What do you mean?" Rivera asked urgently.

"We're not the only ones following Ann and listening in on her," Z said. "We've been watching a man in an SUV eavesdrop on your session tonight. I think he heard all about the basement, the drawings, the meth lab theory, and the fact that Rivera and I are involved."

Stoker knew better than to look out the window to catch a glimpse of the person who had spied on his session with Ann. "So, You heard all of that, too, Z?"

"No apologies, Troy," Z said. "I was listening for Ann's safety."

"What do you think this guy heard?" Rivera asked.

"He has a pretty good microphone, and he muttered a few things under his breath that tracked with your conversation," Z said. "I think he heard pretty much everything."

"This is a game changer, people." Rivera was now speaking as if he were a battlefield commander. "Tomorrow we talk with Ann and the lieutenant governor."

"What about security?" Stoker was asking the question cryptically, hoping that he could eventually help Rivera and Z to understand that Ann was about to hire private security.

"She's already got security, and in thirty minutes it will be tripled," Rivera said.

"Well, she's about to call and look into it on her own," Stoker said.

"Do you mean she's about to hire private security?" Z asked.

Stoker remained cryptic. "Very good."

"I'll call Ann on a secure line and tell her about the arrangements we've made for her safety," Rivera said.

The short man in the SUV felt alarmed as he listened to small patches of the phone call going on in the doctor's office. He could only hear Stoker's contribution to the conversation, and the psychiatrist was not saying much.

"We've got work to do men," Rivera said. "Let's start tomorrow at 0800."

When the eavesdropper in the SUV heard Stoker end the phone call, he crawled into the driver's seat and started the car. He hastily threw it into gear and drove off as he reached for his phone and dialed Harry Klein.

"Higgins knows a lot. She saw the plans, and she's guessed it's a lab."

"Who else knows?" Klein asked the question with no emotion. He was so frozen with fear. His mistake was costing the commander, and he was considering disappearing into the night and running for his life.

"No cops, yet."

"Really?"

"No, Stoker doesn't trust them and neither do two other guys. One guy's name is Rivera, and there's some other guy who they just call 'Z'. And, they have connections with the feds."

Klein chose not to respond. He just ended the phone call. His next call would be to the commander, but he had to stop his hands and voice from trembling before he hit the speed dial.

CHAPTER 18

The intense man with striking blue eyes was gliding along on his cross-country skis and enjoying South Dakota's brisk winter air. He stopped every few seconds and tossed a small piece of pork onto the snow. At each stop he removed a small device from his pocket that looked like a stubby cigar with two reeds sticking out of it. Cupping the device in his hands, he blew into the reeds as he opened and closed his hands around it with an almost artistic technique. The device emitted a horrible noise that sounded like a suffering animal. About a mile away, a pack of coyotes heard the wretched sound from the jackrabbit distress call. Their hunger raged in the frigid, barren month of January. Ravenous deprivation drove them toward the false shrieks and the sham of sustenance.

While these vicious mammals did not starve in the winter, right now food was less available. The coyotes also expended more calories keeping themselves warm as they roamed the plains bordering Minnesota, Iowa and South Dakota. Traveling a few miles for a meal was an easy endeavor for a canine predator living through a Dakota January. Coyotes had always intrigued the commander. He had summoned them this way hundreds of times. On a few occasions, he had even allowed a lone animal to take a piece of raw meat from his hand. But, he would never dare hand-feed a coyote that was with his pack. The commander would be much too vulnerable to the strength-in-numbers and increased confidence of the pack.

Checking his watch, the man with the intense blue eyes estimated that it was time to be getting back to the trailhead to await his guests. He usually loved his solitary hours of watching coyotes, buffalo, elk, deer, antelope, rabbits, bobcats, weasels, owls, falcons, and dozens of other majestic animals. However, today he would likely be initiating a naïve man into the world of the wild, and the misery of the day's critical lessons would far surpass the majesty and sport of admiring raw nature.

CHAPTER 19

At 1:55 p.m. a Chevrolet Suburban with tinted windows, and bearing the state symbol of South Dakota, arrived at the home of the lieutenant governor-elect. Because of his new elected office, nobody was surprised to see such an automobile pull up at the home of Kent Higgins. It pulled inside the garage, and the occupants waited. This car was actually an armored vehicle Rivera occasionally accessed for official business. Z had applied the unauthorized state seal, thirty minutes earlier, to make anybody who may be watching think that this was just routine transportation for a soon-to-be state executive officer.

From the driver's seat, Z activated auditory counter measures through the car's stereo system that sounded like and out-of-tune radio mixed with a mild hum. Once the garage door had closed, Rivera got out of the car and climbed three steps to the door separating the garage and the house. He knocked two times, just as he had explained he would during his secure call with Ann Higgins last night. A moment after the second knock, Kent and Ann Higgins emerged from the house and quietly followed Rivera to the car. They climbed inside the Suburban and waved hello to Dr. Stoker, but said nothing. Z was driving and he also remained silent. Once they closed the car doors, Ann removed a garage door opener from her pocket and pushed the button to make the garage open. As the large SUV backed out of the driveway and pulled away, Rivera and Z noticed the white Ford Explorer parked just down the street, and the man sitting inside of it. Fortunately, the snoop in the Explorer did not know that Ann was in the car.

The group traveled another block before Rivera opened the meeting. "Thank you everybody for getting together this morning. Meeting in person like this is much better than a secure phone call." Rivera turned to Ann. "Since you're the only one who knows everybody, why don't you make the introductions?"

Ann took Kent's hand. "Everybody knows who Kent is, and I suspect he's the one with all the questions." She motioned toward her psychiatrist. "Darling, you know Dr. Stoker."

"Hello, Troy," Kent Higgins said.

"Mr. Lieutenant Governor. It's good to see you again."

Ann introduced Dr. Rivera and Z. "Dr. Rivera is a physician at the Veteran's Administration hospital, but he also has some other kind of . . . " Ann struggled momentarily for how to explain Rivera.

"I have a military background," Rivera said. "I was an active warrior before medical school, and I continue to fill special TAD, or temporary active duty, due to my diverse skill set. That's all I can say right now. Z and I work together when special crises surface. Last Friday a serious issue surfaced, and your wife landed right in the middle of it."

Kent Higgins looked at his wife with a grave look on his face. "Ann, what does Dr. Rivera mean?"

Ann looked her husband in the eye as the Suburban entered a freeway onramp. "I've had some strange and disturbing experiences in the last few days, and I'm sorry I did not, and perhaps could not, tell you. You will understand in a few minutes." Ann took out her cell phone and showed her husband the graphic she had made from all of the pictures she had taken in the basement on Bryant Way. "Kent, this is a picture of a construction drawing for a meth lab." The lieutenant governor-elect looked concerned. "This plan is for the basement of a home in Chelsea Crossing, which I stumbled upon last Friday. Here, look at these pictures, too." Ann showed him pictures of the basement of the home on Bryant Way."

"You say you stumbled upon this," the lieutenant governor-elect said as he examined the drawings closely. "How did you stumble upon such blatant criminality?"

"I did not know this particular home was sold, so I erroneously showed it to some prospective buyers. When we went down to see the basement, there was some strange plumbing, electrical work, and drainage. I also found those construction drawings there."

Kent's brow was furrowed as he continued his line of questioning. "How do you know it's a meth lab?"

"Oh, it's going to be a meth lab," Rivera jumped in. "I showed the drawing to some experts, and they're sure."

"So, can't we just wait until they fire up the lab for the first time, and then swoop in and arrest them?" asked Kent Higgins.

Ann looked her husband in the eye. "It gets more complicated. This is where I need your support." She was showing remarkable composure. "Whoever owns that house saw me there, and they've been following me. Last night they learned exactly how much I know. They found out that I know those properties are future meth labs. That puts me, and perhaps us, in a dangerous situation."

"She knows too much," Dr. Stoker said.

"I want you to take us straight home." Kent Higgins issued the command in a serious tone of voice. "Our kids are in danger as we speak. We need to arrange for around-the-clock protection, now!"

"That's already done," Rivera said. "Right now there are three highly skilled people watching your house and family. We'll be happy to introduce you to them when we take you back home."

"So, why are we talking with the three of you and not working with the police?" asked Higgins. "I just say the word and we'll have those houses crawling with deputies and crime dogs."

Stoker sat forward in his seat and began to speak. "Frankly, Mr. Lieutenant Governor, there is something amiss in Sioux Falls law enforcement right now, specifically in drug enforcement. I'm a consulting psychiatrist to the narcotics teams for Minnehaha County and Sioux Falls City. We keep showing up to bust dealers and meth houses, but the criminals are gone. They know we're coming and they bug out."

"So, there's a mole," Kent Higgins said.

"Exactly," Rivera said. "Somebody in high places has been tipping off the crooks—"

"We need to use authorities outside of the greater Sioux Falls area, instead." Kent Higgins finished Rivera's thought. "It's time to uncover our internal corruption."

Stoker, Rivera, and Z were thrilled to hear the soon-to-be lieutenant governor *suggest* unconventional measures. So often, politicians insisted on playing by the rules. But, Kent Higgins had already seen the big picture and he recognized that somebody was gaming the system. He knew the good guys might have to work outside normal rules and constraints.

"What can Ann and I do to support you?" Kent Higgins asked.

"Accept our security and don't tell anybody else what is going on," Rivera said.

"No problem." Kent Higgins replied. "Anybody from a police detective to the governor himself could be embroiled in this situation. You have my cooperation and silence." Then Higgins glanced out the windshield and thought for a moment. "Honestly, at this point, nobody would believe all of this anyway. This is a wild story." He smiled for a moment and then added, "Imagine if I walked into my office this morning, called the police or the attorney general, and said, 'So, I was driving along in the car this morning with my wife, her psychiatrist, a military doctor and some guy named Z. They told me about a meth lab in a basement in Chelsea Crossing, the planned community my wife is developing." Kent Higgins laughed and then sarcastically quipped, "That sounds *really* believable."

CHAPTER 20

SIOUX FALLS

Robert Nichols, the farmer from Arkansas, parked his rental car under the portico that hung over the main entrance of the Sioux Falls Quality Inn. Six hours was his goal. Nichols harbored an intense psychological desire to be in and out of Sioux Falls in six hours. Sure, it would be ideal to be far away from the scene of the upcoming crime, to which he was about to be an accessory. Yet, crime scenes did not vex Nichols. He had been a criminal, and an accessory to felonies, more times than he cared to count. Instead, it was the cold of the upper Midwest that disturbed him. Robert Nichols seldom set goals in life, and achieving a goal was an extremely rare phenomenon for his underachieving psyche. However, today the farmer from Arkansas had a goal. The cold was motivating him to finish his mission in Sioux Falls in less than six hours. Nichols had landed at 2:15 p.m. that afternoon after a brief flight from Arkansas. A few hours in Sioux Falls in January constituted more time than he wanted to spend in the area's constantly freezing temperatures. Nichols could only tolerate mild Arkansas winters where ice and snow were sporadic.

As the farmer put the car in park, Harry Klein emerged from the front door of the hotel with two pieces of luggage. He was dressed in hardy winter hiking boots and denim jeans. Nichols popped the trunk, but did not get out to help with the suitcases. Klein stowed the luggage and then jumped into the front seat.

"Thanks for coming up to Sioux Falls," Klein said as he extended a handshake to Nichols.

Nichols returned the gesture with a brief, lifeless handshake. "No problem. Let's get this meetin' over with and see if we can fly out of here before nine o'clock tonight. That's the lowdown."

Klein strapped on his seatbelt. "Good plan. It's been a long time since I've been to Arkansas. So, where's our meeting?"

Nichols put the car in gear and taxied out of the hotel parking lot. "It's a casual little get together. We'll mix some business and some pleasure. With them jeans, you're dressed perfect for the occasion. The commander loves to visit this little place west of town. It's got lots a' critters and wildlife. He says it's a downright slice a' paradise." The farmer continued to drive the car, as prompted by a GPS unit, down Granite Lane and then asked, "Have you ever met the commander?"

"I met him for the first time, in Reno, a few months ago," Klein responded. "Before that, I'd never even heard of him. I thought you and that accountant in Reno were the bosses."

"Oh, no. Let me tell you somethin' buddy. Hardly anybody ever meets *the boss* 'cause he's so busy. Green Growth Ventures is not his only line of work," Nichols said. "But, the commander just happens to be in town. Rumor has it he's involved in a lot of businesses and stuff."

"More money than you or I could imagine?"

"Yup. He makes money, but I don't think he's like a Sam Walton, a George Bush, or rich like a rock star. For him, it's more about the hunt, the adventure and the power. I think the commander just loves playin' the game."

Nichols navigated the car onto Interstate 29, and the two men remained relatively quiet. Klein had not mentioned his new assignment to the farm in Arkansas or the disappointment he felt at his demotion. He knew better than to complain, because it was contrary to the culture of the company.

As a manager in Green Growth Ventures, you never made excuses. Ann Higgins had uncovered Klein's operation. He was in charge, so the buck stopped with him. That was the spoken and oft-reinforced rule. And Klein certainly preferred being reassigned to being fired. Green Growth Ventures often reassigned people to teach them lessons. After a few months the firm and its leaders seem to forgive and forget. In his six years with the company Klein had never been reassigned. He had also never needed this magnitude of forgiveness.

Nichols anticipated Klein's disappointment. "Don't take it so hard, Harry. If it's any consolation, we're going to take the long way to Arkansas and relax a little this morning. We're meetin' the commander to do a little wildlife spottin'. He'll have all his scopes and binoculars. It's quite the show."

"Wildlife spotting?"

"Yup. He don't hunt animals. He just likes to watch 'em in their natural environment," drawled Nichols. "And, remember to whisper, that is, if you have to talk. Besides scarin' the critters away, I think this is also some kind of a religious experience for the commander. Also, now you listen to me good here, Klein. The commander's no idiot. Staring at animals through scopes and binoculars ain't everybody's idea of fun. If you pretend to like it, he'll know you're fakin' it. He has a sixth sense for detecting two-faced behavior."

"What if I *am* bored? Then what do I do?"

"Try to find something interesting about the animals. Ask a question. Then ask another."

"Okay."

"You know how it goes. Business with the commander can be full of surprises, like today's little adventure." Nichols said with a little sarcasm mixed into his southern drawl. "Surprise."

Despite the fact that Harry Klein was being demoted for the discovery of the houses on Bryant Way, the drive into the snowy countryside was serene and relaxing. Ann Higgins had uncovered the operation on his watch, so he accepted the fate of the demotion. Because he had been relieved of all of his duties in Sioux Falls, his nagging "to do" list and overflowing email inbox had vanished as instantaneously as his management title. For a few short hours the weight of the world was off of Klein's shoulders. Thanks to that relief, the welcome sight of the blue sky, and a beautiful blanket of snow-covered prairie, he was experiencing a tranquility that he had not felt since his last weeklong vacation two years ago.

Klein's recent assignment in Sioux Falls wound his emotions up so tight and caused him so much stress that he felt like he lost a little bit of himself. These few minutes of stillness opened his eyes to just how far the constant pressure had pushed his health and sanity.

A few minutes later, as they exited Interstate 90 near the town of Montrose, Harry Klein committed himself to finding a therapist in Arkansas who could teach him to manage his stress and help pull him out of his current emotional abyss. But, for these next few hours, he was looking forward to some serene time admiring wildlife and soaking up the sun. He was hoping the adventure would further improve his outlook and mood. He wasn't worried about appearing bored or disinterested.

Nichols navigated south on 451st Avenue and ambled the car into a small parking alcove near the edge of Lake Vermillion. The only other car in the parking area was a burgundy Cadillac Escalade SUV with its rear hatch open. Nichols parked the car, opened his door, and said, "Grab your coat, Klein. Let's go meet Mother Nature."

As Klein got out of the car, the driver's door to the Cadillac Escalade opened, and a man emerged wearing expensive sunglasses, a ski cap, and a striking, sophisticated long suede coat. "Hey Commander," said Nichols. "This is Harry Klein."

"Great to see you again, Klein," the commander said. "Thanks for your willingness to mix some business with some pleasure."

"Nice to meet you, sir." It dawned on Klein that he did not know the commander's name. "You know sir, I've never actually had anybody tell me your name. You know, so I can address you properly."

The commander appeared not to hear Klein. "I see you've got good shoes, a coat, and some gloves. In the back of my car here, you'll find snowshoes. Why don't you each grab a pair? Have either of you ever used snowshoes?" Neither man had—most certainly not the man from Arkansas.

Klein had failed to learn his boss's name. He concluded that he would just keep calling the man "commander" and "sir" until he heard Nichols mention his name.

"If you can walk, you can snowshoe," the commander said as he picked up one of his snowshoes and began to put it on. Klein and Nichols imitated the commander and strapped the snowshoes to their boots. Soon, all three men were wearing snowshoes and holding poles for additional stability.

The commander took charge. "All right, men. Let's go. This little trail is not well defined. Luckily, somebody skied here in the last hour or two. Let's just follow these tracks. I only anticipate that we'll be walking in a mile or so."

Despite the fact that the commander's hair and eyes were covered, there was already something familiar about him. Klein couldn't put a finger on it. However, as his brain tried to connect with the signals of familiarity, it dawned on him that it was the commander's voice. The intonation was familiar. *Where have I heard that voice?* Klein thought. *I think I've even heard it recently. Maybe even on TV?* But, the concentration required to clumsily walk in the snowshoes made him forget his curiosity about this man's familiar voice.

The commander toted a large backpack, which Klein assumed contained scopes, binoculars, and other gear to accomplish the task of wildlife viewing. Thanks to the complimentary breakfast at the hotel that morning and his recent lunch, Klein was not at all hungry. However, in this tranquil environment, he was wishing he had brought a flask. A shot or two of Scotch would've opened the sky a little wider and magnified the warmth of the sun by a few degrees.

After ten minutes of walking in silence, the commander spoke. "A friend at the Department of Game, Fish and Parks dropped me a little tip today as a special favor. He gave me the latest location of a healthy pack of coyotes right here at Lake Vermillion. He learns about the coyotes' whereabouts from farmers near

Montrose and Humboldt." The commander looked up to the sky and let the sun kiss his face as he continued to lead the small expedition. A minute later he declared, "I really love the canine species. I love their bravery, their strength, and their fight." The commander stopped and turned around. "I'll give either of you fifty bucks if you can tell me one of the nicknames of the coyote species."

Nichols responded first. "Commander, I have no idea. I'm from Arkansas and we ain't got no coyotes there."

"Wrong, Nichols!" The commander began walking again as he explained. "Coyotes roam almost everywhere in the Lower Forty-eight. As a matter of fact, their range extends all the way to Panama. I bet you've had coyotes roaming your farm for years, right under your nose. But they're so sly that you've never seen them. They lurk in the shadows and do their dirty work while you sleep."

"Sure, Commander. They hang out with the Boogie Man and Bigfoot," joked Nichols.

The commander stopped walking, and he looked toward Nichols. "You don't have to believe me. But, next time there's a fox in your henhouse, take a shotgun big enough for a coyote."

The commander turned to Klein and began walking through the snow again. "Do you have a guess, Harry? What's a nickname for coyote?"

Klein remembered how Nichols had coached him about the commander's awareness of fake, two-faced behavior, and he decided to respond honestly. "No, sir. I'm not going to even venture a guess. I don't know any nicknames for coyotes."

"I respect your honest response, Harry." He was now acting as if he were a college professor, lecturing a class about a subject he found most enthralling. He reached up to his face and grabbed onto his sunglasses and exclaimed, "My favorite nickname is the American jackal." Swiftly removing his sunglasses, the commander made intense eye contact with the man who had botched the meth lab job in Chelsea Crossing.

As Harry Klein looked into the commander's deep, piercing eyes, his mind instantaneously connected the man's face with the voice that had been so familiar. It took every ounce of his strength to keep a straight face and mask the shock he felt. With all of the recent news about the elections and changes in state leadership, as well as the shift in power from Democrats to Republicans in Pierre, Klein had seen this man. He saw him speaking on TV. He had perused the free paper provided by the hotel during his weeks in Sioux Falls, and the commander's picture had graced its pages on few occasions.

Klein gathered his composure. "Look. I'm not a good liar, and I don't follow South Dakota politics religiously. I'm just going to say it flat out. You've been in the papers lately, but I can't quite place you. Don't you hold a post in the new administration?"

"I will soon," the commander replied. While I've had my specific reasons for working in government, and I've had some aspirations, I never imagined that I would end up in my new office. Frankly, I'm shocked. Of course, I'm pleased to be here, too."

Klein's adrenaline was pumping a little and it overrode his ability to think before he spoke. "I'm shocked as well. The boss of our little drug cartel will soon wield a mighty sword within the halls of power in the state of South Dakota."

The man with the intense eyes, looked piercingly into Klein's eyes, and said directly, "Watch out for the jackals, Klein. We lurk in the shadows, and we do our dirty work while you sleep." Then, he removed the jackrabbit distress call from his pocket and handed it to Nichols who knew what to do with the device.

"Tell me about Ann Higgins and the two houses in Chelsea Crossing," the commander said.

Nichols held the call up, pursed his lips around the open reeds, and blew into it while opening and closing his hands rhythmically around it. The sound was blood curdling. Klein felt a surge of adrenaline as his primal instinct to loathe bloodshed kicked in. The commotion sounded just like a suffering animal's hideous cry. He did not know which animal the call mimicked, but he knew the sound closely imitated the impending moments of death.

"You know, Commander, we never thought that Ann Higgins would visit our construction site late on a Friday afternoon. We got clumsy and made poor decisions," Klein explained.

"What were the instructions?"

"We were supposed to work on those basements during non-business hours."

"Exactly," the commander said. Then he lowered his voice to a whisper to acknowledge they had approached the coyote area. "Let's take the next few hours to observe the laws of nature. Let's see how careful these real, wild American jackals are. Despite the cold and their hunger, they are extremely careful to avoid certain risks. However, there *is* a tipping point where coyotes abandon their fear. As tame observers in their environment, we want to avoid being in their presence at that instant. When they abandon fear, they are completely consumed with violence. We're here today to learn a lesson about caution."

The commander stepped toward Klein. "If you work for me, you need to be keenly aware of the tipping points. Avoid all tipping points, Harry."

It was Nichols's turn to speak, and he whispered in a voice that was almost silent. "You broke one of the big rules, Klein. You crossed the line." Despite the softness of Nichols's voice, his words pierced Klein's heart with panic.

"Yes I did, and I am responsible," Klein said softly. "That's why I'm going to Arkansas."

Neither the commander nor Nichols uttered a word in response. The commander just placed an index finger over his lips giving Klein and Nichols the signal that it was time to be quiet. The trio walked another two hundred yards and then stopped behind a row of chest-high brambles, beside some trees, at the edge of frozen Lake Vermillion. The commander removed his snowshoes. Nichols and Klein instinctively followed his lead and removed their snowshoes. Again, Nichols put the open reed coyote call to his mouth and shrieked out a vile call of demise.

The boss opened his backpack and took out two pairs of binoculars. He handed one to Klein and whispered, "Let's just watch beyond the horizon over there. That distress call will bring the coyotes in."

The three men stood quietly for nearly ten minutes. Only Nichols broke the silence with an occasional blast from the artificial distress call. Klein followed their lead and chose not to speak. The afternoon began its surrender to evening and a slight hint of pink sunset danced with distant cirrus clouds on the horizon to the west.

The commander took the distressed jackrabbit call from Nichols. "Now you try." He handed the call out to Klein.

Both the commander and Nichols's mouths had moistened the call's reeds and wood where they had wrapped their lips around the device. Klein wanted to wipe some of the saliva off of the gadget with his coat sleeve. However, he also had a suspicion that wiping off the coyote call might make him appear less of a man. *Perhaps worrying about germs would offend them*, thought Klein. He remembered a time in his youth when he offended a friend, and potential blood brother, by refusing to participate in the ritual of pressing two bleeding wounds together.

With these concerns in mind, Klein took the coyote call and wrapped his lips around it, all the while willing himself to ignore the ample moisture he immediately sensed. A hint of whiskey further heightened all of Nichols's senses and shot a little more adrenaline into his system. He blew on the coyote call and a loud, punctuated blare escaped the device that promptly ended with an anemic wheezing sound.

The commander did not react to the failed call. Nichols, however, smiled in ridicule, but did not laugh. "Now there, Harry. Give 'er another try. For starters, wet down them reeds a little more. Just give 'em some of your spit. Also, blow a little softer until you get 'er figured out." Klein tried again, and the noise sounded somewhat like the way it imitated death when the commander and Nichols had blown on it. "There you go. Now you're gettin' it." Nichols was more encouraging now, and Klein tried a few more times. "Much better. Now cup your hands around it and flutter those fingers to make it sound like a jack rabbit in the jaws of a mama wolf." Nichols followed the instructions, and the call let out a wretched sound. At first he was disgusted that he could produce the primal, heinous scream. "Perfect. That's just perfect. Keep going there, Harry. In a minute, you'll be bringing in them coyotes." The praise of the man from Arkansas chased away the primitive repulsion Klein had felt only moments earlier. Now he was enjoying his newly mastered skill of imitating coyote prey, and he assumed that he was now accepted into this small band of three saliva brothers.

But, at that moment, a potent dose of terazosin was crossing the membranes in his lips, tongue, sublingual tissue, cheeks and gums. Within seconds Klein would inadvertently swallow small amounts of the potent blood-pressure lowering medication. Within minutes he would feel its effect.

Klein cupped his hands around the coyote call and blew again while quickly fluttering his hands around it. He was broadcasting convincing sounds of severe misery into the surrounding acres. Every thirty seconds or so, he repeated the commotion, while the commander and Nichols used the binoculars to search the horizon.

After another few minutes of calling and waiting, the commander tapped Nichols on the shoulder and pointed to the horizon on their left. Nichols held the binoculars up to his eyes and looked in the direction the commander had indicated. He silently spent a few seconds admiring the commander's discovery. Then, the commander used hand signals to inform Klein that it was his turn. He took the binoculars from Nichols, held them up to his eyes, and adjusted his vision. He was looking out at a pink, sunset-tinged horizon illuminating the plains of South Dakota. In the silence, Klein suddenly became aware of his breathing. It felt unusually heavy, and he assumed that he was experiencing some anxiety from the conversation about accountability along with the anticipation of being in such close proximity to violent predators. As he drew in a deep breath through his nose, he caught sight of the first wild coyote he'd ever encountered. Klein estimated that it was about a thousand yards away. He was surprised at how spry and content the animal looked through the binoculars. Its snout almost smiled as it jogged in a random weaving pattern of travel in the general direction of the three men.

Without saying a word, the commander took the coyote call from Klein and put it up to his mouth. Neither the germs nor the moisture bothered him. The commander blew into the call. But now, the results were different. This time the call was not as distressed and desperate as his previous calls. It sounded as if the expiring animal was resigned to the fact that it was indeed dying. The commander was mimicking the call of a wild beast sharing its last moments of lament with any creature that would hear its sorrow. The commander was a brilliant imitator. Klein sensed a vile thrill from the presentation he was witnessing. The false laments and suffering were a splendid class of evil.

The farmer was still looking through the binoculars. He was sweeping back and forth across the horizon, when he stopped and held up two fingers and pointed out to the majestic snow-covered plain. Klein aimed his binoculars in the direction that Nichols pointed, and saw a second coyote coming toward them. The animal approached with the same casual pattern of an occasional zigzag in one direction or another, all the while making progress toward the commander and his guests.

Klein lowered his binoculars and glanced over at Nichols who was holding up three fingers for the commander to see. The farmer pointed to the horizon. The commander responded to the prompts and looked through his binoculars sighting the third coyote. The man with the intense eyes gazed out across the South Dakota prairie and took in the majesty of the American jackal. "Come to papa my little wolves." In an intense, profound way, the commander wanted to understand the psyche of this incredible creature that could survive in the freezing temperatures of the Canadian tundra or thrive in the barren deserts of the Mexican *Frontera.* In part, the commander felt as if he understood—even empathized—with the coyotes' lust, caution, hunger, motives, thirst for survival, and long-suffering cunning to eventually reach alpha status.

The commander lowered his binoculars and gestured for Klein to take another look. Klein brought the binoculars up to his eyes and focused on the closest coyote. It was closing in patiently and now was about 700 yards away. He felt a thrill from the approaching canine, a peril he scarcely understood. He knew that the thicket camouflaged the men from the animals, but he suspected the coyotes could smell them and perhaps even hear their movements and whispers. The danger thrilled him tremendously.

A sharp pain abruptly interrupted Klein's thrill and serenity and he felt his right arm violently ascend to his neck while the rest of him was enveloped in a powerful set of arms. He sensed brutal force on his neck, and a stark realization of his helplessness against a violent sleeper hold. Klein's vision blurred and breathing was impossible. As panic set in, his ears began to ring and his instinct to fight kicked in. Inside his head he tried to scream as he attempted to struggle against his captor. But, all his efforts were in vain. He was caught off guard, and his assailant had immobilized him in under a second. His brain broadcast the pain of primal, failing survival, and then all went dark.

CHAPTER 21

First he perceived pain, and then cold, and then light. As his consciousness returned, his eyes focused and their gaze rested on the commander's deep, penetrating eyes.

"I'm the guy who's building two houses in Chelsea Crossing. You're the idiot who made a mess and exposed us to the lieutenant governor's wife." The commander's whisper was a rage-filled snarl. "Now I must clean it up."

Klein was sitting on the ground and leaning with his back against a tree. He and the tree were situated right on the bank of frozen Lake Vermillion. He was bound with his hands reaching behind his back and arms stretching around the tree. He felt a dozen or more strands of a slimy, leathery and stretchy material holding his wrists in place. His ankles were bound with the same peculiar bands.

The commander never took his eyes off Klein as he called softly to Nichols. "How many coyotes, now?"

"Six, boss."

"How far away?"

"Closest one's about 300 yards. They're finding the meat you left. A couple of them are even fighting over a piece."

"Okay. His medication's wearing off," the commander said, "but this pig intestine should hold Klein here for a few hours, and the coyotes and other predators will eat the evidence. Let's get moving." The commander then moved his face closer to Klein's. "You are accountable, and you and your men put my whole operation at risk. This could cost me millions of dollars. Also, my operations have never been investigated. I've always been able to lurk in the shadows by night." The commander spat in Klein's face, just a little, each time he pronounced an s. "With this Ann Higgins incident, those guys Stoker, Rivera, and

Z are onto us. We may be skipping over a local investigation, and jumping right into dodging the feds. All thanks to you."

Klein was groggy, and he struggled to process what the commander was telling him until he recalled how the commander had used the phrase "eat the evidence." Adrenaline surged through his body and his mind became vibrant with panic. "I take full responsibility! Words cannot express how sorry I am—"

The commander interrupted. "Shut your mouth. You're too loud! You'll scare away the coyotes." He paused for a moment and glared at his bound victim. "Why didn't you attempt to express your sorrows to me an hour ago? You didn't seem so remorseful then."

The bound man struggled for an answer. He was sorry. "I have been sorry since the moment I heard about Ann Higgins touring the house on Bryant Way." Klein was whispering with as much emotion as he dared. His eyes were bulging with fear. "I hated the idea of going to Arkansas. I didn't beg for forgiveness because I thought that actions spoke louder than words. I was accepting my punishment with a 'no excuses' attitude. I am truly *sorry*, and my plan was to show that by going to the farm in Arkansas and working my butt off."

"You know what, Klein? I actually believe you. That makes some sense." The commander stood and looked out toward the coyotes. He did not need binoculars at this point, and making a little noise was not about to dissuade them. They smelled blood, and the coyotes were at the tipping point. "But, this goes a little deeper than that."

"Deeper?" Klein's panic was intensifying. "What do you mean?"

The commander abandoned whispering altogether. "For all the evil the American jackal gets blamed for, people forget how much this beautiful creature helps keep us strong by culling out the weaklings." The commander rapidly packed binoculars and other items into his backpack. "Ann Higgins did not happen to you by coincidence or some sort of accident. This all happened because you're weak. It's just too bad you never recognized it."

"Recognized what?"

"Watch out for the jackals, Klein." The commander reached into his backpack and removed a large, domesticated rabbit. He held the gentile animal up by the scruff of its neck as it sniffed the air. The moment the rabbit picked up the scent of the coyotes, it sprang to life and attempted, in vain, to escape. "We lurk in the shadows and do our dirty work while you sleep."

The commander removed a small knife from an internal pocket within his fine coat. With a swift chop, he gashed the hind leg of the innocent rabbit, and tossed the now screaming and panicking bunny up over the thicket that was still camouflaging them from the coyotes. It landed about twenty yards away from them. The coyotes zeroed in on the rabbit immediately and made a beeline for their newfound prey. They had now passed the tipping point where hunger overtook caution. The commander quickly advanced on Klein with the same knife and grabbed the collar of the bound man's jacket. He made a swift but delicate slice in Klein's coat right down the front of his chest, destroying his coat but sparing his shirt. The commander tore away portions of the coat and grabbed the trembling man's shirt. Again, he made another swift slice cutting away a portion of Klein's shirt. Klein screamed out in desperation. "I'm sorry, Commander!" The coyotes responded with hungry yips and growls. The commander ignored Klein's desperate apology, grabbed the dangling cloth of his shirt and tore it open, exposing his chest and shoulders.

"Get those boots off him and grab his wallet," the commander ordered. "They're really the only things the coyotes or winter will not obliterate. Nichols ran over, took the knife from the commander, sliced through Klein's laces, and removed the boots with no regard for the desperate man's comfort. He quickly stuffed them in the commander's pack along with Klein's wallet.

"Let's go!" The commander was getting down on his hands and knees and crawling out from behind the thicket to avoid attracting attention from the coyotes. Nichols followed. After scampering on their hands and knees about a hundred yards, they put on their snowshoes and commenced a quick march back to the cars.

The pink, orange and purple hues of a perfect sunset celebrated the conclusion of another day. The commander and Nichols were barely out of earshot when *nobody* heard the blood-curdling wretched call of demise. This time it was no imitation. Only his canine assailants and a few other wild beasts heard the last moments of lament for any creature that would hear his sorrow.

CHAPTER 22

At 7:25 p.m. Nichols boarded a commercial flight back to Arkansas. The blazing sunset was gone and night dominated the sky completely. As he sat in his seat reading a magazine, his phone vibrated. The brief text came from an undisclosed phone number.

> *Consider yourself trained in the jackal intervention.*
> *You'll need it.*

At 7:55 p.m. Nichols was airborne, and he had achieved his goal to spend less than six hours in South Dakota. As a matter of fact, he beat his goal by a few minutes. As the flight ascended up through seven thousand feet, it occurred to him that it was the first time in many years that he, Robert Nichols, had actually achieved—no, surpassed—a goal. But, more importantly, he was just pleased that he was the "go to" guy for the jackal intervention. It meant a little more job security. Having Harry Klein out of the way didn't hurt his odds of keeping his comfortable job, either.

CHAPTER 23

FALLS PARK, SIOUX FALLS

The inauguration was on a perfect January day in Sioux Falls. At noon, it was seventeen degrees and the sun was reflecting brilliantly off the perfect backdrop of flowing water and crystalline ice formations of the Big Sioux River. Park rangers had prepared a gathering area at Falls Park, just down the hill from the Queen Bee Mill ruins. About four feet from the edge of the river, stood a modest stage, which would hold about twenty people. A gallery of 300 plastic chairs in semi-circle rows allowed the audience to take in the beauty of the moment and witness their new governor taking his oath of office. After his ceremony the lieutenant governor, attorney general, secretary of state and a few additional Constitutional officers would also be sworn in.

The governor-elect was all smiles. True to his word, he had selected his clothing from the Cabela's catalog. His had chosen a sky-blue, heavyweight chamois shirt. His jacket was a canvas ranch coat and his grandfather's bolo tie shined in the sun as it rested on his chest.

At the appointed time, the Chief Justice of the South Dakota Supreme Court invited the governor and his immediate family to the stage. The entourage barely fit on the small platform. "I, Richard Horton, do solemnly swear that I will support the Constitution and the laws of the United States, and the Constitution and the laws of the State of South Dakota, and that I will faithfully perform the duties of Governor of the State of South Dakota. So help me God."

The audience applauded. From his seat in the front row, the commander witnessed the event and the people. Some treated the moment as solemn, while others obviously felt festive. He sensed deep pride and a sinister thrill. Now he shared the inner circle of power with men who would crush him if they knew who he really was, and if they were aware of his treachery. As the wind picked up, the commander folded up the collar of his custom-made trench coat. The rugged luxury of the coyote fur that lined the collar amplified the thrill of ascending into the higher realms of the double life he led. As a psychopath, he harbored no mental distress, and his secrets fueled his ongoing risk-taking and covert activities. As he glanced at Governor Horton's beautiful thirty-one-year-old daughter, she shot him a slightly salacious smile. He allowed a long, satisfying howl to reverberate inside his head as he buried himself deeper into the fur of his collar. He barely acknowledged the glance from his potential prey. The hat trick of pride, evil, and lust warmed the commander and he felt his skin produce a slight sweat in the middle of a seventeen-degree afternoon.

A few minutes later, they called the commander's name. As he stood to take his oath of office, he could hardly focus on the moment. As the chief justice prompted him through each phrase, he could barely follow the words of the oath. His mind was intoxicated with the power that he would wield in the State of South Dakota. When he imagined what his new perception of power meant to his illicit activities, his adrenaline surged like he had never felt before. This further fueled the illusions and fantasies of endless possibilities occupying the malevolent thoughts of his warped mind.

CHAPTER 24

SIOUX FALLS CONVENTION CENTER

It was only 6:30 p.m., and less than half of the 3,000 invited guests had arrived to the South Dakota inaugural ball. Yet, the energy was already coursing through the crowd, and the elbow rubbing was already in full swing. Beverages were flowing and music was blaring. Everyone was laughter and smiles.

Ann Higgins spent the first thirty minutes alongside her husband as they mixed and mingled. They exchanged hundreds of handshakes and hugs with friends and acquaintances. But most of the people they met were perfect strangers. On a night that should have been one of the most exciting and rewarding of Ann's life, she felt tense about circulating among so many people she did not know or trust. With all that she had learned during the last few days about the illicit drug trade and possible government corruption, she feared for her life and her family's safety. As she looked around and made eye contact with people, she could not help but question each stranger's motives. Her paranoia even extended to people she knew. After all, it appeared that somebody in power—somebody the community generally trusted—was behind the financing and operations of a silent and powerful methamphetamine cartel in Sioux Falls. *I love our city,* thought Ann Higgins. *It's not big enough for traffic jams during rush hour, let alone a major drug cartel.*

Since election night, Ann and Kent Higgins had been assigned to the governor's security team, but only for public appearances. The governor's security team, however, had no idea about how well Rivera's team was always protecting the Higgins family during the rest of the time. Tonight, Ann and Kent each had an individual security officer assigned to them. In a briefing the director of security services for the state explained that the security detail would be within four to eight feet at all times. They would only intercede if they sensed a threat. Rivera's team would defer to the governor's security team this evening. They would remain outside, in the dark, and keep their eyes open for people who did not match the profile of the inauguration attendees. It was a tough situation for Rivera's team. They could make much more of a contribution to security if they were inside the Sioux Falls Convention Center. However, they could not risk being discovered, either. If the corrupt officials who were protecting the drug trade in Sioux Falls learned the magnitude of the investigation, they might just disappear.

Ann appreciated her security detail tonight and she had every reason to feel that way. She correctly sensed danger because of the meth lab she had stumbled across. At 6:45 p.m. she exchanged a congratulatory hug with the commander, the head of the cartel that posed such a threat to her. Without knowing it, Ann entered into deeper peril at that moment. She looked into his striking blue eyes with full confidence and trust, while she was oblivious to the evil this man directed and bankrolled on a daily basis.

The commander was still feeling the euphoria that swept over him a few hours earlier at the inauguration ceremony. He felt a raw, angry thrill as he greeted Ann Higgins. She reached her arms out to hug him, and he graciously embraced her as he yearned to squeeze a little harder and crush the life out of her. If only her ongoing curiosity would fade away. If only she had not engaged Stoker and his friends to snoop around a little bit more, dig a little deeper. She was fast becoming a damning witness, and the concern was eating away at him subconsciously and occasionally interrupting his sleep. But for tonight he would try to put it out of his mind.

Tomorrow morning he would kick off his day with an aggressive meeting schedule. In those gatherings he would delve into the details of some of South Dakota law enforcement's most deeply held secrets. Police chiefs, sheriffs, and prosecutors from all around the state would update him with all of the information he would need to manage his secret empire. When he asked intelligent drug enforcement questions in these meetings, attendees would be impressed. "This new guy is really aggressive about drug crime," they would say. Nobody would ever question his motives or credibility. Not with his new title.

Over the next few minutes, he found it impossible to stop worrying about the mystery that was Ann Higgins. He couldn't put her out of his mind. She knew too much. Yet, while he was far too insulated by his layers of minions to ever be linked to his crimes, Ann Higgins may now be in a position to do serious damage to his people and systems. She could cost him millions of dollars over the next two or three years. She knew too much.

The commander noticed when Ann turned to the lieutenant governor and whispered in his ear. "Darling. I'll be back." Then Ann gave her husband a peck on the cheek. As she walked away from her husband and his awkward throng of congratulatory admirers, her security officer, Michelle, followed her from a comfortable distance. Michelle was also dressed formally and she fit in among the dignitaries, lobbyists, and who's who of South Dakota.

Ann exited the main ballroom and suddenly she felt vulnerable in the open area. She turned down an exhibit hall corridor and took her cell phone out of her handbag. She turned on the camera app and chose the user-facing camera. She pretended to talk into it like a speakerphone, but Ann was really using the phone's camera to look over her shoulder. She was looking to see if anyone followed her. With every few steps she traveled down the corridor, the crowd thinned a little more. Michelle was still following her dutifully from about ten feet behind. After a few more paces, Ann noticed one man who indeed stood out. He stayed along the fray of the crowd and did his best to appear disinterested in her, but she had seen him take many glances in her direction. The man who was stalking her was a thick-necked, short guy with dirty blond hair, who still suffered the indignation of the scars that acne had left on his face as a teenager.

Ann took four or five clumsy pictures of the man in an over-the-shoulder fashion. She hoped that she had captured the man's face in at least one of the shots. Without turning toward her security detail, Ann asked her a question. "Michelle, do you know where the closest ladies room is?"

"The closest will be too busy, Mrs. Higgins," she replied. "If you're willing to walk for sixty more seconds, there is one near the kitchen that is likely to be almost deserted."

"Perfect."

As they made their way to the bathroom, Ann noticed how the thug continued to hover on the edge of the crowd instead of following them. "Okay, Michelle. When we get into the bathroom, I want to show you some pictures of a man. I think he's been following me and I don't know why. Can you just check it out?"

"Sure," Michelle replied. "Just tuck your phone away so you look more natural and relaxed. Let's just stroll over to that bathroom."

"Do you think I'm paranoid?"

"Honey, I'm paid to be paranoid. You listen to that intuition. Even if it's not right this time, it's teaching you."

As the women rounded the corner they left the dirty blond man's line of sight. Ann reached for her phone.

"Not so fast there, Ann." Michelle was coaching her on one of the finer points of security. Leave your phone put away. Why don't you just pull out some lipstick or something? Those cameras can see everything until we can get into the privacy of the bathroom."

"You mean you think that man might have connections to corrupt security or police?"

"I doubt it, but let's just be suspicious about the possibility for a few minutes."

As the women approached the bathroom, Michelle opened the door for Ann, but slid in sideways with her. Michelle performed a sweep of the area and found only one other woman occupying a stall. Michelle would watch the stall and the bathroom entrance carefully.

Using hand signals, Michelle instructed Ann to produce the phone. As they scrolled through the photos, they found one picture that did a reasonable job of capturing the potential thug. Michelle took the phone from Ann, found the text-messaging app, and forwarded the picture to her own phone. She did all of this between glances around the bathroom. Ann was impressed.

Two seconds later, Michelle's phone vibrated as the picture arrived there. Then, she quickly forwarded the picture from her phone to her squad leader with a message.

Man may be following Ann Higgins. Please watch.

Michelle leaned in toward Ann's ear and whispered. "My squad leader is sitting in the control center where he can see more than two dozen security cameras. Within seconds he'll find the man and assign somebody to watch him."

Michelle pointed toward the door. Ann followed her gesture and they exited the bathroom. In the corridor, Ann saw that there were no other people around, so she spoke openly with her security escort. "Michelle, thank you. You've calmed an anxious woman's heart."

"My pleasure ma'am," replied the security detail as they approached another corner. Michelle sped her pace to ensure that she turned the corner first. As she rounded the turn into the corridor she made a wide turn and gave Ann plenty of personal space. Ann's intuition told her to respect the distance. It made it less likely that the stalker with semi-blond hair would know they were on to him.

As Ann approached the crowds and the entrance to the banquet hall she could no longer see the man who had concerned her ten minutes earlier. But she suspected he was there, hiding. This low-level thug, who had never met the commander nor looked into his deep, intense eyes, had buried himself just inside the throng of people. People were his camouflage and from his perch behind three or four other inauguration attendees, he saw Michelle approaching just a few steps ahead of Ann.

But Ann was not defenseless because Michelle was managing the situation. She was one of South Dakota's best bodyguards. Thanks to the small speaker in Michelle's ear, she knew exactly where the thug was. She soon spotted him with her peripheral vision. As Ann reentered the throng, people resumed giving her hugs and handshakes. Fortunately, she had the presence of mind to let each interaction take her deeper into the hall and closer to her husband. Michelle continued to get reports from the surveillance team; and the acne-scarred man was indeed following Ann wherever she went. He maintained a distance of ten or fifteen feet. Michelle inserted herself between the stalker and Ann and kept track of him with short glances. Updates from people watching security cameras also flowed into her earpiece.

Ann had almost made her way back to her husband when a plain-looking man in a tuxedo gently intercepted her. "Congratulations Ann." The stranger leaned in and hugged her, but also used the opportunity whisper into her ear. "I'm on Michelle's team. That man is indeed following you. We have a plan."

He released her from the hug, congratulated her again and then melted into the crowd.

Plan? I don't want a plan! Ann thought. Fear gripped her as she imagined an exaggerated perception of her current danger. *I need an exit strategy!*

Adrenaline surged through her body and her fight or flight instinct kicked in with shocking vigor. The feeling was primal and it suddenly overrode her trust in Michelle and her security team while overwhelming all her judgment and logic. Because she could not see the thug, she had nobody to fight. An instant later her desire to run overwhelmed her. Ann impulsively kicked off her two-inch heels, causing her to shrink into the crowd even more. Michelle lost sight of Ann, but the thug did not.

Like a frightened animal in a burning meadow, Ann began to run and to dodge. Mostly she darted around people. She didn't care that she was causing a scene, and she ignored the guests' confused looks and surprised reactions. She dodged an ice sculpture, a wet bar, members of the wait staff, and even a piano before she found open space where she could accelerate to a full sprint.

Michelle searched frantically through the crowd for a few moments. When she could not see Ann, she retraced her steps to the edge of the crowd and looked down the corridor. There she saw Ann Higgins disappearing back down the hall with her stalker closing in fast.

As Ann ran her adrenaline continued to surge through her body and through her mind. Within seconds, her panic was replaced with focus. *It's safe in the kitchen*, she thought. As she ran back down the corridor where she had been just minutes ago, she recalled hearing the sounds and smelling the scents of the kitchen on the way to the bathroom. She took an abrupt left and burst through two swinging doors. The sight before her was a sea of carts containing salads, entrées, and a plethora of food. Fortunately, she was able to nimbly make her way through the kitchen and exit into the bowels of the building. Now, she was jogging through the dimly lit storage, custodial and shipping and receiving area. While she had managed to elude Michelle, the one person who could guarantee her safety, she knew she could find plenty of places to hide amongst the darkness of this place. She would call for help on her phone once the danger had passed.

Ann continued in a sprint down the cement floor of a dimly lit corridor, until she found a door labeled "Janitor." She twisted the handle and the door opened. She let herself into the large office, which contained two vacuums, four custodial carts, shelves of chemicals, brooms, mops, a desk, and two chairs.

As Ann sat there, she contemplated her next move. *Had the thug followed her? If so, what did he want with her?* The adrenaline was wearing off and anxiety was setting in.

The last time she had felt this level of anxiety in her life Troy Stoker had helped her through it. In her current nervous state she failed to consider calling the police. Yet, it did not even occur to her that her phone now contained Michelle's number, thanks to the picture the security agent had texted between their phones earlier. Instead, Ann instinctively pulled out her phone and with now-trembling fingers managed to find Troy Stoker in her contact list. She pushed the call button and raised the phone to her ear with a hand that shivered so violently she was afraid she might brush the phone against her cheek and disconnect the phone call. "Answer, Troy. Answer," she whispered in barely audible tones.

Outside the convention center, in a high-tech van, Rivera's men were tapping into Ann's phone call.

On the second ring, Stoker picked up. His voice was cheerful because he assumed Ann was calling him from the inauguration ball. "Ann, this is a surprise. Are you butt-dialing me from the big party?"

"Just stay on the line and don't say anything!" Her whisper was fierce. "I'm falling apart here and I need your help. Also, I may need you to hear this. It could be evidence. But wait, here comes a picture on your phone." Ann somehow managed to find the presence of mind to text Stoker a copy of the same picture she had sent to Michelle. Rivera's men in the van intercepted a copy of the picture as well.

Stoker was confused and he needed clarification. "What do you need me to listen for, Ann? What's going on?"

"Shhhhh!" But, Ann had said it too loudly.

All of a sudden, the door to the closet cracked open. After a brief delay, the thug slinked into the closet with his outdated cell phone pressed to his ear. "Tell the boss we found her." He slipped the phone into his pocket.

"Hello, Ann. I'm impressed. You caught onto me even before the pros in your security detail."

"What's this about?" The ferociousness in Ann's voice surprised her and she grew even bolder.

"I don't know," the thug said. "I only know that someone's paying me four hundred bucks to keep track of you tonight. I really don't know who it is."

Stoker was straining to hear the conversation. All he could make out, amidst the assortment clear and inaudible words so far, was a man saying something about four hundred dollars to Ann. Rivera's men in the van had better technology. They heard almost every word, and the team leader assigned a man to get inside and find Ann Higgins.

"You say you don't know who hired you?" challenged Ann as she hid the phone between two bottles of glass cleaner. "Then, who's building meth labs in my planned community and listening in on sessions with my psychiatrist?"

"Somebody way above me, Ann. I've never met him. I probably never will."

"Actually, you're wrong." The words came from the confident baritone voice coming from a man standing at the doorway of the custodial closet. His voice was so clear that Stoker heard it perfectly through the phone.

Just then, the commander, with his striking eyes, walked through the door. He was dressed in his tuxedo and everything about his appearance was perfect. Both Ann and the thug were shocked beyond belief to hear one of South Dakota's top officials admitting such crimes.

"Listen, Ann. I'm *almost* sorry about all of this," the commander said.

Ann took two bold steps toward the man—whom she had greeted and hugged minutes earlier. She looked him directly in the eye. "What's going on here?"

The commander was not intimidated by her assertiveness. His voice was calm. "I need a little information about an issue that's heating up and I was hoping you could help me out." He motioned for the thug to close the door. "I'm hoping you can keep this real hush-hush and off-the-record. It's extremely sensitive right now and we would not want to tip our hand in any investigation."

"What are you talking about?" asked Ann. "Just be straight with me. Did I screw up somebody's investigation?"

The commander firmly placed his hands on her shoulders in a paternal and condescending gesture and backed her toward the shelf where she had hidden her phone. "What can you tell me about 5644 and 5660 Bryant Way?"

Every hair on Ann's body stood erect, and she momentarily forgot to breathe. From his home, Stoker was listening intently, trying to memorize details from the conversation and recognize the man's voice.

The blond thug, obviously confused, was standing silently and blocking the door.

Out in the van, one of Rivera's men exited the vehicle wearing a banquet server's uniform. In sixty seconds he would be entering the convention center through the kitchen by posing as a banquet worker to keep his team's presence a secret.

"I visited one of the houses on Bryant Way a few days ago. I did *not* know that the owners had closed and taken possession. The lockbox was still present and had a key inside, so I got in."

"What did you see?"

The way he asked the question bothered Ann. He was not speaking like an investigator. He was badgering her, as if she had done something wrong. "I found some suspicious stuff. There are things I have questions about."

"Did you find anything else?" the commander asked.

Ann wondered why she was being questioned about this. *Why here? Why now?* It occurred to her that he might have heard, in new government circles, that she was a suspect. "Why are you asking me this? How are *you* involved in all of this?"

Stoker could hear almost everything because the man and Ann had moved so close to her phone. As he profiled the man who was talking, he detected definite psychotic tendencies in his voice. Ann was in trouble. This man, whom she apparently knew, was an extremely dangerous man.

The commander spoke slowly and loudly. "Ann, what else did you see?"

"I found a crude drawing of a meth lab," Ann said. "What is all of this about? Why all the questions? Is this an investigation?"

"I'm making those properties, and others like them, a priority," replied the commander. "You see, your little paradise planned community was so appealing, that my best chemists wanted to, let's just say, live there."

At that moment, Ann Higgins grasped the horrid truth. The man standing before her was not talking to her as a South Dakota official. He was talking to her as a criminal mastermind. "Wolf in sheep's clothing," she said in a soft, pensive voice.

The commander smiled. "Thank you." In his deluded mind, Ann's reference to a wolf was a high compliment.

Ann closed her eyes and leaned back against the shelf behind her. "Those are your houses."

"My chemists just love them. You know, they like to be so close to the water."

"Chemists! So, it's true! Those houses are being fitted to produce meth in the basements."

"Ann, Ann, darling. Meth is so 2013. Sure, we'll start with meth. But heroin's back, baby doll! The synthetic stuff certainly has its problems, but we're working on it." The commander was animated now. "Coming soon to a basement near you, synthetic smack." He continued on with his showmanship. "New and improved! Will not melt skin away!"

The thug laughed.

Ann couldn't believe what she was hearing. "I never thought I would walk my real estate clients into a meth lab."

"Two labs actually," the commander said. But that's just the basement. The upstairs bedrooms in those homes make tidy little offices for the clerical folks to listen in on cell phone conversations and hack into Wi-Fi signals all around Chelsea Crossing. You would be amazed how casually people say or text their Social Security numbers, usernames, passwords and PINs. It makes it so easy to *borrow* the identities of your fine residents. Yes, those people may be house poor, but they are often credit rich. They never see us coming."

"Identity theft? You would stoop that low?"

"Oh, I would not call it stooping. I would just say, well, you know what they say about inquiring minds. I still cannot believe people are stupid enough to broadcast their Social Security numbers on a cell phone call to their banks. You know if you only get the last four numbers of their social security, stumbling onto the remaining five is simple. Get a little information on an employer, intercept a friend's resume, capture a phone conversation with a relative who happens to bear your mother's maiden name on their caller ID, and you're in. We don't want to rip off everyone in Chelsea Crossing. The authorities would eventually be onto us. However, if they give us a toehold on their friends, family, and relatives who live outside of your little development, we can spread our risk out across this great nation. We've even made some headway into Canada and Europe lately. We're really into diversification. Next stop, Japan."

Ann was appalled by what she was hearing. "Elaborate but not elegant. I'm not surprised by your creativity. You've always been brilliant. But, I am shocked and disgusted at your depravity. How did you hide such profound selfishness all this time?"

The commander liked her question, and he pretended an embellished look of concern on his face. "I like how you used the word 'hide.' That is exactly what I do. I hide behind titles, façades, and the thick office doors of government bureaucracies. People in my little side-ventures only know me as 'the commander.' It's a throwback to my Navy days, and I kind of like it.

"Commander," Ann scoffed. "That explains a lot—even to us non-psychologists. What are you compensating for, *Commander*?"

The commander took immediate offense and his rage was obvious in his piercing blue eyes. Even his speech became angry and irrational. "Oh Ann!" The commander was now speaking in mocking and sarcastic tones. "I'm sensing some psychotic vibe from you. Perhaps some of the issues Dr. Stoker's been medicating you for are re-emerging." He shook his finger at her. "Have you been neglecting your meds?"

"How do you know about Stoker?" asked Ann. "You have *no* idea what I discuss with him! It's none of your business."

"Ah. Paranoia!" The commander smirked with a wild smile. "This is serious." The commander pretended to hold up his hands in a defensive position. "No need to get violent now, Ann. Are those fists? Are you threatening us?"

"Oh, no, no, no. You're not fabricating these lies and spinning some of my perfectionistic tendencies into a sham of deep mental illness," Ann retorted. "What is this all about? Why are you here? Why are you confronting me tonight?"

Rivera's man had successfully entered the kitchen. He picked up a tray of finger food and walked into the main banquet hall. At first, he noticed that all of the guests were having a great time. It appeared that none of them knew about the emergency. However, he saw security guards and police officers scurrying in many different directions. He overheard one radio blaring out, "We need eyes on Ann Higgins."

Rivera's man put down the tray of finger food, and sent a text to his team in the truck.

> *Security scrambling to find Higgins. Most guests unaware of prob. Police helping but not convinced Higgins in trouble.*

Rivera's man hunted for Ann Higgins. He guessed that most police and security would look in the public areas of the convention center, so he considered looking around in the back hallways and less traditional areas. It occurred to him that the portion of the conversation he heard transpired in a smaller room where Higgins and her assailants were less likely to be interrupted. Rivera's man jogged toward the loading dock and started to search the surrounding areas. Besides, he needed to stay away from the main crowd and out of sight of the Sioux Falls police — a mission imperative if they were going to investigate secretively.

"Why am I confronting you tonight?" The commander pretended to collect his thoughts for a moment before responding. "Ann, this is not really much of a confrontation. Frankly, you know too much about our little plans. But, we can't just *get rid* of you in a messy fashion."

Until this moment, Ann never considered this man, who she now also knew as the commander, capable of murder.

From his home, Stoker was hobbling to his kitchen to pick up his landline and call 911.

As the realization of Ann's true danger entered her mind, the commander pounced on her and covered her mouth so she could not scream.

"We are deeply concerned witnesses of your erratic behavior." The commander was now hissing into her ear. "Look at you, Ann. This suicidal state is troubling indeed." The commander looked at the thug. "Wouldn't you agree, kid?"

"Suicidal?" asked the thug. He was confused.

"Yes." The commander coached the thug to agree with his exaggerated voice and gestures. "All of this public pressure. Don't worry, Ann. People will understand." The commander spun her around, and put her in a headlock.

The thug suddenly understood, and he joined in on the sarcasm. "How did we miss your cries for help, our dear Ann? The signs were there the whole time, and we chose to ignore them. Oh, poor Ann Higgins. South Dakota mourns for its native daughter."

The commander pointed at one of the vacuum cleaners and barked out an order. "Get that vacuum cord." Responding with the speed and obedience of an elite soldier, the thug yanked the cord off the vacuum housing. Reading the commander's mind, the thug whipped up a makeshift noose. The commander loved when people anticipated his needs. "You're good, kid. I think I can use you after you finish this gig."

Ann struggled to free her mouth for just a moment, and screamed briefly. Stoker was horrified by what he was overhearing as he waited for a response from 911.

"911. Where is your emergency?"

"Yes. I'm Dr. Troy Stoker, a psychiatrist here in town. I'm on a cell phone call overhearing a murder at the Sioux Falls Convention Center. Could you please understand how urgent this is? This is not a joke."

The operator was skeptical thanks to thousands of prank calls she had fielded in the past. Nevertheless, she decided to initiate the protocol for distinguishing false calls from real calls. "Sir? Will you please explain that again?"

While the commander covered Ann's mouth with a gloved hand, the thug managed to get the noose around her neck. Then the commander took a needleless oral syringe out of his coat pocket. It contained roughly ten doses of a potent pain opiate. He knew that hanging her would kill her long before the overdose poisoned her liver, kidneys, heart and brain. Nevertheless, it would make Ann's death look more like a suicide. With a few violent motions the commander pried Ann's mouth open, inserted the plastic device down her throat, pushed on the plunger, and forced the fast-acting drugs into her stomach. But, amidst all of the struggle and fight, shoving the syringe down her throat triggered her vomit reflex, and she threw the liquid painkillers back up, with most of the vomit landing on the bodice of her formal gown.

"No matter." The commander set the empty syringe aside on a shelf. "It will just look like you couldn't hold your poison, Ann. But, being the butt-kicking, determined person you are, you still went through with it and ended it all."

Stoker was using every ounce of his determination to get help to Ann Higgins "I'm a psychiatrist and a patient has called me in a desperate moment."

"Uh huh." The operator was growing increasingly skeptical. "Is this some sort of prank?"

"No ma'am. I would not prank you from my own home land line."

The thug quickly climbed atop the office desk and wove the other end of the vacuum cord up into the frame of the false ceiling. "Just let me know when you're ready, Commander."

"Heave!" The commander was lifting Ann's quivering body up into the air.

"My patient is calling me from the Sioux Falls Convention Center," Stoker said feeling completely helpless. "Her cell phone number is 605-555-4877. Please tap into it any way you can. I am doctor and psychiatrist. This is a true emergency. Please send police and paramedics right now!"

Ann was full of fight and kicked and punched violently landing a fist blow to the back of the commander's head as well as a kick that surely left a bruise on his back. But, all her fighting was in vain. Soon the intense pain faded to numbness, and then all went black for Ann Higgins.

The thug took up the slack and tied off the vacuum cord using an impromptu concoction of unskilled knots. The commander grabbed a rag and wiped down the electric cord to remove any prints either of them may have left. He also sanitized the desk and doorknob.

"I need ten seconds," the commander said. He grabbed Ann Higgins's lifeless hands and lifted them up to the cord around her neck. "I'm pressing her fingers on the vacuum cord a few times to transfer fingerprints." He also pressed her fingers against the medication syringe, taking care to touch her right index finger to the plunger. Then he slid a chair to the side of her dangling feet.

"Poor Mrs. Higgins," the thug chuckled. "All the pressure of being a big-shot CEO and a politician's wife. How come nobody heard her cries for help?"

"You do good work kid." The commander tied the vacuum cord off once more, this time to the base of a shelf that held a number of heavy chemical containers. "Congratulations. You're getting a promotion, a bonus, and a hefty raise. Welcome to the wildest ride of your life."

"Promotion and raise? What do you mean? I was just doing a quick four hundred dollar gig."

The commander scribbled a phone number on an inaugural napkin and handed it to the thug. "Just call this number and tell my guy, Nichols, that you met the commander. Tell him you need to get out of town now and make a visit to the Reno offices. I'll have him arrange a stop for you in Denver, first. We'll mix up your appearance. You'll love how our surgeon erases those scars on your face. New clothes, and a new hairstyle, and we tan you up like an Italian stud. Nobody will ever recognize you, but the women will love you!"

"Just like that? Off to Reno?"

"Get moving kid. If you stick around here, I'll have to make sure my guys get you before the cops ever do. Now, please, I appreciate your help. You've got potential. Get on the phone with Nichols and get out of town."

Just then, the thug and the commander heard the first siren. With pretend dignity and calmness, they ducked out of the janitors' office. "My name's—"

The commander cut him off. "I don't care about your name, kid. I don't *want* to know just yet." The commander and the thug turned the corner and walked back down the corridor, separated by fifteen feet and acting as if they did not know each other. Behind them, they heard a horrendous commotion. The false ceiling in the custodians' office had failed and Ann Higgins and the rest of the ceiling had come tumbling down. Ann Higgins's 137 pounds had eventually overwhelmed the cheap aluminum ceiling rails. Both of the men ignored the ruckus, and casually made their way back toward the evening's celebration.

"Dr. Stoker. We've verified your home phone and the cell phone connection to your patient. We're sending police and EMS now. Can you tell us the name of your patient?"

"Ann Higgins."

Fortunately, this 911 operator was not politically aware, and she had no idea that Stoker had just uttered the name of the new lieutenant governor's wife. "Alright doctor, I'll alert the police and security at the facility to be on the lookout for one Ann Higgins."

Stoker was gathering his car keys and wallet while waiting to get off the phone with the 911 operator. His cell phone was still connected to Ann's phone.

A few moments later, the 911 operator came back on the line. "Dr. Stoker. It appears as if they have already been searching for an Ann Higgins for a few minutes. Do you know why—"

Stoker interrupted the operator. "Yes, but I'm sorry. I think the best thing is for me to just get over there. Goodbye."

Stoker hung up the phone, limped with astounding speed out to his Bronco, and made a hasty drive to the Sioux Falls Convention Center.

As Stoker pulled up to the convention center he directed himself toward the sea of flashing police lights and parked his car illegally next to them. He ignored his pain and ran toward the closest entrance.

"I'm Dr. Troy Stoker. I have critical evidence into the incident with Ann Higgins this evening," he said to a youthful appearing police officer who was guarding the entrance. Stoker ignored the officer's gesture for him to stop and continued walking toward the convention center doors.

"I've got a Dr. Stoker here," the young officer said into his radio while running to keep up with the determined Stoker. "He says he may have information about Ann Higgins." Seconds later the officer yelled to Stoker, who had outpaced him by twenty yards. "Dr. Stoker, I'm supposed to tell you to double-time your butt to the main entrance. My captain will take you to the command center."

Stoker yelled back over his shoulder. "Well it's a good thing we wasted no time, son. We're practically there." With his cell phone in hand and still connected to Ann's mobile phone call, Stoker dashed thirty more yards to the convention center doors.

"Troy. I've got a situation with a missing lieutenant governor's wife; and now you show up telling me you know something about this?" Captain Stan Brown of the Sioux Falls Police Department was waving him through the doors. "Start talking. And talk fast."

"I got a call from Ann on this phone just minutes ago." Stoker held up his cell phone for emphasis. "I'm still connected to her phone."

"Okay. So where does the alleged murder come in the play?"

"That's what I just overheard. Now let's find her quick and hope that, at this point, we're just looking at attempted murder. "

Police were already fanned out over the whole building. But Stoker knew that Ann had been in a location with a vacuum. When he divulged this clue, the convention center security guard radioed for three police officers to get over to the custodial office. "If she's not there, proceed to search every possible closet or room that contains a vacuum."

Rivera's man had already been looking through the loading dock and had just arrived at the door marked "Janitor," when he heard the noises emitted by police radios and the unmistakable sound of oxford police shoes running in his direction. As a member of Rivera's team he needed to stay off the police radar, for now, so he took off running in the opposite direction. As he made his hasty exit he reasoned that, if Ann was in that janitors' room, the approaching rescuers would be more helpful to her than he could be at this point. Picking up his radio he contacted his team. "We've done all we can here. I'll be back in two minutes. Capture as much video of people leaving the building as possible. Whoever did this, they're out there somewhere."

Stoker and the police captain were running toward the housekeeping office when they received a radio report that some officers had arrived before them. They were sifting through the menagerie of the completely collapsed false ceiling.

"Mrs. Higgins! Mrs. Higgins!" Stoker and the captain could overhear officers calling to her through Stoker's cell phone.

"That's the right spot. They're there!" Stoker yelled. "I can hear them on my phone."

When Stoker and the captain arrived, the first responders had already sifted through ceiling tiles and aluminum grid. Two police officers were prepared to administer resuscitation CPR. But so far, they were having difficulty removing the makeshift noose from Ann's neck.

"Who's got a knife or some scissors?" demanded Stoker.

Just then, paramedics arrived, and one of them produced a heavy-duty pair of scissors from one of his many pockets. Within moments the noose was cut free and the paramedics began CPR while Stoker stabilized Ann's neck. As Stoker looked at Ann's throat he was gravely concerned. Her larynx was obviously crushed, which was possibly a death sentence.

"Doctor Stoker. Take over bagging for me here, one of the paramedics said. I'm going to try and intubate her."

"Intubate? On a crushed larynx? You can do that?"

"I'm two months away from taking my respiratory therapy boards, Doc. I just might be able to pull this off."

Over the next forty seconds, Troy Stoker experienced yet another of the hundreds of miracles he had witnessed during his lifetime. This paramedic who was almost a respiratory therapist, just happened to be in the right place at the right time. Using some special instruments she was able to establish a modest airway. While Stoker bagged the patient, and the other paramedic performed chest compressions, they were able to provide Ann Higgins with life-sustaining oxygen.

The paramedic, who was performing chest compressions stopped for a moment, took out her stethoscope and listened. "Her heart is beating on its own." She removed a penlight and checked Ann's eyes. "Pupils are equal and reactive to light." Then the paramedic removed a reflex hammer from yet another pocket and tapped lightly just below Ann's knee. Ann's leg jumped slightly. "Patellar reflexes are equal bilaterally and are approximately plus two."

The intubating paramedic flashed a smile of relief. "That's all great news. Go ahead and see if she'll breath on her own, Doc."

Stoker paused his bagging, and a moment later Ann Higgins gasped. Then, she started to take shallow, life-sustaining breaths. "Wow. She's breathing on her own and her vital signs are okay for what she's been through," Stoker said. "I'm guessing she's avoided a cervical fracture."

"Let's put the back splints on her, stabilize her head, and get her to the hospital," one of the paramedics said.

Twenty minutes later Ann Higgins occupied trauma bay one at the emergency room. Two hours later she was in the intensive care unit in critical condition. As newly inaugurated lieutenant governor, Kent Higgins, stood over his wife, he allowed the tears to flow freely down the front of his tuxedo. The love of his life was in a coma and he was struggling with so many questions. He knew tonight's trauma was not a suicide attempt. The new lieutenant governor could only wonder, how had an enemy done this? The explanations about who caused Ann's injuries were almost as vague as the prognosis the doctors had given.

CHAPTER 25

MINNEHAHA COUNTY PUBLIC SAFETY BUILDING

The next morning, South Dakota and the nation were shocked at the events that had unfolded in Sioux Falls the previous evening. Because the scene of the crime, the convention center, was also centrally located and close to hotels and restaurants, it became the default media epicenter. The satellite trucks from Fox News, Telemundo, CNN, CBS, NBC, ABC, PBS, and dozens of other news outlets dotted the wide sidewalks in front of the main doors of the convention center. Hundreds of reporters broadcast the heinous details surrounding the discovery of a nearly lifeless Ann Higgins. The convention center was the backdrop for their reports.

"Little is known at this hour about the events that occurred here in Sioux Falls last evening," one talking head from a national morning news show explained. "Eyewitnesses tell us that Ann Higgins, wife of the newly inaugurated lieutenant governor, Kent Higgins, was seen running from the inaugural ball. They found her a few minutes later after an apparent failed hanging in a janitor's utility room. Now, South Dakota authorities are wondering if they have a suicide on their hands or if this is something more criminal?"

The news reports generally concluded that neither the governor nor the lieutenant governor had made any comment so far. However, at eleven o'clock a.m., the Sioux Falls City mayor and police chief, accompanied by the newly elected state attorney general, would hold a press conference in the Minnehaha County Public Safety Building.

At precisely 11:59 a.m., the three men walked into the press conference room and stood side-by-side behind the podium. "Ladies and gentleman of the media, my name is Edward Best. I am the Chief of Police here in the city of Sioux Falls and here with me are Mayor William McCleary and Steve Hewitt, the newly inaugurated South Dakota Attorney General. We'll be sharing prepared statements with you and then we'll take questions." Cameras snapped incessantly and reporters held smart phones and other recording devices in the air attempting to capture every word and intonation.

"Last night, during the South Dakota Governor's Inaugural Ball, Ann Higgins, wife of Lieutenant Governor Kent Higgins, was found in a utility closet in the Sioux Falls Convention Center. Fortunately, police and medical professionals found her. They were able to provide first aid and transport her to the hospital. Mrs. Higgins is now in the intensive care unit at Sioux Falls Regional Hospital. Her condition is critical and she is in a coma. Lieutenant Governor Higgins has given us permission to release that information. The governor and lieutenant governor have asked for the prayers of South Dakotans, Americans, and citizens of the world.

"We've had about seventeen hours to investigate this situation. Because Mrs. Higgins was found after an apparent failed hanging, there has been speculation that this may have been a suicide attempt. While we've not ruled out suicide, we've certainly *not* ruled out foul play. Our tireless police officers have collected information from witnesses, video cameras, and the scene that will help us clarify in the days to come. Therefore, we have designated the convention center a crime scene and we will continue to process evidence," concluded the chief as he stepped away from the microphone.

Then, as he had rehearsed, the attorney general stepped up to the microphone. "The Attorney General's office has seen some of the preliminary evidence, and we are proceeding on the assumption that this is a crime." Then there was silence while the attorney general looked out at the news cameras, and his voice choked up. He stopped for a moment to gain his composure. With a quiver in his voice, he continued. "I've had friends who have been victims of serious crimes in the past; and now my dear friend Ann Higgins is in a hospital ICU, hanging onto life. As your attorney general, I'm allowing the emotion of this incident, the emotions of this day, to burn into my heart and mind. We in South Dakota will stand up to crime. Justice may be blind, but your attorney general is not."

Hewitt was not done with his statement. "I'm convinced this is an attempted murder and while it's the responsibility of the police to investigate, and not the attorney general, I will be supporting the police on this case with all of my energy. The case of Ann Higgins is my number one priority."

"We will now take questions," the mayor said. He pointed at a reporter he knew by name. "Miss Long."

"Marnie Long. NBC News. Attorney General Hewitt, why isn't Governor Horton here with you today?"

"Governor Horton is at the hospital with the Higgins family," Hewitt said. He is spending his time doing two things. First, he is supporting his friend's family during a time of severe personal crisis. Second, he is running the state of South Dakota. I met with him this morning at six o'clock for thirty minutes. He worked until about ten-thirty this morning and then went to the hospital. He'll be back to work by lunch. He'll likely visit the Higgins family again today for an hour or two, and then he'll work into the evening—and probably into the hours of the morning. That's just how hard your governor works. I assure you that the only thing the governor is neglecting is an hour or two of sleep."

"Oliver Miner. National Public Radio. Mr. Attorney General, you say you're convinced this is an attempted murder. What else can you tell us?"

"There are inconsistencies at the scene, and we may have identified a person of interest on video footage. However, the most important factor is Ann Higgins has not been depressed or otherwise prone to suicide. We've spoken with family, friends, work associates, and medical professionals. They cannot point out a single precursor or suicidal stress source. She just has not exhibited any suicidal behaviors."

"Emily French. Fox News. What does the video footage show?"

"Last night at 6:53 p.m. we have video footage of Mrs. Higgins attempting to elude and detach from her security detail, which she does successfully," explained the attorney general. "Shortly thereafter she is seen on a surveillance camera entering the kitchen. At 7:09 p.m., Mrs. Higgins is found in the housekeeping office with a noose around her neck. There are no cameras in that area of the convention center."

"Where does the person of interest show up in the video?" asked the same reporter.

As the attorney general started to answer, the chief of police covered the microphone and whispered to the attorney general. "I don't want to give out this information yet," the chief said. "I'm already nervous that we've given a few extra details that could compromise our investigation."

Hewitt nodded in agreement with the chief. He leaned into the microphone and said, "That's a part of the investigation that we're not ready to share. We're analyzing it as we speak."

"Who called 911?" a reporter blurted out without identifying himself.

"There are only a certain facts we can provide at this point in the investigation, and we cannot reveal who made that phone call."

The mayor, chief of police, and attorney general answered questions for another ten minutes. When the inquiries became redundant, the mayor informed the reporters that it was time to end. "No further questions. Thank you for your time. We'll let you know immediately when there are substantial developments in this case."

The three men exited the room hastily and went to their respective meetings. Within ten minutes the commander was getting an update from the police about the investigation, and he was thrilled. The person of interest was the man with dirty blond hair, who was probably going to arrive in Reno at any moment. Again, the reports noted that Dr. Stoker was the person who had called 911 and overheard the conversation in the housekeeping closet. *This Stoker's going to be a tricky problem, which will require a bit of an elaborate solution*, thought the commander. His confidence was growing that he would, yet again, get away with another serious crime.

CHAPTER 26

Brian Berg loved investigating. Almost without fail, he found something out of order in a physician's office. He rarely visited a clinic that did not have some kind of infraction having to do with medical records or medications. He particularly loved to investigate doctors in private practice and found it much easier than inspecting doctors who were employed by the health systems. Offices containing one or two doctors who were self-employed were easy to overwhelm and manipulate. These small practices did not know due process laws and they often allowed Berg to seize medical records even when he had no good reason for doing so. They were powerless, from a knowledge point of view, as they tried to stop him from demanding logbooks, patient records, compliance documents, and employee files. If doctors, nurses and other people tried to stop one of his "investigations" he would often refer them to Title 36 in the South Dakota code. Rarely would anybody dig in deep enough to see that Berg overstepped his mandate when he manipulated and made demands.

This morning, Brian Berg had arrived at the office and finished his report about the minor problems he found at the clinic in Aberdeen the previous Friday. With a little bit of luck and virtually no skill Brian Berg, *chief* investigator, had yet again figured out how to exaggerate the gravity his findings. He'd placed another petty letter of concern into a physician's licensing file. The office of Harold Slade, M.D. had failed to keep the proper documentation on narcotics; and his nurses had failed in their duty to perform the counts themselves. Furthermore, an expired vial of morphine was presumably a cause for concern. These offenses would need to be remedied by issuing a letter of concern—a supposedly corrective bureaucratic tool.

Letters of concern were the lifeblood of the South Dakota Medical Board. The doctors and staffers who served on the board justified their existence by pointing out the increased numbers of letters of concern that they had written, delivered, and documented year over year. While generally addressing meaningless or petty concerns, the robust volume of letters of concern supposedly proved they were productive. Their statistics wrongly suggested that the board and its staff were looking out for the state citizenry.

But, the reality was that the medical board did a poor job of looking out for the true best interests of the people South Dakota. They rarely managed to find and correct legitimate offenders and practitioners who made harmful mistakes or consistently showed poor medical judgment—especially if they practiced in one of the hospitals or a large physician group. In fact, they recently turned a blind eye to blatantly obvious evidence of a surgeon who was performing grossly unnecessary surgery. Board members and staffers were also aware of a doctor with horrific surgical outcomes. These conclusions were not based on rumors, but on malpractice cases and numerous punitive jury awards. Hospital administrators also had statistics that proved how poorly these doctors performed, yet they kept them under wraps. And, the medical board opted to busy itself in the safe, petty world of issuing letters of concern. They turned a blind eye to physicians who had fathered children in their exam rooms. The hospital system tended to handle such peccadillos by shifting the guilty doctors out of their clinics and into high paying administrative positions where walls of corporate attorneys would insulate them from medical board sanctions and paternity suits.

When the board brought actions against doctors from the Dakota Falls Medical Group or another large clinic, their specialized healthcare lawyers were more skilled at navigating complaints and bargaining with the board to minimize penalties and embarrassment. But, physicians who practiced alone or in a small group were easy targets for the board. Too often doctors in private practice hired the wrong council—lawyers who had no experience before the board. Most attorneys usually lacked the knowledge to effectively rebut the petty issues the board brought up with these "easy target" doctors. Only a few attorneys in the state excelled in this niche law practice of defending physicians against the often cloaked and mysterious workings of the South Dakota Medical Board. The few doctors wise enough to seek out these legal "specialists" were rewarded by closed-door sessions with the board that usually uncovered the truth and concluded in the physician's favor. There were hushed apologies by the medical board that never left the "cone of silence" of the third floor office on Main Avenue.

Berg's lust for power was borne of his own failures. Perhaps the low point of his life occurred when he was dismissed from the Pierre, South Dakota police force. Berg still remembered it like it was yesterday. He recalled his boss walking him through the paperwork and pointing to the space on his termination form that described him as incompetent. "Let me clarify, Berg. A better translation of the word 'incompetent' would be 'utter and complete doofus,' but human resources would not let us put that in your paperwork."

It was the darkest moment of Brian Berg's life. The days that followed were a drunken span of two weeks which may have turned into suicide had it not been for March Madness basketball. His team made it to the final four and it gave him something to live for.

When he sobered up, he realized that he'd drunk away half of his five-week severance. So he took the remaining $2,000, and checked himself into rehab in Sioux City. While in rehab, Brian tried to find the Lord, but he concluded that being a Christian was not for him. Throughout his life his favorite pastime was *hating* his enemies and he could not imagine loving an enemy as the Bible taught. Love was in short supply in Berg's heart at the moment. As a matter of fact, by the time Brian had read through two Psalms and then flipped through the Sermon on the Mount, he had also plotted revenge on his shift sergeant, two detectives and his father. The Bible taught that you should pray for people who spitefully use you. Brian Berg did not want to be a Christian because he enjoyed finding ways to do evil to those who spitefully used him. Revenge, manipulation, and transferring his anger through his newfound perceived power motivated him even more than money, thrills, or even sex. This was Berg's way of proverbially "kicking the dog" to express his self-loathing.

Brian's rehab hospital was progressive about linking its patients up with jobs. Because Brian was a police academy graduate, he eventually landed a job as a night security guard at the hospital in Dell Rapids. Berg was surprised how much he liked working in the hospital. When patients or visitors got unruly, Berg was the first to respond to the call. He could use extreme physical force because after all, he was defending the hospital and its patients. People rarely questioned his violent methods, because he was so quick to point out how he had saved a baby, an old lady, or a recovering accident victim.

One night at the hospital, another security guard was bragging about how he had an inside track on a job with the state medical board. The position came open under somewhat peculiar circumstances. "I heard they let the last guy go after he bungled some simple investigations," the security guard said.

Berg searched online and found the job opening. He noticed that he met most of the criteria so he applied. Three weeks later he interviewed for the position. The interviewing committee concluded that he was their fifth, or perhaps sixth, best candidate.

When the state medical board extended an offer for the position of state board investigator to its top candidate, the man politely declined the job. He was moving to Colorado to be close to his mother, who had just been diagnosed with Parkinson's disease. The next promising candidate for the position withdrew her application. In her email she explained that her boyfriend had just proposed to her, and she had decided to follow him to graduate school in North Carolina. Candidate number three declined the job after explaining that he had done his homework on Larry Stintson. "I have too much self-respect to work anywhere near that shallow, trite man." The fourth candidate got a better job offer.

In the offices of the state medical board the hiring committee could not decide whether to extend the job to Brian Berg or to another candidate. Both were unimpressive. After ten minutes of inconclusive hand wringing and a lively debate, a coin toss selected the next investigator. Two minutes later, Larry Stintson made the phone call. "Hello, Mr. Berg. This is Dr. Stintson at the South Dakota Medical Board. We would like to offer you a job." Two weeks later, Berg arrived for his first day of work. His office manager accompanied him to his cubicle and welcomed with a cupcake, balloons, and a Hallmark card. He did not meet Larry Stintson, in person, for more than a month.

At 10:30 a.m., Berg finished his report on the Aberdeen clinic, submitted it to his boss, and then walked over to the state motor pool and checked out a car. Fifteen minutes later, Brian Berg was traveling along Interstate 90. He was on his way to Pierre to investigate a radiation oncologist, Mary Wright, M.D. Their 2:00 p.m. meeting was rather routine. During Berg's conversation with her, he quickly concluded that the complaint against this doctor was frivolous. After Berg finished his interview with Dr. Wright, Berg asked his usual treacherous question. "May I swing by the nurse's station and introduce myself?" Berg felt that initial surge of adrenaline as he set his trap.

"Well, we're not your typical clinic, and we don't really have a nurse's station per se," the doctor replied. "One of our nurses is in a treatment room with the patient. She won't be out for another fifteen minutes. Let's not interrupt her, or we might get blasted with a few billion particles of radiation," Dr. Wright joked. Berg felt a little disappointed. This question had rarely failed before.

"But, come right this way. I'll introduce you to Michelle Stevens. She's our head nurse, and she really makes the place hum like a well-oiled machine."

Dr. Wright led Berg into a space that looked like an x-ray room, with a table for a patient to lie on, and a large piece of machinery that hovered above it.

After clumsily introducing himself as the *chief* investigator, Berg asked Stevens if he might take a moment to look at their narcotics inventory? Again he felt a surge of excitement as he resumed his hunt for infractions.

Dr. Wright jumped in and answered the question instead of allowing the nurse to respond. "Sure, I've got it right here." The physician walked over and took a seat at a nice computer. It startled Berg that the *doctor* eagerly jumped in to help instead of allowing the nurse to answer. He was also not prepared for this record to be on a computer. He was used to nurses pulling out three-ring binders and showing him paper records that he could control and copy. His adrenaline switched off yet again, leaving him disheartened.

"Here's where we keep track of our narcotics every morning and night." Dr. Wright pointed to the screen. "It cross-references every vial of medication to a dose and a patient. We also have a log right here for when we have to waste a dose or a little bit of a vial. A nurse signs off on it every morning and night, no exceptions. But, really Mr. Berg, our narcotics count is reconciled at any given moment."

As the doctor clicked the keyboard new screens appeared, and Brian Berg had no idea what she was talking about. But, he pretended to be keeping up. He acted as if he absorbed every little bit of data that passed onto the screen. However, he sensed his chances of achieving an adrenaline fix, from one of his power trips, fading quickly.

"Your inventory looks great. Very impressive," Berg said. He had no idea if his statement was accurate or not.

"So where do you keep your inventory?" Berg asked. All he needed to find was one expired medication vial. He wanted so desperately to find an infraction and use his government power to take control, intimidate, and harass.

"Oh, that's right over here," Michelle replied. She gestured toward a high-tech cabinet as she walked over to the device and punched in a code. It opened the first compartment revealing a single vial of morphine. "We keep a limited supply on hand—a just in time inventory, really."

Berg had no idea what a "just in time" inventory was, but he still managed to keep that official look on his face bureaucratic minions don habitually when they have to fake understanding. With his barely ninety IQ, he could keep up with a count of "one" just fine. He noticed that the morphine vials expiration date was still months away. Brian Berg felt dejected.

"We just refuse to have more than one vial on hand at a time of any controlled substance," chimed in Dr. Wright. "We run virtually no risk of theft or employee abuse, because it would be detected immediately. There's no way our medication would ever expire because we use each vial in a week or less."

Berg continued to pretend he understood this seemingly complex system. He tried to look mildly impressed. But, all he really knew was Dr. Wright had no expired medication and this system was way over his head.

The nurse continued to explain. "Yes. It costs us an extra fifty dollars per month to receive our two JIT shipments each week, but we figure it is worth it." Michelle continued to enter codes and open individual little compartments for each narcotic—each producing just one vial. "I mean, can you imagine if the DEA or a state inspector walked in and we were out of compliance?"

Berg felt severely depressed at the moment. "A most impressive system you have here. I've been encouraging doctors to adopt technology like this that helps them be compliant," Berg lied. "I appreciate you showing it to me." Berg hesitated for a moment and tried to think of any other trap he could lay. But, his mind went blank. "Do you mind if I ask other doctors to call you? You know, they might like to compare notes."

After the doctor and nurse both indicated that they would welcome the phone calls, Berg said an awkward goodbye, showed himself to the door, and exited the practice of the technologically advanced Dr. Mary Wright. He would again treat himself to a Big Mac Extra Value Meal, but this time he would super-size it out of discouragement.

As Berg drove, he thought. Naturally, his thoughts turned to scheming. *It's a new day in South Dakota*, he thought as he remembered that there was a new governor. *So, today should also a new day for me, Brian Berg, chief investigator of the South Dakota Medical Board*. He actually had been introducing himself as the "chief" investigator for more than a year now and he'd met no resistance from board members or other staffers. He sure liked the sound of it.

The reality was, Brian Berg was the *only* investigator who worked for the South Dakota Medical Board. The additional reality was that his job entailed reading a lot of complaint letters submitted by patients. He started his investigations by calling patients to gather details about their complaints. He visited about three doctor's offices or clinics per week to collect documentation and conduct interviews. The reality was Berg pushed a lot of paper and he had collected a lot of signatures validating the fact that he indeed, pushed a lot of paper. However, thanks to this *new day*, his job had just become much more dynamic and exciting—in his mind at least.

But really, Brian Berg started his big transition a month ago. He had decided that he had been on his medication long enough. In his mind, he was cured of his past illnesses. It was time to stop taking his anti-psychotic drug, aripiprazole. He had taken fifteen milligrams each night obediently for more than eight years now, along with fluoxetine for depression. He was certain that the combination of time, maturity, and medication had cured him of his delusions and depression. He had not felt this great in years. It was time, in his opinion, for Berg to put aripiprazole and fluoxetine in his past. He had been shrinking his doses every few days. On Inauguration Day, Berg's new day, he completed his perceived transformation. On Inauguration Day, he didn't take any medication—no ceremony required. Goodbye pills, co-pays, and trips to the pharmacy.

Unfortunately, the schizophrenia and depression were creeping back. This time they were manifesting in a new way. Delusions of grandeur were building up in the mind of Brian Berg, *chief* investigator of the South Dakota Medical Board.

Yes, Inauguration Day would mark the dawn of a new day in South Dakota and Berg would share it. His job was important. In his mind the job was getting bigger. Doctors were getting out of control. They needed to be kept in check and he loved being the one who kept them in line. It was his duty to rough up a physician practice by turning its paperwork upside down or threatening to revoke licenses. And, the word "chief" sounded so snappy while giving him that extra clout when he went into a doctor's office or other medical facility to check on a complaint. It was his job to fix wrongs perpetrated by a lazy nurse, greedy administrator, or pompous physician.

Berg started taking aripiprazole when he was nineteen years old. He had participated in a psychological screening during the early interview stages for a spot on a United States Forest Service firefighting team stationed in northern Minnesota. After filling out a fifty-item multiple-choice questionnaire, he was rejected. When he got the form letter dismissing him as a candidate, he was furious. He jumped in his mom's old hand-me-down Mazda, drove to the Forest Service office and demanded to speak to the hiring administrator.

In most cases, the Forest Service never revealed the results of psychological screenings. However, this administrator was a compassionate man. At great peril to his career, the administrator spoke openly and frankly with Berg. "I'm no psychologist, Brian. But, I think you should seek some counseling for some issues that came up on the test." Berg was furious at the man's comments and he stormed out of the office in a fit of rage.

That night Brian Berg got his hands on a fifth of Jim Beam, called up some buddies and suggested they play Poker. By 8:00 he was drunk and at 8:45 he passed out. At 10:00 his friends noticed that he was barely breathing. At 10:20 he was a patient in the emergency room of a northern Minnesota hospital.

After he sobered up a little, he shared his story with the emergency room doctor, including the forest ranger's recommendation that he see a psychologist. The events of the last twenty-four hours prompted the doctor to order a psychiatry consult.

Dr. Emily Teasdale arrived at the emergency room at 3:27 a.m. She took psychiatry call at the hospital two nights per week. She was working hard to build her practice and make some money to pay off $137,000 in student loans. She was also three weeks post-op from her tummy tuck. The surgical procedure had helped her shed the last thirteen pounds to get her pre-residency body back.

She was a beautiful woman eight years ago. When she walked into Berg's exam room wearing a conservative mid-calf skirt, a fashionable and modest blouse, and plain one-inch heels, Berg's delusional mind perceived a woman who was dressed to kill and on the prowl.

"Hi Brian. I'm Dr. Teasdale, but you can call me Doctor Emily or Doctor T."

"You can call me Brian," Berg said in his alcohol-induced stupor.

"Yes. I just did." Dr. Teasdale was joking with him a little, but she managed to keep a slice of authority in her voice.

"So, I understand that there's a forest ranger practicing psychiatry here in town?" Teasdale quipped.

Her beauty and wit won Berg over instantly. Needless to say, any treatment she suggested, he was willing to follow the plan.

"Uh, yeah," Berg replied. "You mean that Forest Service guy I interviewed with. He likes his little quizzes. He thinks he can judge people with them. I hope he's better at fighting fires then he is at getting to know people. He could've at least spent twenty minutes asking me more questions. Then he might get to know me."

After a short conversation wherein Berg pointed out how he had wanted to fight fires since he was a kid, Dr. Teasdale suggested that he come to her office to follow-up. Berg accepted the invitation from Dr. Emily Teasdale, who was his new obsession.

"When we talk tomorrow, I just want to make sure that everything is okay. We'll run some tests to see what we find out," Teasdale said. "Besides, you'll probably learn something about yourself. You know Brian, try to think of our visits as learning about your strengths and weaknesses. It will help you now and in later life."

Berg readily consented. He even showed up fifteen minutes early for the appointment. During the first visit, Dr. Teasdale introduced Brian to a neuropsychologist. "This guy's a brain expert, Brian. He's going to have you take some tests to find out more about who you are. You'll like this, Brian. I can almost guarantee it."

Berg liked anything that involved Dr. Teasdale. When the results of the assessment were back in the hands of Dr. Teasdale, they substantiated some of her concerns. The evidence showed strong suggestion that Brian Berg was schizophrenic; and it was notable that Berg's overall IQ was in the eighty-five to ninety range. To Berg's psychiatrist's dismay, she realized that Brian Berg was unfortunately much less intelligent than roughly seventy percent of Americans.

Not only did the valid testing and interviews with Dr. Teasdale show strong evidence of schizophrenia, but also Berg was depressed. Dr. Teasdale prescribed aripiprazole, an antipsychotic, to treat the schizophrenia. She also had him start taking fluoxetine, or generic Prozac, to address his depression. She had nothing to offer to compensate for his below-average IQ, so she decided not to address it for now.

Unfortunately, Brian Berg was also a raging narcissist, which greatly concerned Dr. Teasdale. A man with a low IQ was likely to struggle to fulfill the unreasonable self-expectations he harbored as a self-proclaimed heartthrob, smart guy, athletic exemplar, and charmer. She was concerned that a young nineteen-year-old Brian Berg, in light of this psychiatric pathology, would experience a series of failures in his lifetime. This was a man who had "perpetual belly-flop contest honorable mention" written all over his face. And that was another reason why she knew he would need the anti-depressant medication coursing through his brain in the near and distant future.

Fortunately, the smitten Brian Berg took his medications as prescribed and at a follow-up visit a month later he was a new man. "So many of my cobwebs are gone. I don't worry about war or a comet destroying the earth anymore. I think more clearly and I can keep up better," Berg said. He thanked Dr. Teasdale at least a dozen times during their visit.

"Thank the U.S. Forest Service," she joked.

With his newfound zest for life, Brian Berg moved back to his parent's home in Pierre, South Dakota. Then, he took the next big step in his life by driving to a strip mall that housed an Armed Forces recruiting office. He walked in the door at 4:27 p.m. one afternoon and said, "My name is Brian Berg and I want to join the Marines and be a firefighter."

After a little clarification about the type of firefighting Berg wanted to do, as well as some probing questions about his potential as a Marine, Berg settled on joining the Army. On his application he dishonestly left out his schizophrenia and depression. Thanks to his medications, the condition did not show up in his pre-service testing or medical exam. The Army did a urine test on him; but back then, it did not check for aripiprazole or fluoxetine. Instead it checked for the usual narcotics, benzodiazepines, amphetamines, and barbiturates. The Army also gathered medical records from his internist in Pierre, but it had no idea that Berg had seen Dr. Teasdale in Minnesota. Furthermore, Berg had no insurance, so he'd filed no claims related to his schizophrenia and mental health.

He was still off the mental health grid, and he intended to stay that way. Using his mom's computer one night, he searched Google for information about how to keep your medical records a secret. He concluded that by paying cash to Dr. Teasdale and a mom-and-pop pharmacy outside the state, he would be safe into the foreseeable future. It was indeed a brilliant—and lucky—conclusion for the not-so-bright Brian Berg.

Two weeks before entering basic training, Berg called Dr. Teasdale and requested a refill of his medications. She kindly consented to thirty-day supplies and six refills on each. He asked her to call them into a small, local pharmacy in Worthington, Minnesota—where the Army would be unlikely to detect his medication use. The next day he made the four-hour drive to Worthington and picked up his 30-day supply. For the next four years, his mom drove to Worthington, Minnesota each month, picked up his medications, and mailed them to him. This kept his schizophrenia and depression in check and off the Army's radar.

The Army had other plans for Berg and the decision-makers there concluded that he would be an excellent fit for the infantry and a poor fit for fire-fighting duty. Four years in the Army and a tour in Iraq taught Brian Berg to own a battlefield, keep watch, guard prisoners, fire rifles, machine guns, and pistols, and to engage in hand-to-hand combat. He also learned to ask a few basic investigation questions. The military was a great fit for Berg, but he had greater ambitions. After four years of service to Uncle Sam, he completed his obligation and exited perhaps the only role in the world, basic soldiering, where Brian Berg could continue to succeed.

After an honorable discharge, Berg's basic military skills were enough to qualify him for a spot in the South Dakota Police Academy. After completing police officer training, he landed a job on the Pierre South Dakota police force— successfully concealing his schizophrenia yet again. However, the toxic combination of his sub-par IQ, narcissism, and poor judgment emerged almost immediately. After six unsuccessful months as a beat cop, Berg was removed from his responsibilities and assigned to "investigate" theft. His job basically entailed fielding phone calls from people reporting stolen bicycles and other items valued at less than $500. He would fill out the forms on a computer as he asked a series of rote questions. He then filed the police report electronically and the digital document would go into a database. Berg never got to actually investigate any of the crimes. He was basically a data entry clerk in a police uniform.

After three years of frustrating his superiors and creating headaches, he was put on final probation. Still, he continued to field phone calls, in his inconsiderate style, from city residents. He often messed up the details he entered into the computer. The day that he told the mayor's wife that she would, "just have to hold her horses," was the last day of his police service to the good people of Pierre, South Dakota.

CHAPTER 27

SIOUX FALLS

It was 12:33 p.m. and Dr. Stoker had just finished visiting with his last patient for the day. He had scheduled the rest of the day off to get caught up on paperwork. But today, with all that weighed heavily on his mind about Ann Higgins, he could not fathom the thought of one more moment in the office, so he picked up his phone and called Allie.

"Hey Troy babe," she answered.

"Hello, love. Are you ready for a good, old-fashioned spontaneous date?" Stoker asked her out, spur-of-the-moment like this, once or twice each month. On some days, her work as the most sought after interior designer in Sioux Falls had her overwhelmed and she would decline. In those instances he understood. He knew that Allie loved the surprise date invitations, whether she could make them or not.

Today Allie's staff was running at peak efficiency, so she decided to make time to break away with Troy. But, she wanted to tease him a little before she jumped in her car to meet him. "No way. I was just going to watch Dr. Oz on TV. Dr. Stoker is not getting between me and my TV crush."

"Great. I'll be there in five minutes. Tell that Oz guy he'd better slip out the back door."

Allie laughed. "Oh, he's already gone. He's scared of you, Taser man."

Twenty-five minutes later, Stoker and Allie were sitting in a movie theater laughing at a shallow comedy. This usually intense couple made it a point to break up stressful weeks with these mini-escapes. It prevented burnout. This is exactly what Troy needed as he processed the events of the last few hours. He did not care about the movie much. He just appreciated holding Allie's hand and simply spending time with the woman he loved.

After the movie, the couple walked down Phillips Avenue, occasionally stepping into a clothing store. But Allie was feeling more frugal than fashionable today, so they bought nothing.

Just north of 11th Street, they happened upon a new café, Ruby's Coffee Spot. "A healthy place," the slogan on the window read. Allie, the nutrition enthusiast, was curious. "Let's grab a bite, honey."

So Stoker opened the door for his bride. It was still a few minutes before 4:00 p.m., so the crowd was small, and nobody was in line. "What do you recommend?" Stoker asked the barista as he and Allie walked up to the counter.

"Our dirty chai is the best in the Dakotas," the friendly girl behind the counter replied.

Allie winced, and the girl behind the counter noticed. "Not a big chai fan?"

"No. It's just not my thing, but your dark chocolate macchiato has me curious. I'll try that."

"And, I've already had too much coffee today," Stoker said. "I'll take one of your cranberry muffins and I'll have that barley grass, grape, and orange drink with a thumb of ginger."

The clerk smiled with approval. "I had you pegged as a burly man who only drinks whole milk."

"You're right on, actually," Allie replied. "Emphasis on burly."

The Stokers walked over to a table that faced a southern window where they could witness the remaining moments of a winter's day sunlight, and they sat down to await their order. The table was far away from one of the TVs hanging from the rafters that was blaring a local news station, KELO. "Sorry, Troy. You know how I dislike chai. It's just not my thing."

"That's fine. I feel the same way about some of the green tea concoctions the coffee shops are coming up with these days. As he bit into his cranberry muffin, he promptly pulled a napkin to his mouth, turned his head, and ejected the muffin bite into the napkin. "That's the worst muffin I've ever tasted. Wow." The look on his face reinforced his displeasure. "Whoever came up with that recipe is much too enthusiastic about bran, fiber, whole grains, and soy-based dairy substitutes."

"Well, it looks like Ruby's is turning out to be our favorite little dirty chai and muffin hot spot," Allie joked sarcastically.

"Yes," Troy said with similar satire. "The next time we have a deep and burning yearning to eat like health zealots and drink confused espressos; we'll come here and cuddle in a booth together."

Troy and Allie each took a sip of their drinks. Dr. Stoker leaned back and looked up into the sky that was now losing its blue hue and turning to a dusky gray. Allie looked over at him and concluded that it was time to broach the subject of his experience with Ann Higgins on inauguration night. "So Troy, how are you processing everything you witnessed with Ann?"

"I'm doing okay." Troy took a look at the muffin, realized he was getting hungrier, and considered trying it again. "I'm naturally bothered that someone would actually try to hurt a person as kind and sincere as Ann Higgins. I'm also bothered that this meth element made its way out of the slums and into a suburban paradise. We're losing this war, Allie. I think this is a wake-up call about just how poorly we're fighting it."

As Troy put his arm around his wife, he looked out the window and appreciated the beauty of the last moments of the day. But, he failed to see the man sitting in a white Ford Explorer who had managed to eavesdrop on their whole conversation. He knew plenty about Troy and Allie from the information he'd gathered from their work websites, LinkedIn pages, and some other paid background check services. But now he had at least two-good pictures of both of them. His superiors would be pleased.

Troy spoke up again. "I'm mostly concerned for Ann and her family. Like all of us, I hope she pulls through."

Allie reached out and took his hand. She chose not to say anything else. She was not trained in psychiatry or any other mental health discipline. She remembered Troy mentioning, early in their relationship, the importance of silence in some conversations. He pointed out the benefits of allowing people time to process. Allie just let him think.

In the background the TV was airing yet another news story about the Ann Higgins assault on inauguration night. The couple was getting tired of hearing the same recycled reports, and they were automatically filtering this one out. However, Stoker subconscious mind caught a short, audible sound bite on the TV from one of the local politicians. A voice he heard through his phone on inauguration night had embedded itself within Stoker's subconscious. Now, this voice emitting from the television imperceptibly drew his attention away from Allie and awoke something in Stoker's brain.

"Troy? Are you okay? You look so far away." Allie gave his hand a subtle, supportive squeeze.

"There I go," Stoker responded, as he looked her directly in the eye. "Typical male. Getting sucked into the TV again." Stoker turned toward his wife. "Honey? Can I try a sip of your dark chocolate macchiato?"

CHAPTER 28

WESTWARD HO COUNTRY CLUB, SIOUX FALLS

Larry Stintson looked ridiculous, but his wife could not bring herself to tell him. The spray-on tan he had purchased at the beauty supply store had turned his skin a comedic tone of orange when he applied it two days ago. To make matters worse, he had re-applied it this morning. Mrs. Stintson was terribly embarrassed to be out on the town at a big event with her husband. She almost faked a sudden illness after overhearing a state senator mockingly label her husband the Annoying Orange.

Attending tonight's event was yet another perk for Larry Stintson, M.D., the politically appointed president of the South Dakota Medical Board. He was seated at a table near the front of this evening's Republican Party fund-raiser dinner. Since the Republicans were now in office, Stintson was supporting them. Democrat, Republican, or Ralph Nader in a tutu. He didn't care. He went with the flavor of the month. For the next four years it was Republican—even if they had to tack on the holier-than-thou champion of the Constitution, Kent Higgins, as the lieutenant governor.

Dr. Stintson had already shaken Governor Horton's hand and hugged Mrs. Horton. Now Stintson sat at his table enjoying a surprisingly tasty dinner salad with a mysterious vinaigrette dressing. While others were enjoying wine or whiskey, Larry Stintson stuck to ice water. He was not willing to drink on a night when he would rub shoulders with so many people. He needed to be at his sharpest, and a small hit of methamphetamine was helping his social skills.

Dr. Stintson and his wife had been assigned to share a table with some boring lobbyist, a political social media strategist who was trolling for her next tweet, and Judge George Silverton. A mysteriously attractive woman, who was most likely his wife, accompanied the judge.

"It's nice to meet you Dr. Stintson," Judge Silverton said. "Perhaps you can tell us what it's like to bring rogue doctors to justice. It looks like we're both in the business of facing down hardened criminals."

This simple sarcastic joke would've delighted just about any reasonable person. But it missed its mark on synthetically enhanced hypersensitivities of Dr. Larry Stintson. When Judge Silverton recognized how the comment had fallen flat, he tried to explain the joke. "Look Doctor, I'm sorry that I didn't effectively communicate my humor and ridiculous facetiousness. I meant no disrespect."

"Hey Judge," Stintson said. "Let me tell you what I can do with the stroke of my pen. I think that a mighty judge like you might even get a little jealous." Stintson glared at the judge and his wife in equal doses. "For example, can you as a powerful judge, even on the ridiculous hearsay of some psychotic stoner, send a posse of five or six police officers to sequester and search the office of a physician—an individual who represents the pinnacle of societal success? Can you demand the immediate duplication of pages upon pages of their medical records?"

"Absolutely not. The Constitution strictly demands due process and prohibits illegal search and seizure."

"Oh really? Now, where is that in the Constitution?"

Unmindful to the mockery, Judge Silverton offered up the legal explanation with the zeal of a Wheel of Fortune contestant solving the big puzzle. "Due process is introduced in the Fifth Amendment, and reinforced again in the Fourteenth. Illegal search and seizure is the Fourth Amendment."

"Interesting," Stintson mocked. "Sounds vaguely familiar from high school—and perhaps a little mention of it at the University of Minnesota, too. For all I know, all those amendments and second-hand legal stuff could be part of the Mayflower Compact."

"The Bill of Rights, actually."

"Whatever." Stintson's meth-fed anger was intensifying. "Have you ever heard of South Dakota—codified whatever they call it— I suppose, 36 dash 4 dash 22 dot 1?"

"I'm sure I've reviewed it somewhere along the way."

"Actually, I suspect you haven't, or we would've met by now to haggle over it in your furniture polish palace of a courtroom. Besides the Pledge of Allegiance, this little paragraph or two is the only patriotic thing I've ever memorized. I committed it to memory because—well—it kind of turns me on.

Cutting out all the boring legalese that so thoroughly fascinates the comb-over crowd, it goes like this.

"The medical board or any of its officers, agents or employees so authorized, may enter and inspect, during business hours, any place where medicine or osteopathy is practiced."

Stintson looked smug as he quoted the law that gave him liberal access to physician offices and medical clinics. "With a stroke of my pen, I send my favorite stooge, Brian Berg, out to exact utter terror upon doctors. Sometimes it's because they're idiots, and other times it's just bad luck that a patient filed a complaint. Of course, there is occasionally a case when some piece of medical equipment maims grandma. Either way, I get to sick the dogs on them."

Stintson's chemical-fueled mind raced, and his rant started to slip off on a tangent. "If a doctor's practice is too specialized or technical, we farm out the review to one of our anonymous 'ghost docs' to scour their practice. Even when these outside reviewers have no idea what they're reading, who really cares? We can't afford to really know how to put a corrective action plan together and let the legal system eventually wear them down with malpractice suits. A fine of a few thousand dollars usually satisfies everybody—and we're protecting the people of South Dakota! Our staff hasn't grown fast enough to keep up with the huge influx of specialists, so we focus on these docs who are 'easy pickings,' usually close to Sioux Falls. I mean, the travel expenses are horrendous now, and we need to justify the board's existence with the cuts coming down the pike with this economy."

Judge Silverton was confused and disgusted by the self-serving zeal Dr. Stintson exhibited. He wanted to interrupt him, but without his gavel in hand, he found it difficult to arrest the ranting of a crazed person. Stintson's speech continued.

"Do you think I laugh my butt off as I admire photos from the little raids Brian brings back to me? I absolutely do."

"Oh, come on now," Judge Silverton retorted. "You're not quoting the whole law and you're overlooking intent and—"

Stintson rudely interrupted. "Such inspection may include any medical or drug records and the copying thereof, and inventories relating to drugs and controlled substances." Stintson sipped some water. "What do you say about that? Does that clarify your *intent*, Judge?"

"Hardly, Doctor. Your interpretation is way out of step with any law out there, except perhaps military law."

"No. I think the statue—oh yes, that's your fancy word for law—I think the *statute* is quite clear. We get to snoop around and inspect all we want. We copy papers, count pills and potions, question trembling medical assistants, cajole dirt out of secretaries, and write down anything we want. We've been experimenting with making little movies of our escapades—you know—to cut down on the 'he said she said.'"

Cutting in on Dr. Stintson, Judge Silverton scolded him. "You're trampling patient confidentiality and the right to representation. And be careful with making movies, especially in the confidential, direct outpatient care environment."

"Hah! When an occasional attorney shows up and starts making demands, this little piece of the legal framework shuts up the schnauzer like an electrified muzzle," Stintson said. They ask Brian their stupid questions, and they try to issue bravado-laden commands. Brian just tells the attorney to direct any inquiries, in written form, to the board. We rarely see any follow-through on those threats from inspection day. They do their fifty-nine seconds of homework on Statue 36 dash 4 dash 22 dot 1, and I suspect the plain language takes the wind right out of their sails."

Larry Stintson craned his neck around. Now he was ready for a drink, and he flagged down a server. After ordering a vodka gimlet he continued on with his tirade. "The whole law, its intent, or whatever you want to call it, is plain and simple. As long as we're there during regular business hours, we can go wherever we want and turn the doctors' offices on their ears. And, we always find something. Between incomplete medical records, idiotic billing practices, safety, fire code violations, infection control, sexual harassment, privacy, and even taxation, or OSHA, nobody's ever in complete compliance. We call it our own little flavor of shock and awe."

By this time, Judge Silverton had pulled up the statute on his phone. It took him much less than fifty-nine seconds to review and he was at a loss for words. Right then and there, Silverton determined to get some other judges' opinions about this law, especially in light of the new federal healthcare privacy laws. Silverton opened the email on his phone and sent a simple message to his law clerk.

> *Please provide me with recent cases wherein SD 36-4-*
> *22.1 is cited. Please set up judicial review conference for*
> *key judges overseeing state medical board.*

By now, the judge was sick of the argument. "Honey," he said turning to his wife, "you look smashing this evening. Would you like to dance?"

CHAPTER 29

SIOUX FALLS POLICE LAW ENFORCEMENT CENTER

It was 3:57 a.m. and four degrees Fahrenheit as Troy Stoker turned off Fourth Street and pulled into the parking lot of the Sioux Falls Law Enforcement Center. As he killed the engine in his old Ford Bronco and set the emergency brake, he pondered what children and other innocent victims he would be meeting during this morning's drug enforcement raid. For the last six years, Dr. Stoker had been participating in early-morning drug raids with the Sioux Falls Police Department and the Minnehaha County Sheriff's office. He accompanied the teams out of concern for the welfare of the innocent. Drug dealers often had children, wives, friends, parents, and in-laws. The line was often gray between who was blameless and who was guilty within the family or micro-community of a drug dealer. Nevertheless, Stoker worked with whomever he could to try and shore up shattered lives. Family victims often suffered financially after a drug bust, because some drug dealers actually used a portion of their earnings to support one or more family members.

Stoker entered the government building, walked down a hallway, and entered the police briefing room. There he met thirteen police officers arrayed in SWAT protective gear. Sgt. Paul Harrison and undercover narcotics detective Deanna King were also standing at the front of the room. Stoker quietly took a seat on the back row. The last time he had seen this many police, he had been helping to revive Ann Higgins on inauguration night.

"All right people. Listen up," Sgt. Harrison said. "Unlike other recent meth labs and dealer's we've been watching, this one has *not* disappeared." The sergeant was referring to how drug-related criminals and meth labs seemed to vanish lately. This was a Sioux Falls phenomenon that had the police baffled. "This is how it's going to go. We'll rendezvous on Eighteenth Street and Third Avenue. On my command, we will approach the home in a stick formation. I need Randall and Millet to cover the back door. Lee will be the eyes on the west windows and Cole on the east. Brooks and Lewis will bring down the front door with the battering ram, and I'll be the first one through. The rest of you follow me."

"The target is one Ray Vincent." It was detective King's turn to speak. "You should find him upstairs, asleep in the master bedroom. As expected, the surveillance team reports silence in the home since about two-thirty a.m. Vincent should be asleep, and it's likely he won't see or hear us coming. We don't expect a lot of resistance. This guy's a slick salesman who's put a lot of heroin and meth on the streets. Vincent's no ninja, so his fight should be minimal."

"I'll be handling Mr. Vincent," Sgt. Harrison interjected. "But, he also has an on-again off-again girlfriend, Lorraine. She's a big unknown. First, we don't know if she'll be there at all. We haven't seen her for a couple days. Second, she's not rational and she might fight us. But Lorraine's nothing we can't handle. I just want everyone to be aware."

"When Sgt. Harrison gives the all clear, I'll enter with Dr. Stoker," Detective King explained. "We have two kids to worry about here. Both of them are female. The big sister, Gracie, is thirteen years old and little Samantha just turned nine. They share an upstairs bedroom. It's the second door on your right. I don't need to tell you they'll be scared. I need Peterson and Green to secure that room and keep those kids safe. Those girls know me well. I've been working undercover as the neighbor next door for seven months. The family now trusts me to do some occasional babysitting and the kids come over and play on the swing set in my backyard."

"All right team! Let's load up!" ordered Sgt. Harrison. The goggled and gear-clad officers stood, shuffled out of the conference room, and headed for their assigned vehicles.

An hour later the battering ram hit the front door. The raid went off somewhat as planned. However, Vincent was not in his room because Lorraine had kicked him out. Instead, the SWAT team found Vincent asleep on the living room couch. About a half second after Vincent instinctively reached for his gun, his judgment overruled his instincts and he slowly raised his arms to the sky. Lorraine did not resist because she was in no condition to do so. She was about six hours into a post-heroin slumber that would've lasted for about seven hours more, had the Sioux Falls police department not barged in and interrupted.

As Stoker waited for the SWAT unit to secure the house, he noticed a commotion in one of the top floor windows, and Detective King immediately removed her baton and started jogging toward the window. Stoker's instincts told him to follow the detective. As they neared the window, a man about six and a half feet tall jumped from the window aiming his feet toward Stoker's head. Stoker reacted by rolling to his left and pivoting up on his left leg in a crouch position. Just as the jumper was landing, he barely moved his left leg when Stoker caught the back of the man's left heel with a forceful right-leg swipe. The jumper was sent sprawling backwards with his feet flying up into the air. The fall caused the man to extend his right hand behind himself in an attempt to break his fall. A loud crack rang out as the radius and ulna bones in his right arm snapped and protruded from his skin. A gush of blood stained and melted the snow below him.

"Oops!" Stoker mocked. "I think you might have a compound wrist fracture. Congratulations scuz bag. Most wrist fractures don't break this bad. Don't mess with Stoker. I don't take kindly to people jumping on my head."

Then, terrified screaming from above drew Stoker's attention back to the window.

"I'm not going back to prison!" yelled a second man above the screams of a girl whom he was lifting up above his head. The man was noticeably overweight and in an obvious state of drug-induced mania. All of a sudden, the crazed man hurled the girl from the window and toward the ground to create a diversion so he could escape. Stoker lunged to his left and caught the girl lengthwise with his left arm cradling her legs and his right arm and shoulder absorbing the impact of the girl's torso. The crazed man then jumped from the window to Stoker's right, landed on the ground, and ran for his life. One of the SWAT team perimeter guards pursued the jumper. But, laden with the weight of his body armor, protective helmet, and Colt nine-millimeter submachine gun, he struggled to keep pace with the portly, amphetamine-propelled criminal.

Stoker's attention remained fixed on the hysteric teen as he brought her to rest on the ground. "Listen Gracie, I know you're pretty shaken up. I want you to talk to this nice lady here," Stoker said motioning for Detective King. "I'll be back in a minute. Your crazed amusement park ride operator is in huge trouble. What's that lunatic's name?"

"W, w, w, w, Willy," stammered Gracie before returning to a well-justified sob.

"Thanks. I'll be back!" Stoker said. Then he took off after the portly Willy, who had managed to get fifty yards down the road and turn into an alley. Stoker knew that he could never keep up with a healthy person who was high on meth. They could sprint for miles. However, he was confident that he had a chance to catch up to Willy. The extra seventy pounds Willy was carrying would considerably hinder the pace of his sprint. During the first thirty seconds of Stoker's run, he closed the gap by more than twenty yards, so he decided to conserve his oxygen by slowing his pace a bit. The next thirty seconds produced a ten-yard gain and he passed the SWAT team member who was fading fast. After two minutes of pursuing Willy, Stoker was only a few yards back. Now that his prey was within earshot, Stoker wanted to send him a message.

"Hey Willy. Thanks for running, man! I'm so glad you put so much distance between all of those police officers and us. The further we get from witnesses, the more options I have for bringing you down," Stoker taunted. This is really opening up some good possibilities for when I catch you." Willy pretended to ignore him. "If you would've surrendered back there, I would've had to treat you all nice. But now that you've pissed me off, you're going to learn a lesson that I could never teach you back in mixed company." Willy briefly held up his right arm and flipped him the bird.

"You know what, doofus?" Stoker said. "The bleeding-heart liberals back at the house would've been all concerned about your rights — the rights of a white trash sewer rat who throws a young girl to a back-breaking encounter with the ground," snarled Stoker.

Willy said nothing, but he reached quickly into his pocket. When Stoker saw the pistol emerge, time instantly slowed from spans of fractional seconds to a period that felt like the warm month of July, and his lightning-fast reflexes and precision training took over. Stoker grasped his telescoping baton and cocked it backward. With a quick snap of his wrist the baton launched from his hand — spinning — just as Willy fired an errant, pathetic gunshot that missed Stoker by a nonsensical distance. In Stoker's state of perceptual slow motion, he watched the baton elongate by the centrifugal force of spinning through the air. He serenely appreciated its graceful arc toward Willy's chubby leg. The blow struck the side of Willy's right thigh at full force as perceptual time sped back up for Stoker.

"Ahhhhh!" shrieked Willy in pain as he released the gun and instinctively clapped his now-empty hand onto his battered thigh. As his hand shored up the injured leg, Willy stumbled but did not fall. Willy's stride changed from a run to a gallop to accommodate the spasms in his thigh. While the meth masked the pain, it could not offset the interrupted flow of glucose, pyruvate, ATP, and fatty acids that fed his leg muscles during his anaerobic, oxygen-deprived footrace with Stoker.

Willy was in trouble and he knew it. He was losing his footrace against this bizarre man — presumably a cop — who wasn't giving up. He needed a new tactic, so Willy changed his course and exited the street for a small city park. Stoker saw his chance to overpower Willy in the invigorating open space of the park. The doctor lunged at Willy's legs and knocked them out from under the large man. Willy spun in the air and fell to the ground landing smack on his back and knocking the wind out of him. Stoker rolled up onto one knee, drew his nine-millimeter Beretta on Willy and allowed him about five seconds to get a few shallow, scarce breaths of air.

"Please don't move. I'm much more accurate with a bow at this distance than I am with this pistol, and I don't want to kill you."

Stoker was skeptical that a man on a meth trip would think with much logic about his precarious position looking down the barrel of a gun. Moreover, the good doctor did not want to put a bullet in anyone's head today if he didn't have to, so he made a judgment call. Stoker holstered his weapon. Then he pounced on the criminal, subduing his arms and legs. With a few quick moves Stoker clearly took charge of the situation. For a few moments Willy did not resist because he was more concerned with trying to breathe. But, after Willy felt a hint of recovery, the meth in his head canceled out his fear and told him to fight. Thrashing with one arm, kicking both of his legs, and searching with his fingers for something to grab for leverage proved fruitless in his quest for escape. His hand tried to grab Stoker's hair, but failed. He swiped for Stoker's eyes and nose, and pawed desperately for an ear.

Swiftly, Stoker wrapped his right arm around Willy's neck, placing his antecubital space, or the crease inside his elbow, right over the hyoid bone, or Adam's apple of Willy's neck. While applying a slight squeeze, Stoker joked, "You should feel lucky, Willy. Today a highly qualified medical professional is subduing you. I bet the last time you got restrained like this, it was some amateur thug who never made it past the sixth grade. I guarantee you that you'll be much more satisfied with today's results. The side effects will be minimal, but I suspect you'll have a beast of a headache for the rest of the morning as they process you at the jail."

Willy continued to reach and attempted to grab at anything at all. One swipe of his left hand glanced against Stoker's cheek and drew a small amount of blood. "Come, on Willy," Stoker grunted. We're all here just to have a little fun. Let me sing you a little song. It just kind of came to me."

It was true that Dr. Stoker had spikes of creativity during times of intensive physical activity and stress. As he struggled with Willy, the ridiculous lyrics flowed in his mind.

"The elbow bone connects to the hyoid bone", sang Stoker between the groans and grumbles of exertion. "The hyoid bone connects to . . . no bone."

With deep gasps and heavy steps, the SWAT team member finally arrived at the takedown scene. With his gun drawn, he looked on at the two wrestlers in the snow. He was too winded to speak, which was fine with Stoker because he was pleased with his bizarre song.

"The bonehead connects to the . . . " Stoker thought for about five seconds. "Oh yes. The big home! Did you hear that, Willy? You're going back to the big home!" At this point Willy could only paw at the air with one slightly mobile hand. Stoker had him wrapped up so tight that his arms couldn't reach behind him anymore. "Hey! That reminds me of another song! Willy won't go, try tellin' everybody but, oh no," Stoker sang at the top of his lungs. "Little Willy, Willy won't go home."

The SWAT officer looked utterly confused. "I heard a shot," he wheezed before panting four more times. "Are you okay?"

"Oh, we're great," Stoker replied. "No bleeding. Only bruising."

"Who fired the shot?"

Stoker ignored the question and resumed his singing. "Of course, you know from recent experience, Little Willy, Willy, the big home connects to the half-way home. The half-way home connects to the methadone."

Acting uncharacteristically cheesy was one of Stoker's coping mechanisms. Usually his wife Allie was the only audience for his narcissistic improvisations. He discovered his odd coping mechanism during the dark days of his military tour to the former Yugoslavia during the 1990s. Constant tension, stress, terror, depression, and anxiety permeated the air in the war-torn area. Sometimes bizarre humor created an escape, and he was not the only one who reacted this way. At first, he noticed that quite a few of his fellow-American soldiers flexed into odd comical behavior during firefights and intense standoffs. He assumed the humorous conduct was the result of television-rendered classical conditioning by the Hawkeye Pierce character on the American television series M*A*S*H. However, his hypothesis crumbled when he noticed how many of the Bosniaks, Serbs, and Croats, who knew nothing of M*A*S*H, would also interject humor into the most precarious of situations.

Willy could not think rationally through his methamphetamine-induced high. He was listening to the drugs, which trapped the neurotransmitters dopamine and norepinephrine in his brain. As the neurochemicals barraged the pleasure sensing brain structures, Willy's brain had little capacity left to register pain. Stoker knew he could not win with pain, so he skillfully squeezed a little harder on Willy's neck. He needed to temporarily limit blood flow through both of Willy's carotid arteries and subsequently restrict circulation to his temporarily supercharged brain. This classic sleeper hold would render him unconscious, eventually. "You're making this too difficult, Willy!" Stoker grunted. "I usually just prescribe a sleeping pill, but this little treatment will be much faster acting."

As Willy felt his consciousness slipping away, he panicked and attempted one last desperate attack. His feet flailed urgently. He threw his head backward hoping to head-but Stoker, but failed. His hands tried in vain to reach back and snag his assailant as Stoker taunted him with more medical speak. "I need to give you a little disclaimer on this medical treatment called *sleeper hold*. I need to tell you about some of the possible side effects. First, Willy, do not use sleeper hold if you take nitrates for your heart, as this may cause a sudden, unsafe drop in blood pressure."

The SWAT officer looked on in disbelief.

"Also, please discuss your general health with your doctor to make sure you're healthy enough to engage in sleeper hold activity. If you experience chest pain, nausea, or any other discomforts during sleeper hold, seek—no better yet— blame the immediate medical help.

The SWAT officer slowly lowered his weapon and caught onto Stoker's humor. "Hah! You're a walking drug commercial, Doc. Hey how about this one, Willy?" the officer said. "In the rare event of a sleeper hold lasting more than four hours, seek immediate medical help to avoid long-term negative side effects."

"Now you're getting it. I love when the police and medical community cooperate on these important matters," Stoker quipped. "If you are taking protease inhibitors, such as for the treatment of HIV, which is a strong possibility judging by those needle marks on your arm, your doctor may limit you to a maximum single dose of ninety seconds of sleeper hold within a forty-eight-hour period.

"If you have prostate problems such as—oh wait. Your sudden wet-groin syndrome tells me your prostate's just fine."

The SWAT officer laughed out loud. "Hey Doc. Can sleeper hold protect against sexually transmitted diseases, including HIV?"

"An excellent question, officer." Stoker said, "considering that Willy here is going back to the big home."

"Hey Willy. It looks like you're doing really great with this treatment," the SWAT officer said as Willy's eyes rolled back in his head and his body went limp in Stoker's arms.

With Willy now asleep, Stoker laid him down on the snowy ground, checked his breathing and heart rate, and declared him stable. The SWAT officer radioed for EMTs, holstered his gun, removed his handcuffs from his belt, and stepped toward the unconscious criminal. "Nice work, Doc! Your patient is resting comfortably. Why don't you let me take him from here? I'll get him to the recovery room," the cop said as he cuffed Willy. "There are two scared little girls back at the house who could really use your help."

"Thanks, officer," Stoker said as he turned and started his jog back to the scene of the drug raid.

When he arrived back at the home of Ray Vincent, Stoker noticed Gracie, the thirteen-year-old. She was terrified as she watched her home being transformed to a crime scene. Her chattering teeth dramatically impeded her speech, and tears streamed from her eyes. She was no longer wailing hysterically and she had regained enough composure for her mind to start putting all the pieces together. Everything going on at this early hour started to make sense to her. The nine-year-old, Samantha, was so confused that she did not know which emotional response to choose. She just buried herself into the arms of Detective King who had reunited the girls back in the warmth and shelter of their bedroom.

"Samantha honey," King said. "This is my good friend, Troy Stoker. When I learned what was happening here this morning I invited him to come over because he's a doctor. I know this is all confusing and you're being brave. So, Dr. Stoker and I will stay with you while we get this all figured out."

Samantha remained surprisingly calm. It was obvious that she knew little about the events of the morning. Moreover, she was used to odd events, such as screaming and yelling, occurring in her house at odd hours. Today's situation only seemed slightly out of place to nine-year-old Samantha.

Gracie was older and wiser, and she had known for months that something was not right in their home. Her dad no longer went to work. Frequent talk about "the cops," strict prohibitions on entering one of the bedrooms, and strangers coming and going at all hours of the night, were all signs that their house had become less of a home and more of a trouble spot. After occasionally seeing her father tucking a pistol into his pants and counting large wads of cash, she was certain that her dad was somehow involved with drugs. Gracie knew that she lived among criminals. She just didn't know what to do about it.

Gracie had been brave. She had kept her internal anxiety continuously managed for months. After her mom left the family, she had to mingle her grieving with assuming the motherly role for her sister Samantha. Together they played, cooked, did their homework, and ran loads of laundry. Gracie made sure that Samantha got to school in time for the free breakfast each morning. She was also there to pick her little sister up each afternoon. The girls often escaped the confusion and sorrow that now permeated their home by going next door to play on the swing set. Even on a freezing cold January day, it was worth enduring the elements to bundle up and escape. Their neighbor, Mrs. King, often treated them to hot apple cider and warm cinnamon rolls, but only if it was okay with their dad.

Now, with this morning's loud interruption in her sleep, and police pouring through her house, Gracie felt intense anxiety. She also wondered about her father's future. But deep inside, she knew that she was safe for now. For just a few minutes she could unleash the pent-up pressure inside herself and have a good, long cry. She took solace in the arms of her kind next-door neighbor—whom she had no idea was a cop—and unleashed a new torrent of tears from a mix of so many emotions she could not categorize. Her tears drenched the shoulder of this kind compassionate woman who somehow had managed to make it over to the house within seconds of hearing the commotion next door. And, while Gracie had no idea why this doctor friend spontaneously appeared during a profound moment of need, the title he bore gave her confidence to embrace this cathartic moment.

Down on the main floor, police officers had Ray Vincent and his marginally alert girlfriend, Lorraine, handcuffed and sitting on a couch. Ray was strictly exercising his Miranda rights to remain silent. Lorraine also remained silent, but her brain would not be exercising Miranda rights or any other thoughts until after it recovered from her recent trip. Thanks to the drugs, paraphernalia, and meth manufacturing materials the police had discovered, there wasn't much to say. Ray and Lorraine were not getting out of this tough situation without a long trip through the prison system. All of the new evidence gathered this morning would combine with weeks of surveillance and indict Ray and Lorraine with an airtight case.

So far, however, it appeared that this home had just served as an ingredient warehouse and distribution point. This particular house never housed a lab for making any of the meth that had taken over their lives. This was a relief to Stoker. If sisters Samantha and Gracie had been exposed to the methamphetamine cooking process, it could've compromised their physical and mental health substantially. Moreover, while Ray Vincent and his daughters would be separated during the next few years, the lack of manufacturing in the home made it possible that this family could coexist again in a future, hybrid form.

After a few therapeutic moments, Gracie experienced an emotional rebound. She was psychologically hearty, especially for somebody who'd lived through months of neglect while experiencing firsthand the effects of the drug culture on her broken family. "Come here, Sammie," Gracie said. "Everything's going to be okay."

Samantha buried herself deeper into the hug with Sgt. King and Gracie. "Girls. I have some things to tell you that I think will help you understand a little more. First, I want to tell you about Dr. Stoker. He's the kind of doctor who helps people when they go through really hard challenges in life."

"Is he a psychologist?" Gracie asked.

"Yes I am," Stoker replied. Although he was actually a psychiatrist—a medical doctor with special training in medical mental issues of the mind—it was not the right time to explain the difference between psychologist and psychiatrist.

"Like Dr. Phil?" asked Samantha.

"Well, sort of," Stoker said. "But, I'm not on TV."

"My dad doesn't like it when I say, 'How's that workin' out for you?'" Samantha said. Unfortunately, her dad was downstairs coming to grips with the reality of the decisions he made during the last six months or so. They were not working for him at all.

"Sammie and Gracie, your daddy's going to have some really big challenges and they're going to last a long time," Stoker said. "That's going to create challenges for both of you. But, I want to you know that you're not in trouble. You've done everything right and you should be proud of yourselves."

"Is my dad in trouble?" asked Samantha.

"Well, I think you know the answer to that," Stoker said. "What do you think?"

"I think we live in a crack house," Gracie said.

"What makes you say that?" Stoker asked.

"I think all those people who come here are buying drugs from my dad. I think that's why he always has a gun."

Even after all of these years, it still stunned Stoker how much children and adolescents perceived about their parents when the adults were involved in destructive or illegal behavior.

"Sergeant King, why don't you explain?" Stoker requested.

"Gracie. You're exactly right. The police have been watching your dad. They know that he has been selling drugs—but not crack—to lots of people. So, while he works with the police, you're going to stay with your Aunt Lucy."

Both of the girls lit up. They loved their Aunt Lucy. She loved to do hair and fingernail polish with them. When Stoker noticed their enthusiasm, he decided that they should take advantage of the positive momentum. "Right here we have a suitcase for you to share. Can each of you put enough underwear, socks and clothes in it for three days?"

The girls produced the clothing almost instantaneously. Moments later, Sgt. King and Dr. Stoker whisked them out of the house quickly enough that they did not see their father handcuffed or perceive what was happening in the rest of the house. Stoker would explain all of the necessary details to these two innocent children later in the day. But first, he was going to work with their Aunt Lucy and others to establish as much stability as possible. In a few hours he would be explaining to a nine-year-old that her daddy was going to jail for a long time. The

13-year-old, Gracie, already knew. However, it was important that Samantha hear the facts from an authority figure and start processing the pain and discomfort.

Stoker was impressed with the thirteen-year-old, Gracie. Whenever drugs or any other evil broke up a family he always looked for the miracle child of the family. Most families had an amazing child who emerged as the golden link, held the family together, and got them through the next months or years. They substituted for the dysfunctional parent or parents. He was sure Gracie was that golden child. She had already assumed the role months ago in the absence of her mother.

Stoker hated emotional pain. He loathed the discomfort sufferers tolerated. Helping people heal from misery was the reason he elected to become a psychiatrist. This morning at 5:30 a.m., while many of his talented colleagues were still asleep, he was out living his life's mission. This activity made psychiatry satisfying. As Gracie and Samantha drove away in the police car with Sgt. King, Troy Stoker briefly closed his eyes. He was deeply satisfied that Gracie and Samantha had made it successfully through the first few minutes of trauma — and he was thrilled that he had gotten a piece of the action with the white trash Willy guy."

CHAPTER 30

SIOUX FALLS CONVENTION CENTER

The second press conference to inform the state, nation, and world about Ann Higgins's condition as well as the progress of the investigation was due to start in five minutes. Again chief of police Edward Best and attorney general Steve Hewitt would be leading the press conference. The mayor decided not to participate.

For today's event, they had chosen the Sioux Falls Convention Center, because it had a hall large enough to house all of the reporters, photographers and camera operators. As Chief Best and Attorney General Hewitt prepared their final thoughts in a room a few steps from the press gallery, the door opened and in stepped the Minnehaha County sheriff and his leadership team. "The governor asked us to join you," the sheriff explained. The door opened again and four state senators, seven house members, three judges, and the Sioux Falls assistant chief of police entered. "We got a call from the governor this morning and he asked us to be here."

"Well, thank you," Chief Best said. "We appreciate the show of force. It reinforces how serious we are."

"It's a nice touch and a critical statement," chimed in the attorney general as the door opened again and governor Richard Horton, his secretary of state Allen Miller, and their entourage majestically entered the room. Just as the door was swinging closed, a final individual caught it just in time. Through the door walked Larry Stintson, M.D., president of the state medical board, but nobody noticed because Governor Horton already owned the room. He was shaking hands and expressing appreciation to everyone. "Mr. Chief of Police and Mr. Attorney General. This is your press conference. We're just here to support Ann Higgins and to support both of you in your efforts to find her assailant."

"How would you like to proceed, Governor?" the attorney general asked.

"No change in your initial plans. May I please just have two minutes toward the end?"

"Of course, sir." attorney general Hewitt responded. "Well, it's time to get started. Let's just have everyone file onto the stage behind us. Executive branch members directly behind the podium. Senators to the right of the cabinet and judges to their left with the house members on the back row. Let's intermingle uniforms in between every other person in a suit. Taller law enforcers on the back row, please."

"Let's move out," chief Best said. "The media awaits."

Twenty seconds later the group filed out onto the stage. Reporters were pleasantly surprised to see police officers mingled with politicians. When the attorney general entered the room the camera operators focused their lenses on him. When the secretary of state entered many of the surprised photographers shifted their lenses toward him. When the governor entered the room, every camera focused on him. The surprised reporters surged toward the front of the room.

An aggressive magazine writer was overcome with ambition and blurted out, "Mr. Governor. Are you in touch with the lieutenant governor?" The governor ignored the question and three other reporters stepped in front of the questioner giving him the painful hint that he was out of line. He had just been demoted to the back of the room.

Chief Best stepped to the microphone and attorney general Hewitt fell back in line between the governor and secretary of state. "Ladies and gentlemen of the press, thank you for joining us here today. We want to start out by telling you that Ann Higgins's condition remains critical, but her doctors see slight signs of progress and healing." Some of the cameras still remained trained on the governor, but most of the camera operators shifted their focus to capture the chief's words. His message would become news copy and web content in a matter of seconds. "Lieutenant governor Higgins sends his deep appreciation to the people of South Dakota, the United States, and the world. The Higgins family wants you to know they have felt your prayers and well wishes. The Higgins children visit with their mom two times per day. They've been reading to her. The kids are showing remarkable strength.

"With respect to the investigation, our crime lab collected a few fingerprints and we suspect that some of them will be useful. As we speak, computers are scouring databases for a match."

The commander looked on. He was not concerned about the fingerprints. He knew that they would only match to Ann Higgins. Perhaps prints from Troy Stoker, the paramedics, and responding police officers would also match. Prints would be useless.

"Later today, we should get some forensic results from our medical investigator who has worked closely with Mrs. Higgins's doctors. Her family has given me permission to report that laboratory tests collected in the emergency room revealed no illicit drugs or alcohol in her system," Best said. The police chief reached for a computer mouse on the podium and a large projector screen above him illuminated. "Our investigators provided me with a picture of a person of interest."

The commander tensed as he anticipated the picture. His government position had placed him close to the investigation. Emails about the investigation came to him and other select state officers within minutes of new findings, so he had already seen this picture.

Chief Best clicked on the mouse, and the picture of the man with dirty blond hair appeared. The commander remembered how the man had helped him hang Ann Higgins. "This man is five feet seven inches tall and approximately one hundred and sixty pounds. We estimate that he is twenty-seven years old."

The commander's heart pounded as he stared at the picture. He had been relieved to see that the picture was shot from a distance. It provided few useful details. The commander was also proud of himself for taking the route through the back hallways and bowels of the convention center to get to the custodian's closet that night. Lurking in the shadows saved him from being photographed. Nevertheless, he worried that this small clue about the blond man could help somebody identify the guy he had just put to work at Green Growth Ventures in Reno. For now the man with dirty blond hair would be safe, as he remained hidden deeply in the office in Reno while learning the art of identity theft. As the commander willed himself to remain relaxed, he felt a deep thrill that came from fooling the hundreds people in the hall at that moment. As he stood on the stage in front of the many cameras, he thought, *Look at this throng of reporters – people who thrive as journalists because of their perceptive skills – and none of them have an inkling that the criminal is right here in front of them!* To hide his excitement, he wrinkled his forehead and frowned slightly, creating a convincing illusion of concern and distress.

The chief of police continued his explanation. "This man was spotted by Mrs. Higgins's security detail, we captured him in a number of security camera images. Prior to her assault, he was often in close proximity to Ann Higgins and we don't think that was a coincidence." The chief raised his eyes, and looked out at the cameras. "I will now turn the time over to Attorney General Hewitt."

The attorney general stepped to the microphone, glanced up at the screen projecting the person of interest and stated passionately, "We want to talk to this man. We think that he can help. He can help the police in their role as investigators. He can help Ann Higgins as a victim. And, he can help you, the citizens of South Dakota as freedom-loving people."

Hewitt turned to the reporters and scanned the audience briefly. He found the TV camera from the station with the highest ratings. Staring directly into its lens, he continued his speech. "Think about it. The last time Chief Best and I met to inform you of the *few* facts we had so far, there was not much to offer. Thanks to the tireless efforts of our police officers and investigators, we have a critical lead. Please help us talk to this man."

The commander felt deep relief that he had instructed the man in the picture to change his appearance. The picture was not clear enough to reveal much information about his facial features, such as his acne-pocked skin. He would make it a point to reacquaint himself with the man the next time he was in Reno. Perhaps he would even learn his name.

Continuing to stare directly at the news camera, Hewitt continued. "Our men and women in uniform are investigating with energy and zeal. I appreciate their professionalism. We, the people of South Dakota, are experiencing the deep emotion of this crime. We've branded into our souls the terror of these days. Please, help us find and identify this man."

Hewitt believed in the people. He had served as a prosecutor and assistant attorney general for many years. In the cases he'd worked, more often than not, he'd caught his big break when a friend, family member, or neighbor stepped forward to identify a crucial witness or the criminal himself. It was people who provided the most crucial clues in most cases. The forensics usually fell into place thereafter.

"As you know, our best information comes from the Sioux Falls police," Hewitt said with a tone of conclusion in his voice. "In the attorney general's office, we have been scouring and cataloging every piece of police evidence and information possible. We have also assigned two seasoned prosecutors to scour arrest records, crime databases, and court cases for any similarities between other cases and Ann Higgins's attempted murder. They update me four times per day or when they find anything substantial." Hewitt pointed at the projection of the blond man on the screen. "I look forward to interviewing this man, learning what he knows, and solving the attempted murder of your friend and mine, Ann Higgins."

Reporters never applaud, and today was no exception. However, it was obvious that South Dakota's new attorney general had captured his audience with the rare gift of passion and persuasive power that only occasionally arose in politicians. The governor was obviously moved and he sprang to his feet, slapped Hewitt on the back, shook his hand vigorously, looked him directly in the eye, and thanked him. Then he took his turn at the podium.

"When I met Ann Higgins," spoke the governor, "I knew right there and then that she was a remarkable, self-made individual. I will not list her accomplishments. Recent news stories have already catalogued those well. But she's a person whom you long to get to know, but you cannot because she is in a coma. You need to know that Ann Higgins writes large checks to people in need. More than a dozen members of her church congregation lost their jobs last year. Ann Higgins wrote checks, through her pastor, to ensure that they did not miss mortgage or car payments. She paid medical deductibles and gave her friends cash for medications they needed. I learned this from her pastor. Ann would never tell me such a thing. The world needs to know that a kind, generous, and sincere woman lies in a coma in the hospital mere blocks from here, fighting for her life. Now, will the fine people of Sioux Falls, or anywhere in South Dakota, please help us figure out why?"

The commander's face remained solemn but his mind was screaming, *Because Ann Higgins was nosy and got herself into a mess!*

"Help us find this man," the governor said. Then he paused and looked out at the sea of reporters. "I'm here to announce that there is a one-million-dollar reward for information leading to the arrest of Ann Higgins's assailant!"

The reporters gasped at the size of the reward. The police leaders exchanged questioning looks. The politicians stood there smiling nervously as they wondered where they would find the money in the state budget. As the commander concealed his fear with a Joker-like smile, he felt his face going flush. Moisture accumulated under his collar, while drops of sweat ran down the small of his back.

"Now, Chief Best, Mr. Hewitt, jump up here and answer these questions," the governor said.

Best and Hewitt approached the microphone.

The first reporter they called on asked, "Where can we get a copy of the picture?"

"We're placing it on our media web page as we speak," the chief said. "My apologies for not providing advanced copies. We decided to go public with this potential lead just a few minutes before we started this meeting."

"Do you have any more pictures of this mystery man?" the same reporter asked.

"Yes. We will release them once our analysis is complete. This is the best picture we have, however."

The next reporter directed his question to Hewitt. "Mister Attorney General. You say you've been cataloging cases and crimes similar to this one. Have there been any interesting cases?"

"Yes. There are currently more than fifty we are examining. It would be unfair and unwise to release those now. When we find anything that is compelling to a grand jury, you will be the first to know."

"Have you issued any search warrants?'

"No. People have cooperated freely. We've been allowed access to all locations we've requested to search. All witnesses have participated willingly."

The commander seethed as he thought about the most helpful witness so far, Troy Stoker, M.D. For the first time in the commander's underworld career, there was a potential witness who was not on his payroll. In this case, Troy Stoker had heard his voice and overheard his conversation with Ann Higgins.

The police had debriefed Dr. Stoker on inauguration night and they continued to call him and ask him questions to seek clarification. The commander was privy to all of this information. But, the commander did not know if, that night, Stoker had heard his voice clearly enough to identify him. He wondered which facts Stoker had connected from the housekeeping closet, Ann's therapy session, and any other meetings or conversations with Ann.

However, even more mysterious to the commander was the fact that Stoker had *not* reported anything about the houses on Bryant Way. The commander had clearly admitted to Ann Higgins that he planned to use both of the houses as labs and identify theft offices. But, Stoker had withheld that information from the police.

"What can you tell us about the source who called 911 on inauguration night?"

"We cannot tell you anything. The source is protected by numerous laws at this point," the attorney general answered.

The commander laughed to himself as he thought about how everybody in the police department and attorney general's office assumed that the laws protected Stoker. This doctor had no idea that Ann Higgins's assailant was contemplating a plan to eliminate this *protected source*.

"What have the Higgins kids been reading to their mother?" a reporter asked. This unexpected question came from a woman who lacked the typical tenacious tone of her journalistic peers. It was a sincere question of substance, and it caught the politicians off guard.

With a hint of charm, Hewitt interjected, "You must be a human interest reporter." The attorney general happened to be taking a rather keen interest in the stunning reporter who asked the question.

"Yes, I'm Maria Stephans, a freelance feature writer for a number of publications. "Do you know what they are reading?"

The politicians paused, and looked baffled. But, Secretary of State Miller stepped forward to the podium. "Yes. They are reading the John Steinbeck novel, *The Pearl.*"

The hair on the back of the commander's neck stood up immediately. His memory shot back to his high school English class where he had read the story of *Coyotito*, or the little coyote, infant son of an oyster diver in Baja Mexico. The commander's phenomenal memory recalled the details of the trauma that befell *Coyotito's* family when his father found an exceptional pearl that made them rich. *Things didn't work out so well for Coyotito*, he thought.

Secretary Miller continued to address the reporters. "The Higgins family selected a short book in anticipation of a speedy recovery. I'm sure the message of the book is particularly poignant right now as well."

Maria Stephans remained standing as she recorded the voice response with her cell phone, and then typed furiously on her phone tweeting:

> *South Dakota #AnnHiggins family reading The Pearl to*
> *mom in coma. #Steinbeck*

After two more questions from aggressive reporters chief Best ended the press conference. Immediately, a concerned Secretary of State Miller caught the governor's attention before he could leave the stage and exit. "Richard, where do you plan to get that million dollars? How are we going to shoehorn that kind of cash out of the state budget? The legislature will have to appropriate it. You're about to burn a bunch of good will to come up with that reward money, Mr. Governor."

"An excellent question, Allen. "I'm sorry I wasn't more explicit," the governor said as he walked to the front of the stage.

The attorney general remained at the back of the stage and exclaimed, "I'm just not sure you should be making spontaneous million dollar commitments." The governor continued his walk to the front edge of the stage and started searching the media gallery, seemingly for a specific person. Horton looked out over the sea of reporters. Some were packing bags and walking out. Others were typing furiously into computers or talking tenaciously into their cell phones. Within a few seconds Horton found who he was looking for.

"Miss Stephans?" the governor called out. Maria Stephans did not hear the most powerful man in South Dakota call her name, and she failed to look up from her computer. However, other reporters noticed, and a momentary hush fell over the front of the gallery. "Miss Stephans?"

Maria looked up and as her eyes registered on the governor, mild shock graced her face. She closed her computer, and stood. "Yes, Mr. Governor. What can I do for you?"

"May we speak with you for a moment?"

In one fluid motion Maria loaded her computer and phone into her bag and stepped toward the stairs on the side of the stage. As she climbed the stairs the governor met her at the top. "I appreciated your question, Ms. Stephens. It was refreshing."

"Thank you, sir. What can I do for you?" By this time, Attorney General Hewitt and Secretary of State Miller had flanked the governor.

"I've learned to never grant an exclusive interview. I did it one time and all of the other writers in town maligned me for a month or two. I learned my lesson—or so I thought."

"Yes. I agree with your policy, Governor Horton," Maria replied.

"Well, because you're a freelance writer, does that mean you can write a story and share it with everyone at once? Can you syndicate a story and give it to everyone?"

"Sure. With a single email, I can get the story in front of thousands of editors and reporters."

"Great. Do you have a camera?"

"Better than that. I have a photographer," Stephans replied. She turned toward the gallery. "Hey Kyle, I've got a couple more shots for you." A man who had been meticulously folding up a tripod looked up in response. "Come on up here."

"Perfect," the governor said. He reached his hand into his suit coat pocket and removed a leather-covered checkbook. "Do you want to record this, Ms. Stephens?"

"Yes, thank you," the writer said as she punched a few icons on her phone. "You're now being recorded."

Kyle arrived with his camera. The activity around the governor had attracted five of six of the politicians, the county sheriff, and Chief Best.

"No pictures yet, Kyle," the governor said as he opened the checkbook and revealed the next check in the sequence. "You see, Secretary Miller informed me of a critical detail I overlooked at the press conference, and it would be a little odd to call all the reporters back." The governor wrote "Ann Higgins Reward Fund" on the check's payee line. "So, I'm hoping you can get the word out with your single email."

Secretary of State Miller was slightly interested in the governor's conversation, but his instant fascination with Maria Stephens was overwhelming. The secretary's well-hidden weakness was women. A thrill traveled up his spine as he admired her cheekbones, lips and eyes, and then let his own eyes travel downward. Despite her modest, respectful, and confident style of dress, the secretary took a moment to ponder the possibilities.

"You see," continued the governor, writing "initial deposit" on the check's memo line, "I neglected to mention how we would fund this million-dollar reward. I cannot commit state funds without respecting the balance of powers and working with the legislator to earmark them."

Kyle the photographer's eyes expanded in disbelief as he saw the governor write "One million dollars only" on the amount line. Maria was also visibly surprised, while the politicians only let a little shock show. "However, I can commit my own money," the governor announced, "and, I'm sure that I can get some of my friends to kick in a chunk while news readers throughout the world will do the rest."

The governor filled in the rest of the check and ripped it out of his checkbook. "Okay, Kyle. Please take a picture of this." The governor covered the bank name with his left thumb and the account number with his right thumb and held it far from his face. "Just get the check, not my face."

Secretary Miller was still checking out Maria, and she quickly glanced at him. He smiled when their eyes met and he tried to pretend that the meeting of their eyes was a coincidence. It was a moment too late. Maria detected the secretary's gaze, but she ignored it outwardly. Then she turned her attention back to the unorthodox photo opportunity. Internally, she made a mental note that Secretary of State Miller would be a potential target for negotiating access and information. As much as she enjoyed feature writing, she sensed that she would spend the next few days on a stint as a crime reporter with a political spin. Secretary Miller would help her out.

"Now what questions do you have for me Ms. Stephens?" the governor asked.

"Governor, some news stories have published estimates of your net worth, and you're not as wealthy as many politicians. This check represents a substantial percentage of your nest egg, allegedly. Why give this much away?"

"This is America. This is a land of wealth and abundance. We are at a dangerous turning point, and I prefer to sacrifice my money instead of other people's blood. We need to beat back criminals and keep this state peaceful, and we need to do it as individuals."

"Do you think you will earn that money back someday?"

"Not unless I'm the first to come up with the information that leads to the apprehension of Ann Higgins's assailant," he said with wry humor.

Stephans was not detoured by his humor. "No, I mean in your future work."

The governor smiled at her, and she realized she had taken him too seriously. "I'll never see that money again. But, it's the least I can do."

The commander looked on with concern. In his secret and public lines of work money always got results. Money always gets the bad guy. Again the heat around his collar returned and the sweating resumed as his heart rate increased. However, the commander would never allow himself to show fear. Instead he willed himself to respond by sublimating his fear and rage and disciplining himself to hide his panic.

CHAPTER 31

It was the first day of her rotation with Dr. Stoker, and Sarah Haslam, psychiatric resident on probation, was miserable. It was 10:00 a.m., and so far they had only seen three patients. One visit lasted an hour while Stoker listened, asked questions, and dispensed counsel. At the end of the hour he did a little bit of medication adjustment and accepted a sincere hug from the patient. This slow pace was driving Haslam crazy. Before today, when she had worked in the hospital, she would routinely round on a dozen patients and perhaps admit a person or two by 10:00 a.m.

Furthermore, it had occurred to her that for the next few weeks most of her waking hours would occur within the few square feet of Dr. Stoker's office. She felt claustrophobic. She realized how much she appreciated working in a hospital where she would admit patients in the emergency room, then roam up and consult on the medical and surgical floors and then meander over to treat patients on the psychiatry floor. She had been so free in the vastness of the hospital.

Haslam was enduring a dull twenty-minute medication check on a patient with bipolar disorder, when the receptionist, Tamara, knocked sharply on the therapy room door. A moment later, she opened it uninvited, stuck her head in the room briefly. "Dr. Stoker. We have a code blue and you have time at noon."

Stoker responded, "Thanks, Tamara. We're on." Then he went right back to visiting with his patient.

Haslam was confused about the phrase code blue. She expected Stoker to jump up and run to rescue somebody experiencing a code blue. In the hospital when they called a code blue it meant someone's breathing or heart had stopped, and a team of medical professionals would converge with fierce intensity to save the patient's life. Obviously, here in the office of Troy Stoker, code blue did not mean the same thing.

Stoker and Haslam took ten more minutes and finished the visit. After saying goodbye to the patient, Haslam's curiosity got the best of her. "I noticed that the term code blue did not send you sprinting to administer heroic CPR on a patient."

"Oh no. Around here the term code blue refers to our strategy for getting through the new ObamaCare regulations. You know, the ones meant to cut healthcare spending."

"Okay. You've lost me. What's a code blue?"

Stoker looked at her and explained. "Well, you know the now infamous ninety-day rule the government put in place to try and slow healthcare spending?"

"Sure I do. All of the ObamaCare regulations brought the insurance companies to the brink of bankruptcy, so the government let them set a ninety-day waiting period on certain non-urgent conditions."

"Exactly," Stoker said. "If you have one of those conditions, the insurers and the government are hoping that you'll get better in the first ninety days or pay for your treatment out of your own pocket during that time."

"Stupidest thing I've ever heard," Haslam replied. "If you have a cold, seasonal allergies, depression, stress, back pain, or one of about twenty-five other diagnoses, you can't see the doctor unless you're willing to pay out of pocket." Haslam started to walk out to the waiting room to get the next patient. "But, why do you call it a code blue?"

"Blue is the color insurance companies are famous for using in their logos and other advertising. It was a dominant color on HealthCare.gov for the first couple of years. Psychologically blue is supposed to inspire confidence, so they use it. It's just our little way of poking fun at government and insurance," Stoker explained. "Insurance companies have been denying patients the opportunity to see a psychiatrist, at least for ninety days, in quite a few instances. Frequently, patients will call us and want to be seen. We will attempt to pre-authorize their visit . . . " Stoker motioned for Dr. Haslam to finish the thought.

"And, they pre-authorize the first visit, but only *after* a ninety-day or sometimes six-month waiting period."

Stoker continued to explain. "So, by the time they get to you, patients are either in a deeper crisis, or they've worked through the problem enough that they cancel or blow off the appointment. Why should health insurance be a disadvantage?

"Too frequently people end up in the ER with a major acute psychiatric episode," Haslam said. "I've seen dozens of cases that could've been prevented with a simple doctor's visit."

"A code blue is how we address the ninety-day system," Stoker said. "Instead of explaining it, let me just show you. Let's see two more patients and then we'll go on our code blue run. If we're lucky, we'll get some lunch, too."

Ninety minutes later, they finished treating the last two patients of the morning. Stoker hobbled out of his office on his recovering knee and walked toward the door. In an almost mechanical fashion, the receptionist handed him a blue three-ring binder. And Stoker exited the door, calling out, "Come on Sarah. The code blue is on."

Sarah followed him out the door and hesitated for a moment before jumping into Stoker's bizarre car, the matte black 1976 Ford Bronco. As it roared to life, she tried to put on her seatbelt, but it was an old system she did not quite understand. She glanced over at Stoker, and mimicked him. After realizing the Bronco had a harness system instead of just seatbelts, she successfully secured herself in.

As they traveled through the streets of Sioux Falls Haslam continued with her questions. "Where are we going?"

"The St. Francis clinic."

"You mean that free clinic in the armpit of Sioux Falls?"

Stoker smiled. "Yes, indeed. That's the one."

"May I ask why?" Haslam was a little annoyed by the fact that she might encounter the poor and destitute in a place where they could come and go as they pleased.

"Because somebody needs us."

Sarah Haslam had no reply and could not formulate a follow-up question. She loathed the idea of working in the clinic that was often referred to as "the homeless clinic." She changed the subject to the patients they had seen that morning. She pretended to care about them by asking questions about each of person. She barely listened to Stoker as he answered her questions. There was nothing Sarah Haslam wanted to learn from this eccentric, private practice psychiatrist.

Stoker and Haslam pulled into the parking lot at St. Francis and parked. After locking the car, Stoker hobbled toward the main door as fast as his injured knee would allow, with Haslam dejected and following him from behind. Instead of checking in at the front desk or the nurse's station, he walked down a hall and found exam room number eleven. When he and Haslam entered the room there was a young woman sitting there who appeared to be in her mid-twenties.

"Hello Ms. Crowley. I'm Dr. Stoker and this is Dr. Haslam. She's a psychiatry resident in training. We're your team today. Would you mind telling me how you are feeling and how we can help?"

Yes! Now those are the right questions, thought Haslam. *None of this 'How are you doing?' garbage. At least Stoker does something right.*

"Doctor. I'm at the end of my rope," explained Pauline Crowley. "I've been having immense stress at work. I started my job as a computer programmer about four months ago and I'm going crazy. I sit there in my cubicle and I want to go crazy. I struggle to do programming and quality assurance. That little cubicle is my prison."

"Is your work suffering?" Stoker asked. "I mean, are you getting in trouble or do you feel like you're not doing a good job?"

"My boss just wrote me up for missing deadlines. He calls it a first verbal warning."

Stoker validated Pauline's concern. "That's serious stuff. In America using a first verbal warning is how employers try and help you succeed, while also making it easy to get rid of you if you don't respond. Let's help you respond the right way."

Relief came into Pauline's eyes. "Yes. Thank you. That's where I'm a little baffled."

"Tell me what happens at quitting time," Stoker asked. "What happens at five or six o'clock or so?"

"I always stay late. It's the only time I can concentrate and get the stuff done that I can't finish when I'm getting interrupted and feeling freaked out during the rest of the day." Pauline got tears in her eyes as she continued to explain her experiences. "When I come home at night I can't get rid of the tension. What's going on with me? I used to be so happy. I thought when I finished college, got a job, and started making decent money, my life would get even better. How come I'm more miserable than I've ever been?"

"I think I know what's going on here, but I can't be sure, so here's the plan," Stoker said. "Your insurance company won't let you see me for ninety days, thanks to the Affordable Care Act. That's why we're meeting here at the free clinic. No insurance claim will be filed and you don't owe me a cent. Due to some other weird laws I cannot treat you for free at my office. And, asking you to pay out of pocket introduces other problems, including asking you to pay for everything when I don't think you should."

Stoker made notes in the blue three-ring binder. "Who is your primary care provider?"

"Marcus Parsons"

"Great. He's a good doctor. We share a few patients and we collaborate a lot."

"Are you drinking these days? You know, stress makes people drink more."

"Yes. I drink a little wine at night, sometimes."

"How many eight-ounce glasses do you drink per night?" Stoker asked.

"Just one glass with dinner."

Stoker would make it a point to follow up with her. Medical studies had shown that patients tend to under-report their alcohol consumption by fifty percent or more.

"Do you smoke, or use any illegal drugs?"

"No."

"Are you on any other medications?"

"No. I occasionally use some ibuprofen or Tylenol after a long run."

Stoker jotted all of this down, shut the blue binder, and looked directly at his new patient. "Okay, Pauline. The medication I want you to try is called mixed amphetamine salts and we should know within a day if it helps. If it doesn't help, please call me. We will need to make a change." Then Stoker smiled at her and looked her in the eye. With a casual tone in his voice he said, "Are you ready for a possible diagnosis that will shock your socks off?"

"I guess," Pauline said. But I don't know how to answer that."

"Don't worry," the doctor said. "It's nothing horrible and there are great treatments. It just surprises people when they hear what I'm about to tell them. You're fifteen seconds from a good dose of denial. Are you ready?"

Pauline nodded. "Okay, wow me, Doc."

"I think that you have been living with something for your whole life. You've compensated with your intelligence and a somewhat flexible work ethic. My strong suspicion is that you live with attention deficit hyperactivity disorder and you never knew it."

"What? ADHD? Like hyper kids and Ritalin?"

"Yes. And *also* like frustrated, creative, energetic, and intelligent adults. And Ritalin is just one of many medication options for treating ADHD. It's somewhat similar to the mixed amphetamine salts I just suggested for you."

"You've got to be kidding me." Pauline was skeptical, defensive, and slightly defiant. "Are you some kind of weird psychiatrist who has weird adult ADHD theories? I've never heard of this. Is this the strange stuff that you get when you meet psychiatrists at the homeless clinic?"

"Are you sure you've never heard of adult ADHD?" chimed in Haslam. "You said you're a computer programmer, right?"

"Yes."

"So, do you read the *Wall Street Journal*?"

"Yes. We pass a copy around the office."

"Okay. What's your email address and I'll send you a link to a story from the *Wall Street Journal* about adult ADHD. It's from a few years back. I'll also throw in a link to an NPR radio story, just so you don't think it's a right-wing conspiracy."

The political joke made Pauline laugh. "Okay. I'll check it out."

"And, Ms. Crowley," Haslam said. "You're meeting Dr. Stoker at the homeless clinic because he's the only doctor in town who's figured out a way around this ludicrous ninety-day rule—and he's the only psychiatrist in town who cares enough to go out of his way to treat people for free. If he wasn't so proactive, you may lose your job before ninety days rolls around. It happens all the time with young adults who have no idea they live with ADHD."

"So, while you're still justifiably contemplating ADHD denial, let me lay out a plan," Stoker chimed in. "You decide if you want to follow it. First, I want you to make an appointment with Dr. Parsons. I'll send him a letter and tell him all about today's visit. Since he knows your general health, I want him to manage your medications for the next ninety days. Your insurance will cooperate better that way, too."

"Okay, so step one is for me to get with Dr. Parsons," Crowley said. "What's step two?"

"Here is a prescription for a one-week supply of mixed amphetamine salts, a stimulant. This is a starting dose of ten milligrams. Fill it at any pharmacy. It will probably cost you about thirty-five dollars. I suggest you start with one pill. After you take it, wait for two hours to see how it affects you. If it makes you hyper, or it makes it harder to concentrate, it means that I'm probably wrong about my diagnosis or dosage." Stoker paused for a moment and smiled. "And, you can have the therapeutic moment of calling me and telling me just how wrong I am."

Again, Pauline Crowley picked up on the humor and smiled. This funny gesture had disarmed her defensiveness.

"If this medication helps, however, take another pill four to five hours later. You should take no more than three pills per day; and don't take it after five o'clock in the evening. Dr. Parsons can provide you a thirty-day prescription if this medication helps you."

Stoker turned to Haslam. "Can you counsel Miss Crowley about alcohol consumption during the next few weeks, Dr. Haslam?"

Haslam was pleased to jump back into the conversation. "With this medication we need you to cut out the alcohol for a while. Can you do that?"

"Yes," Pauline said.

"Ideally, you would never drink while you're taking this medication," Haslam explained. "But, we live in the real world and I recommend that we start with no alcohol while we adjust the medication. If you cannot do this, please let us know right now, and we'll adjust your care plan."

"No, it's not a big deal. I can do that."

Haslam finished her alcohol-related counseling. "After we titrate your medication I suppose you could do some occasional drinking—like one drink per day or less—if you must drink."

Stoker then removed three business cards from his blue binder, and handed them to his new patient. "Third, I want you to go see a psychologist. Here are three who are excellent with ADHD. Please choose any of these three professionals. You will have to pay for this out of pocket and it could cost you a pretty penny each month for the next three or four months. But, it's a small price to pay to keep your good job that will lead to bigger and better promotions.

"Finally, I want to keep in touch with you. Please call my office within four to twenty-four hours after taking your first dose of the medication. Tell the receptionist your name and I will call you back within three hours to get your update. I cannot interrupt another patient, however.

"The other way to keep in touch is by journaling. Go to my secure website on this card here. Your username is 24Nov#93. Your password is right here on the card. The username and passwords are mostly randomly generated characters. You and I are the *only* people who have access to your journal entries. They are completely confidential, and I do read them. I need you to journal at least twice per week. If you are at your desk and cannot concentrate, take five minutes and write in your journal about the experience. Tell me what's going on in your environment and in your mind. It will help me immensely and it will provide increased clarity for you. The information I read and learn from you during the next ninety days will help me consult with your primary care doctor. It will help both of us improve your treatment. Are you game?"

Pauline smiled. "I'm still in denial." Then she laughed at her own comment. "But seriously, I'll try the medication and call you with the results."

"Great," Stoker said. "If you have a little healthy denial, that's understandable for a lot of reasons. Will you call me within the next two days, and update me on your denial and your experience with the medication?"

"Yes."

"Okay. Now, I'll have my receptionist call you and make an appointment in the next, oh shall we say, ninety days or so?"

"Sounds like good timing, at least according to my insurance company," Pauline joked.

"Thank you for meeting us here. If you get into deep frustration again before the ninety days are up, please call me and we'll figure out how to see you. I acknowledge that these circumstances are bizarre, but I did get you in within twenty-four hours—and my discount is pretty fantastic is it not?"

"Phenomenal."

"Oh, Ms. Crowley, one last question. Why did you become a computer programmer?"

"My dad really encouraged me to." Crowley stopped and thought for a moment. "In college I loved political science, sociology, and Spanish, but he insisted I study computer science. He kept talking about all the doors he could open for me and the huge growth he saw in the industry."

Stoker smiled a little bit while nodding his head. Pauline Crowley had never gotten to know herself or identify her strengths. "An insightful history. Will you please journal about how you arrived at your career decision? I'll make a note to discuss it more. Let's work on getting you feeling better."

With that, they showed their new patient the way out and then elected to exit a side door. Nobody likes to be seen exiting a clinic with his or her psychiatrist. Stoker understood this, but did not like the worn-out stigma it implied.

Back in the car, Stoker drove while he dictated a note, hands-free, into his phone about the visit and instructed his transcriptionist to forward a letter to Dr. Parsons. Haslam used her iPad to email the links to the stories from the *Wall Street Journal* and National Public Radio, as she had promised. She also marveled at how simple and effective Stoker's code blue solution was for getting around the red tape.

All too frequently, patients like Pauline Crowley only reached a mental health professional when it was too late—such as after they had lost their job, destroyed their marriage, damaged their children, or attempted to take their own life. Stoker would not stand for it.

In her short eighteen months as a psychiatric resident Haslam had treated countless people after spiraling from stable or reasonably happy to profoundly depressed—in less than ninety days. She'd seen a factory welder, nurse, customer service representative, bank teller, graphic designer and a few other cases of people with ADHD lose their job because they could not concentrate and their work suffered. Even after getting help and medication, the patients struggled to find a new job. Their job history was blotted with the failure of their first job and producing a reference usually proved impossible.

ADHD was not the only condition that could wreak havoc on people's lives. There were dozens of ailments that, if treated early, could be greatly improved. Stoker had a formula for saving jobs, families, and lives. It was brilliant and Sarah Haslam was intrigued.

CHAPTER 32

As Stoker and Haslam arrived back at the office a man met them in the waiting room. He appeared to be in his late thirties, and he had a head of long, dark, and curly hair. The man reminded Haslam of pictures of Kenny G, a musician she remembered from her parents' collection of CDs from the 1990s.

"Rod. Thanks for swinging by," Stoker said. "This is Sarah Haslam. She's a psych resident rotating with me for the next few weeks."

"Good to meet you, Sarah," McArthur said."

"Rod's a pharmacist who consults with the police, DEA and FBI," Stoker explained. "He's our methamphetamine scorekeeper. We keep track of the stuff that's out on the streets by purchasing samples here and there—unbeknownst to the dealers, of course. Rod does the analysis and keeps track of the latest recipes and ingredients. He lets us know about the potency of the stuff on the streets and the latest combinations and cocktails the fans are screaming for."

"Yup. Straight meth is so boring these days," McArthur said.

"So, what can you tell us about the smack we pulled out of Ray Vincent's house yesterday?"

"It's that mystery mix." The pharmacist took a document out of a file folder and handed it to Stoker. "We don't know if it's local or if it's coming in from hundreds of miles away. It's still too new to the streets of Sioux Falls and we can't map it back to any chemical purchases locally. The potency is high and the purity is pretty good, too. Whoever this is, they take pride in their work."

Stoker turned to Haslam and explained a little more. "Just to bring you up to speed, Sarah, we've got some new ice in town. Whoever's making this stuff is either trying to impress their clients, upstage other meth labs, or thumb their noses at law enforcement. The quality is high and they lace it with just a touch of cocaine to really catch our attention."

"Mixing drugs is not that unusual, is it?" Haslam asked.

"No, it's pretty normal. But cocaine is so expensive to bring in from outside the U.S., and the quality, in this case, is so high. We think there's some sort of brag factor on the part of the chemist here. We're pretty sure the motive goes beyond profit. Some drug baron is trying to mess with our heads."

"What did Errol Rivera say about all of this?" Stoker asked McArthur.

"His friends at the DEA don't know what to think of it. Rivera's frustrated because he can't get his hands on those first clues he needs to start getting any traction in an investigation." McArthur changed the subject, as he often did, almost midsentence. "When do you see those two girls, Ray Vincent's daughters, who you removed from the home yesterday?"

"We saw them this morning. The social workers say they're doing great with their aunt. However, they did not respond well to the news that their dad's probably going to prison. Their hearts are understandably broken. They walked in with an 'on vacation' attitude and walked out mourning the loss of their father."

"Those poor, poor girls. Just look at what life has handed them," Haslam commented with as much artificial sympathy as she could muster.

Stoker thought he sensed insincerity in Haslam's comment. "What do you mean?"

"I mean it was hard to see them cry. They were in so much pain this morning."

"So, what do *you* as a psychiatrist propose to do about it?" Stoker asked with a challenging tone in his voice. "What should we, the mighty healers, do with our supernatural powers?"

Haslam barely gave it any thought before responding. "I think with some therapy they should be able to get through the grieving process and lead normal lives."

"And, how would you like it if somebody boiled down your crisis—the ripping out of your heart—to therapy and a hopeful platitude of a normal life?"

Haslam responded to the challenge with a professional but confident tone. "It is a *clinical* observation."

"Yes. And I'm sorry that professors, doctors, and mental health professionals have fed you that limited, hands-off load of beetle dung. I'm not picking on you, Sarah. I'm challenging you, as a student and as your current preceptor, to innovate beyond therapy—or to innovate therapy.

"I am profoundly bothered by our inability as psychiatrists to respond to society's ills and I count myself as one who has not yet figured out how to usher in our next renaissance. My theory is that too many doctors and psychologists want to be coaches and nobody wants to get in the game and be players. I support drug raids and execute 'code blues' as my way of *trying* to graduate our work and create more positive results." Stoker took a seat in his own waiting room and crumpled up the report Rod McArthur had just handed him. He leaned back and ran both of his hands through his hair and exhaled in frustration.

"I'm not bragging because I'm not ready to call my efforts a success," Stoker continued. "I believe in counseling and related biological, social and psychological therapies. However, as you can see, I choose to be more eclectic than that. I use different types of therapy for different types of people. Sure, counseling has its value. Still, this world as we know it today, contains much more trouble than counseling, therapy, and medication can counteract. We've got to find that next level of success."

Dr. Haslam was silent. Thinking about patients in this complex and sometimes difficult manner, was too philosophical and empathetic for Haslam to fathom. Inside her mind, this conversation was only generating anger and confusion and churning her borderline tendencies. As she had done so many times in her life Haslam pretended not to be bothered while she seethed with rage inside her heart and mind. *Who was this doctor to jump on her back and task her with solving society's ills? What was this esoteric psychobabble he was discussing?*

"You'll have to excuse the good doctor," McArthur said. "He wants to save the world with a mix of spirituality, kindness, right-wing talk radio, and psychiatry—probably in that order."

"Sounds like a good order to me. God created the truth and kindness. The AM airwaves own the truth. Someday we psychiatrists will catch up."

Haslam emitted a fake laugh. However, in the back of her mind, she was already scheming about how to knock this opinionated, right wing doctor off his high horse. *If Stoker were truly an excellent psychiatrist, he would not have to go combing the homeless clinics or acting like an ambulance chaser at an early-morning drug raid*? Haslam thought. No, she had nothing to learn here in this rotation with Stoker, but she had plenty to practice. These patients were an excellent rehearsal for the real world, and Sarah Haslam was so excited for the real world.

CHAPTER 33

SIOUX FALLS REGIONAL HOSPITAL

The story about Governor Horton's sizable reward check appeared in every daily newspaper in the country. Instantaneously, the unknown, twenty-four-year-old freelance writer, Maria Stephens, was granting interviews on morning television talk shows and telling the story she captured moments after the press conference. Yet, Stephens knew that she must produce another big story to prove that she was a legitimate news writer and not just a one-hit wonder.

The self-imposed pressure was eating at Maria, even as she was enjoying the buzz of catching a big break in the political and criminal reporting world. Nevertheless, her heart was in writing features and human-interest stories. She loved getting to know the personalities behind the stories. She loved poignant photographs. When the people she interviewed faced tragedy she extended true friendship and absorbed their pain with them.

This perspective had cost her in college. Professors continually emphasized the importance of aseptic "just the facts" writing. Once a professor gave her a failing grade when she submitted a story to the school newspaper that chronicled a football player's downward spiral after blowing out his knee. He no longer played football or attended college, and his depression was a stark contrast to the glory he had enjoyed just months before. Maria's teacher berated her for the piece she called "sappy," and insisted that the newspaper's student-editor pull the article. However, Maria submitted the story to the local paper, where the professional editor printed it in its Sunday edition.

As Stephens thought about how to get her next story, she reasoned that the secretary of state, Allen Miller, was truly in touch with the Higgins family and all that was happening with Ann at the hospital. After all, Miller was the only person who knew that the family was reading *The Pearl*. She hoped that she might intercept the well-connected politician on the way into the hospital to visit the Higgins family.

So this morning, Stephens printed two copies of a brochure about a blockbuster cholesterol drug and set her plan in motion. At 11:00 a.m., she walked into the hospital, wearing her best suit and favorite high heels. She looked just like a representative from a pharmaceutical company as she towed a wheeled suitcase and held the drug brochures in her hand. She found a comfortable seat in the lobby and blended in as she camped out and hoped she would bump into Secretary Miller. As she waited she drafted a story about Ann Higgins and her life's recent parallels to the novel, *The Pearl*, on her computer. But, she hoped that she would never publish the article. She was confident that the secretary of state would help her land an even better story.

CHAPTER 34

At 6:12 p.m. that evening Maria Stephens's patience paid off. Allen Miller walked through the hospital's main doors. "Hello, Mr. Miller," she called out without calling undue attention to him by mentioning his title. "I'm so glad I ran into you. Thank you for the interview a few days ago."

The secretary of state recognized Maria Stephans instantly and he even felt a thrill as he considered the possibility that she had been waiting for him. If Miller had to select a stalker, Maria Stephans would be an excellent choice. "It sounds like the story worked out nicely for you, Miss Stephans."

"Yes, sir. It's a lucky break for a small-time writer with a big heart." She flashed him a smile before she said, "I have a confession. I was waiting and hoping to have another chance to talk with you."

Miller was intrigued. "I'm sorry Ms. Stephans. You're going to have to get in line behind all of my other admirers." He made a melodramatic gesture toward the door where nobody followed him. "They followed me over from the gym."

Maria laughed at his joke and then resumed her quest for her next big story. "Mr. Miller, can I pitch a story idea to you? I think you could really help the Higgins family."

"Well, yes. But only since the question you asked at the news conference was a refreshing contrast. A few of those reporters are canines trying to ferret out any scrap they can dress up and publish as a meal. What are you proposing, Maria?"

"Well sir, I'm hoping you can convince Lieutenant Governor Higgins to let me take some pictures of the family reading *The Pearl* to their mom. I just think it's an amazing moment and I suspect that it could touch the hearts of Americans everywhere."

"What's in it for me, Maria?" asked Miller. The secretary of state had not had a sincere relationship with a woman in years. A woman he loved profoundly had hurt him deeply years ago and he'd never recovered. Since that time, he'd not been able to invest emotionally in relationships. Interactions with attractive women were all just negotiations to Miller. "May I take you to dinner?"

"I'd love to join you for dinner. Do you dance, Mr. Secretary?"

"I washed out of fourth grade square dancing, Maria."

"Excellent!" she said with a wink.

After an awkward moment of silence, Miller asked, "Do you have your camera here?"

"Of course," Maria said. "Why would I come unprepared?"

"Well, then come on," the secretary of state said. He motioned toward the security guards and then joined Maria as they walked to the check-in point.

"She's with me," were the only words the well-known official had to utter to get Maria through security. As the politician and journalist entered the elevator they moved towards the back of the car to make room for two nurses and an elderly gentleman holding a bouquet of flowers. As the doors closed and the elevator ascended, Maria slipped her arm around Secretary Miller's arm as if she were accompanying him to a formal event. Miller's heart raced. He had no false illusions about this young lady. This was a deal, plain and simple. She would flatter him, join him for dinner, and laugh at his jokes for the evening. In return he would help her gather some pictures that would fulfill her professional ambitions. In Maria's mind this was a potentially great story about the Higgins family. She hoped it would help her get more stories in the big papers in Chicago, Los Angeles, New York, and beyond.

After Stephans and Miller exited the elevator, the secretary directed her to the waiting room and asked her to stay there while he went and consulted with Kent Higgins. He assured her that the lieutenant governor would love her story idea before he disappeared behind two sturdy metal doors that led to the intensive care unit. As she waited she took out her phone and opened the digital copy of *The Pearl*, which she had been studying since the press conference that put her on the national stage.

She read about baby Coyotito and his parents *Kino* and *Juana* leaving their hometown, La Paz, Mexico, under the dark of night. The hair on Maria's arms stood up as she read how, " . . . the evils of the night were around them." She could imagine hearing coyotes barking and yelping, while other animals lurked close by. Just as she was reading about *Kino's* warnings to his wife, *Juana*, about the " . . . tree that bleeds," Secretary of State Miller walked back into the waiting room accompanied by Kent Higgins.

"Maria Stephans." The lieutenant governor shook her hand with his right hand and then covered her hand with his left hand in an additional gesture of an implied bond. "I really loved the article you wrote. Thank you for syndicating it so it could get out to all of those newspapers and websites so quickly. Thank you so much."

"You're welcome, sir. I'm sorry about all you, your wife, and your family are going through right now."

"Thank you for your concern," Higgins said. "Secretary Miller told me about the press conference and how your question threw a few of my politician colleagues off their game." He smiled and turned his head toward the secretary of state. "Very unexpected, Ms. Stephans. There are some great journalists out there. I wish a few more of them would think outside the box, much like you did."

"Well thank you, Mr. Lieutenant Governor," Stephans said. "I just think readers want to get into the heart and soul of stories. That's why I've made this request to take pictures of you and your family reading to Ann."

"Well, your request is granted," Higgins said. She noticed how his statement contained none of the pretenses Maria sensed in Secretary Miller's voice a few minutes before.

"When would it be the least bothersome to your family, sir?"

"Well, the kids should be arriving with their grandparents sometime after seven o'clock this evening. Do you mind waiting?"

"Absolutely not."

"Thank you Ms. Stephans," the Lieutenant Governor said. "Let me get back to my wife. But before that, do you have any questions I can answer right now?"

"Well, yes. Let me start with an obvious question because I suspect that the assumptions or predictions that I make about your answer might be a little off base. Why would you read *The Pearl* with your family in a time of such tragic circumstances?"

"So, it's not obvious?" Higgins said."

"I don't know," Maria Stephans replied. "I don't want to assume I know the answer."

"Well, you might be onto something important here," Higgins said. "The day after Ann was admitted to the hospital, I sat down with my kids next to our bookshelf and I pointed to our library of books. 'Out of all of these books,' I asked, 'which one would you like to take and read to your mother?' I wanted a book that would touch the kids' hearts and make them think. I also knew that by doing something to take care of their mom, it would give them strength.

"Our two oldest kids started to debate about a couple of titles that were interesting to them. But then, the youngest, our daughter, kept reading down the shelves very intensely. While the other two kids squabbled, our daughter shot her hand up into the air, as if she were in school, and waited for her turn to speak. Once I quieted the boys, they took notice of their little sister, Joanna. Earnestly, she said, 'We're reading *The Pearl*.' There was no further debate. We just knew that we needed to read *The Pearl*. "

"So do you think when Ann is doing better and she's back at home, you'll cast your pearl into the sea?" Stephans was referring to two instances in the Steinbeck novel. In the first instance, *Juana*, wife of the oyster diver *Kino*, tries to throw the pearl back into the sea because it has overwhelmed their life with danger and trouble. In the second instance, *Kino* himself throws the pearl into the sea, but only after it had cost the life of their precious infant son, *Coyotito*.

Kent Higgins replied, "Ann and I have already cast pearls into the sea, figuratively, many years before. It's critical to know when to cast pearls into the sea and when to embrace the gems life offers you." Higgins pointed toward the intensive care unit. "Now is the time for us to teach our sons and daughter how these next four years could become a financial or political pearl. Yet after all we're going through with Ann, I'm more resolute than ever to use this opportunity to show my kids how to forget about money, popularity, and power. I want us to show them how to serve people. We're just going to do the right thing."

Stephans knew she was keeping the lieutenant governor from his wife, but she asked one last question anyway. "Are you concerned that *The Pearl* has such a sad ending when *Coyotito* dies? I mean, couldn't it be troubling to your kids during this time of crisis?"

The lieutenant governor replied without hesitation. "Absolutely, I'm concerned! If we get toward the end of the book and Ann is still in her coma, I'll summarize it quickly and gently for the kids. But regardless of Ann's outcome, each of my kids will confront the ending, word for word, when the time is right in their lives. They need to know how to avoid coyotes in their life travels."

"Thank you, Mr. Lieutenant Governor. I don't have any more questions. Your wife needs you."

"It's a privilege to meet you, Ms. Stephans. I hope you win a Pulitzer," the Lieutenant Governor said.

"Respectfully sir, I hope *not*," Stephans said. "I live too far from the sea."

CHAPTER 35

After completing the necessary security checks, Troy Stoker walked into the small clinic at the Minnehaha County Jail at 7:15 p.m. He passed the nursing station and walked into a stark exam room with no door. Chained to a metal chair sat Willy, the man Stoker had chased down and put in a sleeper hold just a few days earlier. Stoker stood five feet away from his patient. "Mr. Gilroy. It's good to meet you in a more normal way. I never did learn your last name when we were introduced, quite informally, a few days ago as you tried to shoot me. The guards say you've been a model citizen here while you await trial."

Willy stared at the floor and offered no reply.

"Well, since I'm your doctor, I have the privilege of seeing you here in the clinic instead of visiting with you on a telephone and watching you stare at the ground through the glass."

Willy looked up from the ground, glanced at Stoker, and then gazed off to his upper left, staring at nothing but the white wall.

"So I'm here to examine you. Let's start with your medical record." Stoker opened a folder. "It says here that you're twenty-seven years old, your blood pressure's fine, your heart and lungs sound great, and you don't have any general health complaints."

Stoker sat down on a chair and scooted it forward toward Willy. He used his hands to probe Willy's neck for injuries from the sleeper hold. Everything, including his hyoid bone, felt fine. The doctor also took the opportunity to feel the lymph nodes under Willy's jawbone and in various other positions in his neck.

All were normal. "When they booked you into the jail your tox screen revealed the presence of meth and cocaine in your urine."

"Just a little coke makes a great hit of speed," Willy said with a smirk.

"You're sixty-eight pounds overweight, but so far you've escaped any hints of diabetes. That's fortunate. Also, you're quite the runner."

"That was some good dope. It made me run fast!"

Stoker smiled a little at his comment. At least Willy was starting to express himself. "In doctor speak, I'm a psychiatrist. Also, you should know, I'm not the official jail doctor. This is a special visit just for you. So are you wondering what I'm doing here?" Without waiting for Willy's response, Stoker went on. "I need your help, Willy. We know that you got your junk from Ray. He's admitted that. But we need to know who Ray was working with."

"Huh!" Willy laughed. "Nobody knows that."

"Yes, that's what we keep hearing. I want you to think about this. First, we could say that you were just there, at Ray's house, to get high. Second, you happened to be in the wrong place at the wrong time. But third, we've got evidence you've been selling some of this dope, which would be a huge prison sentence." Stoker paused for a moment and he could see that Willy was listening. "The bottom line is I feel horrible for you because you're in a lot more trouble now." The fear and pain were evident in Willy's eyes, and Stoker knew he could leverage these emotions. "Also, you should've just stayed there and let them arrest you. Why did you run?"

Willy was silent, but Stoker could see that he had hit a nerve. Slowly, the man chained to the chair let the words flow. "I don't know. Somebody yelled, 'Cops!' I just panicked. Panic is different with all that junk flowing through your veins. I should've just sat down and put my hands on my head. Sure, they would've jailed me for a few weeks. But now I'm looking at some serious prison time." Willy looked at Stoker with some anger in his eyes. "I am going to the *big home*," he snarled.

Stoker was not fazed by the reference to the conversation they shared during the combative moments a few days earlier. He felt no pity for how he had handled Willy. "Don't complain, Willy. You shot at me, so I could've returned fire instead of wrestling you down."

"I wish you had shot me. I would rather be dead than go back to prison."

"I might be able to keep you out of the *big home*," Stoker replied.

"Yeah, right!" Willy replied in sarcastic disbelief. "What is this? Are you making fun of me again? Didn't you have enough fun with your little sleeper hold jokes?"

"No pity party allowed, Willy. And, I'm not here to make fun of you. Throwing an innocent girl out of a window was idiotic. Firing a gun in my general direction put another nail in your coffin. You're in a really tough spot." Willy was looking at the ground and avoiding Stoker's direct gaze. "Those were your bad choices," Stoker said. "Lucky for you, I caught the girl, which actually helps you. You're also lucky that I'm a doctor who knows that roughing you up while you're high is not going to teach you much. In your state that day the jokes sunk into your memory and taught you more than any amount of pain."

Willy glanced up at him for a moment. "I'm beyond pain at this point, Doc."

"The sleeper hold was my second favor. It kept you from being conscious long enough to do something else stupid. Now, I'm here to offer you a third chance at some help. Are you listening?"

Willy looked back at the floor. "Yeah, I'll listen."

"We need to know more about who's behind all of this meth. We suspect they're the same scum who are circulating this new synthetic heroin on the streets of Sioux Falls."

Willy's eyes got big. "That new heroin even scares me, Doc. I've done a lot of stupid stuff, and there's not much that shocks me. But, that shit messes people up."

"It's out of control, Willy. I've got a friend fighting for her life in the hospital and I suspect there's a tie to her injuries and the Sioux Falls drug scene. Even more frankly, I've got to find a way around the rules, relationships, threats, and conspiracies that are starting to cripple this place we call home.

"Your friend Ray, is the first drug bust in a long time that has actually worked out for us. Usually, when we go in, the criminals are long gone. It's like they know we're coming. There's something bigger going on and I'm going to find out what. Somebody in high places is pulling the strings in the Sioux Falls drug world. They're leaking out facts and details that hurt the cops and help the scumbag dealers."

"Look, Stoker. I'm not saying anything. The game's different now. You don't mess with the new bosses. You don't snitch on them. They silence people in ugly ways, Doc." Willy looked Stoker in the eye with intense conviction. "I'm not saying a thing. If you rat out these guys, they let you live a life worse than death for a few days before they take you to a horrible death." Willy squirmed in his seat and the chains rattled as he changed his position to try and find a little more comfort. "I'm scared out of my mind because these guys already wonder if I'm here in jail singing like a bird. And, damn it, Doc, I beg you. Please, can't you leak that I'm not telling anyone anything? Let it slip that I'm keeping my mouth shut. You go tell them that I'm keeping my mouth shut!"

"Who can I tell, Willy? I'll march right into his office, home, film studio, or cabaret lounge and tell him that your lips are sealed. That Willy has a religion and you are the god. He's keeping all your commandment and secrets. Your holy grail is secure!"

Willy ignored the question. "And for the record, you did me no favors with that sleeper hold. I wish I'd taken another shot. Hit or miss, I'd be better off with your bullet in my brain."

Stoker closed the medical file and stood up. "I walked in here optimistic, Willy. I thought you might finally see straight now that you have all of that crap out of your system. But, I was wrong."

Stoker took an envelope out of his pocket and removed a sheet of paper from it. "Willy, we need to know what you know, and I'm prepared to do *all* I can to find out. This letter here is to a patient of mine, who happens to be in the prison you'll revisit in the next few weeks." Stoker pulled the letter out of the envelope and waived it in front of Willy's face. "Let's just call this prisoner Paul — to keep his identity safe and all that stuff. I've seen Paul as his therapist for years. The root of his problem is schizophrenia, but it was his anger that landed him in prison. He and I exchange a couple of letters each month."

Willy's face bore a mix of curiosity and strain. He was accurately anticipating what Stoker might say next. "So I might run into him? What does this have to do with me?"

"Not much until he gets this letter." Stoker held it so he could read it. "After reading this, I'm sure he'll be waiting for you so you get the punishment you deserve. But on the other hand, if I write that you're cool and you've been helpful to me, he'll look out for you. You've got to play my game or else Paul gets the letter. It's not quite done, but let me read what I have so far."

Stoker cleared his throat a little dramatically before beginning to read the letter.

> Dear Paul,
>> Thank you for your letter last week. I'm thrilled at the progress you're making with the prison psychologist. I sense ample advancement with your new anger management strategies, which is why I'm writing you. I'm concerned that your anger will be tested in the weeks to come. You see, a Mr. Willy Gilroy will be serving some time there, and you may have heard some of the news reports about him. These facts will test your ability to control your violence toward this particular human being.

Now Paul, even though Mr. Gilroy threw a
thirteen-year-old girl out of a second story
window and fired a gun at me, you must contain
yourself. Remember, your bar fight went from a
brawl to attempted murder faster than you could
comprehend. So please, remember your
breathing exercises to help you find the calm that
you will need to tolerate a man who tried to kill
me.

Willy interrupted Stoker and with panic in his voice exclaimed, "You would never send that!"

"In part, you're right. I won't *send* it. I plan to *hand-deliver* it when I go visit him as a doctor. He and I will talk in a clinic much like you and I are doing now. I'll be able to lower my voice to a whisper and encourage him to look for opportunities to blacken your eyes and knock out a few teeth. I think he'll get the picture."

"I'm calling your bluff," Willy yelled.

Stoker calmly responded to Willy's rage. "Soon you'll wish you had told me what you know about Ray's bosses and the Sioux Falls drug scene. I'm willing to let you suffer, if it means we save dozens or hundreds of people down the road."

"I'm reporting you! You can't do this to me!"

"Thanks to your reputation and rap sheet, I can do anything I want. I'm just passing on information." Stoker leaned over and got directly into Willy's face. "Go ahead and report everything I've said. Report me to the guards first and then let's call the media. Perhaps we can expose me on billboards and in magazine ads. Then, everyone will believe *you*. Let's get it on! Let's get me in big trouble, right now."

Willy was in shock. He did not expect this response from anyone, especially a doctor.

"I'm sure everyone will sympathize with you, the desperate repeat offender, who is battling the demons of involuntary rehabilitation while the guards and nurses are neglecting to provide your quetiapine at night," Stoker sneered in an obviously sarcastic tone.

After Willy just looked at the doctor defiantly for a few moments, Stoker continued, "Look Willy, there are lives at stake here! I'm willing to bend a few of the rules and see you suffer if it can help me get any traction on busting up this drug ring."

Willy tried to stand up, but he could only strain against his chains. His face was red and he wanted so desperately to lunge out at Stoker. "You don't get it. You're setting me up for more misery. Still, the hell I'll face is better than ratting out Ray's bosses. Prison torture—even if it includes daily head smacks, loose teeth, and broken ribs, doesn't hold a candle to what they would do to me on the streets of Sioux Falls. I'll take my chances staying quiet and going to prison.

"I'm sorry about your limited options," Stoker said as he stepped toward the door. "You know, I'm trying to prevent you from going to the big home. You just have to tell me who some of the big guys are. It's not a hard choice, Willy. It's now or never."

Willy sat back against his chair. "You already have my answer, Doc."

Stoker pretended to ignore his comment, picked up Willy's medical chart, and wrote a note to the jail doctor recommending that Willy be placed on suicide watch. He had expressed his wish to be dead and all of the data were there to support such an order. Stoker walked out of the exam room, and yelled out to whatever guard might be within ear shot, "Willy Gilroy's ready to go back in the tank." Stoker was disappointed that his little ruse hadn't worked. He couldn't subject Willy to possible bodily harm.

When Stoker got out to the clinic desk he caught the charge nurse's attention. He was a heavy-set man who seemed content to do as little work as possible. "Will you please emphasize to the jail doctor that Willy Gilroy expressed suicidal wishes and displayed suicidal tendencies to me two times during our brief visit?"

"What else is new?" the male nurse retorted insolently.

"What *else* is new?" Stoker replied with a slight edge in his voice. "Why don't you tell me?" The charge nurse was caught off guard by Stoker's challenge, and Stoker knew he had grabbed the man's attention. "Why is there a small city of news trucks parked outside the Sioux Falls Convention Center?" Stoker questioned with calm indignation. "Tell me that."

Stoker's emotion, poise, and conviction voided the nurse's cavalier attitude.

"Because the lieutenant governor's wife is in the hospital?" he responded.

"So would you call that *new*?" Stoker asked.

The nurse's attitude changed instantaneously. "Sure it's new. It's tragic. Things like this don't happen in South Dakota."

"Thank you. I'm glad somebody else sees it. I was thinking I was losing my mind," Stoker said. "So can you please make sure this man is on the proper suicide precautions?"

"Of course, doctor." The nurse took the chart from Stoker, and began writing notes in it. "I'll get that communicated to the jail doctor right away."

"Perfect," Stoker said. At that moment, Stoker had an idea. Perhaps this nurse would have some insight on the Sioux Falls drug mystery and he directed another question toward him. "As a nurse who has worked in the county jail for a few years—"

"Sixteen years," he interjected.

"What's different now with drug offenders than it was two or three years ago?"

"The drugs are cheaper and they destroy people's brains even faster."

"Do you have any ideas about what might be happening out there?" Stoker asked.

The nurse wrinkled his forehead for a second. "I've got one wild theory." After a short, thoughtful moment, the nurse asked, "What's your name, doctor?"

"Troy Stoker. I'm a psychiatrist, who occasionally works with the police on drug cases. What's your name?"

"I'm Aaron West, R.N."

"So, tell me about your wild theory," Stoker said.

"This strange phenomenon has happened three times, so it does *not* make a trend. But it's happened three times in about the last thirty days. We constantly have people coming in all hyped up on meth. As you know, they experience quite a significant amount of paranoia. They fear for their lives and they're severely hypervigilant." The nurse closed the medical record and put it in the doctor's inbox. "And please, don't even ask me about the number of times I have heard about the CIA implanting bugs in inmates' noses, teeth and heads."

"What are some other common paranoid delusions?" Stoker asked.

"People high on meth claim that they are being controlled by extra-long frequency waves that affect their brain and make them crazy. Also, everybody's had Obama in their heads for the last few years. They claim he's trying to control them. We've heard it all many times over."

"Okay, so what's the new phenomenon?" Stoker asked.

"Well, sometimes an inmate comes in and his worries seem a little more realistic–and a little less paranoid. I'm thinking of three cases where patients said remarkably similar stuff. Each of these three guys kept talking about 'Nichols' and how he was going to feed them to coyotes. I thought it might be a movie reference, or perhaps it was a video game or a book I didn't know about. But when I search the Web, I can't find anything about coyotes or somebody named Nichols in mass media.

Stoker was intrigued by the nurse's observation. "This is indeed odd. People don't usually have the same exact fear or paranoia from the same exact person or source—that they can name. This may be what we call fixed delusions. They are one single, specific delusion instead of the combination of hallucinations you usually see. I have a hunch that these three patients were paranoid about real possibilities. Therefore, they are neither delusional nor hallucinating. This sounds like reality — heightened by drug induced anxiety."

"You mean hypervigilance based on reality?" West asked.

"Exactly," Stoker replied. "Under the right stimulant or hallucinogenic dosage, it could lead a normal person to sound like they're delusional, schizophrenic, or both." Stoker thought for a moment. "Did you ask the patients about any other details?"

"Well, I didn't the first time. I didn't think anything of it. Even on the second patient, I didn't feel much concern about the coincidence. But the third time, I did," the nurse said. "I asked the third guy, while he was still high on the meth, all about Nichols and coyotes. He just told me he didn't know who Nichols was. 'Nobody know, man! Nobody know that man! He bad! He bad!' was all he would say."

"What about when he came off of his high?"

"He slept for about twenty hours and then we talked to him," the nurse explained. "He tried to tell us that the name Nichols meant nothing to him. He said he had no idea why he would be talking about coyotes. But, I didn't believe him. For a guy who was supposed to be hung over and exhausted, he sure showed a lot of anxiety during our questions about Nichols and coyotes."

"In other words, the topics scared him?"

"That was my impression. I guess you could call it a hunch, Doc."

"Here, Aaron. I'm going to give you my card," Stoker said while scribbling on the back. "This is my cell phone number, which less than ten people in the world know. If you get any more of these patients talking about a person named Nichols or worried about coyotes, please call me immediately."

"Sure, Doc."

"I want you to call me any time." He handed West the card. "If it's two o'clock in the morning, call me. If it's eight o'clock a.m. on Christmas, call me. If it's during the Super Bowl . . . "

"We'll call you," the nurse responded. "If we're in the middle of a war, we'll still call you."

"Great," Stoker said. "Hey, do you remember the names of any of those people?"

"Only one." the nurse replied. "The last guy was Tony Bernard. But I can do some searching, get you the other two names, and send you an email.

"Thank you," Stoker said, as he turned and nearly sprinted for the exit. He needed to get back through security and get to his cell phone. He had a plan, and Rivera and Z might be the only people with the skills and fearlessness to pull it off with him.

CHAPTER 36

The photography session was short. Maria Stephans took about twenty pictures during the first five minutes she spent with Ann and Kent Higgins and their three children. The youngest Higgins child began to read about the characters *Kino*, *Juana* and baby *Coyotito*. This girl's innocence and earnestness struck Maria Stephans with the force of lightning and she could only take a few pictures before her emotions overtook her. The intensity of the moment compelled her to set down her camera, stand away from the foot of Ann Higgins's bed, and listen to the voice of a twelve-year-old who missed her mom. The first tear trickled from Maria's right eye and ran down beside her nose. Then more tears followed from both eyes. Kent Higgins handed her a box of Kleenexes, and she allowed herself to sit down, absorb this moment, and just let the tears flow freely. The next seven minutes of tearful listening were the most cleansing moments she had ever experienced in her life.

"Do you have any questions for the kids?" the Lieutenant Governor asked.

"No, I don't. Thank you. You and your children have answered everything."

CHAPTER 37

Sarah Haslam was surprisingly good at treating psychotic and delusional patients. She also excelled at treating suicidal patients and people in crisis—as long as she had the resources of a hospital and expert psychiatric nursing staff at her command. It was an easy recipe, according to Haslam. The second day of her rotation with Stoker she explained her interpretation of her psychiatric resident responsibilities. "You admit the patient and prescribe an injection of droperidol, in spite of the *alleged*, possible heart problems. There is not one person I can't treat using two point five to ten milligrams of droperidol, like on some of those huge people. To hell with even the low percentage of possible cardiac events. I know what I'm doing! I'm a doctor, dammit. From little old ladies to huge men, a shot in their shoulder muscle or their ass—if they deserve it that way, always does the trick."

Stoker was slightly amused, but mostly bothered by Haslam's attitude, and he continued to listen to her. "Then, I set up a nationally accepted protocol for four-point restraints, and *voilà*! These hick South Dakota doctors and administrators want results, so there they are. I'm giving them results. Four days later those patients are out of the hospital and the CFO should send me a personal thank you note. Now that's the true meaning of 'treat 'em and street 'em.' Boy, do I kick butt!"

Stoker just smiled and responded diplomatically, "That brings back a few memories from my residency."

The fact was, however, Dr. Haslam was a disastrous psychiatrist because she failed to understand and treat people with borderline personality disorder and other distinct personality disorders; Dr. Stoker was trying desperately to help her.

This morning Sarah Haslam had just finished a phone call with her residency committee chair, Dr. Penny Denning. Two times each week she provided a required status update on her rotation with Dr. Stoker. Sarah reported on her perception of Dr. Stoker's methods for treating borderline personality disorder. "This Stoker guy has some strange ideas about how to look at these people, and how to, quite frankly, figure these weird people out. Sometimes, I don't even think he knows what he's doing. I mean, what's the meaning of these patients pulling us into their lives as doctors and then rejecting us and pushing us away? They simply must learn to be compliant and listen to the doctor. We know what they've got. They don't.

"I mean, how much history do you need? So what if they were abused — sexually, emotionally, physically. Why should that make such a big difference? I'm not babying these patients like that idiot, Stoker. They don't need to really understand their esoteric, voodoo-like disorder. All they need to do is get better. And that's the bottom line. Why mess around with all of this gobbledygook psychobabble?"

Dr. Denning was not impressed.

"I always favor a direct approach with any patient," Dr. Haslam droned on. She rarely let Dr. Denning talk during these calls. "It's honest, and people deserve honesty. Extraneous information, such as theses lab results and capturing extensive histories, are ridiculous — almost always. Why make a mountain out of a molehill? This Stoker guy needs to live in the real world. Come to the hospital, Stoker, and see some *real* sick people, who actually know how to take their medicine and get better without all this hocus pocus voodoo. Why waste time diagnosing these patients' hormone issues? Give me a break. Testosterone? Thyroid hormone? Low cortisol levels? Leave that to the internist. I'm not going to be bothered with that stuff."

As a preceptor, Troy Stoker already had strict instructions from Sarah Haslam's residency committee to give the struggling resident as much exposure to borderline personality disorder patients as possible. "Don't hold back, Troy," Dr. Denning had told him. "She's got to work on correctly diagnosing these personality disorder patients and implementing an effective treatment plan that will provide a reasonable chance of a good outcome." Stoker took his mandate seriously. After the disappointing phone call with Haslam this morning, Dr. Denning sent a pleading email to Dr. Stoker, asking him to do everything possible to help Sarah Haslam.

Stoker had started the day by spending time talking directly with Haslam about some of the more common Axis II psychiatric diagnoses such as narcissistic, antisocial, histrionic, and dependent personality disorders. "Obviously, treating people with borderline personality disorder is the most challenging Axis II diagnosis. Actually, it's among the most difficult of all psychiatric conditions to treat."

Stoker introduced some of the diagnostic criteria such as a painful history of abuse and dissociative states these patients experience. But it was obvious that Haslam was only tolerating the discussion rather than participating. So Stoker decided to ask Haslam questions that would compel her to participate more actively. "Why do these patients cut themselves, Sarah? And, how does that relate to disassociation?" Stoker asked.

Haslam gave a textbook answer. "Borderlines deal with deep feelings of abandonment. This results in push-and-pull relationships because they want to push you away before they get pushed away. They create high expectations of family, friends, co-workers, and even doctors, which can never be met. In my already *extensive* inpatient experience, there is only one way to treat this mental health condition." Haslam continued her memorized oratory with bravado. "These patients and their reckless behavior, unstable relationships, and ill-regulated thoughts and emotions never have any luck with therapy. It just doesn't work. Some respond to medication, but for most borderline patients the only treatment for them is the school of hard knocks."

Stoker took a deep sigh and composed himself. "Really Sarah? The school of hard knocks is your treatment for borderline personality disorder?"

"Absolutely."

Stoker continued, "Actually, Sarah, years of therapy can help some borderlines. Also, medical studies have proven again and again that borderline personality disorder does not readily respond just to medication. If they have other psychiatric conditions, medication can help them treat those conditions, and sometimes their borderline symptoms will deescalate to some degree."

Haslam said nothing for a few moments. "Yes, Dr. Stoker. I'm familiar with all of the most recent literature. We're all working out of the same cookbooks here. However, I realize that you know much more than I do." She was appeasing him, only to move the conversation along.

Stoker ignored her strange compliment. "Okay, Sarah. Whether or not we're professors in the school of hard knocks, or chefs working out of famous cookbooks, we're psychiatrists. We're still practicing the art of psychiatry, since I last checked, instead of blindly and strictly following protocols."

Stoker looked at Haslam and he could sense that she was no longer capable of listening, so he changed the subject. "I have an interesting patient for you to evaluate. She should be here in about twenty minutes and I would like you to do a full evaluation on her. Mrs. DuVall is a thirty-nine year old unmarried female. She's been divorced three times. I've been currently seeing her weekly for the past two years. She has some difficulties with cutting herself and abandonment issues. I want you to tell me about how you feel about some of her other symptoms that she may present you with. You know how to perform a psychiatric evaluation, and I'd like a full assessment with complete diagnosis to include any new criteria you find. As you know, we all don't agree with a lot of this supposedly updated diagnostic material in the new DSM-V. We like to think of it as the bible of psychiatry. But, I want you take a good objective look at this woman in terms of a differential diagnosis, to include any possible physical problems. And then complete a full psychiatric biopsychosocial plan, which will determine how we will treat her.

"As you know, we're only looking at issues that may cause physical problems that may cause or exacerbate mental health issues. We do not necessarily have to treat the physical problems. We just have to get this patient to the right specialists. But in terms of the psychodynamics, I want you to be crystal-clear with me about what your plan is with this interesting woman. Before you refer her to another specialist, I want you to discuss this patient with me in detail. How does that sound?"

Crap! Now, I not only have to do everything for Stoker, but also I have to explain everything to this hick doctor, Haslam thought as she decided to placate Stoker. "Sure, Troy, I'll look forward to reporting and gleaning insight from you," Haslam lied. Dr. Sarah Haslam was sure she would get this patient better than Stoker would ever believe. She would show him a thing or two.

Stoker had been treating Melanie DuVall, a patient diagnosed with borderline personality disorder, for more than five years. When Dr. Haslam sat down with Melanie DuVall, the patient took over the conversation immediately. "Why am I seeing you instead of Dr. Stoker? Doesn't Dr. Stoker want to see me anymore?"

"No, no, no. I'm a doctor training with Dr. Stoker. He is your psychiatrist and will continue to be your psychiatrist. Today you can talk to him for a few minutes at the end. He did say he wanted to talk to you after I see you. Are you comfortable with this?"

"Yes. Dr. Stoker told me I would be seeing you," said DuVall. "I'm okay seeing you." *Okay, if Stoker's going to abandon me and mess with me, I'm going to mess with this Haslam for a while here,* thought DuVall.

Haslam began the psychiatric evaluation. "So what brings you here today?"

DuVall stared blankly at her.

Haslam repeated the question, "So what brings you here today?"

Again a blank stare as DuVall thought, *If Dr. Stoker is going to push me away, I'm going to do the rejecting before he ever does it to me. And this young doctor is going to leave me, too. So, I'm going to push her away and she won't even know it.*

Dr. Haslam was struggling with how to handle the patient's silence. *What in the hell am I going to do with these wacko Stoker patients? They're not only dumb but they are mute!* Haslam failed to recognize the psychodynamics of this woman's non-response. Then she remembered a technique Dr. Penny Denning had taught during the first year of her residency. Dr. Haslam decided to ask the question, in approximately five-minute intervals, three additional times. Each question was met with no response and a continued blank stare.

Melanie DuVall continued to think, *I'm doing the rejecting before I get pushed away. I'm doing it! I'm winning! I'm doing it! I will push her away before she can push me away.*

DuVall paused for a moment and then reached down to her purse pulled out a small razor blade and promptly cut herself superficially on her lower abdomen, just under her belly button. "So now what do you think? Am I nuts? Am I crazy? Is Doctor Stoker going to see me now or is he done with me now? What's the matter, honey? Haven't you seen any crazy people before?"

Haslam was paralyzed and mortified. She had no reaction. *I'm too good for this hick doctor and his crazy patients*, she thought. *Who knows what's going on with this woman? Because it's not my fault!*

DuVall continued her rant. "Why don't you get the hell out of here? If Doctor Stoker won't see me, I'm done. And I mean really done. I am done. Do you understand what "done" means? I don't deal with young, dumb, lesbian quacks!"

Sarah Haslam stormed out of the therapy session and into Stoker's office. "Dr. Stoker! This woman's about to kill herself and we don't have any support staff whatsoever! What are we going to do in your backwoods clinic in the middle of nowhere with whatever this woman is—a psychopath, a schizophrenic, or just plain wacko?"

Stoker was calm because he knew this patient well. Even though he was going to check on her immediately, Stoker felt strongly this was not a serious suicide attempt. Always the sage, the doctor simply asked, "What are you going to do next, Dr. Haslam?" This was a great teaching moment for her if she would accept it.

Haslam refused to consider solving the problem. "Where do these people come from that come here? She's all yours, Dr. Stoker. There's something with this woman I can't fix. I refuse to deal with her!" she said as she made a hasty exit through the front door. Haslam almost ran out of the clinic, jumped in her car, and sped off down the road. She had no idea where she would go, but she just needed to drive.

Back in the clinic Stoker calmly walked out of his office and down the hall into the room where Melanie DuVall sat with a smirk of deep satisfaction on her face. The bottom of her shirt and top of her sweatpants were covered with blood.

Stoker looked her in the eye and said, "Melanie, I just need to know approximately when your last tetanus shot was."

"About two years ago when I accidentally cut myself a little too deep on my arm."

"Perfect. Good to hear." Stoker knew exactly how to approach this patient. "Melanie, Melanie, at least you could've drawn a little bit nicer picture on your tummy there." This was Stoker's way of acknowledging that he did notice her actions while also allowing her a little control. "I mean last year, that nice picture you did for me was a lot better. I really appreciated how you carved the stick-figure picture of my wife and me on your belly. It was more interesting." However, Stoker refused to respond with anger, fear, disgust, disapproval, or shock. This minimized DuVall's satisfaction at this form of acting out. This classic paradoxical approach was critical in helping her extinguish these negative coping mechanisms on her part.

"I'm glad you remember, Doc. It shows me that you care."

Stoker reached into a credenza drawer, grabbed some sterile gauze and some bandages, and carefully examined the cuts. He saw that all of her wounds were superficial and concluded that she would not need stitches. "Well, I don't think you hit any arteries or large veins. I'm positive you're okay — and I think you know that, too."

By doing his due diligence and treating Melanie DuVall's superficial cuts, it further showed her that her doctor cared. This provided an essential sense of security for her, which was critical for patients with borderline personality disorder. Stoker knew that people with this diagnosis needed that constant feeling of caring from both their psychiatrist and other people close to them.

There was a long pause before a renewed smile came over DuVall's face. "I thought you had abandoned me there, Dr. Stoker. Thank you."

"Melanie. I'm sorry. You know that I have to take that razor from you. Do you have any others in your purse or on your person?"

"Actually Doc, I do keep one hidden for emergencies, but I left it home today."

"Okay. You'd better be telling me the truth." Stoker paused for a moment as he reached or some antibiotic ointment and applied it. "And you know I have to ask you this question. You can tell me what this question is, right?"

"I'm not damn suicidal. You know that, and I know that," DuVall said contemptuously.

"You know. If I weren't such a nice guy, perhaps it would be good therapy to make you wait for three hours in an emergency room for some of my doctor buddies to take a real good look at your wounds. I could give them a call and make sure that you wait at least four to six hours."

"Okay, mister mind-reader psychiatrist man. You win—at least this time. I get it. You've proven again that you're not getting rid of me. You're still here for me. I'll see you next week. I'm good. I'll listen."

"All right Melanie, here's the deal. You tell me exactly why and what was going through your mind when you did this. Or, if you don't feel like doing that, I would be happy to have my buddies in the emergency room take a look at you—after you suffer a three hour wait."

"Dr. Stoker. I'm really sorry. I felt like you were abandoning me. I wanted to push that fake, stuck-up bitch out of here, and I wanted to pull you back in here, I guess. It's my way of coping and it's really hard. I don't know why sometimes I do that. You know my history of horrible hell with my father, and when I cut, it helps distract me from the pain in my head. I know, that *you* know, that I know that's the wrong way to cope."

Stoker finished applying the bandages. "Okay. Thank you for being honest. It looks like these cuts are superficial. Let's hold off on the ER, but let's talk some more. The more we understand your abandonment issues, your abuse issues, your coping mechanisms, and your difficult relationships with people, as I've said before, that's when you will *begin* to feel better."

For another thirty minutes, Stoker and DuVall dissected the psychology and dynamics of today's visit. They started with the first moments Dr. Haslam was trying to engage DuVall. Then they walked through the breakdown with Haslam, and reiterated the conversation she had with Dr. Stoker as he bandaged her wounds.

"Melanie, before you leave, I need to know if you are having any suicidal thoughts now?"

"I know the drill, and you know I'm sincere when I say, I'm not going to hurt myself. Is that the right answer, Stoker?"

"It is for me, if it is for you." Stoker looked at her for a moment, and she nodded as she stood up.

"I'm fine. I will not hurt myself."

Stoker stood up with her and accompanied her to the door. "I'll see you in two weeks, and we'll check your meds then. Remember, most of therapy—"

"I know, I know. Most of therapy does *not* take place in the office," DuVall said. "But at least I know I won't be seeing your Amazonian girlfriend, Dr. HAZMAT, next time."

CHAPTER 38

MINNEHAHA COUNTY JAIL, SIOUX FALLS

Dr. Connor Corbit walked onto the clinic floor of the Minnehaha County jail to round on inmates who have medical concerns. Dr. Corbit had a contract with the county to provide services to the people in jail. He liked the work because he billed the county, and nobody ever questioned which codes he chose to bill. He also appreciated the diagnostic challenges he confronted at the jail. He was sick of his regular family practice. Most of his cases there, in his opinion, were boring and routine. He could explain a viral infection that required no medication—and frankly no doctor visit—in his sleep. At the jail the cases often challenged his diagnostic and treatment skills. It was ironically refreshing to work in a jail.

As he stepped into the nurses station to collect some documents, he noticed the business card of Troy Stoker, M.D. taped to the wall. "Why is this here?" asked Dr. Corbit.

"Oh, Dr. Stoker wants us to call him if any more patients mention somebody named Nichols or express paranoia about coyotes," one of the nurses said.

Dr. Corbit's hands, forehead, and armpits broke out in a profuse sweat. His colleague and friend, Dr. Stintson, had mentioned how Stoker had been a thorn in his side, lately. "Stoker could connect us all and bring us down," the shady orthopedic surgeon had mentioned.

Dr. Corbit picked up his briefcase and said, "Excuse me. I'll be back as soon as I can. I just remembered something important I must attend to."

CHAPTER 39

It took Dr. Corbit about ten minutes to make his way back out of the Minnehaha County jail. His agitated state caught the attention of the guards who had seen him enter and exit the facility hundreds of times. This time they were a little more thorough because the doctor's abnormal behavior triggered some additional search protocols they had to follow. The guards aggressively explored his briefcase, patted him down, and passed the metal-sensing wand over his body. Once the abnormally painstaking security inspection was finally over, Corbit walked to his car as fast as he could while simultaneously dialing a telephone number he rarely used.

"Dr. Stintson's office," answered the voice of Andrea. She was the highest paid medical secretary in Sioux Falls. Stintson had hired her away from another doctor when he learned that she was charming with referring doctors and a fail-safe secret keeper. Dr. Stintson's wife loved her because of her plain, homely appearance.

"May I please speak with Dr. Stintson?"

"I'm sorry. He's in surgery," replied the personable Andrea. Can I get him a message?"

"Absolutely. This is Dr. Corbit." He could not restrain the desperation in his voice. "I've never asked for an urgent call back from him."

"I agree, Dr. Corbit. What's going on?"

"Can you please ask him to call me as soon as humanly possible?"

"Sure. I'll text him right now." Corbit could hear her fingers dancing over her keyboard keys. "I just told him to call you at this number and I told him it was urgent."

"Thank you, Andrea! Bless you, child!"

"You're welcome. Thanks for sending us that well-insured patient from the jail—you know, the banker's drunk wife. He really loved putting her back together after her car accident. I'm expecting her auto insurance payment any day now."

"Sure. No problem," Dr. Corbit said. "I'll send you every auto wreck I see."

"As long as they have insurance or significant assets, darling," Andrea said with a joking tone. But Corbit knew she was not joking. "And, Dr. Corbit, let me know when you want to use Dr. Stintson's cabin in the Black Hills, honey."

"Sure. Thanks," replied the doctor in short, cold words. Right now, the cabin was far from Corbit's mind. His thoughts were completely occupied by the possibility that Troy Stoker knew two small bits of information. The nosy psychiatrist knew the last name Nichols. He was also aware that coyotes were somehow significant. Right now, those facts probably meant nothing to Stoker. But with a little more snooping and some luck, he just might uncover the truth.

"Hello?" Andrea said. "Dr. Corbit?" The doctor's concentration had shifted so much to the issues at hand that he had momentarily forgotten he was in the middle of a phone call.

"Oh, yes. Sorry. That would be great. I love Hill City. My kids are getting old enough to hike Harney Peak. I'll come up with some dates. Thank you. I appreciate your help. I'll just wait here for his call," Corbit said as he clumsily ended the phone call.

As he sat in his car his hands shook, his anxiety escalated to intolerable levels, and his head pounded with a headache he had never felt before. Nausea washed over him and he panicked and considered the embarrassment if he threw up in the parking lot in front of any people. He quickly started his car, shifted it into reverse and began to back up. The blaring of a horn made him slam on his brakes. Two rednecks in an old pickup truck glared at him as they proceeded behind him. The slight adrenaline surge from the startling truck horn temporarily suspended his nausea and calmed his nerves, and he took advantage of the moment to finish backing out of the parking spot, put the car in drive and resume his rapid exit from the parking lot.

When the adrenaline started to wear off, the nausea and anxiety returned with a vengeance. He pulled out of the parking lot and accelerated to fifty miles per hour. He just needed to find a little solitude so he could puke. The vomit kept rising in his throat, and Dr. Corbit kept forcing it back down. He knew he could not win this battle much longer. Finally, he decided that he would never find an ideal place to empty the contents of his stomach, so he abruptly pulled his car over onto the side of the road. He slammed the gearshift into park, leapt from the vehicle, sprinted fifteen yards into a field, hunched over and threw up the last meal he had eaten plus a little bit more.

Sweat dripped down his face and neck. His antiperspirant had completely failed him and he felt like he was burning up as he sat outside, without a coat, on a frigid January day in South Dakota. Everything he had worked toward in life was at risk now that Stoker was investigating. Sure, there was his medical practice that he worked hard to keep compliant with all laws. He also bent over backwards to take excellent care of his patients. However, Dr. Corbit knew that he could end up in huge trouble if law enforcement officials ever learned the secrets he kept just to hide his little meth habit.

Corbit picked up some snow and swished it around in his mouth to clean out some of the unpleasant taste. Then he turned and walked back to his car. As he slid along the snow in his leather dress shoes he wondered how he had ever propelled himself across the snow at such a rapid pre-puking velocity.

He crawled back in the car and decided to ignore the Stoker issue. He found some soothing new age music on a satellite radio station. As the sounds of synthesizers, waves on a beach, and harmonious string instruments mixed together, Corbit felt some relief. His empty stomach seemed to help, too. About half way through the third song, Dr. Corbit's phone rang, and his blood pressure and anxiety surged again.

"This is Dr. Corbit."

"Hi, Connor. It's Larry. What's going on?"

"Troy Stoker is what's going on."

"What do you mean? What is the problem?"

"Stoker came to the jail and left his business card. Somehow he knows there is a person named Nichols involved and that some people are afraid of coyotes."

Stintson's adrenaline surged and his problem-solving skills came into focus. "Just tell the nurses and guards down at the jail that Nichols is one of the real ruthless dealers in Minneapolis, and the phrase 'coyote attack' is just new slang for a drive-by shooting. Feed them the line." Stintson enjoyed being the one who was giving the advice this time. *The commander would be impressed*, he thought. "Reassure the staff with a story. Just say something like, we've heard of this Nichols guy, and he's staying out of South Dakota. He likes the bigger market in Minneapolis. Tell the folks at the jail a big yarn. How about this? The liberal judges and all the rules the police have to live by in Minnesota make a criminal's job so much easier. Sioux Falls will never be an interesting place for this Nichols guy to do business."

"Okay, Larry. Got it. Now, just for clarification, is this Nichols guy in Minneapolis for real, or did you make him up?

"Oh, no. That's just how convincing I can be when it comes to lying, cheating and stealing. We're criminals now. Don't act so surprised."

"What if Stoker comes poking around, again?"

"I guess if he returns, there's not much you can do to keep him from visiting. Tell the jail staff not to worry about calling him if a patient talks about Nichols or coyotes. Tell them to call you. Again, here's where you get creative. Just tell them that you've referred a few patients to Stoker, but you rarely liked the results. You don't refer to him anymore, and he's not your first choice for psychiatric care." Stintson paused for a few moments and cleared his voice. "Look Dr. Corbit, it's your job to marginalize Stoker, just a little bit, in their minds. Your words will go a long way."

"Okay, Larry. Thanks."

"Sure, Dr. Corbit," responded Stintson. "And, thanks for sending me that drunk lady with great insurance a couple of weeks ago. I think I cleared about eight thousand dollars off of her."

"No problem, Larry. Glad she was a goldmine," Corbit said with feigned sincerity. He hated doctors who treated patients as financial instruments and evaluated them based on the their collection value. As a matter of fact, he realized that he hated Larry Stintson. He hated the fact that Stintson had trapped him by uncovering his recreational meth use.

At that moment, Dr. Corbit realized it was time to come clean, voluntarily report to the proper authorities and recover. If Larry Stintson threatened him with arrest or sanctions on his license, he was ready to accept his fate.

Corbit drove back to the jail. As he pulled back into the parking lot, he still felt some anxiety over Stoker's snooping. But, he also felt confidence now that he had a plan in place. In the next hour, Dr. Corbit made his way back through the security checks and rounded on his patients. Once he'd seen all patients, he sat down with the medical assistants and nurses and told them his lies.

"Every few weeks I, as the official doctor for the jail, meet with a Sioux Falls and Minnehaha County police drug task force for an update," Dr. Corbit lied. "That name, Nichols, sparked a memory from a recent meeting and you may have noticed that it concerned me a little."

"I think I saw a bead of sweat on your forehead, Doc," replied Aaron West, the nurse who had recently met Stoker.

"I stepped out to make a few phone calls to my police contacts, and this is what I learned. First, Nichols is a known dealer in Minneapolis. Occasionally, some of the people who land here in jail will know him from their travels to Minnesota. He's not interested in working in South Dakota. Being a drug dealer in a more liberal place like Minneapolis is easier. The police have to abide by more ridiculous rules that slow down their investigations. Also the judges are more lenient. The police doubt this Nichols guy would shift his attention from a city of a few million to build a satellite operation in Sioux Falls. It just doesn't make sense."

Corbit was quite proud of himself. His story sounded convincing, and his success bolstered his confidence as he spun a few more lies. "I also asked my sources about the term 'coyote.' It turns out that 'coyote attack" is the new slang for a drive-by-shooting in Minneapolis, Chicago, Detroit and Milwaukee. The latest threat on the urban streets is, 'I'm feeding you to the coyotes.' It's a death threat."

"So, do we still call Dr. Stoker if another inmate mentions Nichols or coyotes?" West asked.

"No, call me. Please let me talk with Dr. Stoker. If the issue re-surfaces, I would like to work closely with him on this. I'm happy to pass the information on to the authorities first and I'll consult with Stoker second." Corbit lowered his voice and leaned in a little closer as if he was about to share a secret. "Look, I like Stoker as a person. But I used to send him patients and I never really saw great results from him as a psychiatrist. So now, I send my patients elsewhere."

Corbit waited for a moment and then asked, "Anything else you want to ask?"

The nurses and medical assistants had no more questions. Corbit was certain they absorbed his lies. He had convinced all of them — except one

CHAPTER 40

"If you hate your patient, she must be a borderline," Haslam said to herself. It was the fourth time in the last ten minutes she had uttered this catchphrase. She had heard the saying from a perpetually grumpy nurse who worked on the psych floor. The cruise control was set at a consistent sixty-five miles per hour as she drove down Interstate 90, which was wise considering her current state of mind. She was slightly buzzed after downing two daiquiris with a plate of large nachos at some Mexican restaurant she'd never visited before.

Doctor Sarah Haslam did not believe in taking time out to cool down. Sometimes her patients needed to, but not the accomplished professional Sarah Haslam, M.D. Her wrath was justified and logical. Haslam believed in taking time to scheme and she did it well while traveling at freeway speeds. She made a quick plan to put Melanie DuVall in her place. She did not care that she was a borderline patient. She needed to learn a lesson and grow up like all the rest of the borderlines in the world.

She had remembered that Sarah DuVall worked as a waitress at TGI Fridays. Certainly, her employer knew little to nothing about her mental illnesses. Haslam would change that. Later that evening she would write a letter from a fictitious doctor from another clinic. It would be easy to create fake letterhead. The letter would outline her diagnoses, medications and treatment plan. "Despite the new development of desires to act out violently toward your co-workers, I am confident that you can use your coping techniques successfully." It would be accidentally slipped into a file folder and deposited into the manager's inbox with some junk mail.

Now that her scheming was complete, Haslam decided to return to Dr. Stoker's office. She did not know if he would be disappointed, sympathetic, or even angry that she had abruptly ended the session with Melanie DuVall. Frankly she didn't care what this one-man, right wing, Constitution enthusiast thought. She just wanted to get through the next few weeks of this rotation, move on, and forget Troy Stoker.

When Haslam walked through the door Stoker was in a session with another patient, so she went back into the staff kitchen, brushed her teeth to rid of any scent of alcohol, and popped some spearmint breath mints in her mouth. While she waited for Stoker to finish his session, she checked her email from her phone. When Stoker emerged from his current session Haslam took the opportunity to slip into his office and sit down on the chair that she often occupied while they were seeing patients. After Stoker said goodbye to the patient he came back into his office and closed the door.

"I'm not going to apologize about the circumstances earlier today with the young woman who's a borderline patient. I acknowledge they can be tricky to work with in therapy, but you need to learn to deal with them and successfully treat them. I will support you as you wrestle through that."

"Oh, come on, Troy. There is no good treatment for borderline personality disorder. She was a waste of time."

"What makes you say that?" Stoker asked.

"She would not engage with me about her therapy. She expressed anger over seeing me instead of you. She thought you might be giving up on her, or passing her off to a new doctor. Even when I explained that I am just here for a few weeks, she did not want to process that thought. She crossed the line and you crossed the line."

"That's what borderlines are supposed to do. That was classic splitting behavior. You failed with her."

"You set me up for this disaster," Haslam accused.

"I arranged a great training session. You decided not to participate. You excel at helping people for the first few days of short-term episodes and illnesses, but you need to develop some skill at establishing relationships that help patients for months and years. When I first met Mrs. DuVall she treated me like that, too. It took time to get to know her and to get her to have some slight trust in me. That trust and respect has created a safe place for her to come and work with me to keep her life on track."

"You mean to keep her crappy waitress job and remember to feed her dog?"

"Those are critical aspects of her complicated life. A dog is about the only relationship she is capable of maintaining right now and her job is a saving grace. She can go home between lunch and dinner and get that dose of security she needs from her home and dog."

"So you're saying that I should've just listened to her?

"In part, yes. I think that you should've looked for opportunities to understand her heart and mind. You could've asked some probing questions to show that you're interested in her as a person. Reaffirm her when she makes good choices. Ask her to critique herself on the bad choices. A borderline will not respond favorably to criticism from you even after you've met with her five, ten or a hundred times."

The rage brewing in Haslam's mind reached new heights. "Troy, I can't believe you would set me up to fail like that! It's unprofessional and I won't stand for it!"

"Why not?"

"Because I don't need some two-bit psychiatrist, who probably graduated near the bottom of his class, to manipulate me for some kind of sick thrill."

"Think about that statement. How much of it do you know to be true?"

"I've worked with you long enough now. I see right through you."

"Two-bit psychiatrist. I plead guilty. But, I graduated near the top of my class in medical school. If it helps you to feel better, I was not particularly celebrated during my surgical rotations, however."

"That's irrelevant and you know it. Remember, I'm a psychiatrist, too. I know what you're doing with all of these leading questions."

"Of course you do. Leading questions are helpful for everyone. But since you've tired of questions, let me be rather direct with you. Your professors specifically asked me to help you learn to treat borderline personality disorder. I suspect you've had frustrations with borderlines before?"

"I'm a good psychiatrist. I follow the best treatment protocols for borderlines and I follow-up methodically until they're discharged. My discharge planning is superb."

"This office is not a hospital. So what about after the hospital? What about those patients who never get bad enough to land in the hospital?"

Haslam was silent. The best arguments she could formulate in her head were weak. She was not tired of arguing. "Look, Troy. I'm not going to sit here and have you nit-pick at me. That patient was out of line today and so were you."

"There is another borderline patient on the schedule for tomorrow. Let's see how you do with her. I agree that you know the medications and treatment protocols. In that regard you are superb. But you need to develop this empathy element and it's going to take some extra effort. Take the rest of the day off and do something you enjoy. By the way, what do you do to relax?"

CHAPTER 41

CARNAVAL BRAZILIAN GRILL, SIOUX FALLS

"Finally, I get to meet the big shot in the flesh," Dr. Larry Stintson said aloud to himself as he pulled up to valet parking at Carnaval Brazilian Grill. "Dinner with the commander. How in the hell did this get on my schedule? What sales pitch or dog and pony show am I in for tonight?" he muttered to himself.

Stintson got out of his newly leased Infiniti M35h, and gave the keys to the valet. He drove the fancy, left wing hybrid so people would think he cared about the environment. In reality, Dr. Stintson was a man who would gladly care about the environment—if he could profit from it. So far he had managed to impress a few of his liberal friends.

As Stintson entered the restaurant, the incredible scents of Midwestern beef, prepared with Brazilian spices, lifted his mood considerably; and all of a sudden his concerns about tolerating a sales pitch were gone. He approached the *maître d'* and she recognized him right away. "Dr. Stintson, your host has already arrived. Let me take you to his table. Right this way," said the curvaceous Brazilian twenty-something with a stunning smile that was remarkably sincere.

Carnaval, the Brazilian style *rodízio* steakhouse, was arguably the most popular restaurant in Sioux Falls, and Stintson loved everything about the establishment. The décor and linens were exquisite. The ceiling was a flowing fabric imitation on a Brazilian sky moments after sunset, with subtle lights placed to perfectly imitate the position of the emerging stars during the annual *Carnaval* celebration. With all of the extra media in town to cover the Ann Higgins incident, the restaurant was extremely busy catering to reporters, camera crews, producers and technicians who charged their meals, complete with wine and exotic drinks, to corporate credit cards. Waiters dressed as Brazilian cowboys, or *gaúchos*, traveled throughout the dining room carrying swords loaded with succulent grilled top sirloin and other beef, as well as varieties of chicken, lamb, pork and sausage. Stintson reveled in the energy as he gazed out at the crowd and recognized a few talking heads from national news programs. He was disappointed when the beautiful Brazilian woman led him away from the main dining room and into a private room with six tables decorated in festive Brazilian style.

On Stintson's third step into the room he froze in his tracks and found himself looking into the intense eyes of one of the most powerful men in South Dakota. Almost without thought, Dr. Stintson shifted into his politically conservative mode. "So, *you're* the commander!" he said with a little more awe in his voice than he had intended.

"Ever since serving the US of A as a naval officer," said the voice Stintson had heard speaking at a black-tie political fundraising event just a few weeks before. The commander extended his hand for a handshake. Stintson didn't know what to say next. This wolf in sheep's clothing had managed to claw his way to the top of political and social circles while also making a name—or a nickname— for himself in the Sioux Falls underworld.

As the waitress approached the commander turned to Stintson and said, "I'm ordering for a couple other people. They'll be here in a few minutes. Would you like a minute to take a look at the menu, Larry?"

"No need. I'm ready to order." Dr. Stintson turned to the waitress. He knew the menu well. Furthermore, he knew the commander was a bit of a fitness nut, so Stintson decided to order something healthy to make the right impression on his host. "I'll have the salmon with coconut-cashew sauce and a side-salad with your mango-pineapple vinaigrette."

"Would you like anything to drink?" asked the waitress.

"A San Pellegrino sparking water."

The commander gave him a look of disapproval. "Are you on call, doctor? Is there something wrong? You're not having a drink with me? This is what we Navy boys do."

"No, I'm not on call. I am still considering a vodka in a few minutes with my salmon."

"I'm quite certain that you will," the commander bellowed with a serious tone that was deeply unsettling to Stintson. "I'll have the beef ribs, but hold that blueberry barbeque sauce, and bring me some real sauce! Does your bar have anything from the Dakota Spirits Distillery in Pierre?"

"Absolutely," replied the waitress. "And you strike me as a Coyote 100 Light Whiskey kind 'a guy."

"You read my mind," the commander said. "How did you know?"

"Three fingers, straight up?"

"Damn straight!"

The waitress smiled and said, "Yeah, it's strange. I work here, but I also tend bar downtown at a club. Nobody used to ask for the coyote whiskey here in Sioux Falls. But now I see a lot of guys drinking it. I don't know what it is, but I can usually guess the coyote guys a moment or two before they order it."

"We're a tight pack and a rare breed, darling," the commander said. After pausing for a moment to let her laugh, the commander finished the order by requesting Brazilian coconut chicken for the two guests who had not yet arrived. "And, bring my guest, the good doctor, a Smirnoff vodka — double shot."

As the waitress walked away, the commander appreciated her thighs for a moment and then returned his complete attention back to Stintson. "Our fair capital city, Pierre, has some good restaurants, and if you stick to your favorites, you'll eat well there. But here in Sioux Falls? Let me tell you. The food here keeps on surprising me. I can name twenty good restaurants and I'm sure there are ten more I've not yet discovered."

"This one's owned by a doctor," volunteered Stintson awkwardly.

"Let me guess," the commander said. "Is the owner a gastroenterologist, fattening us up now so he can shrink our stomachs?

"No, he's not," Stintson replied. "But, wouldn't that be something? Turning us into obese diabetics and then fixing us up." Stintson laughed at his version of the joke. "He gets us coming and going."

The commander held up his menu and said, "Thanks for ordering off the menu, Larry. Normally here at Carnaval, the waiters, those *gauchos*, bring in food faster than you can eat it. But I've asked them to give us our privacy."

"That's fine," Stintson replied. "Normally I welcome the waiters' interruptions. I mean, this place is every man's dream. Cuts of juicy marinated meats piled on your plate. And, they almost beg you to take more."

"Oh yeah! I'm a big fan of those little chicken hearts they bring in on the little swords in some Brazilian restaurants," chimed in the commander. "So, occasionally I'll yell out, 'Bring me some hearts on a sword!' Why do you think I like to yell that out so much, Larry?" The commander's eyes opened wider and there was a little wildness in his voice. "Actually, I don't really like the taste of chicken heart meat that much. I just love to demand hearts on steel swords. I admit it, Larry. I wish I could demand the hearts of some of the idiots I have to tolerate in state government. Do you know what I mean?"

"Yes. There's a striking contrast," interjected Stintson. "My employees at my medical practice are scalpel-sharp. The staff at the state medical board is okay, but they wouldn't survive one minute in the real world."

"I agree. My minions in my side-ventures work four times as hard as most of my government employees. There are exceptions, of course. But I frankly admit that I lust to see the hearts of a few of those government idiots on the tip of a spear—raw or cooked. Believe me. I've thought about it. But, you know. There would just be a trail of evidence a mile wide." The commander glanced at his menu, and tried to show some interest in it, but his thoughts distracted him and he set it down again and looked at Stintson. "I don't think I would last long in a South Dakota prison, so I hold my temper. I must suffer and endure the idiocy of government employees." He picked up the menu again as he said," But, I digress. Can I get you some chicken hearts?"

Dr. Stintson squirmed in his chair. The commander's bizarre behavior was different from the composed, passionate and debonair political candidate who had so persuasively spoken at the fundraiser dinner a few weeks earlier. "Um, no. Uh, no thank you. I'll wait on my salmon. But I may ask the waitress to send in one of those gauchos with the grilled pineapple."

"Oh, yes! I love that pineapple," the commander said. "We'll bring some in after our additional guests arrive."

"Who are we meeting with this evening?" Stintson asked.

"That's a surprise. I'm sure you'll be astonished." The commander smiled wryly at Stintson. "But, here's a hint. It will be a reunion of sorts." The commander took a sip of his drink and continued, "Larry Stintson! This is your life!" Again, the commander was acting bizarre. "Did you ever see that TV show?"

"You mean the one where they bring on a guest and then re-acquaint them with an old friend they've not seen for years?"

"Yes, yes, yes. That's the one. I can't say too much more about our guests, however. But rest assured, we will not be reaching too far into your past. Sorry, Larry. It's not your high school prom date," the commander said with a laugh.

Stintson laughed, too. But his laugh contained obvious signs of anxiety and discomfort. In his mind he scrambled for another intelligent thought that would propel the conversation into a more casual and comfortable direction.

"You mentioned some side-ventures," Stintson said. "What are you invested in?"

"A perceptive question, Larry. That *is exactly* why I brought you here this evening. I want to tell you a little bit about my main venture. I want you to invest in it—but not with money. I need you invested emotionally," the commander said as he swirled his drink. "Actually, you're already emotionally invested, and you don't even know it."

"Really? You have me intrigued," Stintson replied naively. People often approached Dr. Stintson to participate in business ventures. Normally he would take a defensive posture, but this evening, one of South Dakota's powerbrokers was inviting him into some sort of an investment conversation. His mind was completely open to the dialogue and potential business relationship. "The only things I'm invested in emotionally are money, power, the New York Yankees, and occasionally my wife."

"Oh, Larry, Larry, Larry. You underestimate yourself. You're a complex man, Larry. I know there's a lot more depth in there." The commander was pointing at Stintson's chest. "But, let's wait until our food arrives and our guests join us to get into the details."

"Very well," Stintson said, deciding to play things as cool as possible. When talking business, Stintson did his best keep his composure and remain unemotional. He didn't want to give anything away in this prelude to negotiations. The doctor needed to keep his options open, put on his poker face, and avoid acting too interested. If he was too eager, it may cost him dearly. He needed all the negotiation power his emotional neutrality could muster.

The waitress brought the commander's whiskey as well as Stintson's side salad and mineral water, the vodka, and some fried bananas. Stintson poured his mineral water into a tall glass.

"Thank you my dear," the commander said to the waitress as he lifted his glass in the gesture of a toast while looking Stintson directly in the eye. Stintson returned the gesture raising his vodka double shot and maintaining the commander's gaze. As Stintson looked into his new friend's eyes, the commander just paused and said nothing. Stintson was overcome by a feeling of deep evil that emanated from the commander's intense gaze.

The commander thought for a moment and then decided to test Stintson by saying something completely out of character. He needed to rattle Stintson. The commander disrupted the silence with his odd toast. "Here's to the disciples Mark, Luke and John."

The men clinked glasses and with a wink the commander brought the Coyote 100 whiskey to his lips and threw back the glass's entire contents into his throat with a deep but effortless swallow. Stintson enjoyed a drink of his vodka.

"Bravo," Stintson said. "You wisely left out the tax collector, Matthew," the doctor blurted out with a laugh. Stintson assumed his host would laugh with him. He was wrong. The commander just continued to stare into Stintson's eyes, which further confused the doctor. Now the commander was pleased that his psycho-dramatic game had left Stintson puzzled. The politician had the clear upper hand in the relationship.

Stintson was perplexed. For the last few minutes he had tried to engage in meaningful conversation with his host. However, the commander was obviously setting conversational traps and playing intimidating mind games. Stintson was feeling quite uncomfortable with how the dinner encounter was digressing. As a solo-practice orthopedic surgeon and president of the state medical board, he was accustomed to being in control. Just that morning, the large-and-in-charge Stintson had flung a bloody clamp across the operating room in outrage. The hospital scrub tech had failed to respond quickly to his request for irrigation of the surgical field.

That afternoon, Stintson had stripped a neurologist of her license after she missed the yearly deadline for her renewal. He didn't care about the many patients who were going to suffer without access to their doctor. There were no exceptions. This talented physician would have to shut down her practice for months while she completed a new application and collected the voluminous documentation for the process. While Larry Stintson should've cared, he actually got a slight buzz when he signed the order and slammed the "revoked" stamp on a symbolic copy of her license. For the rest of her life the neurologist would have to explain to the numerous hospitals, health plans, government entities and other organizations the reason her license had lapsed in the state of South Dakota.

Why did her license really lapse? Her thorough, efficient staff submitted a perfect application to the South Dakota Board. However, Brian Berg spilled decaf on her paperwork and he could not bring himself to own the error. Instead he took the application with him on his lunch break one day. With a panic similar to a schoolboy disposing of pornography before his parents caught him, he flung the coffee-stained application into a restaurant dumpster. Then he stepped inside and treated himself to a super-sized triple cheeseburger meal.

That same day the neurologist had left town hastily to participate in the relief effort for a typhoon in Southeast Asia. But she left instructions for her staff to follow up on the application. One week before the deadline, the doctor's secretary called the medical board to check on the application. Nobody at the medical board could find the application and the staffers immediately accused the doctor's office of failing to submit the application. Even after the doctor's secretary produced the certified mail documentation with a board clerk's receipt signature, the state board refused to acknowledge the error or extend her deadline.

Larry Stintson was used to being the actual fabricator of the power plays. Now that he was falling prey to the commander's power play, he was completely out of his element. He had not felt this way since his supervising surgeons had dressed him down during his residency. He decided to try to work his way back onto the offensive with the man who sat before him.

"I'm going to level with you, commander. This dinner already feels like a negotiation with an HMO," asserted Stintson while shifting into his snooty surgeon tone. "You call yourself the commander and I learn that you're really one of our state's highest ranking politicians. You've been purposefully vague about this so-called investment, which you have labeled emotional but not financial. That actually sounds like ObamaCare. I'm now expecting you to hand me a thick document and ask me to sign it. That is what the health insurance companies do. They assure me that all of the information is 'in the contract,'" Stintson said while making air quotes. "I guess that's what they did with a few thousand pages of ObamaCare, too. 'Trust us. It's all in there,' the politicians said."

The commander pursed his lips and stared Stintson in the eyes and he let a few moments of awkwardness pass before responding to the doctor's aggressive comments. He knew the silence would give Stintson's mind a moment to consider retreating from his most recent comments. Just as he saw a hint of regret in Stintson's eyes, he said, "I did not bring any documents and I am not asking you for any signatures."

"Okay," Stintson said hastily. "But, I've got to tell you that this relationship is getting off to a bizarre start, and that's simply because you're not putting much information on the table." Stintson was feeling good about the way he had asserted himself. He was pretty sure he had dodged the commander's intimidation tactics—which was exactly what the commander wanted him to think.

"You're right, Larry. I've been vague," the commander said with a perfect Zen-like calm. "Within the next five minutes or so, our guests and common friends will provide you all of the details you could ever desire—and you will not have to review a single document." The commander then reached into his attaché case and removed a few items. "Speaking of our guests, I don't want them knowing my real identify, for obvious reasons. So give me a moment."

The commander took out a small mirror and slipped in some contact lenses that transformed his intense blue eyes to a more mellow shade of brown. Then he applied some subtle makeup around his eyes and forehead to emphasize his wrinkles. "I hired a Las Vegas disguise expert to teach me all of this stuff. You wouldn't believe how many people in Las Vegas are living in disguise to hide from the authorities or others who would like to find them."

His next face-altering props were two devices he slid into his mouth, one into each cheek. They made him look heavier and older. He slid a set of slightly crooked false teeth over his perfect bottom teeth. The device made his bottom lip protrude slightly. "The pieces in my mouth also alter my voice a fair amount," the commander explained. Stintson could hear the difference. Finally he slipped on a pair of glasses and some shoes that made him two inches taller and the transformation was complete.

"You don't do anything to your hair?" Stintson asked.

"Not a thing," the commander answered. "Do I need to?"

"Well, you don't look at all like the politician who I met a few minutes ago."

"Right, and remember that our guests have no idea about my political role. One of them has never seen me outside of my disguise and the other guest has never met me. Don't blow my cover, Larry. The last person who divulged my identity ended up cleaning up the mess he made. It included gallons of his tears and the blood of the person he told."

The commander was definitely in control of the conversation again. "As I was saying, before I put my game face on, our guests will explain everything. The conversation will be so short and the details so clear, that your medical transcriptionist could fit it on a single sheet of paper—double-spaced. I request a few more minutes of your patience. Will you please enjoy your salad and the bread? Let's talk about the New York Yankees, the restaurants here in Sioux Falls, and your new car."

"How did you know about my new car?"

"You pulled up just before they called me back to our table here. You went the tree-hugging hybrid route did you?"

"Not the tree-hugging hybrid route," Stintson said defensively. "I took the acceleration-loving hybrid route. You would be amazed by the immediate acceleration of an electric motor off of the line. A few days ago I blew away a Chevy Camaro at a stoplight—at least for the first two seconds."

"Then he caught up and left you in the dust?"

"Well, not in the dust," rebutted Stintson. "But the Camaro did recover and pull away from me. We ended the race at around seventy miles per hour."

"Don't tell me about your reckless driving. With my new job, I may have to report you," joked the commander in a cheery, insincere tone.

Stintson waited for a moment to make sure it was okay to laugh, and then he emitted a safe, short laugh. "So, are you a car enthusiast?" asked Stintson.

"Oh, you know. All of us guys think we're car buffs. It's a strange thing, though. Now that you ask, my greatest consideration when I purchased my last car was having some good room in the back for my dogs."

"Really? What did you buy?"

"I went for the Cadillac Escalade. I fold down the rear seat, and Imelda and Ferdinand just love it back there."

"So Imelda and Ferdinand are your dogs' names?" Stintson asked as he picked up his fork and eyed his salad. "You named them after Filipino politicians?" Stintson took a large bite of salad.

"Yup. Imelda has this golden coloring on her paws, and it reminded me of the shoe-hoarding Imelda Marcos," the commander said as his eyes grew passionate. "She's such a beautiful dog. I've always loved wolves, coyotes and other powerful, majestic canines. Imelda and Ferdinand are the closest I can come to owning domesticated wolves."

"And, why is that?" Stintson asked while trying to disguise the fact that he still had salad in his mouth.

"Well, you can technically own pure-breed wolves. It is legal in some states, and you can buy them from breeders," the commander explained. "Sure, you can fence them in, and feed them, and try to care for them. But, they will never let you domesticate them completely. You can't have a long-term relationship as their master or even really as somebody they care about. They just aren't genetically programmed to be mastered by a man. Only another wolf, the alpha wolf, can demand any sort of respect from a wolf."

"I'm sure people try anyway," Stintson said.

"Indeed they do. But after a few months of disobedience and destruction, the wolf owners surrender the dream of owning true wolves. They usually turn the majestic beasts in at an animal shelter. But, some frazzled owners turn them to the wild, and a few people just shoot them, stuff them in a plastic bag and set them out with the trash."

"So, Imelda and Ferdinand are somehow different?"

"They're a wolf hybrid. Sort of like me, I guess."

"What do you mean?"

"By breeding a gray wolf with a Siberian husky, I got most of the majesty of the wolf, but it also infused an acceptable amount of discipline and strength from the husky."

"That much I presumed," Stintson said. "What I really want to know is what you meant about *you* being a hybrid?"

"Well, Larry. Let's just say that the military and law school bred some much-needed discipline into my soul," the commander explained. At that moment something else caught his eye and distracted him from the conversation. Looking toward the entrance to their private dining suite, the commander exclaimed, "Our meals are here, and so is one of our dinner guests. This will explain a lot."

Dr. Stintson turned his head to see two Carnaval servers walking toward them carrying food. The restaurant employees were shrouding the mystery guest, a short man, who followed them. But as the servers neared the table they stepped to the side to place the meals on the table and Stintson instantly recognized the guest. An emotional collision of nausea and panic gripped him. Somehow he found the strength to control his anxiety reflexes, including fighting back the urge vomit the few bites of salad and sips of mineral water he had just consumed. The man he knew only by the first name Cody, who occasionally sold him a little recreational speed or ecstasy, stood before him. And now, the commander was here to bust him. He was sure this was a sting.

It was Stintson's natural reflex to deceive in panic situations. He immediately attempted to pretend Cody was a stranger. "Well, who's this?" he attempted to ask as his voice box tightened and constrained his sounds to a mere whisper. "I mean, um, won't you please introduce me, um, Commander?" His feeble, shaking and husky voice betrayed him. It occurred to him that these two men had information that could make him lose his medical license, his job as the president of the state medical board, and possibly even his wife, house, and medical practice.

Cody and the commander stood silently just looking at Stintson with emotionless stares while the servers finished their work. The commander pointed the servers toward the door and they exited hastily. Stintson broke the silence by standing and extending a trembling handshake toward Cody. "I'm Dr. Stintson." It was his final attempt to mislead. "What's your name?"

"Oh come on, Larry," the commander said. "Give it up. I know how you and Cody go way back. Enough with the pitiful charade."

"I want my attorney!" Stintson lashed out. "Right now! I want my attorney. Am I being clear?" the doctor raged as he reached for his phone. With trembling hands, he tried to operate it and find that app that would record the conversation. "I'm recording this, and I am making an official request for my attorney!"

The commander snatched the phone out of his hand with a speed that stunned Stintson and again tested his gag reflex. Stintson fell back into his chair instead. Cody was confused about why the doctor would want his attorney.

"You're not in any legal trouble, Larry," explained the commander. "I don't invest my time hunting down recreational MDMA users like you. That does not fit my political mandate. No, Larry. I'm not here tonight as the politician." The man with disguised intense eyes paused for a moment and he leaned in toward Stintson a little more. "I'm here as the wolf!"

Stintson felt a horrible mixture of emotions. Terror gripped him as he looked into the commander's vicious eyes. But the fact that this was not some sort of a setup to arrest Stintson for his drug use also caused him deep relief. "You mean this won't be in the papers?"

"It's not like that, Larry," the commander said calmly as he signaled for Cody to take a seat. "Larry, I need your help—no, I need you on my team," he said winding up with emotion like a backwoods preacher. "Dr. Stintson, I need you more than on my team. I need you emotionally invested." His tone was fervent now.

"What do you mean?" Stintson stammered.

"I need to know! Can you do that for me?" The commander's energetic request filled their private dining room. "Will you be on my team?"

Stintson understood that this was not really a question. The commander had just issued an order, disguised as a question, in front of his recreational drug dealer. Now Stintson knew why he'd been intimidated just minutes earlier. He also knew if he didn't give the commander his allegiance, he could eventually end up exposed, arrested, unlicensed as a doctor and embarrassed.

The panic subsided and a little more reason crept into the doctor's mind. At that moment, he realized that it went deeper than being arrested or embarrassed. *If I don't get on board with the commander, I'll end up dead*, he thought. Stintson only had one option, and he realized that he'd better be convincing as he exercised his option. He would do what it took to survive today, even if he had to do some acceptable acting. "I'm all in, commander," Stintson said. He looked up and locked eyes with his new partner. "I look forward to learning more about the upside to this whole venture."

"Oh, Larry!" the commander bellowed. "You've already tasted the sweat nectar of working with the commander."

"Yes, that ecstasy is a pretty sweet ride," Stintson said with a convincing smile.

"Ecstasy?" the commander asked with obvious exaggeration in his voice. "Sure, that's part of it." He stood with dramatic flair, turned to the door, and signaled for someone else to enter. In walked the curvaceous Katerina Baker, Larry Stintson's lover. This time, Larry fought back his urge to deceive. He could never deny knowing her. Instead he embraced the moment, smiled wide, and channeled his panic into wherever this next emotional investment might take him.

"Would you like another vodka, now?" the commander asked as Katerina sauntered up.

"I'm beyond vodka. Just get some of that coyote whiskey inside of me."

Katerina approached Larry, leaned in with a light hug, and a kissed him on the cheek. "Welcome to the *pack*, Larry," she whispered in his ear as she took a little nibble on his lobe.

CHAPTER 42

On this particular evening, Troy and Allie had worked out in their home gym and then enjoyed cooking and eating dinner together. They tried to do this at least two times per week, which was hard for a psychiatrist who needed to offer evening hours to patients.

After dinner, Stoker went outside, chopped some firewood and brought it inside to the wood-burning stove that sat in the middle of the office the couple shared. Allie was already at work preparing a proposal for a longstanding client. Dr. Stoker started the fire and sat down at his small desk. As his computer came to life, he immediately noticed an email message bearing the subject line "Coyote data." When he opened it, there was no greeting or signature but he knew it came from Aaron West, the nurse at the Minnehaha County jail. It contained the names of three people. Gary Watson and Jake Clark were new names; but Tony Bernard was the name the jail nurse had already provided. Rivera and Z were trying to locate Bernard. The email also explained how the staff physician, Dr. Corbit, had reported that Nichols was the name of a drug dealer in Minneapolis with a reputation for violence, and how phrases such as "coyote attack" or "being thrown to the coyotes" were alleged slang used to describe drive-by-shootings. West's message concluded stating that he was highly skeptical of the jail doctor's explanations and how something just didn't seem right.

With a few keystrokes Stoker copied the content out of the email from West and pasted it into a message addressed to Errol Rivera and Z. Stoker explained that these were the three people who expressed concern about "Nichols" and coyotes and he asked them to call him to discuss this issue.

After sending the email Stoker's curiosity drove him to search out information on Nichols and coyote attacks on his own. He started out using Google to search the terms, but found nothing. He also searched the Urban Dictionary. While he found funny references to coyotes, coyote attacks and related phrases, he found no references to drive-by-shootings. Stoker searched for references to coyotes in pop culture and literature, but found little. He was quite convinced that the Dr. Corbit had fabricated his story for some reason.

When his phone rang it interrupted his train of thought about coyotes. Because the caller ID labeled the call source as "restricted," Stoker answered in a neutral tone. "This is Stoker."

"Hey, Stoker. Z here. I'm calling you back on this coyote email. Sorry Rivera could not join us. Sometimes he just has to delegate to me."

"No problem. I'll tell you what I know," Stoker said. "I just got that email from a nurse who works inside the county jail. There is a trend of inmates coming in under the influence of some pretty powerful chemicals that put them in a paranoid state. These three individuals expressed a deep-seated and credible fear of an individual named Nichols as well as the threat of being thrown to the coyotes. Can you do some checking to find out if these three know each other or are otherwise associated? Also, can you verify a pill pusher named Nichols in Minneapolis and check out the story behind the 'coyote attack' slang?"

Stoker could hear Z typing on a keyboard at an incredible rate of speed, just before he said, "Give me a second here, Doc? I'm accessing their data now." Stoker waited for a few moments.

Z spoke up. "All three of these men were released on bail and all three of them skipped their hearings. Now nobody knows where they are."

"Is it like they've fallen off the face of the earth?" Stoker asked.

"Not really. Usually, when we refer to people who have 'fallen off the face of the earth' we are making the statement that their family, friends and employers have not heard from them. But what I am seeing here raises red flags in our world of investigation. In the case of these three men, none of them have any close ties to family or friends. Their telecommunication, social media and email profiles all suggest they are each loners who distanced themselves from their parents and siblings some time ago. People like this often end up working in the crime world and it's not by accident."

"Okay, what about employers and last known addresses?" Stoker asked.

"None have recent last known addresses; and these guys haven't worked using their Social Security numbers for a least a year."

"Wow," Stoker said.

"Wow is exactly right, Doc. "We think you and Ann Higgins stumbled onto something pretty big here, Troy. Watch your back."

Stoker chose not to address Z's warning, but he made a mental note to harden his and Allie's defenses once he got off the phone. Then he asked, "Are those three from around here?"

"Bernard and Clark are. They grew up here. Watson's from Omaha, and he's lived here for about three years. He used to work construction. But, all of these guys are estranged from their families. It's like they made a conscious decision to go underground."

"You can see all of that from data you collect?" Stoker asked.

"We don't collect it, Doc. We just access and analyze it. There are statisticians out there who turn all of this into accurate profiles."

"Isn't that an invasion of our privacy, Z?"

"It sure could be. I only looked at these three guys because they've jumped bail."

"Shouldn't you have a warrant?"

"Yes, I should," Z said. "That's my honest answer." There was a short silence while Z typed at lightning speed. "There, I just sent an email requesting one. Before I dig any deeper, I'll get one." Z sighed and said, "Hey Doc, Rivera never told me that you're so by-the-book, man."

"I'm not so by-the-book, Z. You can just go ask that guy named Willy who's sitting in the jail awaiting trial courtesy of my sleeper hold. I brought up the warrants because I don't want any loose ends if this is as big as you say it might be." Stoker redirected the conversation back to sorting out the issues he'd discovered at the jail. "What about this supposed Nichols fellow in Minneapolis and the drive-by-shootings? I'm really leery about the drive-by-shooting explanation by the way."

"Yes, let me see here," Z said. "I'm chatting with one of my counterparts in Minneapolis. Give me a second." Z's fingers were flying over the keyboard yet again. Ten seconds later he said, "You're right, Doc. That's all bogus. Our guy in Minneapolis says that there is really only one guy worth mentioning named Nichols up there who happens to be associated with the drug trade. But he went to prison about five years ago and he's still there. Apparently he's found Jesus and is a model prisoner," Z sneered with skepticism. He typed a little bit more and then said, "My colleague and I in Minneapolis are completely convinced that 'throwing people to the coyotes' and 'coyote attacks' are the sole creative property of somebody right here in Sioux Falls, South Dakota."

"Great. I'll copyright and trademark those coyote phrases right away," Stoker joked. "Let's see how the convention and visitors bureau can use our newest slogan to attract tourists?"

"Sounds great!" Z kidded. "Test marketing amongst the riff-raff of the world has been overwhelmingly positive. We count dozens of meth cookers and pill pushers that have come to town based on the coyote mystique."

"Very creative," Stoker said. "At the same time I'm fueling this flippant conversation, I'm remembering that Ann Higgins is fighting for her life thanks to the *tourists* we've attracted to our city."

"Well Troy, I'm completely serious when I say that we will find and arrest these rogues. You've given us our best lead, yet. Tell your contact at the jail to keep listening. We think he's onto something."

Stoker ended the phone call, turned back to his computer, and typed a simple message asking Aaron West to contact him about any new people talking about coyotes or Nichols.

CHAPTER 43

Dr. Larry Stintson had no appetite. He was just pushing salmon and vegetables around his plate. But he had indulged in a second vodka martini as he listened to his drug dealer explaining the events that led up to this evening. "Yes. I connected you to the commander," Cody said as he shoveled away food with a healthy appetite. "I would never rat out any of my customers to the cops. But I tell the commander's guys anything they want to know." He took a huge bite of chicken, but somehow managed to keep talking. "They asked me who my doctor customers were. I named four doctors—who they found rather uninteresting— before I named you. Then their eyes lit up."

Stintson pretended to resign himself to the fact that he would have to accept the explanation. But deep inside he was livid with the man who occasionally sold him a few hits of different junk. Stintson had never balked at the price. Even if everything turned out okay, Stintson would never forgive Cody for what he had done. Turning to his mistress, Katerina, Stintson asked, "How did you get recruited, or were you a plant all along?"

"No, no, baby. You and I met way before any of this. I became, let's just say, emotionally invested, about three months ago. Cody here introduced me to one of the commander's guys, Nich—".

Cody interrupted her. "Let's not worry about naming too many names, here sweetie."

Katerina was a little shaken. She knew that mistakes with Cody could be painful or deadly. With a quiver in her voice she said, "I had never met the commander until tonight when they picked me up a block down the street from my apartment. It was Cody and, um, someone else, who recruited me a few months ago. One morning I was slipping out of our favorite downtown hotel — you and I had partied until about three in the morning, baby. Anyway, I guess they were waiting for me in the lobby. I left the hotel and was walking toward my car when they intercepted me in the parking lot. But they didn't take me to a nice restaurant," joked Katerina. "No, the little people like me just get hauled out to some field west of town, where you can hear the coyotes yapping. You didn't even offer me coffee," she teased Cody hoping to use a little charm to help smooth over her recent near-mistake. "But the big-shot surgeon gets the red carpet treatment at Carnaval."

"Yes. I thought about just relegating you to a Caesar salad here tonight," Cody snapped back, arresting Katerina's flirtatious humor and subtle attempt to endear him to her.

"Cody threatened to have me arrested," Katerina said. "He said that I wouldn't like it much in jail. As the coyotes yapped and the cold winds blew, they told me I had three options. The first one was to get arrested and take my chances I could explain the stuff they would find in my urine and blood tests. The second one was to call in the coyotes and hope they weren't too hungry. The third choice was to cooperate with them."

"You made the right choice, Katerina," Stintson said. "You stayed alive, you kept us together," Stintson pausing for a moment and smiled at his nervous girlfriend. "When you really think about it, darling, you may have just opened the door to a great opportunity."

"What do you mean?" Katerina asked.

In a confident and menacing voice, Stintson answered, "Katerina, my darling, believe me when I tell you that the commander here is someone who can take us places in South Dakota. He's got our backs, he's got resources, and he's got a future. The more I think about this, the more I like it."

Stintson's mind was racing. He thought about the options. He imagined the power he could amass and the riches he could access if the commander would let him in on his ventures. Perhaps he might even be able to parlay this experience into a high-profile government appointment. This just may be the big break he was looking for. Next stop Pierre to head up the Department of Health, thought Stintson. All of a sudden Stintson's appetite returned and he yearned for the grilled beef circulating freely out in Carnaval's main dining room. Tonight, the salmon would have to do. He took a bite and his hunger amplified. He took another quick bite and then added some vegetables to a third bite.

Unfortunately, the rest of the group had already finished dinner and the commander suggested that they go for a drive. "I've got some investments I would like to show you," the commander said. "Katerina, you come with me. Larry, why don't you drive your car to the hospital and park in the doctor's lot, walk through the ER, and meet me about a hundred yards from the ambulance bay. None of the hospital's cameras reach out to that point, so nobody should capture us traveling together."

Stintson shoveled four more bites into his mouth as fast as he could. He was conflicted between his momentary hunger and his lust to be part of this mysterious new world.

The commander stood from the table and turned to Cody. "Thank you for joining us this evening. I know your band has a gig tonight, so I won't impose on you any longer."

"Thank you, Commander."

Just as the commander turned to leave, he had new idea. "Hey, Cody. Before you go, it occurs to me that you've been pretty visible here in Sioux Falls for the last few months. You've done some good work recruiting Larry and Katerina, so I think it would be wise for you to lay low for now."

"Okay, boss. I can introduce my regular customers to one of your other guys and ask them to take over for a while. I'll concentrate on my music and hide behind my drums in the clubs."

"Better yet," the commander countered, "call my main man, tomorrow." He wrote down Ron Cunningham's name and phone number on a napkin, and handed it to Cody. "Tell him I need you to go to headquarters." The commander was cautious not to mention Reno or Cunningham to Stintson and Katerina. They may never need to know about Reno and Cunningham. "I think you'll like the music scene near headquarters, Cody. And, you'll love the work."

The commander dropped two hundred dollars on the table, turned to Stintson, and gave him his next set of instructions. "After we leave, wait here for three minutes. Then, walk to the bathroom. Take your time in there for about five minutes. At that point you can leave."

The commander walked to the side of the room, where there was a fire exit to the back parking lot. "Right this way Katerina," he gestured. "We'll creep out the back."

Two minutes later Katerina and the commander were traveling on 26th Street. Tonight the commander had a driver, so he elected to sit in the second row with Katerina. While Katerina occupied the spot just behind the driver, the commander sat behind the empty passenger's seat. Just out of curiosity and perhaps for the thrill, she displayed her long, elegant legs and watched out of the corner of her eye for any reaction from the commander. He didn't acknowledge her subtle ploy. Instead he said, "Excuse me Katerina. I need to make a call." The conversation was short but sweet. He had called a woman named Amanda, and the flirtatious nature of the call was obvious. "I'll be home around ten," the commander replied to this Amanda woman. "Yes, darling. You will have my undivided attention. Tennis? Of course I'm up for tennis. Have the maid turn on the lights and heat up the court. A fabulous suggestion."

The commander ended the call. Katerina had decided not to hide her legs because the retreat could catch his attention and further expose her fear and insecurity.

The commander instructed the driver to stop at a big box electronic store. Once in the parking lot the commander told Katerina to wait in the car. He put on a plain navy blue baseball hat. "I'll be right back," he said as he jumped out of the car and ducked into the store.

Katerina remained alone with the driver, who immediately struck up a conversation with her. "Are you an attorney?" asked the driver once the commander was inside the store.

"No. I'm a massage therapy school dropout who started waiting tables a few years ago."

"There's good money in the right restaurants," the driver replied.

"I was pretty good at restaurant work, so I kept getting better jobs. In Chicago, I used to make two hundred dollars a night in tips. That was on a slow night. Weekends and holidays could be double that."

"I'm sure it helped that you're drop-dead gorgeous," the driver said. Katerina smiled. She sensed that the compliment was sincere and only a touch flirtatious. This guy was not creepy. He was actually muscular and had the potential to be handsome.

"Thank you," she replied. "You're sweet."

"I *am* sweet. I also admit I like the rush of telling a striking woman that she's beautiful. But I'm strong enough not to push it." Now his comments made Katerina a little uncomfortable. She said nothing. But the driver continued on. "My fiancé would kill me."

"When's your wedding date?" Katerina asked. She had to determine if this was a real engagement or if this guy was just semi-engaged.

"One hundred twelve days," replied the driver. "The commander is performing the ceremony at the Chelsea Crossing Country Club."

"Well congratulations," Katerina said. "You have one hundred eleven days to figure out how to stop flirting."

The driver laughed a little too hard and Katerina decided she did not want to reveal more about herself to this odd stranger.

"Who's Amanda?" Katerina asked.

"I'm not quite sure," the driver replied. "But I'll bet you her real name ain't Amanda. I think it's a code name for his wife or his girlfriend. Of course I haven't asked him. You know, we don't ask the commander a lot of questions, especially personal ones. He likes to keep his information close to his chest."

"And he has a tennis court at his house?"

"I think so. I'm pretty sure it's indoors. I bet he plays a couple times each week. He also does some cross-country skiing and he drinks a lot of juice and eats a lot healthy stuff out of his own garden."

"Good for him. I would weigh fifteen pounds less if it wasn't for my boyfriend's constant craving for steak dinners."

"Are you complaining?"

"Of course not," Katerina replied. She changed the subject by asking, "So how did you get a job with the commander?"

"You know," said the driver, "it was a friend of a friend introduction. How long have you known him?"

"About forty-five minutes now," Katerina replied. "We're coming up on our one-hour anniversary."

"And who introduced you to the commander?" the driver asked.

"Well, it was like you just said. It was sort of a friend of a friend situation."

"Are you seeing the pattern here?" the driver asked.

"A few patterns, actually. This is a 'by invitation' club here and, it's best to volunteer minimal amounts of information."

"Smart lady. You catch on fast. By the way, it's okay to ask a question here and there. It shows you're thinking. Just be patient if you get a vague answer."

"Thanks for the insight, um," Katerina hesitated. "What's your name?"

"Just call me the vague answer guy."

"Right, gotcha. And my name isn't Katerina. Just call me 'lady' or 'miss.'"

"Not ma'am?" asked the driver.

"Not for another three or four decades, vague answer guy."

They sat in silence for another minute before they saw the commander emerge from the store with a bag. He jumped in and casually tossed the bag into the back seat. Katerina quickly caught a glimpse of the boxes that were slightly shrouded by plastic bags. He had just purchased two sleek, compact laptop computers.

"I love the look on people's faces when you pull up to the cash register with thirty-six hundred dollars of product and you hand them cash, including tax, before they can ask you all of their little questions."

The driver smiled and nodded. "Are you a member of our rewards club?" he asked in a mocking tone."

"Bingo," replied the commander. "I asked her, in my charming voice, if her store would like to join the Benjamin Franklin Club? She didn't quite know what to say, so I explained that I give her store thirty-six Benjamin Franklins, plus tax, as I pointed to the money. They give me a receipt and product and *viola*, they're members. I punch their card with a bunch of Benjamins."

"How did she react to that?" Katerina asked.

"Well, as you've discovered, people respond well to my good nature," the commander quipped. "She caught right on and she was pretty charming herself. The cashier said that they would be pleased to join the Benjamin Franklin Club. She took my money and started counting it. She was pretty talented because she hit me up for their credit card offer without losing track of her bill count."

"I assume you declined the offer?" Katerina asked.

"That's when I asked her, 'Do I *smell* like I need a new credit card?' Of course she didn't know how to interpret my question, so she covered her confusion with a laugh."

"Did you have her down for the count, or did she recover and hit you up to buy an extended warranty?" asked the driver.

"I cut her off half-way through her speech and told her that I only needed them for ninety days or so. After that we would be smashing them up in my neighborhood monster truck rally. 'If your warranty covers that, I'm interested,' I told her. She was pretty sure it didn't, so of course, I lost interest."

Both Katerina and the driver smiled, but they did not feed the conversation further. They could tell the commander's attention had shifted. "Okay. To the hospital," the commander said. Katerina's missing her boyfriend."

Five minutes later, they were waiting across the street from the emergency room. "Let's see how well Larry follows directions," the commander said as he jumped out of his seat and relocated to the front passenger seat. "Come on, Larry. It's your big tryout. Don't keep us waiting too long, buddy."

Two minutes later Dr. Stintson emerged from the emergency room. He had a stethoscope around his neck and a coffee cup in his hand. He walked briskly to the commander's car and followed the driver's signals to get in through the door behind him. Katerina slid over as Stintson opened the door and the doctor jumped in next to her.

"Did you really stop for coffee?" the commander asked.

"No. I don't need any more stimulation. But I did duck into the staff kitchen, just briefly, to grab a paper cup. I thought it would lend credibility to my presence there. That's why I added the stethoscope, too."

"That stethoscope is nice camouflage, Larry," the commander said in an underwhelmed tone. "Do orthopedic surgeons even use stethoscopes?"

"If we can bill for using them, we do. I use a stethoscope in the ER with trauma patients. If I know that somebody has cash or assets, I will use the stethoscope on an ankle sprain patient. If I listen to their heart and lungs, I get paid more. It's called Review of Systems. Just the other day, I thought I heard an abnormal heart sound, so I called it a heart murmur due to a septal defect and I billed for it. I actually got paid. Of course I sent the patient to the cardiologist to handle it, and he subsequently disagreed with my diagnosis. Either way, I got a few hundred extra bucks for three minutes worth of work with my stethoscope.

The commander actually liked Stintson's story, because it showed the doctor was readily corruptible. "We're on our way out to visit Chelsea Crossing," the commander explained. I have some investments there that I want you to invest in emotionally, Larry. I'm kind of a fan of real estate and I really like to get creative with my real estate."

"Great. I can't wait to see your investments. Are these rental properties?" Stintson asked.

"Yes they are. But I also add a little twist," replied the commander. "Again it is easier to show you than it is to explain it."

"The last time you said you would show me something instead of explaining it, you ushered in my turncoat recreational drug supplier."

"No more reintroductions tonight, Larry," the commander said. "I'm just showing off some business operations." The commander changed the subject to better engage Stintson's mistress. "So, Katerina. How did you and Larry meet?"

"I came to Sioux Falls to visit my cousin about a year ago."

"She was only supposed to be here for five days," Stintson interjected.

"My cousin is really into yoga, so she insisted that I go to her class with her," Katerina continued. "Well, I've never done yoga, but I am quite the competitive soul."

"So naturally, you had to keep up with your cousin," the commander chimed in.

"Yes, naturally," Katerina affirmed. "Thirty-three minutes into a sixty-minute class, I was contorting and stretching into some horrible pose, when I heard a pop—no it was a crack—in my neck. I collapsed right to the ground."

"A vertebrae or a disk in your neck, I presume?" the commander asked.

"I later found out it was a terrible disk injury. But before I could get diagnosed, we had the horrible challenge of getting me out of the yoga studio. You see, I didn't have insurance. I insisted they not call an ambulance or take me to the hospital. It took me twenty minutes just to slowly walk out to the car. It was so painful that I cried all the way there. Later Larry explained to me that back and neck injuries are almost as painful as child birth or kidney stones."

"Okay, so how does Larry tie into all of this?"

"My cousin knows Larry. She's a drug rep and apparently he owed her a favor. So she called the doc and asked him to help us out. He admitted he could not be helpful on the phone and suggested we Skype. I think that introducing the element of sight helped him diagnose better."

Stintson had been thinking about how to make up an excuse not to treat Katerina—until he saw her on Skype. His interest level rose when he saw how gorgeous she was.

"Well, after about five minutes on Skype, sweet Larry drove over to my cousin's house. He diagnosed me right then and there with a herniated disk. He was so kind and tender and reassuring. He promised me that in two days I would be much better. He brought me some oxycodone for the pain and made me promise not to move."

"She kept her promise and listened to the doctor instead of the pain medication," Stintson interjected.

"He checked on me every morning and evening. When I cried he held my hand and messaged my legs to help distract me from the pain. He was generous with the pain medication and always made sure I was ahead of the pain curve."

"I know pain," Stintson interjected. He was nervous about leg touching and references to pain medication. "I felt empathetic to her plight," Stintson said. "And did the pain subside after two days, darling?"

"Yes. True to your prediction," Katerina responded. "After five days I was feeling so much better. So I asked him how much I owed him."

"'Three million dollars,' I told her." Larry and Katerina laughed at the memory of the joke. The commander did not. Stintson continued, "Katerina's cousin has been great to work with and I owed her at least two huge favors."

"So, Larry just sort of forgot to bill me. He also didn't make any records because he didn't want an insurance company to ever deny me coverage or for a future employer to discriminate against me."

"Go Larry," the commander said with just enough mockery for Stintson to recognize—and for Katerina to overlook. Stintson knew the commander saw through his sham. He also sensed that he approved of his scheming. There was more wolf in Larry Stintson than the commander had given him credit for.

"So you stayed in Sioux Falls instead of going back to Chicago?" the commander asked.

"It's funny how things just kind of worked out. I got a job housesitting Dr. McKinley's home. He even pays his house sitters."

"I've not heard of McKinley, Larry," the commander said. "What does he practice?"

Stintson scrambled to answer the question. "Oh, he's a retired endocrinologist. You know, diabetes and stuff like that. Thus the *small* house. He travels a lot."

"But he's got a generous house sitter budget," replied the commander.

Stintson didn't care what the commander thought or said. Between criminals and schemers, their mutual secrets were safe. The fact was, there was no

Dr. McKinley, and the commander knew it. Larry Stintson rented the house Katerina was occupying. He told the landlord he would pay the rent in cash six months in advance if he would forgo the application process. Stintson was also funding the so-called housesitting wages.

"And then when it was time to get me off of the pain medication, Larry was there for me again."

"Fast-forward to summer time!" interrupted Stintson nervously. He did not want Katerina to divulge any details about his overtures to 'help' her kick her dependence on pain medication, so he took control of the conversation. "It had been a while since we'd seen each other. And, well, Katerina's cousin invited me and a few other doctors to her pharmaceutical company's big summer party. Imagine my surprise when Katerina was there!" Stintson had actually bribed her drug-rep cousin into inviting her. He had written more prescriptions for her company's medication in the last three weeks than he had written the whole year prior.

The commander was mildly impressed with Larry Stintson, but he was even more impressed with Katerina's cousin. He made a mental note to have Larry track her down. Anyone who would betray a cousin so deeply to achieve her business goals was somebody worth recruiting into his venture. He was sure he could double or triple her salary. The question was, would she relocate to Reno?

Katerina scooted even closer to Dr. Stintson, grabbed onto his arm, and latched onto him with a renewed admiration. It was the bad-boy effect that was turning her on tonight. It was a new dimension to her secret boyfriend. As the commander fielded a phone call, Katerina turned to Stintson and whispered in his ear. "Okay stud. You've always been good looking and I love your charm. Before today you were also sexy-powerful. But this new bad-boy thing's making you completely irresistible." She was whispering exactly what Cody and Nichols taught her to say. But as Katerina thought about it, she was convinced that she really felt some of it.

The SUV pulled into the Chelsea Crossing planned community and then wound through the streets to Bryant Way. The unnamed driver pulled into the garage and immediately closed the garage door. "Welcome," the commander said as he stepped out of the car. "Come in, come in," he encouraged as he held open the door to the house and gestured his three guests through it. "I can't imagine that you're hungry, but would anyone like a drink?"

"Got any coyote whiskey?" Katerina asked.

"Of course! Three Coyote 100 Light Whiskeys coming right up. None for the driver, however. Come to think of it, perhaps the driver can make the drinks." The driver busied himself at the wet bar.

"That's a great view," commented Katerina.

"Yes, as you look across the pond there, you see the Chelsea Crossing Country Club," explained the commander. "I'm a big fan of the water. I really wanted this home to be close to the water. Actually, it was a necessity."

"I know what you mean," Stintson said.

"Give me five minutes and then you'll *really* know what I mean," the commander said as he flipped a switch that made a fireplace roar to life. Strangely, the fire provided quite a bit of light to the room, but almost no heat. Gesturing to a huge television, the commander gave his instructions. "Katerina, will you please wait here while I have a private conversation with Larry? There are hundreds of channels and thousands of pay-per-view choices." Turning to the driver, the commander said, "Katerina gets to decide what to watch. No insisting on ESPN, you." As the commander walked toward the stairs with Stintson, he spontaneously called out over his shoulder, "No yoga channels for you, Katerina!"

Gesturing toward the upper floor of the home, the commander said, "Let's start upstairs because that's where I could really use your help." The men climbed the stairs and Stintson immediately noticed that all of the bedrooms were missing their doors. As he stepped into the first bedroom on the left, he saw that it contained two desks with computer monitors and two people were working at those desks. "This is where my people listen. They sit here all day and night using technology to listen to phone calls, intercept emails, and spy on online interactions, just waiting for people to divulge their personal data, their Social Security numbers being the most valuable. Right now these two are applying for loans using the data we've managed to uncover."

"So you're not only a high-profile elected official, but you're also the ringleader in an identity theft cartel?"

"Cartel is such an ugly word. We prefer *enterprise*," the commander said. "But as I was saying, people are careless with their information and we're pretty good at waiting in the wings and intercepting it when they share it."

Stintson thought for a moment and then said, "Name, date of birth, address, telephone number, and even employment history should be pretty easy to find, I suspect."

"Yes. All of that data's easy to uncover. People share that information in cell phone calls, text messages, and through smart phone apps. Have you ever texted a PIN to your wife?"

Stintson squirmed and then answered, "Well, um. Well, yes, I—"

"Don't worry, Larry. We all have. And I love it when someone in Chelsea Crossing does it. If they send a little extra information along, then we know it's for a bank account, cell phone account, or even the cable TV provider. Sometimes we drain an account. Other times we just snoop to uncover other useful data."

"Everything's a lead? Everything's a clue?"

"Exactly. Sometimes we can hack into their computers via their Wi-Fi signal. We're patiently 'listening' to about thirty percent of Chelsea Crossing right now."

"And it's the Social Security number that's the real catch?"

"Yes. Those nine numbers are the mother lode, and that's where I'd like your help. Patients divulge that data to you without even batting an eye."

"I must have thousands of Social Security numbers in my records," offered Stintson. "But if a bunch of my patients get hit by your scheme, some data analyst somewhere is going to notice."

"Right. So start by looking at some old paper records. Find three people you treated in the ER six years ago. The kind you treat for a sprain or simple injury and you never see them again. You'll be the last person they think of, if they even remember you."

"Actually, I have to keep kids' records until they are twenty years old — and we collect their parents' Social Security numbers."

"Larry, I'm impressed," the commander said. Very cunning. Very canine."

"If I look back at some records from fifteen years ago, I bet we would find a gold mine. I've got some ex-employees I would love to see cleaned out as well. Come to think of it, there's a computer consultant who charged me about thirty-five grand for a computer system that never worked. Let's start with him. I'll email his information in the morning."

"No email, Larry. Never email in this business. We always hand-delivered paper or digital pictures of the documents on an SD card. You take the pictures with a digital camera, but never use a smart phone. You just bring us the SD card. We take care of the rest."

"I'll swing by the office tonight and pull the files on the first three."

"I can't wait to see them," the commander said. "Now, if you happen to hear of the death of one of your past patients, send that data over right away. It's a great time to steal somebody's identity." The commander walked out of the desk-filled bedroom. The commander walked Stintson into a larger room that contained four desks. Employees occupied all of them. "This was obviously intended to be a master bedroom, but I like it so much better as an office. My guess is the people we have working in here will bring in about two million dollars this year. Of course, I have expenses. They get a commission of about ten percent, and that's half of the same commission I'm offering you," the commander said. Of the money we make on the data you bring to us, you get twenty percent."

Larry Stintson was ecstatic, as the commander explained more. "Now, let's think beyond your practice, doctor. Your office at the South Dakota Medical Board contains some excellent data on a wealthy cross-section of our society."

"Yes," Stintson said slowly and softly. "We license about two thousand doctors."

"What about physician assistants?"

"A few hundred of those, too. We're also in charge of physical therapists, dieticians, athletic trainers and respiratory therapists. We process paperwork for dentists, but nobody has done much work on policing them yet."

"What about physicians who completed their residencies here and then moved on to other states? They would never suspect you."

"Wow, Commander. You really know how to slice and dice the data."

"I'm a small businessman, Larry. I have to think outside the box to stay ahead of my larger rivals," the commander joked. "If we tapped into the identities of three doctors in Sioux Falls this year, we would never show up on the radar. Let's also tap into three from Rapid City, two from Pierre, and two or three from smaller outlying towns."

"Sounds good," Stintson said. He was thinking about all of the people who had held professional medical licenses in South Dakota in the last few years or decades, and he liked the possibilities. "Let's be highly aggressive with doctors who have moved out of South Dakota. There are a few big storage areas down at the office with those old paper records. I can hit that one night with a camera. I can collect a hundred records in an hour."

"Great, we'll cherry-pick the best ones, and we'll make sure we spread our work around the county," the commander said. "Okay. You've seen enough of the top floor. Let's go look at the basement. You know how important a diversified investment portfolio is, don't you, Larry?"

"Sure. Let's see what you're doing to spread your risk, Commander," the increasingly greedy doctor responded. "First we have legitimate and legal real estate investing. Second, you showed me some highly criminal identity theft operations. I can't wait to see what's next." The two men left the room and started down the stairs. "Let me guess. Are you completing the hat trick with a little uranium enrichment in the basement? You know, uranium's kind of neutral because it can be used for good and evil." Stintson thought his humor was phenomenal.

"No, but I like the sound of that," the commander said in a serious tone. "Let's explore that. You had to take a lot of chemistry and physics in school, right Doctor?"

"Yes. I took honors physics and got straight A's," Stintson said as they descended the stairs. "My professors called me in and begged me to declare physics as my major. They talked to me about graduate school, internships and potential employers."

"You didn't bite?"

"Never. I've had my eyes on being an orthopedic surgeon since a weekend back in 1985 when ten of us high school kids went on a waterskiing trip on Mark Twain Lake in Missouri," reminisced Stintson. "We were guests of my friend, Vince Bernd. I had no idea what his dad did for work, and I didn't care, initially. We had two boats; we skied all day, and we ate like kings. His dad was really cool, driving us all around the lake and improving his suntan by the hour. He had an ice chest filled with those Bartles and Jaymes wine coolers and he let us each drink *just one* out on the lake that day. Those drinks were brand-new and all the rage.

"Oh, yes, I remember. The wine coolers of the eighties. God bless the Reagan Years!" the commander said as the stairs reached the basement and the men stepped into a plain, unfinished space. "So you saw the good life and found out this guy was an orthopedic surgeon?"

"Sort of. That's only part of it," Stintson said. "The money and the lifestyle was just the tip of the iceberg. Remember I grew up in a wealthy home, too. We had a boat, but my dad would never let teenagers drink. Money was only part of it," continued Stintson. "When we got back to the lake-side cabin that night, we docked our two boats right next to two others. It turns out that my friend Vince had a twenty-one-year-old sister, and she had brought ten tan, bikini-clad friends. Of course, they wanted nothing to do with any of us high school boys. But you should've seen how they threw themselves at Vince's forty-something dad."

"Wasn't his wife around?"

"No. She couldn't make it down for some reason, but she should've been there. Six of those college girls were sitting around that big kitchen table. They were sitting there in bikinis, clinging to his every word, flashing smiles, making jokes and laughing."

"Sounds like they were drinking."

"Not as much as they had hoped. The under-aged guys had taken all of the wine coolers out onto the dock and the girls were glad to let them have the drinks. It meant they would keep their distance. But I was so interested in what was going on with Vince's dad, I stayed in the cabin, put on my Sony Walkman and pretended to listen to music while I read Hit Parade magazine. But, I was really listening like a hawk to everything those girls said."

"So what was it?"

"His mystique, plain and simple. The first ingredient was confidence, not money. But he also had money and some charm. More than anything he was so accustomed to having the world revolve around *him*. The man just knew how to make it happen. That night, I learned just how much women love mystique."

"So, how did he decide which of those college girls to sleep with?"

"None of them! He insisted that Vince, his teenage son, sleep in the master bedroom room with him that night. Vince got the king-size bed and his dad opted for a pullout sofa. They watched MTV until two in the morning," recounted Stintson. "It was Vince's job to answer the door. The first knock came about a half-hour before midnight. When Vince answered the door, the bikini-clad girl's eyes went from wild and horny to confused in about two seconds. It took her an additional second to hide the four wine coolers behind her back. After claiming she had the wrong room, she retreated."

"How many more girls knocked on his door that night?" the commander asked.

"Only one," Stintson said. "But still, not bad considering the twenty-plus-year age difference. The second girl didn't bring any booze, but she had put on a *negligée*. When Vince answered the door she was so eager to sneak in she started to, you know, just kind of slide in through the door so the other guests wouldn't notice. She was in the room before she realized that a teenager had answered the door, and not Vince's dad. She had the audacity to ask Vince where his dad was. He responded, 'Oh, he's on the phone with my mom.' That shut her down, and when Vince opened the door she looked at him defiantly and then stormed away."

"An entitled little princess, eh?"

"I guess."

"I hate entitled people, the commander said flatly. "I've worked for every cent. Sure, I've had some amazing breaks and I had the good fortune of the military to teach me discipline. But I've never just expected something. I don't mean to be offensive to you, Larry. I know the trust fund has treated you well."

"Yes. I admit. It paid for school and an Audi I drove around campus. I didn't have to pay back student loans."

"Oh, come on Larry. I asked around. You're still drawing fifteen thousand dollars a month from it. That's on top of what you make as a surgeon."

"I just sock it away into savings and investments," Stintson said. " I clear about thirty-five thousand a month from my medical practice, and that's taking most Fridays off."

"Well, let's see if we can tack on another hundred thousand this year with what we've been talking about," the commander said. "By the way, not a word of this to your dear Katerina upstairs. Are we clear?"

"Yes. I keep a lot of secrets from her."

"Like the true identity of the owner of the so-called McKinley home she lives in?" the commander asked.

"For starters, yes." Stintson surveyed the subterranean level of the home. He was more curious to understand this final investment than he was about bragging about his girlfriend. "Now tell me why you call this barren basement an investment. I'm dumbfounded."

"Do you see all of this extra plumbing?" asked the commander as he pointed to sets of hot and cold water spigots and extra drains.

"Sure. And now that you mention the plumbing, as I look around, I can see a whole bunch of electrical outlets in here. If I didn't know better, I would say you're planning for hot tubs and big-screen TVs. If this is some kind of Jacuzzi sports bar, I'll invest emotionally tonight. Then I'll invest financially when I deliver the check tomorrow!"

"Again, a brilliant idea, Larry," the commander said somewhat condescendingly. "But it has nothing to do with hot tubs or TVs. But, we will be moving a lot of water in and out from that pond out there. It's critical to be close to a good water source like that. This will actually be a manufacturing facility of sorts in the near future."

"Really? What's your product?"

"Pharmaceuticals," the commander said as he produced a little baggie with a dozen pills and slapped them in Stintson's hand. "This is for you. It's that MDMA Katerina likes. There's enough there for both of you to have an amazing time."

Stintson thought about whether or not he would have time to party with Katerina this evening. "Thanks for the junk," Stintson said as realized that he wouldn't have enough time to indulge tonight. Not if he wanted to be clear-headed in the office tomorrow. It would have to wait until the weekend. No matter. The way Katerina had held onto him in the Commander's car, he knew he would still have a lot of fun.

"We have one other property close by that's already manufacturing a lot of product," the commander explained. He omitted the fact that the second property was the house next door. "We have a high-quality lab that produces some good meth in our own special recipe. Also it's safer; you know I don't want anybody getting hurt in my little venture—unless they deserve it." The commander squared up his shoulders and stepped to within inches of the doctor's face and stared him straight in the eye. "I hope, for your sake, Larry Stintson, that you understand what I mean."

"Nobody needs to get hurt," Stintson said with a surprising amount of confidence.

"The lab in this house will have to wait, perhaps for six months or more, to be operational," the commander said. "Somebody on my team got a little sloppy, so we have to endure a delay. And when my guy got clumsy, Ann Higgins started poking around and passing along clues to people. He has paid for his mistake and he got hurt, completely hurt."

Stintson knew exactly what "completely hurt" meant. He did not want to dwell on the grim subject, so he steered the conversation. "Who did Ann Higgins pass on the clues to?"

"Troy Stoker, that psychiatrist," the commander said.

Stintson responded with a smirk of confidence on his face. "Well, that's interesting. He recently used a Taser on one of his patients. Let me work this angle for you, Commander. We may be able to shut him down in a matter of days." Stintson thought for a moment and realized that yanking his license may harm Stoker, but it would not shut him up. Who knows, if the psychiatrist had more time on his hands, he may use the time to dabble even deeper into the Ann Higgins investigation. "Are you talking about eliminating Troy Stoker? It might be the only way to go."

"It's too risky," the commander said. "As much as I would like to take him to meet the coyotes on Lake Vermillion, I can't. First, most people would put two and two together and intensify the search for a person brazen enough to kill two respected community members. But more importantly, Stoker has a good friend, Errol Rivera, a doctor at the VA Hospital. This Rivera guy makes me nervous. First, he would stop at nothing to avenge Stoker's death. He would hang onto every clue like a leach; he has access to resources and friends that you really don't want to get involved with. Some of my people are carefully digging around on this Rivera guy. We can't find much about him. We know some of his military history. Of course he went to medical school and completed a residency. But after that, there are lots of question marks. Sure he works at the VA, but a nurse there tells us that there are weeks and months when Rivera is away on assignment. She doesn't know where these assignments take Rivera, but she also knows that she should never ask."

"I've never heard of Rivera," Stintson said. "We don't monitor activities at the VA much."

The commander ignored his comment and continued, "One of my guys talked to a friend who shoots out at the Garretson Sportsmen's Club. He said Rivera used to spend a lot of time out there. He's a great shot—with both hands. Do you know what that means, Larry?"

"Somebody in the military taught him to shoot with both hands? He's had some special kind of military training?"

"It goes a little deeper than that." The commander started walking toward the stairs. "I think Rivera's training is a few notches above standard military grade. We're not going to awaken that Cuban dragon."

CHAPTER 44

SOUTH DAKOTA MEDICAL BOARD OFFICES, SIOUX FALLS

As Brian Berg stood to leave a victorious meeting of the South Dakota Medical Board, he was celebrating the four letters of concern and $10,000 in fines he had been able to report last week. The board also suspended a paramedic's license for thirty days because he was recently convicted of driving under the influence of alcohol. He had to commit to counseling and participating in a recovery program. However, the board had failed, yet again, to bring up the issue of the surgeon who had lost his fourth big malpractice lawsuit in six years.

Brian Berg carried a pager because the state had refused his request for a cell phone for the last nine years, always re-affirming that a cell phone was above his pay grade. Nevertheless, the state did issue him a two-way pager that he would use to send and receive texts. And, as he walked down the hall he felt it vibrate in pocket.

Urgent meeting in board president office now

The message came from a phone number he did not recognize. Berg hurried to the office expecting to find the awkward Larry Stintson sitting there. As he rounded the corner he was shocked to see the intense blue eyes of a man he recognized but had never met. He was sitting in the chair behind the desk and Larry Stintson was nowhere to be found.

"Brian, we have an urgent issue and I need your expertise. It's so hush-hush not even your boss, Stintson, can know about it. All he knows, is you've been temporarily reassigned to work directly with me."

"Okay," was all Berg managed to say.

"Troy Stoker. What do you know about him?"

"Psychiatrist. Doesn't like to give up psychotherapy records." Berg's sentences were short. He was nervous as he sat in front of one of the most powerful men in the state. "Actually, Stoker sends incomplete records. He *hides* the psychotherapy notes. He says his action comply with the law."

"Well, we have a new complaint about him and it opens up a whole new world.

"I want you to get some officers and go to his office. Take a photocopy of the South Dakota Codified Law, chapter thirty-six, with you. It will definitely get you in the door. He has a new complaint against him. We're saying we received it from the state disability office." The commander stood from Stintson's chair, came around to the front of the desk, and sat on it. He handed Berg an envelope with a copy of a trumped up complaint letter. "Here's that letter." The commander paused for a moment and then he said, "You're telling me that he's refused to give you medical records recently?"

"Yes," Berg replied. "He says they're psychotherapy notes and claims there's another process for handling them."

"I don't care what he says about the law or his interpretation of some fabricated loophole. I want you to seize *all* those patient records. Don't take no for an answer. This is life and death, and use non-lethal force if you must. If Stoker complains, I want you to waive that chapter thirty-six in his face and tell him to call his attorney."

"Got it," Berg grunted.

"This Stoker's a dangerous man," the commander said, "so, I have here three surveillance devices I need you to place in his office." The commander held up the first device as he smiled wildly. "His receptionist's desk should be easy to bug. Just get this device stuck under the counter as close as you can to her." The commander held up the second small device. Your goal is to get this bug right in his office. Just stick it under the front of his desk or on the bottom of a chair. Just put it somewhere where it will not be seen."

"And the third one?" Berg asked.

"That's in case you lose one of the other two." The commander then stepped to the door and closed it. Turning back to Berg, he said, "Brian. I need to make this abundantly clear. It would be a violation of legal protocol for you to tell *anybody* about our meeting, especially Stoker. If you tell a single soul that we have spoken, you will end up unemployed and indicted for obstruction of justice. Do you understand?"

"Of course," Berg whispered as he swallowed hard. He believed all the lies the man with the intense eyes told him.

"Okay, Brian, Sheriff Stewart is assigning the men as we speak. Get over there, pick up your deputies, and go get us some ears on this Stoker character."

Berg started to leave the office, when he had a question come up in his mind. So, he stopped, turned back and asked, "Oh, sir? What do I call you? Do I use your name or do I call you by your title?"

"I'm an old Navy vet. My friends call me Commander."

CHAPTER 45

Dr. Stoker's 1:30 p.m. patient had failed to show up, so it gave him an opportunity to get caught up on some administrative tasks. As he opened his email and scrolled down through his messages for urgent matters, he noticed a new email from Aaron West at the Minnehaha County jail. He opened the message and began to read. The nurse reported that they got another 'coyote' patient last night. He had mentioned the name, Nichols, at least six times, too. The new person's name was Michael Briggs. West finished the email by giving Stoker a phone number and asking Stoker to call him.

Stoker picked up his phone and called the number. West picked up on the fourth ring.

"Hey, Stoker. I really think we're onto something here. Is there a reward for me if we catch these bad guys?"

"If there is, you're going to want to receive it anonymously," the doctor responded. "Can you meet me this evening? We need your help to track this guy once he makes bail. These guys are disappearing and we want to know where."

"Sure, Doc. Where's the secret meeting spot? West asked. "The earlier the better. I work the night shift."

"How about the Dawley Theater, the southwest corner of the parking lot? Does five o'clock work?

"Sure thing. I'll be the guy wearing sunglasses at night and wearing a Kansas City Royals baseball cap."

Three hours later, Stoker and West met as planned. Stoker drove Allie's car because his classic Bronco tended not to blend in. Aaron West jumped into the passenger's seat of Allie's Dodge Durango and Stoker said, "Thanks for meeting me, Aaron." Stoker handed the nurse an old pen from a pharmaceutical company. "Unscrew it. Go ahead and take a look. See what's inside."

As West emptied the contents of the pen, out slid eight small, white pills, a colored medication capsule, and a device that looked like a sophisticated medical injection system.

"Okay, Stoker. Are you really asking me to drug this guy?"

"Only a little! But I'm actually asking you to *bug* this guy!"

"You really want me to bug this Briggs guy? Is that even legal?"

"Don't worry. We've got all the warrants covered. Besides, I'm *not* a cop. This is just my little experiment. I want to see where this guy goes when he gets out of jail. Don't you?"

"Absolutely," West said with conviction. "We need to know."

"Stoker held up one of the pills. "This colored capsule is a GPS location device. It would normally give us about forty-eight hours to track him."

"Actually, with the lack of fiber in the jail food, you'll get seventy-two hours," replied the nurse.

"Well, that's good. We want to slow down his digestion. And just to make sure we get the full three or four days, we'll also have him take these eight pills, too. They contain diphenoxylate hydrochloride and atropine sulfate."

"To constipate him," the nurse confirmed.

"Give him four tablets before bed tonight, and make sure he gets a little snack, too."

"And then four more with breakfast?" chimed in West. "I bet you get a few extra hours of pleasurable constipation for our friend, Briggs."

"Exactly," Stoker said. "It's a little bit higher than the normal dose, but I want to make sure that you understand, Aaron, that it's a fraction of the amount that could ever possibly kill this man. As you may know, the dosing is usually four times per day. But we only have two chances to get these pills into this guy. So, I'm simply doubling the dose for two administrations and that should be fine."

"So, what's this injector device?" West asked. "Does it go in his shoulder, butt or thigh?"

"Actually, we have two tracking devices in case he loses one of them or one of them fails. This one needs to go in his shoe," Stoker said. The nurse looked dejected. He loved to give tricky shots and he loved to see the supposedly tough guys at the jail cower and squirm when they got their shots. Stoker noticed his disappointment. "We thought about letting you inject it in a more permanent place, like his butt. However, we have no idea which bastards this guy works for and what technology they have for bug sniffing—even if they have to do some sniffing around the anal pore. If he works for some really bad guys, they would kill him if they find out he's bugged. That would alert this Nichols scumbag, his coyotes, and whoever else is behind all of this. Right now, we don't want them to know that we're on to them. After four or five days, we'll know where he is and we'll want him to get rid of the bugs so the bad guys don't find out we're onto them."

Stoker further explained, "To get this device into his shoe, just roll him over onto his stomach and tell him he'll feel a pinch in his thigh. As you pinch his leg hard to distract him, just inject this into the heel of his shoe. It's a GPS tracking device about the size of a large sewing needle with an array of microchips and nanotechnology in the slightly larger diameter blunt end."

"Cool," West said. "Tonight, I'll pass medications and give him his so-called shot. I'm sure Briggs will make bail in the morning so you begin tracking him. But we'll feed and medicate him first."

"Great. Thanks, Aaron. Let's see where they're hiding these guys. Let's just hope it's not in a bone yard."

CHAPTER 46

At 6:57 p.m., Aaron West, RN, arrived at the Minnehaha County jail, walked into the clinic, and started his normal activities. Distributing medications was one of the first tasks the nurses completed during each shift. West called in Michael Briggs as his third patient.

"So, Briggs. Tell me about your fear of coyotes. What is that all about?" asked the nurse. The patient's tired eyes immediately filled with fear. "It's just stuff," Briggs lied. "You know, sorta' like the boogeyman."

"Okay. Here are some medications that should help you get all of the junk out of your system." The inmate downed a multi-vitamin, acetaminophen, and the GPS tracking bug Stoker had provided. Of course, West also administered the four diphenoxylate hydrochloride and atropine sulfate pills.

"Okay, Briggs. Let me have you jump up on this table right here and roll over onto your stomach." The patient obeyed. "I'm going to give you a little shot right here in your leg. It's about the most painless shot you've ever had." The patient said nothing, but he closed his eyes in anticipation of the pain. West grabbed the injector and shoved the device into the rubber heel of Brigg's high-top Nike basketball sneaker as he pinched the back of his thigh. The inmate winced momentarily, as West said, "All done! That wasn't so bad was it?"

"No, it was barely a pinch. Nice touch dude. What is that stuff you're injecting into me?"

"If you really want to know the details, it's called cyanocobalamin. We give you a thousand micrograms to reduce the risk of a certain type of brain damage you can get from chronic alcohol use," West lied. "I heard you make bail tomorrow."

"Yes. I'm outta here!"

"Great. That's mission accomplished for you then, right?"

"Mission accomplished!"

"Me too!" West said as he smiled.

CHAPTER 47

It was 4:00 a.m., and Troy Stoker had healed sufficiently from the assault-related injuries in his office. It was time to hunt and Errol Rivera was more than ready. Stoker did not hunt like most people, and he was passing along his methods to the insatiably curious and adventuresome Rivera. Stoker's main hunting tools were his compound bow, arrows, and backcountry skis. He would ski for miles, into vast prairies of South Dakota – into places others never thought to access on foot or four-wheeler. Stoker did most of his hunting within 150 miles of Sioux Falls, but occasionally he would make a pilgrimage to the Black Hills on the western side of the state.

A year ago he had invited his friend and fellow physician, Errol Rivera, to join him. The two became acquaintances after meeting at a medical association meeting. However, when they bumped into each other on the rifle range at the Garretson Sportsmen's Club, the acquaintance evolved into a sincere friendship. After guiding Rivera on one of Stoker's skiing and bow-hunting expeditions near Watertown, South Dakota, the two became enduring friends. They filled Rivera's deer tag on that hunt in November. However, the busy schedules of two doctors had prohibited them from bagging Stoker's deer and they only had a few days left until the season ended on January fifteenth.

Rivera was a refreshing personality. He was independent, fiercely patriotic, and a student of history. His studies of dynasties, revolutions, wars, and cultures had taught him to see patterns and processes, which he consistently pointed out in medicine and politics. He was also quick to point these patterns out in human behavior—including his own. While Stoker, at forty-three years of age, was still a relatively young doctor, Dr. Rivera was in his mid-fifties. He had seen a lot of war, pain, and suffering in his time—a lot more than Stoker had ever fathomed. Rivera loved Stoker's hunting strategy because the process was more engaging and more successful than traditional rifle hunting. More importantly, it was more primal. Taking risks to go deep into the woods for days at a time rekindled Rivera's zest for life. Stoker *stalked* big game—instead of waiting in a tree stand for his prey to happen by. This invigorated certain senses and an essence within Rivera that had slumbered for more than two decades.

At 4:00 a.m. Stoker and Rivera exited Interstate 29, again near Watertown, in Rivera's 2008 Chevy Silverado pickup. They had parked the truck and removed their backpacks, skis, and bows from the truck bed. Each strapped on a pistol—to only be used against the coyotes, which were a real threat, as Stoker had learned through personal experience a few years back.

As they locked into their backcountry skis, Rivera hit his keychain clicker and locked all the doors. "Okay, Troy. I just locked her up. There's no turning back now."

"We're saying goodbye to shelter, food, electricity, and fuel in six degrees below zero!" Stoker said. "I love it."

Rivera smiled as he pulled on his jacket and headwear in a winter camouflage pattern. "I wouldn't have it any other way. The testosterone is recharging already."

The two doctors set medicine and the world behind them and became scientists, survivalists, and students. The winter environment was the instructor and they paid attention with all of their senses—including intuition—the famous sixth sense.

During the first few miles of their ski neither man said much. They enjoyed the solitude, the beauty of the snow-covered landscape, as well as the majesty of the stars in the sky. In fact, between Stoker and Rivera, the hunt was mostly silent, until after the kill. In part, it was because tracking game was a silent activity. However, there was something about bagging an elk or deer that opened Rivera up emotionally. After hours of delicate and challenging work, the neurochemistry of success unbolted Errol Rivera's psyche and allowed him to talk about life, failure, success, God, country, and love.

On their last hunting expedition, the final twelve hours had shocked Stoker. He gained deep insight into the experiences that had shaped the man, Errol Rivera. In the frigid winter winds of South Dakota Stoker burned a deep and abiding respect for the man who kept pace with him for miles of grueling skiing—despite a decade of age difference.

Errol Rivera became a doctor to atone for his sins. He spent four years as a black ops helicopter pilot in Central America in the early 1990s. He witnessed nightly scenes of grizzly violence and blood curdling mayhem. "It was a little war nobody knew about and I was tired of killing people," Rivera told Stoker as they silently skied through a pristine thicket of pine trees. "That's what I did for a living. I killed people. I killed a lot of people. The bottom line was, I came back to the states and I was mental protoplasm of pandemonium, bedlam, and chaos. A lot of people who got killed were not combatants. They were just collateral damage.

"I'd get in a UH-1 Huey aircraft that had no seats in the back and we would strap on night vision goggles. Thanks to my time in the 82nd Airborne before pilot training, I was one of the top-rated night vision pilots in the U.S. military. I'd strap into the aircraft, and right behind me would sit an El Salvadorian Air Force officer, because this was an El Salvadorian helicopter. It wasn't U.S. marked even though it came from the U.S. And for all intents and purposes, it was American. But for legal purposes, it belonged to the El Salvadorian Air Force. I was just the officer's advisor. Sure, I was the pilot in command of the aircraft, but only as an advisor."

"So, you were walking a fine line as you took orders in the jungles," Stoker said.

"No Troy, I did *not* walk the fine line. We crossed it and we knew it. In the back of our helicopters, attached to a big cable, were four to six El Salvadorian paratroopers with a variety of weapons, like grenade launchers, M16s, stubby sixties. Those soldiers also wore night vision goggles. Our job was to fly about two to three hundred feet above ground level, over the tops of mountains, and find the guerillas either carrying out their operations or in their basecamps, and we would do I and D."

"Interdiction and destruction," Stoker said.

"Thanks to bladder tanks or wing tanks I could stay in the air and harass them for up to six hours. The soldiers would drop four-millimeter grenades on their targets. We killed a lot of commie guerillas, but more than anything we made them move along. That's what eventually broke their backs. They couldn't find any sanctuary and they had to give up in Central America.

"The problem is when you're wearing night vision goggles you can pick up camp fires, lanterns, or anything that emits heat. But night vision goggles can't tell the difference between an enemy's kerosene lantern and the innocent civilian villagers' cooking fires. Sometimes we were wrong. Too often we were wrong.

"The commanding officers would try to make us feel better by pointing out how the Air Force flew their A-37 Dragonflies and dropped their daisy cutter bombs. They would claim that those guys did twice the damage to innocents that we did. Well, I wasn't doing the math. I was thinking about the real people—the babies, moms, and teenagers—who were innocent, peaceful human beings."

It was at this point, back during Stoker and Rivera's November hunt, when Stoker's psychiatrist wisdom kicked in. He sensed that Rivera had told him enough for that first trip. Rivera's history was on the surface now and processing that history while doing battle with nature and the elements was more therapeutic than any psychiatrist's office or anti-depressant.

This January day was a new day, however. Rivera had said nothing so far about the mental scars he bore from his time in Central America. The plan was to ski the first two or three hours in the early morning darkness. Their course started in a straight line to the East for two miles across the prairie until they came to a little-known Sioux Indian war shrine. Few ever visited it in the summer and nobody visited it in the winter. After paying their respects they changed course to the northeast and began to ascend a hill while entering a forest, which contained a surprising outcropping of pine trees in the middle.

The smell of the pines was invigorating and Rivera belted out *Oh Tannenbaum* with a jovial tone of sarcasm. Christmas had passed a few weeks ago, but the trees were still just as glorious. "That's some excellent German for a speaker of *español*," Stoker joked. Rivera knew every word in German and Stoker could not help but wonder if Rivera's history included extensive language training.

By mile six, the pre-dawn sky revealed some soft hues of pink and orange, and the two men knew it was time to watch for game. They stopped to check out deer tracks and scat. As they wove their way silently through the trees and across vast expanses, they came to a spot where the snow was packed down. "It looks like a dozen deer bedded down here last night," whispered Stoker. "This must be home base for this little family."

"Perfect," Rivera replied. "Let's figure out where to set up, then let's start making sure we have food and firewood for the next thirty-six hours or so."

Stoker and Rivera skied downwind about two miles from the site where the deer had endured the cold of the previous night. The sky was now completely light and the sun was about to make its first appearance. They would return to this spot later hoping to intercept a big buck as it returned to its bedding site. After skiing across a small frozen lake that Stoker knew well, they settled on a camping spot next to a patch of trees. They removed their skis and backpacks and set up their tent. Rivera prepared a small fire ring.

"Let's go get firewood and food," Stoker said. He slung on his lighter backpack. In the trees there were plenty of fallen branches that would fuel a small fire for two or three hours. Stoker knew just where to dig in the snow to uncover certain plants. "If you know where to look, you will find a few select pockets where nature helps certain plants to winter over."

Over the next two hours, the men found Miner's lettuce, wild mustard, some roots, wild fennel and other greens. They filled individual pockets in Stoker's backpack with each plant. The vegetation would be a major staple for lunch and dinner that day.

"Time to fish!" exclaimed Stoker.

"Fish? That wasn't part of the plan. I hate fishing."

"Well then, I guess starving is now part of the plan," Stoker joked.

"Lead the way," Rivera said with a slight murmur in his voice. "Are there any rivers around here?"

"Nope."

"Where are we going to catch these fish?"

"Do you remember that small lake we just skied across a few hours back?"

Rivera gave a slight nod.

"There are some hungry fish under that ice just waiting for a morsel of food."

"Well, Doctor Genius. I did not see an ice auger in any of our gear."

"Ah yes," Stoker said. "Nature has already taken care of that."

"Now this I've got to see. Lead the way."

The sun was now up in the clear blue sky and its rays bathed the solitary acres of expanse that were Stoker and Rivera's hunting ground for the next thirty-two hours. As they arrived back at the lake Rivera skied toward the middle.

"Hey, Errol. Something opened up our fishing hole over there." Stoker pointed to a bank on their right." Even from a distance the men could see that a small fragment in the lake was not frozen over.

Stoker and Rivera proceeded across the lake and ascended its modest bank, which was barely discernible in the snow. They removed their skis and walked another twenty yards where there was a gaping twelve-foot hole in the lake right next to the bank.

"A hot spring?" River asked

"Perhaps a lukewarm one," Stoker responded. "A hot spring would emit steam. But, this one is warm enough to keep this small section from freezing over. Its warmth also appeals to the fish. I think they congregate here a little more."

Stoker removed his backpack. He opened it and removed a long silver tube, which caught Rivera's attention yet again. "It's a two-weight fly-fishing rod," Stoker said.

Rivera looked disheartened. "That looks complicated. Does this mean that I'm going to sit here picking my nose for hours while you do your fly-fishing ballet?"

"No," said Stoker. You are going to catch the fish. It's quite simple, especially with these short casts. The fish can't see us because of the ice. This will be almost too easy."

Rivera watched as Stoker assembled the seemingly complex system of rod, real, line, leader, and tippet. But, he left the fly off. "Let me teach you how to use this. The physics are simple." With two minutes of practice, Rivera was maneuvering the fly-line gracefully. Stoker observed that Rivera was a natural. He wondered if Rivera had fly-fishing skills he was hiding from Stoker. Taking the rod back from Rivera, Stoker tied on a small fly.

"How do fish see that little thing?" Rivera asked.

"I don't know. Ask a veterinarian," chided Stoker. "Now take this rod and just give it a little flip out toward the water. A light flip mind you."

Rivera sent the line gently sailing. "I can't see my bait."

"We never call it 'bait' in fly-fishing. It's a fly. I can't see it either, but I know you sent it out to gently land in the water. I put a fly on it that will sink slowly and does not need much finesse. Let's just wait."

"Not much finesse? You mean a dumb guy's fly?"

"No, it is a beginner's fly. You wouldn't start out my helicopter training with a Blackhawk would you?"

"No way," Rivera said. "I'd start you off with five hours using a remote control, small-scale model and a bunch of hours in a flight simulator. Then, just maybe, I would let you into the co-pilot's seat of a basic training bird."

"Right. It's the same idea. Give it just a light twitch with your wrist," coached Stoker.

Rivera followed the instructions.

"Okay, now just wait."

In a flash the line went tight and began dancing around. "What do I do? What do I do?" Rivera asked as he instinctively pulled up on the rod to set the hook.

"Just keep the rod tip up and let it bounce around a bit. Some of these little fish have delicate mouths. We want to tire them out first, and reel them once they're exhausted."

Rivera continued to hold the rod with the clumsy curiosity of a teenager driving a car for the first time. "Keep that tip up," Stoker said. "You're doing just fine." After thirty seconds the fish had exhausted much of its battle strength.

"Bring him in slowly, just a little," Stoker coached.

Rivera reeled gently and the extra pressure on the line re-awakened the fish's fight. The rod bounced vigorously again and Rivera stopped reeling. After fifteen seconds the fish had again lost its energy.

"Okay, Errol. Bring him in gently."

As Rivera pulled the fish toward them, it fought a little, but it was far too spent to offer any more challenge.

"Well, you've managed to land yourself a medium sized crappie. You'll need a few more for a meal; but that's a good start."

Stoker removed the hook and laid the fish on the snow. The fish flopped a few more times before Rivera picked up the fish and slapped it over the top of its head with the butt of his hunting knife to kill it quickly.

"Okay," Stoker said. "Let's wait a minute or two for the remaining fish to forget the frenzy. They forget about the excitement if you give them a minute," Stoker said. "Let's see if we can get a few more for a meal. With ten of these fish we're set. If we catch any trout that's a bonus. I brought some great spices, plenty of butter, and some breading to make our meal satisfactory. I'm not gourmet, but for two guys trying to survive, it'll be all right."

Rivera cast his imperceptible fly into the water again. This time, however, no fish responded. Stoker began to coach him on recasting and a few other matters of basic technique. However, Rivera was growing impatient with Stoker's mentoring and he casted a few times with an obvious increase in skill. *He's done this before*, thought Stoker

"Let me guess," Stoker said. "They taught you to fly fish in the Army?"

"Yes," Rivera replied. "It was after medical school." Rivera paused for a moment and recast his line. "I received some amazing training from some talented people, just to keep me in the military. Ironically, I really liked the military and didn't need the extra incentives. However, that singular training experience changed my life." Rivera did a quick double-haul cast and landed the fly within six inches of the edge of the ice. Then Rivera smiled and with an emphasized Cuban accent he said, "They made me offers I just couldn't refuse."

Rivera gave the line a couple of twitches and the rod came to life. He began reeling in his second fish of the day. "Your rod is much more predictable than the bamboo fly rods we learned to make in survival school."

Over the course of forty-five minutes Rivera refused to allow Stoker a turn to fish. The mysterious Rivera caught seven more crappie and a surprisingly large trout. Just a few yards from the edge of the water, Stoker built a small fire and began to prepare and cook the fish. To complete the meal, Stoker made a tea of roots. He concocted a salad from the Miner's lettuce and other ingredients; and then he topped it with some rosemary croutons and a little balsamic vinaigrette from his backpack. "Thank you, Troy," Rivera complimented as he ate. "A phenomenal survival meal."

The doctors spent the afternoon on their skis and with their bows at the ready. As they scouted for big bucks they occasionally saw them off in the distance. They were confident that their patience would pay off. As the sun began to sink in the late afternoon they made their way back to the deer bedding area they had identified that morning. They sat quietly about ten feet within the tree line and waited for the herd to return. During the hour when the sunset painted the sky with brilliant hues of orange, purple and yellow, they counted seven doe and several fawn returning to this place that provided them shelter during the night. Just minutes prior to sunset, a majestic buck appeared on an edge of the bedding area, about fifty yards from the hunters. Rivera nocked an arrow, but Stoker touched his shoulder and shook his head. "He's too far," whispered Stoker. The men waited motionless and hoped the buck would choose to move in their direction. Watching this beautiful mammal, Stoker reflected on the tenuous position of the prey. Right now the buck was safe. However, if it came toward them another fifteen yards, it would be well within range of the hunters' arrows.

The buck took a dozen tentative steps around the bedding area from the hunters' right to their left. This lateral movement brought the target about ten yards closer. "Five more yards is all you need," Stoker whispered.

Rivera nocked his arrow and sighted in on the buck, just before a light wind gusted to the right of the hunters. Two seconds later the buck raised its nose and Stoker heard the unmistakable swoosh of Rivera's arrow leaving his bow. Traveling at two hundred and sixty feet per second the arrow arrived with a thunderous clap. It pierced the buck's sternum dropping the animal to the ground immediately. The hunters stayed silent and still while the rest of the herd scattered. After thirty seconds Rivera whispered, "The wind betrayed us. I had to take the shot."

"Sure, the wind changed; you compensated for it in a split second," Stoker said. "Your archery skills are also further along than you led me to believe, *asere*."

"Well I sensed your stinking B.O. during that split second when the wind changed. I surely couldn't ignore that. The adjustment for the wind is all instinct, *amigo*."

Stoker and Rivera were atypical hunters. This was a serene, sacred moment. They had taken a life to improve their own. They refrained from the rowdy celebrations they had often heard from other hunters. They approached the buck, taking the necessary precautions, poking and prodding it from a distance to ensure it was dead. Rivera walked up beside the beautiful, calm, majestic animal, picked up its head and held it up so Stoker could take a picture. Rivera did not smile. His face was serious due to the respect any good warrior would lend to a righteous kill.

"Excellent shot, buddy," Stoker said.

"Thanks." Rivera gently laid the animal back down. "Until a few months ago about the only living things I'd ever killed in my life were Nicaraguans, El Salvadorians, and anybody stupid enough to fight for communism in Central

America. Most of the ones I killed deserved to die, but it's the innocents that still disturb me."

Stoker and Rivera worked together to field dress the deer. They then secured the buck to an ingenious sled that Stoker had built by hand a few years before. Both men stepped back into their skis and made their way back to camp. Rivera took the first turn pulling the deer sled, which created a deeply satisfying fatigue. Now that Rivera had helped Stoker fill his deer tag, his outlook had changed and he was open to talking about the painful past. "Stoker, I know you also spent time in Central America. Tell me about your time in Guatemala. What were you doing down there?"

"Our orders told us it was a humanitarian and medical training mission during a time of local suffering due to a small, local guerrilla war. We actually did plenty of goodwill work," Stoker said. "But I think we were mostly a diversion to distract people from seeing other things our government was trying to accomplish there. American leaders were none too excited about having Guatemalan communists in power, with Guatemala being just one country away from the US."

"Yes," Rivera said. He was slightly winded as he pulled the sled, but he kept up with the conversation with seemingly little effort. "Guatemala was definitely a country we were not willing to see switch over to communism for any significant period of time. There was more clandestine work back then in Guatemala than in many Middle Eastern countries. You did extremely important work by winning over the locals. You also forced the communist spies to divert resources to watching you. And, it made it harder for them to track the CIA."

"So Errol, you're saying my buddies and I were setting the screen so the CIA could get the big dunk."

"Sort of," Rivera said. "But the CIA never dunks; they score silently."

"My few weeks of war in Guatemala were really a Cold War effort, Errol. You were in the real bloody battle a little further to the South with constant bullets and bombs."

Again Rivera started to talk about his experiences. "In El Salvador, Nicaragua, Honduras, and even for a short time in Guatemala, we enjoyed the technology of those new second or third generation night vision goggles. Their clarity was amazing. My boys and I were always looking for those heat signatures."

Stoker decided to be a psychiatrist for a moment and draw out a little more from his friend who had lived with decades of pain. "But, you pointed it out yourself. In the thick jungle, not every heat signal belongs to the campfires and lanterns of communist guerillas."

Rivera did not respond immediately. The pain and memories returned in a flood. He needed a moment to sense the silence and cold that surrounded them. He needed the winter to subdue the memories of the damp, musty, hot jungle of Central America. He needed to be sure that he would not hear helicopter blades, grenades, and machine gun fire. Even though those experiences were decades behind him, he could remember the scents, the sensations, the sights—and especially the sounds—of war. He still remembered hearing the screams in his native tongue. Sometimes the screams came from soldiers during their last moments of life. These were men who had chosen foolishly, men who believed in a communist utopia they would never experience. But too often the screams would come from women and children. They were screams affirming that Rivera and his men had chosen the wrong target.

"How do you break it down to math, Troy?" Rivera asked. "Sure, eighty or ninety percent of the time we were hitting the communists and moving them along. But I had innocent blood on my hands because ten to twenty percent of the time we were just confirming that the poor, innocent people had nowhere to hide." Rivera took a moment to consider his next words before saying; "We flew at night, so logically we were supposed to sleep during the day. But the Air Force spent all morning and afternoon dropping their bombs, so the carnage interrupted and invaded my sleep, as well. I never got a break."

Stoker decided to grab onto one side of the sled to help push. Rivera did not comment on Stoker's help; he just moved aside and accepted it. Both men continued together in silence to their small camp.

When they arrived at the camp Rivera and Stoker used a rope to hoist their buck ten feet up into the air, where it would be out of reach of other carnivores. Then they lit a small campfire and prepared dinner. Conversation was somewhat sparse and mostly based around preparing the meal. By 7:45 p.m. the only thing left to do was sleep. Slumber came easy to the hunters who had arisen before 4:00 a.m. Despite temperatures that dipped to sixteen degrees below zero, Doctor Rivera slept in superb warmth inside his mummy bag. However, his dreams that night took him back to the humid nights in El Salvador when he could achieve no relief from the heat. He still craved liberation from the memories of a soldier conflicted by his love of people and his country, and the orders he received from his superiors.

CHAPTER 48

SIOUX FALLS REGIONAL HOSPITAL

Larry Stintson, M.D. was on call. Tonight when an orthopedic injury came through the door of the emergency room, they would call Stintson to treat the person. And tonight a few minutes before dinner, he got his first phone call. An automobile accident created yet another opportunity for the doctor to go into the OR and fix a man's broken femur. Surgically speaking, the procedure was routine. Soon the patient was in the recovery room and Dr. Stintson was talking with the family. "The procedure went exactly as planned," the doctor reassured. "In a few weeks he'll be as good as new."

After settling the family's concerns and checking back with the patient again, Stintson navigated up to the orthopedic wing of the hospital, found an empty patient room, and sat down in a chair next to the window. Removing his smart phone he accessed an app that allowed him to make a secure phone call to Reno where it was just a few minutes after 7:00 p.m. "Hi, this is Larry in the Midwest." Green Growth Venture identified people only by their first name and vague geography. "I sent you ten profiles a couple days ago." Within the lingo of Green Growth Ventures, a "profile" was the name, Social Security number, and other key data of people who were likely to become victims of the commander's identity theft cartel. "I'm following up to see if you've made any progress?"

"Yes, Larry. I'm looking those profiles up right now," said a clerical person on the other end of the line. "Okay. Here they are." The person assisting him did not know that Larry was a doctor and it bothered Stintson that he was not afforded special status amongst his fellow identity thieves. Being treated with common courtesy ruffled his ego, which was so dependent upon people kissing up to him as a surgeon. The clerical person came back on the phone and said, "It looks like three of them had LifeLock, Larry."

"Doctors often do," he pointed out, subconsciously hoping the person helping him from Reno would assume he was a doctor, and start pandering to him.

"But the other seven profiles look great. It looks like we've applied for sixteen credit cards, so far, among this group. It will be another few days until we can pull cash out of those accounts. We've already used the profile of that woman who now lives in Memphis, Tennessee. Earlier today one of our ladies used her name and a fake ID at a payday loan center in Jackson, Tennessee. She walked out with five thousand dollars in cash. We'll repeat the process in Memphis tomorrow."

"Excellent!" Stintson replied, calculating the money he had already earned. After finishing the phone call, Stintson walked back down the hall toward the elevator. Suddenly, a new thought hit. *I could cut out the middleman and keep all of the money for myself on a few of these!* He thought. *I could pay some crazy fool to walk into a payday loan business, defraud the people who work there, and walk out with cash, without even involving Green Growth Ventures.* Stintson considered using Katerina as an identity thief, but he doubted that she would be willing to do something so scary. Perhaps after the right medications, however, she might be a little more willing and a lot more convincing? No, there were better liars and cheats out there. Eventually, he would come across someone who fit the bill.

CHAPTER 49

While Stoker and Rivera were off on their hunt, Z was responsible for getting updates on Ann Higgins's condition, watching Stoker's email for messages from the nurse at the jail, searching for clues about who might have tried to kill Ann Higgins, and a few dozen other items. However, his most important task was monitoring Michael Briggs's movements using the GPS tracking devices in his intestines and shoe. Z was hoping Brigg's next moves would provide clues about the grand mystery of Ann Higgins, coyotes, and a man named Nichols. Despite the nine-degree temperature on the streets of Sioux Falls this morning, Z waited comfortably in the warmth of a plain white Ford Crown Victoria. The car faced east on 5th Street, offering Z a perfect vantage point of the doors to the Minnehaha County jail. While Z waited for Briggs to make bail and exit, he executed his techie duties by auditing the security of his team's information systems throughout the Dakotas and Minnesota.

He would not have to follow Briggs too closely, however. His military-grade GPS technology and tracking software could track him almost anywhere and know his precise location within inches. At about nine twenty, Briggs emerged from the jail and jumped into a taxi. Z followed by remaining a block or two behind the cab as it drove north on Minnesota Avenue. Ten minutes later Briggs's taxi stopped in front of the terminal at the Sioux Falls Regional Airport. Z had to split off from the cab and take his car into the short-term parking area. Even though he lost track of Briggs visually, he could see exactly where he was on his computer's screen. Three minutes later, Z had parked his car and entered the airport. He casually tracked Briggs's signal until he saw him at an airline kiosk trying to check in for a flight. Z closed his sleek computer and stepped closer to Briggs who seemed to be having trouble with electronic check-in.

Z eavesdropped over Briggs's shoulder so he could see the kiosk screen and read that Briggs would be flying to Denver. As the kiosk printed out Brigg's ticket, Z stepped back a few feet so Briggs would not notice him. Briggs took his documents and walked toward the concourse. Z casually followed. He watched Briggs pass through his security screenings. The security screeners did not detect the GPS trackers in Briggs' intestines or shoe. "God bless the USA, and God bless carbon fiber nanotechnology," Z said to himself and he saw Briggs putting his shoes back on. A few moments later, the criminal who had just made bail walked around a corner and out of Z's sight.

Z returned to the parking lot, opened his computer, and waited for just over thirty minutes. The entire time he watched a small icon as it sat on a map rendered on his screen. He watched the dot representing Briggs move onto the plane. Next, the icon progressed toward the runway. Then, all of a sudden, he noticed that Briggs began to travel rapidly down the runway. Within seconds he had reached a velocity of one hundred twenty miles per hour; and Z watched the readings from the bugs in Briggs's shoes and intestines transmit his ascending altitude. On the map, Z watched Briggs's location-specific dot as it departed Sioux Falls air space. The icon further accelerated as the plane shot higher into the sky. Z closed his computer and headed back to his office where he would further monitor the flight and all of Michael Briggs's movements.

The flight lasted another hour and thirty minutes before touching down. By the time Briggs's icon left the airport on the outskirts of Denver, Z was enjoying breakfast in his office while lending his occasional attention to football highlights on ESPN that were playing on one of his many monitors. Z was waiting for Briggs to show him where the final destination was. Eventually he would settle into a hotel room, apartment or home; and that location was likely to be close to the masterminds behind the mystery of the houses on Bryant Way, Ann Higgins brutal assault, coyotes, and a guy named Nichols.

Briggs's first stop was a clothing store. He spent about forty minutes inside the store before exiting and walking about a block. Next, he entered a high-end hair salon. Z watched his icon remain in the salon for an hour. "Wow, you must really be doing some major work, Briggs," Z said aloud. "You're really changing up your appearance. I can't wait to see what you've done with yourself. We'll bust your ass as your ugly old face or your new pretty boy identity."

An hour later the icon that marked Briggs walked out of the hair salon. However, the bug in Brigg's shoes remained behind. Still, the bug he had swallowed appeared to get in a car and proceed down the road at automobile speed.

"Congratulations, Mr. Briggs," Z said. "It looks like you've got yourself a new pair of shoes. Good for Stoker and his insistence on operational redundancy. Now just show us where in Denver are you going to stay? Take us to your home sweet home, Mr. Briggs."

Z continued to watch Briggs's icon, but the taxi traveled further and further away from Denver. Instead of exiting in the suburbs, Z watched the GPS icon travel right back to Denver International Airport. Briggs appeared to check-in, and then proceed through airport security and onto the concourse to await a new flight. Forty-five minutes later, Briggs got on his plane. "I think he's on the flight to Reno," Z said. Sometimes his work was solitary, and Z often talked to himself.

Briggs' plane pushed back from the gate, taxied and took off. Z observed the first fifteen minutes of the flight's trajectory and matched it to the Federal Aviation Administration data, he could easily access, which confirmed that Reno was Briggs's next destination.

Two hours later when the plane landed in Reno, Z watched the icon walk out to the curbside pickup area. Apparently a taxi or other car picked him up, because Briggs appeared to leave the airport at about forty miles per hour and traveled through the south part of Reno until his trip ended at the curb in front of a two-story office building on Kietzke Lane.

As Briggs walked into the office building, Z, from more than 1,200 miles away, observed him getting on the elevator, ascending to the second floor, and entering a space, which he assumed was an office. While Brigg's on-screen map icon remained relatively stationary within this supposed office space, Z worked furiously to find out who owned or leased the area where Briggs was spending time. As Z dug into his research he found the most recent blueprint of the building on Kietzke Lane filed with the City of Reno Community Development Department. Only one company occupied the second floor of this building.

With a few more keystrokes he found that a firm with the simple name, Rental Reserve Limited, leased the second floor. He dug deeper into this company with a bland name, and he learned the Rental Reserve Limited was a Nevada corporation. Z knew his research would probably not get him much further, because Nevada had laws that made it quite easy for business owners to hide their identities. Even with the elaborate database and information systems that Z and his team could access, he could not unravel a Nevada corporation. However, thanks to a few connections, Z was able to make a phone call and find out that a conglomeration of six different corporations owned Rental Reserve Limited. Two of the corporations were based in the Philippines, two in Nevada, one in Mexico, and another in Panama. It would be completely unpractical for Z to take the weeks or months to do the research and find out who was behind each of those corporations. Moreover, Z was pretty sure that he would just find more layers of corporations owning corporations.

Instead of spending any more time in such a futile search, he decided he would be better off having his team insert some NanoBUGS, a relatively new surveillance technology, to see what was occurring on the second floor of the building on Kietzke Lane. With a few more keystrokes he started the process of obtaining a warrant that would allow him to place microphones, tap phones, and hack computers in this office that was holding the fugitive Michael Briggs.

CHAPTER 50

At 6:30 p.m., Michael Briggs and three other men exited the office building on Kietzke Lane and stepped into the dark of a winter night in Reno. Their shift that day in the Green Growth Ventures office involved working the names and Social Security numbers that Larry Stintson had sent from Sioux Falls. One of their victims was an unsuspecting general surgeon who now lived in North Carolina. Stintson had found his information in an old file from ten years earlier, when this particular doctor had been practicing in Rapid City, South Dakota. Since lunchtime one of Briggs's new co-workers had shown him how to secure two credit lines in the surgeon's name totaling $19,000. Tomorrow, one of the other workers would use those credit lines to take out cash advances of a few thousand dollars. Over the next four days the intricate plots of Green Growth Ventures would extract the balance of the $19,000 – and anything else they could get. Briggs would soon earn handsome commissions on the stolen funds.

As the four guys exited the building and walked to the parking lot, two *Espada Rápida* elite warriors, under Dr. Errol Rivera's remote command, watched them from their Chevrolet Suburban. Z had dispatched them from Sacramento. The innocent looking automobile was actually an armored mobile command center. One of them was snapping as many pictures as possible with a cutting-edge infrared camera beam that was completely invisible to the Green Growth Ventures employees. As the four men approached the car they shared, the warriors captured some excellent photos, which Z would use in the next few minutes to identify the men. As the carpoolers pulled away, the *Espada Rápida*

Suburban waited for a few extra seconds, and then followed the car at a reasonable distance.

It was a short three-minute drive as the car traveled under the freeway and made its way to an apartment complex across the street from the Meadowood Mall. The Green Growth Ventures employees, parked their car, got out, climbed some stairs, and slipped into one of the top-floor apartments. The warriors parked on a road just outside of the complex, where they still had a good vantage point on one of the apartment windows. Without saying a word, the warrior who took the photos removed his laptop, opened an email, and attached the photos he had just taken. He wrote a few lines requesting that his team leader see what he could make of the pictures. He also requested wiretap and surveillance warrants, before hitting send.

Three seconds later, Z received the email in Sioux Falls. After reviewing a few of the photos, he picked up his phone and called the warriors in Reno. When they answered, Z simply said, "Excellent work. That's Briggs. No doubt about it. I can tell with the naked eye. We don't even need to run that mug against the face-recognition software." Z was silent for a minute as he fed the other three pictures into a website that gave him access to databases of South Dakota criminals. Immediately his computer reported success with another picture. "At least one of the others is a bail jumper who was paranoid about being fed to the coyotes in jail. Another of those faces is also bugging me. I can't remember where I've seen him, but it'll come to me."

"What's next boss?" asked one of the warriors.

"I'll get you that surveillance warrant," Z said. "I'm so sure I'll get it, why don't you use your time to insert some microphones and cameras right now. We'll turn them on after we get the warrant. Then after that, drive back to Green Growth Ventures and start figuring out how you want to get ears into those offices."

"It'll be a little challenging," one of the warriors said. There's always somebody in that office. It looks like it's a twenty-four hour operation."

The second warrior smiled wryly and pumped his fist in the air. "I think it's finally time to use some of our NanoBUGS to creep around, listen, and look."

"I'm deeply jealous," Z said. "Everybody but me is getting all the action." NanoBUGS were small robots that looked and behaved like insects. They had microphones and cameras that transmitted to the *Espada Rápida* warriors. The acronym BUGS stood for Better than Uncle Sam's Government Surveillance. When it came to urban surveillance, *Espada Rápida* was even ahead of the CIA, NSA, and other government agencies. "Send me back as much of that NanoBUGS footage and audio as you can, you lucky son of a guns—you get to play with the great toys. I've wanted to use those NanoBUGS for so long. Now, I've got to live this experience through you guys."

The phone call ended and the warriors went to work plotting how to best get their NanoBUGS and cameras into the apartment and office building without being detected. They considered numerous options for getting into the apartment. They were debating attaching microphones to the windows, when the four men emerged from the apartment, got in their car and drove away.

"Or, we could wait until they leave, pick the locks, and walk in," one of the warriors joked.

"Brilliant," the other replied with a laugh.

The men grabbed their backpacks and walked up the stairs to the front door. One of them used a scanner to search for burglar alarm sensors. "Dang! If we open this door, they'll know we've been here."

He took out his phone and sent Z a text informing him of the alarm. Fifty seconds later he got a response back from Z informing him that the alarm was disarmed.

"Amazing," one of the warriors said. "Back in the old days, a black bag alarm job took a lot more time, and the technology guru had to be right on site. Now Z brings down the system from more than a thousand miles away in a matter of seconds."

The warriors simultaneously picked the lock in the doorknob and the deadbolt. They entered the apartment and bugged the living room and kitchen, while also placing hidden cameras strategically throughout the rooms. There were two bedrooms. A smaller room contained a bunk bed while the second, larger bedroom contained a bunk bed and a twin bed. It appeared that five people shared this space. The bedrooms were equally as easy to install the small cameras. They hid the first of three NanoBUGS in a corner of the living room. The surveillance device was smaller than a common housefly and the batteries would power flight for two hours. The device had a standby listening and video transmit time that exceeded twenty-four hours. The corners of rooms tended to capture and focus sounds better than any other spots in the room. Then the warriors also put NanoBUGS in the bedrooms, again choosing the best corners to capture the voices of these men. Three minutes later the warriors had finished and stepped back outside. One warrior re-locked the deadbolt while the second man sent Z a text reminding him to reactivate the alarm system from Sioux Falls.

The warriors went back to their mobile command center. "Next stop, Green Growth Ventures," the driver said. The team of two drove back to the office building where they had been earlier, but they elected not to park in the parking lot to reduce their risk of detection. They parked on a frontage road about fifty yards from the building and they went to work setting up recording equipment and unidirectional microphones. They aimed the microphones toward the office where Briggs had spent time that day. As they zeroed the signal in on the voices, they heard one woman talking on the phone. She was applying for a credit card using an address in New Jersey. Another voice, belonging to a man about forty years old, was also talking to a bank. He was applying for a line of credit in the name of a physician and his practice in Rapid City, South Dakota. He claimed to be the doctor and he promised to guarantee the line of credit personally. The bank approved a line of $100,000 and provided him a username and password where he could start using his line of credit immediately. "Oh, thank you," the scammer said. "I'm going to purchase a small ultrasound machine immediately, so please don't be alarmed if you see me transferring large amounts around as early as tomorrow morning."

While one of the warriors continued to listen and the technology continued to record, the other warrior sent Z an email that included attached recordings of everything they had just heard.

> *I think we've stumbled into an identity theft ring here,*
> *Z. Can you get those warrants? Our NanoBUGS need*
> *to get to work.*

An hour later Z had secured the warrants. The judge in St. Louis was persuaded by the fact that two bail-jumping criminals were apparently living and working together, and there was a significant probability of highly organized, bold, and sophisticated identity theft going on from Class A office space in Reno.

One of the *Espada Rápida* warriors stepped out of the Suburban. He had four different swarms of NanoBUGS hidden in his coat pockets, and flyers for a local pizzeria in his hands. He walked down the sidewalk as if he were a common citizen, turned the corner, and walked to the main entrance of the building. Fortunately, the door to the lobby was not yet locked, so the warrior entered, took a quick look at the directory of businesses, and then showed himself to the door of the first office. He shoved one of the pizzeria ads under the door and then continued to the next office, where he shoved the same ad under that business's door, too. Then he found the bathroom. Once inside the bathroom, he released his first swarm of NanoBUGS into the wall near a vent. They formed a single-file line and climbed into the vent. At some point Z would remotely control the NanoBUGS through the ventilation system until they made their way into the mysterious second floor offices.

The warrior exited the bathroom and deposited another swarm of NanoBUGS into a planter near the base of the building's main staircase. This swarm would wait for hours or days until becoming active. They were part of the backup plan if the others failed.

The warrior then took the elevator to the second floor. During his ascent he released the third swarm onto the wall of the elevator car and they crawled up and disappeared into a vent that led to the elevator shaft. Finally, in his boldest move yet, he walked right up to the front door of the second floor office. He tried to shove the pizzeria ad under the door, but it had a metal plate at the bottom that insured that nothing could pass under the crack, so he simply left the flyer on the floor in front of the door—along with the final swarm of NanoBUGS. They instantly began to crawl up the wall to the top of the doorframe. There they would hide and wait for somebody to exit so they could crawl in one at a time.

With the pizza flyers delivered and the NanoBUGS disbursed, the warrior took the stairs back down to the main floor and left the building.

Back in the mobile command center, the other warrior was navigating the first swarm from the bathroom and through the ventilation system. Back in Sioux Falls, Z was controlling the swarm in the elevator shaft and having good success sending his NanoBUGS through a conduit of server wires and into the mysterious second floor office.

Arriving back at the Suburban, the warrior climbed back in the car and said, "Mission accomplished. I think we can do the rest of this from the comfort of our Embassy Suites hotel rooms."

"Amen, to that, brother. Let's grab some dinner along the way. What would you like?"

"Anything but pizza."

CHAPTER 51

Errol Rivera awoke in darkness, immediately wriggled himself out of his warm mummy bag, and took profound solace in the freezing cold that invaded his lungs, rushed over his skin, and froze the sweat in his hair. He would sleep no more this night and he needed the contrast of the South Dakota winter to sear out the painful memories of jungles, bullets, blood, and screams that still lingered in his mind after almost two decades. "Troy, it's five o'clock. Let's go."

Stoker awoke immediately. The anticipation of a satisfying ski back to Rivera's truck, and a hug from his wife, Allie, obliterated any traces of grogginess. Within ten minutes both men were dressed and breaking camp. It was dark, the temperature was eighteen degrees below zero, and the only food that remained were two MREs, along with a Cuban blend of some special coffee. Rivera set it to brew on a small stove. The distinguished doctors had completed the transition from civilized to survivalists. The next few hours would test their mettle and invigorate their souls.

They loaded their gear into their backpacks and took a few minutes to drink their cups of black coffee and eat their MRE breakfast burritos. Stoker decided to put the tin-foil-wrapped cracker and its accompanying peanut butter and jelly into one of his pockets to eat later on the trail. Once they had consumed 1,300 calories each, the doctors lowered the buck from the tree onto the sled and left the campsite that had shielded them from the cold January winds. Rivera had set up a rope he could put over his shoulder as a harness so both he and Stoker could pull the sled more efficiently.

Stoker had heard Rivera's fitful sleep the night before, and he did not wait for long to bring up the issue. "It sounded like you were having nightmares last night. What's the deal?"

"I go back to the jungles in my dreams a few times per week," Rivera said. "I would rather be dreaming about the jungles than actually living the hell in person, though."

"So, what can you tell me about your experience leaving Central America, and transitioning back to stateside?" Stoker asked.

"At the end of it all I was pretty jacked up. I was screwed up and I couldn't sleep. Basically, Jack Daniels would sort of get me to sleep. When I got back to the States, I knew the bottle was taking me in the wrong direction, and I made good on a smartass remark that I was going to check into a mental hospital."

"Were there any sleep medications that worked for you back then?" Stoker asked.

"I tried a bunch of them, but they didn't work," Rivera responded. "The docs didn't have anything that could help me achieve REM sleep. So the bottom line is, I was suffering from PTSD long before PTSD was considered PTSD." While Rivera told his story, his skiing was more aggressive than ever. "But, the thing was, I was active Army so that saved my butt. I had a savvy commander who had cut his teeth in Vietnam. This guy was a pilot. He was a major and he had survived three tours in Vietnam. During his last tour he flew CH-47 Chinooks and he was one of the last of about a dozen people who survived a total hydraulics failure in a CH-47. This commander of mine came out with a broken humerus and a couple fractures in his lower back, but he survived. Out of his crew of three, two of them survived. Needless to say, my commander was savvy about the experience of returning from war. He was good at diagnosing his soldiers on their path to self-destruction."

"So how did he shrink you?" Stoker asked.

Rivera laughed at Stoker, the shrink, calling a military officer a shrink. "He came to me one day and he said, 'Mr. Rivera, come here.' He brought me into his office and said, 'You're grounded.'"

"Wow," Stoker exclaimed. "That's an extreme measure."

"Yeah," Rivera said. "Being grounded as a captain is a big deal.

"My commander looked at me and explained, 'Rivera, I think you need to rest. You've been working hard, and just between you and me, you're grounded. No one else will have to know about it. It's not official but you're not going to be getting any flights."

"So what was he expecting you to do with your time?" Stoker asked.

"He told me that all I had to do was show up once a day. He didn't care if I spent twenty minutes or two hours there. He wanted to just show my face and then after that, I could go home and relax. He also insisted that I go talk to this chaplain. So I did."

"You know, Troy, we didn't have any psych people to talk to, at least once they discharged me from the VA. The chaplain more or less talked to me. I'm a Christian. I always had been. So we talked about my problem. I obviously had a big issue with killing kids and women, and flying over dead bodies every day."

"I had some great chaplains in the military, too," Stoker said. "They are special people and they help a lot of people effectively."

"My chaplain was patient and logical," Rivera said. "Through a period of about two and a half or three weeks, this commanding officer of mine was able to open up that path to redemption. Through that, I came to understand that I wasn't going to go to Hell for my actions as a soldier. Then he brought my wife and my young children in, and we educated them about what I was going through. That was right when I was thinking that I wanted to become a doctor and it all clicked for me. After all I had done, I needed to pay humanity back."

"But didn't you still have to do a bunch of medical school prerequisites?" Stoker asked.

"Even though my dad had pushed us to study history in college, I had graduated with a degree in biology. On top of that I spent a lot of time flying flight surgeons around. One day I was flying this guy who was from an intelligence unit and he happened to be a doctor. I commented how he must have been really smart to go to medical school. He looked back at me and told me that getting into and completing medical school was more about being determined."

"You and I both know exactly what he was talking about," Stoker said. "We each saw a lot of smart people fail to make it into medical school."

"I understood that way back then, too. Determination was something I'd learned from being in flight school. You have to be determined during that full ten months and just persevere through it."

"So flight school was an ordeal and flight school in the military has a lot of parallelisms with medical school?" Stoker asked.

"Exactly," Rivera said. "If you decide to have tenacity, you'll reach your destination."

"It's one of the biggest failures I see among my patients," Stoker said. "It's their short-lived determination. If I can just help them hang on as they go through something challenging in school, work, or a relationship, they usually end up the victors."

"I found that I just had to live and breathe the subject matter in flight school as well as in medical school. If you get on the train tracks in medical school and you stay on the tracks, you're going to succeed. Sure, medical school is much longer than flight school, but succeeding was all about sticking with the program."

"So what happened after medical school?" Stoker asked.

"Keep in mind, all through medical school and even coming out of medical school I was still in the Reserves. Also I had promised that I would stay in the Reserves and serve my country and be the only medical doctor with a 1,000 hours of night vision goggle time in the United States Military. I came out of Case Western Reserve Medical School in Cleveland and during my residency the National Guard told me that I could be a *commissioned* officer simply because I had graduated medical school. I was supposed to officially attend a two-week watered-down basic training for new docs, but they waived that for me at that time thank God! I decided to take the option of going and working on an Indian reservation here in South Dakota"

"So you paid back Uncle Sam by working for Indian Health Services," Stoker said. "How did you like that?"

"Of course, the money is not that good, but my patients were wonderful. The job also gave me some freedom to do some defense-related consulting on the side. Also they sent me to some great conferences, which was another perk I welcomed."

"You mean the ones with fabulous food and amazing entertainment?" Stoker asked.

"Exactly! And, that's where it gets interesting," Rivera said. "I got sent to some big, amazing conference in Phoenix. They were giving everything away. Free textbooks, free food. I think I survived on mostly lobster for those few days.

"I remember attending conferences where sponsors gave away dozens of laptops at drawings every day," Stoker said.

"Yes, but now with all of the new government oversight of healthcare, you're lucky to get a free squishy ball or USB drive," said Rivera. "Anyway, the Army had this booth and they were giving away coffee mugs so I walk into the booth and said, 'Hey, I want to get my coffee mug. After all, I *was* in the Army. The least I can do is get a coffee mug.' This full-bird colonel turns around and started asking me questions."

"I can envision the conversation now," Stoker said. "I bet his jaw dropped when he heard about your combat experience, night vision pilot hours, and fourteen years."

"That colonel told me that he could get me in as a commissioned officer. To make a long story short, sixty days later I'm swearing back in as a captain in the medical corps of the United States Army."

"So did they ever get around to making you do your basic officer training?" Stoker asked.

"Yes," Rivera said. "They sent me down to San Antonio where I ended up basically babysitting most of these kids who were doctors and had no idea what was going on."

"And then what?"

"After that I was in the Army Reserves and they wanted me to come back and do a three-week stint at my old stomping grounds, Ft. Hood. There I bumped into this guy, General Sommers, whom I had known many years earlier in Central America. All of a sudden, I was his doctor."

"Do you mean General Arnold Sommers?" Stoker asked.

"The one and only!" Rivera said. "Do you know him?"

"I don't believe in coincidences," Stoker said. "As an eighteen-year-old medic on maneuvers in southern Texas, I called General Sommers's plane back to evacuate a paratrooper who was fighting for his life after losing about half of his blood volume."

"You have got to be kidding me," Rivera said. "This is just too good. You know Sommers?"

"Well, I don't really know him, but I did meet him once and he wasn't happy with me," Stoker said. "But I had just saved a life, so what could he do?"

"Well Troy, I am going to take this moment and break one of our rules. We turn off cell phones for these hunts, but I don't believe in coincidences either and I'm turning on my cell phone for ten minutes." Rivera reached into his backpack, pulled out his phone, and turned it on. Opening a new text he typed in the name of General Sommers and then added the message.

> *I'm sending you hardy greetings from a friend of mine*
> *who called back your helicopter in Southern Texas to*
> *evac a paratrooper. Since when have you let medics*
> *order you around?*

Stoker and Rivera laughed as Rivera hit the send button. "He started to place me under arrest," Stoker said.

"Started to?" Rivera asked. "How did you persuade Sommers to change his stubborn mind?"

"A twenty-year major, and trauma expert, stood up to him."

Just then Rivera's phone beeped. Rivera read the message aloud.

> *You tell Corporal Stoker that we're going to make a hero*
> *out of him, yet.*

What does that mean?" Rivera asked.

"The major who stood up for me that day told the general that if I wasn't a hero yet, I have the potential. It was something like that."

"So were you a hero, Troy?" Rivera asked.

Stoker thought about how to answer the question for a moment and then said, "Someday I'll tell you my stories and I'll let you decide, Errol."

"Well, as a man in your early forties," Rivera responded, "I suspect there still may be some heroics left in you."

"I'm not sure what your brand of heroics is, Rivera," Stoker said. "From what I've seen, I'm sensing that your heroic adventures extend beyond the typical weekend warrior stuff. Your responses to the Ann Higgins incident and the resources you've been able to pull together smack of snake eater to me.

"Look, Troy. I want to make if clear. I've never been to The Farm in Virginia."

"But you have friends who have."

"Yes, dozens of friends," Rivera said. "And again for the record, I once had to turn down the opportunity to instruct those young thoroughbreds at The Farm. Those guys need to know how to duct tape, superglue and sew themselves back together. I've had some good first-hand experience with that."

"But you didn't accept the teaching assignment?" Stoker asked.

"I was already committed to another mission. Twenty-four hours later I left for a little place that some people call the Baghdad Central Prison."

"You turned down steak dinners on Lake Anna for MREs while overseeing Abu Ghraib?"

"Trust me. They needed me more in Iraq." Rivera turned his face to the sun as he skied on aggressively. "Anyway, back to medical school."

Stoker was seeing the story of Errol Rivera slowly emerge. The friendship was allowing Rivera to further process some issues that he had buried deep in his soul many years ago. "Yes, take me back to Cleveland. Something tells me that by engrossing yourself in the rigors of medical school helped you get over Central America."

"Absorbing gross anatomy, biochemistry, pharmacology, and histology let me block out the bullets, flames, bloodshed, and screams that haunted my mind," Rivera said. "The deep freeze winters and snow-covered plains of the upper Midwest were a stark contrast to the heat and humidity of Central American jungles that had been the hell of my life. I welcomed the opportunity to do a residency here, too. Working at the VA has let me help men and women who went through some of the same stuff. I make a lot less money than I would in private practice, but it kind of lets me atone for my sins."

CHAPTER 52

It was Wednesday morning at the building on Kietzke Avenue in Reno, and Ron Cunningham, the commander's right hand man, was working hard and doing his job—and so were the NanoBUGS. As Cunningham looked at online bank statements, Z watched through the tiny NanoBUGS camera that was spying from the ceiling. He learned the business that operated there was called Green Growth Ventures. The firm banked with a financial institution called the Security Commercial Bank, based in Las Vegas. The balance on this particular account exceeded $4 million. Z could see everything.

When Cunningham talked on the phone he sometimes spoke with somebody he called "commander." In conversations with other callers, "the commander" also surfaced frequently. When Cunningham made accounting entries and updated reports, Z was privy to those figures. When Cunningham tallied the results of the identity theft team's $45,000 haul from the previous day's work, Z was mildly impressed.

Cunningham's phone rang at 3:30 p.m. and Z again listened in on the conversation. The conversation centered on a farm in Arkansas as Cunningham engaged in an argument with the person on the other end of the phone. "Look here, *Nichols*! How many times do I have to tell you? It's not about how much money we make, it's about how much money we can clean!"

The name "Nichols" instantly riveted Z's attention. Now he had a lead on this mysterious Nichols person. But the conversation ended abruptly and Z learned no more. He concluded that he would start his search in Arkansas.

The NanoBUGS also took pictures of employees. These clear images confirmed the identifications of Tony Bernard, Gary Watson, Jake Clark and Michael Briggs. But more importantly, one image showed the face of John Freeman, the dirty blond, acne-scarred person of interest in the Ann Higgins assault. All of the men had new looks, and they were working hard from their cubicles. Freeman seemed to have a leadership or supervisory role over the other men. Over the next few hours Z would learn the ins and outs of their work and gather the evidence he needed to lock away these minions. But it would not be any fun springing a trap on Green Growth Ventures, unless he could ensnare either this Nichols person or some guy they called the commander.

CHAPTER 53

OFFICE OF TROY STOKER, M.D., SIOUX FALLS

Troy Stoker was back from his big hunt, and he was refreshed and ready to pour his heart and soul into helping the dozens of patients he would see over the next few days. Seated before him today was a new patient, John Abbot.

"Okay. So you're fifty-one years old. You've been looked over for a promotion four times now, you have an adult child who is an alcoholic, and you're feeling the pressures of some significant life setbacks?" Dr. Troy Stoker asked the man in his office who sported an admirable goatee of ivory white.

Dr. Haslam was also present, but said nothing. She loathed "psychologist" work. *Just medicate this guy and send him to a psychologist for hours of useless crying,* she thought. Sarah Haslam had always downplayed the medical evidence from studies that showed how powerful therapy was. She always delegated counseling work. "Send them to bawl to the lesser mortals," she had joked with nurses on the psychiatry floor on many occasions. Then she would write out orders for psychologists or social workers to do the counseling.

The patient leaned forward on his chair and answered Stoker's question. "Those are the two greatest weights on my shoulders. Yes, I gave my heart and soul to my family and my work and I feel like I should be further along in both instances."

"Okay. Let's see if you're really what you say you are. Let's see if you're really failing."

Mr. Abbot looked back at Stoker and said, "All right, Doc. Shoot."

Stoker paused and bowed his head down in a brief moment of deep thought. He closed his eyes. Then he looked up at his patient and said, "I want to ask you a serious question. And, I want a serious answer. If your wife went out your front door, walked across the street, and was struck accidentally by a car —" Stoker lifted his hand abruptly. "Now stop! I want you to think about this for one second now."

Immediately Abbott took notice and looked quizzically and right into Stoker's eyes.

Stoker continued. "How would you feel at the moment that you saw her in the casket at the viewing?"

Stoker saw immediate devastation in Abbots face as the man responded, "I hadn't really thought about that. Come to think of it, I would be shattered."

This Stoker guy is nuts. How much longer must I suffer? Haslam thought. *Just get the guy an anti-depressant, and let's move on.*

"Now one more thing," Stoker continued. "If someone broke into your house with a shotgun and was going to shoot your wife, would you jump in front of her and take the blast?"

There was an uncomfortable pause by Abbot. His mental wheels were turning.

Then Stoker said, "What are your thoughts, John?"

"Wow. That's interesting, Doc," Abbot replied. "I can honestly say that I would feel horrible seeing her in the casket and I would not have a second thought about taking a bullet for my wife. I've never thought of it that way. This is wild. I'm surprised at myself — at this whole thing. I guess I'm more in love with her than I thought."

"So what exactly did you say?" Stoker asked.

"I guess I have stronger feelings for her than I thought. This is interesting."

"Well, I want you to keep that thought in your mind because most of therapy takes place outside of this room, after our discussion. I want you to think about this and we'll talk some more. Now let's go on and talk about your workplace issues.

Suddenly Dr. Stoker heard his receptionist, Tamara, yelling, "Subpoena or no subpoena, you can't go in there. He's with a patient right now!"

All of a sudden the door to Dr. Stoker's office opened — an event that was only supposed to occur if Armageddon arrived. Dr. Stoker did not allow interruptions for other doctors, suicidal patients, his wife, senators, kings, or presidents.

"Dr. Stoker. I'm Deputy Harris."

"I don't care who you are. I'm with a patient in a highly confidential setting and I will not be interrupted."

"Sir. I have a subpoena."

"I understand exactly what that means, Deputy Harris. You will have to wait a few minutes to serve me. Please close that door. You're violating patient confidentiality and putting this patient and me at significant risk. You're also on the verge of violating the Fourth Amendment. I'm activating cameras in that hallway, in the waiting room, and around my office. You are being recorded."

"I'm here with Brian Berg from the state medical board and Jason Moore, a social worker from the state," replied deputy Harris.

"Instruct both of them to wait. I'll be out in twenty-five minutes. Please close the door and have a seat."

"I'm afraid I can't do that, sir."

"What? Do you have a *warrant* for my arrest or something?" Stoker asked with obvious sarcasm in his voice.

"No. I have a subpoena and I'm filming now in your office with my handheld camera here."

"Of course. I am happy to address the subpoena in twenty-five minutes. Now I am informing you that my security cameras are rolling. They always are. Moreover, I'm now turning on the camera in my phone and this conversation is being recorded with video and audio in *all* areas of this office—every single area with the exception of where patients are sitting. Do you understand, deputy?"

"Sir. You can't record me."

"I most certainly can. I can record a *public* employee—especially on my own private property. You're being recorded. I have this little app here and I just pressed this little button. Every camera in every room is now recording you. There are also cameras recording you in the hallway and outside. Now leave my office this instant and wait in the waiting room or I will interrupt my session for two minutes to call the best civil rights attorney in the Midwest. I know my patients' rights and I am deeply concerned for your career right now, deputy."

With that the deputy closed the door. Stoker turned directly to face his patient, who was terrified.

"John. I am so sorry. I have never had this happen before. This should be a fortress for you and your confidentiality. By the way, I've gone out of my way to ensure that no camera captures your space. You are *not* being recorded." Stoker smiled for a moment and then said, "But my cameras in the waiting room are still recording that deputy."

"Don't worry, Doc. The deputy only saw the back of my head. I didn't turn around."

"I'm deeply shocked. South Dakota deputy sheriffs often pride themselves on being the first line of defense for Constitutional rights," Stoker said turning toward Sarah Haslam, who had secretly enjoyed seeing Stoker in a potential scuffle with the law. "Dr. Haslam, as a psychiatrist, you need to know your rights. More importantly, you need to know your patients' rights. You must have a plan in place. My responses to that deputy were researched and planned. Tamara and I have even rehearsed for these situations. Remind me to provide you a copy of my civil rights plan.

Stoker turned back to his patient. "Again, John. I'm sorry for the interruption. My sheriff friends all go out of their way to respect due process and—"

Just then the door burst open and Brian Berg stepped into the room insisting that the deputies follow behind him. "Dr. Stoker—"

Stoker roared as he jumped to his feet, "Leave now! Leave the premises!" The doctor stepped between his patient and Berg to protect his identity. "Leave your subpoena and I'll comply quickly. Now exit my office."

Berg disregarded Stoker's orders. "I'm Brian Berg, with the South Dakota Medical Board."

"I don't give a rat's ass, even if you're the president. My patient will have his privacy and I'm asserting my Fourth Amendment rights. Now leave!"

"I'm serving you this subpoena for the records of one Al Taylor," Berg said.

The commander had fabricated the complaint letter using one of Stoker's patient's names without the man's knowledge—a change that Stintson insisted upon to avoid direct finger pointing toward the board. Moreover, Stintson thought it left open the option to hide behind HIPAA laws to protect the patient's so-called identity. Even Berg didn't know the complaint was a forgery.

"Mr. Taylor filed a serious complaint against you and people in high places are watching this case."

"Exit my office this instant and take Mr. Moore with you. I am recording this interaction and I strongly protest your presence here and your invasion of this person's privacy," Stoker said gesturing toward the patient who had turned his back. Sarah Haslam was thrilled and she had subconsciously stood up and gravitated toward a spot alongside the two men. Her position allowed her to fully absorb the intensity of the moment and hope for Stoker's defeat.

"I need these records now, sir," Berg persisted. He continued to wear his smug, idiotic smile. "We're recording this, too."

Stoker looked behind Berg and noticed that one of the deputies had a video camera trained on him. "You will *not* get the records now," Stoker said in a low, slow, and menacing voice. "My cameras are rolling. You will turn off your cameras and leave this instant. You will go back to your cubicle and look up the terms 'due process' and 'unreasonable search and seizure.' It's called the Fourth

Amendment. Also, you should ask around about patient confidentiality laws, which you are violating severely."

"Dr. Stoker, I need these records and I need them now," Berg repeated. He grinned like the Cheshire cat from the movie Alice's Adventures in Wonderland. Three deputy sheriffs filed into Stoker's office behind Berg. Each man had his hand on the handle of his holstered gun. Haslam continued to stand next to the feuding men and watch the dispute with the body language and intense interest of a boxing referee. She was hoping to see Troy Stoker get some sense knocked into him, compliments of the South Dakota Medical Board.

Stoker turned toward the deputies. "Sirs, have you ever served a subpoena that has to be fulfilled immediately?"

None of the deputies answered. They were thinking about the question. It was apparent, from the confused looks in their eyes, that they were struggling with the answer. Then one of the younger deputies said, "No, sir. We drop them off and it's up to the recipient to respond in a timely manner. I suspect that a time-frame of a few days is reasonable."

"And for you to come into someone's office uninvited, what is the required legal document?"

"A warrant," replied a muscular deputy with a shaved head, "unless there's probable cause."

"Exactly," Stoker said in a cordial voice. "So deputies, will you please leave the paperwork and exit the premises? Also provide the receptionist with each of your names and badge numbers. I may need to reach out to you as witnesses against this man here." Stoker pointed at Berg. "I appreciate your service and I'm confident you were misled about the gravity of this *non-situation*."

"Brian Berg said you have guns and a Taser, sir," interjected the muscular deputy. "He expressed concern that you might use a weapon."

"I do not have a gun here in my practice," Stoker said. "But let me ask you, deputy. This is private property. What are my firearm restrictions?"

"You can have them, sir. A Taser is fine, too," the deputy said.

"What about making a video recording of a subpoena on private property? Stoker asked. "Have you ever done that before?"

Immediately one of the deputies reached over to Brian Berg. With surprising force, he took the camera out of Berg's hand, turned it, off and said, "We're sorry we bothered you, doctor."

As the deputies began to exit, Haslam's shoulders fell and she frowned in deep disappointment. Berg had failed to put Stoker in his place. Still the pigheaded medical board inspector remained standing in the same place.

Suddenly Berg remembered that he was supposed to place one of the commander's bugs in Stoker's office and he leaned to one side and craned his neck around to see if he could get closer to Stoker's desk.

Stoker took an additional step toward the obstinate man from the medical board. "What did you say your name is again?"

"My name is Brian Berg, sir." He quickly surveyed the room. "And where are your weapons?"

"Where is your warrant for weapons, Captain Subpoena?" Stoker asked in total mockery. "Besides that, you're not even a sworn-in law enforcer."

"Actually," responded Berg, I went through the police academy just over five years ago."

Stoker was specifically trained to recognize when people were using pieces of truth to lie about their current status. He knew that Berg's comment about "going through the police academy" was a shroud for failure somewhere along the way, and the doctor took advantage of it. "Great," Stoker said with escalating sarcasm. "And how did that work out for you?"

Berg froze. Stoker had called his bluff. Haslam, still about four feet from the two men, also recognized Berg's attempt to deceive. She anticipated that Stoker would make him pay dearly for using tattered remains of historical truth, and she lost all hope that Stoker would be defeated.

"Don't share partial truths with a psychiatrist, Mr. Berg," Stoker said. "Your deceptions betray you and suggest that your complete story is that of a loser."

"I loved my police job on the Pierre—"

Sarah Haslam interrupted Berg. "Before you got fired, Mr. Berg." Then held up her hand to prevent him from talking. "Save your breath." Haslam was secretly trying to keep Berg from losing more ground in this argument. Perhaps, by some miracle this Berg fellow could rally and make a comeback. "We're trained to know the stories behind half-truths. Don't dig your hole any deeper."

"You're a doctor, too?" was all Berg could manage to ask. Haslam just nodded.

Stoker waited a moment in silence, hoping that Berg would ignore Haslam and keep talking. Berg appeared tongue-tied and befuddled, so Stoker went on the offensive. "Your friends there just explained that your entry here today was wrong. This is yet another episode of tyranny, compliments of a bureaucracy headed by a number of highly educated doctors who should know a thing or two about the rule of law," Stoker said with distain. "Mr. Berg, are you a medical professional?"

"I'm a *chief* investigator from the South Dakota Medical Board!"

"So you know about confidentiality laws?"

"I'm fully trained on HIPAA."

"Well, you're now a HIPAA-trained, wannabe thug from the medical board who's having his completely illegal interactions and intrusions recorded with video and audio." Stoker pointed to the door. "Look Berg, your deputy friends have wisely, legally exited. They know how wrong you are. You had better follow their lead before you find yourself up against a civil rights lawsuit, that's way above your pay-grade."

Berg didn't know what to say. He really did not understand what a civil rights lawsuit was. He did remember from his short few months as a police officer that warrants were indeed the norm, however. He also remembered getting some civil rights training. But, in his mind, it was all quite vague and foggy at this point.

Berg decided to assert himself again by walking around the room. Perhaps he would catch sight of a gun, or detect some infraction of a miniscule rule. At this point he would be content to cite Stoker for something as trivial as improper cleanliness. After a few steps to one side he glanced over and caught sight of Stoker's patient. He instantly recognized John Abbott, who was the big brother of one of Berg's friends. He was shocked that John was a psychiatry patient. *Is John mentally ill?* he thought.

"Brian!" John said terrified. "You can't tell anybody about this. I mean people can't know that I'm seeing a shrink!"

"Hey John," Berg panicked. "Don't worry. I won't tell anybody. Your secret's safe with me."

John stood up, looked Dr. Stoker in the eye, and said, "I just lost my faith in your fortress of privacy." Then he stormed out of the office.

Stoker walked toward Berg purposefully. "Out!" was all Stoker said as he moved toward the state investigator. Berg remembered how Stoker had previously handled Moore and he instinctively cowered and reversed out of Stoker's office.

"Dr. Stoker. I need those medical records right now," Berg said as he continued retreating toward the waiting room."

"Nice try, Berg," Stoker said as they arrived at the waiting room and met up with Jason Moore. "Your social worker buddy here momentarily understood why you can't just barge in here."

Moore said nothing but stared Stoker in the eye with contrived bravado.

"I've asked you twice," Stoker said. "What happens when I ask a third time, Mr. Moore?"

Moore was silent.

"My knee is much better now. I promise I can remove both of you at once," Stoker growled. "I'm now within my rights to use reasonable force on my private property."

Moore turned and walked toward the door in fear. Berg hesitated and then panicked. His adrenaline kicked in and all judgment escaped him. Berg balled up his right fist. Remembering his Army training, he swung directly at Stoker's throat. Stoker sidestepped the swing, spun around on one leg, and brought his right arm around backhanding Berg in the side of the head with his muscular limb—making sure to place the blow on his jaw to avoid the middle meningeal artery in his temple—which would have most likely killed him instantly. Berg spun like a top with his jaw leading the way.

"Smile, Brian. You're on Candid Camera. I can't wait to show that to your bosses. They will thank me for using my carefully placed backhand with great restraint. I could've used my elbow or fist. A twig like you would've snapped. I would definitely accept a 'thank you', but I don't feel that you're emotionally or physically able to express that now. Being an understanding and empathetic professional, I will not charge you for this unorthodox therapeutic approach today."

Berg stood up, yelled, and charged Stoker again. Stoker placed a light and merciful punch to his stomach, which caused pain but do no physical damage. The police had heard Berg's yell, and they came rushing in to see Berg lying on the ground, moaning in the fetal position. Stoker had backed away and posed no imminent threat, but the deputies still stood between the two men.

"What just happened here?" the deputy with the shaved head asked.

"Come over here and I'll show you," Tamara responded from the receptionist desk. I bet we captured a clear shot."

The deputy walked over to her computer. In less than ten seconds, she pulled up a digital video of Berg attacking Stoker. The deputy stepped over to Berg who was now getting slowly to his feet.

"I'd like to press charges against Dr. Stoker," uttered Berg

The deputy leaned down and whispered in Berg's ear. "Actually, I saw the footage. You better get lost before I arrest you. You've got ten seconds."

Berg dropped the subpoena on the floor and scrambled for the door. "Consider yourself served Stoker!"

For the first time in years, one of Dr. Stoker's psychotherapy sessions had been interrupted. Little did Brian Berg know he had begun his descent into Dante's circles of hell. This small-time investigator had no idea what hellfire would be showering upon him. Berg jumped into the car he had checked out from the state motor pool. He inserted the key into the car's ignition and was about to start the car when he realized, *I forgot to place the bugs!* His hands began to tremble. He had also failed to get the medical records. Berg barely knew the commander, but somehow he was keenly aware that his failure would conjure severe consequences.

CHAPTER 54

SIOUX FALLS

It was 5:30 a.m., and Dr. Sarah Haslam was fulfilling her destiny. She needed the freedom to be the kind of psychiatrist her narcissism convinced her she could be. However, Troy Stoker had not trusted her. He had actually stood in her way. He kept her on a short leash, only occasionally allowing her to see patients without him. The babysitting had to stop, today.

As she walked down the darkened sidewalk, her shoes crunched on the briskly frozen snow. Each step contained a nerve-racking element of squeaking snow that reminded her of nails running over a chalkboard. She quietly approached the carport. There, Haslam spotted the car that dutifully transported Dr. Stoker's receptionist, Tamara, to the office each morning. She unzipped her coat and removed a hunting knife from the inside coat pocket. She had purchased the weapon from Walmart the night before for fourteen dollars. As she walked up to the front driver's side tire she held the knife firmly by the handle in an attack position. As she zeroed her attention in on the front tire and raised the knife, something stroked the back of her left calf. A surge of panic enveloped her whole body as she jumped to the front of the carport while her eyes scanned and her brain quickly processed fight or flight impulses and a surge of adrenaline.

"Meow." A sleek gray and white bicolor cat was seeking Haslam's attention by rubbing up against her. The cat ignored the knife as well as the intruder's defensive body language. The animal was so desperate for companionship and warmth that it continued to approach Haslam with that "pet me" look in its eyes. The cat did not seem to notice nor care that it had startled

Haslam, but it certainly cared about making every effort to secure her company. The unabashed cat sauntered over to Haslam and again arched her back to rub up against its new friend's leg. If the cat was desperate for friendship, touch, or warmth, it had looked to a source that was completely incapable of providing them.

Haslam ignored the cat and gave no thought to petting it. Instead, with a swift forearm motion she put the knife through the front tire of Tamara's Mazda. "Oh, little ten-dollar-per-hour receptionist. I'm so sorry about your bad fortune this morning," Haslam whispered mockingly under her breath.

Haslam knew that Tamara was resourceful and diligent. If she punctured just one tire, the receptionist would tenaciously put on the spare and come ambling into work only ten or fifteen minutes late. Haslam needed more time to hatch her plan, and she wanted Tamara to have a good hour or two of delay this morning. So she had to inflict a little more damage to the peppy-looking little car.

Most vandals would care about being detected. But not Sarah Haslam. Her narcissism and its resultant blind confidence pre-empted her from even looking around to see if anybody might identify her. Instead, she walked toward the rear of the car. With another rapid motion, she swiped at the back tire. But rather than impaling itself into the Dunlop steel belted radial, the knife glanced off the tire and slashed sideways across Haslam's calf, narrowly missing the cat. Haslam glanced at her leg and noticed a two-inch superficial gash that bled immediately.

The doctor-turned-vandal cursed softly at the pain and the fact that she had just put a sizable hole in her workout tights. She ignored the blood and instead took a second swipe at the tire. This time she scored a direct hit and sank the back corner of the car to the ground in a matter of about four seconds.

A few moments later, Sarah Haslam—now a non-convicted criminal—crossed the street and jogged down the snow-covered sidewalk for about thirty yards. The little gray cat was following her and begging for attention with an incessant stream of meows.

Haslam stopped, bent down, and picked up some snow, which she applied by pressing on her small wound. The instant cold, in combination with the pressure, put an almost immediate stop to the bleeding. The cat caught up to her and again rubbed up against Haslam. As she brushed alongside the injured leg, a small patch of red blood transferred to the cat. Haslam found it amusing and she allowed the cat to rub up against her several more times and then lick her bloody wound. After a few moments she smeared her bloody hand on that cat, and it did not seem to care. Haslam was patient, and she rested for about two minutes in the darkness as she knelt amidst the modest 1960s brick homes in the middle-class Sioux Falls neighborhood.

Once satisfied that the bleeding had stopped to the point that it would not stain her car, Haslam stood slowly and walked back to her small SUV which she had left running about 100 yards down the block from Tamara's modest home. The bloody cat continued to follow her — this time with an increased confidence that she had found a friend.

Sarah Haslam arrived at her car and she got in without giving the cat additional acknowledgement. She then put the car in gear while simultaneously making the conscious decision to skip her morning workout. As she drove away, the cat sat in silence as she watched yet another stranger abandon her in the cruelty of the winter cold.

Haslam returned to her apartment, let herself inside, and began to attend to her wound. Had she still been rotating at the hospital, she would've gone there and helped herself to sutures and other related supplies. The wound could've used three or four stitches. Nevertheless, all she had in her apartment was some Krazy Glue, which was an acceptable alternative to stitches.

Twenty minutes later Sarah Haslam had cleaned her wound and closed the gash, but she still had some time before she needed to meet Dr. Stoker at his office to begin another day of boring outpatient work. She missed the days of consulting on the ICU with a patient who was grieving the fact that a recent car crash had left her paralyzed to some degree or another. She longed to be on the psychiatry floor prescribing anti-psychotic medications and watching patients transform from raging schizophrenics to rational and calm human beings — usually within just a few days. All of this outpatient depression, ADHD, bipolar disorder, and the other garden variety of people she considered only slightly ill, was deeply boring for Sarah Haslam as a second-fiddle resident to Dr. Stoker. Now, thanks to Tamara's delayed arrival this morning, she would change her destiny a bit.

CHAPTER 55

SIOUX FALLS REGIONAL HOSPITAL

Governor Horton certainly did not want the administration at Sioux Falls Regional Hospital to know that he was going to visit that day. Attorney General Hewitt, who was accompanying him, shared the sentiment. Hospital administrators were notorious for turning a quick patient visit into an opportunity to lobby for additional Medicaid reimbursement or turn the event into a big public relations opportunity. Today, all the governor and attorney general wanted to do was visit their friend, Ann Higgins, in the intensive care unit. However, protocol demanded that the dignitaries at least inform administration of their intent to visit. So at 7:43 a.m. the governor's executive assistant called the hospital and left word with the administration, the security department, and public affairs offices that the governor would be there that morning.

At 8:27 a.m. the governor and attorney general walked right through the main doors with little fanfare and wearing somber and resolute faces that projected concern for Ann Higgins. The director of security met them in the main lobby and accompanied the dignitaries and their staffers to the intensive care unit.

Once inside the unit, Horton and Hewitt stepped to Ann's bedside where they found Lieutenant Governor Higgins with his eyes bloodshot and swollen. Kent Higgins had never been such an emotional man; but he had never been this close to losing somebody he loved so much.

Francis Bandettini and Matt Nilsen

"Governor Horton, Attorney General Hewitt," the lieutenant governor said as he rose.

"Don't get up, Kent," said the governor.

The lieutenant governor ignored the request, and he shook each man's hand vigorously. "Thank you for coming."

"You're welcome. We won't stay long," the governor said. "How's Ann doing? What can you tell us?"

"She had a lot of trauma to her neck, but miraculously it did not break," Higgins explained. "The big question is, does she have any brain damage? It's just too early to tell. We estimate that she didn't breathe for four to five minutes, but we can't be sure. So it's a huge unknown. Currently, she's breathing with a ventilator and the doctors have her right on the edge of a medication-induced coma. That helps manage swelling and a number of other factors, and it gives her brain a rest so it can heal."

"So when do they think they will bring her out of the coma?" Hewitt asked.

"There is a protocol based on many factors. But we can't go wrong by reading to her and providing verbal stimulation. If you talk with her, it may be beneficial. They've just backed off her medication a little bit, so she just might hear you."

"So can she hear us?" asked the governor.

"Maybe. Would you like to say hello?"

"I suppose," the governor said with a touch of discomfort in his voice.

"Come over here where you can lean over and speak directly into her ear, sir." The lieutenant governor then turned to Attorney General Hewitt. "You can come around to the other side. One of you speaking in each ear. Politicians in stereo. They do everything to reduce the stress and tension on the brain, and here we go getting ready to mess that up."

The governor and attorney general took a moment to process the humor and then both emitted uncomfortable laughs that contained a flavor of disbelief. Each awkwardly leaned over toward Ann.

"Good morning, Ann. Richard Horton here. I bring you greetings from Linda, my wife, and I hope that these difficult days get easier and more encouraging."

Ann's eyes slowly opened and she looked toward the governor with a hint of recognition. Then suddenly her eyes started to dart around.

"Wow. That's new," Kent Higgins said. That's more active than I've previously seen her. We'll have to tell the doctor. Very encouraging. She must be a true Republican."

Steve Hewitt leaned in and took his turn saying his hellos. "Hi Ann. Everyone in South Dakota is praying for you." Ann's eyes continued to dart around wildly as if she were excited or alarmed. "We're all hoping that you return home soon with Kent and your children. We pray for your comfort and recovery, Ann."

"Now *that* right there is new," Kent said pointing to Ann's left hand. It was trembling and twitching quickly. And then her right hand began to shake, too. With IV's, tubes, and lines running from her arms, nose, and mouth, the men sensed that she was in danger of pulling or tugging some critical device and harming herself.

"Nurse!" called out the lieutenant governor to the woman who was typing into a computer terminal a mere five paces away. Two minutes earlier, she had been watching over them like a hawk.

"Let's see what's going on," the nurse said in a calm and soothing voice. "Hi Ann. I'm Alisa, your nurse. I'm just going to talk to you while we get through these next few minutes." Alisa was obviously talented. With her deft and well-trained hands she gently moved the menagerie of life support lines away from Ann's hands. She also monitored the screens and instruments that were displaying elevated readings just to the left of Ann's head. "Oh my, these bilateral tremors are a new development," she said. Ann's blood pressure had reached 153/95. "We're going to have to watch that. Her heart's racing, too. If these don't go down in the next minute or so, we'll need you to clear out so the doctor and I can work with her a bit more."

"Perhaps we should give her some space right now as sort of a preventative measure," Hewitt suggested.

"Yes," agreed the governor. "Kent, we'll wait outside the doors. If she gets through this in the next five minutes, come on out and we'll say goodbye. If not, don't worry about us."

"One sixty-one over one hundred," Alisa said. "Still going in the wrong direction."

The governor and attorney general exited right away and walked into the waiting room to reconvene. "Ready to go, sirs?" asked one of the staffers who had been making phone calls.

"Not just yet," replied the governor. We're going to wait for Kent for just a few minutes. Ann had a bit of an, um. Well, what would you call it Steve?"

"Well, her blood pressure shot up and her hands started to shake," the Attorney General replied. "I don't know. Perhaps I would call them spasms?"

"Yes. An episode of some sort," the governor said. Then he turned to his aide and asked, "Any phone calls?"

"Senator Waneta," reported the aide.

"Republican from Rapid City suburbia," chimed in the governor. He prided himself on keeping abreast of all of the South Dakota lawmakers and powerbrokers.

"He wants to talk to you about the federal lands fight that's boiling up again," the aide explained.

"Well, he delivered the vote in November, so I'll get right back to him as soon as we're in the car."

Just then Lieutenant Governor Higgins came through the ICU door into the waiting room.

"Kent, how is Ann?" Hewitt asked.

"Much better. A few moments after you left, she stopped shaking and her blood pressure returned to normal. She seems a lot more comfortable now. It looks like it was just one of those things."

"We'll let you get back to your wife," the governor said. "You're in our prayers."

After exchanging handshakes, the governor, attorney general, and rest of the entourage returned to the elevator, ascended to the main level, and exited the hospital with no fanfare.

Back up in the intensive care unit, Kent Higgins was slightly concerned, and he asked himself, *what just happened here?*

CHAPTER 56

Sarah Haslam was waiting outside Dr. Stoker's door when he arrived at 7:50 a.m. "Oh, Sarah. I'm so sorry. I should've called or texted you. Tamara usually gets here before me, but she's going to be in late today."

"Wow. That's a surprise. That woman is more reliable than Japanese cars."

"Yes. Funny you should say that," Stoker said. "She had car trouble this morning."

"With that little Mazda of hers? It's too new to have car trouble."

"You would think. I guess even a new Japanese car can go on the fritz in this cold."

"Well, how can I help out?"

Stoker was surprised by Haslam's cheery disposition. Her new attitude put him on guard a little. "No, we can just let the calls go to voice mail. I don't have patients this afternoon because I need to get through a mountain of paperwork. Tamara can just pick up the messages and get back to people once she gets in."

"I've got a crazy idea," Haslam said. "How about I answer the calls and do some scheduling and triage. I need to know how to do this so I understand how to run a practice someday. Also, I'd hate to miss out on a code blue. If I catch one I can let you know."

"You want to do receptionist and clerical work?"

"Not forever, but I can pitch in today. Like I said, I'll do some good triage and study up on some of our patients."

"Suit yourself," Stoker said. "If you get stuck, send me an instant message."

"We'll have to see if my pride lets me admit if I'm stuck. I don't like admitting when I'm stuck."

"Sorry, I can only offer you empathy," Stoker said good-humoredly. "I have no solutions for pride. Admitting when I'm stuck or lost is not something that works for the male psyche." Stoker walked behind the reception counter and turned on Tamara's computer. "Who's first on the schedule?"

Haslam waited for Tamara's computer to finish booting up, punched a few keys on the keyboard, and said, "Samantha Gail. She should be here in the next five minutes."

Stoker rolled the phones over from the answering service while Haslam pulled a stack of documents off the fax machine.

"Hey, Troy. Can I stick around here and have a study afternoon rummaging through your psychiatry library? You've got some interesting books that have caught my attention, and I've just not made time to dive into them."

"Sure. Just pull the door closed behind you when you leave."

"Great. Thanks"

Five minutes later, Stoker was in his office with patient, Samantha Gail, a woman who was suffering profound depression after learning that her husband was having an affair.

At 8:15 a.m. the phone rang.

"Dr. Stoker's office," Haslam answered.

"Hi, this is Lonnie Stewart."

"Hi, Mr. Stewart. What can I do for you?" Haslam was hoping that the person on the phone was a potentially new patient instead of a patient who had seen Dr. Stoker before. She was scouting for new patients.

"I just need an appointment to see Troy."

Because the patient used Stoker's first name, Haslam assumed that he had been seen at the clinic before. Indeed, Mr. Stewart was a regular patient who worked with Dr. Stoker on issues of anxiety and outbursts of anger. A small dose of oxcarbazepine at night and some talk therapy had calmed his anger. His depression was helped with a daily dose of bupropion, which was also a very mild stimulant that could help rekindle his libido. His wife was thankful for the changes—usually. She welcomed the new romance initially, but it was getting to be a little much lately.

"Mr. Stewart, this is Dr. Haslam, a resident working with Dr. Stoker," she explained. "Tamara, our receptionist, is not here quite yet, so can I have her call you back to make an appointment?"

Mr. Stewart readily agreed and provided his phone number. Haslam wrote out the message on a stereotypical pink message slip and set it to the side of the desk where she intended to make a pile of the messages.

While she waited for the next call to come in, she opened a new Microsoft Word document on the computer. Within five minutes she had managed to fashion a prescription pad that included her name, credentials, and proper legal data. She used Dr. Stoker's address and included her cell phone number on the pad. While she was confident that she had a license to prescribe medicine and could legally do so, it was only her pride that caused her to overlook the school's policy that she was supposed to only use prescription pads supplied by her residency program. However, she planned to only occasionally use the prescription pad. For most medications Haslam would call in the prescription on the phone, under Dr. Stoker's name. Any pharmacy would fill the prescription if she simply said; "This is resident Sarah Haslam, working closely with Dr. Troy Stoker as a physician in training. Please put the following prescription in his name. Dr. Stoker wants it in his name, because this is his own personal patient." In the case of a schedule two drug such as amphetamines, she would just write the prescription. She could probably talk most ADHD patients into using the non-stimulant Strattera to further curb her risk.

"File and print," Haslam said under her breath. "Forty copies should be a good start." And with one final click, the laser printer came to life and produced a small stack of prescription sheets, which Haslam quickly filed in a manila folder and slipped into her fine walnut-colored leather messenger bag.

Then, Dr. Haslam opened the computer's web browser and typed in the search query, "Sioux Falls homeless clinic." Up popped the St. Francis clinic. "There you are. Let's see what we can set up there for the good Dr. Stoker."

Dr. Haslam picked up the phone and dialed the main number for the clinic. After a few rings she reached a receptionist. "Oh, hello. This is Dr. Haslam, an associate of Dr. Stoker's, one of the psychiatrists here in town. Can I please speak to the manager there?"

A few moments later she was greeted by a new voice. "This is Ron Fowler. How can I help you, doctor?"

"Hello Mr. Fowler. My name is Sarah Haslam, and I'm a resident working with Dr. Troy Stoker. I'm calling to see if the clinic would happen to have some space Dr. Stoker and I could use one evening per week to see psychiatric patients. Do you have any evening capacity?"

"Well, we're open until eight o'clock on Thursday nights. I'll need to check with my nurse managers. While I know all of our treatment rooms will be in use, I suspect that one of our small conference rooms is available on Thursday nights. Could that work for you?"

"Actually, it would work better than a treatment room. Patients would just check in with me directly. They get a little nervous about checking in with a stranger for psychiatric care."

"Let me take down your number and get back to you," Fowler said. "Of course, I would have some paperwork for Dr. Stoker to fill out."

"That's no problem. I can swing by and pick it up, if you indeed confirm that you have space."

"Great, Dr. Haslam. Let me get right back to you with an answer."

As the phone call ended, Dr. Haslam closed the Internet browser. She then opened Dr. Stoker's electronic medical record program and pretended to busy herself looking interested in the medical histories and psychiatric notes of the other patients whom they would see this morning. But in truth, Sarah Haslam was waiting anxiously for Ron Fowler of St. Francis clinic to call her back. She needed to field that phone call before Tamara managed to repair her car and get into the office. Dr. Haslam would never be able to hatch her little scheme under the perceptive eyes of the ever-so-diligent Tamara.

A few minutes later Dr. Haslam answered another call.

"Hi, my name is Ed McCall and I need to know if Dr. Stoker takes South Dakota Medicaid. My mom and I are already on disability. My mom's depressed and on dialysis, and I keep losing my job because I have anxiety—just like my mom, but worse. We both need to see someone."

Bingo, thought Sarah Haslam. She was going to get a new patient in her own little private practice. "Dr. Stoker has voluntarily opted out of both Medicaid and Medicare, so he cannot see you at his office. However, as volunteers, we see Medicaid and uninsured patients at St. Francis clinic on Thursday evenings. We do not charge for those visits. We provide the service as part of our mission to the community of Sioux Falls."

As with most lies, Sarah Haslam's deceit contained a strong element of truth. Dr. Stoker had opted out of Medicaid and Medicare, early in his career. It was not out of greed. He generously treated many patients with Medicare and Medicaid, but he preferred to see them for free instead of taking government money. While it was a matter of principle that he did not accept government money, it was also an issue of sanity and efficiency. Even during his time in the Army, Stoker noticed that working with government programs often opened people up to more layers of scrutiny and ongoing documentation of ridiculous minutia. Moreover, government case managers were famous for second guessing doctors' decisions. He preferred to dedicate the time he saved by opting out of government programs, to giving free care to people in need.

The single element of truth, that Dr. Stoker did not treat Medicaid patients in his office, had helped Sarah Haslam set off her scheme, which was increasingly fueled by her narcissistic personality disorder and the disassociation from reality caused by her borderline personality disorder.

Haslam continued wooing this potential patient. "Well, first Mr. McCall, let's talk about you. Then we'll talk about helping your mom." She was trying to be charming, and did not realize that she sounded like a salesperson instead of a doctor. "Are you available this Thursday evening?" asked Haslam. She had the audacity to assume that the clinic would be calling her back to grant her the patient space.

"I am. You mean this Thursday?"

"Indeed I do," Haslam confirmed. "I have an appointment available at seven o'clock that evening. How does that work?"

"Okay. Wow, I'm surprised to get in so quickly."

"We pride ourselves on being accessible, Mr. McCall," Haslam lied. "Now, what would you like to talk about on Thursday?"

"Well, I have some issues that I need to discuss," said McCall. Haslam could hear how uneasy he felt. He was about to unload a little bit of his burden. "I mentioned the anxiety already. But in the last few months I've been starting to hear some voices in my head."

"I know that we can help you." Haslam had just made a promise to Mr. McCall that few doctors would ever make, but she didn't care. She was putting on her façade of charm, and she succeeded at convincing this man that she was a warm and caring individual. "How much we can help you remains to be seen. I do know that there are many medications that are new and effective."

"They are mumbling-type voices in my head, and it's bothering me."

"Well, as a doctor, I also like to look for other physical problems that could cause these mumblings in your head. Lots of people hear voices and you will be surprised how easy treatment is," boasted the overly confident Haslam.

"Really?"

"Indeed. If you're like ninety-nine percent of people who hear voices," exaggerated Haslam with the false bravado of a full-blown narcissist, "you're just a few days away from understanding it and fixing it, Mr. McCall."

"And, I thought I was crazy."

"If you did not treat it, you could reach that stage, Mr. McCall. Don't worry. We all have our little issues to iron out. I look forward to meeting with you on Thursday at seven o'clock. Do you know where the St. Francis clinic is?"

"Oh yes. I grew up just a few blocks away from St. Francis. Those were better days for that part of town you know."

"That's what I've heard," Haslam said. "Oh, by the way. Let me give you my direct phone number in case something comes up. Please call me direct instead of calling the clinic. I don't want you to have to go through the receptionist red tape. As a new patient she won't recognize you yet."

After Mr. McCall had found a pencil and a piece of paper, Sarah Haslam provided him with her cell phone number. Then she reminded him again that it was best to call her only on the number she had just given.

"We'll see you Thursday at seven," Haslam said ending the phone call. She was proud of herself, even though she had neglected to capture his phone number and his date of birth. She was oblivious to her errors, such as forgetting to ask McCall about his mother, too.

"Congratulations Dr. Haslam," she whispered to herself. "You have your first patient – and with nobody looking over your shoulder, telling you what to do, while insisting what you write in your progress notes." Her whisper had escalated, and now she was having a full-voiced conversation aloud with herself. "Finally, some independence to practice excellent psychiatry. I'll show them." Hearing her own words soothed her mind. Her narcissistic delusion of destiny was controlling her decisions and emotions now. Disassociation from the pain and stress of her reality was quickly edging out rational logic.

At 8:53 a.m. Dr. Stoker opened the door to his office and escorted Samantha Gail to the front desk. She emerged from her session with puffy, red skin surrounding her tearful eyes. Her weeping had washed away her eye makeup, blush, and base. "Thank you, Doctor Stoker. I will be strong. I insist on respecting myself," Samantha said.

"You've done an amazing job of demanding that your husband start respecting you again," pointed out Stoker. It is powerful. Is it working?"

"You know the answer to that."

"Of course," Stoker said. "But it's my job to help you remind yourself. Let's talk in two weeks."

With a smile, Samantha Gail walked out the door with just enough time to make it to work by 9:15 a.m.

"That sounds like it went well," Haslam said.

"Yes. She's a strong person. She just needs some supportive therapy. A few months ago, she wasn't sleeping. So, we started there. Now that she's getting good REM sleep, we're making a lot of rapid progress."

Haslam looked at him with condescending doubt on her face, and Stoker picked up on it right away.

"Sleep is so fundamental, Sarah," Stoker said. "You can't fix much else until you fix sleep. A good psychiatrist is always aware that there are many different causes for mental conditions, including physical problems. We have to use many different modalities to solve psychiatric problems."

"Of course, Samantha also needs to stay medicated for her depression," Haslam said.

Stoker was disappointed that Haslam had defaulted back to her shortsightedness. She was overly concerned with medication. He replied by saying, "Who wouldn't? Medicine is critical for her. But, I want you to look more at the big picture, Sarah." Stoker looked down at the schedule. "Who's coming in next?"

"It's Sid Eliason," Haslam said. "I'm glad you're warmed up."

"Yes. Sid has not made much progress. He won't own his anger or embrace his ADHD. Let's see how persuasive I can be today. You don't want to take this patient do you? I'll answer the phones for a while," Stoker kidded.

Haslam panicked. *What if the Saint Francis Clinic called back while I was in session with Sid?* she thought. "No, Troy. Normally I would, but I'm in the middle of reviewing some of your literature now. I'm kind of on a roll, here. Why don't you take Sid?"

"Okay, Sarah. Suit yourself," Stoker said. "Sid will probably be ten minutes late for his appointment. It's part of his modus operandi. I'll be in here spending the next few minutes working on the never-ending paperwork. Send Sid in when he gets here."

"Oh hey, Dr. Stoker?" Haslam asked. "Can you please give me Tamara's cell phone number? I'll just text her to let her know that she doesn't need to rush."

"Oh, yeah. It's 605-555-1432," Stoker said over his shoulder walking back into his office and leaving the door open. "I know that one by heart," he said as he sat back down in his chair and spun around to his desk and delved into the paperwork.

Haslam sent a quick text to Tamara:

> *Take your time, Tamara. I've got the phones and desk covered… at least as well as you can expect for an over-qualified temporary office worker. ;)*

And then Haslam looked down and began perusing another patient chart. She was only pretending to be interested in it. Really, she was waiting for the next patient to arrive and distract Stoker, so she could continue answering the phones and diverting patients to her own little private practice.

When the phone rang again, Sarah Haslam picked up the handset and brought it to her ear. But before she could answer she heard Dr. Stoker's voice fielding the call. "Dr. Troy Stoker's office. May I help you?" Because Haslam and

Stoker had answered at the same time, the call became an instant three-way call between the caller, Haslam, and Stoker.

"Hi, Dr. Stoker. This is Ron Fowler over at the Saint Francis Clinic. How are you?"

Haslam panicked and her heart raced. If Fowler mentioned her request to use some space in the clinic, Stoker would find out about her scheme. Stoker answered Fowler's question. "I'm great, Ron. What can I do for you?"

Haslam envisioned the whole domino effect. Stoker would uncover her intricate plan. In his disappointment, and possibly anger, he would inform her residency committee of her attempt to set up valiant, and uncompensated, moonlighting. If she did not get control of this situation in the next few moments, she would be packing her bags and trying to figure out how to rescue her medical career.

"Well, I was just calling you back about—"

"Hi, Ron," interrupted Haslam with a calmness in her voice that betrayed her racing heart and shaking hands. "I just happened to pick up simultaneously with Dr. Stoker." She saw Stoker spin around in his chair and look at her through the opened door with a look of surprise on his face. "I suspect you're returning my call?" asked Haslam into the headset.

"Yes. Thursday nights—"

Again, Haslam interrupted Fowler. "Sure! Let's visit about Thursday nights. I have a few questions and I bet you have some, too." She paused briefly. "Any resident would."

"Okay, well we have—"

"Hey, Troy. I can take it from here," cut in Haslam—this time with a little less calmness in her voice.

"Okay," Stoker said with a pause. "Nice to talk to you, Ron."

"You too, Doc."

Dr. Stoker hung up the phone. But his intuition was informing him—as it often did—that something abnormal was going on. So the good doctor returned his gaze to the paperwork set before him and picked up a pen. However, his attention was set on Sarah Haslam and the conversation she was having in the reception area.

"That sounds great, Ron," Haslam said. The rest of her answers were short. She suspected Stoker was plenty curious about the phone call. "Certainly. Documents. Of course. I will. Perfect. Thank you. You, too."

Stoker knew that a conversation between a resident and the manager of a low-income clinic could be about any number of issues. Perhaps she was doing some paperwork for a future rotation? Maybe she was participating in a meeting or conference? She could even be covering for another resident or picking up a

Thursday evening moonlighting shift diagnosing ear aches and strep throats, stitching up wounds, treating sprains, and referring strange rashes to dermatologists. Even a surprise birthday party for a resident or staff member at the clinic was within the realm of possibilities. Nevertheless, Stoker made a mental note to keep one eye open for Sarah Haslam's Thursday evening plans. His intuition was telling him that something was amiss and that Sarah Haslam was hiding something.

Haslam continued to do her pretend work, while Stoker also tried to act convincingly interested in the paperwork stacked before him. Haslam concluded that Stoker was not trying to monitor her, but she was wrong. Moreover, Stoker was aware that Haslam was trying to figure out if her phone call had piqued his curiosity. Stoker's peripheral vision and sense of hearing had picked up on a few clues, but his behavior gave nothing away.

At 9:04 a.m., the front door opened and in stepped Allie Stoker carrying a box of pastries.

"Hi. May I help you?" Haslam asked. She had never met Allie Stoker, and the young doctor already assumed the attractive person bringing food into the office was a drug rep or other medical salesperson.

"Surprise! I come bearing gifts."

What drugs is this bimbo trying to push on us today? Haslam thought.

From his office Stoker bellowed, "What are you doing here?" Rushing out from his office, he took Allie by the hand and playfully led her back to the office. As she passed into his office with him, Stoker slapped her on the butt. "People are going to talk if they see you here. What will they say?" Stoker said as he semi-slammed the door shut and gave his wife a one-second kiss.

But, Sarah Haslam did not pick up on his ruse and playfulness. She had seen doctors do a good job of hiding affairs, and she also knew of doctors who did a poor job of keeping such secrets. She was beginning to conclude that Stoker was in the latter category with this apparent drug rep. She was quite surprised because Stoker had spoken so fondly of his wife. During the brief time they had worked together Stoker had never even made an offhanded sexual comment.

A moment later Stoker's office door opened again and he emerged still holding Allie's hand. "Sarah. Can I ask you for a moment of discretion?"

Haslam's eyes met him directly, failing to detect Stoker's horseplay with his wife. "Yes. I don't lie, but I don't disclose, either."

"Well, this woman you see before me has recently captivated me and taken virtually all of my attention. I must confess. She is the love of my life. I cannot tell a lie. We're having torrid love affair!"

Haslam blushed, and she awkwardly responded, "Well, it's nice to meet you. I'm Sarah Haslam, a resident rotating with Dr. Stoker."

"Troy has told me all about you. You're a University of Chicago graduate, I hear."

"Yes, I am. I'm pleased to be enjoying your balmy Sioux Falls winters," Haslam said before she laughed at her own joke. "And what is your name?"

"I'm Allie. Allie Stoker."

At first, Haslam felt a rush of relief flow through her body. This Dr. Stoker wasn't this cheating philanderer after all. But about three seconds later, her emotions changed. She was livid that Stoker, and his wife would pull yet another prank on her. *How dare they!* she thought. Fury tightened within Haslam's chest and surged outward to her extremities. She was outraged that Stoker would, yet again, play some kind of joke on her. The petty and hypersensitive Sarah Haslam sorely lacked the ego strength required of a good psychiatrist. Again, her face blushed profusely, but this time the crimson was borne of wrath. Sarah Haslam just couldn't handle her own misperception of having her intelligence insulted in any way, shape, or form. Furthermore, she was deeply jealous of any couple that enjoyed emotional intimacy.

"Oh," Haslam replied. She could think of nothing else to say. She was using all of her energy to maintain poise and self-control in front of her new acquaintance. Neither Allie nor Dr. Troy Stoker realized that they had profoundly insulted Sarah Haslam. She deserved better treatment than this. It was already beneath her to be answering the telephone in the office of the two-bit psychiatrist. She did not understand why her preferred residency had not chosen her at Georgetown University. There she would have treated a diverse population that truly needed her extraordinary psychiatric skills. This insult by the Stokers wasn't quite the straw that would break the camel's back. However their little spontaneous stunt had moved her one step closer to seeking vengeful retribution against the many psychiatrists who had harmed her in this pissant town.

By now, Allie was opening the box of baked goods from the Cookie Jar Eatery. "I brought you coffee, Sarah, but I don't know how you like it. There is cream and sugar in the bag. I myself am a Macchiato fan," Allie was saying. Haslam could not have cared less.

"For some reason, today I just feel like black coffee," Haslam said. No cream or sugar this morning. Just black." She continued to seethe inside. And then she began to plot. *In this era when bullying and hazing were so discouraged, plotting a subtle, or not so subtle, revenge is critical*, thought Haslam. *I will be vindicated!*

"The caramel rolls from the Cookie Jar Eatery are amazing, but I will only eat one, and it has to be before a long ski. I have to know that I'll burn it off," Dr. Stoker said.

Sarah Haslam prided herself on nutrition and discipline with the food she ate. *I despise pastries, you idiots!* she thought. *Do I look like donuts and cookies are a regular part of my diet?* She looked at the box of pastries in a somewhat aloof fashion.

"I brought a few choices," Allie said. "I heard you're little shorthanded until Tamara gets here. There's also some banana nut bread and a few different muffins.

"No lemon poppy seed for me?" kidded Dr. Stoker.

"No way, Troy. All I need is a scone-shaped husband who strokes out on me when he's fifty-nine years old."

To disguise her anger, Haslam selected a blueberry muffin—the most healthful of the offerings. "Thank you," she said with as much sincerity as she could falsify.

"How are you enjoying this rotation outside of the hospital?" Allie asked. Before Sarah Haslam could answer, the telephone rang.

"Oh, hang on, Allie," Haslam said. "Let me get this call."

The caller was another physician wanting to talk to Dr. Stoker about a patient they both treated. Haslam handed off the phone call to Stoker, who took the call shortly after closing his office door.

"Back to your question, Allie. I'm really enjoying the contrast of outpatient private practice work," Haslam lied. "Your husband has really shown me a lot. I'm learning so much, and I really appreciate his strength."

Haslam's false statements were interrupted when the front door swung open. In walked Sid Eliason, the 9:00 a.m. patient. As predicted, he was just over ten minutes late; and he wore a scowl that made it clear that he was unenthused about his visit to the psychiatrist that day.

Despite the many shortcomings Sarah Haslam's residency committee had pointed out about her clinical skills, judgment, and interactions with other doctors, Sarah Haslam shined at winning over difficult patients. "Hi, Sid!" Haslam said in a warm voice that reflected just a touch of flirtatiousness.

"Hi, Dr. Haslam."

"Are you doing horrible today?" Asked Haslam sarcastically flashing a grin at Sid.

Sid properly detected her sarcasm. "Oh yes, dear. The sky is falling and the state's making me sit down with the shrink, yet again."

"Fascists!" Haslam joked.

"Actually, they're Commies," Sid said.

Already, Sarah Haslam had wiped the scowl off of Sid's face. "Oh, sorry!" Haslam said with ample melodramatic flair. "I always get those two mixed up. I often fail to see the different shades of gray when analyzing control freak totalitarian bureaucrats. Can you ever forgive my naïveté of the political spectrum?"

Sid responded with equal theatrical ease. "In my mind I'm ready to forgive you; but my heart will need some time. I'm just being honest. Check back with me in a week or two."

"I only have baked goods from the Cookie Jar Eatery to offer you as a peace offering," Haslam said. "Could a pastry possibly soften your heart?"

"Did you say pastry?"

"Indeed. A staple of a healthy diet."

"I never turn down banana nut bread."

Sarah placed a slice on a paper towel and delivered it to Sid with a melodramatic curtsy. "Coffee?"

"No thank you. I'm already two cups into the day."

"Let me get Dr. Stoker for you. I'll tell him to get off the phone."

"Yes. Tell him to make his 1-900 number calls when he doesn't have a patient waiting."

Haslam laughed, and this time it was almost genuine. She appreciated the fact that Dr. Stoker's wife had just overheard that joke. "Oh, you should see our phone bills. We've had to limit him to thirty minutes a day."

Haslam opened the door, walked into Stoker's office and handed him a note informing him his next patient was ready.

"Doctor Phillips, I need to go. My next patient just got here," Stoker said. With a few more formalities, he ended the call, came out in the hallway, and welcomed Sid into his office.

"Well, I hope you don't mind that I offered him your banana nut bread, Allie," Haslam said.

"No, not at all. I'm glad you did."

"It was so nice to meet you, Allie, and I really appreciate the muffin." Now that the two women were alone again, Haslam's emotions smoldered anew. The feeling of deep insult reemerged and she quickly concluded that she hated this Allie Stoker woman, although she knew little about her.

"I'm sorry that I'm not so social today. In addition to my spontaneous receptionist duties, I'm also studying a great deal of material that I need to dominate for some upcoming exams. So if I seem a tad aloof, I hope you'll understand why."

"Oh, you're fine, Dr. Haslam. Not aloof at all. I'll let you get back to everything."

Haslam was pleased that Allie had taken the hint. With any luck, she would be out of her hair in just under thirty seconds. And indeed, luck was with her, because the phone rang. The women exchanged goodbyes and Sarah Haslam picked up the phone. "Dr. Stoker's office. Can I help you?"

"Oh hi," said a voice full of nervousness and anxiety. "I've lost my job, I have no insurance, but I think I need to see a psychiatrist. I can pay you a little bit now and then pay the rest once I find a new job. Do you see patients like me?"

"Of course. As a matter of fact, if you're going through a really hard time, we can see you for free at St. Francis clinic. Once you get back on your feet, you could consider coming to our main clinic. How does that sound?"

"You do that?"

"We do. It's important, too. Crises often hit when our wallets are starved. Are you available this Thursday night?"

Sarah Haslam scheduled her second Thursday night appointment. By the time Tamara arrived at the office at 10:15 a.m. Haslam had booked yet another. She had three appointments this coming Thursday night. Her little private practice was off to a stunning start.

During the rest of the morning, Haslam spent time taking notes from a number of Dr. Stoker's books and medical journals. Because today was an early day, Dr. Stoker finished with patients just before 1:00 p.m., and Haslam had a plan.

At 1:30 p.m. Dr. Stoker left the office for the day, and Tamara was only about ten minutes behind him. Before leaving, however, Tamara forwarded the phones to the answering service. When the answering service fielded a phone call, the operators would follow the instructions previously issued by Dr. Stoker. In a few situations they would forward the call to Dr. Stoker. If they sensed the patient was in danger, they directed him or her to the emergency room. If it was a routine issue, such as someone needing an appointment or a medication refill, the answering service simply passed on an email message that Tamara or Dr. Stoker would address the next day.

Five minutes after Haslam saw Tamara's car leave the parking lot, Sarah Haslam redirected the phone calls from the answering service to phone at the front desk. Since she was the only one at the clinic, she would field every call.

The first phone call came from an existing patient. She lied and stated that she was the answering service. "Will you please call back tomorrow morning any time after eight o'clock?" When potential new patients with insurance called, Haslam asked them to call back in the morning and speak with Tamara. But, when patients with no insurance or Medicaid called, they got Haslam's full attention—and fake compassion. They also got appointments to see her at the free clinic.

By 3:15 p.m., Sarah had scheduled three more patients for Thursday evening appointments at St. Francis clinic. Now she was content to re-forward the phones to the answering service. Each of her soon-to-be new patients had her cell phone number and strict instructions to use it rather than calling the main clinic.

Haslam packed up her bag, set the alarm, and locked the door, leaving the clinic at 3:30 p.m. At 3:45 p.m. Sarah Haslam dropped in at St. Francis clinic to collect the necessary paperwork and shake hands with Ron Fowler, the clinic manager. "Ron, this is really great. Troy really appreciates this," Haslam lied. "You know, with some of these Medicare, Medicaid, and self-pay patients, he also detects problems with their family members, and he may want to treat them right then and there. There's just such a need. I'll return these documents with Dr. Stoker's signature by tomorrow."

The next day, she returned the documents, complete with Dr. Stoker's forged signature. Sarah Haslam was in business.

CHAPTER 57

Larry Stintson, M.D., was obsessed. He loved being a white-collar criminal and he had already supplied the commander with more than a dozen profiles of previous patients and seven profiles of doctors who lived in other states and no longer held South Dakota medical licenses. Stintson had left the commander almost a dozen messages over the last five days requesting a meeting. His zeal for his new criminal ventures had filled his head with questions and fueled his morbid curiosity and desire to entrench more deeply in his newly discovered secret life.

Finally, the commander had relented and granted him some time outside of normal business hours. Ron Cunningham, his right hand man from Reno, called Stintson and set up the get-together. The commander had agreed to meet him this evening. At first Stintson suggested they meet at his doctor's office. The commander quickly decided against the idea, and he more-or-less commanded the doctor to meet just outside the hospital emergency room again. The commander pulled up in his burgundy SUV at just after 7:00 p.m. and Stintson jumped in.

"Thanks for meeting with me, Commander. I just have so many questions." He heard a stirring from the back of the vehicle and turned his head to see two beautiful dogs with wolf-like features. Stintson thought for a moment to recall their names. He remembered how they were named after the Filipino leaders, Ferdinand and Imelda Marcos. "So you brought Ferdinand and Imelda with you today?"

"Sometimes we get some evening time to spend together. I feed them with attention and exercise, and they feed my soul. Let's run them out to Palisade's State Park and let them have some fun," the commander said. It also left him the option of calling in coyotes to scare Stintson into complete obedience if necessary.

"Great," Stintson said as the car left the parking lot. "I'll ask you all of my questions as we drive."

"Okay. The floor is yours. What is your first question?"

"What about people who have huge debt loads or have declared bankruptcy?" Stintson asked.

"Sometimes we can still get financial institutions to lend to them," the commander explained. "Post-bankruptcy is a nice little sweet spot. With those who are not currently credit-worthy, we mark them in our database as a future opportunity." The commander got on the freeway and began traveling north." For example, we've been watching this dentist in Illinois who declared bankruptcy about three years ago. Well, he's been doing some credit repair with secured credit cards, and his new wife has been co-signing on some small loans."

"So when do you make your move on this guy?"

"We did. My people at Green Growth Ventures hit him on Tuesday. One bank gave him a ten-thousand-dollar credit card, and another one let us pump him for eight grand. We sent a guy in a disguise and fake ID to a payday loan place. He walked out with four thousand dollars in his hand. The dentist is still at least fifteen days away from any type of alert."

"Wow," Stintson said. "Twenty-two thousand dollars on one bankrupt guy, and he doesn't even know it yet. So aren't they going to notice that a bunch of people in Chelsea Crossing have been getting hit?"

"Banks look at that type of thing a little. Law enforcement is only starting to look at geographic trends like that. Remember I get some pretty good information these days from my friends in government and I know what they're looking at. But it's a good question. We have been spreading our geographic risk a lot more. That kind of concentrated activity to one neighborhood could sooner or later prompt investigators to start snooping around Chelsea Crossing. We would just move on. I'm really good at moving my operations many days or weeks before somebody is onto us."

"So, do you think you'll eventually have to close this place up and sell it?" asked Stintson.

"I hope not. We'll change our operations and maybe even slow down with the identity theft. By that time, the downstairs meth lab operations could be operational," the commander explained. "What other questions do you have?"

Stintson asked him four or five other questions before they arrived at Palisades State Park. The dogs had obviously been here before because they were starting to get excited. They knew it was time to get out and run. The commander parked in an empty parking lot and the two men got out of the SUV and liberated the dogs. The commander handed Stintson a LED LENSER headlamp and then put one on his own head. The two men walked with their lights illuminating the area ahead of them for dozens of yards. The dogs were thrilled to be running around in the parking lot on a twenty-one-degree night. The commander took out two tennis balls and threw them out about thirty yards. Ferdinand and Imelda sprinted toward the balls.

"Let me change the subject, Larry," the commander said. "Let's talk about Troy Stoker."

"Yes. He's been snooping around on some things, I hear," confirmed Stintson.

"Larry, I want you to keep your eyes and ears open for Stoker. If you hear that he's asking any more questions or trying to act like a private investigator, please let me know."

"No problem, boss." The dogs had reached the tennis balls, but they quickly lost interest in retrieving them. They continued the frolicking, territory marking, and exploring with no regard for the two people a few yards away. "Stoker actually called our office this week and requested a hearing."

"Fascinating," the commander said. "You had better grant it to him quickly."

"Really? Why?" Stintson asked.

"Check your rules, Larry. I bet you are bound by some clause to issue the request within a few weeks or close the case. Ask your attorney," coached the commander. "But right now, we're working on a plan to shut Stoker down," he said in a determined and aggressive tone. "After that, just give us six more months and we'll have that other lab on Bryant Way up and running. Our plan will be back on track."

"So what are you going to do with Stoker?"

"Well, your boy Berg has been of zero help. He walked in to plant some bugs and get some records for me and he walked out getting his ass kicked. It's all on video."

"Berg's an obedient soldier, but you asked him to do something new. He's not a quick study, commander. We'll need to corral Stoker some other way."

"I hope we can just distract him enough that he doesn't have time to snoop around. If that doesn't work, I have some friends on the police force who can find drugs just about anywhere."

"You mean you'd plant drugs on him?"

"In his medical office. It would be so much more sensational in the media if they found the drugs in his practice." The commander whistled for the dogs.

They stopped their animated explorations and frolicking, raised their ears, and half-heartedly started trotting back toward their master.

Larry Stintson couldn't help but empathize with the pain Stoker might feel. Just days earlier, at the restaurant, Carnaval, he had thought he was about to be arrested on drug-related charges. He'd felt the terror that accompanied the realization that his desk contained a few hits of Katerina's favorite recreational meth and MDMA. "That would be amazingly persuasive, sir," he said while experiencing a momentary nervous shiver.

"But I'm not beyond removing him from the picture completely." The commander had to whistle again. The dogs had been distracted before they could make it back to their master. "These half-wolves have to constantly be reminded to obey."

"Are you talking about killing Troy Stoker?"

"It's really up to Stoker."

Strangely, Stintson felt euphoric with his new experiences in the world of the criminal. He'd never been bad-to-the-bone before and he loved the new thrill. Never had Katerina or any other woman, held onto him like he'd experienced during the last few days. The excitement far exceeded the buzz he got from strutting around the hospital, accelerating in his new car, or kicking around his minions at the state board! "All of this is like an aphrodisiac with pure adrenaline coursing through my veins!" exclaimed Stintson to the commander. "Now I live *this* way. If I cannot tap into this power, money and thrill, I don't want to be alive! And hunting Stoker is just another bonus in this game!"

The commander looked at Dr. Stintson. He was concerned about the manic behavior his new doctor associate exhibited. Larry Stintson's eyes were uncharacteristically wide open—a clear instance of sunset eyes. The commander had learned about sunset eyes when he lost a case on an insanity plea. The commander knew something wasn't right with Stintson. It reminded him of that semi-crazy-looking, blond, Sunday-morning news show female host. The commander liked to mock her—but he did not like seeing these symptoms in his new recruit, Larry Stintson.

The commander pulled some dog treats out of his pocket, and immediately Ferdinand and Imelda came to complete attention. "Heel," insisted the commander. Immediately, the rambunctious dogs assumed a position at his side and took on a placid demeanor. "It's all about the incentives, Larry." The commander shared a treat with each dog, and the snacks consumed their attention for the next ten seconds, as he walked toward the ignored tennis balls. Stintson followed.

"Bring me up to speed on this Dr. Davis, the guy with all the malpractice suits. What are you guys at the medical board doing about it?"

"Ah, yes. Dr. Davis. He's a guy who did his general surgery residency, and then completed a vascular surgery fellowship. He's been making a mint doing the same tedious vascular procedures over and over. He got bored about five years ago and started fishing around for general surgery cases. You know, he needed a little variety. With a few winks and some undocumented gifts, he got some other docs to refer gall bladders, hernias, and appendix stuff his way. Run-of-the-mill procedures for most surgeons, but he was a bit rusty."

"So when did things start to go bad?" asked the commander as he continued walking. Imelda appeared at his side and rubbed against his leg. "Crazy bitch. She doesn't want my love. She wants another treat."

"Well, I'm not sure things ever went bad. I mean, technically, all of the work we've reviewed as a board falls within the standard of care."

"Oh come on Larry. You know how low that 'standard of care' actually is. Do you want your doctor to guarantee that he or she will treat you at least to the standard of care? Are those the last words you want to hear as the anesthesia takes over?"

"Well, um —."

"No, Larry! You would fight back the gas mask and get out of the operating room. At that point, you wouldn't care who saw your butt hanging out of your gown as you sprinted out of there."

"Well sir, it's hard for us, as a medical board to take any action against the doctor, unless his work falls below what we feel is the standard of care."

"Larry, Larry, Larry," the commander said. "Have you and I ever worked on a single state medical board issue together? Do you think I'm really approaching this from a governance perspective?"

Stintson thought for a moment. "We've never even shared a phone call, meeting, or email about a single board-related issue."

"Think bigger, here Larry! Think like Rahm Emanuel, President Obama's first chief of staff. Never let a good crisis go to waste, Larry!"

"Of course! We've got leverage on Davis! If we could get some dirt on him, we would be in an even stronger position. I bet he's got some good Social Security number data," Stintson realized aloud. "By the way, I've heard that Rahm Emanuel and the Clintons stole that quote from Winston Churchill."

"Actually Larry, let's think about this. If you subpoena a bunch of complete medical records, would you ever have to bring him in on the scheme?" the commander asked rhetorically.

"Well, no. I suppose we would not."

"I'm no medical records pro. But I recall that there is a financial section in each record," the commander said as they approached the tennis balls. "You know, the place where they have a copy of the insurance card and there are all of those documents where they agree to pay their bills and stuff."

"Yes! A lot of those older insurance cards contain Social Security numbers! They also write them on the patient financial services agreement." Stintson paused for a moment. "We'll re-open the inquiry on Monday and subpoena a cross-section of at least fifty records."

"Great idea, Larry. But, why wait until Monday," the commander said as he kicked a tennis ball toward Stintson, who took the hint and picked it up like an eager canine. The commander decided at this moment that calling in the wild coyotes would be completely unnecessary. Stintson would do his bidding out of power-lust—and out of fear. "I suspect you already have heaps of records down there at the medical board offices, from previous cases, just waiting to be mined."

"Absolutely," admitted Stintson. But he wasn't even sure which cabinets contained the old medical records. At the moment, Stintson couldn't recall where they keys to those cabinets were, either. He would do some snooping in the morning.

Stintson noticed that the other ball was still sitting atop the snow three feet in front of his new boss, who just stood there silently. It was clear that the commander was in charge, and Stintson only cared slightly. So he did not hesitate to pick up the tennis ball and hand it back to the obvious alpha male.

"Frankly Larry, I really don't care what you and the medical board do when it comes to controlling doctors," the commander said with a slight tone of disrespect as he began to walk briskly back toward his car. "I honestly think that the state gets little bang for its buck out of your lackluster crew. I just love what your night and weekend efforts there can do for my night and weekend business ventures."

"I share your perspective. My service to the state has come at a cost to me. When you total up the hours I work and divide it by the eight hundred dollars a month they pay me, I think I make about fifteen dollars per hour. That's six dollars per hour less than I pay my assistant in my private practice."

The commander turned toward Stintson and removed his headlamp. "In sixty days, our side-venture should net you about fifteen hundred dollars per hour, Larry. Welcome to government work. You've got to make it pay."

The commander whistled for the dogs, but they ignored his call. As he approached his burgundy SUV, he whistled again and then yelled, "Get over here!"

The two dogs came bounding up and they rubbed their noses against their master's hand. When he failed to reward them with a treat, they tried to wander off. Then the commander ordered, "Come on. In the car!" The dogs hesitated and bowed down on their outstretched front legs in a sign of subservient protest. The commander walked to the back of his car and opened the rear door. With a hand-signal he motioned them into the back. "In the car," he insisted. The half-wolves shifted into playful mode and started bounding around as if they now wanted to chase the tennis balls. "In the car!" stated the commander firmly and loudly as he removed a small device with a red button on it from his pocket. Immediately, both dogs snapped to obedience and jumped into the back of the Escalade.

"Is that a shock-collar device?" asked Stintson.

Nodding his head, the commander said, "I just get them to focus, Larry." After closing the back door, the commander walked up to within a few uncomfortable inches of Stintson's face. "I think we need to put one on Berg." This statement was not a joke. The commander was deeply disappointed by his failure. "By the way, Larry. I appreciate your focus." Holding up the device, he continued, "You just stay focused and you'll never get shocked."

The commander drove Stintson back to Sioux Falls and dropped him off at the parking lot outside of the hospital emergency room. After the commander drove away, he called a cell phone number with a Reno, Nevada area code. "How did it go?" he asked the person who answered.

"Stintson's office is bugged and we've got a few cameras in place, too. We'll know everything that goes on in there."

"Great work," said the man with the intense eyes. "Have a great flight back to Reno."

CHAPTER 58

SIOUX FALLS REGIONAL HOSPITAL

Patricia Owens was the latest patient to occupy exam room number four in the emergency room at Sioux Falls Regional Hospital. Her husband had driven her there and he almost had to carry her through the doors. She complained of a splitting headache, a racing heart, and uncontrollable shivers. The triage nurse noticed her goose bumps and her sweaty, clammy skin and immediately ushered her back to exam room four and insisted on the immediate presence of the doctor.

Accelerated exam revealed a blood pressure of 163/109 with a pulse of 96, and the ER noted that Patricia was confused.

"It kind of all started a few hours ago," Mr. Owens said. "She was confused about things, and she was, well, I just . . . She was kind of restless, she complained about a headache, and she had shivering. I just had her take a rest. I thought she might be coming down with, you know, a cold or the flu or something like that. But this just feels different to me."

"Has she started taking any new medication or having any other changes to her medications?" asked the nurse.

"Yes, I have all of her medications right here. These are the new ones," Mr. Owens said as he produced three new vials of pills. "She's been taking fluoxetine, or generic Prozac, for a year or two now. But then we saw this new doctor – I can't remember her name at the homeless clinic. You see, we have had to go to the homeless clinic ever since I was laid off two months ago."

"They've got some really good doctors there at the homeless clinic," chimed in the nurse.

"And what are these new medications?" asked the doctor.

"Well, she gave her this one that starts with a V." Mr. Owens handed the bottle to the doctor.

"Venlafaxine," the doctor said.

"Yes, that's it. She gave her this one to help battle her depression, and this other one ami-something."

"Amitriptyline," interjected the ER doctor as he examined another small bottle.

"Yes, that one also. She said that one would be good for Patricia's depression, and it would help her get some sleep. She hasn't been sleeping well lately, and it worked pretty good."

"All right, then. So really, these are the three antidepressants, correct?" the doctor asked.

"That's right," Mr. Owens said.

"Does she take any other medications?" asked the doctor.

"Oh, only the regular stuff, like Motrin and Tylenol when she needs it. In the spring and summer she takes some hay fever medicine, but she hasn't taken that for months now that it's winter. I think that's about it."

"Does she take any supplements, you know, like pills that she takes that contain any kinds of oils or herbs or anything like that?"

"No, she doesn't take any of that stuff. We just eat what the Good Lord puts on our plate."

The doctor turned to the nurse and said, "Brent, will you please start an IV on Mrs. Owens, and let's also get her some oxygen. Just start with a two milligram IV push of Ativan to help calm down her agitation, and then let's follow that up with a four milligram oral dose of cyproheptadine syrup. If she even has a mild case of serotonin syndrome, we'll see a cessation of most symptoms within one to two hours."

"Mr. Owens, now you said that the doctor your wife saw at the homeless clinic was a woman; but the doctor's name on the amitriptyline and venlafaxine pill bottles is Troy Stoker, who is a man. He's a psychiatrist we all know. Here in the ER we respect him a lot. But there are some obvious possible problems with this particular medication combination, and frankly I'm surprised that he allowed your wife to take these three particular antidepressants at one time. Perhaps he was not aware of the fluoxetine?"

"No," said Mr. Owens. "We told her all about it."

"I'm assuming the reason your wife's having these symptoms is because she's taking these three medications together," the ER doctor explained. "We are going to treat her, and we'll find out within the next hour or so if our diagnosis is correct. But my question is, were you only seeing Dr. Stoker, or were you seeing a different doctor than Dr. Stoker?"

"Oh no, she was definitely a woman at the homeless clinic."

"What was her name again?"

"Oh, I'm sorry I just don't remember. She was kind of a young girl. Frankly I couldn't believe she was old enough to have finished medical school. It looked to me like she may have just been graduating from high school."

"Have you ever seen Dr. Stoker?" asked the doctor. "Have you ever met him?"

"No, Dr. Stoker's not familiar at all to me," said Mr. Owens.

"Well, I'm going to get on the phone with Dr. Stoker right now and get to the bottom of this. Give me just a few minutes and I'll get back to you."

As the doctor left the room the nurse started setting up Mrs. Owens's IV. The doctor walked down the hall to the nurse's station, and with a few strokes on the computer keyboard, he found Dr. Stoker's cell phone number. After a quick dial and two rings Stoker answered. "This is Dr. Stoker. How can I help you?"

"Dr. Stoker, this is Dr. Wallace down at the Sioux Falls Regional Emergency Room. How are you this evening?"

"Well I'm doing fine. I suspect I owe this phone call to one of my patients?"

"Well, in part, that's what I'm calling to find out."

"What do you mean?" Stoker asked.

"Well, I'm treating a Patricia Owens here in our clinic. She's claiming that she saw a woman doctor, a young woman doctor at the homeless clinic. But right here on the prescription vials they brought in with them this evening, it has your name and phone number."

Stoker's heart began to race. All at once the nightmare of his resident working behind his back came into focus. Stoker knew what was going on and he knew how all the facts would line up as he investigated over the next few hours. "Well, Dr. Wallace, I think I know what's going on here. This must be a patient whom my resident saw; and I am still waiting to sign off on her report. I will probably need to get after my student, quite frankly. Tell me a little bit more about what's going on there."

"Well, Mrs. Owens showed up about fifteen minutes ago with a wicked headache, high blood pressure, rapid heartbeat, confusion, and agitation. She was even sweating and shivering."

"Serotonin syndrome," Stoker replied. "It should never happen."

"That was my diagnosis too," interjected Dr. Wallace.

"Give me ten minutes, and I'll be right there. This is serious enough that I want to be there."

Stoker hung up the phone, threw on his coat and called out, "Allie, I've got to run to the hospital." Within a minute he was starting up his Bronco. As it roared to life he fumed at the theory he was entertaining in his head. He imagined that Sarah Haslam had taken it upon herself to see patients at the homeless clinic. Her narcissism and independence had pushed her, yet again, to the brink of idiocy, even in spite of her high degree of textbook intelligence. This time as Dr. Stoker strode through the doors of the Sioux Falls Regional Hospital Emergency Room, he was pleased to be walking under his own power. He never knew how good it would feel to make this walk on his own again. But his return was stifled by the circumstances that brought him.

After a quick, ten-second consultation at the nurse's station he was directed to room four, where he introduced himself for the first time to the strangers, Mr. and Mrs. Owens, who had apparently been his patients for a few days now. "My name is Dr. Stoker. I'm a psychiatrist here in Sioux Falls, and we've never met. Nevertheless, my name appears on your prescription bottles, and you'll certainly want to know why. You recently saw a female doctor at the homeless clinic?"

"That's right," said Mr. Owens.

"When was that?"

"Oh, just last Thursday. What would that be, four or five days ago now?"

"Okay," Dr. Stoker said. "Just enough time for your new medications to kick in a little bit."

"Yes, but Patricia slept great the first night she tried that ami . . . , um, whatever it is."

"Amitriptyline?" asked Dr. Stoker.

"Yes, that's the one."

"Well, let me ask you about the doctor you saw. Was it Dr. Haslam?"

"Yes, that's right, Haslam. Thank you. Now I remember Dr. Haslam. She was so nice."

"Oh yes," Stoker said. "So did she ask you about the medications you are currently taking?"

"Yes. Then she just asked us a bunch of questions, you know, like you'd expect a psychiatrist to ask, about feelings and being in touch with yourself and things like that. But we only talked about medication for a second."

"All right, I'm going to shoot straight with you here," Stoker said. "Having your wife take three antidepressants has created a temporary situation that I think we can solve called serotonin syndrome. To be even more honest with you, I'm concerned that Dr. Haslam did not ask about your wife's fluoxetine use or she failed to remember your response. Had she taken the fluoxetine into account, I suspect that she would not have written prescriptions for these two medications—especially at these doses. How much fluoxetine does your wife take each day?"

"Well, our family doctor started her out at just twenty milligrams a day, but that wasn't working, so maybe last summer or so, they bumped her up to forty milligrams. But then, just a couple of months ago, it just wasn't working so they bumped her up to eighty. They say that's a pretty high dose."

"It is a high dose," Stoker said, "but not incredibly high. On its own it should be just fine. However by introducing 150 milligrams of long-acting venlafaxine and a moderate dose of amitriptyline, it most likely caused an increase in serotonin that I'm not comfortable with. That's why she began having headaches and started acting confused and agitated. She was sweating so much tonight, and her blood pressure was so high, because there's just too much serotonin in her system. Now Dr. Wallace already started an IV and he is administering two medications that should help us reverse this."

"I'm already starting to feel a little bit better," interjected Patricia. Those were the first words she had uttered since entering the emergency room earlier that evening.

"Great," Stoker said. "That Dr. Wallace is a pretty great psychiatrist, for an ER doctor. I better watch out or he'll be putting me out of business. Now, I'll work with Dr. Wallace and I suspect we'll be holding your wife here for another few hours. If her symptoms come under control, we will probably be able to send her home around midnight. That's my guess, but Dr. Wallace gets to decide. If he thinks we should wait a little longer, I'll gladly support his wisdom. What questions do you have for me?"

"Well, frankly, Dr. Stoker, we're a little confused about why you're our doctor but this is the first we've heard of you."

"Like I said before, I'm going to shoot straight with you. My residents usually see patients *with* me. In rare cases, when they do not, they are required to provide me with a little bit of a documentation of that visit within eight hours of seeing the patient. Furthermore, they are required to provide me with their dictated patient encounter note within twenty-four hours of seeing the patient. Honestly, I have not received either of those pieces of documentation from Dr. Haslam. Now, you say that you saw her at the homeless clinic. Is that correct?"

"Yes it is.

"Well, she and I occasionally work at the homeless clinic together. I need to ask her some direct questions. However, from this moment forward, I would like to see you at my office, for free until you get insurance again. You will no longer see Dr. Haslam. We need to straighten out a few issues," Stoker said.

"Okay, Doc. It sounds like the price is right," Mr. Owens said with a smile.

"I'm just being responsible. I don't hide behind legal language and lawyers, and I don't like this situation. I need to be honest with you. Your wife should not be in the emergency room right now, and my resident and I are accountable to you for this inconvenience and potentially dangerous situation. I would like to see you in my office either tomorrow or the next day, free of charge. We need to do a good review of why you came to a psychiatrist, and we need to follow up and make sure that there are no lasting effects from today's episode. I don't think that there will be. But if there are, I'm the one who is ultimately responsible for my resident's actions."

"Well, sure, Dr. Stoker. We'll see you, but we don't have insurance right now, and that's why we went to the homeless clinic."

"I'm not concerned about your insurance. I have plenty of patients without insurance. Don't worry about insurance for now. I'll see you free of charge for the next few weeks or months. We can talk about that when we meet. Do you know when you can come by?"

"Well, I'm not working right now, so my schedule's pretty wide open," Mr. Owens said. I just got laid off two months ago."

"And how are you doing with that?"

"Oh, you know. It's hard. But it's mostly hard on Patricia. She really worries. I've got some good job leads. I've already had five or six interviews."

"That sounds good. I'm glad you're making progress and I'm glad you're on the warpath," Stoker said. "Problems come up when people fall off the warpath. Let's talk about that at length when we meet. Are you available tomorrow afternoon?"

"Sure," Owens said.

"Okay, here's my card with my address on it. How about two-o'clock?"

"We'll see you at two, Dr. Stoker."

"Perfect. I'll be back in to check on both of you, oh, in the next half hour or forty-five minutes. I suspect that the doctor and the nurse here from the ER will be checking on you more frequently than that." Stoker shook both Mr. and Mrs. Owens' hands and then dismissed himself. He walked back to the nurse's station, and picked up the telephone. Dr. Stoker dialed the homeless clinic's number from memory. On the fourth ring the receptionist answered in her normal, frazzled tone.

"Hello, this is Dr. Stoker."

"Well, hello Troy. What's got you calling us at night?"

"Hey, I don't suppose your administrator is around?"

"Ha, ha, ha, ha," laughed the receptionist with a belly laugh that Dr. Stoker could appreciate even from the telephone. "Having the administrator around past

4:30 or 5:00 is even rarer than having a psychiatrist call us in the evening. No, he's not around."

"Well I have a bit of an emergency administrative situation. Is there any way you could give me his cell phone number or get him a message in the next few minutes to call me?"

"Well sure Dr. Stoker, I'll tell you what. I don't have his cell phone number right handy with me here, so I'll check with the charge nurse and have her get your message to him. My guess is that we can have him call you back in the next five to ten minutes."

"Great. Will you just have him call the emergency room at Sioux Falls Regional?"

"Emergency Room? Are you okay Dr. Stoker? Who've you been fighting with this time?" the receptionist laughed. Apparently, word of one of more of his altercations from the last few days had gotten around.

"Oh no, I just happen to be here consulting on a patient. I'm all right. But my pride's still a little wounded. If I wasn't already perceived as such a tough guy, I would never get over it."

"All right, tough guy. We'll have our administrator call you ASAP."

Stoker hung up the phone and turned his attention to the hospital's computer terminal. He had noticed that the prescriptions came from the grocery store pharmacy across town, and hoped that the pharmacy was still open. After doing a little searching on Google, Dr. Stoker found the number and dialed adeptly. The pharmacy would have the "smoking gun" documentation to confirm his suspicions

CHAPTER 59

When the automated telephone pharmacy answering system greeted Dr. Stoker, a cheerful, artificial voice listed his options. Stoker loathed these phone systems. He delegated this inconvenience to his receptionist, Tamara, whenever possible. But tonight Stoker was calling from the emergency room of the hospital, and he was on his own to endure the prompts and wait time. After working through a few selections a live voice finally answered. "Pharmacy, may I help you?"

"Hello, this is Dr. Stoker. Last week, you filled prescriptions for Mrs. Patricia Owens written under my name. One was for venlafaxine and the other for amitriptyline. Can you please provide me with a copy of those prescriptions? I need to do some double checking on some of the work my office has done." "What did you say your last name was, doctor?" "That's Stoker. S-t-o-k-e-r."

"Oh. You're that psychiatrist who goes on the drug raids."

"Yes," Stoker replied. "They're really important." Stoker waited while the pharmacy tech looked up the data.

"Yes, here they are. Mrs. Owens."

"Were those written prescriptions or did somebody call them in?"

"They were called in by Sarah Haslam. It says here she is your resident, working closely with you as a physician training in your clinic, and she asked us to put these in your name."

"That's pretty unusual, isn't it?" Stoker asked.

"Sure. Residents write their own prescriptions, and they rarely defer to supervising doctors. It's just not necessary. Why did you have her use your name, doctor?"

"After I've seen your notes, I may have an answer for you," Stoker said. "Can I get a copy of that documentation?"

"Sure, Dr. Stoker, we can fax these right over to your office."

"Oh no, please don't do that. I'm here at the hospital seeing a patient. Can you fax them over to Sioux Falls Regional?"

"Well, we have this new policy in place, thanks to yet another new hackneyed law. As ridiculous as it is, we can only fax things to doctors via the numbers they have arranged in advance."

"You mean you can't send it over to Sioux Falls Regional, a place that probably writes dozens of prescriptions for you a day?"

"No, I'm sorry Dr. Stoker. We can only send information to your own secure fax line, in your name, and at your office."

"Well, could I come and pick up a copy?"

"Interesting you should ask. As long as you show us your driver's license when you get here and present some other form of ID such as a business card, that shouldn't be a problem. Do you really want to come all the way down here though?"

"Well, your pharmacy is closer than my office. I'll get a better copy of the document than I would by fax."

"Okay, Dr. Stoker. So will we expect you this evening?"

"I suspect I'll be there in about thirty minutes. Thanks." Stoker hung up the phone and wondered why Ron Fowler, from the homeless clinic, had not called him back yet.

After a few moments of consideration, Stoker redialed the homeless clinic. "Hi, this is Stoker again. I have a question for you."

"Sure, Dr. Stoker. What's your question?"

"Do I have any other clinic time or appointments that I am supposedly seeing patients at your clinic in the next few days?"

"Well of course, Dr. Stoker. You've got that one conference room every Thursday night now. Dr. Haslam was here covering the appointments Thursday night. I think she was pretty busy. She even let us slip in a quick referral of our own."

"Okay. Well, this Thursday and next Thursday I'll be there. Haslam's not going to be able to cover it."

"All right, we'll keep the coffee warm for you."

"Thank you."

The mention of coffee prompted a craving in Dr. Stoker and he made his way back toward the staff break room. After filling up a Styrofoam cup with a fairly fresh brew, Stoker sat down, pulled out his iPhone, and checked his email. About half way through his first email he heard an overhead page announcing that he had a call waiting at the nurse's station. With a few strides and in a few seconds, Stoker made his way to the nurse's station and picked up the phone, line three.

"Hi Troy, this is Ron Fowler, from the homeless clinic. What's this administrative emergency I'm hearing about?"

"Well, I'm here at the emergency room treating a patient, and it seems to me that she may have been first seen at your clinic by Sarah Haslam."

"Well, sure. Residents at our homeless clinic are constantly seeing patients under the indirect supervision of our attending physicians."

"Yes, indeed, but I think the circumstances with Sarah Haslam might be a little different, so I'm in a bit of an investigative mode."

"Oh? Please tell me what you mean."

"Well, I saw this patient tonight who had prescriptions in my name, but I have never seen her. It appears to me that she saw Dr. Haslam without me knowing. Has she set up or made any type of arrangements with you to see patients?"

"Well of course. A few days ago she called and said that you wanted to set up a time on Thursday nights, and so we lined it all up."

"You'll be shocked to know, Ron, I never knew about those arrangements. I think she's been working behind my back."

After about five seconds of silence, Fowler said, "Oh, Troy. It's all coming together so clearly now. Do you remember that phone call a few days ago where you initially answered the phone, and she intercepted it?"

"I remember it all too well. She was awfully anxious to get me off the phone, wasn't she?"

"Yes, Dr. Stoker. She made quite the effort. I think both you and I have been had."

"Well Ron, thank you for being so forthright with me. I will let you know what happens and I will include you in discreet communication about this situation. I would appreciate it if you didn't bring it up with anybody for a day or two. My next move is to bring it up with her residency committee."

"Very well, Dr. Stoker, I will make a note of it in my administrative files but will not communicate it with any of my staff or our board until we have more solid information."

"Thank you," Dr. Stoker said. He concluded the phone call, and made a beeline for exam room number four. "How are you feeling, Patricia?" Stoker asked.

"With every passing moment I feel a little better. Whatever they put in that IV, I think is really doing the trick."

"Okay, perfect. I'm glad that you came in when you did. Serotonin syndrome can be very dangerous. It can even be fatal. I'm going to make a run to your pharmacy to pick up some documents so that we can use this as a teaching moment. I don't see any reason why a single patient should ever suffer from serotonin syndrome in this day and age. I'll be back to check on you in about thirty minutes."

Stoker exited exam room four, walked back through the emergency room doors, jumped into his Bronco, fired up the engine, and made his way to the grocery store pharmacy that would be holding precious pieces of evidence in the case he was assembling against Sarah Haslam.

As Stoker entered the grocery store his only focus was making his way to the pharmacy. The scents that wafted from the bakery failed to catch his attention—a rare phenomenon that could only be attributed to his anger, concentration, and determination to find out what had gone on in the last few weeks. As Dr. Stoker approached the pharmacy counter there was already one patient ahead of him, so he waited patiently. He marveled at how many products could array the areas beneath, beside, and around the pharmacy counter. He estimated that there were more than 1,000 products trying to catch his attention. On most days, Stoker would consider a candy bar or packaged pastry. But tonight he had no appetite.

"Can I help you, sir?"

"Yes, I just spoke to somebody about twenty-five minutes ago. My name is Dr. Stoker. Can you ask around and find out who I spoke with on the phone?"

"Yes, just a minute, Dr. Stoker."

A few moments later a girl named Margie came walking up to the window.

"Hi Dr. Stoker. I'm Margie, the pharmacy tech. I have your documents for you. May I please see your driver's license and perhaps a business card? I've asked the pharmacist to come over and just say hello. We'll both initial the paperwork that we provided this to you."

Although it felt like government intrusion, Stoker produced his driver's license as well as three copies of his business card.

With a few initials and signatures on some ubiquitous confidentiality document, Margie passed over two color copies of prescription documentation he had never seen before. On the top of the small sheet was Dr. Stoker's address, and at the bottom there was a line where it indicated that Sarah Haslam had called in the prescriptions, but filled them under the name, Troy Stoker. Now the doctor had all the evidence he needed.

As he left the pharmacy he was already formulating the letter in his head that he would write to Dr. Penny Denning, chair of the Department of Psychiatry and overseer of Sarah Haslam's residency. Within the hour he would fax copies of his letter and the documentation of the prescriptions Haslam called in. But first he needed to make one more stop at the hospital to check on the status of his surprise patient.

CHAPTER 60

OFFICE OF TROY STOKER, M.D., SIOUX FALLS

Dr. Penny Denning, chair of the department of psychiatry at the University of South Dakota, arrived at Troy Stoker's office at 7:50 a.m. During her brief drive that morning she had orchestrated the upcoming conversation where she would confront Sarah Haslam. It would be pretty easy to simply ask questions about her experience seeing patients at the homeless clinic. She would work in questions such as: Did Doctor Stoker know about these patients? Did Doctor Stoker know about the Thursday evening clinics? How did the practice of seeing patients there on Thursday night begin? Where did you get these prescription pads? If Haslam lied, she would simply ask follow-up questions such as: If I call Mr. Fowler at the homeless clinic will he relate a different experience? Doctor Denning also had copies of the prescriptions that Dr. Stoker had retrieved from the pharmacy. She had managed to hunt down rogue prescriptions for other patients in the Sioux Falls area, too. She had serious questions about potentially fatal drug interactions on one particular patient.

There was already a pot of coffee brewing when she walked through the door and into the reception area. Dr. Stoker greeted her, accompanied her to his office, and asked her to have a seat. He served her coffee with sugar. Stoker still remembered, from his residency days, exactly how she liked her coffee.

"I see no reason for Sarah Haslam's residency to go on any further," Dr. Denning said. "This is the last straw. I'm deeply sorry about all that has transpired, Troy."

"You never could have anticipated that Sarah would do something like this," Stoker said. "There is no need for an apology."

"Do you have the prescriptions she issued and records from the hospital?"

"I have the ones I've been able to hunt down so far," Stoker said. "Who knows how many patients she has treated?"

"That should be the first thing we ask her about," Denning replied. "Let's ask for a complete list of all of the patients she saw at the homeless clinic and their contact information. Any charts or visit documentation would be of additional help." Dr. Denning opened a folder and pulled out some other copies of prescriptions and a few other documents. "I hunted down prescriptions from eight other patients. Look at this one." Denning slid a copy of the prescription along the table to Stoker. "Dr. Haslam prescribed an MAO inhibitor for depression, as well as oral meperidine for pain."

Stoker reached for his phone, "What's her number? That's a surefire kill shot! I need to call this patient right now."

Denning was calm. "I hope you don't mind, Troy." I picked up the phone the moment I saw this and called her myself. She stopped taking both medications last night. She had only taken one dose of the meperidine. She's calling you this morning for a new appointment." Denning shifted uneasy in her seat. "You know Troy, I also asked the patient if she had started a tyramine-free diet. She didn't even know what that was. She didn't know that she was supposed to avoid aged cheese, wine, pepperoni, and things like that. I don't think Haslam talked to her about tyramine-laced food at all."

"Did you talk to her about it?" Stoker asked.

"Yes, I told her to avoid all aged foods for one week."

"Either way, she wrote a prescription that any first-year medical student would label as foolish," Stoker said. "This resident was out of control—and on my watch."

"Once we've captured all of the patient information from Sarah," Denning said, "we can present the prescriptions and ask for her response. I cannot fathom a reasonable explanation. From there, I will proceed to dismiss her from the program."

Dr. Denning removed a letter signed by all of the members of the residency committee dismissing her from the program. It was short. Only four sentences. Very efficient. The school's attorney had drafted it saying that short and direct would be the best approach. No explanation, other than "ongoing evidence of insufficient progress," should be provided in writing.

While they waited for Sarah Haslam to arrive, they discussed their mutual experiences with patients, illegal methamphetamine abuse, and the dynamics of Dr. Stoker's practice. Dr. Denning tried to talk Dr. Stoker into coming back and practicing with her group at the hospital, which she did almost every time they talked. Recruiting doctors was part of her job. Stoker politely declined and told her how happy he was as an independent physician.

"I can make all of my own decisions and practice medicine with less outside influence," he explained. "I'm sure I would make a little more money with you and the hospital, and I admit that I would love to delegate to more secretaries and social workers. But I've just got to maintain my independence."

"I'm always looking to increase market share," Denning said.

Stoker flinched. He hated how the big players in town treated health care like a war. One of the downfalls of being the chair of the Department of Psychiatry was that Dr. Denning had to kowtow to administration and worry about market share, productivity, profit margins, and a number of other business measurements that gauged how well she was progressing in the little war of dominating medicine in Sioux Falls.

"You could certainly help us bring in new patient volume, Troy," Dr. Denning said. But when it was obvious that Stoker had no interest in leaving his private practice, she gave up by saying, "Well, at least if you don't come join us at Sioux Falls Regional, I won't have to stress out about integrating a Libertarian into our left-wing club."

"Libertarian? I might be fiercely independent and pretty right wing. But you dare label me as Libertarian? I simply volunteer proudly to stand among the ten or fifteen percent of psychiatrists who aren't liberal tree huggers that look to the so-called 'Huffington and Puffington Post' for their latest treatment modalities. Do you guys get CME credit for reading left-wing rags or the Communist Manifesto?"

Dr. Denning laughed at the political barb. She had debated politics, in jest, with Stoker for years. "You can't blame a girl for trying to recruit you Dr. Stoker." The sound of the front door opening interrupted their conversation and caught both of their attention. Sarah Haslam entered the reception area and stepped back into Stoker's office. When she saw her professor, Dr. Denning, she looked genuinely surprised.

"Hello Dr. Denning. Are you collaborating with Dr. Stoker?"

"As a matter of fact, I am. And on a most interesting case, I might add," said Denning.

"Yes. Very interesting," Stoker said. "Come on in my office, Sarah. I'm sure you will appreciate this patient's circumstances."

Sarah entered the office and took a seat. Her hands were wrapped around her drive-through coffee cup absorbing the warmth.

"This is one of my patients who was admitted to twenty-three hour observation at the hospital last night," Stoker said. "She had previously been diagnosed by another psychiatrist here in town with a major depressive disorder. However, her husband tricked her into coming to the emergency room after she experienced a number of strange symptoms." Stoker paused for a moment. "Sarah, what do you think would've caused this patient's severe agitation, blood pressure problems, and mental status difficulties in this fifty-six-year-old woman? The ER doctors treated her last night because her behavior was so erratic. She's never had these symptoms before."

"The rapid onset is indeed remarkable, but so far I fail to see why this case is so fascinating," Haslam said as she set her nearly full coffee cup on Dr. Stoker's desk. "Sounds like textbook serotonin syndrome to me. I bet some idiotic primary care doctor—tell me it was a nurse practitioner—just amped her up on a couple of antidepressants in a desperate attempt to chase away the blues for some ailing depressed housewife."

"No, Denning said. "Did you hear me explain that it was a psychiatrist?"

"Okay," Haslam said. "So what medications did this psychiatrist prescribe?"

"These three," Stoker said as he laid the copies of the prescriptions created and called in by Sarah Haslam, M.D.

The surprise on the resident's face was horrific, and her hands began to shake.

"Dr. Haslam. We need to know all of the details about the St. Francis Clinic patients you've seen," Dr. Denning insisted in a firm, calm tone. She knew that a sharp tone would set off the narcissist Sarah Haslam. The only chance they had to find out who all of her mystery patients were was to appease her narcissism. "Dr. Stoker needs to contact them and have them come in for a visit to further establish the doctor-patient relationship. Can you please help us with that?"

"Of course. I've been keeping painstaking records of all of my St. Francis Clinic patients," Haslam said as she reached down into her leather messenger bag and pulled out a stack of charts and handed them to Stoker. "It's all right here."

Stoker looked at each of the charts and read out the names. "Now think with me here, Sarah. Is there any patient you've seen who is not included in these charts?"

By now, Haslam had recovered a bit and she had put on her poker face. "No. They're all right there. I'm up to seventeen patients, and I have four more scheduled for Thursday."

"Why Sarah? Why did you go out and start your own clinic?" asked Dr. Denning.

"I'm a good psychiatrist and nobody *ever* lets me practice complete psychiatry. I had to prove to myself that I could do it. It was not money. It was just about—being a doctor."

All three doctors sat silently. Haslam neither showed nor expressed any remorse. She issued no apology nor accepted any fault. Dr. Denning removed the dismissal letter from a file folder.

"Sarah Haslam. Effective immediately, I am terminating your residency."

Haslam's face showed no emotion. After a few seconds of silence, Sarah reached out to her coffee cup atop Dr. Stoker's desk and with a single finger slowly and deliberately tipped it over. Creamy brown liquid covered the admitting notes, prescription copies and medical records they had just discussed. Then she stood up and hoisted her messenger bag over her shoulder. "It's so cliché to say, 'You'll be sorry.' So let me just say that extraordinary misery awaits both of you."

Haslam turned her back on Stoker and Denning and walked toward the door. As she reached up her hand to push the main door open, she paused and took a look back at the doctors who had tried so hard to help her. It appeared as she was going to say something else, but then she turned back toward the door and exited the building.

Stoker and Denning cleaned up the coffee mess and then Denning explained that she needed to be getting back to the hospital.

Stoker spoke up. "I need to call all these people and offer them free appointments to come in and meet their psychiatrist."

Denning smiled and said, "Don't tell the Obama people," she joked. "They will love the 'meet your psychiatrist for free' day, and they will roll it into ObamaCare."

Stoker laughed. "Yes. Socialists get a lot of propaganda mileage out of that word *free*, but they sure seem to underuse the word *freedom*."

"*Touché*!" Denning said picking up her purse and paperwork.

Stoker thanked her for her help over the last few hours and showed her to the door. After Dr. Denning had pulled out of the parking lot, Stoker picked up the phone and made his first awkward phone call. "Hi, my name is Dr. Stoker, and I'm calling to clear up some confusion about your visit with the psychiatrist at the homeless clinic last Thursday."

CHAPTER 61

Sarah Haslam just drove. She chose to travel eastbound. The cruise control was set at sixty-five and she occupied the right lane of Interstate 90. Anger was her only emotion. Revenge her only thought. As she drove eastbound, all of her energy was dedicated to thinking and plotting. As a scientist, she was used to creating a theory, and then she would gather the evidence to support or refute it. She knew that she could think through dozens of revenge scenarios and choose the one that was most likely to succeed. Her first revenge scenario involved vandalism. However, she quickly dismissed it because it would not inflict enough pain on Stoker or Denning. Moreover, she could easily be prosecuted for it. She ruled it out.

She needed to come up with a retaliation that would inflict deep emotional pain. The outcome also needed to vindicate her from the emotional damage inflicted that morning in the office of the brute, Troy Stoker. By the time she crossed into the state of Minnesota, she had dismissed two possible vengeance schemes. That was fine with her because she knew that her awesome mind would eventually figure out, better than anybody else, how to plot and scheme against these hick-town, second-rate doctors. She remembered her days playing high-level chess in high school and she associated that experience to her present dilemma. Now, as an analytical psychiatrist, her strategic thought processes would serve her well. In chess, it was wise to dismiss a move after analyzing and exposing its flaws. It was the same with revenge. You had to consider the endgame.

Since her high school chess team days she was brutal on the attack. She always employed a few key strategies such as the Queen's Gambit. She celebrated when defeating opponents by crushing the classic Scholar's Mate. She lived for those moments. But now that she was a doctor, she knew that a scientist rarely finds the right solution within seconds, minutes, or hours. No, Sarah Haslam would think like a scientist and rule out dozens of scenarios before arriving at the perfect revenge scheme. In her narcissistic and psychopathic mind she justified breaking a few laws to get her revenge. But she drew the line at killing or maiming. Beating somebody up was fine, she concluded. But she would stop short of putting Stoker or Denning in the ICU. That would be overkill.

After two hours of scheming, she had developed a theory she really liked. It involved getting Stoker's wife in trouble. Could she make her lose her job? Could she set her up to look like a criminal, cheating wife, or drug addict? Perhaps. But she *really* liked the idea of getting revenge on Stoker through his wife, Allie. After all, she was involved in that ridiculous practical joke where Allie posed as Stoker's mistress. Allie deserved a little pain, too. *My mother gave me pain,* thought Haslam. *Why not spread the pain around a little bit?*

By her fourth hour of driving east on Interstate 90, Sarah's bladder was screaming for relief—which also reminded her to look at her gas gauge. At a gas station she found relief, fuel, snacks, and a Colt 45 Raspberry Lemonade Blast. *This will camouflage nicely as can of pop*, thought Haslam. *Besides, I'll only drink about half of it.*

CHAPTER 62

Stoker's intuition was bugging him again this morning. For the last twenty-four hours he had sensed that he needed to be proactive about Brian Berg and the South Dakota Medical Board; so he picked up the phone and dialed Errol Rivera. "Hey, Rivera. I don't think this Brian Berg guy's going away. His psychological profile is pathological. Here we have somebody who is used to wielding his perceived power without any restraint from his bosses. Considering his double-digit IQ and unchecked, significant narcissistic traits, he's going to come back and swing at me with anything he can."

"Absolutely! Now he's a viper that's gone back to his lair," Rivera said, "and he's strategizing—in his delusional, low intelligence, reptilian-like primal areas of his brain—to bring you down. He's after revenge and you know the medical board will back him. History shows that the board listens to their boy, Berg, while ignoring doctors, solid facts, and reason."

"So I want to be proactive, but I don't know how to get an audience with the board. I'll figure that out."

"It's lawyer time, Stoker," Rivera stated. "Call Holly Glover. She'll know what to do. She's the best healthcare attorney in South Dakota. With her civil rights passion she'll take the tapes of Berg's failed raid and turn them into a Federal lawsuit if you want. "

"You're right. That petite half-marathon runner sure is *large and in charge* in the courtroom."

A few minutes later, Stoker had Holly Glover on the phone. "Well, Troy. I must say that you are the first client who has ever wanted to proactively initiate an inquiry from the board," commented Glover after hearing Stoker's explanation of recent events.

"Can I just go down to their offices, walk in and say, 'Hi, I'm Dr. Stoker, and I'd like to schedule a hearing.' Or do I ask you, as my attorney, to request a hearing, set up a meeting, or file suit against the board on my behalf?"

"While it is completely unheard of, you have every right to walk in and request a hearing," replied Glover. "I can make the request for a hearing or an informal meeting. But I don't recommend filing suit against a state government entity. They are typically immune from prosecution."

Stoker thought for a moment and replied, "I'm going to handle this for now, Holly. Please consider yourself retained as my attorney. But, I want to show a good-faith effort at transparency and present overtures that I want to solve this thing instead of turn it into a public relations nightmare. I'm going to write a letter to the board president, what's his name?"

"Larry Stintson."

"Right! Stintson, the orthopedic surgeon," Stoker said. "I'll write the letter, hand deliver it, and request that they open up their calendar and we find a hearing date that works well for both parties."

"I love it!" said Glover. "It is completely refreshing. I wish I could be a fly on the wall."

Fifteen minutes later Stoker printed off his letter explaining that he wanted to participate in a hearing with the board and satisfy their concerns. He put on his tie and suit coat, exited his office, and jumped into his Ford Bronco. After a short drive, Stoker parked on 9th Street, entered the 1st Dakota National Bank Building, and ascended the stairs to the third floor. He entered Suite 301 where he found a small reception area with a panel of glass separating visitors from the receptionist desk. Stoker grinned and wondered why gaining entrance to talk to the board felt like buying a movie ticket. Perhaps this would be a bit of a wild ride. On the wall hung a doorbell. Stoker pressed the button but heard no chime.

After thirty seconds nobody responded, so Stoker pressed the doorbell again—hoping that it actually rang somewhere. As he considered pressing it for the third time, a door to the reception desk area opened, and Brian Berg walked through with rote unawareness. "May I help you?" Berg asked a moment before he lifted his gaze from its customary default fixation on the floor. As Stoker began to speak, Berg looked up and froze."

"Yes, Brian!" Stoker said seizing the moment. "I need to talk to the person with highest authority who is here at the moment."

Berg slumped into the receptionist chair and hesitated as his eyes darted toward the floor, back to Stoker, and then to a few other places in the little box-office-like receptionist area. "Well, Dr. Stintson is the president of the board, but he's not usually here."

"Sure, Brian. I anticipated that he would probably be practicing a derivative of orthopedics today, so I chose my words carefully. Can I please speak to the highest authority person *who is here at the moment*," repeated Stoker.

"Well, I am a *chief* investigator," Berg said. "Can I direct you to the right place on our website or something?"

"Let's do a little double-check here, Brian. I asked for the person with the highest authority," Stoker clarified. "Do you have a boss?"

"Yes."

"Is he or she here? I mean, the person you report to. This is the person you ask for permission to take the day off, so you can watch a whole season of *Lost*."

The subtle play on the word "lost" went over Berg's head. "That's our office manager, Kira."

"Is she here?"

"Yes."

"I need to discuss an issue with her, deliver a document to her, and make an appointment. Will you please inform her that I would like a moment of her time?"

"Does this have anything to do with me?"

"Brian, I've only met you one other time. Granted, I am a psychiatrist, so I'm trained to notice these things. Let me point out that you seem to think that a lot of things have to do with you." Berg did not know how to respond to Stoker's observation. "Will you please let Kira know that a physician would like to speak with her?" Stoker removed his business card from his pocket. On the back he wrote the words "appointment" and "document," and then he handed it to Berg. Stoker was fairly certain that the mini-meeting agenda on the back of his card would compel an office manager who was conditioned to respond to "action items," to engage in the short conversation.

"I'll see. She's pretty busy."

Stoker ignored the weak initiation of an excuse. He chose not to facilitate it by simply looking Berg in the eye and saying nothing. Berg walked back through the door mumbling something about how he didn't know if she would be available. Thirty seconds later, Kira appeared through the same door.

"Hi Dr. Stoker," she said through the box office glass. She was wearing a large grin. "How can I help you?"

"Yes, Kira. I'm a psychiatrist who practices here in town and I've recently had some interaction with your board. Are you aware of my case?"

"Yes. I was briefed a few days ago."

"Good," continued Stoker. "I am here to schedule a hearing so that we can come together and resolve any concerns the board has and discuss other issues. Do you have access to the hearing calendar?"

"Well, yes," said Kira. "But that's not how it works."

"Yes. I suspect not," Stoker said. "Let me ask you, do you ever get hunches about things? I mean, call it intuition or your conscience suggesting that you do something. Does that ever happen to you?"

"Yes." Kira thought for a moment. "Occasionally, yes."

"Does it ever pay off?"

After another moment of brief introspection, Kira replied, "Sure. Sometimes my brain just kind of puts stuff together for me, I guess."

"Yes. Our subconscious is observant and deliberate. If we listen, it's powerful," explained Stoker. "My intuition is telling me that I need to meet with the board. If you point out any malfeasance on my part, I'll take responsibility for it. I just want to work it out."

Kira's grin disappeared and her eyes became angry. "You mean like assaulting our investigator?"

"I would love to discuss all of the events of that encounter. You know what happened. How are we going to resolve this, except by a hearing?"

"I probably said too much," Kira said in a much calmer tone. "This is not how it usually works. Doctors never come in here and ask for hearings."

"I know. This is new," Stoker said as he rolled up the letter and slid it through the hole to Kira. "This is a letter to your board president. I'm formally requesting a hearing. Can you please schedule that with me now, Kira?"

"You just don't get it, Stoker," the office manager said with a hint of distain. Her body language and demeanor became confrontational. "We come after you!"

"Excellent," Stoker said in a calm voice while he looked Kira in the eye. "Let's schedule that."

"Oh, we'll schedule it, Stoker," Kira said. "Let us finish digging up the dirt on you. Then we schedule your little thrill ride—on our terms, not yours."

Stoker paused for a minute to deescalate the drama that Kira had worked so hard to generate. "So does your hearing calendar have any openings in the next week or two?" Stoker asked calmly. "Between now and then, I'm happy to provide you with names, addresses, and phone numbers of all of the people who have dirt on me."

"No. We're all booked out," Kira sneered as she turned toward the door. "You'll hear from us," she said as she exited and left Stoker alone on the other side of the glass.

CHAPTER 63

Sarah Haslam couldn't remember the last time she'd bought a man lunch, dinner, or any meal for that matter. It was probably a girl's-choice dance in high school. But today was different. Her motive was far from romantic. It was exciting however, because she had finally settled on a plan that was sure to exact a glorious revenge on Troy Stoker. And she had identified just the man with motives to help her. As always she arrived just a few minutes early for her lunch appointment. It let her have a fair amount of control over the table where she ate. It also allowed her to choose the seat that would give her the best vantage of the whole restaurant. It put her in charge of her surroundings. She was less likely to be surprised. Of course, she had chosen the restaurant, Tinners Bar and Grille, which she appreciated because it had some healthy options that were always delicious.

As her guest approached, she noticed that his appearance was somewhat more disheveled than the first time she had seen him at Dr. Stoker's office. As the hostess gestured the man toward Haslam, the spark of recognition was only vague. "Hi, Dr. Haslam. I'm Brian Berg."

"Brian, thank you for meeting me here. I think you'll find my information and little idea rather interesting."

"Okay. Good. Let's talk," Berg said. By the way, this is the first time that a doctor has ever invited me anywhere."

"Are you suspicious of my motives, Brian? Do you think I'm trying to get in good with you or the board?"

"No," Berg stammered with a deeply unconvincing lie. He was disappointed. He had incorrectly assumed that Haslam's interest and invitation was more of a personal nature.

"Well, when I tell you my little story, you'll see that I do indeed have a motive. Don't worry. My desire to keep a lousy psychiatrist in check is healthy."

Berg said nothing as he sipped his water and then fidgeted with the menu.

"I'm having the turkey avocado wrap, but I wouldn't expect that to be man-fuel. I hear the Rib eye sandwich is great. I'm sure everything here is pretty good.

Berg flipped the menu to look at the back page. "Rib eye sandwich?" He scoured the menu, but could not find it. He clumsily flipped back to the front face of the menu and scanned it some more. "Oh. There it is under sandwiches."

"Brian. I just spent the last few weeks of my residency with Dr. Stoker — if you can even call him a doctor. Frankly, what I experienced has driven me over the top. I've had such a poor experience that I've suspended my residency. I've filed a number of complaints with the school, the American Psychiatric Association, and a few other entities," Haslam lied. "I may file one with the South Dakota Medical Board, but we'll have to see. I'm concerned that such a complaint would not get much traction. He would just end up with another . . . What do you call it? Complaint? Concern?"

"Letter of concern," interjected Berg.

"That's right. Letter of concern," repeated Haslam. "I'm afraid that those letters may change behavior on mild or moderate issues. However, with such deeply challenging issues, like those I've lived with during the last few weeks, I cannot, in good faith, let him get away with a little slap on the wrist."

Berg leaned in and held up his menu to shield his words and prevent others from overhearing. "Look, doctor. This Stoker's a guy we've got our eye on. There are, shall we say, concerns, from people even higher up than the board."

"Who do you mean?"

"I'm not saying a word about who. Just trust me when I say that Stoker and his stunts have angered some people. We would be happy to see him out of practice or even in jail."

"Really? Jail time?" Haslam was intrigued. "Finally, someone gets it. I'm no lawyer, but in my book, Stoker's a felon."

"What were some of things that you witnessed while you worked with him?"

"He's a pervert. It's bad enough that he completely disregards American Psychiatric Association guidelines and is constantly hugging patients. But believe it or not, I walked in on him and a patient in a compromised situation," Haslam lied. Fueled by her hate, pride, and narcissism, her imagination ran wild. Her list of false accusations grew larger. "Let's cut to the chase here, Berg. The wolf in sheep's clothing, who goes out on these saintly drug busts, often comes back with the spoils of victory. He has a stash of crank locked up in his little safe there, along with illegal firearms. And while he uses a little of the smack himself, he's mostly supplying some contacts down in Omaha. And, while I've never seen Allie, his wife, actually touching or using the stuff, people who know her whisper that she's lost about twenty pounds. Her skin looks horrible, and she's not the same person she was a year ago."

"Does he ever distribute to patients or anybody else here in town?"

"Never!" replied Sarah Haslam while considering how the best lies are laced with obvious truths. "He's too smart for that. He knows how quickly he would get busted going retail. He's purely a wholesaler—but he gives it away for free to his little wench."

"Are you ready to tell a grand jury what you're telling me?"

Haslam was slightly surprised that Brian Berg knew how to access a grand jury. From what she'd learned about him, Berg only knew how to write pathetic letters of concern and fill out government forms. "Look, Brian. Give me two or three weeks and I will bring you the evidence that you need on drugs and his exaggerated insurance company billing practices. You will be a hero in the Argus Leader and other local papers. Who knows, they may even pick up the story in Minneapolis."

"Great," Berg said. "Get me anything you can. I have a good feeling about this. It's been a long time since I've come into a case this huge. Let me know what I can do for you. As a *chief* investigator, I can usually get stuff." Berg acted pretty cool as he mentioned his title and self-proclaimed powers. "This is serious stuff. It's important to make the investigation look like it is by the book. But the people I work with don't give a damn about playing by the rules. You didn't hear that from me." Berg glanced at his menu, and then said. "If they want Stoker down, he's going down."

"By the book," scoffed Haslam. "I don't even want to know what the book says. I just want to see Stoker's embarrassed eyes and pale skin as he hears the words, 'Your license is revoked.' Actually, I'm now starting to envision him in an orange prisoner's jumpsuit and handcuffs."

Just then, the waitress came over to their table. "Are you two ready to order lunch?"

With clumsy enthusiasm, Brian Berg interjected his order before Haslam could speak up. "I'll have a deluxe burger. Make that a combo with a Coke. And, super-size me!"

CHAPTER 64

OFFICE OF TROY STOKER, M.D., SIOUX FALLS

Tamara, Dr. Stoker's receptionist, sealed the envelope and affixed the certified mail sticker on the outside. As instructed, she was mailing a daily letter to the South Dakota Medical Board. While the date changed each day, the content remained the same. It simply requested that Dr. Stoker participate in a public hearing with the board to explore his alleged misconduct. Stoker specifically requested a "public" hearing. He wanted to leave the option open to invite people who would support him as well as interested members of the media.

After Tamara affixed the stamp and placed the letter in the outgoing mailbox, she picked up her cell phone and dialed the number for the South Dakota Medical Board. As she had done for a few days now, she asked to speak to the board president's secretary, Lucille. She used her smart phone so that it would be easy to record the calls.

"President Stintson's office," Lucille answered.

"Good morning, Lucille," Tamara said sincerely. "I'm calling to set an appointment for a hearing with the board and Dr. Troy Stoker. Will you please help me make that appointment?"

"I'm going to leave a message for Dr. Stintson to call and schedule that with Dr. Stoker," responded Lucille just as she had yesterday—as well as a few other preceding days. "What is the best number to reach Dr. Stoker?"

Tamara dutifully provided the secretary with Dr. Stoker's office number. "Thank you, Lucille," Tamara said reading from the script Dr. Stoker had provided. "This is an urgent and important matter for your board. When can Dr. Stoker expect a call from Dr. Stintson?"

Although Lucille had no script, her answer was consistent with yesterday's response. "Dr. Stintson returns as many calls as he can as quickly as his busy schedule will allow. However, he does not return all calls and I cannot commit that he will return this one."

"Will you please note that Dr. Stoker has requested a hearing in your message?"

"I will."

"Will you please retain a copy of this message? It has a reasonable potential to become evidence in procedural or legal matters."

"At your request, I will."

"Thank you, Lucille," Tamara said. Then she decided to break away from the script. "Lucille, can I ask you something from way out in left field?"

Lucille did not miss a beat. "Of course?"

"Do you think my daily phone calls and letters are a ridiculous pain?"

"Absolutely not!" Lucille said with a conviction that surprised Tamara.

"You mean, you don't think we're playing a manipulative little game?"

"It is a manipulative little game you're playing," Lucille said calmly. Then her voice became quiet. "Tamara, let me tell you something." Her hand was obviously cupping her phone. "Keep playing it. I'm keeping meticulous notes of your calls. I've catalogued every letter. This is exactly how you have to act to get results around here."

Tamara immediately read between the lines. *Stintson's secretary was on their side!* "Well, thank you, Lucille," she said with a little shock in her voice. Returning to her script, Tamara said, "We're here expecting President Stintson's phone call."

"I'll see that he gets the message," said Lucille.

CHAPTER 65

CHELSEA CROSSING, SIOUX FALLS

At 7:30 p.m. on a cold South Dakota night Brian Berg turned his pickup truck into the driveway of 5644 Bryant Way. As his front wheels passed over the sidewalk the garage door began to travel upward, and Berg noticed a person standing in the garage. As the door completed its ascent, he saw the commander standing there with two majestic dogs sitting perfectly obedient at the side of their master. The commander motioned for Berg to pull his truck into the garage and Berg followed his instructions. Berg turned off the engine and secured the emergency brake. He looked momentarily at the dogs and felt a flash of anxiety. The dogs looked like wolves and Berg's instincts told him to stay in his truck.

"Come on out, Brian," the commander said. "As long as you're friendly with me these dogs will treat you well."

Berg opened the door, hesitated, and then stretched his left foot out onto the ground. His right hand trembled a bit as he climbed out of the truck, so he closed the door and then immediately stuck his hand in his coat pocket.

"What are their names?" Berg asked as he walked toward them.

"This guy here's Ferdinand," replied the commander, "and the bitch here is Imelda. Aptly named for the golden colored fur on her paws." The reference to the former first lady, Imelda Marcos, of the Philippines was lost on Berg. He looked at the commander with a confused expression.

"Sorry, Brian. I forget that I'm getting older. Not everyone lived the history I remember," the commander said. He pushed a button to close the garage door. "I spent a few of my military years in the Philippines. It's an amazing country with strong, fascinating people, and it holds a special place in my heart. Imelda Marcos was a world-famous political figure from the Philippines and she was fond of shiny shoes. So it was a perfect name for my female dog with golden fir on her feet."

"Oh," Berg said showing a glimmer of comprehension. "What kind of dogs are they? I mean, are they wolves?"

"Indeed." The commander beamed with pride and his voice became passionate. "They are part wolf. But I would never own purebred wolves. They are notoriously bad pets. Wolves need to roam. They respond poorly to training. So these dogs are a grey wolf and Siberian husky mix. It's a manageable breed. As you can see, these two are reasonably obedient, thanks to that set of genes. They're also fiercely loyal. If anybody were to attack me, their master, they would fight to the death in my defense. That's how I've trained them."

"Do they follow your commands?"

"Almost always. But remember, the wolf in them wants to disobey, so I exercise a little mercy with these two. If I'm trying to get them to roll over or do any of those goofy tricks, they have a sense that those commands are for play and not for survival and they may or may not obey. However, they have yet to disobey a command to attack."

"You've had them attack someone?" Berg asked.

"Well, mostly I'm talking about in practice and the drills we go through during our morning workouts. When it comes to aggressive or domineering behavior, they *want* to obey. They want to please me, their master."

"Their commander," Berg said.

"Something like that." The commander motioned for Brian to pass through a doorway from the garage to the home. "Welcome to our little place here in Chelsea Crossing." They walked into a well-appointed living room. Large, glass windows looked out onto a frozen pond as well as the Chelsea Crossing clubhouse on the other side of the water. A fire was crackling in the fireplace and Larry Stintson was standing up from a couch and walking toward them. The dogs were nudging Berg's hands and requesting that he pet them, but he just folded his arms and ignored them.

"Hello, Brian. How are you this evening?" Stintson asked while shaking his hand, smiling, and looking him in the eye. "Would you like a drink?"

"Sure. Um, I'll have a, well, how about a Scotch?" Berg had no idea which drink might be appropriate in the company of two powerful men. Berg had consumed plenty of beer and whiskey in his life, but he'd never savored Scotch.

He just remembered a lot of sophisticated people in movies drinking it. *Or was that gin?*

"On the rocks?" Stintson asked.

"Yes. Um, on the rocks. Of course."

Stintson started preparing Berg's beverage and asked, "So what do you think of Chelsea Crossing, Brian?"

"I've never been here before. I couldn't see much because it was so dark. This home is really nice. Is this where you live, Dr. Stintson?"

"Oh, no," Stintson said. "We just hold meetings here every once in a while."

"Yes, we rent this home from a friend," chimed in the commander as he picked up a half-consumed drink from a table. He then snapped his fingers and pointed toward a rug in front of the fireplace. Ferdinand and Imelda sauntered over and laid on the rug. "We like to call this place our laboratory. It's where we cook up some of our best ideas."

"It's a nice little out-of-the-way place for us to get together," Stintson said as he brought Berg his drink. "It's just far away from cameras and nosy people. And Brian, we're going to ask you not to tell anybody about our meeting here tonight. It's just too important to disclose. If knowledge about our plans got out, it could really harm the progress of all that we're working for. We want you to be part of this success. Understand?"

Berg nodded his head.

"So I propose a little toast here this evening," the commander said raising his glass. Stintson followed suit immediately and Berg also raised his glass after catching on a second later. "To doctors. May we celebrate the many excellent physicians and ferret out the ones who just suck."

"To doctors," Berg said as he held his glass a little higher with perfect timing and grace.

"I can drink to that," Stintson said, as the three men looked each other in the eye. Stintson and the commander tipped back their glasses and took a sip of their respective drinks and Berg followed right behind without missing a beat. The potency of his first swallow of Scotch surprised him a bit, but he hid the shock and drank it down with some well-disguised discomfort. Berg made a mental note to ensure that his next swallows would just be modest sips.

"So Brian, we've got to get this Stoker issue under control," Stintson said. "The commander here has taken a special interest in this particular psychiatrist, and we're going to bring him down, even if we have to frame him." Stintson took another swig from his glass. "If you dig up a little dirt and we exaggerate it a lot, it should be pretty easy to dispense with Stoker." Stintson took a much smaller sip from his drink. "What did you learn from Sarah Haslam?"

"She caught Stoker kissing a patient and she says that he practices bad medicine."

"Bad medicine?" Stintson asked. "What does she mean by bad medicine? Is he crazy? Does he do things that are unconventional or different than most doctors?"

"Yes. He is different, but she didn't explain much about why he's so, um, well uh, bad."

"Does she give examples?" asked the commander.

"She calls him a felon."

"Okay," the commander said. Why? What felonies has he committed?"

"She says he has drugs and illegal firearms, but I really don't know."

Stintson perked up. "That's excellent, Brian. It looks like we don't need to frame him after all. Let's just use Haslam's testimony, get in his office, and blow this thing wide open."

"Why don't we all meet with her?" Berg suggested. "Then you and the commander can ask her all of your specific questions."

"No way, Brian," Stintson insisted with enough directness in his voice to cause the wolf dogs to raise their heads a bit. "We don't want to *ever* talk to Haslam." Stintson reached up, securely placed his hand on Berg's shoulder, and looked him directly in the eye. "Did you tell her who you were working with?"

"Absolutely not," Berg said like a good soldier. "I told her that I was working on behalf of the board. I don't know if she knows that you're the president."

"Right," Stintson responded. "I'm not concerned about that. We just can't let people know that I'm investigating with the commander. It would raise unnecessary suspicions."

"Compromise the investigation," inserted Berg in an attempt to show that he knew what he was talking about.

"If I met with this Haslam," the commander said, "she's smart enough to put the pieces together. That's just one more person who we would have to let in on our dirty secrets."

"This crazy Sarah Haslam is really screwed up," Stintson said. "I talked to Dr. Penny Denning, her residency chair. Haslam has little skill as a psychiatrist. She needs some strings pulled to have any chance of getting her career back on track," Dr. Stintson explained.

"How hard is it to get into a new residency after you've been kicked out?" asked the commander.

"It depends. If an Ohio State graduate gets kicked out of an orthopedic residency at Johns Hopkins because of poor evaluations from other surgeons, he'll recover," explained Stintson. He will probably get a new spot in a reputable family practice or internal medicine residency, but at a less prestigious institution. However, Haslam's idiotic misconduct in a lesser-known South Dakota psychiatry residency could end her career. With some luck and perhaps a favor from me, she can probably get into a non-competitive family practice residency. She'll have to edge out foreign medical graduates with low test scores."

"So with a little persuasion from one of the state's most visible doctors—"

"She'll say whatever we ask her to say," interrupted the impulsive Brian Berg.

"Here in South Dakota, there are basically two behaviors that can get a doctor's license suspended or revoked," the commander outlined. "First, if they are deemed to be incompetent, we can yank their license. But this Stoker guy is a menace and his behavior falls squarely in the realm of the second behavior, unprofessional conduct. His misdeeds are going to earn him some time in the penitentiary in Yankton."

"In my mind's eye, I was envisioning Stoker in the Springfield prison," joked Stintson. "Let's see what this Haslam says. Perhaps she'll have enough dirt to give him an extended tour with numerous stops at state penal facilities."

"I'm going to ensure Stoker never lives to see the inside of a jail cell," muttered the commander inaudibly."

"What was that, commander?" Berg asked.

"Oh, nothing. Not important."

"So it will be your job, Brian, to help her recall some of these moments of unprofessional conduct," continued Dr. Stintson. You know, the felonies. You really need to focus in on misconduct. The times Stoker touched people inappropriately, abused prescription powers, used his psychotherapy skills to grossly manipulate patients, or used or moved drugs."

"I'll have some people look into his banking and tax records," the commander said. "I suspect there are some nuggets of interest there. I wonder what his records of patient co-pay cash deposits look like. We know doctors who just pocket the co-pays and never report them as income."

Stintson's hair stood up on the back of his neck and his face turned beet red. On most patient days, he walked out of his practice with more than three hundred dollars in patient co-pays and deductibles they had paid in cash. He never reported this income to the IRS. But the commander never saw the surgeon blush.

"At least our investigative record requests can slow Stoker down and mire him in paperwork," continued the commander. He'll need to use extra time to answer our inquiries, so he can't see as many patients. If he sees fewer patients, the odds of him hugging, kissing, Tasing, or committing other crimes drops significantly. If we learn anything significant, we can also get a warrant. The search can include getting a dog into his office to sniff for gunpowder and firearms. We'll choose a dog that is also amazing at sniffing out drugs; we'll find them."

"Let's send him to the Acumen Institute in Kansas," Berg blurted out. The commander looked at Stintson seeking clarification.

"The Acumen Institute is a place where doctors and other professionals can go to get training on certain issues, "explained Stintson. "We occasionally require doctors to go to their professional boundary training. You know, if a doctor cannot keep his hands off of a curvy little receptionist or if the board finds that he's been inappropriate with a patient, we'll send him to the Acumen Institute to help them learn to be appropriate."

"So you cannot suddenly require Dr. Stoker to go, based solely on the rumor that he's inappropriate?" asked the commander. "There has to be due process and much more evidence than the word of a disgruntled, dismissed resident, right?"

"Sure, there is always due process," Stintson said. "But often doctors do not want to go through the painful formalities of due process. Despite our best efforts to stay confidential, word gets out. People who file complaints with the board are not bound by any sort of gag order. So doctors quickly accept letters of concern, limitations on their license, and recommendations that they attend the Acumen Institute. They just want to get it behind them, so they accept the correction plan and move on. With Stoker it's different. I would like another witness before I considered sending him away for special training."

"Sure, that makes sense." The commander said.

"We'll definitely find a patient who will say Stoker is a pervert," interjected Berg.

"No, Brian. That's so tired," snapped the commander. "Thanks to Clinton and Lewinski, we're all too jaded to care about affairs. Besides, these cases never quite go how you want them to. Consenting adults rarely get in trouble for mutually getting a little crazy." The commander finished his drink, called the dogs to his side, and motioned toward the garage. "This is what we're going to do. It's simple. We're going to find out who his patients are and we're going to steal their identities."

Brian Berg did not know about the company named Green Growth Ventures, so the commander chose his next words carefully. "I have some friends who will destroy them financially. After that, our investigation will lead us right back to Stoker. If this Haslam woman is right, and he's moving drugs, we'll bust him for that, too. He'll be in jail so quickly, he won't care about his license or how his rights were violated during your visit, Brian. It'll all go away."

Stintson chimed in, "Rivera will back off, because he'll doubt his friend's character and story. If Stoker decides to be difficult while he's in prison or he keeps his attorneys investigating, we'll get some help from your friends on the inside, where they'll find him hanging in his jail cell."

CHAPTER 66

A courier delivered the letter containing the summons for a hearing with the South Dakota Medical Board at 12:15 p.m. It specified that the hearing would be closed to the public and Stoker was immediately unhappy with that decision. In addition, the envelope contained a letter of concern signed by Brian Berg and Larry Stintson, but Stoker didn't care. Thirty minutes after receiving the summons from the South Dakota Medical Board, Troy Stoker sent a fax response to the board's president, Larry Stintson. His response accepted the invitation to meet, requested that the meeting be held as soon as possible, and asserted his right to open the meeting to the public.

At 2:30 p.m. Tamara hand-delivered a hard copy of Stoker's previously faxed letter to the office of the South Dakota Medical Board. At 4:50 p.m. Larry Stintson called Dr. Stoker's office for the first time ever. "Hello, is Dr. Stoker available? This is Dr. Stintson from the South Dakota Medical Board." He was speaking quickly and it was evident that Stintson was nervous. "May I please speak with Dr. Stoker?"

"Dr. Stoker is with a patient right now," Tamara said. "What's your number Dr. Stintson?" Tamara asked. She knew Dr. Stintson was the president of the South Dakota Medical Board, but she didn't want him to think he deserved any special treatment.

"Can't you just interrupt him? I step out of exams all the time to take quick phone calls from other doctors."

"Well, Dr. Stoker does not. He's actually a psychiatrist and his patients are not as tolerant of interruptions. His sessions are often intense. Patients are the center of what we do here. We never interrupt a session. Now what's your number, doctor?" Tamara listened to the doctor repeating his telephone number, but she didn't bother to write it down.

At 5:05 p.m. Dr. Stoker walked his patient to the door and wished her well.

"Dr. Stintson called," commented Tamara as Stoker returned to the reception desk.

"Oh. I suspect he's referring a patient," Stoker mocked. "I'll call him."

At 5:28 p.m. Dr. Stoker reached Larry Stintson on the phone. "Say Troy, thank you for your speedy response, but there's no need to have a public meeting. I mean, this is just a little informal conversation that we have with doctors ninety-five percent of the time. We almost always conclude with a meeting of the minds, Troy. You know, seeing each other's points of view, doing a little fence mending, and clearing up misunderstandings."

"Dr. Stintson. There has been no misunderstanding here. Will you please schedule a public meeting as soon as possible? I believe in open government. I believe in our republic. I really look forward to airing out the situation."

"But Troy, there is your patient's confidentiality to be concerned about."

"Yes. Let's refer to her as a Jane Doe in all comments and remarks and documents that might be heard or observed by the public or the media."

"I really doubt we can do that."

"Actually, it's simple. My attorney informs me that there is precedent with your board and all over the United States."

Stintson had no idea what to say.

"When is your next available hearing time?" Stoker asked. "I'll be there."

"Troy, I'm getting an emergency call," Stintson lied. "We'll get back in touch with you," he said with a click.

CHAPTER 67

"If Stoker wants an open hearing, get him a date as soon as you can," the commander ordered Stintson. "Do it next week. Get it over with quick. Don't give him time to prepare or to rally the media. Just be done with it." The commander slammed down his phone, and it startled Stintson.

Stintson picked up his cell phone and sent a text message to his assistant, Lucille, at the medical board offices.

Get Stoker on the hearing schedule ASAP

Ten minutes later, Lucille printed the letter setting the hearing date and filled out the fax cover page.

CHAPTER 68

OFFICE OF TROY STOKER, M.D., SIOUX FALLS

Stoker knew he was close to getting his hearing, and he was determined to make sure it happened. He composed a quick letter to fax to Dr. Stintson. In the body of the letter he thanked Dr. Stintson for his call, requested a speedy hearing date, and re-affirmed his desire to resolve the issues at hand.

Stoker printed the letter and filled out his cover sheet. The doctor walked over to the fax machine with complete intent to transmit the document to the state board. As he reached down to insert the fax, he noticed the final page of a two-page fax arriving. He picked up the new fax, read it, and then he tossed his recently prepared document in the trashcan and exclaimed to himself, "We'll see you in five days, Larry!" Then he called his attorney, Holly Glover on her personal cell phone.

Glover answered on the second ring. "What's up, Stoker?"

"I have a hearing with the state medical board in five days. Can you find at least eight non-consecutive hours of time in your schedule to help me prepare?"

CHAPTER 69

OFFICE OF LARRY STINTSON, M.D., SIOUX FALLS

It was a late-night celebration at Larry Stintson's office. The commander had sent Katerina to surprise him with his commission from the portfolios he'd sent over to Green Growth Ventures in Reno. "Eleven-thousand dollars, baby!" Stintson said."

"Look at you go, you sexy bad boy," Katerina whispered in his ear. "There's also a little bonus from the commander. But, I won't share it with you until you take me someplace nice."

Stintson took out his phone and sent a text to his wife that included a simple lie about one of his patients going bad. He concocted a story that he was going into surgery, and he would probably be there most of the night.

"Sheraton, here we come!" Stintson grabbed Katerina by the hand. "Now, what's that bonus, Katerina, my love?"

"Oh, Larry." Katerina was stunned and elated. "That's the first time you've ever called me your love."

"I kind of liked it, too" Stintson said. "Let's get out of here, so we can talk about the bonus."

Katerina reached into her purse and pulled out a sealed plastic bag that contained three pills of two different colors. "You know which ones are my favorite, don't you Larry?"

"Katerina, you like the psychedelic. The ecstasy has always been your thing, my love."

"I'll show you some ecstasy, sexy man. Get me to the Sheraton!"

CHAPTER 70

Troy Stoker had a hard time making his way to his seat at the front of the boardroom at the South Dakota Medical Board. There were two television stations setting up cameras, and getting past all of their equipment in the tight room was a bit of an acrobatic maneuver. But Stoker did not mind at all. Holly Glover was already in her chair at the table and Stoker eventually made it to the seat beside her. Sitting down he asked, "How are you, Holly?"

"I'm great, Troy. We've worked hard in our prep sessions and I'm invigorated and ready to go. Plus, I just ran seven miles, so my mind is sharp and focused. How are you feeling?"

"Razor sharp. Thank you for the prep sessions. Do you feel like I'm ready?"

"You know the Constitution better than half of the ham-and-egg lawyers out there, so I think you'll be okay with a handful of doctors."

"Thanks. I wouldn't be surprised if there are one or two people on the board who are history buffs or passionate about America. I deeply hope there are."

"I am more skeptical than you, Troy," said Glover. "If there were board members who knew about civil rights and due process, we wouldn't be here. This board thinks it can do what it wants and trample on people like Hitler's Brownshirts. Stintson, Berg, and the rest have abused people's rights and they don't even know it. I've worked with them through dozens of inquiries and I've often pointed out Constitutional matters. They've closed a few cases after I pointed out their blunders."

"Don't they have an attorney who assists them?"

"Technically they do, but he's not been in a court room for years. Sure, he attends these hearings, but they're less formal than a courtroom. He just doesn't know the law. He does some part-time work for the board at a hundred and ten dollars per hour. The medical board is kind of like a freelance gig for him. His main job is his private law practice, which mostly involves writing underwhelming wills and closing small real estate transactions. I sent him an email when we learned about this hearing. He said he would try to re-arrange his schedule to make it. That's the last I heard from him. I'm not sure he's going to be much of a resource to them."

"Well, let's create a little teaching moment and illuminate the board and their attorney," Stoker said. "Of course, if I've done anything wrong, I'll plead guilty and accept the sanctions."

"You know, Troy, contrary to what you see on TV, hearings and trials usually don't contain much drama. In real world trials and hearings, surprises don't exist. I've never seen unplanned witnesses take the stand or surprise evidence admitted at the last moment—like you might see in a movie or read in a thriller novel. Legal rules in the real world do not allow such tactics, and judges would be crazy to make exceptions."

"So is tonight different?" Stoker asked.

"Yes!" Glover said. "There is some potential for surprises. You see, usually in legal matters we've had meetings, phone calls, and information exchanges for weeks before the main event."

"Like pre-trial hearings and discovery?"

"Exactly," confirmed Glover. "But in this case, everything happened quickly. To do our best to satisfy the discovery process, we sent copies of recordings and other documents we may choose to use tonight. I sent them four days ago. That's how it's supposed to work. But the medical board has sent us nothing. Today we're sitting here with very little of that information on the table. The medical board has ignorantly overlooked those rules or courtesies and ignorance is no defense."

"So this could turn out to be some great courtroom drama." Stoker smiled as he thought of the possibility.

"Technically, boardroom drama. This is a hearing. It is less formal, too. Stintson can bend the rules a bit, but everyone must answer questions completely and truthfully."

"Well, part of being a psychiatrist is using a technique called psycho-drama. I'm a pretty good actor—but usually my audience is one or two people."

"I think you've identified a nice transferable skill, Stoker. Use it to your full advantage tonight," said Glover as a door at the front of the room opened. In stepped Larry Stintson and Brian Berg. Glover and Stoker both waited a few moments before acknowledging and greeting them.

"I trust you reviewed the documents and recordings we sent over, Dr. Stintson?" asked Glover. "Oh, no. I've not had time. I'm sorry. Busy surgery schedule and all."

"What recordings?" Berg asked with a confused look on his face.

"Oh, I really don't know," replied Stintson to Berg. Awkwardly he turned toward Holly Glover. "What is on the tapes?"

"They're actually not tapes. They are digital recordings," Glover clarified. "We will introduce them completely if the hearing warrants," she said with a pause. "But Larry, let's save the recordings for the actual hearing. We don't want to get too far ahead of ourselves and taint your proceedings."

"Fine," Stintson said failing to comprehend the gravity of the recordings as evidence. However, Brian Berg was visibly panicked as color drained from his face and he braced himself on the table.

Six other board members arrived through the front door and said brief hellos to Stoker and his attorney. Then Dr. Stintson's secretary from the medical board, Lucille, also filed in and chose a seat three down from Larry Stintson. More people had occupied the seats around the boardroom table. Two newspaper reporters filled chairs; and the medical board's office manager, Kira, occupied another seat. Stoker did not recognize the other people seated around the table. There was also a small gallery toward the back of the room. It contained about thirty other seats, most of which were taken. Errol Rivera was sitting in the second row of the gallery and he gave Stoker the thumbs-up sign.

As the board members at the front of the room engaged in informal pre-meeting conversation, a slight commotion arose toward the back of the room. A man with a spray-on tan and neat haircut was making his way toward the front of the room and apologizing in contrived sincerity to people as he stepped over and around them.

"Is that the board's attorney?" Stoker asked Glover.

"Uh-huh," Glover replied. "That unopened envelope in his hands contains his copy of the discovery documents and recordings."

"How do you know it's unopened?" Stoker asked.

"Just watch," said Glover wryly. "I use really strong, reinforced tape."

The attorney eventually made it to the front of the room. He gestured for Berg to scoot over so he could sit next to Stintson. While pretending to show interest in the pre-hearing huddle, he wrestled, in vain, to open the envelope. He reached for his keys and used one as a crude letter-opener. Benson and Stoker both enjoyed the spectacle.

Behind them the gallery was now full, and people were starting to stand against the boardroom wall. Stoker took a break from watching the board attorney failing to open the envelope. He turned around and noticed a few of his patients who had come to support him. He also sighted the representative of his legislative district in the South Dakota Legislature. The news camera operators activated some lighting, which Larry Stintson took as a cue that it was time to begin the hearing.

With the bang of a gavel Stintson called the meeting to order. "Welcome everyone to this hearing of the South Dakota Medical Board," he said in a voice with extra bravado. "I am Dr. Larry Stintson, president of the South Dakota Medical Board, and I will chair this meeting."

The attorney finally freed the contents of the envelope and interrupted Stintson by spilling them on the table. Even though everyone present observed the small debacle, Stintson pretended not to notice it and continued on. "First and foremost," continued Stintson, "we need you to turn those cameras off," he said with an authority that mirrored his command-and-control style in the operating room. "This hearing is about a sensitive matter and cameras are not appropriate," he insisted arrogantly.

A confident reporter stood, "This is an open and public hearing, Dr. Stintson. Cameras are allowed." Stintson lifted his gavel, then hesitated and thought for a moment. She seized on his indecision and said, "In a hearing where evidence may surface about alleged First Amendment breaches by this government entity, how will it look if you attempt to curtail freedom of the press, Doctor?" Stintson was stunned. He was not used to objections.

"This is a different set of circumstances," Stintson said with failing bravado. "The media is welcome but the cameras must be turned off. Don't make me remove the cameras, or you Miss, from these proceedings."

"Dr. Stintson, I will protest," continued the reporter. "I strongly suspect that the other journalists here will join me." Eight other people nodded their heads and stood. "My competitors here would gladly report on my forceful removal from the premises tonight and my editors will file suit in the morning."

Stoker stood. "My unequivocal preference is for full media coverage." Glover made no attempt to quiet him. She was already thrilled with the direction of the hearing.

"Order!" Stintson yelled as he banged his gavel to contain Stoker. Stoker responded with a good-natured smile but said nothing. Stintson turned to his attorney and they whispered together for a few moments. "Very well," he said with a suddenly cordial voice. "Please keep the cameras rolling. Thank you for your patience regarding this matter," he stammered clumsily.

After sipping water and gathering his composure, Stintson continued, "We're here, um, in this, uh, hearing, to discuss an infraction of South Dakota South Dakota Codified Law, Chapter Thirty-six, by one Troy Stoker, M.D., a psychiatrist who practices here in Sioux Falls. The board alleges that Doctor Stoker failed to provide the complete medical record to a patient who requested it in a timely manner. Because this is an open hearing, we will simply refer to this patient as Jane Doe, and we inform the audience that the patient may actually be male or a female. However, we will use female terms for this meeting tonight.

"The patient filed a complaint with the South Dakota Medical Board. We subsequently shared the complaint with Doctor Stoker and mailed a subpoena for those records. Dr. Stoker did not comply with that request, so we subpoenaed the records again. But this time we sent out a staff member to issue the subpoena in person. We also issued a letter of concern to Doctor Stoker. To date, he still has not complied with that subpoena and provided records to the patient or the board."

Stoker sat quiet and relaxed. He saw hostile gazes and glares toward him emanating from board members, reporters, and people in the gallery. He knew the hate was temporary.

"As a result," continued Stintson in a preachy tone, "this hearing may result in another letter of concern for Doctor Stoker, further legal action, or limitations on his license to practice medicine. Let's begin by getting some perspective from Brian Berg, a staffer from the state medical board," Stintson said turning to Berg. "Brian, why don't you stand up and introduce yourself and explain what you do."

Berg stood before the crowd. Stoker noticed how Berg seemed to like the attention and the cameras. This rather unremarkable man was suddenly poised. "My name is Brian Berg. I'm an investigator with the South Dakota Medical Board. When we get complaints I start the process of gathering facts. Usually the facts end up clearing the doctors, so I recommend the case be closed. If those facts add up, I continue the investigation and report my findings to the board regularly. In some cases there is enough evidence to write a letter of concern about an issue and place it in the doctor's file. Sometimes, like today, there is enough evidence for a hearing. At that point, I become more of a witness and the board members become sort of like a jury with their medical knowledge."

"So you've been investigating Dr. Stoker?" Stintson asked.

"Yes. But it has been really hard. He's been uncooperative. His non-compliance is why we're here this evening. He wouldn't give us the records."

"How many times have you requested them?"

"Two times."

"What does he state as his reason for not providing the records."

"Oh, Stoker's made up his own little process which has left the board and his ex-patient in the dark."

"So the patient still does not have the records, either?"

"No."

Someone in the crowd gasped and a couple of people murmured. Stintson paused and let the moment produce its intended result.

"Well, that is the experience of the board with regard to Dr. Stoker," Stintson said. Then he turned to Dr. Stoker and Holly Glover. "Miss Glover. Do you have any question at this time?"

"My client does," said Glover as Stoker stood.

"Mr. Berg. A few minutes ago you stated that this hearing was a result of my non-compliance."

"Well, no. I was just explaining the typical way these things work, and —"

"I wrote down your words verbatim. You said, 'He's been uncooperative. His non-compliance is why we're here this evening. He wouldn't give us the records.' Those are your words are they not, Mr. Berg?"

"I really don't recall the exact words I used."

"That's fine. The news cameras can back us up if we ever need to get down to a word-for-word accounting. But I bet you can remember the answer to my next question precisely. Berg just grinned a nutty, narcissistic smile. "Who first requested this hearing?"

"Last week I recommended it, and Dr. Stintson scheduled it."

"Actually, I requested the meeting eight days ago for the first time. Do you remember when you introduced me to Kira, your boss and office manager?"

"Yes."

"What did I come here to request?"

"I don't remember."

"Did I have a letter with me?"

"Maybe. I don't know."

"Let me dispense with the twenty questions game here Mr. Berg and just get straight to the point." Stoker directed his attention to the board members. "Members of the board. My fellow physicians, I requested this meeting eight days ago. I came here in person and Mr. Berg introduced me to the office manager, Kira. I asked her to schedule the meeting and provided her with a letter, addressed to Dr. Stintson, re-affirming that request. Kira refused to schedule the meeting and I did not hear back from Dr. Stintson, or any board member or staffer, that day. The next day I sent another letter, certified mail, to Dr. Stintson requesting a hearing. I was not trying to be a thorn in your side. I wanted to talk about these issues and work things out. It is the board that has refused my requests to meet."

"Do you remember that Mr. Berg?" Stintson asked.

"No, I don't see it that way at all, Dr. Stoker. I think you are trying to elude the issue." Berg replied.

"Dr. Stintson, did you get my numerous letters and phone messages over the last few days."

"I don't recall seeing them," Stintson lied. "I get a lot of calls and correspondence."

"Do you have a secretary here at the board? Is there somebody who helps you organize, prioritize, and document your communication?"

"Yes."

"Is she here tonight? I suspect she is helping you arrange and manage this meeting?" Stoker knew that Lucille was here. Tamara had asked her to attend.

"Yes." Stintson said.

"Could you please ask her if she has any records of those letters and calls?"

Stintson looked over at Lucille who was opening a file folder. "Here are the letters that I had forwarded to your office every day, doctor. I can print copies of the phone message emailed and sent to your cell phone via text message," said the secretary with a buttery voice that implied she was trying to be efficient and helpful.

Stintson was visibly flustered. "Well, there must be something wrong with our systems. I'll look into that. But I can guarantee my fellow members of the board that I recommended this meeting and put it on the calendar."

The other board members had heard Stintson and Berg lie before and the look of disbelief on their faces convinced many of the audience members that they should at least consider what Dr. Stoker was saying.

"I can guarantee that this meeting would've never happened if I had not been persistent," Stoker said speaking directly to the board again. "You see, doctors, the story that Brian Berg just told you is largely incomplete. Let's fill in a few holes, starting with the assertion that I never provided the medical records."

Berg's stupid grin still graced his face and he kept an uncharacteristically composed demeanor. Stintson was obviously uncomfortable and he kept folding and unfolding his arms.

"Mr. Berg, which of Jane Doe's records has the board received so far?"

"A few, limited pages. Most of the information is still missing."

"What kind of information is redacted from that record?"

"Some of your, um, psychology notes or something like that."

"Yes," Stoker said as he lifted a single finger into the air. "As a point of clarification, they are actually called psychotherapy notes. Mr. Berg, Why did I exclude them?"

"How should I know? I'm not a mind-reader."

"You *should* know because I explained it clearly in the letter I sent you. I also called and spoke with you to clarify my medical and legal rationale. What did I explain to you on two occasions? What was my reasoning for excluding psychotherapy notes?"

Berg's grin was now completely out of place. Many board members and audience members were sensing that something was wrong with the medical board investigator. "I don't remember all of the details, but it has something to do with how this patient should not see her own medical record."

"Another point of clarification for members of the board," Stoker said. "I wanted her to know what was in her medical record and psychotherapy notes, but I knew that it would be harmful to this patient to just give her a stack of her records. So I arranged for the assistance of a mental health professional to interpret them for her. I went above and beyond." Stoker stepped closer to Berg and looked him in the eye. "The law is clear—the *only* person who makes this decision and manages this process of sharing, or not sharing, psychotherapy notes is the psychiatrist. Period. End of story. "Why do we do that, Mr. Berg?" Stoker asked him as he pointed at him.

"So you and the other psychiatrists can make more money," Berg stated foolishly.

"I charged nothing to pull those notes together and create those copies. Zero dollars, Mr. Berg. If you would like, we can all send each other bills for zero dollars for this session, too."

"I'm *losing* money on this meeting," blurted out Larry Stintson. Immediately he realized how foolish it looked for an orthopedic surgeon to complain about money.

"It has nothing to do with money." Stoker turned to one of the board member doctors, a neurologist. "Dr. White. You see patients who confront serious mental health issues every day. Why do psychiatrists sometimes elect to not provide psychotherapy notes to patients?"

Larry Stintson jumped in. "Dr. Stoker. You cannot call a board member as a witness."

"Dr. White deals with this issue, all the time, Dr. Stintson. I can ask her for her input," clarified Stoker. "She can refuse to provide it." Stoker paused for a moment, but raised his hand thoughtfully so nobody interrupted him, and then looked back and Stintson and said, "So, let me be clear, Mr. President, I'm not asking Dr. White to be a witness. I'm asking for her input and experience as a physician. Does any board member have an issue with that?"

All of the board members were silent, and Dr. White shook her head.

"I didn't think so," Stoker said.

Dr. White jumped right in. "Larry, I'm answering the question. It's critical enough." She looked down the table to the other board members. "According to state law, a psychiatrist, psychologist, or other mental health professional may withhold psychotherapy notes from a patient, if the mental health professional judges that the patient would be harmed by reviewing his or her own psychotherapy notes. The mental health provider can review them in person with the patient. If this is unacceptable for the patient in question, the next step is to transfer the patient's record to another mental health professional who would be acceptable by *that* particular patient, *and* who would be willing to take over that patient's care. That psychiatrist, psychologist, or social worker then meets with the patient and can interpret the notes for him or her. That has been state law for many years, but now the federal laws are changing for greater protection of the psychiatrist's own psychotherapy notes," Dr. White said allowing a momentary pause. "But when you look at HIPAA and other federal laws, now they cancel out the requirement for another mental health professional to interpret the records for the patient. So the psychiatrist does not have to give psychotherapy notes to anybody, according to this new federal law. So Dr. Stoker went out of his way to satisfy the patient."

"Thank you, Dr. White—" Stoker said, before she unexpectedly cut him off.

"This is a critical process," she asserted. "The crux of this issue is whether or not we want our patients to kill themselves over something they see in their medical record. Can you imagine how horrible it would be for an abuse victim who has made a decade of progress, to go back through those notes and digress—in a matter of hours—back to where they were years ago?"

Stoker chose to be silent and the silence prompted Dr. Stintson to search for words and find something to say. "Well, um, thank you, Dr. White. A fine clarification, there, um, for the record."

"Mr. Berg," interrupted Stoker. "Did I provide those records to any other mental health professional?"

"Not that I'm aware of."

"Actually, you were completely aware," Stoker rebutted. "I explained it on the phone to you and in a letter I sent you. Would you like to see a copy of the letter to refresh your memory?"

"I have it right here," volunteered Lucille. Her zeal drew an evil look from her boss Larry Stintson, but she was not too concerned. State jobs were amazingly secure.

"I'll take your word for it, Dr. Stoker," interjected Berg.

"Good. Because I provided the complete record to an excellent psychiatrist, Dr. McGill. We had an extensive conversation about the patient in question. I wanted her to know what was in her records, so I went above and beyond to make sure it happened. Dr. McGill still treats her, and I hope she continues to progress."

"Very well, Dr. Stoker." Stintson banged his gavel, but nobody knew quite why. "I trust you're done with questions for Mr. Berg?"

"No, Mr. President." Stoker liked to remind people that Stintson was the president of the mismanaged medical board. "I have more questions for him."

"Make it snappy, Dr. Stoker." Stintson said.

Stoker ignored his command and continued on. "So Brian, tell us about the day that you came to my office to get those records. Will you tell the board that story?"

Berg was still smiling but he was showing signs of discomfort. "Yes, I will. I will also ask Sarah Haslam to witness to what I say."

"Delightful," quipped Stoker. "This should be illuminating. Please tell us the story then, Mr. Berg." He had not seen Haslam in the gallery. He didn't care what she said.

"Well, when I had not seen the records from Dr. Stoker—"

Stoker interrupted. "Wait, Brian. Are you telling the board that you had never received any of this patient's records from me?"

"Okay. When I had seen the *incomplete* records from Dr. Stoker, I went out to his office and subpoenaed the rest."

"Don't you mean *we*? You brought a few people along with you, Brian."

"I brought the police along with me because I heard that Dr. Stoker had weapons, stacks of ammunition, and a Taser in his office."

"I had no fire arms or ammunition, Brian. Where did you get that information?"

"You used a Taser on Tom DuPont!" Berg interjected.

"I object," Stoker said. "Dr. Stintson. Will you please inform your staffer about the latest confidentially laws? He should not be naming one of my patients in a public forum."

"Brian!" scolded Stintson as he banged the gavel. "Tomorrow morning. Eight o'clock a.m. in my office. We will talk about this seriously."

Berg's smile disappeared. Stoker's questions had weakened the investigator and his credibility, but Brian Berg was the victim of his own knockout blow when he broke confidentiality laws. His hands started to shake visibly.

"Mr. Berg, let me clarify. I have no firearms or ammunition in my office. But if I wanted to, I could. Which Amendment is that?"

"The Second Amendment," Berg said.

"Do you own any firearms?"

"Yes."

"Which ones?"

"A hunting rifle," Berg said.

"Is that all? Any pistols or shotguns? Let's tell the whole truth here, Brian"

"Sure," Berg said. "I own a few."

"Right," Stoker said with a smile. "I'm glad you do. Most people in South Dakota own firearms. So where did you get the idea that possessing firearms was the basis for raiding my office with five or six deputy sheriffs?"

Stintson banged his gavel. "I object to the inflammatory language such as the word 'raiding,'" Stintson said.

"Okay," Stoker said. "Hold that thought, and tell me if you still object to it in a few minutes."

"Because you shocked a patient with a Taser," interjected Berg.

"Yes! I did. After being struck twice. I was a minute or two from bleeding to death. I used a Taser on a patient who was attacking me. My actions were completely within the law. I should've used the Taser ten seconds sooner. I wish I had. But for now, Mr. Berg, please tell us the story of your visit to my office to subpoena medical records."

"When we got to your office, I asked to speak with you. Your receptionist told me I would have to wait."

"Did you wait?"

"As a state official, my business was *very* important, so I sent an officer in to interrupt you. You still refused to visit with us, so I interrupted. After that, you became irrational. Next you became violent and you ended up hitting me."

"Why didn't the police arrest me?"

"Well, the point is, you were rude and unprofessional. Your non-compliance was off the charts and your violence is unacceptable. That is why we needed this hearing. That is why I recommended it, and that is why Dr. Stintson wanted it to happen so quickly. We can't have violent doctors out there. You've shown a pattern of violence with your Taser and by physically throwing people out of your office."

"And, Sarah Haslam can attest to this?"

"Yes. She'll confirm everything I said."

"Would it be okay to call on her now, Dr. Stintson?" Stoker asked.

"Maybe," replied Stintson. "Do you have anything else to add, Brian?"

"No. If I think of anything else, I'll raise my hand," he replied.

"Okay, Dr. Haslam," Stintson said. Why don't you stand up and tell us your side of the story. Will you introduce yourself to the board?"

Haslam stood in place in the gallery. She decided not to climb over people and television equipment to stand closer to the board. But the TV cameras swung around and shined their lights on her. All of a sudden, she seemed content to have so much attention.

"My name is Sarah Haslam, medical doctor. I was doing a rotation under Dr. Stoker's mentoring at the time of the incident, so I was there in the room with him when Dr. Stoker went ballistic on Mr. Berg. I couldn't believe the yelling and disrespect. And then when Dr. Stoker punched him, I was aghast. I've never seen anything like it in my whole medical experience."

Stoker sensed that Haslam was done with her speech, so he asked, "Was my so-called violence provoked?"

"No," Haslam responded. "You just went crazy without any warning."

"*Warning* is an important word. Thank you for bringing it up. Did I issue any warnings to the officers, Dr. Haslam?"

"No. None."

"Actually, I did. And they listened to them respectfully. They knew I was within my constitutional rights. Did I issue any warnings to Mr. Berg?"

"No. You just attacked him."

"Mr. Berg," Stoker said turning to Brian. "Did I warn you to leave my office?"

"You never did."

"Okay. Let's check the testimonies of Brian Berg and Sarah Haslam," Stoker said as he clicked a remote control. A movie screen began to descend from the ceiling just behind the board members, as Stoker opened his laptop computer. "The day of Mr. Berg's visit—which the board may or may not decide to label a raid—I had security cameras running in my hallway and reception area. I always do. I also have additional cameras in my office where I treat patients, in case of emergencies, I can instantly activate with the click of a button. I've rarely used them; but I did that day."

"You can't use those recordings in this hearing," objected Berg. "You never told me I was being recorded."

"Okay, Brian. First, I did inform you, and you'll see that within the first few seconds of this recording. Second, you had an officer pointing a video camera at my patient and me. You can see that on my recording. Where is that recording?"

Stintson was clearly out of control of the situation. He was speechless and his gavel was motionless.

"Wait" stumbled Berg in a panicked voice. "You can't just spring this on us. You have to share recordings and documents beforehand."

"We did," Stoker said. We sent a copy to the board president and the board's attorney just hours after the meeting was scheduled. What did you send us, Brian?"

Stoker pushed the play button. "You sent us nothing." The first shot was Berg and the police officers at the reception desk insisting that they see Dr. Stoker right away. Tamara was objecting strongly and authoritatively. "First, we are recording this whole interaction both video and audio. Second, nobody interrupts Dr. Stoker when he's with patients."

As Berg looked up at the screen he sunk into his chair. His hands resumed their shaking as he witnessed an image of himself protesting, "But we have a subpoena."

"Great leave it here, and we'll respond in a timely manner," Tamara said. We know how subpoenas work. Do you?" Two board members snickered. They saw how ridiculous Berg's logic was, and they were impressed that Tamara was so poised and prepared.

"I'm an investigator from the state board and I demand access."

"You may get it when Dr. Stoker finishes his session," Tamara said. "What are you investigating?"

"Medical records."

The on-screen debate went on for another minute or so before Berg ordered one of the six sheriff deputies to go interrupt the session. As the officer knocked and stepped into the office, the board members and audience witnessed Stoker instructing the officer to wait and informing him that he was being recorded.

As the officer retreated on the screen Stoker interjected to the room of people, "Is there anybody here who objects to this recording on the grounds that Mr. Berg was not informed of the recording?" Stintson sat still while the rest of the board members shook their heads vigorously. A few seconds later, the screen showed Brian Berg bursting into Dr. Stoker's office. The boardroom filled with gasps. Larry Stintson was too shocked and too embarrassed to even lift the gavel.

On the screen Stoker was instructing Berg to leave the premises, and then Berg ignored him and began to say, "I'm Brian Berg with the South Dakota Medical Board."

Stoker paused the recording and said, "Let me point out that I was with a patient at this moment. You can't yet see him or her because I've carefully positioned the cameras." Stoker pressed play. People in the audience covered their mouths and shook their heads as they saw Berg trample patient confidentially and refuse Stoker's requests to leave. They witnessed Berg's on-screen indifference as Stoker called him to task for overlooking due process and unreasonable search and seizure.

Some people in the boardroom audibly laughed as one of the officers explained the difference between a warrant and a subpoena. Then Stoker paused the recording. "Brian, were you informed of the recording?"

"It seems as if I was," Berg said. "With so much happening, I must have mentally overlooked it."

"Did I warn you about the consequences of failing to leave the therapy session and my private property?"

"You threatened me with a law suit and told me you would remove me."

"Exactly! That's how we protect our rights from idiots!" Stoker said in a deep, authoritative voice. "What happened next, Brian?"

"You pushed me out of your office."

"No! Let me ask a more specific question. Did you recognize my patient?"

The remaining color drained from Berg's face. "I, um," Berg stammered. "He was my—"

"Say no more," interrupted Stoker simultaneous with Dr. Stintson bringing down the gavel.

"Brian, you must not share details about patients," Stintson said. "Tomorrow, eight a.m. Now just a simple answer, Brian. Did you know the patient? Yes or no?"

"Yes," mumbled Berg.

"Was he or she bothered by your presence?" Stoker asked.

Berg could not lie. The camera would kill him, yet again, if he did. "Yes. He was embarrassed."

Stoker pressed play again. "I've altered the audio of the patient's voice so nobody can recognize it." The odd computer-generated voice came through loud and clear. "Brian! You can't tell anybody about this. I mean, people can't know that I'm seeing a shrink."

As the recording continued to play, people snickered as Berg tried to win control of Stoker. Just as Stoker asserted his right to use reasonable force to remove Berg and the social worker, Stintson banged his gavel, "Okay, enough, Dr. Stoker. We get the point. We will be having a serious discussion with Mr. Berg—"

"I'm almost through, but not yet, Larry," Stoker said. "But you need to see the violence Mr. Berg reports. Trust me. It's in there."

Just then the image of Brian Berg took a roundhouse swing at Stoker. As everyone in the room gasped, Stoker paused the recording. "Brian! How many times have I touched you so far?"

"Zero," responded Berg.

"That's what I thought," Stoker said. All of the board members, including Stintson, were shaking their heads. Nobody could hear a pin drop. Stoker let the silence soak in for a few seconds, then the audience murmured their disbelief. Stoker pushed play, and his image sidestepped the swing. Then, spinning on one leg to his right, a loud slap was heard as the back of Stoker's hand had connected with right side of Berg's jaw. The audience exhaled various single-syllable expressions in support of Stoker's defensive move, until they were interrupted by Berg's image, which was charging Stoker again. The audience gasped as it observed Stoker countering with a shot to the stomach. Then the recording showed the police entering and separating the men.

Stintson banged his gavel to hush the crowd. "I will not have you turning this hearing into a kangaroo court," Stintson shouted at Stoker.

Stoker stood silently and cast his gaze toward the other board members, who were glaring at Stintson. "Who set up this kangaroo court? "Do you understand me, Stintson?"

Stintson was caught completely off guard. He did not expect Stoker to confront him directly. "Well, I see your side of the story —."

Stoker interrupted. "You've done a huge disservice to dozens of people. You owe my patient an apology. This happened on your watch, Stintson." Stoker sat and locked his stare on Brian Berg. When Berg refused to look at him, Stoker threw his stare to Larry Stintson. In the awkward silence, Stintson's mind froze and his eyes darted all around the room, looking anywhere except at Troy Stoker.

"I move to close this case," Dr. White, the neurologist, said breaking the silence. "This is a non-issue. Actually, let me revise my statement. This is a gross error on the part of our board."

Another board member seconded White's motion, and a quick voice vote made Larry Stintson's vote completely unnecessary.

Larry Stintson banged his gavel. "This hearing is hereby adjourned."

The room broke into dozens of conversations, and the strangers closest to Stoker slapped him on the back and congratulated him. Reporters climbed over people and camera equipment to try to get to Stoker. The first reporter to reach him asked, "How do you feel about your big victory tonight?"

Stoker paused for an uneasy moment in time. He slowly looked up at the reporter, and said. "Free." He gathered his materials and confidently strode into the hallway.

Just outside the hearing room, a newspaper reporter had managed to strike up a conversation with Dr. Rivera. "Would you mind if I ask you some questions and get some quotes, Dr. Rivera?"

"Freedom of the Press? Of course. Ask me anything you want. But, I give you fair warning. You'll get frank responses."

The reporter's eyes lit up. She sensed that this might be a great interview. "Why are you here this evening, Dr. Rivera?"

"To support my fellow-physician and like-minded constitutionalist friend, Dr. Stoker."

"So what are your impressions of the results of the meeting, Doctor?"

"I say, *viva* the Fourth Amendment. And the board can stick that where the sun don't shine." He intentionally interjected just a touch of his Cuban accent.

"So this applies to the South Dakota Medical Board, and not just the police?" the reporter asked.

"Look, Brian Berg showed up with numerous police officers. I lived the first few years of my life in Cuba; the behavior that the board has been exhibiting reminds me of the corruption I experienced on a daily basis in Cuba." Rivera was just getting warmed up. "The board must not pay attention to the news. Dr. Stintson and Brian Berg must be completely unaware of the Supreme Court's recent *Riley v. California* ruling requiring reasonable search and seizure and proper warrants for *cell phone* searches. We're not talking about a case from the Jeffersonian era here. Now for something as fundamental as cell phones, wouldn't logic and the law dictate that the state medical board must have a search warrant to enter the highly confidential venue of a *psychiatrist's* office while he's in session?"

"But doesn't the board need to inspect and regulate doctor's offices to protect patients?" the reporter asked.

"How far do you want to take that? Come see what Fidel does with that kind of logic in my home country," Rivera expounded. "Fortunately, our Founding Fathers here in America established fundamental laws against unreasonable search and seizure and the right of the people to be secure in their persons, papers, and effects. Our state's medical board sent its investigator into a psychiatrist's office, and the investigator behaved like a British officer during colonial American times or like the Cuban police who searched my family's home. He was a brute, and the law does not allow that. This corrupt pocket of state government has been exposed, thanks to a doctor who has a spine, understands the law, and was trying to protect the confidentiality of his patients. Do you understand what this good man and physician was trying to do? His job—for heaven's sake. God help us!"

"You seem to be pretty passionate about the Constitution, doctor."

"It's just a matter of remembering eighth grade civics, *chica*, and one of the many reasons I came to this great country!"

CHAPTER 71

It had been a rough morning for Brian Berg. His 8:00 a.m. meeting with Dr. Stintson had involved a lot of direct instructions about patient confidentiality. Berg's office manager, Kira, participated, too. She interjected occasional facts about HIPAA and other privacy laws. She seemed to know more than Stintson about specific regulations that applied to mental health patients and their records.

At 10:00 a.m. Berg met again with Kira. For this meeting, she was accompanied by a human resources consultant from the state. "Brian, we're issuing a written warning for publicly violating a patient's right to privacy."

"What?" Berg asked. "Usually a first offense is a verbal warning and a second offense is a written warning."

"When one of our employees breaches patient confidentiality, we skip right over the verbal warning and issue a written warning," Kira said. The human resources consultant said little, but he nodded his head aggressively in concert with Kira's words. "If this happens again, Brian, you're likely to lose your job. Do you understand?"

"Yes," Berg said. A few minutes later, he was signing the written warning document and leaving Kira's office. As he walked by the desk where Stintson's secretary Lucille sat, she pretended to be deeply engrossed in her work, so she did not make eye contact with Berg. However, Lucille was keenly aware of his presence. She was disappointed, but not surprised, that Stintson and Kira had focused on disciplining Berg for confidentiality this morning, when just last night, Troy Stoker had kicked their butts on basic constitutional issues. Lucille was pretty sure that Stintson and Berg had already chosen to overlook the lessons they had learned about patients and doctors possessing basic human rights, a mere fourteen hours earlier.

Berg returned to his cubicle and busied himself with the paperwork from a number of investigations. If he could just make it to lunchtime, he could get away from the office for a few minutes for a burger, fries, and a drink. Today, out of pure despair, he would certainly supersize.

The minutes and hours dragged on until, at 11:27 a.m., Berg slid out of the office and off to McDonalds. He ate his meal and realized that he'd had little time to think of anything outside of work. Now that his thoughts were his own, his mind automatically obsessed about ways to exact revenge on Troy Stoker. Nothing concrete came to mind, but he did conclude that he wanted Stoker to suffer more than to die. He remembered the plan that Stintson and the commander were hatching to frame him for stealing the identities of his patients from his psychiatry practice and he smiled. He concluded that seeing Stoker go to prison would be awesome. However, Berg wanted to be a part of this process. He wanted to be on the team, instead of just cheering from the sidelines. Berg resolved to quickly find and submit some Stoker patient portfolios to the commander.

Berg walked back to the offices of the state medical board, made his way back to his cubicle, and continued processing forms and routing paperwork. After another hour of work, a new text arrived on Brian Berg's pager.

> *Can you spend the rest of the afternoon working with*
> *me?*

"Of course I can. You're the boss," Brian Berg said to himself out loud as he considered the message. "You're the commander and big shot politician. We'll do whatever you want." Berg simply typed a one-word response.

> *Yes*

Within seconds Berg received another message on his pager with more specific instructions from the commander.

> *Just come out to the parking lot and jump in my car in*
> *20 minutes*

Brian took five minutes to answer an email, three minutes to file a few things, two minutes to lock his desk, and then he walked out to the parking lot with six minutes to spare—to ensure he would not be late for such an important person.

The commander pulled up exactly twenty minutes later in his burgundy Cadillac Escalade. Brian climbed inside the front passenger seat and relished in the fact he was rubbing shoulders with one of the most powerful men in South Dakota. It made him feel much better after all of the turmoil he'd experienced over the last few hours with Stoker and his bosses.

Nevertheless, Berg was not a refined enough person to appreciate the meticulously clean automobile in which he rode. The leather seats did not impress him because he did not have the wherewithal to appreciate the luxury.

"Brian, thanks for breaking away with me," the commander said. "You and I get to play a little hooky today. Actually I sent some bureaucrat a quick email saying you and I were participating in a teambuilding experience this afternoon."

"Okay. Great," Berg replied, thrilled to be away from his desk. He was getting a perk. He was taking advantage of the system—and he liked it.

"You and I are going to be working together a lot in the future, Brian. The bottom line is I need you, I need your trust, and I need your confidentiality. There are a lot of things on my radar screen in the world of doctors, pills, and hospitals. Can I count on you?"

"Of course."

"Good. Because some of this stuff is going to blow your mind."

The two men drove for about twenty-five minutes. They discussed the medical board and shared some bits of each other's life stories. They had both been in the military, so there was an instant bond of brotherhood—at least Berg assumed that was the case.

"I love wild animals," the commander said. "I can't help admire, respect, and even fear the ferocious animals. Have you ever been deep sea fishing, Brian?"

"No."

"Oh. You'll have to join me sometime. The ocean is full of sharks, and pulling one in that is bigger than you," The commander paused for a moment and glanced at Berg. "well, there's almost no greater thrill."

"Do you eat the shark meat? Berg asked.

The commander ignored his question. "Have you been to Yellowstone?"

"Yes. My parents took me to Old Faithful when I was eleven years old."

"In the summer I presume?"

"Yes. It must have been. I don't remember any snow."

"Oh. You must visit in the winter someday, and you'll have to see the wolves. They are like nothing you've ever experienced before."

Berg shuddered inside. He hated dogs and all animals related to them. His mother had taught him to fear dogs as a child, and he heeded that advice to this day.

"They're beautiful," continued the commander. "They seem so happy, pristine, orderly, and dignified. Their team dynamics are magnificent. From the correct vantage point, and with some finely crafted binoculars, you can watch them hunt. When the wolves find that elk, deer, or small buffalo on a frigid January day, the dance starts and the attack rapidly follows. It climaxes as blood gushes from the prey's neck and stains the brave wolves' beautiful white, silver, and gray coats. The wolf teaches us that it's never black and white. It's life, and frequently the beautiful shades of gray must be tinted with red.

"Then it dawns on you, as you watch this majestic animal at the apex of his abilities. Killing is not always evil, Brian. We humans are mistaken; we take the act of killing too seriously. In our age of so-called enlightenment we are conditioned not to kill – and it took us thousands of years to arrive at this erroneous conclusion. When we refuse to kill, we miss out on an opportunity to remove flawed people, flawed powers, and flawed ideas. Remember that, but don't repeat it. Think about it, but don't bring up this subject with anybody else."

Brian Berg swore to himself that he would remember this concept and that he wouldn't talk about it with anybody. Actually he probably wouldn't think about it much. He was not inclined to philosophy and really did not know what ethics were all about. He would just accept the comment at face value from a man far more educated than he.

About twenty miles west of Sioux Falls, the commander parked his Escalade in an empty parking lot on the East side of Lake Vermillion. "Well Brian, we don't have wolves here in South Dakota, but we do have coyotes. That's the best we can do for a quick afternoon Dakota winter safari."

Berg chuckled. He was obliged to appreciate the commander's humor, but internally he was despising the thought of having any type of interaction with coyotes.

"We'll each wear a sidearm. This pack of coyotes is getting a little too confident. I think somebody's been feeding them. I doubt anything will happen, but we'll want to be cautious. Do you prefer a Beretta M9 or a Colt .45?"

"You're the VIP, so you get the big gun, sir," Berg said, doing his best to conceal the tinge of terror he felt as he considered coming into distant contact with coyotes.

"Please don't call me 'sir,' Brian. People I work closely with call me, Commander. It's an old Navy thing. You can call me by my first name or you can call me, Commander."

"Either way, you're the VIP, so you get the bigger gun. I doubt I could hit a dodging coyote, but I suspect the bang will scare them off?"

"Oh yeah. One shot and they'll be gone. I've got snowshoes in the back. We'll only go in about fifteen minutes. I walked in a mile the other day and the view in one of my favorite spots—well, let's just say, the view there is not so nice anymore. I think the coyotes found a feast there. We'll call the coyotes in from a little further away this time."

"Call them in?" Berg asked failing to hide his fear.

"Yes. We use a little device called an injured jackrabbit call. You blow on it."

"Like a duck call?"

"Yes. Same principle, but a different sound."

Berg and the commander put on snowshoes and backpacks and started their short journey. Berg's stomach churned with anxiety. Within ten minutes the commander told Brian that they should only whisper from here on out. "Here's the jackrabbit call," the commander said as he pulled it from his pocket and blew on it. Berg winced at the high-pitched, miserable sound it emitted.

The men walked another one hundred yards, and the commander stopped and took off his backpack and snowshoes. This time he removed a waterproof blanket and laid it on the ground just behind a short bush. Then he removed two pairs of binoculars from his pack and laid down supine on the blanket. Propping himself up on his elbows, he looked through the lenses. "From here we can see almost two miles. We'll see them right off on the horizon." The commander blew again on the injured jackrabbit call.

"How long does it take?" Berg asked in his normal speaking voice.

The commander put his finger to his lips to remind Berg to whisper. "Last time it took about a half an hour, which is about average." The commander continued to search the horizon. "So Berg, what's your favorite part of your job?"

Whispering this time and taking a knee on the blanket, Berg replied, "Busting doctors when they're not in compliance," he said without hesitation. "And they're always out of compliance in one way or another."

"I bet you have a few good stories," the commander said handing Brian a pair of binoculars.

"I have new stories every week," Berg said smiling. "It never fails. All nurses have the same reaction when I find an expired vial of medication. Just last week I was in—"

The commander interrupted him. "So Brian, what are we going to do about Troy Stoker? I think he's manipulative and a criminal."

"Well, we have one serious complaint," Berg said. "We'll have his license in the next few days I suspect."

The commander blew again on the jackrabbit call.

"I'll tell you. Everyone in Pierre knows about him. All the top officials. It seems he's into some deep stuff, and people have been watching him for a while."

After another blare from the jackrabbit call, the commander was scanning the horizon for wildlife again. "There they are!"

"Where?" Berg asked with childlike, primal fear plainly evident in his voice.

"Almost straight out in front of us."

Berg looked through his binoculars and found two coyotes jogging in the general direction of the two men. Instinctively, he lay down on his stomach and propped himself up on his elbows, all the while keeping his sights set on the coyotes.

"Wow. They're fantastic," Berg whispered in a surprisingly convincing tone." It looks to me as if they don't have a care in the world. They look so relaxed."

"Don't let the façade fool you, Brian. Those animals are vicious and hungry, yet cautious. That's part of the mystique of the American jackal. That is one of their names, you know. They have a few names—just like some people who are not who they seem to be. I think this Stoker guy is one of those people."

"Well, what else is Stoker into?" Berg asked.

"Did you know he goes out on drug raids with the police and sheriff's drug teams?"

"Yes," replied Berg. "Rumor has it, he's keeping some of the spoils from those raids. But, are you talking about some other crime or medical violation, sir?"

The commander paused for a moment before answering Berg's question. The approaching coyotes enthralled him. He had detected two more. "Stoker claims he does this to be there for the victims and give them support. But there have been leaks for more than a year now. I think somebody's tipping off some of the drug dealers, and that's why the narcotics teams are often walking into abandoned meth houses. That's why they go into the homes of people we know to be drug dealers, but they find nothing. They know we're coming and they clean up their operations. I've looked at it from a lot of angles, and I think Stoker's our leak. I'll share some documents with you in the next few days."

"Okay. Then let's bust him," Berg said.

"We will. We will," said one of the most powerful men in South Dakota as he lay on a blanket seemingly without a care in the world. "Now Brian. I've just let you in on one of the most confidential secrets in South Dakota right now. You must mention it to no one. This is a huge issue and we don't want Stoker getting wind that we're on to him. Can I trust you?

"Yes. Absolutely."

"Can you trust me?"

"Yes, absolutely." Berg felt a tinge of concern. He had no idea how much he could trust the commander.

"Good," the commander said. "Because I think this Stoker guy's an American jackal, and we're going to be calling him in, so to speak, just like we are calling in these coyotes. We may have to let him get close enough to feel some fear. From your point of view, our tactics to lure him in may seem absolutely crazy in these next few days. But remember Brian, I'm still a lawyer. I know the law and I'll make sure that we're both protected."

"Those coyotes are only about a hundred yards away now," Berg said. "Should we be putting some more space between us and them?"

"Things are *not* always as they seem, Brian. And sometimes you have to let yourself get a little uncomfortable. I'm going to ask you to do some uncomfortable things in the next few days. Are you ready to do that?"

"Like what do you mean? It will all be legal, right?"

"Brian, do you remember when you were a cop?" the commander asked. "The first thing on your mind was nabbing the man and getting him sent off to jail. You know he's guilty, but there are all of these hurdles."

"Arraignments, hearings, the actual trial, deliberation," Berg said. "It was a painful experience to go through it all just to send away a car thief."

"Well, since you're working for the governor, a lot of that stuff doesn't apply," the commander said. "You can bend some rules. You *must* bend some rules. We'll never get the job done if we play by all the rules. The governor has our backs and wants us to be aggressive."

Berg was having a hard time listening and paying attention. With the coyotes closing in he was shaking nervously and his bladder was threatening to give way to the alarm he felt. The coyotes were circling in, lifting their snouts into the air, and considering the risks and rewards of attacking a human. The last time it had been too easy.

"Certainly they can smell us and I know that most of them have heard and seen us," the commander said. "If this was October or November, they would've turned tail and retreated a long time ago." He threw out a scrap of meat that landed only ten yards away. One of the coyotes considered it, but refused to come in that close. Then another showed some interest and fear was displaced by competition in both canines as they charged for the scrap of an easy meal.

Brian's bladder released a small amount of urine—and he did not care. He was also starting to hyperventilate as panic enveloped him; Berg wrestled with the potential social blunder of losing his cool and showing his cowardice to one of the most powerful men in the state. He had his right hand on the pistol holstered on his hip and he was considering drawing it to have it ready in case one of the coyotes came toward the men.

"Brian, for the next few weeks I'm going to ask you to be fearless. I need you to follow orders and execute quickly. With this Stoker guy, there will not be time to think. You just need to act. It may seem dangerous at times, but I promise that I will always have a plan to keep you safe. I can control the danger." With that, the commander took out his pistol and fired two harmless shots rapidly into the air. The coyotes retreated instantly. They forgot their hope for a meal and retreated to save their hardscrabble lives.

"Trust me, Berg. I know what I'm doing," the commander said pretending not to notice the moist spot on Brian Berg's blue jeans. "We'd best be getting back to the car. It'll be dark in about an hour. Let's go grab some dinner. You hungry, Berg?"

"Starving," Brian Berg lied fighting back nausea. He swore to himself that he would start taking his aripiprazole again, the moment he got home.

CHAPTER 72

VA MEDICAL CENTER, SIOUX FALLS

"Troy, This is getting out of hand," yelled Rivera with Cuban passion embodied in his passionate eyes and fervent voice. People at the Veteran's Administration Medical Center were accustomed to hearing passionate yelling from Dr. Rivera's office. "Let's get moving on this now, Stoker. You know that Stintson and Berg are not done with you. Your constitutional rights have been trampled by the state medical board—and whomever they are fronting."

"I've never had a pack of wild dogs breathing down my neck like this and I'm pulling out the guns," Stoker said. "I'm calling Holly Glover right this second. We're filing suit or getting an injunction—tomorrow."

"No Troy," Rivera said. "The American Colonists in the late 1700s appealed to King George the Third and tried working through legal recourse, but nothing got fixed until there was a war. Troy, there is going to be a war of sorts. You need to forget the courts and start preparing for your personal battle of words and ideas with this ghost who has eluded you so far. That board meeting and the raid on your office were not about medical records. That's evident now. We've all got a hunch that your pressure is connected to the fact that you overheard the attempted murder of Ann Higgins; and I suspect that somebody who holds a high office in Pierre is involved. I have a great contact at the state Capitol will meet with me and we're going to smoke out this *cobarde*."

A small surge of adrenaline rushed into Stoker's system when Rivera mentioned his contacts. Besides his full-time job as a physician, Rivera had hinted at other responsibilities. Stoker sensed that Rivera was preparing to let him in on the more of Rivera's reality—the one that had to do with his ongoing interest in liberty, the Constitution, and historical processes that bore themselves out over and over again.

"Great. I like the idea of your contact in Pierre. Let's call him," suggested Stoker.

"We'll do more than call *her*. She's a woman, by the way. Do you still have the day off from patients tomorrow to get caught up on your paperwork?"

"Yes. The paperwork and billing awaits," quipped Stoker.

"Can you be ready at six o'clock in the morning?"

"Sure. But isn't that a little early for your friend to be on the phone?"

"Yes. I'll set something up with her at eight o'clock—at the Capitol in Pierre. I'll pick you up at six. Bring your documents and I'll bring Z."

"Won't we be late for an eight o'clock meeting if we leave at six?" Stoker asked. "It's more than a three hour drive."

"Oh no *amigo*. We'll be early. See you at six."

CHAPTER 73

Troy Stoker was finishing breakfast at 5:56 a.m. and it was still pitch black outside. He lived in a farmhouse on twelve acres of land he had purchased in 2010, just as land prices in the area were starting to inch upward again after some rough years. Three months ago he had paid off the mortgage on his land and in another five years he would own his house outright, too. People in South Dakota tended to rid themselves of debt as quickly as possible. With pro-bank lending laws, most South Dakotans were conservative in their outlook. Farmers, private practice doctors, auto mechanics, or any other business owners who needed to borrow money to get started, worked to get out from under the lopsided contracts that gave more rights to banks than borrowers. South Dakota protected banks better than virtually any other American state.

Real estate had been relatively inexpensive in South Dakota for the whole of American history. Only in recent years had land and home prices caught up with other Midwestern and American cities. Many people attributed it to the pro-business climate in South Dakota, the state's lack of income tax, successful oil and gas extraction in North Dakota, and the renewed success of agriculture as an investment.

As Stoker cleaned his plate and orange juice glass, he heard the whirr of a mechanical engine, but he could not map it in his mind to a car or other machine. If it were summer, he would've assumed it was a large piece of construction equipment. Stoker moved the thick blinds back and peered out the window, but it was too dark to really see the object that was making a moderate amount of noise in front of his home. He suspected that Rivera had modified his truck's muffler as part of a prank, so he walked out of his front door with curiosity. Within five or six steps Stoker ascertained that he was looking at a small automobile that had some interesting lines and a sleek looking exterior.

The unusual car came to a stop right in the center of Stoker's asphalt driveway and the driver's door opened. "Good morning Dr. Stoker," called out Errol Rivera as he emerged from—whatever it was. Z emerged from the passenger side door.

"What is that, Rivera?" Stoker asked. He was curious and amazed.

"This, *amigo*, is the Terrafugia TF-X," Rivera said. He walked around the vehicle while acting out an animated impression of a television game-show model, imitating gratuitous gestures while demonstrating the automobile. "It's also your ride to Pierre."

"I'm not getting inside no stinkin' Cuban plane," Stoker joked.

"Good," Rivera said. "Because we're flying in an experimental auto-airplane built in Woburn, Massachusetts. And by the way, the word Terrafugia is not Spanish, you racist. It's Italian or Latin or one of those inferior dialects."

"Oh, good. I'm glad it's only experimental and not Cuban," Stoker replied sarcastically. "I love being in experiments hundreds or thousands of feet off the ground."

"Look, Troy. My team and I have logged more than a thousand hours in this plane. I've flown about two hundred of those myself. It *is* incredibly safe. It even has a parachute ready in the back. *If* there were any problems, it would deploy and float us back to earth. Not even Air Force One has a big parachute that can float it gracefully to the ground, my friend."

"Okay. Give me the tour," Stoker said. "Convince me you're not crazy—again. Then I'll jump in."

"All right, let's start with the humming you hear," Rivera said referring to the idling engine. "We've been warming up the two highly reliable 600 horsepower electric motors, which will help propel us to altitudes and speeds equivalent with modest Cessna models. A 300 horsepower engine kicks in after we're up in the air a few thousand feet." Rivera pointed inside the craft. "Here in the cabin," Rivera said gesturing toward the driver side door. "You'll find a steering wheel for driving on the road and a helicopter-like control stick for controlling the craft as you fly among the clouds. The wings are currently in their folded position, so that we can fit on a narrow two-lane highway. However, in just a few seconds they unfold and serve the higher purpose of cruising the wild blue yonder. Don't worry buddy. I wouldn't put you in any airplane, helicopter, or automobile that I did not deem safe enough for my daughter. Now where's your briefcase?"

"Just inside the door," Stoker said as he stepped back towards his front door.

One minute later Rivera was in the pilot's seat and Z was in the second seat. Stoker had assumed the back seat behind Z. All three occupants wore LightSPEED Zulu headsets and Stoker heard Rivera request clearance to takeoff from a controller at Sioux Falls Regional Airport. As Rivera accelerated the engines, Stoker asked, "So what's a helicopter pilot doing test driving an air car?"

"Excellent question! Let me show you," Rivera said as he flipped a lever and pushed a few buttons."

Stoker noticed that the skyward pointing propellers started to spin, so he just watched and waited. Within a few seconds he felt some initial lift as he realized that the propellers, at this moment, were actually serving the purpose of rotors. At least for now, he was not in an airplane or an automobile at all. This vehicle was behaving as a helicopter, which explained why Errol Rivera was working as one of Terrafugia's test pilots.

As the TF-X ascended up beyond the trees, Stoker enjoyed the amazing feeling of hovering in such an ingenious craft. His eyes continued to absorb Rivera's actions at the controls and the behavior of the rotors that held the vehicle suspended. Stoker noticed that the rotors had tilted forward about fifteen degrees and created a modest amount of forward thrust in combination with the ongoing upward thrust. The forward momentum continued to accelerate and the rotors continued to gracefully move into a more horizontal position. At the point when Stoker estimated they were moving forward at sixty knots, the three hundred horsepower jet engine took over for the propellers. The car was fully converted to an airplane and it accelerated even faster. Stoker was impressed to see the propellers retract and come to rest.

"Ladies and gentlemen. I would like to welcome you aboard flight 001 of Rivera airlines," chimed in Rivera's voice through the headset. "I'm honored to be your test pilot today; I'm also well compensated for the privilege. Snack and beverage service will be provided momentarily by Z which today stands for Zelda," Rivera said with obvious sarcasm.

"Here you go again," Z said while defending his manhood. "You won't fight me when we're on the ground, but you sure are brave when you're airborne, big boy. A wussy on the ground where I could actually deck you."

"Promises, promises," Rivera said. "Zelda's adjusting her miniskirt before she starts taking the drink cart up and down the aisle. Please avoid touching her legs, at all cost."

Z responded nimbly to the teasing. "Yes, on Rivera airlines the good doctor insisted that we only serve frou-frou drinks and all we have for you today is the Rivera-inspired strawberry daiquiri—virgin, of course."

396 Francis Bandettini and Matt Nilsen

"What can we get you to drink, Doctor Stoker?" Rivera asked.

"Nothing for me, thanks," Stoker replied.

"Good," Z said. "Because we don't really have any drinks. They're a figment of Rivera's imagination, just like the skirt."

"Look," Stoker said. "I'm in an absolutely elegant flying car. This is great! I'm awestruck. I'm not touching a drop of any beverage. I'm already wondering if I'm hallucinating."

Rivera navigated the flying car above Interstate 90. Stoker took out his smart phone and started snapping pictures. Most of his pictures captured images of Z and Rivera inside the cabin. However, he was able to capture a few good images of the peculiar wings and a few other exterior features of the plane. He attached the photos to an email that would transmit to Allie moments after they landed.

"I've flown a lot of helicopters and airplanes; this baby's smooth," Rivera said. "It's like driving a little sports car in the air. If you're ready for some roller-coaster action, perhaps we can make you grab that little bag on the back of your seat, Troy, and fill it with breakfast."

"Good luck," Stoker said. "The Army chopper pilots in Guatemala and the former Yugoslavia failed in their quest to make me puke."

Rivera made a radio call informing air traffic control and other craft in the vicinity of his location and trajectory; then he said, "Troy, today we're going to meet with Jessica Carey, the director of information technology security at the South Dakota Capitol. She's probably not going to tell us much, and I don't blame her. Really, today's kind of a sales pitch. We've told her your story, and right now she thinks that we're planting crazy ideas in her mind. She told me that she thinks my theory is off base, but she's willing to listen a little more. At the end of our meeting we won't be asking her to take any actions or commit to anything. Our goal is to leave her moderately intrigued and curious that something may be awry in Pierre. Let's just leave her wondering and open to future information."

"I've dealt with Jessica before," Z said. "She's fair, and she's smart. I give her credit for being more forward thinking than any of the state IT folks we have in Sioux Falls. I think her career is going places and she has great connections here in Pierre. Rumor has it she's got some friends in intelligence agencies and military posts as well. But I think we should avoid bringing that up."

"So Dr. Stoker, What's our story here today?" Rivera asked.

"First I'll tell her about my experience listening on the phone on inauguration night. Then we'll backfill with the homes in Chelsea Crossing. We can also tell her about the pattern of drug busts turning up dry—as if somebody has tipped them off."

"What about the medical board scrutinizing you?" interjected Rivera. "What about your civil rights being stomped on?"

"Maybe we should bring it up," Stoker replied. "But if we want to raise her suspicions, we have to concentrate on things that mean the most to her. She'll care about civil rights a little," Stoker explained, "but she'll wonder quite a bit if her LAN cables, servers, computers, and Wi-Fi hotspots are transmitting those emails that eventually tip off drug dealers. She'll be more concerned, and hopefully intrigued, that somebody who wanders these halls tried to kill the lieutenant governor's wife. If we can line her up on that, I'll be in an excellent position to defend my rights when the war comes back to town in Sioux Falls."

"What do we have to show her?" Z asked.

"My notes from the telephone call with Ann Higgins on inauguration night, the diagrams from the houses at Chelsea Crossing, and some copies of case files from our vice squad showing how dealers disappear literally hours before a raid."

"Okay," Rivera said. "It's a reasonable start. Z and I have a few things to share, too. Now let's talk about suspects."

During the next few minutes of the flight, the three men made an extensive list of possible suspects. They agreed unanimously that the lieutenant governor was not a suspect. Kent Higgins just did not have it in him. He won his elections based on his strength of character. He was not a political climber. Frankly, he was probably not capable of navigating and manipulating a political system in a devious and criminal fashion. "He wouldn't last a day as a criminal," concluded Rivera. "Most of all, he loved his wife, and he was not inclined to hurt her feelings, let alone try to kill her."

They could not rule out the governor, unfortunately. In his business and political career he had shown a willingness to plow over opponents using just about any means. Perhaps all of the anti-drug campaign rhetoric had been a smoke screen? The same could be said for Steve Hewitt, the new attorney general. He was assertive and had that special something—that Clintonesque charm. But Sioux Falls was new territory for him and it seemed unlikely that he would know the detailed criminal operations in an unfamiliar town. Allen Miller, the secretary of state, drew unanimous votes from Stoker, Rivera, and Z as a potential corrupt politician.

The list also grew to include Larry Stintson, president of the state medical board, and it was impossible to rule out some of the board members. They also considered the Minnehaha county sheriff, as well as prosecutors and judges who would have knowledge of pending drug raids. As much as it pained him, Stoker also had to admit that the Sioux Falls chief of police, Edward Best, his vice squad lieutenant, and sergeant were also suspects.

As the Terrafugia TF-X approached South Dakota's capital city, Rivera reached out to an air traffic controller at Pierre Regional Airport. She directed him with coordinates and vectors and soon they were approaching their destination. Rivera pointed up with his finger and said, "Hey Stoker, can you reach up here to this little control panel?"

Stoker unfastened his harness and inched himself to the edge of his seat. He could reach the small device just fine, so Rivera coached him through the process of entering in the coordinates of the helipad where they had been instructed to land.

"Okay," Rivera said, "Let me bring this baby down to about fifteen hundred feet. I'll need about a minute."

As the plane descended toward Pierre's skyline, Stoker noticed the copper dome and limestone walls of the South Dakota State Capitol. He appreciated the strength projected in the neoclassical architecture. Its close proximity to the blue waters of the Missouri River was a stunning site at sunrise. He wished he had time to stay and hunt in the area or fish on Lake Oahe. Stoker loved South Dakota. He could easily live in Pierre or the Rapid City areas. He and Allie had deliberately chosen Sioux Falls to be close to family, and it had proven to be a wise choice.

"All right, Troy. You're going to land this baby from the back seat. Are you ready?"

"Ready for anything," Stoker said. "Let's land it."

"You've actually done the hardest part by programming in the coordinates," Rivera explained. "Do you see that illuminated button?"

"Affirmative, captain."

"Push it whenever you're ready; I'll instruct you from there."

Stoker pushed the button and the resting propellers came to life and started to spin. "What's next?"

"Now, the easiest and most important part is, just sit back and relax," Rivera said. "Don't you wish we could push a button and our wives would just do what they know they're supposed to?"

"Actually, from what I've heard, your *mamita* says you respond pretty well when she pushes your buttons," Stoker said.

For the last three minutes of the flight, Rivera held his hands up in the air to emphasize that he was not controlling the plane, which was now behaving as a helicopter again. The automatic landing feature slowly glided the craft downward, right onto its designated helipad. Almost instantly after touchdown, the engines began a cooling down sequence. The propellers stopped spinning and returned to their upright position. The wings folded upright and a sensual female voice declared the plane ready to travel in car mode. Rivera shifted the vehicle into drive and navigated toward the security gate. Upon arriving there a guard stepped out of the shack with a puzzled look on his face. "May we please proceed to the fine city of Pierre?" Rivera asked.

"I'm sorry, sir," said the guard. This is a new experience for me. Will you please give me a moment to check with Homeland Security to ensure that we properly document the comings and goings of your flying car?"

"Sure. But first, let me show you this," Rivera said. "It should help you get in touch with the right resources at Homeland Security. I don't think letting us through this gate will be a problem."

The guard examined Rivera's identification and a one-page document for about five seconds, and then exclaimed, "Very good, Colonel Rivera. I'm sorry for the inconvenience. Useful information, sir. Have a great day." The gate opened and the newly converted car pulled out into the streets of Pierre.

As they drove this futuristic vehicle through the streets of South Dakota's capital city, almost without exception, each person they passed took a moment to stop and take a good long look at the phenomenon before them. Smart phones snapped pictures at every stoplight. Some people even rolled down their car windows at intersections and tried to get Rivera to open his window. Rivera was not a snob, but he didn't want his picture taken with this new technology—at least not yet.

As the vehicle pulled from Broadway Avenue into a parking lot just northeast of the Capitol, two police cruisers converged on it. One of the officers got out of his car while the other stayed in his car affixed to his radio and looking nervous. As Rivera got out of the TF-X the officer approached him aggressively. "Sir, I need to see your license and registration."

"What is my crime or infraction?" Rivera asked.

After stammering for a few seconds the officer replied, "This is just such an unusual car. We need to make sure it's not a threat to security."

"Oh, so you get to violate our constitutional rights because I'm fortunate enough to be testing a car that's unusual?"

"Sir, I have the security of the whole Capitol at my charge. There are hundreds of people in that building right now. I think it's a fair inquiry."

"It's not fair and I know it is not constitutional," Rivera responded. "So no you may not see my license or my registration. I have a scheduled meeting in twenty minutes in that building."

"Sir, I need you to stand right there and quit resisting."

"Resisting what?" replied Rivera.

"We're not resisting anything," Z interjected. "And I am putting you on notice that I am recording this interaction."

A third police car arrived, and a muscular officer with bleach-blond hair emerged from the cruiser. "Sir, we need to see your license and registration, and now we need to search your vehicle."

"Let me answer for my friends and myself with a little more precision here," stated Stoker firmly. "Our answer to your unjustified and useless demand for documentation and a search is the Fourth Amendment of the Constitution of the United States. Do you know what that says?"

"Well no, but I don't see why you are resisting—"

"The right of the people to be secure in their persons, houses, papers, and effects, against unreasonable searches and seizures, shall not be violated is the fourth Amendment," interrupted Stoker. "We *certainly* resist encroachment on our rights."

"Now, if you have some probable cause for this debacle, will you please inform us?" Rivera asked in a challenging and firm tone. "Remember, we're recording this." Nobody said anything for a moment before Rivera spoke up again, "Officer, I rowed my way to the U.S.A. from Cuba years ago to escape police and government intrusion. I fought in Uncle Sam's Army, on the ground and in the skies, for more than a decade to preserve the freedoms you're trying to toss aside. I'm willing to go to the mat on this."

The officers lost the stare down in less than two seconds. Without saying another word, the bleach-blond looked at his fellow officer and made a hand motion signaling retreat. Then all three cars drove away.

"I'm not sure what that abrupt exit means," Rivera said. "Let's get to our meeting before they return with reinforcements."

"Or a further distorted viewpoint on civil rights," Z said.

Stoker, Rivera, and Z walked toward the Capitol building and started up the steps. "Jessica's office is not really in the Capitol building itself, but she loves to reserve one of the impressive conference rooms," Rivera said. As they neared the top Jessica Carey herself met the three men. The badge affixed to a lanyard around her neck let everyone know that she was a director of information technology security for the state of South Dakota.

Stoker thought it was odd that Jessica would meet them right at the front doors of the Capitol building. He wondered if it was a gesture of hospitality. She expedited them through security. As they walked through the halls, Jessica was cordial. She even made some jokes toward Z, which seemed to have a slightly flirtatious tone. Perhaps these two techies had a hint of chemistry.

However, once Jessica had entered the designated conference room with them, her demeanor instantly shifted to an icier disposition. "Go ahead and have a seat gentleman," she said. "Doctor Rivera explained a little bit about your concerns on the phone, but I have to be quite clear. Your story has an element of witch hunt to it. It's just not credible in my book. With a newly inaugurated administration I'm just struggling to be suspicious of the state officers. They have a blank slate. What kinds of crimes could they have committed already?"

Stoker dropped a file on the desk. "Take a look at what we have here."

Carey thumbed through Stoker's notes from his phone call with Ann on inauguration night. "So it sounds like she knew this person. She was shocked by who he was. It implies that he may have been somebody in a leadership position. But it doesn't mean this was a leader in government. He could've been a leader in industry." After dismissing the evidence, she turned to new pages in the file. "What's this?"

"That's a picture of the plans for a meth lab in a house that Ann Higgins stumbled across in her real estate work." Stoker then removed pictures of the basement on Bryant Way. "She took these pictures in those homes. The electrical, water heating, and drainage suggest that this place was a few days from becoming a meth lab."

"And it's clear from Dr. Stoker's notes that Ann Higgins's attacker took responsibility for those homes and meth labs." Jessica closed the file. "Okay, but so far I don't see how it applies to IT security at the Capitol."

"Somebody powerful attacked Ann Higgins that night because of what she saw," Stoker said. "Here's another file." He passed it to Carey and she opened it. "These are police reports from attempted drug busts in Sioux Falls over the last few months."

"It looks to me like these were busts that never happened," Jessica said.

"Exactly," Rivera interjected. "Somebody in high places is tipping off these scum bags."

"I'll need more than that," Jessica said.

Rivera spent the next few minutes explaining what his team had learned at Green Growth Ventures in Reno and he showed her the pictures of the criminals who had jumped bail and were working feverishly each day to steal the identities of dozens of people. Pointing at the picture of the dirty blond man, John Freeman, Rivera said, "This man is a person of interest in Ann Higgins's attempted murder. Now he's got a cozy office job in Reno." Rivera took out two other pictures of Freeman that the NanoBUGS had taken in Reno. "There's a connection. Are you interested in finding out who almost killed the lieutenant governor's wife?"

"This is all very far-fetched, gentleman" Jessica said. "Your evidence still has nothing to do with my team or the technology I manage."

"Whoever this is, they work fast," Z said. "They have insider knowledge of what's going on in government and law enforcement. We suspect they are using government channels."

With a slightly playful tone she looked Z straight in the eye and said, "So, gather your evidence and get a search warrant. You're asking me to get involved here when I shouldn't."

"Look," Stoker said. "In Sioux Falls, we're seeing drug labs disappear hours before we raid them. The same thing happens with dealers, too. We're just about to bust them and they disappear off the radar screen."

"These guys are getting information from police insiders, sheriffs, a prosecutor, a legislator on an oversight committee, or somebody in one of the executive offices," Z appealed.

"Wild speculation," Jessica said forcefully. "I'm the wrong person and you're in the wrong place at the wrong time asking me to do the wrong thing. You know your conspiracy theory would not hold up for thirty seconds in front of a judge. You can't get a warrant, so you try and circumvent due process."

"No," Rivera said. "We're just trying to gather evidence."

"I'm sorry. It's not my role. You need to talk to the police."

"The police may be part of the problem!" protested Rivera. "We need your help watching emails, telephone conversations, and web traffic. If you see patterns of calls or communications with Reno, can you red flag that activity and just let me know?"

"This meeting's over," Jessica said as she stood. "I'll walk out with you." She motioned for the door.

Respectfully, Stoker and Rivera followed her gesture and exited the room. Z was the last to leave and Jessica gently placed her hand in the small of his back and subtly guided him out of the conference room door. Z was sure that the touch was deliberate and he strongly suspected that she wanted to get just a little closer. She wanted him to smell her perfume, which was strikingly intoxicating. Stoker's ever-attuned senses picked up on the non-verbal exchange, both visually and intuitively, between Jessica and Z.

As Jessica and her guests neared the main doors of the Capitol building, she exited the building with them. Again Stoker noted that it was odd that she would accompany them so far. This strange behavior meant something, but Stoker could not quite put his finger on it. She was controlling something or protecting something. *Jessica's not brushing us off!* he thought. Stoker realized that they were onto something, and she knew it!

Rivera was the first to reach the bottom of the stairs. As his feet hit the wide sidewalk he took a moment to stop and turn around, which forced the whole group to pause for a moment. "Look, Jessica. I don't want to be abrasive or act like a jerk. I want to be persuasive. Will you please consider this?" He put on some sunglasses and turned his face toward the morning sun. "I'm a Cuban by birth," Rivera continued, "and an American by the grace of God. I've followed orders for this country that should've killed me. I believe in being proactive. I believe in doing something about the wrongs I observe. I live by the old quote, 'The only thing necessary for the triumph of evil is for good men to do nothing.' So please help us do *something*. We really need your help here, Jessica."

"I agree completely," Jessica said. The comment surprised the three men. It was a departure from the closed-mindedness she had expressed during their meeting. Carey pointed at the phone attached to Rivera's belt. "That's a nice phone. I've been researching that model and I've heard good things about its encryption." Then Jessica asked, "What's the number?"

"Let me write it down for you," Rivera said.

"No way," Jessica said. "Not here. I don't want anyone to see you passing me a piece of paper. Just tell me the number."

"It's 703-555-1606."

"Perfect, Colonel Rivera. It's memorized." Jessica began climbing the stairs. "Thank you gentleman," she called out. "I'm sorry if I've wasted your time."

The men walked back to the Terrafugia TF-X. There was still a police car pulled up at an angle to the craft. The officer inside watched them carefully climb in, but he did not try to stop them again. As they pulled away the police car followed them all the way to the airport. Five minutes later as they lifted off from the helipad, they could see the officer standing outside of his car and shielding his eyes from the sunlight while they ascended into the air.

Once Stoker, Rivera, and Z were airborne, the conversation resumed through the headsets. "Hey Z, tell me something," Stoker said. "That tech guru at the Capitol, Jessica, is at least three years older than you, yet I sensed that she captivated you a little. We call that an infatuation in psychiatry. There was some chemistry between you two. What's up with that?"

Instead of dodging Stoker's question, Z was surprisingly frank. "Dr. Stoker. I love strong women. Intelligence, assertiveness, and strength turn me on as much, or perhaps slightly more, than breasts, legs, butts, or high cheekbones. Don't get me wrong, her eyes, her smile, and a few of her other features also caught my eye. But I've got to say, I'm always dying to run a finger up and down a ripped set of female six-pack abs."

"So your idea of a good time is going to an NCAA debate tournament," chided Rivera, "or watching the overgrown woman weightlifters at the gym?"

"That's my vice, Errol. What's yours?"

"Don't tell me you're into she-males," teased Rivera.

"Not in the least," Z said. "I crave emotional intimacy with strong women. There is a legend in my family about my great-great grandma. Someday, when you're not in the mood to mock my family so openly, I'll share it with you. She was a Trailblazer in the American Northwest. I come from a long line of beautiful *and* strong women. In our home we celebrated amazing women. My dad encouraged us to challenge the stereotype of 'the fairer sex' by gathering us around the TV to watch *Xena: Warrior Princess* on TV."

"Now we're talking," Rivera said. "Xena was one hot *mamí*. I think I'm starting to understand where you're coming from *loco*."

"Speaking of amazing Cuban women," Z said, "during the Elian Gonzalez debacle in the 1990s, my dad kept pointing out how it was Elian's mom that brought him to freedom; and his dad that took him back to tyranny. He was livid with Elian's dad. 'You remember that boys! That woman bravely navigated shark-infested waters for her child. Don't you *ever* let your kids take the easy way out—let alone insist upon such cowardice. Honor the names of your strong mother and grandmothers!'"

"I suspect that most people assume that Z is short for Zane," Stoker said. "But I have a hunch that it is not."

"Nope. Not even close," Z said. "You're only the second person to ever think beyond that assumption. How did you conclude that, Dr. Stoker?"

"The world is full of paradoxes. As a psychiatrist they walk into my office every day. I suppose I've developed a sense for anticipating surprises. However, I failed to anticipate traveling in a flying car today. So what does Z stand for?"

"It stands for a lot of things."

"I mean is it an actual name, a title, or a nick name?"

"This is where I jump in and change the subject," Rivera said with diplomatic authority. "Have you studied much history, Troy?"

Stoker decided to reign in his curiosity about this enigma of the person who went by the name "Z." Perhaps, with time, he could understand the working dynamic between Rivera and Z. But that all hinged on whether or not Rivera could share more about his responsibilities outside of medicine. Stoker allowed Rivera to change the subject by responding, "You mean outside of all of the facts they pack into your brain in school?"

"All of that stuff is a great framework," Rivera said. "Sometimes you'll get an amazing teacher who really helps you apply 131 A.D. to our day. So what other historical facts have you packed into your brain, Stoker?"

"Back in the 1990s, I got really curious about economics, which kept leading me back to history. I read a lot about the first four centuries that really formed the United States of America. I wondered why the Virginia Company, which landed before the Pilgrims, didn't get much credit. The Pilgrims deserved most of the credit, but for some reason they got all the glory in many of my history classes. I learned about banking and its roots in Europe and other civilizations.

"When the Mormon missionaries knocked on my door they gave me a Book of Mormon, which sparked some curiosity. I started researching Incan and Mayan history. I think the missionaries got bored with me, because I was more interested in the history and archeology than learning about their religion."

"So considering all that you've read, where would you predict the good ol' U.S. of A is headed right now?" Rivera asked.

"My ears perk up when I hear historians say that few civilizations have lasted more than 200 years," Stoker said. "One of my military heroes pointed out that societies move from courage and abundance into bondage pretty quickly. Usually it's the nooses of apathy and dependence that draw nations into servitude."

Rivera nodded and Z agreed. "My dad always sat us down around our kitchen table to ensure we got our history homework done," Rivera said. "Sure, he encouraged us in math and science, but it was history he harped on every night. My dad taught us about the rise and fall of civilizations when I was a teenager. We were always talking and often debating around the table."

Just then, Rivera's satellite phone rang. Z answered it for him intending to relay the conversation. "Colonel Rivera's phone."

"Is this Z?" The voice was female and familiar.

"Yes," responded Z. "Who's this?"

"You don't recognize my voice, Z?" teased Jessica Carey, the woman who had left them at the Capitol steps. "I'm surprised that your memory is so short, smart guy."

"Miss Carey," Z said with pretended formality. "The last time we talked, all we got from you was a cold shoulder."

"That was by design, Z. I'm sorry. I had to act that way inside the Capitol building. I don't know who's listening there. I needed it on the record that I gave you guys the cold shoulder. Whoever is watching and listening—and I am convinced that somebody is—needs to think that I have no idea that there is a criminal in high office here in Pierre. Something is not right, and what you see happening in Sioux Falls matches some activity I've been tracking here. But the Capitol building, my email, and my office phone are the wrong mediums to discuss these issues. I'm calling you—actually I was calling Colonel Rivera—on my personal encrypted phone."

Z attached the phone to an audio cable. "Okay Jessica, I've got you patched in with Rivera and Stoker. We're all on. Tell us what you've got going on there."

"Hi guys," replied Jessica. "Hey, Rivera, just an FYI, that quote about good men doing nothing? Well, it's part of my mantra, too. But let's be history geeks another time."

Rivera smiled, "Sounds good. Can you tell me what you just told Z?"

"To be blunt, I've been seeing patterns in our data that match those Dr. Stoker presented today. I respect what you're doing and I'm willing to help out any way I can. I have some theories that I've not dared share with the police, my bosses, or prosecutors for many of the same reasons you mention. I want to talk more; evenings and weekends tend to be better than regular business hours, if you know what I mean."

"Don't worry. We won't be reaching out to you during normal business hours or while you're at the office at all," Rivera said. "What does your Saturday morning look like, Jessica?"

"Any time after 7:30 a.m. No earlier, however," insisted Jessica. "Nothing gets in the way of my Saturday morning core and cardio workout." Z could not contain his smile as both Stoker and Rivera pumped their fists at him.

"Let's say eight o'clock on Saturday morning," Stoker said. "Can we use this phone number?"

"Sure. Also anything you can email me would be great. My ultra-secure email is Jessica at —"

"Wait. Hang on," Rivera interrupted. "Z. Can you write this down?"

"I've got it." Z said.

"Well, do you have a pen and paper?" Rivera protested

"I've *got* it."

"Write it down."

"Look Errol, I've got it," Z said looking at Rivera and tapping his index finger on his forehead with emphasis.

"Oh, right. You techie geniuses who memorize everything."

Jessica finished providing her email and said, "I'll send you some FTP credentials, too, Jessica," Z said. "You, Stoker, and I can warehouse all sorts of files there. We may even be able to teach the man with the flying car how to use FTP," he joked.

"Thanks for your call, Jessica," Stoker interjected. "The apathy you claimed really faked us out. We thought we hit a dead end. Thanks for having the guts to do what's right in the grand scheme of this situation."

"Dr. Stoker, I don't give a rat's ass about my job," Jessica said. "I love due process and all of the other rights afforded in the state and federal Constitutions. I'm willing to bend some of those rules when our enemy is most likely a person who has sworn to uphold the law, but who is really using their office to abuse it. Their due process rights are severely compromised in my book. I love this country enough to take a risk to make the right changes *with extreme prejudice*. If we're going to do this right, we're going to have to piss people off and bend some rules, damn it. I've worked a little with that guy Z, but how good is he really? Let's nab this bastard. This is my encrypted phone. Call me anytime."

Rivera, who was always trying to connect with history buffs, spoke up next. "How did you know all that history, Jessica?"

"People who love history have to do something so they don't starve," she replied. "I learned computer programming in high school and took a bunch of math, computer science, and IT classes in college. I was working full-time in programming and IT by the time I was twenty and making sixty thousand dollars per year. I finished off the history degree at night."

"Very interesting," Rivera said.

"Yup. Then I got kicked out of the University of Minnesota while pursuing a master's degree," Jessica said. "I wrote some scathing papers that exposed liberal B.S. ideas that have existed and resurfaced over and over since Egypt. The Saul Alinsky-wannabe professors there had no tolerance for such facts."

"So much for liberal open-mindedness," Stoker said.

"Well gents, I've got to run," Jessica said. "We'll talk on Saturday."

Z hung up Rivera's secure satellite phone. The first thing Rivera did was turn to Z. "Did you really memorize her email address?"

"No. I wrote it down as fast as I could, but I—"

"Wanted her to think you had mad memorizing skills, too," interjected Stoker.

"Yes, Stoker! I admit it. Is that what you want, Mr. Shrink Man?" Z was smiling and joking with Stoker. "Yes! Okay. Are you happy? I admit it. I was posturing. I hate hanging out with a psychiatrist. I can never lie to you guys."

"So, you've hung out with a lot of psychiatrists?" Rivera asked.

Z paused and thought for a moment. "No. I've never hung out with a *single* psychiatrist."

"Well good, I'll just let you continue thinking that our Jedi mind powers include polygraph lie detection and mind reading," Stoker kidded.

"I think we're ready," Z said changing the subject. "We have some decent evidence, we're spying on Green Growth Ventures in Reno, and now we have a connection inside the Capitol who can help us watch the big boys. We're ready to find out who's hiding behind their government office and political ambitions."

"Definitely," Rivera replied. "Troy, if we have you home by tomorrow morning, can you join us for a quick trip to the East Coast this afternoon and evening?"

"Of course. I'll let Allie know."

CHAPTER 74

SIOUX FALLS

Less than an hour later, Rivera landed the Terrafugia craft back in Sioux Falls. Waiting for them on the tarmac was a Gulfstream V. "Let's hop on this plane," Rivera said. "It's much faster. Besides that, the regime in D.C. is not ready for a fresh new idea like the Terrafugia. The current president does not like capitalistic progress that would further free rugged individualists. He envisions us taking school buses to work and the store. He would love to fuel them with fourteen-dollar-per-gallon biodiesel. I'm sure in Obama's America we would all ride bikes and take mass transit."

Stoker laughed. Z did not. They boarded the Gulfstream V and quickly greeted the pilots. "Rocky here can get this bird off the ground alone," explained Rivera. So why don't you take the co-pilot's seat Troy? The co-pilot can hang out back here with us for a while. After we get to cruising altitude we'll bring you back to brief you on where we're going and what we're up to. I'm also going to ask you to sign a critical document."

"No problem. I'll get this bird off the ground," Stoker joked as he climbed into the co-pilot's seat. Stoker had done some limited, non-sanctioned co-piloting in military helicopters and smaller prop airplanes; but he had never been in the co-pilot seat of a modern jet. It was exhilarating to place his hands on the controls and study all of the instruments.

"I would only do this for Colonel Rivera," the pilot said. "You must be some badass from a three-letter agency."

"Just tell me how to fly this bird," Stoker said. "I think we should dispense with the chitchat here, son. Give me some help with the throttle and coach me a bit with the yoke. You take care of the pedals and everything else, okay? Now where are we on that checklist?"

"Whatever you say, sir."

After the pilot had taxied out onto the runway and received permission from the control tower, Stoker grabbed the throttle with his left hand and inched it forward. As the engines responded he felt a thrilling exhilaration. As the plane passed through eighty knots the pilot put his hand on top of Stoker's throttle hand and adjusted the thrust. Stoker felt the yoke in his right hand respond to the pilot's skill and move toward his abdomen as the nose rose gently off the ground. Stoker focused on the pilot's movements as he further manipulated the controls and the jet lifted off of the runway and began ascending into the cloud-covered Dakota sky.

"All right sir," the pilot said. "Not a bad takeoff for a—let me guess—an FBI agent."

"Something like that," Stoker replied. "What's my next flying lesson? It's been years since I had some informal flight training in the military." The pilot encouraged Stoker to roll the plane to the right with the yoke and then he walked him through some small manipulations of the rudder pedals just to get a feel for them. Every few seconds the pilot would coach Stoker to pull up on the stick, veer right just a touch, or gently depress a certain pedal.

As the plane arrived at 28,000 feet the pilot informed Stoker that the next few hours would be pretty boring. Stoker remembered the briefing Rivera had arranged a few minutes earlier, so he thanked the pilot and returned to the cabin. Z and Rivera were enjoying a meal that included grilled salmon sandwiches on sourdough bread, a baked potato, and a colorful green salad. "Troy, come and eat while we talk," Z said. "We've got about two hours to explain a few things. Colonel Rivera and I will also answer as many of your questions as we can."

Stoker suddenly realized he had been ignoring his hunger for hours. The flying car, the confrontation with the South Dakota Capitol police, the bizarrely abrupt meeting with Jessica Carey, her subsequent phone call, and the impromptu East Coast trip had all completely captured Stoker's attention. Hunger had fallen off the radar screen. Now he welcomed the opportunity to refuel and he was pleased that somebody had the foresight to provide them with high-quality nutrition.

"I'm a juice guy, so they know to stock me with fresh-squeezed tangerine juice," Rivera said as he poured Stoker a glass.

"To citrus!" Stoker said raising his glass in a toast. Rivera and Z raised their glasses in a toast and ratified the gesture. Stoker then took his first sip. It was delicious and it further heightened his pangs of hunger, so he reached for his sandwich. It was better than food he enjoyed at restaurants on the ground, which had the advantage of a full-service kitchen just moments away from the diners.

"We're on our way to visit a few people in Northern Virginia," Z explained as he started out the briefing. "You're going to come up with dozens of questions in the next six or eight hours. We'll try to anticipate some of them now and we'll answer some of them on the flight home. However, we need you to ask few, if any, questions in our meetings in Washington D.C."

"Arlington Hall is a building that houses some key National Guard functions as well as a center for foreign affairs training," Rivera said. "Few people know that it houses a specialized and highly secretive team of the Drug Enforcement Administration. But before we tell you any more, we're going to ask you to sign a non-disclosure agreement. We need to be sure that the DEA's VIP unit and Z's identity and skills remain a secret. Whatever you learn about my place in the crime-fighting world needs to stay in your head. From here on out, Troy, you're going to keep some pretty big secrets. Are you ready for that?"

"I've always wondered about you, Rivera. Of course I'll sign your document. Give me a few more weeks running around with you and I'll have you signing one on me."

"I'm already bound. You could become the director of the NSA or CIA and I wouldn't have to sign a thing," Rivera clarified. "Look Troy, we don't want Americans to learn of the VIP unit because it will compromise its effectiveness. The unit has appropriately ended the careers of crooked politicians on dozens of occasions. People have no idea who did the behind-the-scenes dirty work."

"At four o'clock Eastern time we'll meet with the director of the VIP unit," Z explained. "Just call him James. You don't need to know his last name."

"Kind of like I don't know yours?" Stoker replied with a question that was more of a statement.

"We should get those forms signed before we talk any further. You're drawing some valid conclusions and asking the right questions." Z hit a few keystrokes on his computer, and a miniature printer attached to a small desk behind Rivera's leather seat spit out a document.

"All right, Troy. Please sign this," Z said. "Your signature here at thirty-thousand feet is just as valid as your signature in Sioux Falls. But we want you to sign it before we get to D.C., because the promises people make there apparently never have to be kept."

"Let me give it a quick read."

"Be my guest," Rivera said. "But the bottom line is, if you divulge anything about our operation over the next few days, you get to go to prison and forfeit a huge chunk of your assets to pay the fines that start at five hundred thousand dollars."

"It also reminds you that treason will get you the electric chair," interjected Z. "You know, just your standard keep-your-yap-shut-if-you-don't-want-to-rot-in-jail-or-be-executed stuff."

Stoker studied the document for thirty more seconds, signed it and slid it across the table to Rivera and Z. After feeding the paperwork into a scanner, Z turned to Stoker and spun his laptop computer toward Troy.

"The VIP unit has been watching South Dakota government especially closely for the last few years. This is a list of suspects which contains many of the names we tossed around this morning." The list included almost two-dozen people. "We are quite certain that one or more of these individuals are using their knowledge and positions to advance the manufacture and distribution of a little MDMA and a lot of meth. We're also seeing some synthetic heroin starting to pop up."

"The synthetic heroin is a whole new battle," Rivera said. "The old synthetic heroin never took off because it ate people's skin and had other horrid side effects. But the new stuff is powerful, cheap, and almost universally addictive. I'm more concerned about synthetic heroin than I am about terrorists, dirty bombs, or even nukes. This stuff can bring down cities."

Stoker pointed at the list of suspects. "You haven't been able to narrow this list down further?" His eyes scanned the names. "Wow, the governor, secretary of state, attorney general, three state senators, two judges, eight state house members, three sheriffs, the Sioux Falls chief of police, and Larry Stintson of the medical board?"

"Stintson is a new addition, and we confess our lack of progress," admitted Z. "Whoever this person is, he has been careful. Every name on this list is there because of circumstantial evidence instead of substantial facts. We are stunned at how effective he is. But tragically, when this person tried to kill Ann Higgins, we got our biggest break. Now we've got a plan and evidence to share with James and the DEA VIP unit."

Stoker looked up at Rivera and Z and then he sat back in his chair. "So are you telling me that by some great coincidence, one of my patients almost gets killed by a South Dakota VIP, and I *just happen* to reach out to Errol Rivera, who is a member of the DEA's VIP unit?

"Not exactly," Rivera said. "I'm just a person who has some friends in the VIP unit. So for the next few days I'll be tagging along, as a consultant, let's say."

"A highly armed consultant with wide discretion on his operating parameters and access to a wide array of aircraft on a moment's notice?" Stoker asked. Again, Stoker's question was more of a statement. "So, what exactly is it that you do, Errol? I mean outside of practicing medicine and test-piloting aircraft?"

"Whatever needs to get done. We don't put a lot of constraints on our willingness to serve."

"To whom are you referring when you say 'we?'"

"We don't put a lot of constraints and parameters on defining the 'we' issue, either," interjected Z.

"Okay, I get it," Stoker said. "You need to be unclear about your organization or assignment, so let's take a new angle on this. Now I know a fair amount about Errol. I know about his childhood in Cuba and Miami, his time in Central America piloting helicopters for the Army, medical school in Cleveland, and practicing medicine at the VA here in Sioux Falls. I'm also starting to understand why singing *Oh Taunenbaum!* in German came so naturally. Is German your third language?"

"Fourth language, *amigo!*" Rivera said. "Mandarin Chinese is my third."

"I'm sure there is a lot I don't know about Errol. But let's talk about the story of Z," Stoker said in a confident and insistent tone.

"Besides English, the only language I share with Rivera is Arabic," Z said. "I grew up in the Northwest in a modest home. My parents were musical fanatics to a fault. Music was their religion. I was in piano and voice lessons at the age of three. At four they started teaching me the violin. I went to a private elementary school, at great sacrifice to my parents, where the curriculum was based on music. I was expelled in the second grade. For another ten years, I tortured teachers and my parents with my bombastic behavior and intolerance for activities like listening and studying. Music served me well because I played any and all rock instruments. I was playing drums in nightclubs at the age of fifteen. I could hide behind the drums, so the issue of age rarely arose. By eighteen I was playing guitar and singing back-up vocals. Long hair, low lighting, and some painted on stubble helped me camouflage in well enough. Nobody checked my ID. I was making money and buying toys.

"I also loved technology—especially the hardware. My room was a wasteland of computer parts. Ours was the first house within three square miles to have Wi-Fi. That was 1996. In 2004 we actually started paying for it."

"So you're a genius electronically and mechanically and you were ahead of your peers socially," Stoker said. "Naturally, society wanted to punish you. People wanted to hold you back and contain you with rules and norms."

"I have never thought of it that way, but it sounds pretty spot-on," Z said.

"So fast-forward to your life after high school. I have a good therapeutic profile of who you are based on your adolescent years," Stoker said. "But I don't want to talk psychiatry. I want the cold, hard facts about what you did to get you here in this plane with us now. Why are you about to meet with the DEA's VIP unit? Tell me about college or the work experiences that turned you into a covert tech expert and qualified you for this vague job with few 'constraints and parameters.'"

"Covert you allege," teased Z.

"Please clarify my allegation." Stoker smiled and took another sip of juice. "Or, we can talk about your rise to the height of technology aristocracy."

"Community college, man! I am a product of a technology lab at my local community college," Z said. "The lab was open until midnight. I quizzed the teachers, connected and disconnected devices, and then I would figure out the physics behind the scenes. I aced all of my classes and won all sorts of awards. One of my teachers introduced me to some professors at a University in the San Francisco area, and they pulled some strings and got me in."

"Which University?"

"I'm not at liberty to say."

"Stanford," chimed in Rivera. "Come on Z. He signed the documents. Z earned a degree in electrical engineering from Stanford, and then he started a PhD program. That's when he got in some trouble." Rivera didn't mind talking with his mouth slightly full, and in between bites he gave a synopsis of Z's problems. "While Z was working on a satellite communications system, some Air Force officer with big-shot MIT credentials challenged him to compromise the security of a new system he designed."

Z picked up the story from Rivera. "It was Christmas break, so I had all the time in the world to focus on the problem. I sat at my desk and survived on powernaps, delivered pizza, fruit juice and caffeinated beverages for six days. As he requested, I broke into his system. Before I knew it, I was watching the military movements of tanks and troops in the ongoing war in Iraq. I immediately reported what I had done, and I turned over all information to the Air Force information and compliance services."

"Oh boy," Stoker said. "I can see where this is going."

Z shared a nervous smile. "They distrusted me instantaneously. They labeled me a potential spy and took me into debriefing."

"After days of interrogation and confinement—with no decent pizza, I might add—it was obvious that I was just this kid from suburban America who just happened to have the skills, initiative, and pride to fulfill the order the Air Force satellite communications officer issued."

"And that's what we loved about him," interjected Rivera. "He was clean and we knew it. But now the military and CIA were deeply worried. And arguably, they had their reasons. So, I was assigned to get Z off the grid and into a new life."

414 Francis Bandettini and Matt Nilsen

"New life?" Stoker asked.

"We created a new identity for Z and sent him through officer's basic training. Then we sent him to work as a military intelligence and technology analyst in a little office in Fort Meade, Maryland."

"What's in Fort Meade?" Stoker asked. "Something tells me that Z was not doing maintenance on email servers."

"It was a military conglomeration that eventually became the Department of Defense's U.S. Cyber Command. Just to be a bit poetic, we assigned him to the Air Force cyber team."

"They hid me in plain view," Z said smiling from ear to ear. "That same big-shot general didn't know it, but I was now a techy minion on his team. I just had a different name, haircut, and eye color. I used his satellites to watch the Chinese launch their cyber attacks on American defense and commercial computer networks. I also watched the general. We used to watch him while he did what we called 'launch and lunch.' He would launch his temper at his staff and then he would go out and lunch with his girlfriend. I didn't fear him then, because I collected enough dirt on him to really make the general squirm. And now, if our paths ever cross again, I've got video and audio on my smart phone to share with him. If I disappear, Rivera's got a copy, too."

"So, Sioux Falls is a long way from Maryland," Stoker said. "What brought you here?"

"Again, I did excellent work; and again, it got me in trouble. I sniffed out a colonel who had a deal with an Iranian agent to go rogue in his F-22 and shower a few nuclear warheads on the Kansas-Missouri border to divide the country."

"So, *again*, we had to send Z underground!" Rivera chided. "Since that time Z has been living on twenty acres, which he owns outright, near Baltic, South Dakota."

"I'm a marked man, and there's an Iranian-financed contract out on my life. So I did a strategic analysis on the US and I concluded that this area is about as safe as it gets, and it's fairly easy to hide out here. This is where I want to be when World War III—which is already happening by the way—escalates from cyberspace to bullets and bombs."

"I built much of my small home myself, so I have no lease or mortgage. It's hay bale construction with lots of steel and glass. I need lots of sun to stay happy, so my south-facing wall is three large panes of beautiful glass."

"Off the grid, huh? Do you have a driver's license?" Stoker asked.

"Yes, from Hawaii. But I rarely drive," Z responded. "I have a redneck driver, who asks no questions. I fed her a story about a medical disability a few years ago and she still believes it."

"Do you have any other legal documents in your name?" Stoker asked.

"Rivera helped me get a passport for an emergency, but I've never had to show it to anybody."

"How do you pay your bills?"

"My electricity is all solar and wind-generated. My heat is primarily geothermal, but I also have a propane back-up system and a wood stove. I pay for propane and wood in cash. I pay my phone bills in cash. I have other resources, and Rivera introduced me to a bookkeeper who helps me if I ever get stuck."

"How did you pay to build your house?"

"I grew the hay," Z explained, "paid a farmer cash to bale it for me, and turned those bales into the structure. I acquired recycled materials from demolition projects around town. I'm most proud of the large panes of glass I acquired from a demolished hotel. Home Depot, Menards, and Lowes all take cash. So do most handymen. It's a small home — less than 800 square feet and I was able to build about sixty percent of it myself."

"Where did you get all of that cash?" Stoker asked.

"Let's just say that I do a lot of odd jobs for entities that have the ability to pay in cash — and satisfy the IRS by facilitating simple transactions and pulling a few strings," Z said as he leaned forward toward doctor Stoker. "Look Troy, I see where you're going with this, so let me anticipate a few of your questions. I have no property records, financial accounts, or other documents in my name, so I am probably pretty safe. We'll see what the future holds."

"So laying low in South Dakota seems like a good strategy for hiding out. How do you travel? How do you get in and out of airports?"

Z glanced at Rivera and smiled broadly. "I have a Cuban chauffeur who pilots me wherever I need to go."

Rivera smirked. "You'll be parachuting over Cuba in three hours if you don't remember who's in charge here, *Señor Zeta*."

"I could use some time in Florida about now. These South Dakota winters kill me."

"Well, give us another hour and we'll offer you a small reprieve in Washington D.C.," Rivera said. "The temperature there is a balmy forty-one degrees."

"I'll take it," Z said. "Now we better fill Stoker in on a few more key details about Arlington Hall and how the unit there operates."

CHAPTER 75

ARLINGTON, VIRGINIA

Stoker, Rivera, and Z waited inside a modest reception area on the second floor of Arlington Hall in northern Virginia. The man whom Rivera and Z had referred to only as James had made them wait for nearly forty-five minutes. Neither Rivera nor Z seemed too concerned. Stoker reasoned that this James character was probably doing his best to work them in.

The monotony of the waiting was broken when an assistant who appeared to be frazzled and anxious stepped into the office. "Dr. Rivera. Will you please step out here into the hallway with me for a moment? I have a message for you."

"Absolutely," Rivera said, as he stood and walked into the hallway. Two seconds after Rivera disappeared from sight, a commotion erupted in the hallway. Guttural martial arts yells and the slamming of a body against the wall displaced the quiet the men had been experiencing.

"Again Rivera! I pinned you again. Now you must admit that Judo is the superior martial art!"

Stoker and Z ran out into the hallway, where a man, presumably James, knelt on top of Errol Rivera. His face was pinned to the carpeted floor and his grimace was obvious. "Get off of me you ogre!" demanded Rivera. "You know all too well that the only time Judo ever wins is when the element of surprise is on its side – and the assailant can hide behind the skirt of his assistant."

"Ha!" the man laughed. "Are those excuses coming out of the mouth of the overly accountable Errol Rivera?"

"No, those are not excuses. I should have seen this coming. I am responsible. But, we both know that Judo, especially your Judo, is never going to succeed in defeating one opponent in six. I dare you to go up against anybody trained in an Israeli martial arts gym—if you know what I mean."

"Okay we'll see about that," said the man as he stood up and offered Rivera a hand to help him stand up.

Rivera refused the hand, helped himself up, and made a hand gesture towards Z and Stoker. "James, you remember Z."

"Remember him? I've talked to him on a roughly weekly basis for the last four months. It's good to see you again, Z. Your insight has been amazing." James turned to Stoker, extended his hand, and said, "You must be Dr. Stoker."

"Yes, I'm Troy Stoker. It's good to meet you, James."

"Great to meet you, Dr. Stoker. My name is James Furth."

Stoker was surprised. He had just met this man and he had shared his last name. Apparently, the big secret was out. Rivera and Z also looked startled that Furth had shared his last name.

The three men stepped back into Furth's office, and his assistant, without asking, followed behind them and placed a Sunkist soda and turkey sandwich in front of each of them. "Sorry I don't do potato chips, boys," exclaimed Furth. "I gave them up about two months ago."

"No problem," Z said. "Thanks for dinner."

"Yes, thank you," Rivera and Stoker said almost simultaneously.

"Well, let's talk about Sioux Falls," Furth said. "Dr. Stoker, you may not even know that we owe you a debt of gratitude. The information you've provided through Rivera over the last few days has proven invaluable. We've been watching patterns of power in high places protecting the Sioux Falls drug trade now for well over two years. Whoever is pulling the strings in your city knows all the right people in all the right places. He or she has been careful. There are many layers between this individual and the street. It's hard to identify thugs like this, let alone dig up enough dirt on their activities like you did at the inauguration a few nights ago. Now this guy's made a mistake. From what we've been able to gather from your phone call on inauguration night, some of the photographs, and a few little money trails, we think we have a pretty good idea who this person is."

"But that's only half of the equation," Rivera said. "Your work identifying the trends at the jail, the coyote attacks, and the man named Nichols led us to a gold mine in Reno."

Furth looked at Z and nodded at him, so Z spoke up. "During the last few days we've had some little electronic spies, we call them NanoBUGS, crawling around the offices of Green Growth Ventures in Reno. We found some bank accounts that are suspicious to us. We've collected enough information to

Francis Bandettini and Matt Nilsen

establish probable cause. Director Furth will present that to a judge and ask for permission to manipulate some of these bank accounts."

"Well, I'm thrilled I could be of service," Stoker said. "Not a day goes by that I don't treat a half dozen or more people scourged by the products and activities of this drug-pushing jackal lurking out in our community."

"Very well," Furth said as he turned to Z. "Over the next day or two, I want your help hacking into the bank account of Green Growth Ventures. We're going to use some technology and we need your skills."

"Yes, Sir!" Z said with a level of enthusiasm that Stoker had not yet experienced from this young enigma.

"Give me a day or two," Furth said, "and we should have the warrants and technology in place to smoke the foxes out of their holes. I can't wait to see who our drug and identity theft kingpin is there in Sioux Falls."

CHAPTER 76

The commander picked up the phone immediately from his office in the Capitol building in Pierre. The Lieutenant Governor wanted to speak to him. "Good afternoon, Kent," he said with all the friendliness and sincerity he could muster in his voice. "To what do I owe this call?"

"She's really improving! Ann's off the respirator and breathing on her own. I wanted you to be one of the first to know," Kent Higgins said. He was riding in the passenger's seat of an ambulance that was transporting his wife, Ann, to a helipad at the Sioux Valley Regional Airport. "I just wanted to take a minute and thank you. You've been supportive these last few days. Ann is recovering miraculously, and now a man, Dr. Rivera, is flying her on a medical helicopter to get more treatment in Washington D.C."

"Well, that's *fantastic*, Kent. I'm thrilled for you," the commander lied exerting extreme mental energy to cover the panic he felt. "When do they get to see their mom?"

"Soon. Well they've been seeing her, but they have not seen her this alert. We'll have to see how long we stay in D.C."

"What an amazing reunion that will be."

"Yes, they'll be thrilled with her progress, but this is still going to be traumatic for the kids until Ann is out of her coma."

The commander was relieved that Ann was still in a coma and not talking to anybody. But the trip to Washington D.C. would complicate matters. "Oh Kent," the commander said with an alleviated tone that he quickly tried to mask with false disappointment, "I'm deeply touched by the strength of your kids right now. They're in my prayers. Certainly, she'll come out of her coma any day now."

"Thank you. I'm just so thrilled that I was able to give her a hug again without all those tubes in the way. I sensed that she recognized me a little bit. At least I hope she did. I think she knows who I am, and she knows I'm there for her."

"Well, Kent, when can I come and visit again? When would a visit be supportive instead of bothersome?"

"You know you're welcome anytime. We appreciate you more than you'll ever know. When we're back in town, please come visit," Higgins said. "Unless you want to fly to D.C. in the next day or two," he joked. "We'll be at the National Institutes of Health. Stop by and say hello."

Brilliant idea! Thought the commander. *At least I'll send someone on my behalf with a specific message.*

"If she's there longer than a few days, I'll see if the governor can fly out overnight and visit her early one morning," the commander said. "Please send all my love to Ann. I will make an extra effort to visit her within the next few days."

"Sounds good, my friend. I'll see you soon," Kent Higgins said as he hung up his phone. The ambulance came to a stop and parked on a tarmac two hundred feet away from a warming Army helicopter. Dr. Errol Rivera met the ambulance dressed in full flight gear.

CHAPTER 77

Moments after finishing the call with lieutenant governor Higgins, the commander was waiting for orthopedic surgeon Larry Stintson to answer his cell phone. "Pick up you idiot!" he bellowed toward the ceiling of his new and spacious office. However, Stintson was not answering his cell phone, so the commander resorted to calling the direct line for Stintson's secretary.

"Dr. Stintson's office," answered the obscenely overcompensated Andrea.

"Dr. Stintson, please," demanded the Commander from his office in Pierre, nearly two hundred miles away.

"May I tell him who is calling?"

"Yes, just tell him it's the commander, and insist that he hurry up." Seventeen seconds later, Stintson was on the phone.

"Why are you pulling me away from patients?"

"Look here, Stintson, we've got a problem. Ann Higgins is off the respirator and it sounds like she may be getting better!" Stintson had no reply. "She's obviously not talking yet, but I need to know, what's going on? I mean you're the doctor here. When will she be waking up? When will she be talking?"

"I don't know," Stintson said with a touch of irritation in his voice. "There are dozens of possibilities for her. Nobody's even sure what's going on with her. She may never wake up or she my wake up in five minutes."

"What do you mean? You don't know? You're a doctor! You've got to know these things you sniveling twerp."

"Listen, here, *Commander*," Stintson said with obvious contempt. I'm an orthopedic surgeon. I don't know this brain stuff."

"You went to medical school, didn't you? You had to pass tests on brains, neurons, spines, and stuff like that, did you not?"

"I was bound and determined not to be a psychiatrist, neurologist, primary care doctor, kidney doctor, or diabetes doctor. Sure, I crammed all that stuff in my head for the exams. Once the class was over, I promptly forgot anything I would not need as an orthopedic surgeon. I can almost promise you that I slept through any medical school lecture on comas, amnesia, traumatic speech disorders, and the former people, otherwise known as vegetables, that haunt the ICU's and rehab hospitals in comas. I have no idea what's going on or what to expect next."

"Well, get on the phone and find out," the commander ordered. "We need a timetable, and I need an answer in five minutes! I've got to set plans in motion and get this mess cleaned up."

"Sure, boss. Perhaps I'll call Troy Stoker and see if he knows the answer," Stintson said. His scorn was even more obvious. But before the commander could reply to Stintson's insult his attention was completely captured by an alert that popped up on his sleek little laptop computer—the one so few people knew about. His bank in Reno, Nevada was sending him an automated alert about a large transaction within his main account. A large withdrawal, which the commander had not authorized, had extracted an astonishing amount of cash out of his account.

CHAPTER 78

James Furth of the DEA's VIP unit had just punched a few keys on a dedicated banking terminal computer located on the top floor of Arlington Hall. With the permission of a federal judge, he transferred $3 million out of the Reno, Nevada banking account of Green Growth Ventures. Within seconds the digital money made its way to the Bank of New York Mellon on the island of Manhattan.

"How do things look there in Pierre?" Furth asked Z over the phone. Z was watching the events unfold with Jessica from her office in Pierre. They were watching the online and telephone activity of the governor, lieutenant governor, attorney general, secretary of state, state senators, state house members, and judges. In Sioux Falls, Troy Stoker was accompanying one of Jessica's IT analysts as she monitored the Minnehaha County Sheriff and respective members of the county's vice squad. As well, Stoker was watching key Sioux Falls Police Department personnel's telephone and digital activity. Of course, Larry Stintson of the medical board was a primary concern. However, that day he was in surgery and it would be hard, if not impossible, to monitor him in the hospital. The judge who had authorized the monitoring had failed to find sufficient cause to allow wiretaps and electronic surveillance to extend into the hospital and the doctor's private office and cell phone.

The teams in Pierre and Sioux Falls, as well as Furth in Arlington were connected via a conference call. Errol Rivera was listening in on the phone call, too. But he would soon have to drop off of the call. In a matter of minutes, he would be piloting a military helicopter that would carry Ann and Kent Higgins and an accompanying medical team, to a highly specialized lab in Washington D.C.

"No activity yet," Z said.

"We're all quiet here in Sioux Falls," Stoker said.

"Dr. Stoker, welcome to the waiting game," Furth said.

Stoker was familiar with the waiting game on many levels. His military years taught him to be patient with enemies, allies, patients, and medications. With some of his patients, he had waited for years for them to come to the realization that they needed to make the changes necessary for peace in their lives. Stoker could wait for a few minutes or hours for the true identity of a criminal to emerge.

"Guys, it looks like I've got something interesting here!" Jessica said. "One of the state's big shots just cancelled his noon meeting. His intercom conversation with his assistant, fifteen seconds ago, was a command to hold all his calls. There was a lot of stress, desperation, and strain in his voice, which is uncharacteristic for this cool cucumber."

CHAPTER 79

PIERRE, SOUTH DAKOTA

The commander yelled out loud, "Three million dollars! How in the hell?"

Just then his phone rang and he could see from the caller ID that it was his accountant, Ron Cunningham, in Reno.

"You had better have some answers! Are you moving money around, three million dollars?" he bellowed to his financier of more than a decade.

"I have no idea, Commander." That's why I'm calling you. Have you been moving money around?"

"Never! If I wanted to move that much money around, I'd be on the phone with *you*. You'd be the one pulling the strings and doing all the dirty work!"

"Boss, it looks like it was transferred to a bank in New York, which is good news. We should be able to follow that money and figure out what happened. I suspect this is a colossal misunderstanding."

"Well, this is way too coincidental. I've got a pretty good idea what happened to that money. I'm just putting two and two together. Call me the second you have more info. Better yet, just send me a secure text. I'll call you right back." The call ended abruptly.

The commander gathered his coat, computer, and briefcase, and walked briskly out of his office. "Cancel my meetings! I'll be in the air all afternoon," he barked to his executive assistant. As he walked toward the Capitol building exit he typed in a quick text message to Brian Berg and Sarah Haslam.

> *It's time for Operation Allie. I want Stoker's wife in our*
> *hands in the next two hours.*

The next call was to his pilot. "Can we be in the air in twenty minutes?"

"Yes, Commander. Where are we headed?"

"Sioux Falls," he responded. "And, make sure my wolves are on board. Don't feed them! I need them irritable and obedient."

CHAPTER 80

Ann was keenly aware of her surroundings as the Boeing V-22 Osprey tiltrotor aircraft she occupied landed on the helipad just west of the Walter Reed Medical Center in Bethesda, Maryland. Strangely, she felt serene, despite the fact she had not figured out how to say a word or make a gesture of basic communication. There were so many times she just wanted to smile for yes or shake her head for no, but her body would not follow her mind's commands. Even basic communications mechanisms eluded her. Kent, her husband, sat next to her, two flight nurses were keeping tabs on her, and Errol Rivera was at the aircraft's controls with another pilot. Seconds after landing, Rivera turned the ship's command over to his co-pilot, stepped back between the pilot seats, threw open the door, and signaled for the flight nurses to move Ann's gurney toward the door. "Right this way!" he yelled over the din of the aircraft's diminishing rotors. "You've got a doctor's appointment, Mrs. Higgins!"

Ann and Kent emerged from the Osprey and were rushed into an ambulance by two muscular women and one compactly built man with bulging biceps. All three sported side arms, sunglasses, and black baseball caps. None wore a uniform or any clothing that indicated who they were.

Instead of proceeding to the military hospital, Errol Rivera directed the driver across Wisconsin Avenue to the Mark O. Hatfield Clinical Research Center on the campus of the National Institutes of Health. Within two minutes of arrival they had cleared the substantial security procedures and exams. After a short elevator ride and lengthy trip down multiple hallways, Ann Higgins was sitting on a strange table that appeared to slide into a medical scanning machine of some type. Her husband, Kent, stood by her side and held her hand.

"I need to get back to Sioux Falls ASAP," Rivera explained. "This is Dr. Anthony Bocelli, a PhD neuroscientist and fMRI Section Chief at the National Institute of Mental Health. The initials fMRI simply stand for functional MRI. You may also be interested to know that just a few hours ago Dr. Bocelli was giving the keynote address at a seminar called The Thirty Most Influential Papers in fMRI in the Past Thirty Years. That feat alone is impressive.

"It's nice to meet you Mrs. Higgins, Dr. Rivera, and Lieutenant Governor Higgins. You have some friends in high places, Colonel Rivera." Bocelli turned to the lieutenant governor and explained, "He's not telling you that the conference was in Italy and I finished my talk scarcely nine hours ago. Dr. Rivera pulled some amazing strings with the surgeon general to get me out of that conference and back here to work with Mrs. Higgins. I can honestly say this is the first time I've ever received a call from the surgeon general himself. Two Air Force airmen hustled me out of the conference and thirty minutes later I was airborne in a C-37A. About seven hours later I was landing here in Washington D.C. and they rushed me back to work."

"Sometimes you just need the right person in the right place at the right time, Dr. Bocelli. In this case, this is cutting-edge technology we're using to fight crime. This machine is the next generation of MRI that measures brain activity in specific brain areas, instantaneously. We call it real-time fMRI. One of its very powerful applications, in our specific case here, is that it can give us insight into people's truthfulness and intent, but we use it for *many* other brain-related studies and explorations. Using fMRI on an accused criminal is constitutionally delicate. *But* I predict that using it on a *victim* who cannot communicate will turn out to be brilliant. Dr. Bocelli is going to use it to help communicate with Ann and find out who this evil, scumbag mongrel is. I look forward to terminating him with extreme prejudice."

With his blood vessels bulging from the side of his head and arms, Dr. Rivera was never one to avoid sharing what was on his mind. "I know I'll sleep much better when Ann's assailant is dancing with *el diablo*." An ironic statement from a man whose dreams were plagued with Central American history few people knew about. "I'll even tell my buddy, that shrink, Stoker, that I'm sleeping much better. He won't believe me, though."

When a technician entered the room to assist with the procedure, Rivera realized he needed to get out of the way. "That's my cue," Rivera said, quickly shaking hands with Kent. He exited the scanner room hastily for his Osprey flight back to Sioux Falls.

Dr. Bocelli in this case had to assume that, even in her comatose state, Ann could understand simple directions. "Just relax, Ann," Dr. Bocelli said as the tech situated her on the table. "Because you cannot communicate with us, I will be sensitive of anything that may cause you anxiety or distress. We are all aware that lying inside a tight space with all of that noise may be bothersome. We'll be monitoring your heart rate and breathing. We will also use galvanic skin response detection to anticipate and measure small changes in perspiration."

A few moments later Ann's head and torso were gliding slowly into the fMRI machine. Even with noise-canceling headphones on her ears, she could hear the machine's sounds. At first, she heard grinding and clicking. A few moments later, a high-pitched beeping sound joined the clicks and grinds. She was surprised at how loud this machine was. It was equally as noisy as her recent helicopter flight. She also realized how similar the intense whirring and thumping seven-Tesla magnet — the largest fMRI magnet produced on earth — was.

In the control booth Bocelli and Kent Higgins could also hear the sounds emanating from the fMRI machine. "The beeping means that the machine is actually scanning her brain," explained Bocelli in a professorial tone. "Right here on the screens you can see the images of her brain and you can also see little bursts of color transposed on the image. Those bursts of color indicate more concentrated brain activity in that area. When you see color, it means that specific part of the brain is working a little harder."

Bocelli pushed a button on a microphone in front of him. "Okay, Ann. I'm going to give you some instructions and then I'll ask you some questions," flowed Bocelli's calm voice through the headphones on her ears as he talked into a microphone on the other side of a panel of glass. "I know you cannot answer with your voice. In fact, I'm not even sure you can understand me. But this fMRI will let us see the activity in your brain, which hopefully will let you answer a few questions for us. Dr. Rivera says that he and a few others in Sioux Falls would like to know who attacked you. I assume you would like to let us know. Don't worry. This is painless. Are you ready?"

Ann's face showed no feelings and she had no outward means of answering his question. But Dr. Bocelli could immediately see evidence of her emotions. Images of Ann's brain appeared on the screens before him; specific interpretive colors began to indicate activity throughout numerous structures within her brain.

"As we ask you questions you're going to answer them by trying to move your index finger. When you want to answer 'yes' to a question, we want you to try to wiggle your pointer finger on your right hand," instructed Bocelli. "So now, let's try that with a simple question. Is your name Ann Higgins?" Bocelli asked.

Ann attempted to move her right index finger, to indicate *yes*. But as expected, her finger remained still as it rested on her stomach. However, in the control booth, it was obvious that her brain was attempting to react with her right finger to the *yes* question. As Ann attempted to move her finger, an area on the left side of her brain lit up. Bocelli turned to Kent Higgins and explained, "The left motor cortex area of her brain vividly illuminated on her brain scan when she tried to move her right finger. Also, her cerebellum, which tells the brain what to move, additionally showed modest activity on the same side of her brain when she attempted to move her right finger saying '*yes*.'"

"Excellent, Ann. Your '*yes*' answer came through clearly. Now we know that you can hear and understand us. We're communicating loud and clear, so far," Bocelli said with genuine calm and sincerity. "Let's try answering a '*no*' question by wiggling your left index finger when we ask the question. And, the question is, do you live in Los Angeles?"

Ann attempted to wiggle the pointer finger on her left hand. Again, the finger remained motionless. But, the real-time brain scan showed significant activity in the right motor cortex of her brain as shown on the scan immediately.

"Perfect, Ann. You're clearly answering both '*yes*' and '*no*.' Are you comfortable so far?

The monitors lit up as the previous *yes* response had shown on the scan.

"Excellent! Let's move on," Bocelli said. "Now, let's also add another dimension to your new, temporary communication skills."

Bocelli struck some keys on his keyboard while intermittently clicking a mouse. "Okay, now, Ann. Right in front of you, you see a small screen. I'm going to project some images on the screen and monitor your reaction to those images."

A moment later, and with a few more keyboard clicks, Bocelli produced a picture of her son, Todd, which appeared on the small monitor a few inches in front of Ann's eyes. "Is this your son?" Dr. Bocelli asked. As in the previous *yes* answer, the left motor area lit up when she tried to move her right index finger. Also, the amygdala area was visualized more prominently on the scan and the frontal parietal areas of the scan were more recognizable. "Look Mr. Lieutenant governor. Do you see this pattern here? This shows '*yes*,' this is her son because she said '*yes*' with her right finger. And, it also shows that she '*recognizes*' the person before her, because this is the pattern for the '*yes*' answer and '*recognition*,'" emphasized Bocelli.

With a few more keystrokes and mouse clicks Bocelli produced a picture of a teenage boy Ann had never seen before. "Is this your son, Ann?" As the neuroscientist watched the monitors, Ann attempted to move her left index finger to answer *no*. However, the main response Dr. Bocelli saw was in the right motor area of the brain and much less amygdala visualization and left frontal parietal visualization. "Essentially, Ann shows '*no recognition*' of this person," Bocelli said. "This indeed is the pattern for the '*no*' answer and '*non-recognition.*'"

Bocelli took another ten minutes and went through the *yes* answers and the corresponding *recognition* brain patterns. Then he took another ten minutes and went through the *no* answers and the corresponding *non-recognition* brain patterns.

Bocelli pushed the button on the microphone. "So Ann, I'm going to show you some photographs here to help you narrow down and find out who hurt and hospitalized you. Dr. Rivera provided us with a suspect list, and I will put their faces up on the screen." Bocelli transmitted the first picture. It was an image of the new Sioux Falls vice squad lieutenant, who Ann did not know. Ann's brain scan showed activity in the regions of the brain the signaled a *no* answer and *non-recognition*. "She doesn't know this guy," whispered Bocelli even though the microphone was off.

"Here are the pictures of the chairman of the South Dakota board of realtors you provided," Bocelli said to Kent Higgins. "I understand that Ann dislikes him. Are you sure Ann dislikes him, Mr. Lieutenant Governor?"

"Yes, definitely."

"Okay. Watch what happens here." As Bocelli put an image of the president of the real estate board on the screen, the monitors lit up in a new area of the brain. "Look at this Mr. Lieutenant Governor. See how the insula, this part right here, lights up like a Christmas tree. That's *disgust*. You're right that she dislikes him."

"Wow! It looks like she really hates him," Higgins said.

Bocelli removed the picture from in front of Ann's face. "Let's try some more suspects. Let's show her pictures of the governor and other executive officers," Bocelli said. "Enough beating around the bush, let's catch your murderer." Then the scientist proceeded to fine-tune this interesting machine, and in this case, incredibly accurate lie detector.

CHAPTER 81

WASHINGTON, D.C.

By Robert Nichols's best guess, he had arrived in Washington D.C. about two hours after Ann Higgins. The commander had insisted that he get there as quickly as possible and at any cost. Nichols was on a flight out of Memphis two hours after the commander called and he knew his commercial airline flight traveled faster than the Osprey that brought Higgins.

Nichols had never been to the Maryland or Washington D.C., and he was at the mercy of a taxi cab driver to get him to the National Institutes of Health. Nichols was not used to big cities and the mammoth size of government.

"The National Institutes of Health is a big place, sir," the driver said. "Where do you want me to drop you off?"

Nichols had no idea how to answer. He thought that a government "institute" would probably be in an old building, similar to the science building at the junior college where he took biology 101 during his first and only semester of higher education. "Right at the front door," replied the farmer from Arkansas.

"There are many buildings on that campus sir," the driver clarified. "Which building?"

Nichols stammered for an answer. "Oh, just the main building."

The taxi driver smiled. He knew his passenger was confused. "Very good, sir. I shall drop you off at the front door of the main building."

An hour later, Nichols paid the cab driver with six twenty-dollar bills and stepped out of the cab. As he looked at the main entrance to the building where the cab driver had left him, he immediately noticed a security checkpoint. A large metal fence that he estimated at ten feet high surrounded the building. He was carrying two significant weapons, so he opted to avoid the checkpoint, for now. He remembered many movies where people were able to enter or exit supposedly secure buildings through kitchens, loading docks, and other utility doors. So Nichols began walking around the building in search of other entrances. As he made his way down the sidewalk he came upon a large sign that turned out to be a map of the whole campus. He quickly realized that the National Institutes of Health comprised dozens of buildings. He knew he would never find Ann Higgins on his own, so he picked up his phone and called the commander.

"Boss, this place is huge. Do you know where she is at the National Institutes of Health?"

"Let me do some checking around," the commander said. "I'll call you back."

The commander searched the Internet for a few minutes before he concluded that he did not have the time or skill to figure out where Ann Higgins might be. He sent a text to Ron Cunningham in Reno and instructed him to figure it out and send simple instructions to Nichols in Washington.

From Reno, Ron Cunningham called that National Institutes of Health and simply asked to be connected to the room of Ann Higgins. They had no record of her. So he narrowed down a list of six possible locations where they were likely to treat Ann Higgins. They were buildings where they specialized in neurological and mental health medicine. He sent the list to Nichols.

Back at the National Institutes of Health, Nichols tried to walk to each of the buildings Nichols had suggested, but the intimidating fence never ended, except at the security checkpoints. The security was equally heavy at each potential entrance. But Nichols hesitated to call the commander. He knew that commander did not want another phone call with a problem. Instead he would demand a solution. So Nichols thought. And his thoughts returned him to the map. He walked back to the map and formulated a plan. It only took him a few minutes to create a plan he loved. He was enthused to pick up his phone and share it with the commander.

The commander answered on the first ring. "What do you got for me Robert?"

"Ann Higgins arrived by helicopter," Nichols said, "and the closest helipad is at the military hospital. She'll be returning to that helipad; I'll take her out there."

"Why can't you find her while she's in the hospital and vulnerable?" the commander asked. "Wouldn't that be better?"

"There's no way we're getting in there, boss. Those security people got dogs and they're sweeping under the cars with mirrors and stuff. They're doing full car and body checks. Even the important people with appointments get the full pat-down."

"They'd ask you all sorts of questions about the nature of your visit to try and trip you up," the commander said. "It's also a huge risk for you to be captured on camera."

"These guards look tough. I bet they're retired leathernecks and spooks," Nichols said. "These ain't your TSA minimum-wagers, Commander. That's for sure. These bitches take their body cavity checks seriously."

"So you're going into sniper mode now? Very brave," the commander said.

"I'm going to hide out there and wait for her to return to that helipad. If I can get within eighty yards of her, I know I can bring her down."

"I like it," the commander said. He knew this was a crazy idea. Nichols would almost certainly be caught by the military police in a place like the Walter Reed Military Hospital. But considering the urgency of the situation, the farmer became expendable in the commander's mind.

"I wish we had some shoulder-fired RPGs," the commander said. "I'd have you blow the whole bird out of the sky. The whole world would blame the terrorists and a few key people in South Dakota would fear us forever."

CHAPTER 82

Allie Stoker was on kilometer nine of an exercise ritual she thoroughly enjoyed four or more times per week in the winter. Her Solomon cross-country skis glided almost silently under her feet as she propelled herself forward with discipline and well-timed kicks. Her cross-country skiing workout was exercise, mental therapy, time with nature, and the satisfying tie back to her Nordic roots. She loved the contrast of the freezing temperatures kissing her cheeks while her vigorous activity produced enough heat to make her sweat profusely and crave the cold that mere millimeters of cloth separated from her ninety-eight point six degree skin.

Allie had completed one loop around the Great Bear Recreational Area track and now she was half way around the track the second time. She was feeling good and her head was clear. As she entered into a thick and wooded area, she began a slight hill climb and slowed considerably. Suddenly, Allie heard a muffled explosion. A simultaneously distinct roaring pain screamed from her right hip as confusion flooded her mind; an overwhelming impact made her stumble to the ground. As she lifted herself up from the snow, she turned over and looked down at her right hip; she could not find any clues to help her identify the source of the impact. Her ski tights were intact and she had no apparent injury. However, within three seconds, a delayed, excruciating, and white-hot pain caused the surrounding muscles to spasm as the harrowing agony radiated out to the whole of her body. It felt as if she had been branded on the right side of her hip and then kicked by a mule.

"I suggest you stop right there, Allie," said a sneering and triumphant voice. Allie Stoker looked into the trees and she saw the menacing approach of Sarah Haslam closing in on her with a shotgun drawn. Allie's first instinct was to escape, but the instinct was repressed by the sound and sensation of a second shotgun round missing her by three feet and whizzing over the top of her head.

"*Please* give me a chance to fire again," Haslam said. "I beg you. I love my new toy here. Brian just introduced me to the beanbag shotgun shell. The prospect of maiming you right here and now without killing you, well let's just say it turns me on with a bloodlust I never knew existed."

Allie Stoker held up her hands in surrender. Both she and Troy were familiar with a wide variety of weapons, and she'd heard of beanbag shotgun shells. But she could see that Sarah Haslam wanted to gloat.

A man spoke up and stepped out from behind a tree. "That less lethal shot was made of rubber, but we have some classic lead right here, too," he boasted. "However, I don't think you want to taste our lead, because it's so much less forgiving than your recent shot in the ass."

"You see, Allie cat," Haslam said, I have the power to maim you. But my friend Brian here, well, he has the option of treating you for acute lead deficiency."

Allie Stoker rose to one knee and again held up her hand. Her lower back and upper leg muscles emitted violent spasms. Trying to ski or fight would be useless. As she looked back over her right shoulder she saw the hollow stare of Brian Berg, the man who had attempted to raid her husband's office a few days earlier, watching her through the sights of an AK-47. "Sarah, something tells me that this is much bigger than your average stick-up."

"Oh Allie, there is nothing average about this moment, honey. It is a huge moment in time that has everything to do with revenge. Brian here tells me that it also has everything to do with justice. We've got a few people who want to meet you, *darling*. We need you to help us provide a little persuasive leverage on your husband, my little pumpkin—or whatever it is your little lover boy calls you. It seems like he's been sticking his nose where it doesn't belong."

"Let's see how good you are at following instructions, Mrs. Stoker," said Brian Berg. "Do exactly as we say. We have enough ammunition for six or seven of those warning shots. You're familiar with those rounds already. But we only have a meager supply of lethal ammo, so you can expect nothing but the worst from this Russian dragon I'm holding in my hands. Now let's ski."

As Allie looked around and evaluated her situation, one of the first things she noticed was that the sun had just set below the horizon. In thirty minutes all would be dark and the temperatures would plummet. She got back up and skied in the direction Haslam pointed her. The second thing she determined was Brian

Berg was unsteady on his cross-country skis. He was a weak link as long as he was attached to skis. Sarah Haslam, on the other hand, seemed to know what she was doing. She had crazy confidence in her eyes and she was steady on her skis.

"Any second now, somebody could see us here on this trail," Berg said. "So just keep moving. We need you to stay ahead of us and the first thing you're going to do is exit the trail to the right.

"Just ski a few degrees to the right," Haslam said, "and we'll direct you from there with landmarks."

Allie Stoker was not quite sure where they were intending to take her so she exited the groomed cross country trail and traveled deeper into the trees. As she skied through the virgin snow her skinny cross-country skis, which were meant for groomed tracks, struggled to maneuver. Fifty yards off of the trail she glanced back and noticed that Haslam was a mere five or six yards behind her. Berg was further back. He was obviously struggling to keep up. But he was making due in his clumsy sort of way. During the same glance over her shoulder she noticed two other cross-country skiers coming up the trail behind them. They were about three hundred yards behind; Allie fought back the urge to shout out to them and ask them for help. She realized that asking them to help might possibly save her single soul. Nonetheless, she knew that she would introduce two other souls to potential mortal peril. The next three minutes tried her wisdom, patience, and selflessness as Allie continued to ski silently, further and further from two strangers who might have been her only lifeline.

"Okay Allie *darling*, do you see that rather large tree just off to your left?" Sarah Haslam asked.

"Yes, Sarah. I anticipate that's our next destination?"

"Indeed. You're a quick study, Allie. That's the next stop before we tie up your pretty little hands." With the mention of binding Allie's hands, the look in Haslam's eyes changed. Her eyes widened and took on a distant, unpredictable temperament. Her voice grew more intense and she began to babble on very quickly. "You can say your prayers. Angels will protect you. I'm your best friend. I love you. You damn little Stoker ho. You're looking bitchin' there." There were no pauses between sentences and her thoughts were not clear. "Allie you little slut. I really love you, you little slut. You know Allie, you don't eat yellow snow."

Allie looked at Berg. She could see that Haslam's episode of erratic behavior initially confused him. After she had been babbling for a while the situation made him visibly nervous. Allie wondered how much she might be able to win Berg over?

As Allie steered her next strides slightly to the left, a light snow began to fall. She strategized in her mind about possible ways to escape, but she knew she was defenseless against two guns. She also hoped that a significant storm would not cover the three sets of tracks that might lead her husband and any investigators to wherever it was they were heading. Allie skied on, and she continued to hear Haslam and Berg following her in the background. She knew that she could out-ski either of her captors with little effort, but there was no way she would outrun their bullets.

When they were within fifty yards of the tree, the sound of AK-47 blasts startled Allie, but she tried not to show it. She kept her cool as the crack of a few AK-47 bullets flew above her head by three or four feet. She refused to acknowledge Berg's warning shots. She also knew that Sarah Haslam was now broken by her own misdeeds, like a dangerous cornered animal with a scared little mouse in tow. Allie knew that Sarah Haslam was in control. She recognized that Haslam craved being large and in charge and she suspected that she could get through this ordeal by showing small hints of respect for the unemployed physician's viciously negotiated status.

Allie knew that if she acted a little scared it would actually help keep Haslam from accessing the rage and violence that could be lethal. Allie needed to counteract Haslam and try to force some kind of link or bond with her. Admittedly, it would be difficult. The man that Allie loved more than anyone in the whole world had discovered truths that had finally ended Sarah's residency. Haslam certainly didn't see these facts rationally. Allie Stoker was sure that this whole exercise was part of some deep-seated psychological need to assign the blame for her failure to somebody else. Her bizarre behavior proved that she was also in an agitated, erratic state. It would indeed be hard to connect with someone who hated a person she loved so much; but try she must. Connecting with Haslam could save her life.

In light of Haslam's bizarre thought processes, it would be hard to create emotional bonds with her. However, there were times when brief episodes of lucidity were present within Haslam's mind. As they skied on, Allie noticed that sometimes Sarah's thoughts were clear and she was slightly available to connect with. Allie would need to foster these brief emotional links to save both herself and Sarah Haslam.

"Sarah, you're familiar with cross-country skiing. How did you get introduced to it?"

"I grew up in the snow. Our parents taught us both downhill and cross country skiing."

"What part of the country are you from?"

"Allie, you and I associated together for a number of weeks. You never asked me where I was from. You never asked much else about me for that matter. Why are you asking me now? And just in case you were wondering, that was a rhetorical question."

Allie had to think fast. Her attempt to connect had failed. Haslam wanted it to fail.

"Sarah, I'm just trying to keep myself calm. This is a pretty stressful situation. I'm using breathing and relaxation to keep me as calm as possible. A little bit of conversation is just helping to keep my mind clear. So yes it's small talk. But if I'm going to pull off whatever you need me to pull off, I'll need to talk with the people around me occasionally. I'm guessing you're from the upper Midwest?"

"My family's from Chicago. We prefer to do our skiing in Wisconsin. My father made a living as a project manager for a large manufacturing company. That allowed us to afford some days on the ski hill. Fortunately, the president of the company where my dad worked owned a cabin about a half-mile from one of the resorts in Wisconsin. We got to use it every year or two. In the cabin, he had a nice array of cross-country skis, boots, and all of the other accessories. We would often book a long weekend and ski downhill for two days. But we would always ski one day on cross country skis."

"So was that back in the day of the three-pin bindings?"

"Yes," replied Haslam.

"I still miss the three-pin binding. It always kept my foot perfectly aligned for a sustained and controlled glide. I don't see a lot of improvement in many of these new boot and binding systems."

"Actually, many of my friends go to the Rocky Mountain and Sierra Nevada ranges for back-country skiing, and they agree with you. They won't use anything but a three-pin binding. If they get a chance to come down a big mountain in the powder, the three-pin binding gives them the control they crave. Sometimes an idea comes out ahead of its time. The three-pin binding is one of those ideas."

As they approached the landmark tree Allie asked, "What's my next landmark? It's going to be dark soon and I suspect you two don't want to ski all night under a starlit sky?"

"Can you see just over that ridge?" Berg asked.

"Just over that little hill is our final destination, at least as far as skiing goes."

Allie estimated that they only had a mile left to ski. Haslam and Berg would be foolish to ski with her in the dark. With a little bit of luck, Allie might be able to quickly sprint ahead of them and lose herself in the darkness. Better yet, she could quickly dismount from her skis and run backwards before Berg or Haslam could turn around and get a bead on her. At a full sprint she might be able to find her way in the darkness behind a tree for some cover and then move from tree to tree as Berg and Haslam got turned around and tried to shoot at her.

However, Allie estimated that the snow would be almost knee-deep. Her ability to sprint, dodge, or even hold out a sustained, light jog in deep snow was very questionable. Haslam's plan—to capture Allie during a moment of great strength—was actually quite brilliant. Allie had to admit that escaping seemed like a lethal long shot.

Allie conscientiously sped up her pace little by little. As the party of three arrived within a quarter mile of the top of the small hill, she could hear Brian Berg panting excessively. She supposed that Berg rarely exercised. Sarah Haslam was keeping up and showed no signs of strain. As they crested the hill Allie saw a Chevy pickup.

"Is that your truck, Brian?" Allie asked.

"That there's a 1999 Chevy four by four," Berg said as he panted. "It's my pride and joy. I do all the work on it myself."

"Including the windows he just tinted up really dark," interjected Haslam. "We want you to spend the next few minutes traveling in anonymity."

"Something tells me the back of that pickup truck has seen a few trophy bucks in its time," Allie said.

"Well, I don't know about trophies, but I sure have brought home a number of bucks back there," responded Berg with a hint of enthusiasm in his voice.

"So do you wash the blood out of the truck bed yourself, or do you just let the rain and snow wash it out over the next few weeks?"

"I only let nature wash it out. It's part of the ritual. There's almost always enough snow to clean out the back of a pickup truck in a week or two."

"So are you a rifle hunter or do you like to bow hunt?"

"I've been bow hunting a few times, but my daddy raised me as a rifle hunter. I didn't spend a lot of time with my dad, but he did teach me to hunt. He always frowned on scopes. He taught me how to use my sights."

"Well, Brian, my daddy taught me to hunt also," Allie said before pausing for a moment. She omitted the fact that she was a bow hunter, however. "This year I filled my deer tag on our third trip out. It was a beautiful experience dragging that deer back and dressing it. Fortunately Troy's the better venison cook in the family."

"Let's not talk about Troy," interjected Sarah Haslam with a fiery tone. "I'll decide when we talk about Troy!"

Allie Stoker was pleased. She knew she had connected with Brian Berg. She was confident that, with a few more connections, he would never dare pull that trigger on her.

When they arrived at the pickup truck Sarah Haslam pulled up to within ten feet of Allie. She aimed her gun right at Allie's face and said, "I want you to hold still while I take my skis off. Notice how I can do this while still training this gun somewhere in the vicinity of your nose or your forehead. Sarah Haslam carefully disconnected from her skis and instructed Brian Berg to do the same. Brian clumsily fiddled with his skis for almost two minutes, but he eventually figured out how to disconnect from them.

"I can't wait to get these boots off my feet," complained Berg. "They're killing me. How do you guys do this for hours at a time?"

"It's called toughness, Brian," Haslam said in a tone that left both Allie and Brian wondering if she was kidding or serious. "Now Brian, put these skis in the back of your truck. And grab me two of those zip ties while you're at it."

Always the good soldier, Brian Berg complied. Within thirty seconds Sarah Haslam had put down her gun and was attaching zip ties to Allie Stoker's wrists while Brian Berg had his gun trained in her general direction. Haslam instructed Allie to step out of her skis while Allie unlatched them. If Allie had developed just a little better relationship with Brian Berg, she would have had the confidence to knee Sarah Haslam in the face and knock her out. However, Allie could not be sure that Berg wouldn't fire on her, so she complied. She had no idea what else would motivate a state employee to kidnap a doctor's wife; something told Allie that the motivations were linked to his job and possibly his survival.

"All right Mrs. Stoker. Walk around to the passenger's side of the car, get in, and sit on the passenger's seat with your legs facing outward." Allie complied, and twenty seconds later Sarah Haslam was frisking her. Sarah removed Allie's cell phone and wrap-around sunglasses from her pocket and placed them in a cup holder in Berg's center console. Then Haslam attached zip ties to Allie's ankles and knees. "I'm going to apologize in advance," said Sarah Haslam with snide sarcasm as she lifted Allie's sunglasses out of the cup holder. "Brian. Where is that black gym bag?" Berg produced it from behind the driver's seat and handed it to Sarah. Sarah reached inside and removed a small can of red spray paint and shook it. "Hey. We bought red just for you. If we're going to darken your vision, we may as well give you rose-colored lenses." Then Haslam gave two quick squirts of paint inside the lenses. After allowing ten seconds for the paint to dry, she placed them on Allie's face.

"Hey, sweetheart. It's so much better than a blindfold," she mocked. "We're going for a little ride," Haslam said. "We're going to do some exploration of downtown Sioux Falls. Let's see how you like it."

Sarah Haslam jumped into the shallow backseat of Brian Berg's truck. She left the ski hat on Allie's head. Brian shifted his truck into gear and pulled onto the narrow road. Allie carefully calculated her next question. She had succeeded in connecting the slightest bit with Sarah Haslam. Now she needed to take some calculated risks and attempt to create a twisted relationship with the woman who might be bent on killing her. After all, this was a kidnapping. Allie knew that adult kidnappings often escalate and result in the victim's death.

During the first five minutes of the drive neither Berg nor Haslam spoke much. Allie observed that Haslam appeared resolute, intense, and determined to follow through on her plan, whatever it may be. Berg was nervous. Allie noticed a slight trembling in his hands. His eyes were wide and his jaw vacillated between relaxed and clinched. Brian Berg was having second thoughts, Allie concluded.

"I know there are no simple answers, Sarah, but when did your residency committee let you down for the first time."

The narcissistic Sarah Haslam could not pass up an opportunity to criticize her residency committee. It was a brilliant question for Allie to ask.

"When they started playing favorites. There were four of us starting out in year one. It was obvious that they had their darling, their superstar. Her name was Jana Christensen. She could do no wrong and she was a real know-it-all. She reminded me of that Hermione Granger character in the Harry Potter books. She would never let any of us answer a question or get a word in edgewise. That impresses residency committees, you know? Of course she got to start on all the best rotations. I would say that the first big mistake they made was sticking me with extra weekend call so that Jana could attend all the journal clubs and group therapy sessions that occurred during regular business hours, Monday through Friday."

"And the other two residents?"

"Oh, they hated her, too. The three of us saw right through her. They had to take plenty of weekend and evening call as well. It was all disproportionate thanks to the golden child."

"You went to school in Chicago. Where did the golden child go to school?"

"The University of Virginia. The medical school there is a laugh in my opinion. How can you take a medical school seriously in a town of about 100,000 people?" Haslam was becoming increasingly agitated. "And, Jana always used to talk about Monticello this and Monticello that. It was nauseating. The only thing I found redeeming about her was her love of Washington, D.C. She seemed to know the town almost as well as I did. We both appreciated The Awakening, the Albert Einstein statue, and a few other sculpture gems."

"Yeah, they moved The Awakening over to Maryland."

"I know. The idiots. I don't know who makes the decisions there in Washington, D.C. but I think the Founding Fathers would roll over in their graves about some of the cheap tinsel they've intertwined with the brilliantly laid out city that is Washington, D.C."

"Do you think the Founding Fathers would eat from the hot dog, pretzel, and ice cream vendor vans along the Washington Mall?" Allie Stoker asked with a touch of humor in her voice.

"Madison and Jefferson definitely would. I think they might eat two of their three meals a day there," replied Haslam with some unexpected humor in her tone. "Ben Franklin? Never! I can't speak for the rest of them."

Wow, thought Allie. *This Sarah Haslam may have a sense of humor after all.*

"How did you get to know Washington, D.C. so well?" Allie asked.

"I did an internship at the Department of Health and Human Services," replied Haslam." I never really targeted Washington, D.C. as a college experience, but I had some college friends who were political science majors. It was an almost automatic part of their plan. They knew that I was determined to go to medical school, so they made a few phone calls and asked a few questions and found this internship in the medical world. I applied half-heartedly, and they accepted me with full-scale enthusiasm. I'm glad I did it. It was a great bullet point on my medical school résumé. I think it was one of those things that really helped me get in."

Allie was pleased with how the conversation was going. She decided it would be ideal to share a little about herself and try to find some common ground. "Would you believe that I visited Washington, D.C. for the first time after I got a 3:00 a.m. phone call from my mom?"

"Don't tell me," Haslam said. "It was a medical situation."

"Yup, it was my mom telling me that my dad was in the Georgetown University Hospital" Allie said. "My dad had just retired as a math teacher and he was really craving the idea of spending some time studying history by traveling around the country a bit. You know, he needed a break from math. Mom and dad flew to Washington, D.C., found an inexpensive Best Western Hotel, and started out on an aggressive five-day sightseeing agenda. Well, mom and dad weren't used to the oppressive, humid heat. But of course they could not waste a moment."

"So your dad pushed himself and blew a gasket, huh?" Haslam asked.

"Indeed he did. He actually suffered a small heart attack and was in the hospital in Washington, D.C. for the remainder of their trip. When we got the news my brother and I flew out immediately. For the first two days we spent all of our time with dad in the hospital. But when he improved, we went out and familiarized ourselves with the city. We walked miles each day and saw everything from the Smithsonian to the Bureau of Printing and Engraving."

"What is that?" Berg asked.

"It's where they mint our money," replied Haslam.

"They let you in there?"

"They do. It's actually pretty interesting," Allie said.

"Security is tight," interjected Haslam. "So Allie, how long was your dad in the hospital?"

"Only four days. But his doctors suggested he stay in town and finish a course of outpatient cardiac rehabilitation. Dad was upset because he had to miss his planned flight home. He's such a tightwad and he didn't want to end up paying any rebooking fees. My brother and I paid the rebooking fees. My dad never even knew. Anyway, it took him a number of days at the Georgetown outpatient rehabilitation clinic before they'd let him get on that airplane. My mom and I ended up staying at the Best Western for an extended stay and coaching him through eating the right things, doing the right therapies, and taking the right pills. During that time we just absorbed the city. It is an amazing place, politics aside."

"But this whole Washington D.C. conversation distracted us from the favoritism you experienced from your residency committee," Allie said changing the subject back and hoping Sarah Haslam would run with it.

Haslam seemed more than happy to take the suggestion. "The committee had its favorite resident. The rest of us were second-class. That's the situation in a nutshell," Haslam said in a frigid tone. Then her demeanor changed from frigid to malicious. "So Allie, are you still doing your processing, relaxing, and breathing?"

"Yes. Thank you. I—"

"Don't thank us for enduring your half-witted attempts to bond with us. All of your attempts are self-serving with your talk about Washington D.C. and your family," Haslam said turning to Berg, who had only relaxed slightly as he drove.

Allie thought for a moment and then replied, "I want us all to get out of this alive. I am trying to stay alive. You would do the same, Doctor Haslam."

"Hey, Brian. How much do you want to bet that Allie here is not a deer hunter," Haslam said with obvious disrespect in her voice. Berg just glanced at her with a confused look. "She knows that creating a bond with us makes us less likely to harm her. If she tries to run away, she thinks that we may become good enough friends that we would fail to pull the trigger on her because we care about her."

"So you're not a hunter, Mrs. Stoker?" Berg asked in an accusatory voice.

"Oh, no. I'm a hunter, and my dad did teach me," responded Allie. "I have been trying to connect with both of you. But I've used real facts to do it."

"Okay. Name a popular hunting rifle," insisted Berg.

"I like the 700 Winchester Magnum," replied Allie. "But I admit, I'm a bow hunter."

"What kind of deer do we hunt here in South Dakota?"

"Whitetail, mostly. Hunters also bag some mule deer but mostly on the western side of the state. Whitetail are certainly the majority, especially around here."

"What's a big buck?"

"A male deer with four or more points on both sides," Allie said. "But I would argue that five or more points are a better measure. My last buck was five on each side. Troy's was only four."

"Shut up, Brian!" yelled Haslam. "You half-wit! You're making it worse. Now you're all impressed with your new hunting buddy—who you may have to shoot if she tries anything stupid."

Berg was fumbling with words and trying to speak and his hands began to tremble again.

"You need to *hate* this woman because of her husband. Her husband is the man who booted you out of his office, insulted your manhood, and endangered your position with the state. Allie Stoker laughed about it that night as her husband recounted the tale. She mocked you openly over her overpriced glass of wine and linguini, while you were eating Cup-O-Noodles and watching MacGyver re-runs. Don't let her kiss up to you with hunting talk."

Berg just watched the road and continued to drive. In his mind he renewed his resolve to be tight-lipped while enduring the next few hours or days stuck in the middle of two manipulative women. *Man, even non-girlfriend females are impossible*, thought Berg. He had avoided relationships with women for more than a year now. They were just too complicated. Berg's thoughts and Haslam's tirade were interrupted by an incoming text on Allie's phone. Haslam shot out her hand and picked up the phone.

Hey Babe. How was your ski?

"Oh, Allie *babe*, I've got this one," Haslam said as she began to type.

Still going. Feeling so good, luv. Need few mins more.
Having one of those gr8 workouts

Haslam hit send.

"Do you think he's going to believe I'm skiing in the dark?" Allie asked. "He'll never believe that."

Just then, her phone beeped again. Haslam opened the message.

In the dark?

Haslam's face showed obvious rage. Again, she typed into the phone.

Yes. It's a beautiful night. Let me finish this.

CHAPTER 83

OFFICE OF TROY STOKER, M.D., SIOUX FALLS

Back in his office, Stoker's suspicions were slightly aroused, but he was not too concerned. He made a mental note to check with her again in fifteen minutes as he invited his last patient of the day back into his office.

Five minutes into the session Stoker's instincts would not rest. Something was awry in the last text exchange with his wife. He suddenly ended the session with the patient, explaining that he had a serious family emergency. Despite little actual evidence that there was an emergency, Stoker knew. His intuition told him something was wrong. Mentally he scanned through the possibilities in his mind. He informed Tamara of the emergency and asked her to close up. As he was locking up a file cabinet and preparing to leave, three men walked in the door. They were dressed in slacks and dress shirts.

"Are you Dr. Stoker?" asked a man with a blowback hairstyle and shiny shoes.

"Yes, but I have an emergency, and I'm on my way out the door." Stoker motioned toward Tamara. "She can make an appointment for you."

Stoker stepped toward the door and the three men stepped in front of him. "We're with the state medical board," said a shorter man with a nose that had been broken at least once before. "And we're here because we can be."

The third man spoke up. He had an authoritative voice and the top three buttons of his shirt were unbuttoned to reveal a muscular chest. "The state board has broad powers when it comes to inspecting medical records."

"Yes," Stoker said, "but during normal business hours. It's now almost seven o'clock. Come see me at eight o'clock tomorrow morning and we'll talk." Stoker tried to push his way past the men. But they caught him, one under each arm.

"We need to see your records, now."

"You guys aren't from the state board," Stoker said. "Let's see some ID, some business cards, or pictures of you guys playing pin-the-tail on the jackass with Brian Berg at your office Christmas party."

"You think you're pretty funny," the man with the crooked nose said. "Where do you keep your records?"

"In a server in Florida," Stoker responded. "Leave us a list and we'll begin to respond tomorrow." Stoker walked to Tamara's desk and picked up a pen. Let me write a few things down for you, here." He was grateful to have a lethal pen in his capable hands.

The men walked over to him and two of them grabbed his arms and tried to bring them around his back. Out of the corner of his eye, he could see that the third man had a thick zip tie that he intended to put around Stoker's wrists. Immediately, Stoker spun out of the grips of one of his assailants, distracted him with a fake punch, and drove the ballpoint pen through his cheek.

Attacker number two tried to wrestle Stoker to the ground, but Stoker broke free, stepped sideways, and waited for the man to come at him again. Stoker baited him by holding out his arms. The man grabbed both arms with the intent to subject him with the zip tie. But Stoker quickly flipped his wrists inward and easily broke free. Then, he reached his hand up into his own shirt, removed his neck knife while beginning a spin to his side. Stoker was so swift that the man could not react to his new position. As Stoker thrust the knife into his back, the air rushed out his left lung. Stoker left the knife in place for effect. The panicking man lunged for it but could not reach it. Like a dog chasing its tail, the injured man spun momentarily thinking he could catch up to the metal sticking into his back.

The third man was the only person who concerned Stoker. He had a violent confidence and a lean, nimble physique. Stoker pulled himself up into a boxer's stance to see how the man would respond. The man countered with a karate stance. Stoker loved fighting so-called karate experts. He knew how to draw them off balance. Stoker stepped toward his assailant and threw a jab, which he did not intend to land. The man countered with a punch to Stoker's face, which he wisely let glance harmlessly off the top of his forehead. But the man never had the chance to bring his punch back or regain his balance. Stoker's fingers formed a knife hand and he shot it forward violently. His finger sunk into the man's Adam's apple and the hyoid bone cracked with the sound of a whip.

Stoker turned sideways, raised his leg and threw a violent sidekick into his enemy's right knee, snapping it backwards into a very unnatural position.

"Listen, men. You guys are going to be okay." He turned to Tamara, who had withdrawn a Ruger LCP from her purse. "Call 911," he ordered.

"Oh, I will Dr. Stoker," she responded. But Stoker could see that she was content with her pistol's laser trained on the chest of the man who had just pulled the pen out of his cheek. "On the ground!" she yelled. He was the only man who posed any potential threat, but he complied. "Now, Dr. Stoker's going to rescue his wife, and I'm going to babysit you boys while you sit here and think long and hard about the consequences of your decisions."

Stoker headed for the door as Tamara was saying, "Raise your hand if you want me to call 911 so you can get morphine." Only two of the men were capable of raising their hands, which they did with surprising speed.

"Tamara," Stoker said. "Let's go. Lock them in so they can't follow us. We'll let the sheriff deputies and EMTs find them. Tamara liked the idea. She grabbed her purse and headed out the door. Stoker locked it and they sprinted for their cars.

Immediately Stoker saw a Toyota Tundra pickup truck sitting out on the street with a man inside. "You go First Tamara. If he follows you, I'll follow him." Tamara jumped in her Mazda and sped off down the road unfollowed. Stoker jumped in his Bronco, fired up the engine, and left in the opposite direction of Tamara. As he accelerated through fifty miles per hour, the Tundra was right behind him.

Stoker yelled out a command to wake up his phone. After it beeped that it was ready to obey, he yelled, "Call Z." Moments later his phone had him connected, hands free, to his new techy friend—who had access to impressive critical resources.

"What's wrong, Stoker?" Z asked. There's an alarm going off at your building and your receptionist called in a 911."

"More on that later," Stoker said. "I've got a guy chasing me and I would prefer to lose him without involving the police."

"Can you make it to the granite quarry off of Madison Street?" Z asked.

"Brilliant!" Stoker said. "I like where this is going. Yes, I can get there."

"Perfect. Stay on the line with me, and we'll pull this off together."

Stoker could hear Z jumping into his car and taking off at a high rate of speed. Z spoke up again. "My ETA is about six minutes, but I'll need thirty seconds to get the gates open."

"You can hack through those gates, too?" Stoker asked.

"No, I just pick the locks," Z said. "Hacking can't solve everything!"

"Okay, I'm about eight minutes out," Stoker said.

"Perfect. How well do you know the quarry?"

"I made a few trips there to get granite for my barn's foundation. I know it reasonably well. I know the edge of the road is either a wall of granite or a cliff. There's not a lot of room for error."

"Exactly," Z said. "Do you remember that hairpin turn about half way down?"

"Sure.

"Well, after you flip around it," Z said, "I need you to accelerate like crazy for three seconds. Then slam on those old-time brakes on your Bronco and veer left. Once you're stopped, set your antique parking brake. Trust me on this."

"I trust you," Stoker said.

Just then, the Tundra sped up and slammed into Stoker's rear end. "He just smacked into the back of me. It felt like a warning bump. This guy's not tough enough to do anything brave, yet."

"What's your psychiatric profile of getaway drivers, Stoker?" It was a bizarre question for such an intense moment.

"I have no idea," Stoker responded as he took a quick, tire-squealing right turn onto a different street. "I suspect they're going to send their best guys in to do the job and they leave the weakest man in the car."

"That's what they taught us in training," Z said. "But you get the lonesome loser into a chase and this is his big chance to prove himself. That guy behind you, his adrenaline is flowing and he's willing to take some risks to climb his social ladder."

"Good to know," Stoker said as he slid into a U-turn that temporarily tricked the person chasing him. "Okay, I just opened up a ten-second gap on him."

"Perfect" Z said. "I'm pulling up to the quarry in about two minutes."

The Tundra was struggling to keep up, and Stoker was optimistic that he could stay ahead of him. While both vehicles had a high center of gravity, Stoker's well-tuned suspension was earning him a few moments of advantage at every turn.

"The gates are open, Stoker," Z said over the radio. "Come on in."

Stoker turned right from Kiwanis Avenue onto Madison Street. "I'll be at the gates in thirty seconds. He's almost twenty seconds behind me."

"Let him catch up a little," Z said. "We don't want him to give up."

Stoker dropped his speed to a mere five miles per hour above the speed limit. By the time Stoker turned into the granite quarry, the Tundra was back within ten seconds of catching the Bronco. As Stoker roared past the gates, his headlights lit the way before him. He realized that, even with his studded winter tires, driving on a snowy, frozen, granite surface would be treacherous. Stoker slowed down a little more, but his pursuer did not share his caution and he caught up with Stoker in a matter of seconds.

"This guy has a death wish, Z," Stoker said.

"I don't think that his boss will tolerate him coming home empty handed," Z responded. "Now how close are you to the hairpin?"

"Thirty seconds."

"Okay," Z explained. "Accelerate for three seconds after the turn, slam on your brakes, veer left, and set that emergency brake. After that your phone will go dead."

"Okay," Stoker said. He sped up and put another two seconds between him and the Tundra. "Coming through the turn in ten, nine, eight, seven, six, five, four, three, two, one, now!" Half way through the turn, Stoker stepped on the gas.

"Three, two, one," Stoker said. "Breaking!" Stoker slammed on his brakes, veered to the left almost brushing the granite quarry wall to his side. He set his emergency brake and the Toyota Tundra flew past him. But the truck was surprisingly silent. There was no noise from the engine and Stoker saw that its lights were flickering off as it glided forward fifty more feet and sailed off the edge of the road into the night sky. A second later Stoker heard the metal compressing, bone crushing crash of death. There was no explosion. Ironically, it was perfectly silent again. Stoker was speechless for a moment. Then the urgency to connect with Allie compelled him to turn his Bronco around and start back for the quarry gates.

"What was that?" Stoker asked a few minutes later as he pulled up beside Z.

"That was an electromagnetic pulse grenade that I dropped from a cliff above you. It knocked out the electrical system on that Tundra. Of course, it didn't affect your manly 1976 Bronco engine. But I'm sorry about your aftermarket car stereo and your cell phone." Z held out his hand. "Let me see your phone."

Stoker handed him the phone and said, "So you killed his engine with your toy there, and he lost enough control of his power brakes and steering to send him over that cliff."

Z was working with Stoker's old phone and bringing a new, sleek phone to life. "You got a problem with that, Stoker?"

Stoker's answer was firm. "No, that was a brilliant job of protecting the public from danger by bringing that guy to the quarry. You also spared other cars the effects of damage from your EMP grenade." Stoker carefully turned his car around and started back to the entrance of the quarry. "Tonight I don't have a problem with that at all. Because I think we've got a problem much bigger than the man in the Tundra and his buddies at my office."

"What's going on, Stoker?" Z asked, as he handed him his new phone. "That should be a perfect copy of your old phone, by the way. All your apps, contacts, and all that stuff are exactly the same."

Stoker inspected the phone briefly. "Well, Allie's text told me that she was still skiing—in the dark—but her GPS locator says she's near downtown. My intuition, and the experience with the goons at my office, tell me there's something wrong. We need to find out what it is."

"Then let's dig deeper," Z said.

Stoker used his new phone to send Allie a text message inviting her to dinner. "I agree," Stoker said. "Let's get downtown."

The two men sped toward the heart of Sioux Falls. Two minutes later Stoker got a reply back that puzzled him.

> *No thanks. Just grabbed pastrami sand and ibuprofen*
> *for sore legs. C u @ home*

Stoker slammed the accelerator to the floor. Allie never needs pain medication—and she hates pastrami.

CHAPTER 84

"Okay, Ann," the soothing voice of Dr. Bocelli said through the headphones. She was back inside the fMRI machine. "We're going to show you a few more pictures. We want you to know that seeing the face of a person who tried to kill you will be painful. We also know that you're brave and you would never back down from this opportunity."

After a few more keystrokes and mouse clicks, Bocelli displayed a new image. "Here's another picture." The image of South Dakota governor, Richard Horton, appeared on the small screen in front of her face. "Do you recognize this person?"

Ann's fMRI scan lit up in the areas of the brain that showed a clear *yes* response and *recognition*. "Do you see that, Kent?" Bocelli asked. "Her amygdala is lighting up which is her brain's way of telling us that she knows the governor. You will also notice that the insula—that area that expresses '*disgust*'—is quiet. She does not feel '*disgust*' toward the governor, but her brain recognizes the face, so he's not your suspect."

Bocelli removed the image of the governor and replaced it with a new person's picture. After giving Ann a few seconds to survey the image of the South Dakota secretary of state, Allan Miller, Bocelli asked, "How about this person?" Again, Ann's brain scan results showed that her brain recognized the man, and did not manifest evidence of *disgust*.

"That's not him, either," exclaimed Kent Higgins.

"Correct, Mr. Lieutenant Governor. You're becoming quite the neuroscientist," Bocelli jested as he turned off the microphone.

"Ha, ha," Higgins said. "You should see me as a rocket scientist."

Bocelli laughed softly. "Well, let's show Ann the picture of the South Dakota attorney general. Wouldn't that be a story?" The neuroscientist hit the enter key and the picture of Steve Hewitt materialized in front of Ann's face. Immediately the recognition areas on her brain scan ignited. Bocelli's finger pointed to one of the screens, "There! Right there! Look at how the insula is lighting up! I've rarely seen such a robust *disgust* response so quickly." He turned his head over to another monitor. "Look at her galvanic skin response! She's sweating up a storm. Her heart's racing, too." Bocelli clicked a few more keys. He could not hide the intensity of the moment from his face.

"Her brain must feel some real significant disgust over this picture of Attorney General Hewitt," said the lieutenant governor. "There's our jackal!"

"I agree with you. This person seems to evoke such strong responses, I have to concur that this is pretty significant evidence." Dr. Bocelli removed the picture from the screen. "Look at her heart, rate," interjected Bocelli. "Now it's jumped up to 151 and Ann's galvanic skin response is still quite elevated. Her respirations increased significantly. She's experiencing a 'fight or flight' response, at a visceral level, in the primitive area of her autonomic responses in her brain."

Now that he had finished explaining, Dr. Bocelli sensed that silence was the only appropriate response as the gravity of this moment flooded his customarily objective, scientific mind.

Kent Higgins reached up and spoke softly into the microphone. "Ann, you were amazing. You're so brave. I'll be right back to hug you as soon as they get you out of this machine, my love. Let me quickly touch base with the governor then I'll be right back with you."

As lieutenant governor Higgins stood from the chair he looked Dr. Bocelli in the eye and extended a handshake. "Thank you, doctor. This has been astounding," Kent said. His sincere gratitude moved Bocelli deeply. He and his new technology had really helped somebody today.

CHAPTER 85

The phone call was short and cryptic, because the line was not secure. Lieutenant governor Higgins decided that calling the governor immediately was more important than investing fifteen minutes in finding a secure line somewhere on the campuses of the National Institutes of Health. "Governor, I've just had an amazing experience in Bethesda with this neuroscientist Dr. Bocelli and his cutting-edge fMRI. I'll give you the details later, but after his exam with Ann I'm ninety-nine percent sure that our attorney general is my wife's attacker."

"What? This is unbelievable! Do you know what you're saying, Kent?"

"Yes, Governor. I do. We'll talk about it in detail on a secure line. But we must now, without hesitation, issue an arrest warrant. I'll stake my reputation and office on this. You have to trust me on this one, sir. I'm having Dr. Bocelli send the technical details to our geeks to look at in South Dakota. Will you please start the process of arresting the attorney general?"

"Okay. As long as you're sure about this, I'll go with it. But we need to talk in person when you get here ASAP."

"Thank you very much, sir. We will. I'm going to get back to Ann now."

"How's she doing?" the governor asked.

"Much better than I thought, sir. That's the other amazing thing. You'll be fascinated when I tell you all about it."

"That's great. I'll let you know as soon as I have an indictment drawn up. I'll call you," the governor said, and he was gone.

Back in Pierre the governor sat in his study at the Governor's Mansion and pondered. Normally, in an unraveling case of government corruption his next phone call would be to the attorney general. But that was obviously out of the question. He picked up his secure line and called his overnight, on-call assistant.

"Rosie, get me the Minnehaha county sheriff on the phone. Also get my helicopter fired up. We're going to Sioux Falls, ASAP. File the flight plan to land in the sheriff's office parking lot and notify the building crew there."

CHAPTER 86

It was 3:15 a.m. Kent and Ann Higgins held hands as they traveled in a specially equipped military ambulance for the short drive between the National Institute of Mental Health and the helipad at Walter Reed Military Hospital. Ann's gurney had slid neatly through the back doors and she sat securely during for the half-mile drive. In the wee hours of this morning, they were about to take a short trip in a medical helicopter to a hospital in Philadelphia. They would register Ann under an assumed name and continue her recovery in a secure environment.

A nurse who would accompany them on the flight, sat in the front passenger seat. "On the helipad, we'll keep you on your gurney and move you to the helicopter, Ann. Then we'll just lift you into the helicopter and secure you."

The suburban pulled up to the helipad and the medical team opened the vehicle's rear doors and slid Ann out the back. The co-pilot met Ann and introduced himself. His helmet covered up his shaved scalp and his flak jacket covered a torso of lean, disciplined muscle that had helped propel him through the water as a collegiate swimmer. Once the gurney's wheels were extended and locked into place, the co-pilot pushed her around the front of the car. Ann's body shivered at the momentary cold, and the spasm caused her leg to fall off the gurney to one side. The co-pilot noticed immediately, stopped the gurney, and sprang to her aid. He stepped to her side to push her leg back onto the gurney.

The crack was deafening and the co-pilot's head and torso lunged on top of Ann with a sudden spontaneous force that propelled the gurney backwards until it crashed into the ambulance. Both nurses drew their revolvers and sprung into position between the injured co-pilot and Ann Higgins. They avidly scanned the horizon for the shooter as two men with AR-15 rifles emerged from the helicopter and awaited another muzzle flash that would give the shooter's position away. But the assailant had missed his chance and would not fire again.

As the warriors provided cover, the nurses separated Ann and the injured co-pilot. The first nurse radioed for paramedics as she assessed the co-pilot's wound. He had been hit in the shoulder, and the flak jacket had not prevented the bullet from piercing through skin, muscle, sinew, and bone. But he was alert and oriented, and his complaints about the pain were limited to a few heroic yells.

The second nurse grabbed Ann's gurney and sprinted her toward the helicopter. Kent was running a few steps behind them. When they got to the helicopter, the nurse released the wheels and gently dropped Ann and her gurney to the ground. Then she singlehandedly lifted both Ann and the gurney into the helicopter before pushing Kent into the craft. Then the nurse slammed the door shut from the outside, re-drew her pistol, side-stepped her way in a long arc around the helicopter's perimeter, and boarded through a door on the other side. One of the AR-15-toting warriors jumped on board right behind her.

"Get us outta here, now!" yelled the nurse. "Let the paramedics and Walter Reed take care of the casualty!"

Although the pilot was technically in charge, he accepted the nurse's order and took off with the maximum upward thrust that the laws of physics and the rules of the government would allow.

The nurse knelt beside Ann who was still lying on the helicopter's deck. As the craft ascended the nurse straddled Ann's thighs, put one hand firmly on her forehead, and held onto a handle with her other hand. This was the best she could do to stabilize Ann's spine for the moment.

The other soldier jumped into the co-pilot seat, threw on a headset, and then uncovered one ear so he could communicate with the nurse. "I see the ambulance lights now," he yelled. "It looks like they're about thirty seconds away from getting to our injured guy on the ground. How's your patient?"

"Let me know when you can find me some stable air, so I can assess Ann Higgins and get her gurney strapped down!" yelled the nurse.

"Give me twenty seconds," the pilot said. "We'll be out of sniper range in just a few more clicks."

The nurse looked down at Ann, "I don't think she's bleeding, and she's obviously breathing, so I don't think twenty seconds is going to be a problem."

Kent Higgins was standing and hanging onto a strap with one hand while bracing himself against the helicopter wall with another. As much as he wanted to hold and protect Ann, he knew that it was best to let this brave, remarkable nurse continue to work.

"All right," the pilot yelled a few moments later. "We should have a pretty smooth ride for a while."

The nurse knelt beside Ann, grabbed her stethoscope, and checked her vitals. "Well Ann, your heart's racing like crazy, but so is mine. For somebody who just left a battle zone, your blood pressure's actually okay." She used a penlight to check her pupils. "Equal and reactive. That's good," the nurse said. "You took quite the bump on the head flying backwards into that Suburban. But so far, everything looks okay."

The nurse continued to examine Ann, searching for bruises, broken bones, sprains, strains, and any other signs of injury. She found a small goose egg on the back of Ann's head and declared it a badge of honor.

"Hey everyone," yelled the pilot. "I just got good news." Our guy on the ground is wounded but not seriously. It's too early to be specific, but they think he's on his way into surgery to rebuild his shoulder. That flak jacket slowed down the bullet quite a bit. I guess the surgeons will tell us exactly how much."

Kent Higgins knelt down beside the nurse. "I used to be a respiratory therapist. How can I help?"

"Do you remember your lifts?"

"Absolutely," Higgins said. "But I've never executed a one point six second patient-gurney transfer into a helicopter before like you just did. Go easy on me."

The nurse smiled and her eyes beamed with well-deserved pride. "Well, let's stabilize her spine and lift her gurney over to the wall where we can strap her in."

The lieutenant governor slid his hand and arms into position and then followed the nurse's lead. Together they pulled the gurney to one side of the craft, and locked it into place with straps. The nurse affixed some Velcro straps to her torso and head and reclined her.

Higgins walked toward the front of the craft and caught the attention of the two pilots and the nurse. "Thank you so much. I never imagined that we would put you in such danger. We owe you our lives."

"You're welcome, sir," the nurse said. "These are our lives. And we wouldn't have them any other way."

CHAPTER 87

SIOUX FALLS

The commander's phone vibrated. He picked it up and saw a text from Nichols. He touched the screen, opened the message and read.

> *Got one shot off. Missed. She's gone on helicopter. I escaped into some woods. Caught taxi.*

The commander broke into an immediate, profuse sweat. By the time he stood up his shirt was drenched and drops of perspiration ran from his forehead. He stormed around a desk and kicked his bitch wolf, Imelda. "Damn!"

CHAPTER 88

IN FLIGHT OVER INDIANA

Errol Rivera was cruising at 12,000 feet and traveling at 240 knots, when a twenty-seven year old honorably discharged airborne specialist and reservist, who frequently attached with Rivera for vaguely documented missions, informed him that he had an urgent message from Lieutenant Governor Higgins."

"Thank you, soldier. Please read it to me."

> First, Ann's brain scan shows definite positive response for Steve Hewitt according to Bocelli. Brilliant move bringing her here. Thank you. Calling governor to indict and arrest. Second, we took fire boarding helicopter. We're fine. One man down but not critical.

Rivera's eyes blazed with anger. Through his microphone, he spoke to everyone on the flight who was wearing a headset. "Somebody messed with an *Espada Rápida*! What's next warriors?"

"Justice! Justice! Justice!" they yelled in unison. "The walls of prison or the halls of Hell!"

It was *Espada Rápida*'s code. They would trust the police and the courts, and they would do all they could to find their brother's attacker and have him arrested. But he'd better not put up a fight or he would never live to see the walls of prison.

"Nobody messes with my warriors!" Rivera said into the microphone in a dignified baritone voice. Then he returned to the soldier who had communicated the message from Kent Higgins moments before. "Thank you, warrior. Tell the lieutenant governor that I'm also calling the governor." The soldier returned to his post and relayed the message.

Rivera piloted the plane onward through the dark. Soon there would be glimmers of sunrise in the eastern sky, but Rivera would not see them through his westward pointed windshield. He contemplated the investigation into the second would-be assassin of Ann Higgins. Fortunately he would have excellent access to an investigation that occurred on military grounds.

The same warrior interrupted his thoughts. "You have a message from Z in Sioux Falls,"

"What does it say?"

> *Attorney general on the move. Flight plan says Sioux Falls. Allie Stoker missing, presumed kidnapped. Will advise.*

Rivera radioed a request for in-flight refueling so the Osprey could make it back to Sioux Falls without another stop. Then he turned back to the warrior and said, "Tell Z that our ETA is an hour and thirty minutes." Rivera eased the throttle slightly forward and the Osprey increased its speed to 248 knots. "Also tell Z to secure the rest of the Higgins family. Since Allie Stoker's been kidnapped, we need to safeguard Ann's kids and parents, too."

"Yes, sir!"

"And can you please circulate a few pictures of the South Dakota attorney general amongst the crew? Something tells me we'll be meeting Steve Hewitt real soon."

CHAPTER 89

"Lieutenant, please take over the controls for me," ordered Rivera to his co-pilot. Rivera remained in the pilot's seat and swiveled sideways to take the phone from the communications specialist who was ordered into the cabin. "Send Troy Stoker a secure message. Tell him to keep us updated of his position and developments as he searches for Allie. If he finds her location, we need to know immediately. Now patch me through, securely, to the governor."

A few minutes later, the governor's voice flowed into his headphones. "Colonel Rivera, I pride myself on being in touch with generals and colonels in our state. How come we haven't spoken much?"

"We've only met one other time, sir."

The governor remembered the colonel. "You came to Pierre to brief us about terrorists who might try to use helicopters and crop dusters to terrorize the food supply within our quiet state of South Dakota," the governor said. "Your reputation precedes you Colonel Rivera."

"I lay low and serve, sir. I love my country, sir. I love South Dakota—especially because it is about the only place I can feel some calm anymore. Well, that and the red rock country of southern Utah. I can only exist in places that are the complete opposite of a Central American jungle."

"I can appreciate that, Colonel," the governor said before clearing his voice. "Our South Dakota National Guard Adjunct General says I'm supposed to follow your orders strictly, Colonel. Did you know he calls you Chief Crazy Ass?"

"Indeed, I do. I've never discouraged him from it and I've never had a shred of evidence to refute it."

"In spite of what he calls you, we are supposed to follow your orders to the letter, sir!" the governor said.

"Thank you, governor. I will use my new powers to get you to reverse healthcare reform. Is that simple enough for you, Chief Master Sergeant?" Rivera joked.

"All of a sudden, I agree with your nickname. May I call you CCA for short?"

"Let's just keep it more formal," Rivera said in jest. "You can call me Chief for short if you please. I order you to get your sorry butt out of my site. Thank you. That is all Sergeant Governor."

The governor laughed. He had met untouchable warriors before and he respected them deeply. "I'm about to leave for Sioux Falls, Colonel. Can you please tell me why you've called? I understand that it relates to the Ann Higgins situation."

"Mr. Governor, last evening I accompanied Ann to the National Institute of Mental Health. I had her examined by a specialist in a cutting edge type of MRI, called fMRI. It is able to monitor the brain's reactions to events. We ask people questions and the machine detects the answer, even if the person decides not to respond. We can show someone a picture of food they don't like and the fMRI shows us how the brain registers that."

"Yes, I saw it on *60 Minutes* a few years ago. Very powerful. Very futuristic."

"Well sir, for Ann Higgins it's not futuristic," Rivera said. "For her, fMRI is now."

"So she's been in this machine?"

"Yes. And her mind is very much alert, discerning, thinking, and feeling."

"Amazing."

"Yes," Rivera said. "But what is more amazing is when we showed her pictures of numerous people, including you, she indicated that one of those people was the man who tried to kill her."

"Steve Hewitt." The sorrow was evident in his voice. He had trusted Hewitt and esteemed him as a prosecutor.

"Mr. Governor. I know you got a call from your lieutenant governor asking you to arrest the attorney general based on East Coast science that sounds far-fetched. I'm just calling you to confirm that this is for real. You have probable cause and our attorney general is a crook." Rivera paused for a moment. "Sir, I don't know why, but Hewitt's flying to Sioux Falls as we speak. I think he's coming here to do some damage control. Ann Higgins is getting better, and he's worried that soon she'll be able to talk. Little does he know, she's spoken."

"Colonel Rivera, thank you. I trust Kent Higgins, and I've already started the process of drawing up indictments. This just helps confirm my intuition that I'm doing the right thing."

"Sir, you're welcome. It's a little early to report, but we will have more evidence for you about just how dirty your AG is. It will flow in during the next twenty-four hours or so. But for now, I've got a kidnapping to solve and a jackal to catch."

The men ended the phone call, and then Rivera turned on his microphone so the whole crew could hear what he was about to say. "All right, warriors!" bellowed Rivera. "Change in plans. Let's let air traffic control in Sioux Falls know that we will not be landing at the airport. We will be arriving in their airspace, for reconnaissance, search, and rescue of a kidnap victim. Get those guns ready people!"

CHAPTER 90

The Higgins kids were sleeping comfortably while their grandparents slumbered in the guest bedroom where they had slept most nights since the brutal attack on Ann. Two guards were awake and alert. They videoed and documented every car that drove by as well as every phone call. They also catalogued joggers and dog walkers, but there were few of those during January in South Dakota.

When both of their phones vibrated at the same time, the warriors knew something was up. Their texts informed them that two other warriors would soon arrive, and the whole Higgins family was supposed to climb into the car and drive straight to the airport. Minutes later the four warriors were kindly but firmly awakening the Higgins kids and grandparents. When the warriors gave them a pre-arranged codeword that proved they could be trusted, the Higgins family responded with vigor.

"Where are we going?" asked Todd.

"We'll tell you once we're all in the car," said the armed man behind him. "You never know who's listening."

"How do we know I can trust you?" Todd asked. "Are you police? How come your uniforms don't have any markings?"

"Excellent questions, Todd. I wish everybody were as suspicious as you," said the man who led the group out through the garage door with his pistol drawn. "First, we gave you the codeword. Second, your security detail let us in on orders from Rivera." Todd was more convinced. "Third, did you see your cell phone?" Todd's phone was on silent, which was the norm for his cell phone at night. As he walked through the garage to get in the car he punched a few buttons. There was a text from his dad that had arrived four minutes ago—or about one minute before the men's arrival.

> *You can trust the two men I'm sending, son. Ask for the*
> *codeword. See you soon.*

Todd tucked the phone away and sprinted the remaining paces to the large, dark gray SUV where a driver awaited him with an open door. He leaped inside and assumed the middle seat in the passenger's row. The extraction team also jumped in the vehicle. Once everyone was inside, the garage door opened and the SUV backed out of the driveway and onto the dark, quiet neighborhood street. As the car drove away briskly, the driver introduced himself. "Hi, everyone. I'm Bullfrog."

"Hi, Bullfrog. Where are we going?" Todd asked.

"We're taking you to a secure National Guard hanger at the airport. I'm not sure what the plans are after that, but I suspect it involves a rendezvous with your parents."

"Are you guys police?" Todd asked. He was doing all the talking for the family, apparently.

"No."

"FBI?"

"No."

"Military?"

"Sort of."

"What do you mean, sort of?"

"Look, Todd. We're not in a position right now to give a lot of details. For now just know that we're the men assigned to keep your family safe. We also hope to be the people who capture whoever it was who hurt your mom."

Todd decided not to pursue his line of questioning further and during the rest of the ride the conversation was about the different weapons and gadgets the men had. When they arrived at the airport, the sentries allowed the car through with no scrutiny. As they pulled into the hangar, there were a few other women and men in the same non-descript uniform. The Higgins kids and grandparents, still wearing their pajamas, robes, and slippers, piled out of the car.

"We need to get you out of town and to a safe place," Bullfrog said. "These pilots know where they're supposed to take you."

"Follow me," said a woman who appeared by her suntan to be in her mid-fifties. But by her smile and level of fitness, she seemed much younger. She took them through a door and into another large hanger where a small plane awaited.

"Cool," said the youngest Higgins child. "It's like a small jet."

"That's exactly what it is," the pilot said walking toward the steps. "Climb aboard." Once inside the cabin, the pilot explained, "Kids, you each need to choose a fake name that you'll go by for the next few days. Can you do that?" After two minutes of considering different names and changing their minds a few times, they had all settled on new names. "Okay, your new last name is Smith, and you are from Orlando, Florida. That's your cover story. It will protect your identity and your mother."

The kids found this exciting and they were all going along with it. Todd, whose new name was now Brad, raised his hand and asked, "Are we ever coming back to Sioux Falls?"

"I can almost guarantee it," the pilot said. "Now during this flight you will only use each other's new names. There is a prize for anybody who can go the whole flight without using anybody's true name. Anybody who pulls it off gets to try a flight on a new machine called the Malloy Hoverbike. It's experimental and my team is testing it out at a location near where your mom and dad are. It's sort of like a bicycle that hovers off the ground."

"Cool!" the kids said almost simultaneously.

"We have a super-safe testing facility where you can try it. That is, if you don't use your Sioux Falls names during the flight," the pilot said. Then, she explained about safety in the airplane and showed them where the bathroom was, how to work the onboard computer system and iPads, and where they could find some food.

Thirty minutes later the plane was in the air and none of the Higgins were sleeping. Within a few short hours they would re-unite with their mom in a hospital in Philadelphia. They were all calling each other by their new, fake names, and so far, nobody had disqualified himself or herself from trying out the Hoverbike.

CHAPTER 91

Brian Berg directed his pickup truck off of Interstate 229 onto the Tenth Street exit. Traveling west toward downtown, Haslam ordered Berg to turn right at the Great Western Bank building. Berg veered his truck onto First Avenue. "Pull over right there, Brian. Leave your signal light on. We'll only be there for about sixty seconds."

Berg did as he was told, but he was starting to resent following orders all the time. Sure, Sarah Haslam had gone to medical school. But Brian Berg had been in the military, trained at the police academy, worked for a short time as a police officer, and knew about investigation from his work at South Dakota Medical Board. He was quite confident that he knew more about kidnapping and hostage management than Sarah Haslam.

"I need to get rid of this phone," Haslam said. As Berg brought the truck to a stop, Haslam jumped out of the truck, yanked a ski glove off Allie's hand, and slammed the door. With no hesitation, Haslam walked to the front of the truck and set the phone on the asphalt a few inches in front of Berg's front passenger tire. "Brian. Pull forward!" As Allie Stoker listened to her phone shattering into dozens of bits and pieces, she felt unconcerned. She was confident that the GPS unit would still remain intact and transmit for a few more hours. Troy had chosen that particular phone model precisely for this lifesaving feature.

"If anything bad ever happens to you, just crushing this phone will not disable it," he had said a few months before.

Even if they left it behind, lying on the asphalt in pieces, it would serve as a valuable clue to investigators. Allie was certain that Troy's paranoia would set off his intuition within minutes of her last text. It was a given that he was already suspicious. The question was, did Troy let his courtesy for his patient's time and attention override his conscience tonight?

But Allie's hopes were strained when Haslam scooped up all of the little pieces and narrated her next move. "Listen to this, Allie! Here goes your former phone into the drink," she yelled as she flung the glove, filled with state-of-the-art cell phone components, toward the Big Sioux River. With Allie's vision obscured by the painted sunglasses, her hearing was particularly sharp. She hoped and prayed that she would hear the components hitting a frozen section of the river and remain on the ice above the water. Time almost stood still as she listened for the results of Haslam's lob. The first moment of despair entered her heart as a splash informed her that the technology she was relying upon was meeting a watery doom.

CHAPTER 92

"Only two miles to the 10th Street exit," Stoker said aloud as he observed that he was traveling ninety-three miles per hour. He continuously shifted his vision from the road, to the state-of-the-art LED instrument cluster, then to his cell phone that was tracking Allie. Her phone's position had been stationary for about a minute and with any luck he would catch up to it in another three minutes. "I'm coming for you honey," he said out loud. The road was clear before him and he glanced again to see that he was maintaining his speed. When he looked at the phone she was still just over the 10th Street Bridge. And then, the icon just disappeared.

"No, no, no, no!" yelled Stoker. Grasping the phone he hit speed dial number three.

The response was almost instantaneous. "This is Z."

"I just lost her cellphone signal. That GPS tracking device just quit all of a sudden. That was my lifeline and now I'm out of options. I really need your help, buddy. If anyone can find her, it's you."

"Take your best guess on where she is and then let's meet there ASAP. I'm just minutes behind you with my microphones. They'll be our best tools. We'll listen to every laugh, fart, and argument within a twenty-block radius until we find her. If she speaks, we'll hear her."

"Her last cell phone tracking signal came from just west of the 10th Street Bridge. My guess is they—whoever they are—were taking her downtown for some reason. Let's park at Nordic Hall and we'll go from there."

"I'm also bringing some night vision scopes and thermal imaging equipment for reading heat signatures. Have you called the police?"

"No! That's the last thing I want to do."

"I agree. That's why we've called in *Espada Rápida*!" Z said.

"Who's *Espada Rápida*?"

"Do you remember that confidentiality document you signed on the plane on the way to Washington D.C.?"

"I die if I divulge?" Stoker said.

"That's the one," affirmed Z. "You're going to learn a lot about a band of brothers and sisters, *Espada Rápida*, with amazing skills and backgrounds in the next few hours — and you need to keep our secrets. If Allie was kidnapped, people in high places are pulling the strings to get to you and Ann Higgins. If you call the cops, you'll get disinformation at best. At worst you alert her kidnappers, and she gets moved further underground. That's why we need to rely on *Espada Rápida* instead of the police."

"So you and your band of swift swords are going to help me rescue my wife?" Stoker asked.

"Yes. That's what we do. Over the last seventy-two hours, we've also integrated with the Drug Enforcement Administration and we're about to brief the FBI about the houses in Chelsea Crossing, the men who jumped bail here, and that so-called business, Green Growth Ventures in Reno."

Stoker was just getting off of the freeway, entering downtown, and making his way toward the Nordic Hall rendezvous point. "Thank you, Z. I'll do whatever you need me to."

"I need your permission to start recording all your calls," Z said.

"You've got it. But after we get Allie back, I'm changing my number. I don't trust you quasi-government freaks."

"Go ahead," Z said. "It won't matter."

CHAPTER 93

"Okay, Brian. Let's go show Allie her new place." Brian drove down First Avenue. Allie could not see where she was because of the painted sunglasses she was wearing, but she could judge by the sounds, smells, and frequent stops that she was probably downtown. Berg maneuvered the truck to Mall Avenue. They pulled up into the dark alleyway adjacent to one of the older buildings that occupied the block between 10th and 11th Streets. Before Allie got out, Haslam checked her hostage's hat and sunglasses to make sure nobody would recognize her. Then she removed the zip ties from her legs. She left Allie's wrists bound and threw a parka over her shoulders.

"Hey Brian, why don't you jump out, come around, and put a gun on our little feline friend, Allie cat, here?" Berg jumped out of the truck, and as he walked around, Haslam leaned over and whispered in Allie's ear. "Now listen here you little hussy. We're going to walk into your new little apartment. If you say a word, scream or run, I'll drop you right here and now. I'll shoot Berg in the knee, too, and leave him to take the fall. I'll be four states away before my name ever surfaces. Do you understand me, sweetie?"

Allie nodded her head in agreement, but said nothing. Brian opened the truck door, "Out you go, Allie."

Haslam was livid that Berg would use Allie's name out in the open. "Shut up you idiot!" Haslam whispered her rebuke with fiendish intensity. "What if somebody heard you mention her name?"

As Allie emerged from the car she could only see her feet through the crack at the bottom of the painted glasses. However, the aromas of a bakery hit her like a warm summer's breeze. These were not the scents of sweet rolls, donuts, French bread, or cookies. Allie smelled whole wheat, nuts, and wheat bran mixed in with a little cinnamon and other earthy spices. Instantly, she knew where she was. She was close to Ruby's Coffee Spot, the café that served Troy the unpleasant blueberry muffin just a few days earlier—and claimed to have the best dirty Chai in the Dakotas.

"Up the stairs, missy!" Haslam said as Berg opened the dilapidated back door to the old cinderblock building. "I got a great deal on your rent, honey. I think you'll love the place," Haslam said as she led Allie up two flights of stairs. As they approached a door on the third floor, Sarah Haslam removed a key ring and unlocked two deadbolt locks on a reinforced door. As they turned on the lights and entered the room, it was evident that this space was not an apartment at all. It was an office space with old pieces of cubicle walls, a couple of outdated desks, and four or five office chairs strewn about.

"Welcome home, honey!" Berg said with a failed tone of maliciousness in his voice. "I hope you love what we've done with the place. We haven't had a chance to freshen up much yet, but you'll see that I've taken a minute to board up the windows and install a soundproof reinforced door. That spot over there is yours," Berg explained pointing to an office chair in the center of the room.

As Sarah Haslam closed the door and secured the deadbolts, Allie just stood inside the doorway looking around. She was not going to follow Brian Berg's implied suggestion that she walk to the chair and sit down. But Haslam was much more forthright.

"Get your ass over to that chair and sit down," she demanded while shoving Allie toward the chair. "You've got new bosses now." Allie sat down on the chair as Haslam continued to lecture. "If you listen and obey, you just might live to leave this room one day. But first, we need your help catching a bigger fish. Which reminds me, we need to make a little phone call. But before we do, let's get something straight," growled Haslam as she reared back and brought a full force palm slap to bear on Allie's cheek and ear. "Keep your big mouth shut! While you're here, you'll be quiet."

Berg wanted in on this action. He was trying to re-establish himself as a tough guy. "Quiet. You have to stay quiet!" Berg yelled as his tough guy voice failed and cracked. His hands began trembling again. "You have a place to piss and crap," he said pointing to a bathroom with no door. "Just keep your yap shut."

"Hey Brian, get me that duct tape!" ordered Haslam. She turned back to Allie. "No yelling and screaming or carrying on, or we'll put a bullet in one knee with this silenced subsonic twenty-two," Haslam said removing the gun from her coat pocket. Haslam had crazed look in her eyes. "If you stay quiet, we feed you. Silence earns you bathroom breaks. On the other hand, stunts earn you pain, hunger, and a day or two between bathroom breaks. So just shut your pie-hole, bitch."

Allie Stoker looked up. "I'll keep quiet, Sarah." She continued to look her kidnapper in the eye. "You will hear little out of me." Allie sat up a little taller in her chair. "You need your silence, because I want you to hear every creaking floorboard, every slight breeze of wind against the windows, each opening and closing door on the floors above or beneath us, and each car coming to a stop out on the street. Oh, I'll stay quiet. Don't you worry." Allie paused for a moment and then continued. "Because I want each of those sounds to make you wonder, 'Is that him? Is that Troy Stoker coming to reconcile with you and rescue me?'"

"You keep clinging to that hope there, Allie cat. First, Troy has to find you. But before that, he has to know you're gone. He's probably still in his office consoling some poor sappy housewife who is suffering from garden-variety, suburbia clinical depression. She's probably twenty tissues into the story about how her husband doesn't find her so attractive anymore."

"Troy's a rescuer. He always has been. During his time in Bosnia and the Balkans he rescued families from soldiers and terrorists. In Jamaica he rescued people from a Hurricane. In Indonesia he fought back drug runners masquerading as monks. In Guatemala he went toe-to-toe with a general to save the lives of a band of soldiers. Every day he rescues people from abusers, oppressors, and even sometimes themselves. You've vastly underestimated an exceptional man. He's going to find me. He's going to kick your ass. You have no idea what he's capable of!"

"I can't wait for him to get here!" Haslam shrieked as she slapped Allie across the cheek, knocking her off of her chair and to the floor. With her hands still bound Allie could do little to break her fall. Haslam stepped toward her and hovered over her. "We have the element of surprise!" she hissed as she lowered her voice to a whisper, knelt down, and brought her face eye-to-eye with Allie. "Your little hero will come through that door and your final memories of him will be a hollow-point bullet blowing his brains out of the back of his skull. But don't worry, I'll make sure you survive, so that memory haunts you for decades." Then Haslam turned to Berg. "Allie needs a hug, Brian. Give her a hug," she ordered.

Allie used her bound hands to push herself off the floor and back into a standing position.

Berg looked awkwardly back at Haslam. He was not sure how to handle this strange request. *She's using me to help intimidate Allie*, thought Berg.

"Come on, Brian. Chop, chop! She needs comfort. She's going through a hard time." Berg looked at the floor and quickly ran his right hand through his hair and then rubbed the top of his ear anxiously. "What's wrong?" Haslam patronized. "Has it been that long since you've hugged somebody? Have you forgotten how?"

Berg slowly walked toward Allie. In a moment of mental clarity, Brian Berg realized the dangerous position he was in if he intimidated Allie on this new level. Kidnapping Stoker's wife already made him fear for his safety. As he thought about the consequences of menacing Allie, with a slight sexual overtone, introduced a white-hot terror into his psyche. He couldn't begin to imagine how Stoker would react.

As he awkwardly walked toward Allie, his back was briefly turned to Haslam, allowing him to mouth the word "Sorry!" in an exaggerated gesture toward the woman he had kidnapped. She understood Berg's message. The uncomfortable man tentatively wrapped his arms around Allie embracing her in an awkward hug, mostly squeezing her shoulders and being careful not to embrace her in a full-body hug. Allie was thankful that the zip ties subjecting her wrists made it impossible to return the bizarre hug borne of Haslam's psychotic whim.

Berg whispered, "Allie the last thing I want is hell from your husband. I'm sorry about this."

"Thank you," whispered Allie sincerely as Berg embraced her. It was that moment when Allie Stoker knew she had won him over. Haslam's attempt to intimidate her had backfired and increased Berg's guilt about his actions, as well as his sympathy toward Allie. Brian's healthy sense of fear and vague sense of decency further intertwined to ensure that he would never harm Allie Stoker, a person who was now more than a name. Now that she was a human to him, she was safe from his aggressions.

Sarah Haslam misinterpreted Allie Stoker's thank you as gratitude for the supposedly comforting hug. In a falsely perky voice she said, "Now about that phone call." She opened up a desk drawer and removed a small laptop computer. "I love technology. You can buy anything. I only had to pay three hundred sixty dollars cash for this low-end computer that connects to super-fast Internet. I can talk to anyone in the world anonymously. But right now, there is only one person I want to reach. If anybody traces our call to dear old Troy, it makes it look like the call is coming from a big black hole in Baja, Mexico." Haslam removed a set of earphones from the drawer, plugged them into the computer, and started punching some keys. Two minutes later she was ready to call. "Okay, Allie. How do we reach him if he's in therapy?"

"The only way to interrupt therapy is by sending a text that contains the phrase 'almost Armageddon.' Troy always says that it better be almost Armageddon if we are going to interrupt a patient."

"What's his number?" asked Haslam. After Allie provided her with the phone number that only a handful of people knew Haslam created a text message that read:

Almost Armageddon. I need to give you some disturbing
news about Allie. Rough day skiing.

As Sarah Haslam hit the send button, a disturbed tear of joy trickled from her left eye.

CHAPTER 94

NEAR WASHINGTON PAVILION, SIOUX FALLS

Troy Stoker turned off of 13th Street and pulled into the parking lot at Nordic Hall. He removed his laptop computer from his brief case, turned it on, and brought up a map of downtown Sioux Falls. He knew this city well, but he realized how much he usually envisioned his city in a two-dimensional mindset. The restaurants the Stokers frequented were all on street level. He only ascended to upper floors of buildings when he visited his lawyer. Even when the Stokers went to mass, they worshiped on the ground floor at the Cathedral of St. Joseph. But Stoker knew that most of the buildings in downtown Sioux Falls were multi-story buildings. If Allie was kidnapped and in the immediate area, he needed to come up with a plan to search, block-by-block and story-by-story.

As Stoker was zooming his map in on the area near Nordic Hall, his phone beeped. He quickly retrieved his phone and opened the message.

> *Almost Armageddon. I need to give you some disturbing*
> *news about Allie. Rough day skiing.*

"Thank you, God," Stoker prayed out loud. "It's only a ski injury. How 'disturbing' can that be for a person with perfect superhuman pain tolerance?" He pushed the callback button, and on the second ring, the call picked up. "Hello, this is Troy Stoker. It sounds like you might be treating my wife, Allie there?"

"I guess you could say we're treating her, Troy. This is Dr. Haslam," declared Sarah.

Stoker recognized Sarah Haslam's voice instantly. The relief he felt moments earlier was gone, and the indignation and resolve returned instantly to his heart and mind. Stoker's interrogation instincts engaged, and he thought of a strategy that Haslam would not expect. "Let's get this over right now, Sarah," Stoker said in a strong, calm voice. "Let's cut you an immunity deal. Because you know," Stoker paused for a moment, "we've known each other for a while, so you know I will be straight with you. I will vigorously petition my good friends for immunity if you free Allie right now, and tell us what you know about the commander. If not, you know this may not end well."

Haslam stuttered for a moment. The proposition surprised her and made her forget the clever words she had planned on using to puzzle him. Haslam simply said, "We've got Allie." She was angry that she had forgotten her witty statements that would make Stoker squirm. Stammering she said, "I can't wait to remove a finger, experiment with acid on her skin, or just turn her into my martial arts target!" Her psychosis and rage had taken over and supplanted her intelligent plan with violent wrath and empty threats.

Stoker remained calm. He recognized that she was suffering from some delirium, probably due to sleep deprivation and the disappointment of being kicked out of her residency. "Just make sure you keep her cuffed if you try fighting her. She'll kick your ass."

"Not unless she wants another sandbag shotgun round to her hip," Haslam said.

"So that's how you overpowered her? You tried to shoot her in the butt but missed by a few inches?"

Haslam fell for the unexpected question. "Something like that."

Stoker strongly suspected that somebody had recently introduced Haslam to sandbag shotgun rounds; he used that salient hunch to try and learn more. "Is the G.I. Joe who taught you about the sandbag shells there with you?"

Haslam hesitated and instantly Stoker knew Haslam was not working alone. He leapt on the opportunity to nail down the fact before Sarah could respond. "Is he Army or Marines?"

"It doesn't matter."

"What's his name?"

Haslam paused, decided to ignore his question, and remembered some of the menacing points she had intended to make before Stoker had so effectively distracted her. "You've made all the wrong enemies, Troy. You should know better than to mess with me or with the medical board."

"The state medical board is using kidnapping as an enforcement strategy now?" Stoker asked. "That's dramatically more effective than letters of concern — and only half as crazy."

"Let's just say you're a pilot study, Troy. We'll have to see how it goes," Haslam taunted. Her witty response catalyzed her confidence. "Look, Troy. You've stuck your nose in where it doesn't belong. The people who wanted Ann Higgins dead are not people you want to mess with. You've gotten too close, and they want assurances."

"They want him dead," muttered Berg like an idiot. Stoker had heard the words, but he did not recognize the voice. Haslam glared at Berg.

"Student loans getting you down, Sarah?" Stoker asked. It was another unexpected question to try to throw her off. "There are better ways to make cash."

"No, you idiot. This is about revenge. I volunteered for this assignment," Haslam lied.

"So is this the part where you let me talk to Allie? You do want to prove that you actually have my wife, don't you?"

Haslam realized that it was the next logical step, but it frustrated her that Stoker was in charge of the conversation. She hesitated, but could not think of anything else to say, so she unplugged her earphones from the computer, which activated the built-in speaker. "You're on speaker. Any funny business and I'll treat both of you to the sounds of a sandbag shotgun shell and a whole lot of screaming."

"Hi, Troy," Allie said. She was careful to sound brave despite the fear she felt. "I'm all right. Don't worry about me. No broken bones or bleeding. For kidnappers, they've been semi-civil, so far."

"Allie, my love." He made sure his voice was confident and cheerful. He was even a touch casual. "Thanks for letting me know. Just hold on and pray. We'll work this out."

"Troy. To make it through this, I keep envisioning a simple moment I want to share with you again."

"What's that?"

"Promise me," Allie said, "once we've made it through this ordeal, we'll brew up dirty chai and bake blueberry muffins."

Stoker's adrenaline surged as his mind instantly recognized Allie's clue. "Mrs. Stoker. I hereby promise you that we will enjoy dirty Chai and your *extra-healthy* blueberry muffins." Stoker's calm reassurance disguised the energy and optimism that poured into his soul. He knew approximately where she was.

"I love you—"

Haslam plugged the earphones back into the computer and cut off the communication between the Stokers. "Hey Troy, baby," she mocked. "We all love you. If you've got an extra muffin or two, consider sharing with all of us."

Stoker ignored her mockery as he saw Z pull up beside him in his well-worn Toyota 4-Runner. Stoker stayed focused on Sarah Haslam. "At what point do you tell me not to call the police?"

Again, Stoker was leading the conversation. His suggestion clouded her mind and all she could say was, "No cops, or you never see Allie again!"

"Right," Stoker said. "If what you say is true, Sarah, the powers that be already know that you've kidnapped Allie. The police would be useless to me. If I can promise you one thing, I promise you I'm not calling the cops."

Stoker's comment hit her hard. Until now, she did not realize how quickly and how deeply she had sunk into an intense conspiracy. Stintson and Berg had lured her into a ring of power that could even manipulate the police. Just weeks ago, Sarah Haslam had been an indomitable doctor, but now she was expendable—perhaps even more expendable than Brian Berg.

Stoker interrupted her thought. "Can I ask you one more question, Sarah?"

"Uh, sure," Haslam stumbled. She was distracted by the new vulnerability she felt.

"What do they want from me?"

Haslam spoke close to the computer, lowered her voice an octave, and whispered, "Very soon, you will have an opportunity to show some goodwill." Then she disconnected the call.

CHAPTER 95

"I heard—and recorded—the whole call!" exclaimed Z as he jumped out of his car.

"Oh no you didn't," Stoker said as he stepped out of his Bronco. "You did *not* hear the message between the lines. I know generally where Allie is!"

"What? What do you mean? How did you glean her location from that short conversation about sandbag shells, G.I. Joe, and blueberry muffins?

"It was the blueberry muffins," Stoker said as he reached inside the car and grabbed his bulletproof vest, nine-millimeter pistol, and a weapons belt containing flash-bang grenades, a telescoping baton, two ammunition clips, a multi tool, and a basic first-aid kit. Stoker thought for a moment, removed the first aid kit and Taser, and threw them back in the car. "I presume we're taking your car, since it holds all your gear?" Stoker grabbed his computer and headlamp.

"Yes. And also because there is nothing stealthy about your Bronco," Z joked. "Now explain to me how blueberry muffins told you where she is."

Stoker opened Z's passenger door. "Let's drive up Phillips Avenue and I'll show you. It has to do with a café there." Stoker said as he slid in, closed the door and strapped on his seatbelt. Z followed his lead and moments later the 4Runner was turning left on Phillips Avenue.

"For your microphones to work, how close do we need to be?"

"Here in my Sioux Falls stash, I have a laser microphone that can hear for about a mile. We have more powerful microphones than that in other locations," Z bragged. "But distance is actually a secondary issue. Interference with other noises is our biggest obstacle. While we have ways of compensating for interference, there are an overwhelming number of sounds, which are impossible to predict, coursing through all the spaces in a city. Sometimes you have a great signal and you can hear a robbery, drug deal, or extortion going down. Then all of a sudden, another noise comes into your auditory field and interferes. It can be as simple as an electric heater kicking on, someone cooking a burrito in a nearby microwave, or a toilet flushing. My most miserable experience with interference happened when a voice coach in an apartment building in Dallas started a session with a middle-aged crazy lady who had recently experienced some kind of prophecy that she was going to be the next Lady Gaga."

"There's a diagnosis for that," Stoker said.

Z laughed. "I bet there are a few diagnoses, actually. Where would you start, Dr. Stoker?"

"Schizophrenia is definitely a possibility, along with delusional disorder," Stoker said. "She could also have a brief psychotic disorder, perhaps brought on by substance abuse, lack of sleep, or both. And by the way, when people have prophecies we call them hallucinations most of the time."

"What do you call them when they're not hallucinations?"

"Divine communication," Stoker said. "Sometimes things just line up. Sometimes a mother gets an accurate intuitive signal that her child needs help crossing a busy street. I saw a man last week who worked at his job for fifteen years. He got an overwhelming feeling that he needed to look for another job and he listened to that inner voice. He landed a new job one day before his employer went out of business. In the military I saw people on all sides of conflict listen to an inner voice that saved their lives. I listened to intuition once, a single second before a car crash. The crash still happened, but I walked away from a rollover because I veered right and braked at the precise moment another driver swerved into my lane."

Both men were silent for a second. "I guess it's a bit like microphones," Stoker said. "You have to filter out the bad signals and focus on the good ones. The lady who craved fame may have been listening to an overwhelming and unreasonable desire. Too many psychiatry patients hear voices stimulated by excess dopamine in their brains. Fortunately in most cases, we can help with that."

"Well I don't know much about psychiatry, but I do know that I have PTSD from listening to that lady sing."

"That's too bad. I strongly suspect that medicating her would've helped her out."

"Are you talking about the real Lady Gaga," Z asked, "or the lady in my microphone?"

"Both!" Stoker said with a laugh. "But you and your PTSD are a lost cause, buddy," he joked.

Stoker pointed his finger down the road. "Okay, do you see the sign up there? The one that say's Ruby's?"

"Ruby's Coffee Spot?" Z asked. "Home of the best dirty Chai in the Dakotas?"

"You've been there?"

"I happen to like dirty Chai, and Ruby's is pretty good."

"How do you like their pastries?"

"They should stick to coffee and tea. If that's healthy eating, please kill me now. I'm sure those recipes go over well in certain New York boroughs, San Francisco, and other places where shunning meat and smoking your herbs is the norm."

"Exactly!" Stoker agreed. "I hate their blueberry muffins, and Allie's not a fan of dirty Chai."

"So that was the cryptic code," Z exclaimed. "You married an intelligent woman. She knows that she is close to Ruby's and she let you know. Z parked his car and killed the engine.

"You give us civilians too little credit." Stoker said.

"I give you and Mrs. Stoker too little credit," rebutted Z as he jumped out of his car, opened the door directly behind him, and pulled a bag out of the back seat. "I rarely underestimate the average civilian—but I love it when I do." Z grabbed two bags of equipment and removed them from the car. "Let's go, Stoker. Let's find our way into one of these buildings. From a second or third floor we can start snooping. And please, leave that weapons belt here. We need to blend in, and we should not be barging in on anybody tonight."

"No problem, but don't even think about asking me to leave my gun."

"Never. Please bring two guns. Since you have a coat on, I think you should keep your body armor on, too."

Z closed his door and walked toward a brick apartment building. Stoker closed his door and followed. Two seconds later the car chirped as Z locked it. Stoker smelled the baked goods scents emanating from Ruby's, and the smells reinforced his dislike for the place. When they got to the apartment building, Z tried to enter, but the main door was locked. "I bet we're about to prove my point about the average civilian," Z said as he stepped back ten feet from the door. "Come right over here behind me, Stoker. On my signal just follow me." Z pulled his keys out of his pocket and the two men waited for about thirty seconds while Z watched the doorway patiently. When the door opened, Z whispered, "Here we go." He walked up to the door just as a tenant was leaving the apartment. When she saw Z holding his keys, she assumed he lived there. Z pretended to be pleasantly surprised by the person's arrival. "Oh, hello," Z said as he caught the door before it closed and held it open for Stoker. The tenant continued on her way, and Stoker and Z stepped into the apartment building.

They found a staircase and started climbing upward, as Z explained. "I actually love using the microphones from parking garages instead of buildings."

"Why?" Stoker inquired.

"Because they give you so many options for listening. From one parking garage I can spy on so many more people. You don't have to trespass—like we're doing now. If you pay to park there, you're a customer and you have free reign of the place."

"Would that hold up in a court of law?"

"I'll let you know if I ever find out," Z said. "I do what it takes to nail bad guys. The courts have their place. I concentrate on being effective and I almost always play by the rules. It's worked out really well for me—for the last four or five years at least."

Z and Stoker exited the stairwell on the third floor of the apartment building. They walked to the end of a hallway where there was a large window that looked out onto Phillips Avenue. Z opened one of the bags and produced two white jumpsuits. An iron-on decal on the back of each jumpsuit displayed a logo from a company supposedly called Owen Glass Inspectors. Z tossed one to Stoker and also handed him a hat. "Put these on and try to keep your back turned. I would hate for one of your acquaintances to recognize you." Both men dressed, and then Z handed Stoker a pair of headphones and began assembling cords, cables, and devices. "Give me a minute and I'll introduce you to a few of your Sioux Falls neighbors."

Thirty seconds later Stoker's earphones came to life. There was a lot of static and electronic-sounding noise. As Z played with dials and tapped keys on a small computer, more human sounds came into the mix. The jumble of conversations, traffic, water running, and televisions blaring was overwhelming. Z picked up the microphone and pointed it to his left. He started a slow sweeping motion. In his headphones Stoker heard a more organized and systemic series of sounds that corresponded to the locations Z targeted with the microphone.

"I can see where you're pointing, generally," Stoker said. "What floor are you on?"

"Right now I'm just calibrating, but we'll listen to everything" Fifteen seconds later, Z declared himself ready. "Okay, Troy. There's a system to doing this. We sweep from left to right and from the top down. We also sweep *into* the depth of the building from the back to the front. It's not a perfect science, but we can cover about ninety-five percent of a building. Are you ready?"

"Let's find Allie."

"The computer is going to be listening. We'll be using an algorithm that detects both threatening tones and tones of duress. It can also flag when a person is negotiating desperately. I'm talking about negotiation for your life, not driving a hard bargain on a real estate deal."

"What do we listen for?" Stoker asked.

"You are listening for Allie and Haslam's voices."

"Something tells me that Sarah's state of mind is going to have her talking a lot more than Allie," Stoker said.

"I'm no psychiatrist, but that makes perfect sense to me," Z said. "Allie will be saving her strength and using her brainpower to try and navigate her way out of this. Let's listen," Z said as he pointed the microphone again to the top-left of the window. "I bet we can reach three buildings from here. We can also listen through the very building we're standing in."

Z moved his microphone slowly from left to right. Stoker heard snippets of conversations about homework, bills, love, and anger. He heard televisions blaring twenty-four-hour news, movies, reality TV, and heated politics. He picked up on the sounds of exercise, praying, showering, belching, cavorting, and fighting. But he had not yet heard Allie or Sarah. After ten minutes of searching, a middle-aged man who appeared to be a tenant came walking toward them in the hallway. The instruments that Z and Stoker were using caught his attention and he wondered what they were doing. Stoker glanced briefly over his shoulder and instantly recognized the man, Carl Hunt, who was his patient. Z noticed the man approaching, and he started making up words, phrases, and numbers that he hoped would make him sound like a "glass inspector."

I'm detecting a three point six tolerance, which is well within range," Z said as if he knew what he was talking about.

"That's a good piece of glass," Stoker said while doing his best to imitate a Chicago accent.

"Glass inspectors?" inquired Mr. Hunt. Stoker's heart raced as he pretended to concentrate on a specific section of the window on the bottom right.

"This window has a good seal and it scores a ninety-four, no, make that a ninety-six," Stoker improvised while leaning in closer to the window. He pretended to inspect the caulking that held the glass in place.

Stoker was a convincing actor. Z tried not to laugh as he answered Mr. Hunt's question. "Yes we are. We're glass inspectors from Chicago. It's a mandate put in place by the Obama Administration." Mr. Hunt believed Z's creative cover story, and Stoker exerted tremendous energy to avoid breaking out into peals of laughter as Z continued to explain. "It's serious stuff. President Obama and the EPA didn't want excess energy loss through windows. Also they created twenty-six thousand new government jobs when they mandated glass inspectors. My friend, Carl here," Z said pointing to Stoker, "used to work as a computer programmer. But now we got these interest-free SBA loans from the Obama Administration. We've got our very own business now. We're entrepreneurs."

"You used to be a computer programmer? Isn't that pretty high-demand work?" Carl asked while Stoker still looked at the window with the intensity of an eye surgeon fixing a cataract.

"Well, you know. I guess he's still *technically* a programmer," Z said. "I mean, he's got the skills. We just choose to work as inspectors now. We're slowing global warming and saving the planet. I mean really, what do we need more? Will you die if you don't get another game to play on your phone, or do you want a planet with the right balance of greenhouse gasses?"

"I want a new game on my phone, you idiot!" Carl said. "There *is* no global warming. Do you make more as glass inspectors than you did at your previous jobs?"

"Oh, no." Z continued the charade. "We make about half, but the benefits to the planet are tremendous. We're involved in a much greater cause."

Carl was so incensed and agitated by the nonsensical conversation with these two so-called glass inspectors that he failed to recognize Stoker. "You two might be the most misguided, brainwashed souls I've ever met in my life. Maybe after this you can join AmeriCorps and teach Spanish as a third language to Vietnamese emigrants." Carl retreated to his apartment and slammed the door.

Given other circumstances, Stoker and Z would've laughed their butts off, but Allie was in danger and the comedic approach had all been part of a necessary charade to leave no reasonable trace about who they were and what they were doing. "Okay, Stoker. We're about half way done with this building. Let's keep going."

Z and Stoker swept the building for another twelve minutes. "I don't think she's in here, Troy," Z said. "Every time the computers have picked up duress or threatening tones, we have been able to isolate lover's quarrels and other arguments. Actually, the computers keep hitting on all the people who are watching the O'Reilly Factor. We need to write an algorithm that recognizes the voice of Bill O'Reilly and filters it out as a possibility."

"I agree," Stoker said. "I haven't heard Allie's voice or the voice of Sarah Haslam anywhere in this building. Is it time to move on?"

"Yes," Z said. For the next hour he and Stoker swept two other buildings and then swept the apartment building where they were trespassing. They had failed to hear Allie Stoker or Sarah Haslam, so Z loaded up the listening equipment and they left the apartment building.

A few minutes later Z and Stoker were on the rooftop of another building on Phillips Avenue. It was eighteen degrees and there was a moderate breeze.

This building was further down the street from the apartment building they had just left. "I like the tops of buildings," Z explained. "You don't get a lot of visitors and you have a pretty clear shot to your targets below. However it's obviously harder to hear what's occurring on the first floor, and sometimes the second, just depending on the situation. Much like tonight, we have to contend with wind. But the software can filter out wind and ambient noises."

"Can it filter out the loopers in their revelry on 10th and 11th Street?" Stoker asked.

"A little bit," Z said. "But our directional microphones will actually do a better job of staying in the haystack until we find that needle." As Z aimed the directional microphone at the top of the buildings across the street he began to sweep. The sounds were remarkably similar to the activities they had witnessed in the other buildings they had swept. They swept through the penthouse level and down into some empty offices. On the third floor, the first rooms to the left were completely void of noise. The computer detected nothing unusual as they listened through the center section of the building. *It's all just normal conversation and the sound of somebody eating*, thought Z.

"Wait!" Stoker insisted. "Go back there for just a second."

Z moved the directional microphone and turned some knobs. A man's voice was saying, "I've guarded prisoners in the Army, and I even arrested a full-bird colonel once for drunken and disorderly conduct when I was an M.P.," the voice of a man said with a hint of emotion. "But I've never felt the fear that I felt that day on the prairie west of town as the coyotes circled me, and the commander made it very clear that I was to follow his every order without question."

"How many coyotes were there, Brian?" the calm voice of Allie Stoker asked.

Stoker's eyebrows shot up and all of his senses went on full alert.

"Four or five, which may not seem like much. But, have you seen the teeth on a hungry, wild coyote?"

"No, never. But now that I've heard your story, I'll look it up on YouTube when we get out of here."

"That's her!" Stoker said. "That's Allie! She's talking with somebody named Brian."

Z picked up his radio and communicated the new finding to someone on his team named Abbie.

"Okay, what's next?" Stoker asked.

"Let's listen. Let's see what we can learn," Z said. "Patience and time are our greatest allies right now. Finding out who this Brian person is would also help us out."

Stoker and Z continued to listen to the conversation transpiring on the third floor across the street.

"So how did it all end?" Allie asked Brian.

"Oh, the commander just pulled out his side arm and shot it in the air. At that point all the coyotes hightailed it out of there."

"And what did you do?"

"Besides pissing my pants a little bit? I just watched the commander to see if I could figure out what to do next. I just followed his lead. And then I went home and started myself back on my aripiprazole again. Which reminds me, I need to take it." Berg removed a small pill container from his pocket and popped the pill in his mouth. "It's already helped throttle back my paranoia."

Stoker looked over at Z. "I think I know who this Brian is."

"So how'd you get mixed up in all of this, Brian?" Allie asked.

"Well, the commander's sort of like the Red Baron. He only goes after the easy kills, the easy targets. I guess I'm connected through my boss, Larry Stintson. You see, he's an easy target because he's got a few little problems that nobody knows about."

"That's Brian Berg!" blurted out Stoker. "That's Brian Berg, the guy from the state board who raided my office. We've got Haslam. We've got Berg. Let's get in there," Stoker said, as he stood, removed his headphones and cocked his Beretta out of instinct.

Z held up his hand and signaled for Stoker to stand down. "Keep listening, Troy. Allie's pulling some great intel out of your buddy Berg down there."

Stoker put his headphones back on and listened to Berg as he bore his soul to the woman he had just kidnapped. "He likes the commander's product, and when the commander found out he was a customer, Stintson and his mistress fell right into their little trap." Berg was silent for a minute and it sounded like he took three gulps of a drink. "That's as much as I've been able to figure out." They heard Berg make a deep exhale. "And me? I'm just the next guy down the food chain at the medical board. I was just following orders by going with the commander that day, out to be one with nature. But as you can see, he can become persuasive in a short period of time."

"I'm not excusing what you did, Brian," Allie said. "I'm not excusing what you're doing right now. But I will say that you were put into a catch twenty-two and I recognize that your motives were not sinister. When we get out of this, I will make sure the jury knows that."

Z turned to Stoker. "She's good, Doc. She's got him eating out of the palm of her hand."

The calm voice of Allie Stoker continued, "You were once willing to put your life on the line for the right thing when you fought for your country and served in the military. Now you need to figure out how to do the right thing again."

"If I surrender the commander will kill me," Berg said. "If I don't your husband and his friends might kill me, too."

"You've got to get caught without getting killed," Allie said. "Wait this thing out. I'll tell Troy how you were coerced. I'll tell him how you gave me a cautious, respectful hug when Haslam was trying to create an intimidation moment." Berg and Allie were silent for a few seconds. "Figure out how to survive the first ten seconds, Brian. When the police come busting in here, or our car gets pulled over, all you need to do is survive the first ten seconds and get arrested. It will all get so much easier after that."

"You watch too much T.V., Mrs. Stoker." Berg said.

"No, my crazy husband keeps reading me passages from all of his right-wing survival books. I just happen to remember that one."

Out in the freezing cold of a January night, Stoker smiled and said, "You know Z, she used to tease me when I read those preparedness ideas to her. That rule about surviving the first ten seconds came from a book about urban warfare."

"I know that book," Z said. "*War: Coming to a Neighborhood Near You.*" Z removed more equipment from his bag. "I liked that book a lot. I'll introduce you to the author one day, Troy." Z started setting up another device. "You keep listening, Troy. We're going to look at Allie and her abductors through another means."

In two minutes the new equipment was showing Z and Stoker the thermal images belonging to Allie and Brian Berg as they sat in the office space. "I only see two images," Z said. "This one on the left must be Berg and this one on the right is Allie. You can see that Berg is able to move freely, but Allie must be bound to something or otherwise subdued."

They were still listening to the conversation in the office space, and Allie asked, "Brian, do you remember what you said about bathroom breaks?"

"Oh, yeah. I'm sorry. Do you need to, um, well you know? Do you need the bathroom?"

"Yes, that's why I'm asking."

"Oh, here, hang on," Berg said clumsily. "Let me take off your cuffs." Then his voice turned slightly harsh. "But remember, I do have this shotgun here. If you force my hand, I will use it." Allie was not convinced.

Berg leaned in to remove Allie's handcuffs, and Allie whispered gently. "But, I have to tell you, I don't care what happens to Sarah Haslam. As a matter of fact, I have some preferences about what happens to Sarah Haslam." The cuffs came off and Berg backed away quickly. He was holding the gun at his side but was pointing it downward instead of at his prisoner. Allie stood and stepped into the bathroom, which was remarkably clean for an abandoned office that had not been used for a few months.

Outside in the cold Z got word that some of his fellow *Espada Rápida* warriors had positioned themselves behind the building where Allie Stoker was held captive. Within minutes there would also be a team on top of the building. Z passed on that news to Stoker, and then said, "There's an entryway in the back. My guys say it's probably the best access to the office space. Option number two is a forced entry by rappelling from the roof."

"So how do we support your team?" Stoker asked.

"You and I are the team's eyes and ears at this point. Watch and learn young grasshopper." Z bowed toward Stoker and then he smiled. Stoker laughed at Z, who was at least a decade younger, and Z said, "You will learn much if you are humble."

"I thought I smelled grasshopper." Stoker responded by returning a brief, sarcastic bow. "But, there's no friggin' way I'm waxing your car or painting your fence, Mr. Miyagi!" He was referring to a character from the movie *The Karate Kid*.

Z's laughter was interrupted by another radio communication into his earpiece. He turned to Stoker and said, "You and I will be moving shortly. Since I have the most intel about what's going on in there, I was just put in command of our tactical unit." The enthusiasm on Z's face was obvious. He spoke into his radio. "Listen up, *Espada Rápida*. It's time for us to do one of the things we do best. We must wait." Z continued rallying his team. "We've practiced this scenario hundreds of times, and we've succeeded in rescues much like the situation we're facing today. When the time is right, we'll go in."

A few minutes later the sentries watching the back of the building reported that a woman in her mid- to late- twenties had just entered the building. Z adjusted his thermal imaging and saw an individual climbing the stairway to the second floor and then to the third. Through the microphones they heard two deadbolt door locks opening. When the door slammed Z immediately commented to his team, "That's no ordinary door, warriors. It sounded thick and reinforced. Heads up to the team on the roof. I think the window approach will be best."

The team leader on the rooftop reported in to Z who in turn informed Stoker. "They boarded up the windows, but we think your best entry is still going to be through the front windows on Phillip's Avenue. We'll get some help from a few precisely timed explosives."

Z removed an earpiece from his bag and handed it to Stoker. "I think you should listen in on this. Since I'm in charge now, I can make that decision."

Stoker slipped the earpiece into his ear as Z pulled a radio from his bag, turned it on, and entered a security code into its display. The channel came to life and Stoker heard the semi-cryptic communication of a team in perfect accord.

"We've inserted the NanoBUGS through the ventilation system," confirmed the team member named Abbie. "In about two minutes we'll have them in place with cameras and microphones. We already have two set charges ready to blow those boards off the windows."

In one ear Stoker was listening to the sounds from the office space where Allie was held captive. In his other ear he heard *Espada Rápida* preparing to rescue his wife. He longed to hear the two worlds converge.

CHAPTER 96

"Hi Honey, I'm home." Sarah Haslam was being ridiculously sarcastic. "So how's our little Allie cat?"

With Haslam's arrival Brian Berg tried to act tougher. He held up the shotgun as he pretended to be angry, impatient, and in charge. Berg was back in nasty mode, or at least his best imitation of nasty mode. "She's been a real peach, Sarah," Berg sneered almost convincingly. "I decided she had been quiet enough to earn her piss break." Berg walked over to a metal chair that sat a little closer to the windows and he motioned for Allie to follow him. "Okay Allie, we want to be *so sensitive* of your comfort. We can't have you sitting in the same position all the time. "Come over here and straddle this metal chair with your chest facing the back and we'll chain you up nice and gentle to the front of it."

"Cuff her to the chair, Brian," Haslam said. "Perhaps she can get some sleep that way."

As Berg cuffed Allie to the chair, Haslam carried on. "You know, this is all Troy's fault, Allie." Haslam pulled up a chair and sat down directly opposite her victim. "Did you know that I was scheduled to be on call at the hospital tonight? If it wasn't for him, I would be there admitting patients. You would be asleep in your bed. Your husband screwed that all up for me."

"My husband?" Allie questioned. "Let's think about this, Sarah. I don't know much about what happened before you came on rotation with my husband, but I do know you were already on thin ice. Rumor has it, you know your medications and you have a good sense for when to send someone to therapy.

Sure you knew all your medical lingo and psychiatry speech, but when it came to getting beyond tasks and processes, you had your challenges. Now I don't have the diagnostic skills of you, Troy, psychologists, and social workers. But when a student goes out of her way to set up her own little enterprise and puts patients and fellow physicians at risk, something tells me that's *your* fault."

Sarah Haslam raised her hand and struck Allie again on her right cheek as she had done on two previous occasions. Allie withstood the blow, looked up at Sarah and said, "Why don't you take off these cuffs. Let's get beyond bitch slaps."

"Oh Allie, darling."

Stoker was listening on the microphone, but he didn't flinch. He knew a simple slap was the last thing that would bother Allie. The challenge would actually invigorate his wife's mind and strengthen her resolve to find a way out—and to survive.

"Stoker, she's getting really aggressive," Z said. "Let's get off this roof and join the team at the back door. We're putting together a plan that will send the warriors in through the third-floor windows first, and that reinforced door a few moments later. You and I can block the escape route."

Z packed away the thermal imaging equipment. "You just keep listening, Stoker. Also we just got word that the camera is in place and so are the explosives," Z said. "Sarah Haslam is making plenty of noise, so she made it pretty easy for you, me, and the rest of my team to sneak around without Haslam or Berg hearing us."

"Oh, my little Allie cat," chided Haslam back in the office space. "I'm no self-defense expert. The closest I've ever come to learning how to fight was doing a few Brazilian jujitsu dance moves on a Jillian Michaels exercise DVD. So while you could kick my ass, I used my brain to defeat you. My IQ is among the top three percent in the United States. I would *never* attack you directly. I admit it. I'd lose. But when it comes to outsmarting you, when it comes to manipulating you, I promise you, I have the upper hand."

Allie was in no mood to argue about who was smarter. The winner of this contest would have to survive on patience. "I guess, I can't argue with you there, Sarah. Let me get some sleep, so I have at least a few neuron to try and keep up with you mentally."

In his clumsy fashion, Brian Berg broke into the conversation. "Hey, Sarah, you mind if I step out and get something to eat. I'd really like to stretch my legs, get some fresh air, and clear my head a bit."

"Sure Brian. Don't take too long. And remember, if you're not back soon, I'm calling Stintson and he'll have people out looking for you. Remember we've got to get through the night before we move her out of Sioux Falls tomorrow. I'll watch Allie while you sleep until five or six in the morning. After that you watch while I sleep."

Berg felt the sudden bravado rise up within him. While Sarah Haslam had not issued a direct order, she plainly assumed that she was in charge of the situation. Berg was sick of playing second fiddle. After all, it was the commander who had given him instructions to recruit Haslam. The commander had put him in charge of this mission. "Listen Sarah, have you ever guarded a prisoner? Have you ever arrested somebody? Have you even applied handcuffs to somebody?"

"No Brian. That's why *I* have *you*."

"Listen Sarah, for the last nine hours or so you've been calling all the shots. But need I remind you who put the weapons in your hand? Who taught you how to use them? Who set up that reinforced door and boarded up the windows? Who served four years in the military? Which of us have been a prison guard, military police, and a police officer?"

"So you want to call the shots here, Brian, buddy? You want to determine strategy? When did anybody ever rely on *you* to come up with a plan or consider contingencies? You just followed orders in all your jobs. I'll tell you what Brian. You be in charge for a while, and let's see how it goes. Why don't you boss me around a little bit and tell Allie what she can and can't do. Let us know what the big plan is, Sergeant."

"What is the plan?" interjected Allie Stoker. "What happens to you, Sarah, in a few hours from now when my husband submits to the demands of your bosses, whoever they may be? What happens to Brian Berg? Do you care about Brian?"

"This is a business arrangement for me and a survival arrangement for Brian," Haslam said.

"I'm pretty sure I know what happens to me," Allie said. "It's either me or the man I love. While I prefer to live, I accept the fact that Troy and I might go down together. In your heart, and in your mind, has your little plan included your last breathing moments, feeling the metal ripping through your body, and your own blood staining the floor around you?"

Haslam ignored Allie. "Okay Brian. When you get back you're in charge. And as your minion, might I request a sandwich? Preferably on whole-wheat bread with some lettuce and other vegetables? I vastly prefer turkey instead of roast beef. Chicken is fine too. That's my humble request, *boss*."

Berg walked to the door and began to open the deadbolts. "Hey Brian," Haslam addressed him in a mocking tone, "Do you have any money?"

Berg slowly turned around, walked back into the room to the drawer that had previously contained Sarah Haslam's computer and removed three twenty-dollar bills. Without another word, Berg returned to the door, unlocked the two deadbolts, and left.

CHAPTER 97

As Brian Berg wandered the streets of Sioux Falls on a frigid January night, he had no particular destination in mind. He also had no idea that warriors were following him. They had seen him exit out the back door of the red brick building, and they decided to follow him instead taking him into custody. Berg was just glad to have a moment away from Sarah Haslam's strange behavior. Ironically, he felt more anxious about his kidnapping crime when he was not with his victim.

As Berg walked down Ninth Street he grew increasingly agitated. By the time he had crossed Main Avenue his hands were visibly shaking. Profound hunger propelled him to keep walking toward some restaurant to find food. However, he knew that his uncontrollably shaking hands would cause him embarrassment. It could even draw police attention to him.

Berg was considering all of his options. Perhaps he should just run for his life. He could try and disappear into Minnesota or Iowa. Perhaps he could get to the bus station and take one of the daily buses that traveled to Omaha, Kansas City, or Fargo. He reasoned that he could figure out his next destination once he was on the bus. As a final gesture of good will he could call the police, just moments before stepping on the bus, and tell them all about Allie Stoker being held against her will. Perhaps that would help him feel better—and land him a lighter sentence if he ever got caught.

As Berg neared Minnesota Avenue, a police cruiser rounded the corner. Berg's new paranoid criminal instincts took over and he broke into a run. Turning right onto Minnesota Avenue, Berg continued his run. His skin broke out into a drenching sweat. When he reached Eighth Street, Brian turned. He realized the officer had not chased him, so he slowed to a jog. A flood of guilt, fear, and remorse showered over him and riveted his soul with the depth of the wrongs he had actually let himself commit. He was now a felon. Brian Berg could go to prison, and today's actions may preclude him from ever landing a good job. As his breathing began to follow panic patterns, all he could think about was how to get out of town, find a new place to live, and just lay low for a year. Berg decided to step into the Sioux Falls main library where he could sit down, rest, and think.

Berg entered the library at a race walker pace, passed through the front corridor, and darted back to the book stacks. His odd behavior caught the attention of a handful of library patrons. He walked up an aisle of books where he pretended to act interested in history. He anxiously examined the numerous volumes on the shelves. At random, he chose a book about some European revolution, which he'd never heard of, that happened during the Nineteenth Century. He carried the book to the reading room where he found a powder blue chair. Berg sat down and pretended to read while he tried to figure out a way to get out of his current situation alive.

Berg wanted to run. He wanted to disappear. And, he realized that without his truck, he did not know how to run. He also did not know how to calm his racing anxiety. He reasoned that if he got some food he might feel better.

In the meantime, a dark-haired woman, who was twenty-eight years old, also sat in a chair in the same reading room. Berg had not seen her follow him in because he lacked the mental clarity to survey his surroundings. Her name was Abbie, and any average observer would've assumed that she was reading a book on her tablet device. That's what she wanted everyone to think. In reality Abbie's tablet was a high-powered surveillance device. She was transmitting images of Brian Berg to her warrior teammates.

Abbie had also taken a liking to psychological profiling and what she saw was fascinating. Berg sat in the liberally cushioned library chair, and he was obviously in a panic. Abbie was spot on with her analysis.

Berg thought about what he needed to do, and he realized that the library might have a book about dealing with panic. So he stood and walked over to one of the computer terminals and typed in the search phrase, "Stopping panic."

The list before him included a number of books by mystery writers, psychologists, and self-help authors. Finally he settled on one called *Your Panic Arrested!* Berg's anxiety skyrocketed. *You're panicked – you're arrested!* Berg screamed within his own mind. Then he realized that the book title did not refer to him getting arrested, and the pressure within his mind subsided enough for him to proceed with his plan. He wrote down the Dewy Decimal classification code for the book he hoped could arrest his panic. Then he started his clueless search around the shelves for the proper location. It has been a long time since

Brian Berg had used a library, so he took a detour to the information desk, briefly asking one of the librarians for some assistance.

The librarian was all too eager and helpful. She snatched the paper out of his hand and made a beeline for the correct shelf. By the time Berg caught up with her she already had the book in her hand, "Here you go, sir," said the librarian as she handed it to him and observed the title. "Oh, um, well, I . . . ," she stammered. "I hope it's helpful. Have a great, um, evening."

Berg was slightly embarrassed, but he was still much too panicked to worry about his embarrassment. He returned to his seat and opened up *Your Panic Arrested!* By page seven he had already tried the first breathing exercise and he was shocked at how effective it was. While his panic was not completely gone, he was at least at a functional level. By page eleven his hands had stopped shaking. By page fifteen he remembered just how hungry he was. It occurred to Berg that he would love to take the book with him, but he didn't have a library card. He also thought it would be odd to explain to Sarah Haslam that he had delayed his return because he was, well, applying for a library card. Furthermore, walking into a room with a book on panic in front of your kidnapping victim and partner in crime was probably the wrong message to send. Moreover, Sarah Haslam was, or at least recently had been, a psychiatrist, and he had no idea how she would interpret his book selection under the current circumstances. He concluded that it probably would not work favorably for him, Allie Stoker, or Sarah Haslam. Berg considered the fact that he was now a felon, so stealing a library book seemed almost irrelevant. Nevertheless, if he were to get caught in the act, it could really complicate matters in the next few hours. So, Berg walked into a corner of the library that was almost completely unoccupied, stepped in between two shelf stacks, and looked over his shoulder. He didn't see anyone watching him, so he opened *Your Panic Arrested!* and ripped out of the first few pages. He slid the remaining book back into a random shelf and headed for the door.

From his short career as a police officer, Brian Berg knew that hiding your stolen goods was actually what got you busted. So Brian held the papers in his hand as if he owned them. He held them so the torn edge hid in his hand while the clean edge sat upward. Then he made a beeline for the exit. He realized he was walking hastily so he slowed his pace, stopped at one of the computer terminals for about ten seconds, pretended to use it, took a few deep breaths, and then calmly exited the library. Abbie the warrior caught the whole incident on video.

CHAPTER 98

Z had moved the command station down to Mall Avenue, behind the building where Allie Stoker was a captive on Phillips Avenue. He had asked Stoker to profile Haslam and Berg.

"When it comes to profiling our two criminals here, this one's a slam dunk," Stoker explained. "Ask yourself, why would two people kidnap the bait, Allie, and then wait to hatch an even more elaborate scheme to get to their true target, me? Wouldn't it just be easier to find me in a vulnerable place and take me out with a bullet or baseball bat?"

"Logically, most people would just find the cleanest way to get rid of you," Z said. "If they gave it a little more thought, they would do a reasonable job of covering their tracks, too."

"Exactly," confirmed Stoker. "But that's not how confused minds work. While Haslam and Berg profile with different motives and diagnoses, they share a particularly lethal irrational behavior here. Both of them are so crazed that they fail to have the foresight to consider how much hell is going to rain down on them. Yet they have the creativity to scheme elaborately about some triumphant, thrilling moment when they control the object of their hatred. In this case they hate me. They want to cause me to continue to have deep emotional pain as long as they can accomplish this. This is a self-serving but illogical fantasy, pure and simple. We all have fantasies to some degree or another, but rarely does revenge work out."

"So what do you make of Berg?" Z asked.

"Brian Berg is exhibiting some erratic, disorganized behavior," Stoker said. "But he has some moments of great focus, such as when our warrior, Abbie, saw him reading the book on controlling panic attacks in the library. My guess is that he's come off his medication. Paranoia is starting to creep back in. *But*, he's mostly harmless. He's already thinking about how to get out of this alive. He won't harm Allie unless he's really backed into a corner — or he commits some stupid mistake. At this point, he's actually our ally."

"And Sarah Haslam?" Z asked. "I'm sensing she's dangerous. She'd pull the trigger."

"Sarah Haslam is completely volatile and she's really enjoying brandishing that shotgun. She loves how this weapon lets her maim people and cause them prolonged suffering instead of just killing them. She wants the opportunity to harm Allie as a means of hurting me. It's plain and simple. She's also on a self-destructive path. As a resident she would seek out vulnerable patients and look for ways to be medically and emotionally violent as well as voyeuristic. She likes it. She is enjoying this new flavor of viciousness and she is looking for ways to justifiably escalate the violence."

"Why doesn't she just walk over to Allie and start punching her?" Z asked. "Why isn't she torturing her?"

"Emotionally, she *is* torturing her," explained Stoker. "But for overt and physical violence, she needs an excuse. If we raid that office space, she will look to harm or kill Allie first, and then she'll open fire on your team. She thinks she's justified."

"Are you suggesting we call off our raid?"

"No, I'm just reinforcing how critical it will be to make Allie safe in the first half-second of the raid — and you need to know how much your team is at risk here."

"My team is always at risk, Troy," answered Z with a confident smile. "We've got this."

CHAPTER 99

Allie Stoker sat handcuffed to the metal chair in the middle of the abandoned office that was now her prison. "So, Alley Cat. I'm glad we're going to finally get some time for some girl talk. With Brian out of the picture for a few minutes we can talk about make-up, skirts, and even guys," Haslam spewed with overly dramatic sarcasm. "Who knows, we may even synch our cycles!"

Stoker and Z were listening in. "That's all I need," grumbled Stoker.

"Oh, yes!" continued the delusional Haslam. "It may take a month or two of quality time together. I'm already making my list of chick flicks! Don't you just love Jean-Claude Van Damme?"

"A man who can do the splits," Allie replied. "There's no greater turn-on! I wonder if he can bake?" She decided to meet Haslam's sarcasm with equal sarcasm.

"Oh, yes! He's French isn't he? Of course he can bake!" Haslam said. *Un peu de croissant pour le petite dejeuner! Oo la la!"*

"*C'est la vie!!!"* Allie said. "You know, that Van Damme. I love men who know how to fight with their hands—so much that I married one. I hate to say this, but I think Troy Stoker is more dangerous in a fistfight than Van Damme. He even scares me sometimes."

Sarah Haslam's psychiatry training kicked in. "What do you mean, he scares you sometimes?"

"There are a few things that Troy really loves in life," continued Allie. "His relationship with me, his patients, and his friendships with a few select, capable friends with some common military ties." Allie shifted in her seat and held her head high. "You've already messed with his patients and harmed me," Allie stated matter-of-factly. "I think that your demise is coming soon here, Sarah. And, I think you know that."

Sarah Haslam was silent. She pretended to ignore Allie, but the warning hit her right between the eyes. It was a psychological double-tap.

Haslam stood up and walked to the refrigerator. She took out a bottle of orange juice and drank from it slowly. After she replaced the juice in the refrigerator she walked over and sat on one of the desks. "He'll have to find us first. I suspect he's searching like crazy, but it will take him a while. We'll be moving soon, anyway."

Z heard Haslam's comment; he radioed his team and prepared them in case they had to accelerate the rescue mission timeline.

"Next stop, Arkansas," mumbled Haslam. "We'll depart about an hour before sunrise. You'll like the delivery van we rented. Nobody will see you chained up in the back."

Allie ignored the comment about Arkansas and the van. Instead she decided to confront Haslam and stir her paranoia. "Sarah. I'm just wondering about your last name, Haslam. I must ask you. Is Haslam a Middle Eastern name?" Allie knew that it was probably a British or western European surname.

"No, my great grandparents were from Germany or France or something like that."

"Well, I've got to level with you. In this situation, where you've kidnapped me, it does sounds like you're a terrorist! Is this some larger plot?" Allie asked with a dramatic flair of false concern in her voice. "Did the commander really hire you or did he just activate you? Or maybe he chose you because of your name," Allie asserted. "That's brilliant! He hides his crimes behind the terrorism he's about to pin on you."

Haslam's paranoid, accelerated mind immediately grasped onto the conspiracy idea Allie was hatching in her mind. Thoughts raced—some of them orderly and others disjointed. *Dirty bombs, anthrax. Are my parents sleeper agents? Is that why my brother studied engineering? Oh no! Will the authorities think I'm a terrorist? Did the commander hire me because of my name?*

Haslam sat in silence.

"Oh, sister. You've been played," Allie said acting on Sarah's paranoia. "We got to get you out of this."

"I have a time factor here."

"What does *that* mean?" Allie asked.

Haslam did not respond as her eyes darted back and forth. Her time factor statement was completely was out of context within the conversation—a definite sign of Haslam's increasing anxiety and sleep deprivation were now creating some significant disorganized thinking from her lack of REM sleep. It had been more than seventy-two hours since Sarah had experienced REM sleep and her state of mind was quickly deteriorating. Haslam stood up and went over to the sink. With remarkable efficiency she popped open a can of grape soda and drank half of it. Then she paced back and forth between the reinforced door and windowed wall.

Allie remained silent and just watched her abductor slowly slip into psychosis. Outside the old walls and windows of the century-old brick building, Allie could hear the sounds of Sioux Falls. She smiled as she heard the loopers, teenagers revving their engines as they cruised their cars around downtown. She heard the laughter from the careless high school girls as they flirted with the boys who welcomed their advances and hoped to get them to join them for a ride that would not exceed the carefully police-monitored twenty-mile-per hour speed limit.

Haslam interrupted her pacing and turned toward Allie. Crushing her soda can, she flung it at Allie. "Damn you Allie Stoker! Damn you Brian Berg! Damn the commander! Whoever, he is."

"You've never met him? You've never met the commander?"

"Shut up! Just shut up! I need to think." Haslam yelled.

That is exactly what Allie wanted. *Absolutely, Sarah. You just keep thinking.*

CHAPTER 100

Brian Berg walked west on 12th Street for ten minutes before he ducked into a hardware store. He had concluded that running away would be futile. The commander would find him and feed him to the coyotes. He would wait for the police to swoop in, do his best not to get killed during the raid, accept his arrest, and hope to plea a reasonable deal without exchanging too much information about his new boss. He would also hope for Allie Stoker's safety.

He purchased a razor knife and battery operated stud-finder. He had a plan that just might get him out of this situation alive, and he liked that it involved breaking down walls—or at least breaking through a little drywall. He had seen such an escape on *MacGyver*, in one of *The Matrix* movies, or during an *A-Team* episode somewhere during his life.

Berg then backtracked for ten minutes and found himself back on Phillips Avenue. He was incredibly hungry. Remembering Allie's mention of dirty chai, he stepped into Ruby's Coffee Spot and ordered two *grande* cups of the hot beverage along with a few muffins and rolls that sounded foreign to him. "Do you have any ham or roast beef so I can make a sandwich?" An awkward girl behind the counter snickered before she explained that Ruby's was a vegetarian establishment. "Do you have any cheddar cheese?"

Eventually, Berg settled for hummus as well as some olives in a wax-paper bag.

CHAPTER 101

Stoker and Z were parked in a van on Mall Avenue near the back door to the red brick building where Sarah Haslam was holding Allie Stoker captive. They were taking advantage of the cameras, microphones, and thermal imaging, which monitored the conversations and movements of both hostage and kidnapper. "Haslam's wearing down," Z said. I think our patience is going to pay off."

"Abbie, can you give me a sitrep?" Z asked over the microphone.

"We've got four of us on the roof ready to rappel in at your command and three will come in from the rear. You and Stoker will keep that back door covered. We also have two warriors who will move into position on Phillips Avenue about two seconds after the flash bangs explode."

"Great. I'll keep you appraised of what is going on inside," responded Z. "Where's Colonel Rivera and what are his plans in the next few hours?"

"He's on his way home from Washington D.C."

"Thanks Abbie. Stay warm up there," Z said.

"Roger that."

"All right warriors, listen up," Z said. "This situation's rules of engagement are the same as usual. You have the right to use force if you are attacked or under threat of an attack. We prefer to take the tangos, Haslam and Berg, alive. But if you're fired upon or you meet life-threatening resistance, shoot to kill. We think that Haslam cannot stay awake much longer. When she falls asleep, we make our sweep."

Stoker and Z patiently returned to their surveillance, which seemed unremarkable. The last words they had heard from Sarah Haslam were her yelling about how she needed to think. Since that moment she had remained silent and in deep thought. Or was she asleep? Allie was also silent.

Eventually, Stoker and Z heard footsteps approaching along Mall Avenue. As they watched through the tinted windows of the van, Brian Berg walked right by them. Although they were tempted, they decided not to jump out of the van and apprehend him. Instead they watched as he opened the back door and entered the building. Stoker and Z watched Berg's heat signature ascend to the third floor. But instead of proceeding to the door, Berg's heat signature stopped about eight feet short of the entry and remained there for about two minutes. It appeared as if he was sitting on the floor. "What's he doing just sitting there?" Z asked.

"You mean the way he's just crouched down outside the door? Stoker replied. "What are you hearing with your microphone?"

Z listened intently. "I hear scratching, or something like that."

Then the heat signature extended and his hand appeared to be working on something above his head. "This is strange," Z said. "I hear more scratching."

"Who knows," Stoker said. "With Berg it could be anything."

CHAPTER 102

Brian Berg was squatting in the hallway just outside the office space where Haslam was watching over Allie Stoker. He had inserted the batteries into his new stud-finder. He was using the device to determine where the studs were located in the wall, which he hoped to burst through when the police, FBI, or the commander came for him. After identifying the fifteen-inch space between the drywall studs, Berg quietly and slowly used his new razor knife to slice small cracks in the drywall, weakening it, and preparing it for his big escape moment. Perhaps MacGyver, Mr. T., or other TV characters could break through drywall spontaneously. But Berg wanted to be sure, when he hit the wall, it would give way instantaneously.

Berg then reached about six inches above his head on the wall, and with his razor knife, slowly inserted the device into the wall. He repeated the action numerous times, patiently working it down the wall and creating a dotted-line effect down to about ankle level. He was confident that he would be able to fight his way through the compromised drywall and slide through the fifteen-inch portal to freedom.

Berg then hid all the tools in his coat pocket and turned toward the entry door. He deliberately took careful steps toward the door and counted them to give himself an estimate of the distance from the door to the weakened area in the wall. He would do his best to also weaken the wall on the interior side. But he still had some question in his mind about whether or not he could do it without being detected by Sarah Haslam.

Arriving at the door, Berg unlocked the deadbolts, opened the door, and walked into the room to see the unwelcome faces of Sarah Haslam and Allie Stoker.

"Geez Brian. What took you so long?" Haslam asked waiving the shotgun. It had become her favorite status symbol. "Did you go to a movie, too?"

"No. I couldn't decide what to eat. Nothing sounded good," Brian said. I brought dirty chai, though!" he exclaimed as he set down the drinks and unwrapped the food. "I got some muffins and other stuff here, too."

Haslam walked over, set down her gun, and surveyed Berg's spread. She picked up the tub of hummus, and said, "Nice job Brian. The hummus is a great touch. But you forgot my sandwich." Turning to Allie she asked, "Would you like some Allie cat?"

"Actually, yes. I would love some."

A few minutes later, Allie was gratefully eating hummus on a whole-wheat and sunflower seed roll. Her body was starved for calories and other nutrients and this small meal was somewhat satisfying her hunger. She also drank the dirty chai, but mostly out of courtesy toward Berg. However, it also helped stave off her hunger. Berg tried the hummus but did not like it, so he satisfied his hunger with some of the strange muffins which he did not particularly enjoy either. Haslam finished off the hummus and dirty chai and treated herself to the remaining baked goods.

For no particular reason, Berg decided to assert himself and attempted to seize back a little more control. "Okay, Sarah. Why don't you take a break and go find yourself a sandwich. After that you can take a watch while I get some sleep."

"Okay, Boss!" Haslam again replied in open mockery, as she stood, picked up the gun and handed it to Berg. She put on her coat and started for the door. "Do you need anything while I'm out Allie cat, darling?" she continued in the same disrespectful tone.

"No, Sarah, darling. But I just suggest you stay in the shadows. They're looking for you out there."

"Okay, you're probably right. By now, they know you're missing, *Allie Stoker*," lashed back Haslam. "But they have no idea who has you or where you are. Right now your *Troy* is talking to the police, and the cops are dragging their feet waiting for twenty-four hours before they will declare you a missing person. If they're doing anything, their searching your phone records and querying airline flight manifest databases under the assumption that you've taken off with a secret lover or something like that!"

Allie was confident that Troy Stoker was *not* waiting for twenty-four hours. She was also quite content to let Haslam believe that Stoker would not be thinking outside the box and accelerating the search for his wife. "Good point, Doctor Haslam," she responded in a deadpan fashion.

Sarah Haslam accepted the false compliment with smug satisfaction. "Of course it's a good point. I'm an intelligent person," she said as she threw her scarf over her shoulder.

CHAPTER 103

"Sarah Haslam's coming out!" Z said over the radio to his team. "Apprehend Sarah Haslam on sight!" he ordered.

"Affirmative!" came the response.

Stoker and Z watched Haslam's heat signature with the thermal imaging as she exited the apartment door and moved toward the stairway. Then they saw her image descend the first two stairs and stop. "She's hesitating or something," Z said to Stoker. "What's she doing there?" They sat in silence, watched and waited.

Inside the building, sitting on a dilapidated step, Haslam pondered. Her paranoia, intermingled with her natural cautious emotions, would not let her go any further down the stairs. *Bad idea*, she thought to herself, *to go out onto the streets of Sioux Falls*. Her thoughts were filled with potential perils. She considered that just by some small coincidence, somebody might have seen her with Allie Stoker. It was also possible that the police had assembled a list of Troy and Allie Stoker's known enemies, psychotic patients, and other potentially dangerous people in their life. At this point there was a high probability that her name would be on that list. Perhaps the police had even tried to find her to ask her a few questions. She had not been available at her apartment or reachable by telephone or by any other means. *That could really move me up on the list of suspects*, she thought. Sarah Haslam did not know what to do, so she just sat.

Z glanced over at one of his other teammates. "She's not moving, so now could be a great time to apprehend her. How close do you think you can get before she sees you and retreats to her fortress?"

"Close, Z!" the teammate said with confidence. "I'm sure that outside door has some squeaky hinges, but we can fix that with a little WD40 and a few other tricks before we even open it. That staircase could give us away. It's old and I bet it squeaks. But I might be able to crawl up, keeping my hands and feet towards the outside of the stairs. I bet I can and get within ten feet of her before she sees or hears me."

"I'll tell you what," Z said, "Why don't you take your hat off and throw on Stoker's normal civilian coat here. That way if she does detect you, you can just pretend like you belong there."

"Sure," the warrior said. "If she sees me, I just act as surprised as she does. I admit she scared me, she admits that I scared her, and just as she starts to calm down, I pull out the pistol and order her on the ground."

"Exactly," Z said. "Now get to work."

Z's fellow warrior walked cautiously toward the door and started some work on the hinges, applying lubricants and allowing the chemicals to sink in. After a few minutes he slowly twisted the door handle and pulled the door open two inches. He lubricated the hinges one more time and then slowly opened the door a little more. Z was listening with the directional microphone; he picked up only a slight amount of noise as the door opened. It was not enough for Sarah Haslam to hear.

As Sarah Haslam sat on the step she began to speak to herself in a whispered tone. Z could only hear a word here and there and none of her gibberish really made any sense to him. He handed the earphones over to Stoker.

"Can you make sense of this, Troy?"

Troy listened for about two minutes. "She's perseverating," Stoker said.

"What does that mean?" Z asked.

"Well, in its mild form it's just kind of like people talking to themselves as they pace the floor when they're worried or stressed out. But really in her agitated state, this is just a manifestation of her confusion. It actually works out really well for your guy because she probably won't hear him coming."

As Z watched on the infrared his teammate had made it halfway up the first flight of stairs and he was wisely moving slow. Through the directional microphone Z heard an occasional slight creak from the stairway, but this guy was good. His patience was paying off. Within another two minutes he made it to the first landing.

"He just needs to get to the second floor and then take about three additional steps," explained Z. "After that he can bound up the final six or seven stairs and surprise her before she can stand up, turn, and run the few paces to that reinforced door."

"Remember," Stoker said, "She also has two deadbolt door locks that she needs to undo."

"True," Z said, "But I bet she's got a pistol and she would try to use it on my guy. Who knows she might shoot the deadbolts to speed up the process of getting through that door. We're going to give our warrior a slight margin for error so he doesn't get shot."

A minute later Z's teammate had reached the second floor and he was about to step onto the first step. Within the next thirty seconds he would be close enough to spring up the last few stairs and apprehend Haslam.

"Damn you, Troy Stoker," yelled Sarah Haslam. "You're miles away, yet you're in my head!" she said as she smashed her fists down on her thighs, stood up, turned and walked toward the apartment. She removed the keys from her pocket.

Z's teammate retreated back a step wondering if her outburst had come because he'd been detected. He realized that Haslam had neither seen nor heard him. The warrior also heard Sarah Haslam sliding the key into the first deadbolt. Thanks to the sounds of her ongoing verbal outburst and the jingling of the keys he decided he could climb the stairs more quickly. As he ascended halfway up the third staircase he paused, turned his head to the side, and took a low-profile glance into the hallway just in time to see the top of Sarah Haslam's head walking through the door. A moment later he heard the door close and the deadbolts latch shut.

Out in the alley Z, Stoker, and the other warriors had seen the whole incident on the infrared monitor. They had missed the simple apprehension of Sarah Haslam by less than ten seconds.

"The problem with paranoia," Stoker said, "is it often pays off."

CHAPTER 104

Brian Berg had just walked eight paces from the door and along the wall to measure the approximate location where he had made the scores on the other side of the wall. He removed the stud finder from his pocket and quickly scanned the wall. After he located the studs' positions he removed his razor knife and quickly put two small cuts at the base of the wall to mark the locations. He made five or six cuts into the wall to weaken it from the inside before he heard Haslam's voice emanating from the hallway. She was yelling some partially audible complaint about Troy Stoker. Quickly, Berg returned the razor knife and stud-finder to his coat pocket as he heard Haslam jostling the deadbolt door locks.

As Haslam entered the office space Berg tried to conceal his surprise at her premature return. Fortunately, Haslam's psychotic state prevented her from noticing Berg's awkward demeanor. "Okay, Brian. Get some sleep!" ordered Haslam. She was now clearly delusional and she was re-asserting herself as the alpha and leader. At that moment Berg was interested in avoiding a confrontation with a disturbed person, in getting some sleep, and in weakening the drywall for his escape. His desire to be the leader had disappeared.

"I'll take this spot over here," Berg said sitting down against the area of the wall he hoped to burst through and escape. "It's a tad darker so I'll sleep better."

"Wherever you want, Brian."

Berg quietly removed the razor knife from his coat pocket and transferred it to his back pants pocket. Then he removed his coat, fashioned it into a pillow, and lay down on the floor facing the wall he wanted to weaken. Berg closed his eyes to fool Haslam into thinking he was asleep. Twenty seconds later the illusion became reality and he dozed off.

Berg awoke with a start. He glanced quickly at his antiquated pager and saw that it was just a few minutes after 4:00 a.m. Panic set in and he wondered if he had missed his window of opportunity to create his escape space through the drywall and into the hallway. As he surveyed the scene Sarah Haslam was awake, but paying more attention to a game on her laptop than she was to Allie Stoker who was sleeping.

Berg chose not to move; he didn't want to alert Haslam that he was awake. Instead he listened to her talking to her screen in words that were mostly coherent. However, some of her phrases made little sense and her insight was non-existent. Berg reflected on the last twenty-four hours. In retrospect he wished — oh he wished — that he would've just jumped in his truck, driven to Florida, and gotten a job flipping burgers, selling vacuums, or answering the telephone in a call center. If the commander wanted to chase him down, he could at least take a few days to figure out some countermeasures. Berg concluded that he would be better off enjoying a few, final sunny weeks in Florida before meeting his maker. Right now he was likely to experience a miserable winter death or a prison cell that would be horrible at any time of year. Again his anxiety climbed to uncontrollable levels. The breathing tricks he had read about in the library did little to subdue his panic at this moment. Berg wondered if he could grab one of the guns, surprise Sarah Haslam, and just force her to surrender or die right then and there.

In his mind Berg concocted a story he could tell the police. He could claim that he had secretly heard about the kidnapping of Allie Stoker and learned of her whereabouts. On his own he had heroically decided to check out the situation. He would lie and report how, when he arrived, events escalated. He ended up killing Haslam in defense of his own life and to help Allie Stoker escape.

Then Berg considered his fictional story from an investigator's point of view. He envisioned an officer asking him how he got through two deadbolts? Did Haslam just open the door after he knocked? Berg realized that his story would have too many holes in it.

Finally, Brian Berg concluded that the best course of action would be to admit his change of heart and to explain that he decided not to go through with the scheme to bait and eliminate Troy Stoker. Berg would wait for Haslam to fall asleep then he would take decisive action against her. He would prefer to take her alive and subdue her before he called the police, but he was not beyond using lethal force. It was time for Brian Berg to come clean and take his chances in the courts and prisons.

After thirty minutes, Haslam got up and went into the bathroom. Allie Stoker was still asleep. Berg took advantage of the opportunity. He stood up and reached up high on the wall with his razor knife. The moment he heard Haslam flush the toilet, Berg made a large vertical score with the knife. The flushing water covered the noise. Berg fell back to the floor and hid the razor knife. As Sarah Haslam emerged from the bathroom, Berg was back in a sleeping position with his eyes closed. But Berg was wide-awake. He hoped that Haslam would soon fall asleep so he could get her gun, turn the tables on her, and turn himself in.

Haslam played on her computer for another fifteen minutes, but eventually all went silent. Berg rolled over so he was facing Haslam, but he kept his eyes shut. After two more minutes he opened his eyes slightly and observed with the help of the glow of Haslam's computer screen that she had fallen asleep with her head on a desk next to her computer. Allie Stoker also seemed to be sleeping remarkably well for someone shackled to an uncomfortable chair in an upright position. Brian Berg knew it was time to get up and subdue Sarah Haslam, but he couldn't. He was frozen with fear; he spent the next fifteen minutes mustering up the courage to take on Sarah Haslam. It was fifteen minutes too long.

CHAPTER 105

"Stoker, I want you to listen to this," Z said. "I think Sarah Haslam's sleeping. I just want to make sure she's not faking it. I mean she could be trying to test Berg or Allie to see how they would react to her falling asleep. What do you think, Doc? Can I get a consultation?" He handed the headphones to Stoker.

"Zoom me in on the pattern of Sarah's breathing," Stoker said. "After all, these may be some of her last breaths." As Stoker listened he considered Sarah Haslam's breathing rhythms. "It depends what kind of sleeper she is," whispered Stoker. "We all sleep a little different." Stoker listened for another minute before declaring, "I'm convinced that she's asleep. And she's not a good sleeper. I think I hear some mild apnea. Did you notice how you cannot hear her breathing for a few moments and then all of a sudden you get this dramatic inhaling sound?"

"Now that you mention it, I do remember hearing those type of breath sounds."

"What about Berg?" Stoker asked. "Do you want me to listen to his breathing, too?" Stoker asked.

"No. I think he's awake, but I don't care," Z said. "According to your profile, he's not going to put up a fight. He'll surrender the moment we burst into that space. Besides if Berg was snoozing, he would be talking in his sleep and saying lots of things like, 'I love you too, Mommy,' and 'I want the footie pajamas.'"

Z became serious again, "Look, Stoker. Usually in a hostage situation the police use time and try to negotiate for a release. They wear the kidnappers down with phone calls, negotiations, and psychology. However, this situation is a little different. First, you didn't call the police. You called *Espada Rápida*. We are definitely less diplomatic than the police."

"Second, negotiations with a psychotic person—"

Stoker finished Z's thought. "Will push them to violence instead of settlement. The missing element of logic in the person's brain never lets them consider the benefits of surrender—the foremost being survival."

"Exactly," confirmed Z. "I know I'm preaching to the choir here, Doctor. Finally, in most hostage situations the evildoers entrench themselves and offset the element of surprise by calling up the target of their extortion; then they make their demands. Well, Haslam has not made her demands clear yet, and we still have the element of surprise on our side. She thinks the police are way behind her, but she has no idea that six battle-hardened warriors are perched above her while a few more have her surrounded."

"So it's time!" Stoker said.

"Let's get your wife out of there. This is how it's going down." Z removed an iPad from his duffel bag and began drawing a floor plan of the office space. He labeled the walls as he drew them in and diagramed doors and windows. He sketched the positions of Haslam and Berg and labeled them as the tangos. He drew a symbol representing Allie Stoker's position right in the middle of the office space. A few more arrows represented the planned movements of the rescue maneuvers. "I'm sending this sketch to each team member. We're going to have a brief meeting." Z pressed the button on his radio. "Listen up, *Espada Rápida*. Female tango is asleep. It's time to move in. Everyone check your phones for a sketch I just sent you. Report in when you are looking at the image."

Over the next ten seconds numerous voices confirmed they had the image. Z continued, "As you can see, our package, Allie Stoker, is positioned in the center of the room. She is seated on a chair, to which she is bound. Her safety is priority one. The female tango is positioned toward the southwest quadrant of the room about eight feet from the package. The blast charges are positioned to protect the package from flying glass, but the tango may not be so lucky. The tango is sleeping hunched over on a desk and her gun is off to her left. She profiles as psychotic and delusional; she's also armed. Expect immediate and lethal resistance. Be prepared to respond accordingly.

"Our male tango may or may not be armed, but his psychological profile suggests he will not resist. Nevertheless, be prepared in case he surprises us," concluded Z. "Any last questions or observations?"

One of the warriors voice came over the radio and he asked, "Can you please advise on the status of civilians within close proximity of the office space?"

"This is office and commercial space," responded Z. "Heat signatures pick up an almost empty building. The restaurant on the main floor has one person in that space. It's probably a cook in the kitchen doing prep work. But let me be clear, casualties among innocent civilians are unacceptable." Z paused. "Any other questions?" There was silence. "Great. Everyone into position, inform me when you are ready."

CHAPTER 106

Stoker stood behind the building where his wife was a captive and he looked at the back door Berg had passed through hours earlier. He listened over his radio while three members of *Espada Rápida* jogged to the back door and slipped inside. He envisioned them quietly climbing the stairs, approaching the double-deadbolt door, and applying explosive charges to the locks. Over the radio he heard the tethered warriors on the rooftop report in. In seconds they would be rappelling in through window spaces just tenths of a second after explosives cleared their paths of the glass and boards. Stoker's heart pounded in his chest in anticipation of the impending raid as he heard Z say, "On my count. Five, four, three, two, one."

Even from the back of the building Stoker felt and heard the explosions of charges blowing the boards off of the windows in front of the building. The deafening blasts of the flash bang grenades at 175 decibels accompanied a blinding flash of light that reflected up into the dark morning sky. Then he heard the distinct burst of AK-47 gunfire interrupted by two quick double tap rounds and then all went eerily silent. Stoker was almost certain that the machine gun bursts came from Haslam as part of a desperate, last-ditch offensive effort, while the double tap was the disciplined, trained skill of an operator carrying out a justified kill.

After a moment that felt like hours, Stoker finally heard a voice over the radio. "Female tango down," What Stoker did not know is who the spray of erratic bullets may have hit.

"Please, God. Protect my Allie!" he uttered in the most sincere prayer of his lifetime—and he had uttered thousands of fervent prayers in the last few hours. "And please be with the brave souls on the rescue team."

Stoker waited for another six seconds before the first communication came through. "Are you hit, Turbo?" inquired another warrior.

"I'm fine," replied the warrior, dubbed Turbo. "That psycho bitch just zinged my shoulder. I'm fine."

Stoker heard more static and then he heard, "Clear!" Then another man reported in, "We're all clear in here! The package is safe! The threat is neutralized."

Stoker fell to his knees on Mall Avenue. "Thank you, God!" he prayed in gratitude for Allie's safe rescue; then he bounced back to his feet and jogged toward the back door of the red brick building.

"Hang on, Stoker," Z said. Stoker listened to the radio communication among the warriors as they described how Sarah Haslam had managed to fire eight or nine rounds. They speculated that it was a desperate, psychotic maneuver during her state of temporary blindness and confusion caused by the flash bang grenades.

"Who's got eyes on the male tango?" Z asked into his radio. Nobody answered his question. "I need Berg!" Z yelled.

Just then, Brian Berg burst from the back door of the building. He was so terrified that Stoker could see the whites of his eyes even from a distance of 30 yards.

"Stop right there, Berg!" Stoker yelled as he raised his nine-millimeter Beretta and placed his sites on Berg's left knee. Z also drew his weapon. Berg hesitated momentarily and began to raise his hands.

"We need Berg alive," Stoker said to Z. "The world needs to know what Brian Berg knows."

Berg panicked and leapt for his truck. Stoker made the snap judgment not to fire. Z also held his fire, but chose to purposefully advance on the truck.

"Don't shoot," Z instructed Stoker. Berg fired up his engine. "Let's see where his retreat leads us."

Berg simultaneously threw his car into gear and revved the engine causing it to lurch forward with tires spinning on the frozen asphalt. With a slight fishtail he sped off on Mall Avenue, leaving Z and Stoker behind.

"Sorry, Z," Stoker said. "I'm not chasing Berg down. Allie is my priority."

Z picked up his radio. "I need airborne or satellite eyes on a blue Chevy pick-up truck, probably driving pretty erratically. Our male tango's getting away." Then turning to Stoker he said, "I bet Berg leads us right into the belly of the beast," Z said. "Allie is definitely our highest priority." Z holstered his weapon. "Let's get in there," he said as he started jogging for the back door.

"A momma's boy like that is going to panic, run to the boss and beg for mercy and protection," Stoker said as he followed Z.

"Something tells me that he's *not* going to get the golden ticket to Reno," replied Z.

"No, but I think he'll lead us to our guy," Stoker said as they approached the door. "Perhaps the commander will show up, too."

"I can hear the coyotes howling," Z said. "Berg will be an easy catch."

As Z reached for the back door, the door flew open and out marched two warriors holding Allie in a fireman's carry.

"Allie!" Stoker exclaimed as he rushed up to her. She jumped from the fireman's hold and ran into the arms of her husband.

"Troy! Oh, Troy," Allie cried as she let tears flow freely and trembled in Stoker's arms. "Thank you so much. How did you know? How did you know where we were?"

Stoker ignored her questions. "Are you okay? Where are you injured?"

"I'm fine. Just hold me. Sarah's dead, and Berg got away."

"Did you see what happened with Haslam?"

"No, Those explosions blinded me. All I could do was tip my chair to the floor and take cover."

"I'm sorry it had to come to that, honey." Stoker said.

"But after I regained my eyesight," Allie explained, " I saw Haslam's dead body lifeless on the floor." Allie paused for a moment. "She opened fire and she deserved it.

"That's what happens when you spray bullets with an AK-47."

"Exactly. Now let's go figure out what happens to Brian Berg," Allie said. "Let's get moving, Troy!"

"Hang on, Allie," Stoker said. He was hesitant to let his wife out of his arms just yet. "Let's get you to the hospital and get you checked out."

"No hospitals, Troy!" Allie said as she pushed her way out of his arms. "The best thing we can do right now is capture Berg alive. He's got a lot of info we can extract from him about the big-city problems that have been hanging over Sioux Falls."

"Hey Allie. I'm just going to warn you," Stoker said, "When we meet up with him you may see a side of me you've never seen before. The info you say we need to extract from Berg will only come before the Holy Rollers show up.

"Holy Rollers?"

"Rivera describes them as the fine men in black who rock and roll—and put lots of holes in sorry bastards. But we need to do some aggressive interrogation with Berg before they show up—the kind of interrogation that pisses off the UN or pushes the limits on the Geneva Convention. It's not going to be pretty."

"This is a narrow window of opportunity," Allie said. "We're not going to miss it! Do what you need to do. I'm right there with you. Now let's jump in the Bronco and roll."

"We're only about three minutes behind him," Stoker said.

One of the warriors stepped in and said, "Dr. Stoker! We really should get Allie to the hospital."

"No way!" Allie said. "Let's get that degenerate Berg," she replied. "Get your butts in the car," she said to the warriors. "We're going to need you."

Stoker was stunned by his wife's sudden fiery disposition and he momentarily questioned her fitness for a chase. However, he wisely decided not to lose the momentum. "Everybody in!"

"I'm staying here," Z said and then he instructed two of his warriors to join Allie and Stoker.

Within seconds Allie, Troy, and the two members of the tactical unit were in Stoker's Bronco. "Who's got a radio for Allie?" Stoker asked.

"No extras Dr. Stoker," replied one of the warriors.

"Well, since Z fried my car stereo, we'll have to improvise. Which of you has a radio with speaker mode?"

One of the warriors held out his radio. "This one has a crystal-clear speaker."

"Crank it up, and let's do this whole pursuit in concert!"

Stoker brought the finely tuned engine to life, slammed the Bronco into gear, and roared out of the alley onto Mall Avenue. "My guess is Berg's headed for the freeway. Let's get some help." Stoker grabbed the radio and pressed the transmit button. "Z, this is Stoker with Allie and two of your guys."

"Correction!" interrupted one of the warriors from the back seat. "That's one guy and one woman," she said as she ripped off her tactical helmet, shook out her long mane of silky, dark hair.

"Correction, Z. I have two of your ass kickers, with me."

"What are your names?"

"Abbie and Brett."

"I've got Abbie and Brett here. But more importantly I need a location on Brian Berg and his baby blue pickup truck. The license plate's 1SC087," Stoker said. "How's that air or satellite reconnaissance coming?"

"I'll put out an APB," Z said, "but it's going to be ten or fifteen minutes until we can get a bird in the sky. We're still working on tapping into a satellite, too."

Then a new, but familiar voice came over the radio. "Did someone call for air surveillance?"

"If it isn't Chief Crazy Ass," Stoker replied. "Where are you?"

"I'm in an Osprey, just getting back from Washington D.C. I'll be in Sioux Falls airspace in sixty seconds."

"How about you position your helicopter at eight thousand feet above Interstate 229 and 10th Street and find that truck?"

"Yes sir, Doctor Stoker!" responded Rivera. "I bet my team up here finds Berg's truck about thirty seconds after we get there. We'll let you know when we spot him."

"Rock on!" yelled Abbie, the enthusiastic warrior. "We're riding with Rivera!"

"You're on speaker, Colonel," Stoker said. "We've got Abbie and Brett from your tactical team along with Allie here in the Bronco. The four of us are going after Berg."

"Hi Abbie. I got the sitrep from Z. Great rescue!" came Rivera's voice over the radio. "Now you know why we needed you there instead of co-piloting the chopper with me to D.C."

"Yes, sir," Abbie replied.

"By the way," Rivera said. "You're on the Apache team now, Abbie."

"Sir?" responded Abbie with disbelief intermingled with enthusiasm about her sudden promotion.

"You're flying on our Apache helicopter team, now."

"Thank you, sir!" Abbie said with a grin a mile wide.

"Is that *the* Colonel Rivera?" Brett asked.

"You've got it!" replied Abbie. "Rumor has it he's the only Apache gunship instructor that gets his trainees over the Mexican border for some real world, Chief Crazy Ass experience that nobody ever talks about."

"So Rivera," interrupted Stoker. "We'll take 11th Street out to the Interstate and wait to hear from you."

Stoker shot down the one-way 11th Street and across the bridge toward the interstate reaching a speed of seventy-five miles per hour. 11th Street merged with 10th Street and he found himself at a red light on Cliff Avenue. He skirted all of the waiting cars to the right, approached the intersection cautiously, and waited for a clear moment. When one appeared, he gunned the engine and shot across the red-lighted intersection continuing toward Interstate 229.

"Which way do you think Berg went, north or south on the Interstate?" Stoker asked everyone.

"Troy, be still!" Allie said. "Wait for Rivera. He'll have an answer for you any minute. This is a moment for patience." Allie was right. Rushing in the wrong direction could be a mistake that would only cost precious time in the pursuit. Stoker pulled over just before the onramp to go north on the freeway. There they waited.

"Allie, babe. Where do you hurt?"

"My hip, where Haslam shot me with that beanbag shotgun round. That's all."

"Can you walk?"

"For the next two hours my adrenaline will get me anywhere; after that I'm taking forty-eight hours off."

The voice of Errol Rivera came over the radio from eight thousand feet, "Hey Stoker. We've sighted your bogey. He's headed south on Interstate 229; he's zipping along passing all the other cars. Our guess is he's traveling at about ninety miles per hour."

"Roger that," Stoker said as he checked his mirrors, saw that the traffic was clear, and fired his engine to life. "I'm on my way."

"Don't drive too fast, Troy." Rivera said. "He's not getting away. Let's see if he slows down a bit once he gets further from town."

Stoker entered Interstate 229 and accelerated to eighty-five miles per hour. As long as Rivera could see Berg, Stoker just needed to stay close. Brian Berg did not have the skills to evade Z, Rivera, and all of the other warriors who worked together in their vaguely defined world.

"Allie, there's a bottle of orange juice, two protein bars, some baby carrots, and two sunflower seed bagels in the athletic bag at your feet. I suspect you are hungry?"

"Famished," Allie said as she reached for the food. She started with the orange juice and downed half of the bottle. "Manners count for nothing after so many hours of starvation." She took a huge bite of a bagel. "Kidnapping somebody toward the end of a workout should be a capital crime."

"Agreed," Troy said. "Did they feed you? "If you call two granola bars, a mozzarella cheese stick, and oh — you'll love this — a dirty chai from Ruby's," she said as she took another substantial bite from the bagel.

"Who brought you the dirty chai?"

"Brian Berg. It was a gesture of good will. I drank the whole thing and thanked him heartily. It was part of my act and he sucked it up; it worked."

"When we catch up to him, I'm going to be having that serious talk with Berg."

"Okay just wound him superficially and scare the crap out of him," Allie said. "It was disturbing and bizarre that he was such a gentleman kidnapper. He did not want to hurt anyone — except Sarah Haslam toward the end there. A man he called the commander threatened him with his life and forced him to kidnap me. He went out of his way a couple of times to treat me humanely."

"So he shot you in the hip?"

"It was actually Haslam who shot me. One shot with that beanbag shotgun shell. It's quite the motivational weapon."

"How's it feeling now?"

"Deeply bruised. It's going to take some time to heal."

"I'll get you some oxycodone," Stoker joked.

"Not on your life, Troy. Only wussies like you need the narcotics."

Stoker realized right then and there that his wife was just fine.

Rivera reported in from the Osprey. "He's slowed down to seventy-two miles per hour and he's lucky. About two miles after he slowed, he went through a speed trap."

Thanks, Errol. I'll kick down to eighty. Where's that speed trap?"

"You've got five miles to the trap. After that buddy, it's smooth sailing."

After four miles Stoker slowed down to sixty-eight miles per hour. Once he passed the speed trap, he accelerated to eighty-five for two more miles then brought his speed back to seventy-eight. "How close are we, now Rivera?"

"You're still two miles away. Just take it easy. He just jumped onto Interstate 29." You'll catch up to him soon."

"You've got it," Stoker said as he accelerated to eighty-two miles per hour.

"Okay, Stoker. It looks like Berg is getting off the freeway," Rivera said through the radio.

"Which exit?"

"276th Street."

"He's going to Chelsea Crossing," Allie said.

"I hope so!" exclaimed Stoker. "Brian Berg! Take me to your leader!" Stoker yelled.

CHAPTER 107

CHELSEA CROSSING, SIOUX FALLS

As Brian Berg turned his truck into the Chelsea Crossing planned community, he thought of the perfect place to abandon his pickup truck and make his way to one of the Bryant Way properties. Surely if he talked to the home's occupants, and told the workers there about his little arrangement with the commander, they would give him a place to hide out for a day or two while he figured things out. Berg reasoned that it would be a big mistake to park in front of the houses. He needed to leave his truck somewhere nobody would think to look for it. It dawned on him that the Chelsea Crossing Country Club would be the last place anyone would ever look for Brian Berg or his truck. At that moment, the most brilliant thought of his life hit him. Why not hide his truck by parking it between the two Chelsea Crossing snowplow trucks? The weather forecast for the next three days called for only a slight chance of snow, so nobody would use the snowplows.

As Berg navigated the streets of Chelsea Crossing he was completely unaware of Errol Rivera hovering 6,000 feet above him. He pulled into the driveway of the country club and steered back to the maintenance area. His truck wedged perfectly between the snowplows. He was parked so close to the machines that there was not enough clearance for him to open the door and get out of his truck. So he wriggled himself out of the back window and into the truck bed, then jumped out of the truck bed and started walking across the frozen pond toward the houses on Bryant Way.

From up in the air Rivera radioed into Stoker and his team. "Berg just parked his car in the maintenance lot at the country club. He's walking across the pond toward some homes."

"Check your map," Stoker said. "I bet Bryant Way is close by."

Z's voice came across the radio fifteen seconds later. "The houses on Bryant Way back up to that pond. I think we almost have probable cause to go busting through those doors to find out what's going on in there. Wait until he goes inside, Stoker."

"No way! Then we'll have witnesses," Stoker replied. "Witnesses will not bode well for us if we're going to get the type of information we need out of him."

Stoker parked his car on a neighborhood street that gave him good access to the pond and would allow him to intercept Berg. "You guys hang back here for a minute," Stoker said to Allie, Abbie, and Brett. "Let me have the first *conversation* with him." Stoker jumped out of his truck wearing a utility belt and a .45 caliber Smith and Wesson pistol. He jogged slowly through some trees toward the pond as he reconnected his own radio to his earpiece. As he approached he saw Brian Berg walking across the pond. When Stoker got to the edge of the tree line, he jumped out of the forest and sprinted toward Berg. When Brian Berg saw Troy Stoker running in his direction, he panicked. His adrenaline kicked in and he ran toward the homes on Bryant Way. Unfortunate for Berg, the meth lab in one of the basements had been operating at full capacity throughout the night and it had just belched hundreds of gallons of hot water into the pond, melting the ice. Berg was a mere fifteen feet from reaching the pond's bank when his left foot planted on a soft piece of slush. The slush gave way and Berg tumbled forward into a pool of thirty-eight degree water. The intense cold fueled Berg's survival instinct and he tried to swim to the edge of the ice. His first attempt to grab onto the ice resulted in an armful of slush. He grabbed again, but his arm only slid through more slush. Just as the current was about to drag him under, something yanked him by his coat's collar out of the water and slid him backwards onto solid ice. Berg looked around in disbelief, relishing in the fact that he was back from the brink of death. He looked toward his feet, and saw Troy Stoker crawling toward him on his belly. It was Stoker who had risked laying himself out on the treacherous ice to save Berg's life.

As Stoker inched away from the hole in the ice, he rose into a crawling position and quickly scrambled over to Brian Berg. Leaping on top of the man who had kidnapped his wife, Troy pinned him to the ice. Berg's eyes almost bugged out of his head. Between the cold and fear he felt he was trembling violently.

"Why did you kidnap my wife?" Stoker yelled. "Who put you up to this?"

"I'm not telling you one thing, Stoker."

"I'm going to prove to you that the occipital section of your skull, the back part, is the strongest part of your head," yelled Stoker. He slid Berg closer to the hole so his head was on a slushy spot. "Watch this!" He lifted Berg's head and slapped the back of his skull against the slushy ice. "I'm going to tell you that you're going to get a little docile because this coup-contrecoup injury affects the front part of your brain. That impact slings your brain forward and smacks your frontal lobe against your forehead. Now, tell me why you kidnapped my wife!" Berg refused to respond, so Stoker smashed his head again, a little deeper into the slush. "Welcome to the Headbangers Ball! You can party with Joe Biden and his frenzied frontal lobe!"

Berg looked up at Stoker with a look of complete confusion as Stoker lifted his head one last time and gave it a violent shove toward the remaining inch of ice. As Berg's head splashed into the thirty-eight degree water, Stoker shoved his shoulders a little further back. For a few brief seconds Berg's head was completely submerged in the water. Then, Stoker yanked his head up. "I'll be damned. This South Dakota waterboarding is better than our boys can do in the back alleys of Jalalabad! Of course, ice is a little harder to come by in the desert. Hey look Brian, I bet you wish you were there right now!" yelled Stoker as he shoved his head under the water again and counted slowly to fifteen.

When he yanked Berg's head out of the water, it dawned on Stoker that the frigid water had sucked all of the sensation from his own right hand. He pulled his face up to Berg's coughing, spattering face and whispered menacingly to the semiconscious man, "I've lost the feeling in my hand. How's your head?" Then Stoker roared, "Who's the commander? Three seconds to answer or I'm putting your head back in—and it won't be coming out for a long time, so help me God!"

Berg struggled for air as his eyes darted around violently and he searched for the ability to gasp through his freezing vocal cords. "At, at, attttttttt. Ittt's th-th-the atttttt attorney."

"What's that? Attorney? Which attorney? Some attorney's behind all this? I need a name!" yelled Stoker as he slowly lowered Berg's head toward the water.

"No! No! No! No!" screamed Berg. "It's the attorney general!" yelled Berg with horror. "And, now he's going to kill me. The commander will throw me to the coyotes! I never wanted to hurt anybody! I don't want to meet the coyotes!"

Stoker turned his radio on to non-vox, continuous transmit mode and tossed it to his side a couple of feet. He pulled Berg further away from the slushy area and he signaled for Allie, Abbie, and Brett to join them. Now that Stoker had what he needed, it was time to rescue Brian Berg. Stoker stripped off his coat and wrapped it around the convulsing man. With the forearms of his shirt, he dried off Berg's head. Allie and the warriors knelt at his side. Brett covered Berg's head with his hat.

"You know Brian," Stoker said. "This is where it all went wrong for Ann Higgins. Right over there in one of those houses. Our attorney general decided to build a meth lab in there and she stumbled across it. Now look. Haslam's dead and your future sounds pretty miserable, son."

CHAPTER 108

From six thousand feet in the sky Rivera had relinquished control of the Osprey to his co-pilot and he was watching with concern as he witnessed Stoker, Berg, and Allie on the ice. "Don't push it too far, Troy!" he yelled into his radio. But Stoker had tossed the radio aside to rescue Berg and could not hear Rivera's transmission.

"Colonel! There's a car approaching at a rapid rate of speed. A burgundy Cadillac Escalade."

"Who is it?" Rivera asked.

"We don't know."

"Could you get a bead on them with thermal imaging?"

"Working on it. Thermal imaging in ten seconds, sir."

"Things are getting ugly on the ground," Rivera said. "I need team alpha jumpers ready on my mark! Delta team jumpers on port side also ready on my mark! Copilot, on my orders, take us down to twenty feet." Rivera turned to the person working on the thermal imaging. "I need to know what you see in that car!"

"A driver, plus two more biologicals in the very back. By the way they're moving around they're probably dogs."

"I don't like this. Everyone hold on! Co-pilot! Get us down to twenty feet. The colonel's going in!"

"We're clear. Our landing zone's on the south edge of that pond!" yelled the pilot.

"Ten-four! Get us down!" commanded Rivera.

The Osprey gracefully descended from the Dakota sky as the jumpers yelled their checks.

CHAPTER 109

The commander came to a skidding stop and pulled his Escalade right up to the side of the pond where Stoker was listening to Brian Berg explain his activities with Attorney General Hewitt with every gasp and breath he could muster.

"Troy Stoker! Stop right there and put your hands in the air! You too, Allie! Don't make me unleash Ferdinand and Imelda on you."

Stoker looked up and saw two spectacular dogs, with strong wolfish features, growling and barking ferociously as they fought against their restraints. They were full of fury and bloodlust. Stoker was instantly aware that he was also standing in the sites of the attorney general's FN Five-SeveN.

"You've got some tough decisions to make here, Mr. Attorney General," bellowed Stoker.

The sounds transmitted by the radio Stoker had tossed aside moments earlier came through loud and clear in the Osprey as it passed through two thousand feet. "Attorney general! *Santa Maria! Es el diablo!*" cursed Rivera. "The attorney general is the mark! The devil is mine, and that's an order!"

Back on the ground Hewitt taunted Stoker. "I knew you were a crazy man, Stoker. You're trying to kill a good man there. Berg's a servant to his country and a civil servant to the people of South Dakota. Step away from him!" The commander walked toward them. The warriors held their hands in the air. "Nobody's ever going to know how you crazy SOBs really tried to kill this man. The world will think you killed him—just like Ann Higgins tried to kill herself. And I'm going to kill you in his defense. Everyone will be the better for it. It's all justified! Now stand up, Brian!"

Berg's extreme hypothermia and convulsions overpowered his muscles; his arms and legs would not follow his brain's commands. Stoker knew that Berg would be dead within a quarter hour if he did not get medical help for the hypothermic man.

"I hate to say this, Stoker. But you're really going to make my day. Brian Berg's going to be speechless. You're going to be speechless. And guess what? I think I'll follow suit and remain speechless."

"Get up, Brian!" the commander said as he further closed in on Stoker.

In a split second the aircraft that had been barely noticeable made a rapid descent coming down almost directly behind the commander. The turbulence kicked up and distracted the commander. He turned around just in time to see Errol Rivera and seven other warriors rappelling to the ground and surrounding him. As they landed on the ground the commander lowered his gun and pointed to Stoker. "Officers! Arrest that man," bellowed Hewitt.

"Drop your gun!" Rivera yelled. "We're not officers!"

"DEA!" one of the warriors yelled.

"You're DEA?" the commander asked. He was completely stunned.

"Yes, he is!" Rivera yelled.

The attorney general dropped his gun and began to raise his hands. Then all of a sudden, Steve Hewitt released his dogs. "Imelda! Ferdinand! Attack!" Hewitt ran toward Stoker, Berg, Allie, Abbie, and Brett. Ferdinand advanced instantly. He zeroed in on Allie and sprinted toward her with the bloodlust of his wolf progenitors. Perceiving the threat, Allie engaged every defensive instinct in her body. She bore her teeth in an exaggerated gesture, let out a primal roar, and took off in a sprint toward her canine assailant. Her five-step dash closed the gap on the dog. Allie's counter attack surprised Ferdinand, but he did not relent. When the dog leapt at her in a vicious attack, Allie flung her balled right fist toward the dog's mouth. Her hand entered the dog's mouth, passed its teeth, impacted the dog's throat, and traveled another four inches into the dog's esophagus. The dog's last moments of life were sheer terror as Allie swung her left arm around striking the dog's neck while falling forward on top of the canine. With a loud crack the dog's cervical vertebrae snapped into fragments and severed the dog's spinal cord stopping it's breathing immediately. The dog's mind was briefly aware of its panic before shock set in and a peaceful, permanent sleep befell the majestic half-wolf.

CHAPTER 110

PHILADELPHIA, PENNSYLVANIA

"Kent?" Ann Higgins inquired. She was waking up from a tumultuous sleep, had a splitting headache, and was feeling horrible. "Kent? Are you there?"

"Ann! I'm right here, baby!" Kent Higgins replied. "I've been by your side the whole time! Dear God! Thank you! You're awake. Oh, Ann. It's so good to see you." Kent picked up the nurse call button, pushed it, and said, "Nurse! Nurse! Can you come in here? She's awake!"

"Where am I?" Ann asked.

"The hospital."

"Which one?"

"We chose a special one for you in Pennsylvania."

"Pennsylvania? I don't understand."

"Believe it or not, I'm not sure I do either. We can fill in the details later. Let's start by having you visit with the kids, instead."

"Where are they?" Ann asked alarmed.

"They'll be right back. They're here with us and they're fine. They'll be even better when they get a chance to talk to you."

The nurse came rushing in. "Mrs. Smith. Good morning," she said. Smith was an assumed identity to disguise her true last name. "We just noticed how some of the readings on the EEG and the vitals on your monitors changed dramatically. This is wonderful." The nurse checked more monitors and performed a brief evaluation on Ann. "I have strict orders to notify your attending physician when you wake up. Just stay here and relax. Oh, I'm supposed to tell a Dr. Rivera and a Dr. Bocelli, too."

"Rivera? Bocelli?" Ann Higgins asked. "Who are all of these people?"

"Give us a few days, Ann," Kent Higgins replied. "If we told you the whole story now, you would never believe us."

CHAPTER 111

The commander was paralyzed by surprise and grief. His beloved Ferdinand was dead—killed in the first moments of a fight no less. The commander had never feared a woman in his life. But now, the one hundred and twenty-five pounds of Allie Stoker infused him with alarm.

As the powerful four-footed Imelda advanced on Stoker and Berg, Stoker instinctively hunched down and made himself small, while Berg panicked, screamed, and flailed on the ice in a futile attempt to get on his feet and run away from the dog. Imelda's wolf instinct honed in on Berg and she pounced on him sinking her teeth into his shoulder. Berg and Imelda tumbled backwards into the icy waters. Brett, the warrior, removed a rope from his tool belt and handed one end to Abbie. "Hold onto this," Brett said as he ran his end to the other side of the hole in the ice. Brian Berg grabbed onto the rope and the warriors pulled on the rope to bring him toward the stable ice.

Imelda was panicking to get her footing and pull herself out of the water. But she was still determined to follow her master's commands. She was growling as she swam. She wanted the fight. Stoker knew she was going to attack again as she swam toward Berg, who was struggling to hold onto the rope.

Stoker sprinted toward the hole in the ice and dropped himself down into a feet-first baseball slide. As he was about to glide into the water, he grabbed onto Brett and Abbie's rope and slammed his boot into the dog's snout with full force, pushing her under the water. When Imelda's head emerged one last time and attempted to attack Stoker's foot, he brought his right foot up and kicked her once, which further ignited her fury. Then he kicked her a second time. On the third kick, the enraged Imelda submerged and a gentle current dragged the majestic half-wolf under the ice to her watery grave.

Abbie and Brett pulled Stoker back from the hole in the ice and fished the hypothermic Berg out of the water for the last time.

The attorney general darted toward Stoker "Stop right there, Hewitt," came the authoritative voice of Errol Rivera backed up by the pumping of two twelve gage shotguns. Hewitt hesitated and Rivera caught up to him. "Hands on your head." Hewitt stood still and complied. He slowly moved his hands toward his well-kept hair. When Rivera grabbed his right arm to apply the handcuffs, the commander spun and sent his elbow flying into the colonel's abdomen. Rivera's well-toned muscles withstood the blow. When Stoker saw his friend come under attack, he took two running steps and jumped up into the air. Stoker came down with his elbow on Hewitt's head. The blow knocked the attorney general out cold.

"Hey Stoker!" Rivera yelled. "Never, ever do that again! I really wanted to kick that guy's ass! You've robbed me of a therapeutic moment. You are the anti-catharsis! I'm reporting you to the state board!"

Stoker, Allie, and Rivera laughed so hard they had to drop to one knee. Brian Berg whimpered. The *Espada Rápida* warriors just looked at each other with confused looks.

Just then, Z and Jessica Carey came running to the scene. They saw their three friends laughing uncontrollably. Allie's arm was scraped up, the attorney general was knocked out cold on the ice, and Brian Berg was shivering and crying. A small pool of blood was collecting on the snow under the attorney general's head.

"That was awesome!" Z said. "We saw the whole thing!"

"I captured it all with Google Glass," Jessica said. "Don't worry, though. *Espada Rápida* warriors will not be on the news tonight. But the AG, Stoker, and this crying dude here will certainly be making headlines on KELO."

"Sure, Z. You get here when the fighting's over," Stoker joked.

"Yes, but I saw it all. And I've got to say the way your wife defended herself, Troy, kind of turned me on. Does she have a little sister?"

Jessica overhead the comment and delivered a sharp jab to Z's abdomen. Z winced, but absorbed the blow well. Jessica instantly appreciated that he was humble enough to acknowledge the pain, but strong enough to remain standing. Z even smiled a bit in recognition of her humorous, and slightly violent, flirtation. Then with the hand that had just slugged him in the gut, she briefly ran it over his washboard stomach. "Nice abs for a guy who spends entirely too much time sitting around being a techie all day," Jessica said.

Rivera stood up. It was time to get serious and clean up this situation. Within a few minutes Brian Berg was wrapped in military issue blankets, but his body core temperature was not improving. Hypothermia-induced delirium kicked in the moment they loaded him in the Osprey on a stretcher.

Rivera had ordered Hewitt handcuffed to a seat in the Osprey. A few minutes after they had secured him, the attorney general slowly showed signs of regaining consciousness. He blinked his eyes and struggled to wake up. As the Osprey took off, Rivera sat on one side of Hewitt while Stoker sat on the other.

"Where are we going?" Hewitt asked after a while.

Rivera answered him. "We'll drop Brian Berg off at the hospital. Then we'll refuel and take you to a special doctor we want you to see, Hewitt."

"Doctor?" Hewitt asked. His senses were returning to him now. "Why a doctor? Am I injured that bad?"

Rivera responded. "Worse than you know. This is a special institution where a Dr. Bocelli will put you in a nice little space—I hope you're not claustrophobic—and subject you to his new lie-detection system. We need to take a look into that contorted, scheming, and creepy little brain of yours."

"All in the name of science, of course," Stoker said.

"You'll forget all of this thanks to my friend midazolam here," Rivera said as he held up a syringe filled with five milligrams of the clear pharmaceutical. When he injected it into Attorney General Hewitt's left shoulder, he winced. "I'll explain more once we're in the air—and once this midazolam has kicked in."

"Are we going to Mirandize him?" Stoker asked.

"Absolutely! Somebody will, but it won't be me and it won't be now. I don't have the authority to arrest or Mirandize."

Stoker sensed keenly that he should not further pursue this line of questioning. The midazolam took effect and Hewitt slept like a baby. He would forget almost the whole conversation thanks to the medication.

CHAPTER 112

The FBI's raid on Green Growth Ventures in Reno started with an intense, adrenaline-fueled sixty seconds of agents yelling, guns drawn, employees failing to escape, and everyone being handcuffed and corralled into the office's large meeting room. There was a little more excitement because Ron Cunningham and his assistant had locked themselves in a record room and were shredding key documents as quickly as they could. But it only took the agents another thirty seconds to get into the room and pin both of them to the ground. Nevertheless, the next hours were comprised of almost nothing but silence. Ron Cunningham simply said, "Nobody's saying a thing until our attorneys arrive." Even after the attorneys arrived it still took hours for anybody to say a word.

But the agents didn't waste any time hacking into the computers and digging into the paperwork. They were deeply interested in the deeds and other records pertaining to the two homes on Bryant Way in the Sioux Falls planned community, Chelsea Crossing. They called Z with the news.

When Z heard the report he replied, "I'm not surprised that you found that paperwork there. Ironic that I'm standing about two hundred yards from those homes. Thanks to your work, we have additional probable cause to enter those homes. We'll be knocking down those doors in minutes." Z captured the attention of an FBI agent and he and five other warriors started a brisk jog toward the two homes.

But the most surprising find was an extensive history of transactions and activities in conjunction with a farm in Arkansas. Z was intrigued to dig into this mysterious chapter in the life of a man formerly known as the commander.

CHAPTER 113

SIOUX FALLS REGIONAL HOSPITAL

By the time they had dropped Brian Berg off at the hospital, he had warmed up enough to confess all his misdeeds. As the Osprey touched ground, he begged Stoker, and anybody else who would listen, for mercy and a decent deal.

"Did the AG threaten you with coyotes?" Stoker asked.

"Yes!" Brian Berg was pleading with all the dignity of a sewer rat and all the energy of his heart.

"Well, I'll request that they send you to a prison in Iowa, under an assumed name. With time off for good behavior, my guess is you could be out in three years. I have some friends, and I'll see what they can do. Allie says you were a perfect gentleman as a kidnapper." His comment was sarcastic, but Berg failed to detect the irony.

CHAPTER 114

Dr. Anthony Bocelli had yet another patient in his fMRI machine. He had already walked his patient through *recognition* and *non-recognition* controls and he was ready to start asking him the real questions. But today his disdain for the patient overrode his normally calm and soothing voice and pleasant disposition. "Do you recognize this house?" Bocelli asked in a dry tone as he revealed an image of 5644 Bryant Way on the screen.

"Absolutely not!" came the denial from Steve Hewitt, as he laid tethered to the table that held him inside the fMRI machine at the National Institute of Mental Health.

Dr. Bocelli took his hand off of the microphone and turned to Errol Rivera and Troy Stoker. "What do you think, doctors? Does he recognize the house?"

"Oh yeah," Rivera said. "Look at how his amygdala lights up."

"I concur," Bocelli said.

"Let's try the second house on Bryant Way," suggested Rivera. "Show him the basement, too."

Bocelli displayed the house at 5660 Bryant Way on the screen in front of the commander. "Do you recognize this house?"

"No!" Hewitt said. The fMRI registered his recognition of the property. "It looks a whole lot like that other one you just showed me, though. You're not going to manipulate me into false results. Now get me out of this machine, you sadist."

Bocelli showed a picture of the meth lab in the basement. "Do you recognize this?"

As the commander denied knowing about the meth lab, the scan was showing that he recognized it.

"Tell me if you recognize this?" Bocelli said as he surprised the commander by displaying a picture of the crime scene where he had attempted to murder Ann Higgins. As a prosecutor Hewitt had seen crime scenes hundreds of times, so photographs of blood and gore rarely bothered him. Still, Hewitt was surprised by his own reaction to this crime scene. It occurred to him that it was *his* crime scene, and he had never seen one of his own crime scenes before.

When he fed people to the coyotes he fled before the final dreadful moments. Actually Hewitt rarely provided the punishments or did the dirty work because Nichols was always so eager to carry out the bloody tasks. Instead of answering the question, he just lay there silently thinking.

Bocelli pointed at the monitor. "We don't need his verbal answer. He knows this place."

As Hewitt lay in the fMRI machine, he had no idea that he was in Washington D.C., let alone at the renowned National Institute of Mental Health.

Inside the booth, the three doctors could see that he recognized the crime scene. "Look at that," Stoker said. "His scan shows no signs of disgust."

"No," Bocelli said. "He's probably just jaded as a prosecutor."

"No way," Stoker said. "He's a definite psychopath. His jading happened long before his attorney days," Stoker said. "As a psychiatrist I can diagnose Hewitt, right here and now, as a sociopath and most likely a psychopath. Your fMRI machine confirms it. This guy has no conscience. His insula, that place in people's brains where the fMRI normally shows *disgust*, probably never fires."

"I wish I could publish today's findings," Bocelli said.

"Me, too," Rivera said. "This would be the lead article in any medical journal."

"Or newspaper," interjected Stoker.

"But Bocelli," Rivera said, "If you even think of publishing—or even divulging—this information to—"

"You who can pull my phone number out of the ether," joked Bocelli. "I understand where you're coming from. I'm not the type to fear for my life, Dr. Rivera. I just respect what it takes to get things done sometimes."

"Thank you, Dr. Bocelli," Rivera said. "I rarely have the pleasure of working with people who see the big picture."

The next picture to appear before Hewitt was an image of the farmhouse in Arkansas. Again, Hewitt denied knowing anything about it, but the fMRI showed he knew it well. For twenty more minutes Bocelli displayed pictures of the Reno office, employees of Green Growth Ventures, Larry Stintson, Robert Nichols, Brian Berg, heroin, methamphetamines, and dozens of other images related to his misdeeds.

"Mr. Hewitt. Let's try a new line of questioning," Bocelli said. "Here is a different image." Bocelli produced a recently procured copy of his bank account activities for the last thirty days. The beginning balance was more than $4 million. The funds transfer for $3 million was also highlighted on the page. Bocelli did not bother to ask if Hewitt recognized it. The scanner confirmed that he recognized it and the fMRI also picked up illuminations in the insula of his brain.

"I stand corrected," Stoker said. "This might be one of the only things that can make him feel disgust."

"Losing his money," Bocelli said, "may be the only thing that makes him feel that way."

Then Bocelli put up pictures of Ferdinand and Imelda, his beloved half-wolves. Again, Bocelli elected not to ask a question. The commander's eyes filled with tears of rage. He knew he would never see his beloved dogs again. The next pictures came in rapid succession. His desk in the Capitol building in Pierre, his burgundy SUV, his tennis court at his home, and the farm in Arkansas.

"What do those pictures have to do with anything?" Hewitt asked.

"Nothing that you should be concerned about," Stoker said through the microphone.

Bocelli made sure the microphone was off and he turned to Stoker and Rivera. "What Mr. Hewitt fails to understand is that all of these concur with my controls that I showed him. I can say with high certainty that these are images that show *recognition* within his brain."

Stoker stood up and said, "When I give the signal I want all the microphones off for about sixty seconds." He took off his watch and belt. "We're not going to get to the level of detail we need to reach, or the next level of fact-finding, with pictures and questions. And you don't want to hear or record this." He looked Bocelli in the eye anticipating that he would not like his next move. "I'll give you a hand signal when it's okay to turn recording back on. It's time for some improvised, hard-core psychodrama." Stoker set his belongings in a corner of the booth. "This guy took my wife and tried to kill Ann Higgins, so we're going to play some head games." Stoker continued to remove his crucifix and necklace, shoes, and wedding ring so he could go into the fMRI room without introducing the danger of flying metal.

"What's improvised, hard-core psychodrama?" Rivera asked.

"It's pissed off psychodrama, Stoker style. If this man is indeed a sociopath or psychopath, he really needs some hard-core stimulation to temporarily elicit normal emotions that most people experience. The only emotions Hewitt has are the emotions that manipulate people. To find any other emotions, we need to dig deep, figuratively speaking, to reach his real emotions." Then Stoker stepped out of the booth and into the fMRI room.

"What's he doing?" Bocelli asked.

"He's going to have a little talk with our *amigo*, Hewitt," Rivera said.

"I really hope Stoker doesn't have any other metal—especially like something in his brain," Bocelli said.

"Now that's a thought," Rivera replied in jest. "He may have a little shrapnel floating around up there, especially little pieces." He smiled and looked at Bocelli. "As I understand, doctor, that just might turn out to be a great recipe for a brain smoothie."

Bocelli did not return his smile. Instead the neuroscientist displayed edgy, anxious behavior. "Okay. I hope Dr. Stoker knows what he's doing. Let's just hope he has no shrapnel anywhere near his brain, vital arteries, or major organs."

"Calm down, *amigo*. He's fine. He had an MRI just recently and he did fine," Rivera said as he and Bocelli watched Stoker rapidly approach the man on the table.

The commander was lying, in a semi-agitated state, inside the fMRI machine. He had never been inside any scanner. But, his tendency towards claustrophobia was wearing away at him emotionally, in spite of his intrepid effort to hide his distress from the doctors.

Suddenly, some motion down by his chest caught Hewitt's attention. In horror, he saw Stoker's head inserted into the fMRI machine and the intruder's right arm coming up and violently ripping off his headphones. "Hey, dirtbag. Remember me? The guy in the microphone? I just thought I'd get down to your level and speak to you personally, asshole. Remember me? The guy whose wife you tried to kidnap? Remember me, friend of the Ann Higgins, a woman you tried to kill? But you didn't, asshole," Stoker continued to invade his personal space with extreme prejudice.

"What the hell are you doing in here, Stoker!" Hewitt yelled. "Are you nuts?"

"You're damn right I am!" Stoker replied. "I'm going to be your worst nightmare right now, so shut up and listen."

The commander struggled against his restraints and his instinct to fight kicked in. When he realized how stuck he was, he spit in Stoker's face.

"Don't make me do what I had to do with terrorists in Yugoslavia," Stoker roared. "So shut your pie hole, bitch!"

"First off, your little tennis plaything, Amanda? She's history, and she's singing like a bird right now. Whatever she knows, we know. Secondly, your network is decimated and your assets are seized. Third, with your money and your power gone, you have nothing—and I mean nothing! Do you understand that? And don't get me going on this little thing about taking my wife. Who the hell do you think you are? Do you want me to beat the crap out of you right now? If you weren't in restraints, I probably would. On second thought, Ann Higgins is still in a hospital suffering from brain injuries—which you caused—so maybe I'm just going to pummel you, right now! I'm really not sure!"

Hewitt yelled. "Hey, just wait you—"

"I told you to shut your pie hole, bitch!" Stoker yelled, grabbing Hewitt's right ear and twisting it just shy of the point where the cartilage started to tear.

"Auuuuuuhhh! Are you crazy?"

Stoker continued with his rant. "No! Hold on! Your ear's still attached, Van Gogh. So shut up and listen!"

Hewitt decided to clam up, at least for a while. He thought he would just remain quiet until his lawyers caught up with this nut job.

"Here's one last thing I want to say before we take you down for good. You know your crazy dog, Imelda, that you loved so much? Well, you saw her attack us a few hours ago, and you saw what happened. We turned her into a popsicle! But just for you, we made a recording of the moment to share again, and again, and again. A real special moment."

Stoker pulled his head out of the fMRI for a second and yelled toward the control booth, "Hey Rivera, will you queue up that footage of beautiful Imelda and her last moments? Show the commander, there! Throw it up on the screen!"

For the first time, the commander's eyes showed deep terror and they watered.

"You will love this recording, Commander!" mocked Stoker.

"You are one sick, awful, pathetic bastard, Stoker," Hewitt said in a low, guttural voice. "You and I have more in common than I ever thought. I never thought you had this in you. I've underestimated you. You may have won this battle, but I'm going to win the war. Let me tell you now what's going to happen to you, you sick son of a bitch. You want to know some stuff, I'll tell you some stuff. Let me tell you about my empire, my power, and how I'm going to bring you and your merry band of men down."

"That will be the day!" Stoker said.

"You know damn well that none of this is admissible," Hewitt seethed. "I'll tell you everything, you peon. You're a two-bit psychiatrist from a podunk town. I've got something to tell you, pissant. You really think you can tie me down. I can't wait for all of this evidence to be thrown out because you've not read me my rights or afforded me access to my attorney—even if you've lied to me and did record it!"

"In a week I'll be getting on my private jet. You'll be in shackles facing charges for kidnapping me, your attorney general, and taking me on this crazy, drug-induced trip across state lines. Why don't you add aggravated kidnapping to your list of crimes, you dick?" yelled back Hewitt. "It's you and that Rivera asshole who will be facing jail time!"

"I get it! I understand you now, Big Mac Daddy Attorney General! You call the shots. It's in your court. I get it!" Stoker hissed.

"Hah! You think I really care that much about the money, the status, or that office?" Hewitt asked. "I never intended to be elected, you idiot! My only aspirations in life have been to work as a prosecutor so I could stay ahead of the police and keep my obscenely profitable ventures off of their radar. You have no idea of my assets," the commander said snidely. "And since it will be inadmissible as evidence, let me give you some idea. But first, mighty asshole Stoker, do you own any significant assets?"

"More than you know, skid row."

"Oh! Congratulations!" mocked Hewitt. "I own homes, office buildings, drug laboratories, farms, bank accounts, and safe deposit boxes full of gold, silver and diamonds—many of which the government cannot trace. And now, thanks to you Stoker, they can't even investigate them. This will all be thrown out." Rivera signaled a thumbs-up from the booth, meaning that the fMRI was indicating that Hewitt was probably making truthful statements about his assets.

"False bravado!" Stoker said. "Keep on swinging, while we measure you for your prison jumpsuit. I bet we're going to find that you're owned by loan sharks and cartel bosses much bigger than you!" Stoker accused in an attempt to draw out more anger-fueled information.

"Hah! The only large sum of money I ever borrowed was thirty-two thousand dollars in student loans. It was my seed money for all of this."

"You are not a military man!" Stoker yelled. "I refuse to believe that such scum ever walked among the ranks of the brave."

"The Navy's where I met corruption. That's where I, as a young lieutenant, discovered marijuana. I wasn't a user, but I was profoundly intrigued at the price people were willing to pay for pot in the Philippines and in the United States. I monitored the street prices like a Wall Street stock trader keeps track of the Dow Jones Industrials. I saw huge profits there and my objective was simple: Learn all I could about prosecuting the illicit drug trade—so I could always be a step ahead of it," Hewitt said.

"So when did you start growing pot, Steve?"

In his anger, Hewitt could not help but brag. "Actually, it took a few years. After the military I joined the law firm of Hensworth and Pierce which prided itself as the premier criminal defense law firm in Kansas City. A few months after that I used the thirty-two thousand dollars from my student loans to become a ten percent owner of a farm a few miles outside of Jonesboro, Arkansas. I found a farmer who couldn't make bail for a DUI, and his farm was days away from foreclosure."

"Steve Hewitt," Good Samaritan to the rescue," Stoker said. "Was that man's name Robert?" A few moments later, Bocelli projected a picture of the farmer onto the screen in front of Hewitt's face.

The commander closed his eyes in exasperation, pursed his lips, and exhaled through his nose. "I want my attorney!" he roared. "And get me out of this damn contraption or I will spend every waking hour of my life finding and killing each of you. And then when I'm done, I'll figure out where this place is and I'll devote enough explosives to flattening it ten times over! Do you understand me?"

"I do," Stoker said calmly. "A lot more than you ever realized," he said as he pushed a button and the table slid out of the fMRI. "As you wish, *Commander*."

"Rivera's voice came over the intercom. "The fMRI scan definitely shows Hewitt's recognition of this scuzbag."

"Bulls eye, *amigo*!" Stoker said. "And that includes you commander. Welcome to the technology of the Twenty-first Century."

Stoker walked back into the booth. "So, *asere*, do I receive an Emmy or an Oscar?"

"You've always struck me as a Tony kind of guy, actually. Your performance was live theater, so the Tony sticks. I guess acting every day in your psych office really trains you for this line of work."

Bocelli was speechless. "We call that psycho drama," Stoker said. "Tonight you saw an unlikely, intense form utilizing the unique Troy Stoker improvisation method. In reality it's effective as an extreme therapy also," Stoker explained. "By the way, that's the first time I've ever hurt a dog—but I might bite Hewitt's ear off."

After stammering for a few moments, Bocelli found his words. "Okay, I'm sure I can honestly say, I will never see anything like this again in my career."

Stoker looked Bocelli in the eyes and said, "I have never behaved that way toward anybody. I've never met this level of psychosis intertwined with sociopathic tendencies and just plain evil." Stoker could see that Bocelli was deeply disturbed. "I doubt I'll ever act that way again. But within the cannon of psychiatric ethics this is permissible under such extremes."

Rivera thanked Bocelli. "I appreciate you not leaving a paper trial."

Bocelli looked at Rivera, "When I get phone calls on my personal cell phone, the number that only my wife and my big brother know, I listen *very* carefully." Bocelli shook the doctors' hands. "Have a safe flight back to Sioux Falls."

CHAPTER 115

Robert Nichols sat at the kitchen table in the Arkansas home where he had lived for years. But today he was sitting in handcuffs and he was sharing information liberally with the DEA and Z. "Of course I took the commander's bail. There's no crime in that. What did you say the commander's name was again?"

"Steve Hewitt," Z replied.

"And he's the attorney general of South Dakota?" Nichols asked in disbelief.

"Well, he has been," Z said. "I suspect his term will be coming to an end in a matter of hours though."

Nichols smiled one of those huge grins of disbelief. "Only the commander could live a double life like that and get away with it."

"What did Hewitt tell you his name was?"

"Name? He's got no name. He's just the commander."

"You've known him for all of these years and you never knew his name?" restated Z. He found the farmer's story easy to believe. After all, most people only knew Z by a single initial. Virtually all of Z's financial transactions were nameless as well. "Believe it or not, I understand. I actually kind of like relationships that way."

Nichols just looked at him and said, "As long as he kept payin' me I didn't need to know his name."

"You sold him your farm without knowing his name. You accepted payment from him without knowing his name."

"The checks came from his company, Green Growth Ventures. The bank cashed 'em, and that's all I cared about. It stopped my foreclosure and that's all that mattered."

"Do you know where he got his money?"

"Oh, yeah. Well, he said the first down payment was from student loans. He bragged about that one night on a fishing boat off the Florida Keys. We used to go fishing in Florida about four times per year."

"What about the next payments?" Z asked.

"I'm sure they came out of our profits," the farmer said.

"Well, sir," said one of the DEA agents, "before we seize your farm here, would you mind giving me a little tour? I would like to understand the meth lab you've been running out in your barn there. It can only help reduce your sentence if you cooperate."

"How much do you know about synthetic heroin?" Nichols asked with a prideful smile on his face.

CHAPTER 116

In Reno a number of men were seated around the table in the conference room. Now that the attorneys had cut deals that favored Ron Cunningham and guaranteed long prison sentences for the rest of the Green Growth Ventures employees, he was speaking rather freely about the history of Green Growth Ventures. He seemed to be proud of the criminal enterprise he had helped build, and he loved being the person getting all of the attention all of a sudden.

"It was a brilliant decision to switch from marijuana production to meth," Cunningham explained. "While Hewitt was having a down year, he was certainly not discouraged. He sensed new opportunity. Green Growth Ventures, LLC had managed to amass cash of just over eight hundred thousand dollars—much of it offshore. And it was ready to invest in the world of meth. The farm in Arkansas was also a perfectly pristine place to learn the craft of making and distributing the latest craze in synthetic highs. While the DEA and local sheriff might be searching for marijuana on his farm, they were not searching for methamphetamine. So the first meth lab affiliated with Green Growth Ventures was built in a nondescript barn amongst the corn and soybean fields of Arkansas."

Cunningham continued to explain how the commander loved methamphetamine production. "It was always harvest time. No waiting for crops to grow. The shipments were small and the money was excellent. Even more important, cooking meth was scalable. Starting up new labs was easy, and Green Growth Ventures wasted no time expanding to South Dakota. The commander made it easy to hide production and distribution, misdirect authorities, and cover his tracks."

Over the next few minutes, the accountant's story helped the FBI and DEA put all of the pieces together. Instead of building his new meth business in Pierre, Hewitt chose to start production in Sioux Falls, which was far enough away for the kingpin but close enough for the prosecutor. Rather than purchasing a rundown home in an undesirable neighborhood, the common practice of meth cookers, Hewitt directed Green Growth Ventures to purchase a small piece of land just outside of Sioux Falls.

"Between the South Dakota and Arkansas labs they were able to produce and distribute more than $8,000 worth of product each week," Cunningham explained. "Certainly these labs are not as productive as others. Nevertheless, highly productive labs got busted. They got greedy, and greedy labs are just too easy for the cops to notice. These small labs stayed under the radar. Then by using a series of vague and mysterious relationships, they managed to distribute the goods out on the streets of Sioux Falls and a few other places."

"So when did the identity theft start?" asked an *Espada Rápida* warrior, who also happened to be a DEA agent.

"Now that was not Hewitt's idea," Cunningham said. "The commander was initially against it."

"So what happened to turn him around?"

"He agreed to let us assign one employee to dabbling in ID theft. After a month that employee was bringing in thousands of dollars per week. So we assigned a couple more people to it. That's just good business, people. We just applied MBA thinking to the underworld, and *voila*!"

CHAPTER 117

NEAR BETHESDA, MARYLAND

The government-issue sedan was transporting Hewitt from the National Institute of Mental Health to a location that Rivera would not disclose. He was flanked by Stoker on his right and Rivera on his left. "Here's the plan, Hewitt," Rivera said. "We know that you think you're going to beat this rap because you've not been read your rights. Well, neither Stoker nor I have a badge, so we can't read you your rights."

"But, we're making those plans," Stoker said. "You'll be arrested in Arkansas."

"I don't care where I'm arrested." Hewitt smiled as he looked around and recognized that he was in Washington D.C. "And the two of you will be arrested within hours of me issuing warrants for your arrest."

"Well, here's the thing," Stoker said. "We've been executing a little plan, and we're pretty sure nobody's ever going to believe your little story."

Rivera chimed in, "Yes, just imagine when you say that Stoker and I put you in an fMRI machine at the National Institute of Mental Health."

"You'll sound crazy," Stoker said.

"So when you end up being arrested on your farm in Arkansas five hours from now," chided Rivera, "go ahead and tell the arresting officers that you were actually apprehended yesterday on a pond in Sioux Falls, put on a helicopter by non-descript people from the government, flown to Washington D.C., and put in a mind reading machine."

"Yet somehow," Stoker said, "you were then transported magically to Arkansas early this morning?"

Hewitt flinched. He knew that the story sounded crazy. "There were witnesses on that pond!"

"Yeah, all of them were Rivera's soldiers," Stoker said. "They're not saying a thing. The public already believes our story about picking up a military general who was having a heart attack at the country club."

"You're forgetting about Brian Berg," sneered Hewitt.

"How poetic that you used the name 'Brian Berg' and the word 'forgetting' in the same sentence," Rivera said. "We've really incentivized him to do a lot of forgetting. As we speak, he's being transported, in shackles and an orange jumpsuit, to a Federal penitentiary somewhere in the country. Part of his plea deal is a promise to forget a whole bunch of things. It's a really sweet deal for Berg. I bet he'll be out on parole in two years—and that's after kidnapping somebody. I'm sure you, as the master-prosecutor could've cut a better deal. But we just had to do the best we could as naïve doctors."

"We're covering our tracks as we speak and weaving you back into the timeline," Stoker said. "Your burgundy SUV is en route to Arkansas right now. The driver is using your credit cards to buy gas and food down the whole route. He's even got a little disguise that makes him look remarkably similar to you."

"He'll stop and use your driver's license to get a few drinks at a bar," Rivera said. Your stunt-double will speed through some stretches of road known to have cameras that take pictures of people traveling too hastily. He actually hopes to get pulled over and get a ticket or two."

"So you see, Hewitt," Stoker said, "you're out there buddy. You're *not* here in Washington D.C. You never have been; and suggesting you were here would make you look, well—"

Rivera finished Stoker's sentence. "You would look *loco, amigo.*"

The commander closed his eyes and said nothing more. The three men traveled along a Maryland highway in silence until Rivera's phone vibrated and hummed.

"Well look at this. A young woman Larry Stintson attempted to treat has filed a complaint with the South Dakota Medical Board. It looks like she had a minor wrist fracture so she went to the emergency room. Dr. Stintson wanted to rush her to the operating room and turn her into big surgical case. A couple of board members are going to go visit him at his office tomorrow—flanked by some FBI agents who want to ask him about some interesting findings at Green Growth Ventures in Reno. It looks like he's been funneling patients' financial data into your venture. You're quite the entrepreneur, Hewitt."

"Make sure they have Stintson pee in a cup for a drug test," Stoker said. "If he's been hanging out with a kingpin like Steve Hewitt, he's been enjoying some of the product from Bryant Way."

"Larry Stintson," Hewitt said with a quick laugh. "I guarantee he'll test positive." The commander cocked his head to the side and looked out the windows into the blackness of the night. "That doctor was a suck up; but he had potential. It's too bad. He was just starting to find his place in my world. He would've been good. Not great, but good."

"So when we get him on the witness stand, what's he going to say about you?" Stoker asked.

"Whatever I tell him to say," Hewitt replied. "I think this conversation's over. I'm going to catch a little shut-eye."

"Let me help you with your sleep," Rivera said as he injected Hewitt with five more milligrams of midazolam. Within a few minutes the man, formerly known as the commander, was asleep and completely unaware of the upcoming next leg in his itinerary.

CHAPTER 118

The commander stirred. He vaguely sensed an extremely distant consciousness. His mind was still obscured by the ongoing doses of midazolam that Rivera had been shooting into his shoulder muscle. Hewitt perceived a distant tingling from his butt muscles that had been compressed by his weight and robbed of circulation. He must have maintained practically the same position during the last hours of unconscious flight. A minute later his awakening mind perceived the drone of engines—what kind of engines he had no idea. Frankly, he did not care. His handcuffs cut into his wrists but the pain barely registered in his groggy mind.

Hewitt was still numb and he barely felt any discomfort. The magnitude of his recent capture was completely absent from his mind and he was oblivious to the amount of drool that had drizzled down the front of his prisoner jumpsuit. As his mind slipped into another level of consciousness he experienced a brief, recent memory of Allie Stoker quickly dispensing of his beloved wolf dog. It was a painful memory and it awakened additional emotion that activated another recess of his mind. His next memory was yelling at his accountant through the phone about a sudden $3 million withdrawal from a banking account.

His returning memories were interrupted by a sharp pain pricking him in the middle of his fleshy right thigh. Within seconds his brain whiplashed from groggy to high anxiety. As his mind roared to life, his concerns about the cold disappeared, but he felt a sudden onset of anxiety—a very unnatural feeling.

"That's an amphetamine rushing through your circulatory system," said a familiar voice, a voice that he hated. "It's actually some of your own product."

Hewitt's blood vessels constricted and instantly he felt the cold again which only served to further waken him and feed his anxiety and paranoia. The pain from the handcuffs cut into his wrists and activated an intense flinch. With some adjustment against the handcuffs he relieved the pain in his wrists. His thoughts further awakened to the sound of prop engines of an airplane that he recognized from his days in the military.

He opened his eyes and struggled to focus them. There was a well-lit spotlight illuminating an unrecognizable person four feet in front of him. He blinked and attempted to look to his left and then to his right. He surveyed the space above him, but his restraints impeded him from seeing his feet or the floor. It dawned on him that wherever he looked, the spotlight followed. Then he perceived straps wrapped to his head. *I'm wearing a headlamp*, he thought. To prove the presence of the headlamp he darted his head and eyes around the space a little bit more. The light followed perfectly. Convinced of his ability to control the light, he shifted it back to the person sitting in front of him. The menacing stare of an indignant Errol Rivera looked him straight in the eye with fiery ire. Hewitt slowly averted his gaze and the headlamp to Rivera's right. Rivera moved himself into the newly illuminated area, but continued his silent, intense stare. The commander just closed his eyes as a spontaneous, splitting headache overcame him, and a flood of memories of coyote attacks, a frozen pond, and a vacuum cord in a janitor closet pervaded his thoughts.

"It's probably been a while since you flew in a C-130 Hercules," Rivera said. "Welcome aboard Rivera Airlines. I'm sorry we're not serving any food or beverages, but please accept the complimentary meth injection for our fourth class passengers. I even snuck you in a double dose—just because I think you're kind of cute. I hope you wanted it in your leg. I apologize in advance for the blood pressure spike, cold, tremors, and other side effects. I'm normally not a big amphetamine fan, but for your situation this medication and a high dosage are a great match."

"If you need to use the bathroom, go right ahead! You're already sitting on as much toilet as you're going to get on this flight."

"Who are you?" the commander asked. "I mean, what *are* you, Rivera?"

"Just a warrior and some SOB who's supposed to be flying this plane. Enjoy the ride. We're efficient around here. We'll be expediting your landing."

"Where are we going?"

"The governor just gave me a half-hearted order to get you back to Sioux Falls in one piece."

Rivera exited the cabin and stepped into the cockpit, securing the door between the two spaces.

Hewitt's mind was now racing and all of his senses were moving from high alert to a state of shouting overdrive. Profound agitation overwhelmed his mind as he began to take in the full impact of his immediate surroundings and the loud roar of the C-130 engines. Everything around him was coming alive and exaggerated. Earlier this week, he had been the third most powerful man in South Dakota, while also running his crime syndicate worth millions of dollars. The wealthy respected him, and the scum of the earth feared him. Now he sat shackled and impoverished in clothing he did not even own. As his anxiety began to make him tremble, tears welled in his eyes and he lifted up his shackled wrists. *Hundreds of men and women have worn shackles at my insistence*, he thought. He would almost certainly be joining them in a South Dakota state penitentiary.

The amphetamine fueled his escape instincts, and he realized he still had his intellect. Neither Rivera nor Stoker could take his astuteness from him. He directed his headlamp around the airplane cabin in search of any slight advantage that might help him orchestrate an escape. As he glanced at the floor in front of him he noticed a stray paperclip, and his dread was displaced with optimism. Opening handcuffs with a paperclip would be textbook-simple.

He strained against his cuffs and leg irons with a desperation that caused the chains to cut into his ankles and draw blood. But his attempt brought him no closer to the paperclip. The commander took another minute and thought carefully through a quick maneuver that might make him the owner of the paperclip. It would be his single most important acquisition in his now limited reality.

Slowly, the commander slid off his seat, and then to his right and dropped down awkwardly on one knee. He rotated to one side and dropped down on his right hip. Thankfully the tension in both of his ankle shackles was not that great. The resulting tension in his tibia and his knee was alarmingly painful—but much less concerning than imprisonment with hundreds of men he had prosecuted. He extended his shackled hands above his head, which allowed his trembling fingers to fumble with the paperclip and slide it along the metal floor until he could grasp it clumsily with one hand. While lying on his side, his trembling hands inserted the jerry-rigged paperclip into the key slot. He gingerly worked the lock until an instant click preceded the springing open of the cuffs. Adrenaline surged though his mind and further fueled the amphetamine-induced euphoria.

After a few moments of adjusting his legs, he used the same paper clip to free his leg shackles. "I'm free!" he whispered aloud. "I'm the commander!" he exclaimed, as he looked frantically about the cabin for parachutes. Within two seconds his headlamp was illuminating the paratroop door on the starboard side of the aircraft, and his eyes followed the contour of the door upward until it found a parachute pack secured in a space right above the door. It had been years since he jumped out of an airplane with a parachute, but with an abundance of adrenaline and amphetamine coursing through his veins, he was optimistic he would remember how to complete the jump as perfectly as he had done it more than two decades before.

As he strapped on his parachute he reasoned that his conditions were not ideal. He would not have the benefits of air deflectors, a pilot pitching the aircraft at the right angle, and the consistent and optimal velocity for a jump. He also momentarily wished for a static line that would open his chute for him as he jumped free from the airplane, but he quickly dismissed the idea. Instead he reasoned that he would prefer to free-fall for a few seconds to get him closer to the ground faster. It would also make it harder for search parties to estimate his landing location.

He knew he would have to take a few chances; in his current super-charged mental state he did not care. He tightened straps and attached clips. It all came back to him fluidly, and his confidence and excitement increased accordingly.

After walking through the safety checks, at least the ones he could remember, with his parachute, he stepped up to the paratroop door, grabbed a lever and flipped it counter-clockwise releasing the door. With a slight nudge upward, the door traveled up into the ceiling of the C-130. The commander had the presence of mind to secure the door into place with a small wire-attached pin. He took a brief step backward, folded his arms across his chest, and stepped gracefully out the door falling into the frigid night temperatures ten thousand five hundred feet above the eastern boarder of South Dakota.

CHAPTER 119

As Rivera piloted the Hercules C-130 through Minnesota air space and into South Dakota an alert light on one of the cockpit readouts lit up. Rivera covered the nuisance with his hand. "Hey ladies, look. We've got a depressurization in the back. Let's drop down to ten thousand feet."

"So do you want to continue traveling at 150 knots?" Stoker asked.

"Roger that," Rivera said obviously unconcerned.

"So why are you going so slow?" Stoker asked. "A door is open in our prisoner bay and you don't do anything about it?"

Rivera looked at Stoker with a scowl. "Why do you have to ask me these questions?" Rivera said "It's nothing for you to be concerned about, Stoker."

"Right, right. I know how this goes. I shut up, play dumb, and listen to your tired, old jokes about how disposable I become if I know too much about your spy world."

"No. It's not that. It's just that it's been a long time since I've flown one of these babies. I'm just enjoying this relaxing flight. I admit I also like subjecting that dirt bag, Hewitt, to a little extra turbulence."

"Shouldn't we check on him?" Stoker asked with a touch of impatience in his voice.

"Go ahead," Rivera said as he handed Stoker some foam earplugs to protect his hearing. Stoker put them in his ears and turned toward the cabin door just as Rivera hit a button to open it. As Stoker stepped into the cargo area he turned on a light that threw its rays onto the empty steel handcuffs and ankle irons on the airplane floor. The paratroop door was open and Hewitt was gone. Stoker ran to the door, pulled the pin that held the door open, slid the door back into place, and secured it with the pin. He paced around the cabin, searching between the cargo and in all of the nooks and crannies. Then he thought to count the parachutes.

"Parachutes, parachutes, parachutes," mumbled Stoker to himself. "Where are the parachutes on this plane? Who's running this show? Who would be stupid enough to overlook the parachutes? There have got to be at least ten on this bird!"

Stoker stormed back to the cockpit, stepped back inside, and closed the door behind him. "Rivera, radio it in! Hewitt got away! Get the police on the ground down there looking for him, stat!" commanded Stoker.

"I've already taken care of it," Rivera said.

"Who's the idiot who failed to inventory the parachutes?" Stoker ranted. "I can't believe Hewitt got away!"

"I can," Rivera said remarkably calm. "He's a smart man. He got away. He knows what he's doing. Let's just forget about him. I think we're only twenty minutes from a shot of bourbon."

Stoker was stymied and confused. "Rivera, what's going on? What are you doing?"

Rivera smiled wryly. "I think what this colonel is saying is, it's time for a little celebration."

"Okay Rivera." Stoker was searching for the right words. "You actually set him up? You are one sneaky *diablo*. You just wound Hewitt up like a toy train, put him on the tracks, and sent him precisely where you intended for him to go."

"I'm really glad that I packed that parachute—um, correctly," Rivera said.

Catching on completely now to what was going on, Stoker cut in. "No. You didn't!"

Rivera smiled. "I double-checked it, *amigo*. As Arnold said in that great movie Commando,"

"No! Don't say it!" yelled Stoker. "No more of your cheesy 1985 movie flashbacks!"

"I let him go," Rivera said in a shamefully poor imitation of Arnold Schwarzenegger. "I cannot tell a lie. I chopped down the cherry tree!"

Rivera radioed to air traffic control and requested clearance to approach and land at Sioux Falls Regional Airport. "Actually that *cucaracha* ignored all the signs." The tower granted clearance, and Rivera said, "As a military man, prosecutor, and criminal, he clearly saw that there were some irregularities back there—and he chose to ignore them. Would there really be a paperclip on the floor right in front of him? Just one parachute? Does a prisoner usually get a headlamp on his head? Do we leave prisoners alone in the back of a plane? Especially somebody as recently infamous as him? He chose to ignore those signs and he took a huge risk. That gamble sent him jumping to his death."

"All he was wearing was the prisoner jumpsuit and high-top sneakers. I suspect it was about twenty-five degrees below zero at his jumping altitude," reasoned Stoker.

"That would've been a harsh, cold minute or so before he hit the ground," Stoker said.

"Either way, something tells me the coyotes find him before we do."

Just then, Stoker's phone rang. "This is strange," Stoker said. "I'm getting a call from Ann Higgins's cell phone."

Rivera was insistent. "Answer it, *loco.*"

"This is Stoker."

"Troy!" exclaimed the voice of Ann Higgins. "I just needed to talk to my friend and my shrink!"

Stoker was ecstatic. "Ann, it's so great to hear your voice. I can barely hear you with all this airplane noise. Can I call you back in a few minutes?"

"Of course. I just want you to know that I'm okay. Talk to you soon."

Rivera immediately ordered, "Give me a sitrep on Ann Higgins."

"She's alive and she's talking. It sounds like she's doing great."

"Another reason to celebrate!" Rivera said.

As the airplane completed its final approach, Stoker asked Rivera, "So what's your next mission?"

Rivera flashed his infectious Cuban smile. No *asere*, the proper question is, what's *our* next mission? I need a consulting psychiatrist in a *very* complex situation. Are you game?"

THE AUTHORS

The authors ascending Harney Peak, South Dakota, October 2013

Dr. Francis Bandettini is a private practice psychiatrist and co-author of *American Jackal* and the forthcoming series of Troy Stoker, M.D. psychiatry thriller novels. He graduated from the University of Wisconsin-Madison with a degree in the molecular biology honors program, and earned his medical degree at the University of Osteopathic Medicine and Health Sciences in Des Moines, Iowa. Dr. Bandettini completed his psychiatry residency at the University of South Dakota School of Medicine where he subsequently joined the faculty as an assistant clinical professor of psychiatry. He is a retired Captain from the United States Army and South Dakota National Guard. He lives with his wife in the greater Sioux Falls area.

Matt Nilsen is the co-author of *American Jackal*. He completed his undergraduate studies at the University of Utah and earned a master's degree from the Medical College of Virginia. He lives in Salt Lake City with his wife and four children where he is working on the Troy Stoker, M.D. psychiatry thriller series.

Photography credits: Summer Blackhurst and Naomi Bandettini